A TRILOGY OF DESIRES
MALCOLM & STARR PARTS I-III

STEELE INTERNATIONAL, INC. A BILLIONAIRES ROMANCE SERIES BOOKS 7-9

CHARMAINE LOUISE SHELTON

CONTENTS

CAPTURE MY DESIRES MALCOLM & STARR PART I

EMBRACE MY DESIRES MALCOLM & STARR PART II

CHERISH MY DESIRES MALCOLM & STARR PART III

FREE BOOK

Get the start of the STEELE International, Inc. A Billionaires Romance Series with *Discover My Desires Sebastian & Lola Prequel* **FREE!**

Click Cover Below or visit **bit.ly/CLBooksNewsletter** to subscribe to my newsletter for latest news and launches, books from my author friends, and sizzling reads in book promotions. Plus, start reading the steamy billionaire romance *Series Prequel* of Sebastian Steele and Lola Lewis.

Their stories. Their discovery of unknown desires…

FREE BOOK!

SERIES
INTERNATIONAL, INC.
BILLIONAIRES
ROMANCE SERIES
Discover my
DESIRES
SEBASTIAN & LOLA PREQUEL
Charmaine Louise Shelt

Discover my
DESIRES
Charmaine Louise Shelt

ALSO BY CHARMAINE LOUISE SHELTON

**STEELE INTERNATIONAL, INC.
A BILLIONAIRES ROMANCE SERIES**

Discover My Desires Sebastian & Lola Prequel
(Available Exclusively to Subscribers)

Fulfill My Desires Sebastian & Lola Part I

Heighten My Desires Sebastian & Lola Part II

Ignite My Desires Roger & Leonie Part I

Stoke My Desires Roger & Leonie Part II

Justify My Desires Roger & Leonie Part III

Deepen My Desires Sebastian & Lola Part III

Capture My Desires Malcolm & Starr Part I

Embrace My Desires Malcolm & Starr Part II

Cherish My Desires Malcolm & Starr Part III

A Trilogy of Desires Sebastian & Lola Parts I-III

A Trilogy of Desires Roger & Leonie Parts I-III

A Trilogy of Desires Malcolm & Starr Parts I-III

ABOUT STEELE INTERNATIONAL, INC. A BILLIONAIRES ROMANCE SERIES

Welcome to the titillating world of the multibillion-dollar global company and the love affairs of the family that controls it.

STEELE International, Inc. is a series of interconnecting Billionaire romance. Follow the Steele family as they fly around the world chasing the women they love and their happily ever afters. Get ready for glitz, glamour, and steamy romance books. What's better than that? The Jet-set Lifestyle has never been hotter...

The Desires Series is not for the tea set; it's for the top-shelf vodka straight up in a pretty crystal glass coterie!

Don't miss any of the sizzling romance books in the STEELE International, Inc. A Billionaires Romance Series:

Discover My Desires Sebastian & Lola Prequel
(Available Exclusively to Subscribers)

Capture my DESIRES

Charmaine Louise Shelton

*I dedicate this novel to the thrill seekers, rebels, and free spirits.
Keep doing your thing, baby!*

Fulfill Your Desires.

xoxo
Charmaine Louise

ABOUT CAPTURE MY DESIRES
MALCOLM & STARR PART I

I'm the second son; the rebel; the bad boy billionaire playboy of the family. The one others come to for solutions —The Enforcer. My wild, reckless days help me make my Entertainment Properties Division of STEELE International, Inc. the highest generator of revenue. I'm Malcolm Steele and I always get what I want. And I want the brown-eyed beauty.

I'm the laid-back LA girl who owns a luxury yoga and wellness center; the one with the hippie parents who named her Starr Knight; the one who on a chance encounter meets a sexy as sin man when she closed her heart to love. He brings out a wildness in me I never knew existed. And now fear.

Can he capture the heart of his free-spirited woman, or will one of his former lovers make their fledgling romance collapse?

Travel with Malcolm as he chases his Starr around the skies in private jets, wingsuits, and water jetpacks from Beverly Hills to Rishikesh to St. Barth's in this love triangle steamy romance story.

Their love story is a standalone romance trilogy in the series. Get a glimpse of their dynamism in other books.

Anthem: "Gypsy" Fleetwood Mac
https://www.youtube.com/watch?v=mwgg1Pu6cNg

Playlist:
https://www.youtube.com/playlist?list=
PLXwYvn0e218Bkvniy3AAnyw7o8DMj0geb

Visit CharmaineLouiseBooks.com

PROLOGUE

1 *8 Years Ago*

*S*TARR *— 13, Beverly Hills, CA*

"—YEAH, right! What makes that loser nerd think anyone wants to go to her corny birthday party?"

"Right! And with her weird hippie parents, too! What'll she have there? Unicorns and rainbows?!"

"Did you get a glimpse of her face when we told her we'd go? She grinned ear to ear with happiness braces on full blast… SIKE!"

"With a name like Starr, she's not very bright, is she?"

"That's the problem she thinks she's so smart, knows more than the rest of us—"

My mind reels as their voices fade out behind the closing bathroom door. I hug my knees to my chest while I rock on the toilet's lid. Tears stream down my heated cheeks, blurring my vision.

I don't need to see clearly to know the voices of Sally, Laura, Gail, Connie, and Jessica—the It Girls of Beverly Hills Junior High School. I could envision Sally, their leader tossing her silky blonde hair over her shoulder as she mimed my glasses. Gail, her main sidekick would have fluffed her curly afro to copy my naturally curly hair.

Obviously, I'm not so smart to have fallen for their easy yeses to attend my thirteenth birthday party this weekend. The It Girls at my simple backyard barbecue? Too good to be true.

For a moment I thought their teasing ways were over since we're in the seventh grade now. Who knew they'd carry over their mean-girl antics from fifth and sixth grades to a new school?

Duh!

A drawn-out sigh slips from my lips when I tilt my head back to stare at the ceiling, hoping to stop the flow of my tears. I'm so tired of them being so nasty to me. And for no reason!

Sure, I like to excel in my classes, and I answer the teachers' questions happily—and correctly. But that doesn't make me a nerd. Just interested in my schoolwork.

The whole braces thing is messed up too. I got them this past summer and grew five inches. So along with a mouth full of metal, thick-lensed glasses, and unruly curls, I tower over the other girls in our class.

Gawky much?!

It was bad enough they teased me ruthlessly about my "hippie" parents, clothes, and crystals in elementary school.

So what if my parents changed their names from Jordan and Belinda to Peace and Sun years before I was even born?!

I like my name, Starr Knight. And doggone it, I am bright, and I love my parents—hippies and all!

They're brilliant environmental law attorneys who take on the most challenging cases against big businesses and win billions! The law firm—Knight & Knight LLP—my parents founded years ago after they met at a music festival while at Stanford Law School ranks in the top five of the United States. With offices in LA, Seattle, Denver, Chicago, Houston, New Orleans, Miami, New York City to represent cases in the top environmentally focused cities. They may be hippies, but they're sharks in the courtroom.

And so am I!

After a sniffle, I rise, shake out my vintage, glittery matchstick midi skirt so the layers fall to my Doc Martens' eight-eye, patent leather boots on a whisper. I smooth my off-the-shoulder ruffle top over the white camisole before I grab my well-worn leather crossbody bag.

Loose tendrils of curls fall over my eyes as I bend over. I sweep them back into the big bun at the nape of my neck with a resigned huff as my rose quartz pendant slips along its leather cord. Determined, I straighten my spine and leave the bathroom.

Time to face the music on the school bus ride home.

"Hi, sweetheart, how was school?"

I lift my head from my notebook and smile at my mother. We look exactly alike. Sorrel brown eyes full of love as she peers at me. Smooth chestnut-colored skin glows from healthy eating and regular exercise. Long, curly, dark brown hair pulled up in a topknot. Dimples highlight her sculpted cheekbones when she returns my smile. She's a beautiful woman in her late thirties.

"History class was interesting, and I loved art," I answer as I stand three inches taller than her petite feet-foot-three-inch frame. "But the crew siked me into believing they were coming to my birthday party."

I raise my hand when she speaks. A scowl settles on her pretty face.

"Hey, no worries. 'Be equally thankful for what you perceive to be good and for what you perceive as bad. It all happens for a reason. Either way, you don't let it disturb your inner peace. Strive for tranquility no matter the outer circumstances.' Right?" I ask, reminding my mother of her favorite yogic piece of advice.

She cups my face and beams at me.

"Absolutely, Starr!" My mother exclaims.

"What's the 'absolutely' for?"

We turn to see my father stride into the room. His baritone voice booms around us.

I get my height from him being six feet, five inches. He's opposite of my mom and me, with his obsidian eyes and pecan-colored skin. Equally fit and health conscious, he exudes power at forty-one. He's renowned for his command of the boardroom or the courtroom if negotiations reach that extent.

"A bit of a misunderstanding about my party. But no worries!" I respond as I give him a hug.

It's nearly dinnertime, and they make a point of being home as a family each night if possible. Otherwise the chef makes a meal for me.

"Well, perhaps your gift will make up for it," my father says as his eyes twinkle. "How about you open it early?"

With a shriek, I grasp the envelope and rip it open. An itinerary for a two-week stay at an ashram in Rishikesh, India, the world capital for studying yoga and meditation rests in my hands.

I never thought my parents heard me rambling about the

center for spiritual studies a few months ago when I found it online.

Another of their traits I inherited is their focus on well-being. Whenever I have encounters with the crew, I practice breathing exercises to brush off their meanness. It takes the focus away from them and brings it back to me, keeping me centered and at peace.

I whoop and throw my arms around my father, then my mother. Yup, hippies and all, I'd have them no other way!

MALCOLM — 15, Southampton Village, NY

"OH SHIT! What the hell is that on your back, Malcolm?! It better not be real, bro!"

My head whips around, my mouth twisted as I glare at my older brother—older than my fifteen by two years barely.

Since we're so close in age, everyone confuses me with him. We share the Steele clan traits of wavy ebony hair and dove gray eyes. Our olive-colored skin tanned further by the bright sun of Southampton Village, where our family's compound spans for a mile along our private beach.

Baz has a few inches on my six-foot-frame, so I have to look up at him.

But I don't look up *to* him. Hell nah!

He's Mister Perfect. The supposed leader of the Steele siblings. A role he's taken upon himself since forever. That's cool for Roger who's fourteen and the fraternal twins Harris and Haley at eleven. They freaking idolize Baz.

Me? Not so much. I refuse to be in Sebastian's shadow. I make my own way and don't need his interference in my life. My identity is my own. Screw looking alike.

"Oh, screw you, Sebastian! You're not my father! Back off, *bro*!!" I snarl viciously as my nostrils flare and my face reddens.

I storm off from the party we're having on the beach, sick and tired of his crap. I push past the others ranging from my age to twenties.

Of course it's a crowd. Everyone wants to be around the Steeles. Our multibillion-dollar family has deep roots in New York City with our multigenerational luxury real estate development and management company based out of The STEELE Tower.

Even though it's the summer and we're out in the Hamptons for the weekend, each of us interns at the company. Come Monday, we'll be on Fifty-seventh Street and Fifth Avenue in the heart of Billionaires' Row at our respective divisions, learning our family's business from the ground up.

We have our mother to thank for "not being spoiled rich kids who only lounge around the pool all day." Shelley is a native New Yorker who worked as a shopgirl in one of STEELE's retail spaces. She met our father Morgan when he was on a business call to the store. At the time he was President of the Retail Properties Division and our grandfather was the CEO. Now, our Dad is top dog.

Baz assumes he's next in line, so he runs around barking orders at the rest of us.

Well, to hell with that!

I want no parts of STEELE International, Inc. I plan to start my own company for extreme sports lovers like me. Baz can have it all—Favorite Son and future CEO. I'll continue on as the second son; the rebel; the bad boy billionaire playboy of the family. And billions it will be too. Those I make on my own, not handed to me. Thank you very much!

Who the hell does he think he is telling me how to behave and what to do constantly?! He needs to get off my back already, literally.

That's why I got my tattoo. The wings on my back symbolize freedom from family constraints and the flying as I speed along on my bikes. After I won my latest motocross race, I memorialized it forever in ink. The tattoo artist didn't give me any flack since my height and attitude make me appear older than fifteen. Plus, I flirted with her, then backed it up once she completed my tat. She did a damn good job, and I thanked her royally.

So Baz can shut up with his nagging.

I need to feel the wind in my face to cool down. A quick walk to the garage and I'm astride one of my KTMs, ready to hit the dirt trails outside of the ritzy town. Just as I lift my helmet—I may be a rebel who takes risks, but I value my life—a movement to my left catches my attention.

Damn. Belinda Crane.

Belinda *Baz's Girlfriend* Crane, to be exact.

By her expression, she's not thinking of Big Brother right now. Nor does she mistake me for him. Nope. That heat is all for me.

She twirls a strand of her long silky red hair between her delicate fingers as her eyes travel from my boots to my leather-clad muscular thighs and chest to my smirking mouth. When green meets gray, the lust rolls through us in waves.

I may be fifteen, but this isn't my first rodeo, nor will this be my first ride of this little filly. Poor Baz has no clue. Yeah, height and attitude make all the difference in life.

Belinda sashays over to me, her grip-worthy hips sway, making the strings of her white bikini dance. The round mounds of her tits bounce with each step. Her hooded eyes never leave my face, but my eyes travel the curves of her luscious body. She's a true redhead.

"I love your tattoo, Malcolm… A lot," Belinda says breathlessly as her fingertips skim over my back from shoulder to shoulder, sparks reach through the leather to make my cock jump to attention.

"Do you now, B.?" I smirk.

She nods and licks her full glossy lips.

My eyes dart to them, and I chuckle.

The first time her little pink tongue wrapped around my hardness, I nearly came before she even started blowing me.

I've learned more control since last winter's break. And I plan to use it.

"I'm going for a ride. You wanna cum?" I ask, not missing she picked up on my word choice when her pale cheeks flush bright red.

A quirk of my eyebrow has her nodding and scurrying to hop behind me. The warm, wet folds of her pussy press against my ass.

Yeah, I can't wait to bury my thick ten inches balls deep in her greedy snatch.

The purr of the engine is a precursor to the purrs I'll have Belinda moaning as soon as I get her writhing beneath me.

At times, it's good to be a Steele.

But on my terms.

MALCOLM

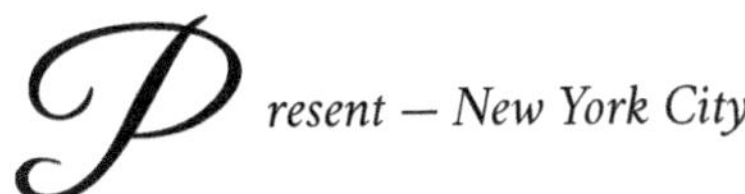*resent — New York City*

"GOOD EVENING, MR. STEELE."

On reflex, my gaze travels over the mâitre d' at LEVELS 4 Restaurant as her whisky-colored bedroom eyes drink in every one of my six feet, four inches. Her sultry smile widens with satisfaction. Unmistakably impressed by my bespoke three-piece suit, custom dress shirt with Hermès silk tie and pocket square, and A. Testoni Oxfords.

I run my hand over the five o'clock shadow covering my firm jaw, partially to distract her heated gaze and to hide my delight in her beauty.

Not one to flirt when in a committed Dominant-submissive relationship, even if it has lost its allure. I can still appreciate a gorgeous woman.

The mâitre d's honey-colored skin glows naturally with minimal makeup. Only ruby-red lips that draw my attention to her lush mouth. My cock—having a head of its own—

twitches at the vision of her lips wrapped around my girth as she kneels naked before me.

I incline the head on my shoulders in response to her greeting.

"Your guest has not arrived yet. Would you prefer to wait at the bar, or shall I escort you to your table, Sir?"

This time I can't contain my smirk at her innuendos. Well played.

"The bar will do, thank you… Tabitha," I answer as I read her name on the tag placed strategically on the ample curve of her left tit.

Her eyes gleam after my gaze lingers on the fullness of her breast.

I give her an appreciative nod, then pivot to stride towards my bar.

Yeah, my bar as in part of my global, luxury, members-only BDSM/dance club LEVELS New York in Manhattan's Meatpacking District. Apropos for the flagship location since men pack their meat into willing women and willing men allow women to pack them with their toys, or whatever combination suits members' fancies.

The decorative theme for the club is minimal and industrial in deference to its warehouse history. The fixtures and furniture that appear well worn are high-end, modern replicas used to add authenticity without the grime of old pieces.

My cousin Lucien Jackson cooked up the idea and told me about it. Lucien literally cooked it up since he thought of it as he finished his hospitality and culinary training at Le Cordon Bleu in Paris.

Of course, when we presented the concept to Sebastian for his approval, his response was typical Sebastian. "Who the hell goes through that prestigious training to come up with a titty bar?"

Well, five years later Lucien's idea proves it's bigger than that and has a high profit margin with additional locations in Paris and London. That's all that concerns Sebastian and me, to be honest: will it add to STEELE International's bottom line? Yes, well, it's a go. No, then no go.

LEVELS is one of many business partnerships that STEELE has with Jackson Corporation. World-renown for their award-winning eateries, choice cigars, and distinguished liquors and wines, their products pair well within STEELE's casinos, hotels, resorts, and residential and retail properties.

On the personal side, my mother is best friends with the Jackson matriarch. They spent most of their adult lives together forming a closer bond than they have with their blood siblings and relatives. Not sharing DNA doesn't keep our families from being a close-knit group.

Growing up, Lucien and I were the deviants, the ones who took the most risks—and won. As the second son of the Jackson clan, he relates to my frustrations, especially as teenagers. He set his course to prove himself within their company, just as I did with STEELE.

As the president of STEELE's Entertainment Properties Division, I oversee our casinos, hotels, and resorts. LEVELS falls within my milieu. I'm the most appropriate sibling to take on the division. My wild ways of pushing the envelope and my love of the challenge extreme sports triggers prepared me for the role to lead our most profitable division focused on pleasure and thrills.

While in my sophomore year at Harvard University—our family's legacy school—I came to terms with my position when Baz saved my ass from being thrown out due to lack of focus. As a Steele didn't get me accepted, I'm smarter than the average guy. But I slipped when once again I was in my older brother's shadow.

My come-to-Jesus moment occurred when Baz laid it all out on the table. He had no interest in competing with me, controlling me, or clashing with me. His purpose being to look after his younger siblings and do well by our family name. He urged me to work with him and not against him as I had for years.

I got everything off of my chest as we shared some Jackson Special Blend Scotch in his off-campus loft apartment one night. The fact he offered the liquor to me despite my age put him in the cool category for the first time in our lives. It loosened my tongue, and we resolved our issues—or rather mine.

The next weekend I flew to New York for a session with a tattoo artist famous for his intricate designs. He morphed the wings on my back into a work of art that wraps around my shoulders to my pecs like a mantle. The wings still represent my freedom and flight, but the additional design elements blend with them to serve as a reminder of my responsibilities to my family and to STEELE International, Inc.

I reapplied myself to my studies from undergrad through Harvard Business School to graduate with honors at the top of my class both times. Combined with my summer internships over the years, I was more than ready to join our family's company upon graduation.

Every one of the successive positions led to my current role, along with being the Second Vice President of the Board.

Each sibling works at STEELE and has board positions: Sebastian, president of the Retail Properties Division and First VP; Roger, president of the Residential Properties Division and Third VP; Harris and Haley, fraternal twins, co-founders of the subsidiary STEELE Technology and Cyber Security and Members.

At the moment, our father serves as CEO and Chairman of the Board. He trusts Baz to carry our legacy into the future and my younger brothers, sister, and I respect him and accept his leadership.

Fortunately, Baz and I grew past my teenage angst to develop a close relationship. We've come a hell of far since my wild days.

Although I still enjoy my adventurous activities. Excursions happen around my work schedule with Lucien, Anton Alexeyev—my Vice President of Development and college friend—and his cousin Borya *The War Defender* Alexeyev, my personal trainer and former MMA champion. Now I control my fighting, no longer chaotic with the MMA fights I take part in regularly to blow off steam.

Harris nicknamed me *The Enforcer* from my lethal fighting skills and for my no-nonsense, take-care-of-it attitude.

So while Baz is the leader and Roger the responsible one, I've become the guy everyone comes to get shit done... Or corrected.

The thought brings my mind back to the present and my reason for being at LEVELS New York tonight and not my usual Dominant/submissive scene with my current sub, Vicky Reynolds. Although who I'm meeting would most definitely be a sub I'd like under my palm.

My guest being Sebastian's former girlfriend/sub Lola Lewis. However, not former in his mind... And I'll use her request to meet as a means of correction for him.

One night six months ago, Sebastian and Lola literally bumped into each other at LEVELS New York. Then by chance Lola turned out to be the owner of the Paris-based luxury lingerie company Baz had a meeting with the next morning at STEELE. Lola's expansion plans for her Lola's

Coterie turned into an expansion of her sexual desires with the Alpha Dom.

Yeah, Baz and I have more in common than our doppelgänger looks.

Somehow he fucked up, and here I am to fix things. Naturally.

My chuckle catches in my throat when I glimpse Lola strutting off of the elevator. She captivates more than my attention as several heads—male and female—turn to track her path across the floor.

Lola stuns in a black, long-sleeved mini dress side knotted with a plunging neckline. Her magnificent tits play hide and seek with the soft fabric. The draping follows the natural curves of her body elegantly. Its hem skims her upper thighs, lengthening Lola's petite frame. Her toned legs end in nude fuck-me sandals.

I slam back my Scotch and rise from the barstool. Time to save the lucky prick's relationship.

"I'm here to meet Mr. Malcolm Steele for dinner—"

"Lola, good to see you," I interject as she speaks to Tabitha, who's eyes dim when she sees my sexy AF dinner guest.

I don't harbor any intimate attraction to Lola. My hard limit of no involvement with my brothers' or friends' partners—current or past—stops my cock from coming to life. Despite Lola's beauty, it's a definite hell no.

She tilts her head back to reach my eyes and smiles warmly.

"Malcolm, good to see you, too," Lola trills.

A less enthusiastic Tabitha leads us to our table in the center of the dining area, perfectly situated with an unobstructed view of the large room and of the bar. A spot from which I can easily observe all the patrons and the staff. I may be here for personal reasons, but I can keep an eye out on my business too.

The bar and dining room bustle as usual with the crème de la crème of society. They hobnob with top-shelf drinks and eat Continental cuisine of pastas, meat, and steaks with favorable sauces crafted by Lucien.

My gaze alights on several recognizable faces enjoying nightcaps at the bar area's high-top tables or savoring the dishes. Tonight, the box office hit action movie actor and his wife, a former senator of Connecticut, and a high-powered female CEO of an online shopping conglomerate represent some members and guests. The club caters to the most wealthy and influential in society. They prefer the relative safety that one can expect from the ironclad nondisclosure agreement that LEVELS requires every member and their guests to sign.

Membership offers two options: Global All Access or Dine/Dance. GAAs can choose from any of the seven levels: 7th Sky Lounge that offers a stunning, 360-degree view of Manhattan and across the Hudson River to New Jersey's shoreline, a bar, restaurant by day dance club by night, a coverable pool that's open during the warmer months, and a glass-retractable roof; 6th and 5th multilevel dance club with two bars and a lounge for food and drinks; 4th Level 4 Restaurant and bar open for breakfast, lunch, and dinner; 3rd has twelve private suites for members to continue their pleasure apart from the BDSM levels; 2nd Peepshow for BDSM with seating alcoves, primary stage, mini-stages, performance rooms, and a bar that serves non-alcoholic mocktails; below ground the Cellar a BDSM dungeon with mocktails bar. The DD members only have access to the party levels— Sky Lounge, Dance Club, and Level 4 Restaurant.

Like the other members, my brothers and I seek

LEVELS New York for the solution our bodies crave. We're Global All Access Members. Other than Haley, who we forbid membership. Our baby sister in a BDSM club? Errr… Hell no!

We're all guilty of not having longstanding relationships. Our work to increase STEELE International's success as the next generation takes most of our time. All of us, including our sister Haley, commit at least ten hours a day on business. In Sebastian's case, it's fourteen hours. We put pressure on ourselves, but he does it even more. I'm not far behind with thirteen. We're not left with enough time a relationship requires.

Although I make time for my sub. I prefer commitments of three to four months at a time or until they get too clingy. As with my current sub, Vicky. Fortunately she's bicoastal, so we see each other a couple of times a month.

Women are more than willing to have a one-night tryst or a few months with one of the STEELE Quaternity, as the media has labeled my brothers and me. They've dubbed us the most sought-after of the world's eligible billionaires. Our near-limitless wealth, power, and good looks attract women like bees to honey. They clamor for a taste, if only for one night.

I dispel thoughts of Vicky to focus on Lola. She slides into the chair I hold out for her, then I sit across the table. We exchange pleasantries before we place our orders.

Once the server leaves, Lola tosses her lustrous ebony hair over her shoulder and leans forward to pin me with her hazel eyes fringed with long lashes.

"I have a business offer for you, Malcolm," she says as her eyes glitter.

For a second, I choke on my sip of Pellegrino. What the everlasting fuck?!

Lola giggles and claps her hands in glee.

"Okay, you have my attention. But do know, I value my life and will not tangle with you, vixen," I tease with a smirk, wiping the sparkling water from my lips. Baz trains with Borya too.

She places a hand over her heart and raises her other hand in the air as she grins.

"I swear to not inflict you with bodily harm by your brother, Captain Caveman," Lola laughs.

We chuckle as the server sets our appetizers on the table between us.

Over our meal, Lola explains her thirtieth birthday trip to Laucala—a private island in Fiji—for a fitness retreat a couple of months ago. She raves about the location, classes, and the instructors.

I listen politely, unsure of the direction she's taking. Does she want me to tell Sebastian to take her back there for a makeup holiday? Does she think I need a vacation? My head nods automatically as I eat my main course.

"—Starr is phenomenal! We're so much alike being driven to succeed with our businesses, in our early thirties, and only kids." Lola gushes.

"Wonderful," I respond, partially in response to Lola and to the delicious Shrimp Oreganata.

Lola narrows her eyes and purses her lips.

"Maybe this will keep your attention, Malcolm," she huffs before she continues. "Starr plans to expand her center, Starr Light Fitness & Wellness Beverly Hills, into international fitness retreats at luxury resorts around the globe and to open a location in the Caribbean to start. She wants a partner. Just like Lola's Coterie did with STEELE International. Get it?"

Lola ends on a triumphant smirk.

Now, she has my attention.

Fitness? Could be conducive to my new venture with

Lucien and his older sister Lydie, who is second in command to their father Connor at Jackson Corporation. Our latest project Jackson Hole at STEELE Resorts concept is a members-only, high-end beach clubs for the jet set. It's my second foray with clubs in co-ownership with Lucien. Basically, Jackson Hole is LEVELS on the beach minus the BDSM.

A fitness and wellness center could offer more amenities for JHSR and placed within one of our STEELE resorts, increase activities for guests. Fascinating.

I thank Lola for the introduction, then it's my turn to lean forward.

"You… Sebastian. Tell me how to make the two of you work again?"

Lola crumbles a bit in her seat. Her eyes lose their glitter as she glances down to adjust the linen napkin on her lap. She sighs and raises her gaze back to mine.

By the time she finishes her side of their captivating story and swears me to secrecy, I have the mind to box Sebastian upside his thick head. Seriously, bro? I wonder to myself.

To Lola, I give her tips on how to handle my brother. Tips I learned from years of being around him and the women with whom he's had brief encounters. He's a playboy who never settles with one woman for longer than a night or two.

I can tell his feelings for Lola are on a different level. Now speaking with her and witnessing the gut-wrenching hurt in her eyes, I know she cares deeply for Baz too.

When we stand outside of LEVELS New York, I give Lola a squeeze and promise to not say a word to Baz and to contact Starr tomorrow afternoon. I help Lola into her chauffeur-driven Bentley Bentayga SUV and wave as they pull off.

I duck inside the back seat of my Bentley Mulsanne Duo-tone in platinum and black as my driver Oscar Carrera holds the door open.

As we weave through the evening traffic of Manhattan heading north along the West Side Highway to my penthouse on the fifty-third floor of The STEELE Tower, I stare out the window. My mind goes over the conversation and the emotions that rolled off of Lola in waves.

I sense she loves Baz truly and neither of them know how to deal with their unchartered relationship as they explore D/s for her. But it's deeper.

If Baz is on the verge of love at thirty-five, should I reconsider my relationship status since it's not as fulfilling as in the past?

A vibration and buzz from my trousers pocket bring me back to the sedan. I withdraw my mobile and glance at the screen. The glow in the dim interior reveals a text message from Vicky.

Sir, I miss you.

I click the video link and my lower head takes over.

Vicky lies on her bed spread-eagle with a blindfold over her cornflower blue eyes. Nipples pointed peaks atop her DD mounds. Her soaked pussy glistens with her juices in the candlelight.

"Oscar, change in plans. Take me to Vicky's, thanks," I say into the sedan's intercom as I adjust my burgeoning erection, then type my response.

Do not touch yourself, or I will punish you, Little Pet...

I chuckle to myself.

Nah! I'm good!

STARR

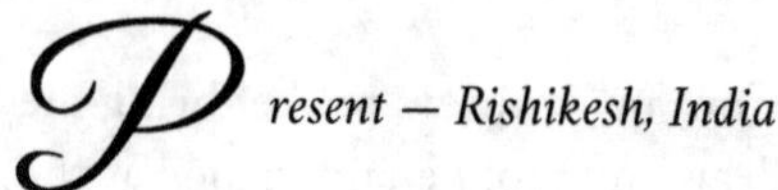

resent — Rishikesh, India

"Starr, you've been distracted since you arrived a few days ago. Do you want to talk about it?"

I lift my gaze from the lunch bowl to Ganika Mishra, my yoga teacher and friend of eighteen years. Her obsidian-colored eyes fill with concern, drawing a frown on her lovely face.

Ganika can read me as clearly as she interprets *The Yoga Sutras of Patanjali.*

We met eighteen years ago when my parents brought me to Rishikesh, India for my thirteenth birthday. Ganika was the youngest teacher at twenty-one years old. So the lead teacher of the ashram thought it best I pair up with Ganika. Since then, we've been close.

Nothing gets past her.

I knew she sensed my concentration was off center. Being polite, she didn't pry.

Now, as we eat lunch on the ashram's terrace overlooking the Ganges River, Ganika peers at me.

My thoughts wander to the night a few weeks ago.

"Damn, Starr, you feel so good, baby. Unh... Unh... Unh."

Quinn Peters, my boyfriend, if you will, of six months grinds and groans on top of me in my bed. His chocolate brown eyes roll back in his head in pure ecstasy.

One-sided ecstasy, that is...

Me? I'm staring at the ceiling praying to God and to every deity in every religion's pantheon Quinn will just cum already.

No matter how many times we've had sex, it's never satisfying for me. Foreplay: kiss mouth, lick one nipple, ram inside my pussy. My barely wet pussy, to be exact.

"Fuuuuck! Yeah, baby! That's how you like it, huh?"

"No."

Holy mackerel, you could hear a dandelion puff drop on the surface of a puddle.

What the heck? Did I just admit it out loud???

Quinn stops in the middle of an unimpressive thrust, the tip of his so-so dick halfway in and halfway out of me. He zooms in on my face with his legal-eagle eyes.

I squeeze mine shut and pray to fall through the mattress. Get swallowed up by the bedding.

A single bead of sweat rolls off the tip of Quinn's nose to land between my eyes.

My lips press together to hold back my groan—not one of pleasure, but one of disgust. Yuck.

After a century passes, more likely less than thirty seconds, Quinn breaks the tense silence.

"What did you just say, Starr?"

He's all attorney in the courtroom with me now.

I take a deep cleansing breath, then open my eyes to face the situation.

"I said, 'No,' Quinn," I respond, staring back up at him. His

scowl urges me to continue before he speaks. "I need more. Let's try something different."

Using the strength of my core and leg muscles, I flip us over. I straddle his narrow hips and grind down on his dick. My eyes close as I throw my head back, then pinch and tug the aching nipples of my heavy breasts.

"Drive up into me, Quinn. Hard! I want you to take me!" I tell him, wishing to ease the pressure built up in me after so many nights of dissatisfaction.

After a moment, I notice he's still as a stone statue.

My bouncing ends abruptly. I squint my eyes to peek at him through my lashes. Yup, he's checked out. Great.

With an exaggerated sigh, I roll off of Quinn onto my back to stare at the ceiling... again. This is simply not working for me.

My parents introduced us years ago since he's an attorney at their law firm. They thought we'd have a lot in common.

I finally gave in to his dinner requests, then to spending time with him. Finally, we started seeing each other. The sex began shortly thereafter. Not at all what I expect or want.

I need more, and Quinn can't give it to me.

Without going into the details of my desire for a man who will take me roughly and satisfy my needs, I tell Ganika Quinn and I broke up.

She listens without judgement, then reminds me how everything happens for a reason. I can't allow myself to lose focus by dwelling on what's not meant to be in my life.

As always, she gives me sage advice. The rest of my stay goes smoothly. I enjoy my lessons and time with my friend and others at the ashram. By the end of my stay, I'm back on track and feeling centered.

✻ ✻ ✻

"Oh, yes, another thing. Anton Alexeyev the Vice Present of Development for STEELE International, Inc.'s Entertainment Properties Division called twice. He wants to schedule a meeting with you and his boss regarding your expansion project."

Adrienne Anthony—my CMO and General Manager of my Starr Light Fitness & Wellness Beverly Hills—tells me with an exaggerated eye roll and air quotes for his title. Mr. Alexeyev must not impress my best friend of eight years.

We met at Stanford Graduate School of Business. Everyone referred to us as Night & Day since we contrasted in our appearances and attitudes. From our long, curly hair with Adrienne's light brown and mine dark brown to her green feline eyes and my sorrel brown angelic eyes to her buttery pecan-colored skin and mine the color of warm chestnuts. I have dimples to her sharp cheekbones. But we're both five feet, six inches with curvy fit bodies from our years of yoga, Pilates, and strength training as certified teachers and students.

Again alike with our hippie vibes, independent nature, and outgoing bubbly personalities. We're loyal and open to a fault. Resourceful and trustworthy round out our traits.

Where Adrienne has a tattoo of a peacock wrapped around her foot up her ankle to symbolize success, I have shooting stars on the back of my neck for wishes.

We hit it off immediately at Stanford.

I followed my parents' footsteps to their alma mater. Undergrad I received a degree in economics from Stanford University, then continued on to the B-School. Not exactly the Law School. But I wanted to forge my path. Health and wellness became my focus after my first trip to Rishikesh. It helped me to regroup from the taunts of the It Girls in junior high school. Then stayed with me through adulthood.

I wanted to combine my love of wellness with helping others. So I opened my center six years ago at 25. It was my initial goal. Now, I want to expand into international fitness retreats at luxury resorts and add a second center location in the Caribbean. The Fiji retreat was a test run.

And a good thing since I met Lola Lewis. As she promised, she made the connection for me to STEELE. So despite Adrienne's eye roll, I'm super psyched!

"Yeah? Awesome! When is he available?" I ask, clapping my hands.

After Lola told me about STEELE, I Googled the company and understood what she meant about the partnership opportunities. Although everyone knows of STEELE, I wanted to get the details on their resorts specifically.

Besides the opulent properties and their many locations around the globe, the corporate headshot of the division's president captured my attention.

Malcolm Steele.

I bet he's a man who can take control of the boardroom and of a woman in the bedroom.

His gray eyes zinged me from my tablet screen, setting my nether regions afire. The full lips and angular jaw coupled with his thick, tousled ebony hair had me squirming in my bed. I researched him the night Lola told me she'd make the introduction.

The tropical temperature of Fiji didn't compare to the heat coursing through my body.

Sadly, I noticed he's with different women in every social photo on the Internet. Labeled a member of the STEELE Quaternity didn't help.

At least my libido cooled when I noticed he's a playboy. I've had enough with self-centered men.

Now, I take a deep breath when I feel the heat rise once again at the thought of Malcolm Steele.

Down, Starr!

"Well, the meeting will be with him and his boss... Malcolm Steele," Adrienne says as she swipes her finger on her tablet to retrieve the boss' name. "But he's traveling out of the country now. Alexeyev said something about Positano—"

Adrienne continues on for another hour, catching me up to the happenings at the center while I was in India.

I listen attentively. But on the edges of my mind, I wonder how a man like Malcolm Steele compares to a man like Quinn.

Malcolm Steele has such confidence and exudes dominance and power. Granted, Quinn is a shark in the courtroom and even in the bedroom, just not enough to satisfy me. His needs come first.

Even now, weeks after I broke up with him, he can't let go.

Ego. Give it a rest.

I chuckle to myself when I remember Quinn's reaction to my vinyasa flow class I invited him to early in our relationship. He couldn't get into the asanas like others around him. So he flounced out of the class before it was over.

Ah well. Let it go, like Ganika said.

"—I told her you may be tired from the return flight, but she insisted on coming in for a private session with you. It's in an hour."

I shake my head to clear my thoughts of men to focus on my business. No more salivating over Malcolm Steele or replaying Quinn's antics.

"I apologize, Adrienne. My mind wandered. Who's coming in for a session now?" I ask sheepishly.

"Vicky Reynolds," Adrienne replies with another giant eye roll.

A giggle bursts from between my lips.

Adrienne cannot stand Vicky. She thinks the Hollywood royalty actress is beyond annoying. She tends to name-drop her great-grandfather the founder of a movie studio, her father a major producer, and her mother a screen siren. At all costs, Adrienne avoids Vicky.

After two years of her being a client, to me she's like a little sister. Albeit a petite, blonde-haired, blue-eyed sister from another mother. Four years younger than my thirty-one, her acting career and travels make her worldly. But she appears to look up to me. Often asking my advice. It could be the yogi tenets I share in my dharma talks. I shake my head and tune back into Adrienne.

I'm surprised they even spoke since Adrienne has instructed the front desk staff to handle Vicky's requests.

"Fine, I'll see her in my studio," I respond with a chuckle. "Let me know when she gets here."

"Namaste."

"Namaste."

No sooner than I straighten from my bow to the light in her, Vicky starts in on her latest "scene" with her Dom.

"Oh, Starr! It's just so incredible the way my Dom makes my body tingle and crave his command! I flew back from New York on a pillow from the spanking he gave to me. You know"—Vicky glances around my private studio as though others may overhear her next words—"I didn't obey his command to not touch myself before he made me come on purpose. I just love the way he punishes me! It's the best fuck ever—"

My mind wanders again as I visualize me with a Dom as incredible as Vicky's.

I've never been in a D/s relationship, but after six months of hearing Vicky brag about her latest Dom made me realize that's what's missing for me.

A man who will control me and bring me the maximum satisfaction possible. The erotic visions that play in my head have a definition. BDSM.

I live vicariously through Vicky since Quinn could never fulfill my desires. She's the only person I know in a D/s relationship. After she told me about it, I had to Google most of the words and activities she spoke about.

My research revealed most active participants in the scene don't discuss their lifestyle with non-players.

But like Adrienne says, Vicky loves to talk about herself. It's all about her.

The one thing she's never disclosed—and she's not in the least bit shy about telling me every minute detail—is the name of her Dom. Vicky told me she had to sign a contract for the terms of their D/s relationship and a nondisclosure agreement. She only hints at him being a powerful multibillionaire who's "to die for" in looks and in the bed. He infatuates her with his "ten-inch cock… The absolute biggest she's ever had."

By the time Vicky finishes, I'm as hot and bothered as she is with her face flushed and blue eyes so dilated they appear black.

However, I dismiss my unrestrained fantasies. No way will I find a man like her Dom. Besides, I'm not so sure I want the commitment she's in. The idea of a contract and an NDA throws cold water over my heated skin.

Vicky and I part ways at the elevator. She heads down to the locker room and spa. I go up to Adrienne's office to close out my day. The jet lag has me ready to crash.

We go over a few more items on her list before I head home for the day.

As I walk through the center, my heart swells with pride at my accomplishments. The classes stay full; clients have standing private sessions; the teachers enjoy being here; the rest of the staff go about their work happily.

The idea of a Caribbean location and regular international fitness retreats excites everyone. Requests for assignments started as soon as I voiced the ideas.

Just as important as my staff's elation, my parents' approval and acceptance of my separate journey ranks high for me.

They would have preferred I studied law and followed in their footsteps, then joined the family firm. But they under-stand my need to take my path. And my need to seek solace from turmoil when it rears its ugly head; something I carry over from junior high school.

It pleases me to hear clients get their relief through the services my fitness and wellness center provides. To extend my peace to them fills me with joy.

I wave to the front desk staff, concierge, and the boutique consultant before I exit the bliss of the center. The valet smiles and opens the door to my silver Tesla Model X Long Range. I bow my thanks with prayer hands, a custom we do each time.

When I arrive at my Benedict Canyon Drive mansion, I marvel at its brick walls, wood-beamed ceilings, stone-tiled flooring, and wood-burning fireplaces. The elements lend to its concrete and stone rustic appeal. The pool with cabana, tennis court, and manicured lawns appeal to my outdoor nature. My favorite pastime of meditation in the side garden amongst the fragrant flowers relaxes me after a day at the center.

But tonight, I bypass the soothing sounds of the fountain to head straight to my steam shower.

During the drive home, my mind returned to Vicky's boasts about her "Dom to die for." The fever ran through me again as my core clenched at the vision of a Dom capturing me with his silks bound around my wrists and ankles. Spread before his hungry eyes, my body quivers with the thrill of erotic possession.

I take a deep inhale under the rain shower's warm water.

The rivulets glide down my heated skin from my soaked curls, between my heavy breasts, over my bare mound. A trickle touches my folds, adding to the moisture of my needy pussy.

A fingertip brushes my engorged clit when I lift my foot to rest it atop the travertine bench. My eyes flutter closed as I tilt my head back and give in to the vision of the Dom spanking my beaded nipples and swollen lower lips.

My full bottom lip nearly splits as I bite down on it with a throaty moan. My Dom grips my hips as I undulate against the invasion of his rock-hard dick pounding my dripping pussy.

His massive girth and length force me to rise onto my toes. I slap the stone wall of the steamy shower for leverage and buck against him, matching each of his powerful thrusts.

"Take it, take it deep, Little Pet. You… belong… to… me," my Dom growls against the delicate shell of my ear, driving me closer to the edge.

The warmth of his skin on mine and the slickness of our wet bodies as he takes me roughly from behind makes me cum with a strangled scream.

As I press my forehead against the stone, my pants slow. But my mind still races.

I don't want to live vicariously. I don't want to just fantasize.

What do I want?

My Dom.

What throws me for a loop?

My Dom looks just like Malcolm Steele.

MALCOLM

The late afternoon sun reflects off the windows of the buildings along Fifty-seventh Street as I take a moment between calls to stare out the floor-to-ceiling windows of my office on the twenty-ninth floor of The STEELE Tower.

The modern, gray-tinted glass fifty-seven story mixed-use skyscraper on the southwest corner of Fifty-Seventh Street and Fifth Avenue. I'm on the executive level where my father, Sebastian, Roger, and I have office suites. Our finance and legal departments along with various conference rooms occupy the remaining space. The other divisions have designated floors below along with my younger siblings', twins Harris and Haley, STEELE Technology and Cyber Security.

From my office suite, the view of Manhattan stretches out before me unobstructed. Central Park to the north, the Hudson River to the west, the East River opposite, and the rest of northern Manhattan from Harlem to Inwood. On a beautiful, cloudless day like this morning, the panoramas are riveting.

The interior of The Tower reflects the metal our name represents. The decor—as sleek as the exterior—features platinum silk wall treatments, ebony wood floors, dove gray and white leather furniture, crystal light fixtures, Lucite tables, steel accents, and original artwork. The reception area has a spacious desk. Three attractive receptionists with headsets in their ears and custom-tailored light gray dress suits and skin-tone heels that serve as uniforms sit behind it.

The majesty of our family's power and wealth awes all who enter SI's offices.

After my respite, I swing my chair back to face my desk. Through the glass wall that separates my inner office from my administrative assistant's area, guests seating area, and conference room, I spy Sebastian with Lola as they walk past in the corridor.

Perfect timing. I can update Lola about the fitness center meeting and fuck with Baz.

With a devilish grin, I stand. Then adjust my navy blue striped suit vest and smooth the Full Windsor Knot of my platinum silk tie. A quick finger combing tousles my thick hair the way women adore. All to piss off Baz.

My long legs make quick work of the distance to the corridor, and I call out to my brother and Lola.

They detour into my outer office.

"Hey there, gorgeous!" I greet Lola with an embrace and Baz with a nod. Then wink at him over the top of her head before giving her a squeeze.

A growl falls from Sebastian's lips, and I laugh, releasing Lola from my hug.

"Good to see you again, Lola," I start with a twinkle in my eyes. "I spoke with Adrienne Anthony, Starr Knight's studio manager. Apparently Starr is out of the country at an ashram in India and unreachable. So, we must connect when she returns."

Baz's expression morphs from annoyed to confused.

"It's so good to see you again, too, Malcolm! Thank you for dinner. The—"

"Whaaat???" Baz yells, his eyes zip between Lola and me.

The cool, in-control Dom now completely off the grid.

Perfect! Just the reaction I wanted from him. He needs to value Lola and not be a giant dick to her. Someone needs to make him see how easily he could lose Lola to another man if he doesn't get his head out of his ass.

While Baz stands gobsmacked, I tell him about Lola's suggestion for me to meet with her friend. It's apparent he's not listening to me, still focused on my hands on Lola and the dinner she had with me. Too bad, bro. That'll learn ya.

He snaps his head in my direction when my words filter through what must be his nightmare—Lola as my sub.

I plow on, behaving obtuse on purpose. Maybe he'll catch up.

"—concept could fit well with our latest Jackson Hole venture. New amenities attract unique guests, while the regular ones find more reasons to keep coming back to stay. Once I meet with Ms. Knight, I'll fill you in."

Since a baffled expression lingers on Baz's face when I finish, I sigh dramatically, realizing that he wasn't paying him the least bit of attention after all.

"Get your head out of your ass, Baz. Lola and I had dinner last week to discuss business. B-U-S-I-N-E-S-S. Got it?" I admonish him "Lola met Starr Knight, the owner of the Beverly Hills-based fitness studio and wellness center Starr Light Fitness & Wellness. She plans to expand into international fitness retreats at luxury resorts and to add a second center location in the Caribbean. Lola told me about

Starr since she had an exceptional experience at her first retreat in Fiji on the private Laucala Island. Are we clear?"

Sebastian appears chastened and risks a peek at Lola to find her hazel eyes glowing warmly with suppressed laughter.

To add to his unease, I drape my arm around her shoulders as I join in her glee. How low can the Alpha male sink? I chuckle.

"Crystal clear, brother. Now, back off my girl. We're going to dinner," Baz chides to regain control.

Lola's eyes widen.

He frowns at her, then realizes he referred to Lola as his girl.

Oh boy.

Instead of addressing the term of endearment, Baz grasps Lola's hand and pulls her from my office.

"Have fun," I taunt with a mocking wave.

Baz throws a glare over his shoulder at me as he ushers Lola through the door.

I can't help myself. My booming laughter carries across the office suite.

Gotcha, big bro!

"Ready for this one, big guy? Or do you want to pussy out for the nine-thousand-foot jump instead?"

A sound that one may consider a laugh rumbles deep in Borya's chest in response to my taunt.

"*Da. Posmotrim, kto takaya kiska.*" He sneers as he slams his massive hands in front of his broad chest.

Anton chuckles and adds, "We all know it'll be Lucien who's the pussy in the end."

I glance over at Lucien *The Sexy Chef* as he's known by

his millions of social media followers. He does seem a bit green around the mouth and his eyes widen at the jabs.

Our crew sits aboard the skydiving plane over Fox Glacier in New Zealand. We're going for a twenty-thousand-foot jump. A glance out the windows and door offers stunning views of rainforests, lakes, mountains, glaciers, snowfields, and the Tasman Sea. The Westland National Park appears in the distance as we make our way to the jump point.

It's been six weeks since the four of us met up for one of our escapades.

The adrenaline pumps through my veins as I check my safety gear. I may be a thrill seeker, but living is my top priority.

The guide gives us last instructions. Then we line up to exit the plane one after the other for the drop zone 300 feet above sea level.

"Yeah, baby! Let's rock!" I yell as I fist bump Anton before he jumps out the door.

I turn to Lucien and give him a thumbs-up to check on him. No need to do something that will cause anxiety beyond the rush.

He nods and gives me the signal he's ready to go. Then gets in position.

Borya jumps next and does a crazy flip in the air. The wild Russian's laughter floats back as he soars through the clouds.

Up next, I go through my ritual to give thanks for my fearless friends, love to my family, and my safe finish. It's what I do before any of my extreme activities, even when I was a pain-in-the-ass teen. My rebel spirit still exists, but it's alongside my duty to family and self.

A thumbs-up to the guide, and I take my jump.

The air rushes past me as I hurtle through the clouds.

My blood races through my veins as my heart pumps with exhilaration.

A shit-eating grin stays plastered on my face as I free fall through the sky at 120 miles per hour. I take in the pristine beauty of New Zealand, awed by the natural landscape free of man's touch. The twenty-thousand feet give me eighty-five seconds to view it all.

I pull on my cords and float safely to the ground under my parachute. Years of experience allow me to land on my feet at a run.

Damn! That was spectacular!

The ground team hustles over to help me with the open parachute. They relieve me of my harness as I remove my helmet and goggles.

Once my heartbeat slows, I thank them for their help.

A screech draws my attention to the petite blonde running at top speed towards me. Instinctively, I catch her in my arms as she leaps into the air and clings to me like a baby monkey. She peppers my face with kisses as she squeals in delight.

"Sir! Are you all right? I was so scared! I hate when you do these crazy stunts!" Vicky exclaims holding my cheeks between her palms.

Her cornflower blue eyes search my face for any sign of distress. A scowl mars her pretty features as her eyebrows pull together and the corners of her mouth droop.

The rush of the jump has more than my blood pumping in my veins. My cock throbs, hard as steel. Nothing gets me more amped than a dangerous encounter. A dance with death. A fight to the end. Bring it.

Instead of answering her question or assuaging her fears, I slam my mouth against her pouty lips and kiss the breath out of her.

Vicky moans and melts into the onslaught of my demanding kiss.

Her soft sounds make my cock twitch and beg me to fuck her raw.

She must sense my need as she squeezes her inner thighs against my hips and rides my growing erection through my jumpsuit.

I allow her to have at me a bit longer before I take back the control. A swift slap to her ass has Vicky squealing for a reason other than my safety. Hers.

"Be still, Pet. Or need I remind you who is in charge?" I ask in my most dominant tone of voice.

Her shudder and the way she drops her widened eyes show Vicky understands her place in our D/s relationship.

"No, Sir," she whispers as her movements grind to an immediate halt.

On the one hand, I hate the loss of the friction against my aching dick. But on the other, she has to realize I'm in control.

Recently Vicky shifted into the realm of clingy and demanding. Asking where I've been if I don't respond to her text messages or phone calls… or emails. She gets surly when I tell her I'm not available to scene with her at LEVELS New York or at my penthouses in New York City or in West Hollywood. Going to her penthouses on Wilshire Boulevard or in TriBeCa are off limits. Too close to partner status.

She has my commitment as her Dom. Even longer than my usual three months now that it's been six.

For one, the bicoastal aspect makes our time together less consistent, so not boring. Then she's busy with her filming schedule and me with my work at STEELE. It's been conducive. But these last couple of months have been taxing.

Her requests for more time with me coupled with her ring innuendos make me want to run.

I may have an enormous member, but I'm not a dick. I can't just dump her because she's heading down the path we both said we didn't want at the onset of our contract.

Yeah. Contract.

I don't get involved with subs without one, plus a nondisclosure agreement. I need them to understand before we start the relationship is temporary—three months typically—and will not lead to marriage. It's to satisfy our sexual needs and proclivities mutually. Nothing more. And never to discuss it with anyone.

The sense that Vicky wants more haunts me, which is why I was hesitant for her to join the crew for our latest outing. I agreed reluctantly when she went on and on about not having gone to New Zealand before.

The sucker that I can be caved to her request. So here we are with Vicky in my arms and my dick eager to fuck her.

Go figure. I'm a virile male, so how can I say no?

"Good, Pet," I respond. "Go to the helicopter and wait for me."

Vicky slides to her feet, and I swat her ass in the tight ski pants that cling to her butt cheeks beneath her parka. She giggles and skips ahead.

"Okay then. Looks like your girl is overjoyed you landed safely."

A glance to my right reveals Lucien smirking at me as he runs his hands through cropped, dark brown hair. His emerald green eyes shine as his dimples pop onto his annoying face.

Not my *girl*.

I swipe at him with my foot, but he jumps and lands his own roundhouse kick. Not enough to harm me, merely to get me away from him.

We laugh good-naturedly then follow Vicky to the Sikorsky S-92 Executive Helicopter where Anton and Borya wait with the pilot.

Still hyped from the exhilarating jump, I sit in the back two seats with my hand between Vicky's thighs. I slip my fingers between her wet and puffy folds to stroke her clit. The tips brush just inside of her pussy, enough to get her juices to flow without an orgasm.

As she moans softly with her teeth in her plump lower lip, I keep her on the edge for the duration of the thirty-minute flight. Vicky thrives on exhibitionism. The risk of being caught proves her adrenaline rush.

The crew and I rented a house nearby as a base for our five-day trip. The less time between the two locations, the better for our plan to sky dive, ice climb, and to hike the glacier. It's only day one, and I can't wait for the rest.

Vicky chokes on a sob when I withdraw my soaked fingers for her pulsating pussy one last time before we disembark.

I smirk at her. Then lick my fingers clean off her sweet juices.

She wanted to interlope on my Guys' Trip.

Well, let's play.

Vicky rushes—beside herself—to the awaiting Mercedes-Benz G-Wagens. Her eagerness makes her hips and ass sway enticingly. They're like a Siren's Song to grip them and bury my thick girth balls deep inside her willing body.

My dick jumps in appreciation. I run my fingers under my nose to inhale the remnants of her sweet essence. Yeah, we'll have some fun as soon as I get her in the bedroom and tied to the makeshift St. Andrew's Cross with a blindfold.

And a crop.

·   ·   ·

"—I know... Yes, not much longer... Mmm hmmm... Mother! I know how much he's worth! I said I'll get the ring, didn't I... No, Malcolm can't hear me. He's in the shower... Hell! I'm doing all the kinky shit he wants me to do! Do not dare talk to me like I'm not doing my part... Well... His giant cock up my little ass for starters—"

In a rage, I snatch Vicky's mobile from her ear and jab my finger on the screen to end the call. The pressure I put on the device almost cracks the screen.

WHAT THE ABSOLUTE FUCKING FUCK?!?!?!

Through the red haze of my vision, Vicky cowers on the bed with her mouth agape. She sits as stunned by my outburst as she is in me overhearing her conversation. A conversation that never should have taken place given the ironclad nondisclosure agreement she signed.

The steam from the shower I just finished resembles a puff compared to the fire streaming from my nose. If this were a movie, I'd be a fucking dragon about to sear the maiden.

Except Vicky is no maiden. The lascivious liar.

Now it all makes sense.

When we first met at a dungeon party, she didn't come across as a sub, but she played coy when I made innuendos about her participation in the lifestyle. Not at all turned off. The second time we did a scene with her bound to a spanking bench for edge play, followed by a rough fuck with multiple toe-curling orgasms for her. All within Vicky's approved limits. She didn't balk. She went into subspace...

I took her word and trust.

Dumbass.

Vicky's recent hints towards a commitment beyond our contract I extended from the original three months then the marriage bomb of "I'm ready to settle down with you" had me on high alert.

But this? Telling her mother about our sexual activities and plotting to bamboozle me?

She's in it for the money. Of course.

Fuck this!

"Get dressed and packed"—I raise my hand to stop Vicky from speaking—"You will leave as soon as the crew prepares the Sikorsky. A ticket to LAX will be ready for you when you land at Hokitika Airport. The crew will give you the airline and your mobile before they leave you."

I stride to the nightstand to grab my mobile, then leave the bedroom without another word. A swipe of my hand over my face brings me back into control.

Down in the living room, a quick call to the pilot and to Miles Crawford—my administrative assistant—finalizes the details for Vicky's immediate departure.

Anton struts into the room laughing with the brunette he met at the bar last night. One glance at me standing in nothing but a towel and a scowl, and he tells the woman to wait for him in the kitchen.

"What happened?" Anton asks, his Russian accent creeping in as it does when he becomes agitated.

In fluent Russian I fill him in, and a string of curses fall from his mouth. His glacial blue eyes turn frostier. Anton runs his hands through his long blond hair and growls.

"Motherfucker!"

A gasp from the entryway draws our attention.

Vicky stands there in my cashmere sweater. She shifts from one bare foot to the other as her wide eyes dart between the brawny Russian and me nervously. She opens her mouth to speak, but I cut her off.

"The car will take you in ten minutes. Unless you want to travel as you appear, I suggest you go upstairs, change, and pack. My attorneys will contact you upon your return to Los Angeles."

By the end, the last word is a growl deeper than Anton's. My control thins.

He glances at me, then turns to Vicky as he points to his Rolex Cosmograph Daytona.

"Eight minutes, *dorogoy*," Anton sneers in a voice dripping with disdain.

Tears pop from Vicky's eyes as a cry escapes her lips. She scans my face for any sign of forgiveness.

I blank my expression and square my shoulders. I will not fall for her melodramatic act.

This shit is O-V-E-R.

"*L*eonie… Hello there… Leonie?"

I use my voice to bring her back to our meditation session gently.

She shakes her head to clear what must be distractions. Then opens her eyes to see me, Lola, Haley, Blair, and Billie peeping at her. Leonie's golden-caramel cheeks redden as she laughs in embarrassment.

The biracial Parisian megamodel stuns in person with her lustrous mane of mahogany wavy hair pulled into a topknot. Feline amber eyes, angular cheekbones, and a sleek body ending in long, toned legs to die for prove she's *The Lion* of the catwalk.

Lola told me she was coming to Beverly Hills for business but was taking some time to hang out with her girlfriends. It's the first time I met her BFF Leonie Beaulieu, Haley Lola's boyfriend and Malcolm Steele's sister, and Blair Thomas and Billie Chandler Lola's administrative assistants.

Their first stop to jumpstart their girls' time was to Starr Light Fitness & Wellness Beverly Hills for yoga and meditation classes. Since Lola and I met at my Fijian Laucala Island retreat, she's raved about her experience and how cool of an instructor I am to her friends and associates. Many who live here and those who are in town come to the center for classes or private sessions with me. So it's a straightforward decision for Lola and friends to come while we're here.

Since they wanted to leave the stresses of life behind, I structured a vinyasa that requires concentration. To focus on the breath synched with the movement of the asanas creates the best means to prevent one's mind from wandering.

Naturally, they tuned into their breath and the sequence of challenging asanas I used in the flow. The vigorous physical and mental workout was just what they needed as opposed to the slower pace of a Hatha class. My dynamic teaching style made it fun.

Lola mentioned her best friend was going through some guy problems, so I won't push Leonie too far. I can understand completely.

Quinn calls and sends text messages to me. He even stopped by here unannounced. Adrienne dealt with him while I hid in the staff room.

I doubt he wants to get back together for us, rather to soothe his ego. He's all, "Come on, Starr, call me back. We can make this work."

Seriously? *Make this work*? Like we're some case he has to win. Give me a break already.

He's really pushing my balance off kilter. Ugh!

Then Vicky has been glum the past couple of months. Her Dom broke up with her unexpectedly. What a jerk! She didn't reveal her usual details, just that their time ended. She seemed so pitiful.

My heart broke for her.

The world of men has gone crazy…

I return my focus to Leonie and offer her a warm smile.

"No judgement…!" I say as I join in her laughter.

What else can women do but take their antics in stride? We sure as hell can't murder them! The ludicrous thought makes me giggle as we leave my studio.

After a few minutes in the steam room and a quick shower, we head to lunch at nearby Crustacean Beverly Hills. The modern Vietnamese fare specialties include delicious seafood that's the perfect light meal after yoga.

We settle on the gray suede seats at a banquette near the Walk on Water. The path runs from the front door through the restaurant between tables. Interspersed with wood and weight-bearing glass, the water below appears to offer a glimpse of the ocean's depths. Aside from the cuisine, the path is the eatery's highlight.

When the server arrives, we order An Sum—Crustacean's version of dim sum—to share and salads for our meals.

"Have you spoken to Malcolm Steele, yet?" Lola asks me.

"No, we keep playing phone tag. Right now he's it!" She laughs. "I was unreachable in India, then traveled a few more weeks. He was away on business, followed by a holiday in Italy."

Lola grins like the Cheshire Cat, and her hazel eyes dance with delight.

I giggle in response. She's so silly! Then I get it.

"Oh, well, you see…"

Exaggeratedly, Lola brushes her left hand against her cheek. She must have removed her ring for the class and locked it in the safe at the center.

Now, it's my turn for my eyes to bug out of my head as the light bounces off of the gigantic diamond nearly blinds me.

"Holy shit! Are you serious with me right now? That's humongous!"

My quiet calm, namaste, om, center your mind blows clear out of the water.

Lola and the girls giggle at my reaction. The server places our drinks on the table with a smile, enjoying our mirth.

Well, all righty then!

"Here's to the woman who got her man!" I raise my sparking water in a toast.

Lola smiles graciously at us as we raise our glasses to her happiness.

The grin on my face spreads just as wide. I'm thankful for her benevolence and for including me in her circle of friends. It's nice to have a group of women who get along, support one another, and have each others' best interests in mind. I raise my glass even higher and offer my cheers.

Once we clamor over her proposal and details of her upcoming nuptials end, Lola explains how I want to expand my business. She tells everyone my plan to include regular fitness retreats at five-diamond resorts around the world, preferably in unique locales. Fiji was just the start.

Then she tells them about Malcolm as head of STEELE's Entertainment Properties Division oversees their hotels and resorts. He could help me with a partnership.

"So at some point, I'd love to get on his calendar. Ha! Or on my mat! Give him a taste of what he's missing."

Suddenly Leonie laughs so hard she snorts.

Surprised at her reaction, I gaze at her, befuddled. And turn to Lola, who also looks confused.

Leonie clears her throat and smiles.

"What you said about getting him on your mat and showing him what he's missing sounds like a double entendre. Especially when the Steele men are involved!"

Lola cracks up and can't stop.

Even I laugh, now clear on the cause of Leonie's hysteria.

She's in a bit of a way with Roger and a guy she dates off and on named Giovanni Mattei. Now there's a story!

"Yes," Haley starts. "My brothers can be a bit much, I must admit. Trust me, growing up with them and observing the hordes of women falling all over them was sickening!"

We laugh some more until the server swaps our appetizers for our main dishes. Silence descends on the table as we replenish our stores after our workout.

"*D'accord*, where do we go for our Girls' Not Out?" Leonie asks.

"The latest hot club to open is the Remy West Hollywood," Billie, who knows all the West Coast happenings responds. "Their It thing is dancers bound by ropes Shibari style suspended from the ceiling. It has a BDSM vibe, if you know what I mean."

She giggles and wiggles her eyebrows up and down.

Lola and Leonie glance at each other, then snort.

I have to hold back on my laughter. Do they take part in such activities? And if so, do Sebastian and Roger? Because being Malcolm's brothers... Does he?

Leonie laughs uncontrollably, and the sound pulls me from my wistful thinking.

"What did I say?" Billie asks, confused.

"Oh, Billie, nothing! It's aah... How do you say... graphic!" Leonie giggles. "Let's meet at eleven in the lobby. *Oui?*"

Billie nods, accepting my save.

"What are you wearing?" Haley asks. "I have a black mini dress or a light blue sequin romper."

Fortunately, the conversation switches to a safer topic. Blair chimes in on how well the light blue would contrast with Haley's gray eyes and ebony hair. Meanwhile, Lola's eyes still twinkle with glee.

* * *

My girls and I sit in the VIP area of the Remy West Hollywood. Billie was right. This is a hot spot. The Shibari tied dancers hover inches above the crowd. The colorful silken cords artfully swathe their long, toned limbs. They blindfolded some. While others stare boldly at the revelers. The dungeon-like atmosphere adds to the BDSM theme. It's first time at any place that resembles a sex club.

As I glance around the room, my body tingles as it wonders what it would feel like to have the silks binding me. No movement or escape from the erotic acts inflicted upon me. My nipples tighten and my pussy clenches just from the thought. Damn…

"Time to get our groove on one more time, Ladies!" Blair announces as she pulls Billie to her feet. "Let's go. No time to decorate the banquette!"

My reverie fades, and the Remy replaces my fantasy. I shake my head to push the vestiges away.

She's right. We've been dancing and drinking for the past three and a half hours. Girls' Night Out is fun. We enjoy each other's company and our drinks. I finish the last of my cocktail and join my friends on the dance floor. I'm going to make the most out of our GNO, too.

I slam back the last of my mojito cocktail, then follow the girls to the dance floor.

The DJ's music and callouts have everyone bouncing to the beat. I throw my hands up and shake my hips in my silver chain-mail micro mini dress. It's front drapes to my cleavage and the back scoops to the top of my ass. Only a tiny g-string covers my bare mound. Silver Swarovski crystal five-inch sandals adorn my feet, making my shapely legs go on forever. I work hard on my body and have no qualms about showing it off.

"The DJ plays the best music!" Blair says as she bumps her hip against Leonie's side.

Blair flips her chestnut brown hair over her shoulder as she twirls on the dance floor. Her cerulean blue eyes like her ice-blue sequin mini dress sparkle in the lights. She catches the attention of a few guys who make their way over to us.

"Hello there, beautiful," one of them says as he bends down to my ear. His warm breath brushes the delicate shell. I shiver in response.

He's taller than me, so I lift my gaze to take him in. He's an attractive model type—strawberry blond hair, jade-colored eyes, lean build. Why hello there…

I smirk and turn my back to him while I continue to dance. No need to appear eager.

Undeterred, he places his hands on my hips and pulls up behind me. His body melds to mine—hard against soft.

"Where do you think you're going, Beauty?" he rasps in my ear. "No getting away from me."

We move to the sensuous pulse of the music. His hands don't wander, only tighten their grip as he bends his knees to align his groin to my ass.

Mmmmmm.

I just want to dance and have a good time. So I let the handsome stranger move us to the beat. After a while, he twirls me around and with bent knees; he grinds his pelvis into mine. The sensation of his hard dick against my ass makes my pussy clench on air and ache for him to fill it.

Already keyed up from my earlier fantasy, I squeeze my thighs together. The need overwhelms me.

We move as one, glued together for a few songs. His lips nuzzle my neck, and I angle my head to allow him more access. My hands rest on top of his broad shoulders, fingers entwined in his shoulder-length hair. His hands flex to grip me possessively. As the next tune begins, he murmurs in my ear.

"Come on, Beauty, time for us to head out."

I glance around to find the other girls. No way will I leave without checking in with them. I notice Lola wrapped in a tight embrace with a dark-haired, sinfully sexy man. It can only be her fiancé Sebastian grinding with her. I hadn't seen him arrive. They look so good together, like they belong with no one else. Lost in their own world.

That's what I want. Not some guy I meet at the club and go home with for a one-night stand. I've only had three lovers, and all in committed relationships. As much as I want to explore my erotic sexual needs, I'm not willing to go the wham-bam-thank-you-ma'am route.

If you believe, it will happen.

So with a deep, cleansing breath, I shake my head and slip from the hottie's embrace.

"Don't leave me like this, Beauty," he groans.

I step away and give him an apologetic smile.

He nods disappointedly and strides away.

I turn and make my way through the crowd to Billie, Blair, and Haley. They're dancing not too far from Lola and Sebastian. The girls cheer when I reach them.

Moments later, Sebastian strides away from Lola. He leaves her standing with her mouth hanging open. She glances from him to us, apparently torn between her man and her friends. She hesitates.

"Go! Be with your boo!" Billie laughs in her Southern Belle accent and shoos her hands at Lola.

With her wavy, medium-blonde balayage hair and pecan-colored skin, Billie reminds me of Tyra Banks' doppelgänger. Billie is curvy like the megamodel, but a petite version at five feet, four inches.

Haley, Blair, and I nod, giving Lola the thumbs up as we continue to dance.

She only hesitates a moment. Blows kisses to us. Then rushes after her man, pushing her way through the pulsating crowd.

Hell, I don't blame her. I'd do the very same thing. In fact, all of us would opt for our sexy fiancé if given the chance. Girls' Night Out is fun. Being with your friends is fun. But it doesn't compare to a night in with your more than fun lover!

"What's so funny?" Haley asks over the bass of the music.

"Girls' Night Out or Lover Night In?" Leonie asks, raising and lowering her hands like a scale.

Haley giggles as her gray eyes shine like liquid platinum behind her glasses. She looks like a female version of her brothers—gorgeous.

"That's a straightforward decision… Girl's Night Out!" She responds.

Leonie's eyes widen in surprise as she stares at her.

Haley giggles some more and claps her hands.

"Gotcha! Lover takes all every time!"

Billie and Blair ask what's the joke, and Haley fills them in. They laugh and high five with us in agreement. Then we dance some more, getting lost in the beat and a fun night with friends—old and new.

MALCOLM

Talk about a crazy week... Roger *The Responsible* loses his stoic cool in a fight with his ex-girlfriend Leonie's Italian boyfriend—fucking prick—at a Lola's Coterie grand-opening party in a STEELE property. Sebastian the self-proclaimed *Never Gonna Marry Playboy Alpha Dom* surprises Lola with their wedding. What the hell else can happen?!

"Oh, oh my! Excuse me!"

The melodious, sultry AF voice slides into my musings as I'm jostled from behind and a pair of delicate hands grab a hold of me.

STEELE Dubai I teems with four hundred guests for Baz and Lola's nuptials. We closed the entire hotel and resort for the extravagant four-day affair. Baz worked his magic with the help of our mother Shelley and two wedding planners to pull it off without a hitch.

I half swivel my body to face the clumsy guest—sexy tone and all—who bumped into me. Hopefully she's not drunk off her ass, or using an excuse to get my attention. I damn sure don't need another Vicky-style deception. Three months free of the conniving broad, and I don't need a setback, thank you very much.

STARR

Damn these marble floors! Who's bright idea was it to gloss them into a giant ice skating rink? Especially when I'm wearing five-inch Manolo Blahnik satin and Swarovski crystal sandals.

To avoid a face plant before I reach the ballroom for Lola and Sebastian's wedding, I grab the closest person in the crowd. One hand wraps around his waist while the other clutches his elbow.

Awkward much?!

Fortunately, he's a tall, solid mass of muscle and doesn't waver as I collide with him. Not yet stable on my wobbly feet—I feel like a newborn foal—I tighten my grip on his waist as I glance up at him.

My mouth falls open, and I freeze.

Holy God and every deity in every religion's pantheon!!! It's Malcolm Steele. And he's even more gorgeous in person, even if his expression is one of annoyance.

Eek!!!

MALCOLM

The face of an angel stares up at me. Her sorrel brown eyes widen in surprise as her lush mouth forms a perfect O.

My cock twitches for the first time outside of the LEVELS clubs I've visited to sate my sexual and Dom needs.

As my eyes scan her, bent at the waist and still holding onto me, a flush of heat races through every one of my cells. From the hairs raised on my scalp to the tips of my curling toes. My heartbeat speeds up faster than my Bugatti Chiron.

I reach out to steady her but jump as though shocked when our fingers touch. Tingles explode. If I 'm not mistaken, she shuddered in response to our connection. Did she feel it, too?

What the hell is wrong with me?! Get it together, Steele!

Then again…

Once she stands, we're five inches apart, and I can brush my lips against her temple. More heat radiates off of her body. And what a body.

She may have the face of an angel, but that body belongs outside of the pearly gates of Heaven. I'd be happy to welcome her to my home. My cock weeps in agreement.

The coral-colored long-sleeved dress clings to her bodacious curves. Padded shoulders highlight the deep vee-neckline where her full perky tits play hide and seek with the draped opening. A mock cummerbund cinches her tiny waist. My eyes follow the light bouncing off of the minuscule crystals sewn onto the material. From the flare of her hips to the asymmetrical hemline cut high at one knee to end in a point at the middle heel of her glittery fuck-me sandals.

Well, fuck *me*…

"Excuse me!" The angel squeaks, then shakes her head to clear her throat.

Her long, curly dark brown hair moves gently along her back. I want to wrap the glossy tresses around my fist to hold her in place while I pummel her from behind into pure ecstasy.

"Hey, are you okay?"

I have to rip my eyes away from the angel to focus on the concerned voice. Another woman takes My Angel by the arm, glares at me, and leads her away from me towards the ballroom.

Frozen in place, captivated by her round ass in that sinful dress, I watch her disappear into the crowd.

The vibration of my mobile in the pocket of my trousers rouses me.

Shit! I'm late and I'm the best man!

THROUGHOUT THE CEREMONY, the picture-taking session, and the toasts at the reception, my mind wanders to My Angel. After these hours, I give up on not referring to the mystery woman as mine.

Why the potent attraction? No clue.

I can't find her amongst the sea of four hundred guests. Damn the need to invite everyone in our social circle, business associates, friends, and family.

Sure, it's a big deal since Baz is the first of the much-wanted Steele siblings to marry and remove himself from the supposed STEELE Quaternity. But the humongous gathering doesn't help me find a needle in a haystack.

As I stand to the side sipping a Jackson Special Blend Scotch with Anton, he straightens suddenly.

"Fuck me! There's the *khlopushka!*" He exclaims.

I frown at him, wondering who the hell could be the firecracker that has him excited. Anton is not one to show such blatant interest in a woman.

My gaze follows his to the dance floor.

Not only is his *khlopushka* shaking her thing, but My Angel shimmies to Beyoncé performing "Single Ladies"—another of Baz's surprises for his new bride.

Once again I find myself stuck in place, unable to move. Damn, she's stunning.

"Hi, handsome."

A figure appears before me, blocking my Angel from my sight. In the time to extricate myself from this female guest's clutches, my Angel disappears. Funny enough, so has Anton and My Angel's friend.

I weave through the crowd, giving brief acknowledgements as business associates want to offer congratulations and women want to snag me next.

Finally, I spy Baz whisk Lola from the dance floor and see Leonie and Roger talking. My Angel stands beside her.

Leonie raises her finger to gesture for a moment. Then turns back to My Angel to whispers in her ear. She nods and smiles at Leonie. A smile that lights the room brighter than her crystal-embellished coral gown.

She must be a friend of Lola and Leonie. Now I can capture My Angel.

Starr

I cannot believe I made such a fool out of myself in front of Malcolm Steele. The man I want to partner with for my business. I damn near rumpled his custom-tailored classic tuxedo—looking fine AF in it, mind you—and he was the best man in my friend's wedding!

All night I avoid him to think of a way to amend the fiasco of our initial meeting. Cue the eye roll…

Then to top it off, a giant sexy Russian makes off with Adrienne. It was okay until Sebastian snagged Lola from the dance floor as expected of the lovebirds. Then Roger swept Leonie away.

Now I surreptitiously exit the ballroom, praying I don't bump into Malcolm Steele again, no pun intended. Thankfully, I make it to my room and pack. After the brunch tomorrow, I'll make my escape to Rishikesh. Since I'm on this side of the world, I might as well stop by the ashram to see Ganika for a week. By then, a plan will emerge.

* * *

FINALLY! Thank fuck!

I spot My Angel from a distance. She's with Sebastian and Lola, chatting with them during brunch. Anton was of no use since I couldn't get a hold of him, or Roger for that matter. Undoubtedly, they booed up with the firecracker and Leonie, respectively…

At last I can catch My Angel, and I make my way over to her with the newlyweds. But a redheaded wedding guest waylays me. A look of annoyance crosses my face when she steps right in front of my clear path. As quickly as I can, I get away from her and rush across the room.

Not fucking again!

"Where did she go?" I ask Baz and Lola agitatedly.

They turn to see me peering over their shoulders in the direction My Angel walked away. They glance at each other and laugh.

"What's so damned funny?!" I demand of Baz.

He chuckles, but Lola answers.

"So you finally met Starr! Did you schedule your meeting?" She asks.

I glance down at her, perplexed. Starr? Meeting?

Holy shit!

My Angel is Starr Knight?!?!

* * *

A TROUGH MUST FORM beneath my feet as I pace back and forth in front of my desk.

Where the hell is Anton?! He's never late for our weekly status meeting.

I don't care if it's ten minutes before the start time. *To be early is to be on time; to be on time is to be late; to be late is unthinkable.* We live by that adage.

Another irritated glance at my Patek Philippe Grandmaster Chime. My life is more complicated than the most complicated wristwatch ever crafted. It's 1,366 pieces may work in perfect harmony, but my one quest to get a hold of My Angel is complete discord.

It's been over a week since I first laid eyes on the beauty. And I'm no closer to seeing her again.

Forget trying to reach Lola during her and Sebastian's no-contact-allowed honeymoon. Leonie could only offer My Angel's mobile number after I explained my need for it. Sure, I said it was to schedule the expansion partnership meeting. I'm not laying my cards out before I get a chance to speak to My Angel directly.

Unfortunately, her mobile goes to voicemail every. Single. Time. A fruitless call to her center in Beverly Hills resulted in the front desk staff not disclosing her whereabouts to a stranger.

A stranger?! Not for long, if I can help it.

Then there's Anton… After he disappeared from the reception, more than likely with My Angel's friend, I couldn't reach him either. Sure, he had scheduled a holiday prior to the wedding and stated he would not be accessible since he was off to Nepal for ten days. I left voice messages and sent texts anyway, beyond desperate.

At first I tried to convince myself the reaction was a fluke. Nothing more than the sight of a gorgeous… voluptuous… mesmerizing… woman. Then I tried to clump her with the other gold diggers I've encountered, including Vicky…

But My Angel is close friends with Lola and Leonie apparently. And they're not at all with Sebastian and Roger for their billions. So, by deduction, neither would My Angel want mine. Plus she owns a thriving fitness and wellness center—has her millions—graduated from Stanford undergrad and B-School—highly intelligent—and her parents are high-powered attorneys even if they have weird names—excellent family background. What more do I need to know?

I freeze mid-stride when Miles announces Anton's arrival over the telephone intercom.

Finally!

Anton strides in with a shit-eating grin on his face as he continues to speak Russian into his mobile. He raises his hand before harsh words tumble from my mouth.

"I've got you covered, *moy drug!*" He chuckles as he lowers his mobile and gestures for me to sit at the conference table.

My molars grind to bite back words of annoyance. But I sit because he must be up to something worthwhile. At least he better be…

"Okay *khlopushka*, we're ready," Anton says in Russian into the mobile as he brings the videoconference up on the wall-mounted television across from the table.

The image of My Angel's friend appears onscreen. She's sitting in an office in what must be the fitness center. Apparently she's fluent in Russian. She scowls at Anton's use of the word firecracker to describe her. Then shifts her bright green eyes to me.

Another beauty who reminds me more of a tigress with her feline features and predatory stare.

"Hello, Mr. Steele. I'm Adrienne Anthony, the CMO and general manager of Starr Light Fitness & Wellness Beverly Hills"—she glances at Anton with a look, then back at me as my heart pounds—"Your veep reached out to schedule the expansion partnership exploration meeting again. Ms. Knight has returned to the United States and is available next Tuesday at ten in the morning or at one in the after-noon Pacific time. Which do you prefer?"

"Thank you for scheduling the meeting. However, I have a suggestion"—I lean forward in my chair and pin Adrienne with my most panty-melting smile—"Ms. Knight wants to open a location in the Caribbean and host international fitness retreats. Let us—Ms. Knight, you, Anton, me—meet at STEELE St. Barth's on Tuesday for five days. During which Ms. Knight will hold a sample two-day retreat with a few of your clients as a demonstration where Anton and I will take part. Then the four of us will meet to discuss the partnership. My administrative assistant will arrange a STEELE private jet for your and your clients' transportation. Kindly ask Ms. Knight if she agrees to my terms. Anton and I will await her answer by the end of day today."

Adrienne sits back, surprised. Her buttery pecan-colored cheeks flush crimson. I can tell she's a firecracker who prefers control, but I'm a dominant who doesn't give up control. At all.

Anton caught how I checked his firecracker and smirks knowing my exact intentions. He can put together my frantic communications to him regarding My Angel easily. His frosty eyes glitter with devilry since he'll have the added benefit of seeing his current interest again.

Pleased with Adrienne's reaction, I lean back and chuckle to myself.

I always get what I want. And I want the brown-eyed beauty.

STARR

Inhale
>*Om Gum Ganipati-ya Namaha*

Exhale
Inhale
Om Gum Ganipati-ya Namaha
Exhale
Inhale
Om Gum Ganipati-ya Namaha
Exhale

With my eyes closed and my aventurine mala in my fingers, I repeat the Sanskrit mantra to remove obstacles and bring success for my japa practice. It's normal for me as a part of my daily meditation. However, today holds special meaning because I meet with Malcolm Steele in two days, at last.

I need all the strength I can get to make it through the next seven days. Well, five since I won't see Malcolm until Adrienne, another teacher, and six VIP clients we selected for the sample fitness retreat arrive the day after tomorrow.

Although I expect a STEELE property to satisfy our

needs, I opted to come ahead of time to make sure all is ready and to get a feel for the property. The classes agenda will feature yoga sessions for meditation, pranayama, and asanas with Pilates and Barre for strength training. We'll gather for group breakfasts both days and for dinner the first night. An excursion around St. Barth's on the STEELE resort's power catamaran will make the dinner exciting. Clients will depart the afternoon of the second day.

Leaving me alone with Malcolm Steele…

How the hell will I survive???

I still don't have a plan to make up for the fiasco of our initial collision, even Ganika couldn't help me. My brain went haywire when I gazed into his soulful gray eyes. At first his expression was annoyance, then a spark ignited followed by a flicker of… lust?

Shivers race through me and my pussy throbs from memories of BOB—Battery Operated Boyfriend—alleviating my ache as fantasies of Dom Malcolm Steele ravished me with a flogger, then fucked me bowlegged.

I sigh and open my eyes to paradise.

The breeze off of the Caribbean Sea wraps around me as I straighten my legs from lotus position on my oversized Hermès beach towel. Salty air fills my lungs, and the warm sun soaks into my skin. It's early morning so no one's out except for a kitesurfer in the distance and two resort staff members watching him by the shoreline.

With ease, the kitesurfer harnesses control of the wind to master the waves beneath his board and to complete front and back rolls in midair. The colorful kite dances above him. I noticed his aerial acrobatics when I stepped onto the sand. He's been at it for almost an hour. This guy must be a hell of strong.

I'm totally impressed by his command of nature and of himself.

As he makes it to the shore and gathers his equipment with the help of a resort staffer, I continue to watch him, mesmerized by his incredible body. He must sense my stare because he turns in my direction, then does a double take.

I glance behind me, not sure if he sees someone else. When he waves, I wave back and clap as he approaches me. Not wanting to appear rude or a gawker, I walk towards him smiling as I continue to clap.

The sun glistens on his olive skin, further kissed by the warm rays. A sexy as sin intricate tattoo wraps around his well-defined pecs. He slicks his longish ebony hair back from his sculpted face where a touch of a five o'clock shadow covers his firm jaw. His broad shoulders taper to eight-pack abs that flex as he rubs a towel over his torso. Biceps bulge with each pass.

My mouth waters when I follow his happy trail past his Adonis belt. Then my gaze takes in his muscular thighs beneath his board shorts... Hold up! There's no extra muscle along the inner thigh...

My mind reels when I realize it's his dick. His incredibly massive, hard dick. Unconsciously, I bite my lower lip and shift from one foot to the other for a bit of friction at my core. This guy is hung and ready!

A deep chuckle draws my eyes back to his face. His knowing smirk makes my cheeks redden in embarrassment.

Great, Starr! Good going...

"Wow! That was phenomenal! I wish I could—"

The words die on my lips when he removes his goggles. Soulful gray eyes twinkle at me.

Holy God and every deity in every religion's pantheon!!! It's Malcolm Steele. AGAIN!

At once I freeze, my limbs stiffen like the goats that faint when startled. However, the rest of my body responds in the opposite. My tongue slips out to moisten my lower lip.

Nipples bead to poke against my triangle bikini top. Lower abs tighten as my pussy contracts and its juices pool in the string-bikini bottom.

"Ms. Knight... How lovely to see you again."

Malcolm

WELL GOOD GOT DAMN!!!

My Angel fails to even reach the first rung of Jacob's Ladder. Her beyond banging bodyody makes my mouth water and my cock thicken and lengthen along my thigh. It's a damn good thing I have on board shorts or my junk would be on full display.

Once again her sorrel brown eyes widen in surprise. But this time her little pink tongue pokes out to lick her plump lower lip.

My nostrils flare and my eyes narrow as I home in on her lush mouth. I want her tongue and lips on my cock. Now!

However, I refuse to speak another word. This time no one is around to take her away from me. The sound of the waves slapping against the shore makes me wonder what it'll sound like when I spank that ass.

"Mr. Sttt—eele, ah!" My Angel starts as her voice stutters on my name and her body shudders back to life.

Yeah, no question. She feels it too.

Starr

No! I will not make a fool of myself again! I simply refuse to lose it.

I take a deep, cleansing breath and feel it course through my body, reactivating my limbs. Then I speak, "Mr. Sttt —eele, ah!"

Just saying his name caused my body to shudder and my voice to stutter. Got damn!

"Pardon, me. Mr. Steele, lovely to see you again, too. Thank you for the opportunity to discuss a partnership," I respond, proud my sentence came out coherently this time.

A flash of lust sparks in his hooded eyes.

I replay my words in my mind and catch the—as Leonie says—double entendre. I must be careful around the Steele men like she told us!

So, it wasn't my imagination after all. The flare of heat that shoots through me at the knowledge he's as taken with me as I am with him makes me feel powerful.

Well, not as powerful as Malcolm kitesurfing…

"I look forward to a conducive and long partnership with you, Ms. Knight. Your eagerness to come early pleases me immensely," Malcolm quips.

More color floods my face even as more juices flood my soaked bikini bottom at his purposeful play on words.

He continues in his baritone voice that captivates me. "Have you eaten, Ms. Knight? I am starving. The breakfast offers a selection of delectable dishes."

I bleat what I hope is a positive response.

Malcolm chuckles and places his hand on the small of my back to guide me towards the sea-front terrace for one of the resort's restaurants. As we pass my towel, he scoops it up and shakes out the sand before folding it under his arm.

I risk a peek up at him since he towers over me by what must be ten inches. An uncontrollable giggle falls from my mouth when I wonder if his dick is the same length!

Malcolm grins down at me, then spreads his fingers further across my back, sending a jolt to my clit. The tip of one finger brushes against the curve of my ass. I shiver and bite back a moan.

When we arrive at the restaurant, the staff trip over

themselves to accommodate Malcolm, particularly the female hostess. She makes a show of guiding us to a table and placing the menu in his hands as she skims her fingers on his.

Mine!

I shock myself at the visceral reaction to another woman touching Malcolm. To hide it, I put my menu in front of my face to study the "delectable dishes."

A finger appears at the top of my menu and lowers it slowly.

"Ms. Knight—"

"Starr," I interject.

The most seductive smile spreads across his face before he starts again, "Starr."

The way my name rolls off of his tongue as though he tastes every letter makes me shift in my seat. If I don't change my bathing suit, it will remain forever destroyed. Sort of how I hope he destroys my pussy…

"I know you're a yogi, but do you have an aversion to meat?" He asks with a straight face.

Again I bite back a giggle. This guy.

"No, Mr. St—"

"Malcolm."

"No, Malcolm," I reply.

"I do not enjoy the word 'no' coming from your mouth when you speak to me. How about, 'meat is definitely on the menu,' instead?" He smirks.

This time, I can't hold back the snort that escapes my mouth. Even when the server arrives to take our order, I can't control myself.

Malcolm grins and offers to order for me. I wave my hand and nod my agreement, still laughing as tears fill my eyes.

Once the server leaves, Malcolm's gaze lands on me. He studies my face for a moment before he speaks.

"It pleases me we meet officially. I did not know who you were in the lobby of STEELE Dubai I. Lola told me she is a huge fan of yours and your plans for expansion"—he raises his hand to stop me from interrupting—"Since the retreat and our business don't occur for two days, I propose we spend the time exploring our sexual attraction."

My mouth falls open at his bluntness. But my mind screams, HELL YEAH! as it recalls my nightly erotic fantasies of Dom Malcolm controlling me and extracting absolute bliss from my body one spine-tingling orgasm at a time.

He reaches over to run the tip of his index finger around my O-shaped mouth with an expression of such longing, I moan.

"You do not know how many times I fantasized about your luscious mouth wrapped around the girth of my cock with you naked on your knees before me. That first sight of you bent at the waist gripping me will forever remain imprinted on my mind," Malcolm murmurs in a voice thick with lust.

I blink and swallow. Hard.

"You feel the same, do you not, Angel?" He asks softly.

More blinks follow a slow nod.

"Let us explore one another. This will have no impact on our business. I am a man who knows a sure thing and will not hesitate to follow through," Malcolm finishes with a simmering smile full of promise.

I know I should stop him and demand an apology for his audacity. But something holds back my indignation.

Why not see where this goes?

It's not as though he's unknown to me. Lola recommended him. He's her husband's brother. She wouldn't marry into a family of crazies!

Sure Malcolm is a playboy. But why shouldn't I have some fun with my fantasy Dom? I have to think he's no different from his Alpha male siblings. Lola and Leonie wouldn't be with them if they were questionable.

"As long as it won't impact our chance at a partnership negatively," I state. "Or else this… interaction ends now."

Malcolm's expression turns staid, "I swear to uphold my promise to you. Our business will proceed no matter the result of our 'interaction.' Agreed?"

I hold my hand out to shake on it.

Without hesitation, Malcolm envelopes my small hand in his larger one. Deal made, we stare at one another, unsure what to say next until the server places our entrées in front of us.

I take a bite of the sausage link and moan around the fork, "Delectable, Malcolm."

It's his turn to shift in need as his eyes darken to a stormy gray.

"We shall see very soon, Angel," he says mysteriously. "But leave room in your belly. I have something even tastier to fill it."

Damn… Every time I think I have the one up on Malcolm, he gets me back in line. I love it!

"Yes… Sir," I whisper more to myself than to him as I absorb his nickname for me.

But when his fork clatters to his plate, my eyes snap to him immediately.

Forget the storm, all sorts of emotions churn in his eyes and across his face.

"After you finish your breakfast, you will return to your villa and wait for me in the bedroom naked, lying supine, legs spread, arms above your head on the bed. Clear?"

I choke on my iced green tea, but recover quickly with a nod.

"Words, Angel. I will have your words," Malcolm demands.

"Yes, Sir," I reply confidently, eagerly even.

He watches me for a moment, then as though satisfied nods to himself as he retrieves his fork.

We finish our breakfast as we chat casually about his extreme sports and my interest in trying some less than heart-stopping kinds. I'm intrigued by his fearlessness and his willingness to take me under his wing. No pun intended.

Faster than expected, the time comes for me to obey his first command.

My heartbeat increases as I rush to the spectacular four-bedroom beachfront villa, the largest of three available to guests. I wondered why Miles reserved such spacious accommodations for me only. No doubt at his boss' request.

Now, I'm thankful for its size and its separation from the primary hotel. How awful would it be for a staff member or other guest to see the company's president entering or exiting my room? Or worse, to hear my cries of ecstasy...

No way do I want anyone to assume the partnership between Starr Light Fitness & Wellness, Beverly Hills and STEELE International, Inc. has anything to do with me banging a Steele. I pride myself on making my own way. Connections formed, great. But no favors, thank you.

All negative thoughts evaporate from my mind when I strip out of my bikini, take a quick shower—no need for sand in my huckus-tuckus—then spread out on the bed. Only five minutes pass—five minutes of my brain envisioning the powerful Dom Malcolm ravishing me—when the man himself appears in the doorway.

Fuuuuck...

"*E*xcellent, Angel."

Malcolm's growl makes goosebumps raise on my heated skin. His gray eyes darken to obsidian as they roam over my naked flesh. A pause at the juncture of my thighs elicits another growl as he licks his lips hungrily; the full bottom one beckons for me to bite it.

"Already wet for me, Little One?" Malcolm asks with an arched eyebrow pointedly.

A shudder runs through me, ending with a low moan.

"Yes, Sir," I respond, knowing the title pleases him.

When he flares his nostrils and a carnal smirk appears on his face, I know for certain Malcolm is a Dom. The question: am I a sub, or better yet, can I be *his* sub?

"Once I finish a shower, we will talk"—he drops his board shorts and his dick springs free—"Until then, do not move. Understood, Little One?"

My jaw drops. What the hell?!

I raise up on my elbows to get a better look. Besides his colossal cock, the glint of silver at its mushroom head shocks me speechless.

The movement of his hand to stroke his turgid member languidly draws my attention to his face where a seductive smirk greets me. His eyes dance in delight at my surprise; whether from my reaction to his size or to the jewelry, I cannot discern.

Malcolm rubs his thumb across his tip from the silver ball above to the silver ball below, then asks, "Any questions, Little One?"

"N-n-no, Sir," I say in awe.

He nods and gives his dick a last tug before he pivots and strides into the en suite bathroom.

When the water gushes from the rain shower, I collapse onto the bed, my mind already spent from trying to make sense of what I just beheld.

Is Malcolm a freaky Dom, too? Why does my body tremble in erotic anticipation of accepting his gigantic dick into my pussy with the added sensation of the jewelry? Am I a freaky sub???

No sooner do I realize the thoughts turn me on to the point my pussy juices drip down the crevice between my thighs and ass to pool beneath me on the bed does Malcolm return. He stands before me with damp skin and hair, his cock still erect.

"Tell me, Little One, what is your experience as a sub?" He asks as he pins me with his unblinking stare.

"I… Uh…" My gaze shifts away from him as I struggle to convey my lack of experience.

After a deep cleansing breath, I face him again. Encouraged by the no sign of judgment in his eyes, I continue.

"None. I.. I've only heard about a D/s relationship from a… a friend who has a Dom or rather had one. I've researched the lifestyle a bit, but I never did anything…"

My ramblings carry on for a bit more. But Malcolm remains expressionless, as he patiently waits for me to finish. I lower my gaze and twiddle my thumbs as I stop babbling, awaiting my fate.

"Are you interested in learning more about a D/s relationship and the BDSM lifestyle, Little One?" Malcolm asks.

"Yes, Sir," I answer softly.

Instantly, I feel the bed dip as Malcolm sits beside me, then lifts my chin with his forefinger. Once our eyes connect, he slants his mouth over mine and kisses me breathlessly. The possessive, passionate kiss makes me reel as his tongue dominates mine.

Malcolm clasps my face between his sizable palms and holds my gaze again.

"Communication and trust serve as the foundation for Doms and subs. Your safewords are green to continue, yellow for a moment, and red to stop all play at once. We will push your limits, so be sure to choose the appropriate safeword. I will respect your wishes. You learn a sub holds all the power, not the Dom. Do you understand, Little One?"

He finishes his first lesson, and I nod enthusiastically.

A rumble comes from his massive chest to reverberate through me, peaking my nipples and making my pussy clench with need.

"Forearms and knees. Ass up towards me," Malcolm commands as he rises to tower over me.

Now his steely gray eyes glint more than the penis piercing.

I scramble into position.

"So beautiful," he murmurs, a single fingertip whispers down my spine. "Your pussy lips glisten. Just as enticing, your bottom hole winks at me. Which shall we play with today, Little One?"

A moan pours from my mouth as I drop my forehead to the sumptuous Egyptian cotton bedding. The sensation of his fingertip stroking my wet pussy lips then rimming my puckered hole, draws a staggered inhalation from me.

"We have time to explore your dirty little hole. Let us enjoy your succulent pussy, shall we?" Malcolm asks with a wicked chuckle when I groan.

"Y-y-yes, Sir," I sputter.

My back bows when his wet, velvety tongue swipes in one motion across the seam of my slick pussy lips. His fingers splay over my pelvis and his thumbs press into my butt cheeks as he grips my hips. Held in place, I can only accept the onslaught of his carnal torturous licks, nips, and pokes as Malcolm feasts on my core.

When my thighs quiver from my impending orgasm, Malcolm pulls back and smacks my ass three times. I gasp as the pleasure recedes, replaced by the sting of his palm.

"Do not cum, Little One" he commands, then returns to his meal with the addition of his thick fingers.

Each time I near bliss, Malcolm withdraws and spanks me, alternating between the pleasure and the pain. The last smack catches my clit, and I yowl as I jerk away from the sting. Immediately, he buries his face between my thighs and sucks on my poor clit.

My body convulses, and fists slam into the bedding as I attempt to stave off the orgasm.

"Yellow! Yellow!" I cry out in anguish. "Malcolm, please! I can't take anymore! I need to cum! Fuck me… Please!"

His only response is to plunge his middle and index fingers deep inside my aching pussy as he leans over me. His chest presses against my sweaty back in dominance while his lips brush my ear.

"Cum for me, Little One! Cum for your Dom! Now!" He roars.

My head explodes as the most epic climax rips through

me. Stars shoot behind my closed eyelids. My greedy pussy squeezes his thick digits, pulling them further inside.

"Aaaaahhhh…" I keen as wave after wave of erotic bliss takes me over the edge to oblivion.

The cool touch of metal to my fevered pussy entrance brings me back from Malcolm's sexual thrall. Oh, my God! The twin balls scrape my G-spot and tunnel through my channel to bring erotic frisson to my very soul.

My core stretches to accommodate Malcolm's mighty girth and the twin balls. He takes no time for me to adjust. Brutal thrusts slam into my pussy as his groin and heavy ball sac slap against my reddened butt cheeks.

More pleasure and pain erupt.

Immediately, I cry out in wild abandon.

"So fucking tight and wet, Little One! Fuuuck!" Malcolm groans between his grunts and slaps of my ass.

"Uh. Uh. Uh. Uh." I respond after each thrust.

Malcolm widens his stance and bends his knees to shift the penetration angle as his grip tightens on my hips. He continues to saw inside of me as orgasm after orgasm over-takes me.

By the time he slams against me one last time with the twin balls bumping against my cervix, I'm a blubbering mass of jelly. Malcolm's passionate growl precedes a torrent of his seed deep in my pussy. He slumps his sweat-soaked torso against my back and drops us to our sides, still connected intimately.

Exhaustion—mental and physical—consumes me. As I drift off, I hear a gasp from Malcolm, and he withdraws his still-erect cock from me. Our combined juices drip from my core as I mewl and give in to the slumber.

MALCOLM

Oh, fuck!!!

So enraptured by My Angel submitting to me and welcoming a D/s relationship, I forgot a condom… I chance a peek at her, but she sleeps peacefully. A satisfied smile graces her gorgeous face.

Fuck it.

I spoon behind her and hope she doesn't lay me out when she awakes. Communication and trust include protection, dumb ass. Since I've never gone bare in my life and take regular tests, I don't pose a risk to her. It's doubtful my health-conscious Angel would not take precautions with her body.

The only concern is whether she's on birth control. The caveman in me is pleased my seed fills his mate's womb, but I have to be realistic.

A contented sigh from My Angel draws me from my musings.

Again, fuck it. We'll deal with it later.

I cuddle—what the hell???—behind her with my face in her soft curls and drift off.

* * *

As ANTON and I wait for the other retreat guests to arrive at the beach for our first class, a Cheshire Cat smile covers my face. My Angel wasn't pissed with me—thank fuck! And she takes a birth control shot every few months. Not sure how my caveman feels about that news…

Female laughter floats through the air from behind us. We turn in their direction. Like a magnet, my eyes find My Angel. She's splendid in a white tank top and matching leggings with sheer mesh panels strategically placed on both pieces. Her long curly hair in a high ponytail—perfect for tugging her head in place. A shy smile flickers across her face as she sees me.

After our two incredible days of delving into our fledging D/s relationship, it's time for work. I reassured her we'll be all right with no one the wiser. Well, as long as no one notices the instant hard-on beneath my athletic shorts.

A flash of golden blonde hair juxtaposed against My Angel's chestnut-colored skin creeps into my periphery.

"*O chert voz'mi, net.*"

Anton's curse comes just as the blonde shifts her blue eyes to my gray ones. She gasps and covers her mouth in shock.

Oh, hell no, does not even cut it.

Vicky Reynolds… You've gotta be fucking kidding me!

Quickly I glance at My Angel. Fortunately, she's distracted by the other participants and Adrienne. Then my gaze moves back to Vicky.

She's recovered and moves forward with the crowd. They take their places at ballet barres set up in the sand opposite each other with some space between them for My Angel to walk.

Anton stands beside Adrienne with a smirk on his face. She ignores him and chats with the woman on her other side.

I hold off until Vicky settles at one barre, and I stand at the other. The women on either side gravitate toward me, like moths to a flame. No thanks.

"Ready to step up to the Beach Barre, ladies and gentlemen?"

So this is how My Angel gets that round fuckable ass…

* * *

Two days later, I've successfully dodged Vicky and gotten my ass kicked by barre, Pilates, and yoga. Go figure. I promised My Angel I wouldn't interrupt her last moments with her retreat guests, so I head to my villa ready for a well-deserved shower and soak in the hot tub.

I'm looking forward to binding her with silk ties to my bed tonight. Her body ripe for the taking, begging for release as she writhes beneath—

"Hello, Sir."

The softly spoken words stop me in my tracks like a sledgehammer to the head. I curse inwardly, but put a stoic expression on my face before I turn.

Vicky.

"I am not your Dom, Vicky. Kindly refrain from addressing me as such. In fact, do not address me in any way. Excuse me," I respond, then pivot to continue on my way.

A small hand grips the back of my arm.

"Please forgive me! I've been so lost without you! What can I do to make it up to you?" Vicky asks with tear-filled eyes.

Drama Queen... I extricate my arm from her hand and shake my head.

"Vicky. It is best for you to move on," I answer, then raise my hand when she speaks. "No. Enou—"

She flings herself onto me, wrapping her arms and legs around my body. Automatically, I cup her ass. Vicky slams her mouth on mine.

Starr

One thing I answered: I am a sub, but unfortunately I cannot be Malcolm Steele's sub.

He's Vicky's Dom. Former Dom or not, he's off limits for me.

When I witnessed their exchange as I headed to his villa since the retreat guests boarded the private jet early, I couldn't believe my eyes or my ears. No wonder Vicky wanted to stay longer. I thought she wanted time away from LA to clear her mind of her failed relationship.

It may be failed on Malcolm's end, but not on Vicky's. She still wants him. And it's too messy for me to get caught in the middle.

Besides, I reminded myself of the Google search results that showed Malcolm as a rebel playboy and of Vicky's description of him. I don't need the heartache she suffers. After Quinn, I swore off men for now, anyway. I must remain true to myself.

The two days of sheer bliss Malcolm and I shared will have to suffice. As much as it pains me—not at all pleasurable—I must let it go.

During the days of our partnership discussions, I kept my distance from Malcolm, only focusing on business. He tried making contact with me or plans to hook up, but I made excuses to avoid being alone with him. When he caught me around the corner from the conference room asking why I was so aloof, I cried red.

Immediately, he jumped back from me.

I told him I changed my mind and hoped he would stand by his word of not allowing the sex to interfere with the business. He reaffirmed his pledge. We came to an agreement and ended the meetings with Malcolm's legal team drafting a contract for my team to review. They'll send it via email next week.

Malcolm remained professional and did not make me feel uncomfortable in any way.

However, I couldn't stay another minute and chose to fly

back to LA a day early. While he and Anton were in a meeting, Adrienne and I headed to the airport for a commercial flight.

Wistfully, I walk across the tarmac to board the plane home.

MALCOLM

"*B*rat, this woman has you hung up. I've never seen you so out of sorts over a hookup. You need to just fuck someone else and move on already. *Da?*"

I finish hammering the speed bag with a four-punch sequence of fist-circle and fist-straight punches. Then turn and glare at Anton, who's warming up with Borya. Along with Sebastian, we're in the full gym on the first floor of Baz's penthouse duplex at The STEELE Tower in New York.

"*Net!* And watch your mouth about Starr Knight, Anton. She's not a hookup, *brother*," I spit out at him.

Baz chuckles and Borya guffaws.

I pivot to glare at them, but Baz holds his taped hands up as he shakes his head in surrender.

"Listen, I'm the last one to poke fun at someone who's bent out of shape by a woman unexpectedly. Look at what Lola did to me. She had me all messed up in the head when we first met… Hell, she still has me going!" He says with his gray eyes twinkling.

"*Da!* And I had to beat his *zhopa* to get his *bashka* back in the game. Come on in the ring, and I'll help you, too!" Borya adds, smashing his fists together. His muscular arms flex from the impact.

"Listen, no disrespect, *da?* Why don't you go see her? She should be back from her latest trip, and the contracts need her signature..." Anton recommends with a conciliatory nod.

THE FIRST COUPLE OF WEEKS, I fought the attraction I have for her. I tried the route of considering her just a hookup like Anton mentioned. Why should I—the bad boy who has women lined up to fuck—care about one stubborn woman who disappeared on me, then denied my calls and text messages?

Later it morphed into me thinking I only want what I can't have. Malcolm Steele gets everything he wants and even more.

But when I went to LEVELS New York and couldn't focus on any of the available ravishing subs, I knew it fucked me thoroughly. I couldn't get My Angel out of my mind. Once again...

Anton's bright idea made up for his stupid-ass comment.

So as I stride into Starr Light Fitness & Wellness, Beverly Hills, my eyes scan the entry for any sign of My Angel—and Vicky, I think with a shudder. One woman I'm desperate to see and the other not at all.

The interior is elegant, tranquil, and beautifully appointed, just like the woman who owns it. A soothing instrumental melody and the scent of rose and ylang yang fill the air. A sense of relaxation fills me.

But my heartbeat increases when I hear someone

mention Starr's name as they pass me on their way out. From the sound of it, they just finished a class with her.

Great! She's here.

The front desk staff directs me to her private studio. Each step closer increases my pulse—and my cock stirs. Too many times whacking off in the weeks since I last saw My Angel. It knows she's near, like a heat-seeking missile.

The studio door stands ajar. Through the opening, I watch My Angel floating in the air. She's draped in some sort of silk hammock—reminiscent of a swing found at any of the LEVELS clubs.

My cock punches against the zipper of my trousers when My Angel flips backwards. Her long toned legs go in the air as her hands reach for the floor. The deep back bend props her open. Just for me.

With no hesitation I enter her studio then lock the door behind me. As I stand before her, she lowers her legs. A wicked chuckle falls from my lips when her calves brush against my hips and she startles.

"Oh! Excuse me! I didn't realize anyone was still—"

My Angel's words trail off when she rights herself and comes face-to-face with me. The swing sways gently.

My smirk widens when her lush mouth opens in a perfect O. Her wide eyes skitter over my face as her cheeks flame with embarrassment. Or do I dare suspect lust?

"What are you doing here, Malcolm?" She demands while she attempts to climb out of the swing.

My hands shoot out to grip the edges of the soft fabric and pull her closer to me. The tiny, fitted shorts cover her pussy barely. Heat from her core ignites my cock.

I groan from the pressure as it hardens further to the point of pain. Tingles ripple down my spine to zap my balls. They grow heavy with the need to fill her pussy with my seed; mark her with my scent.

Mine!

"You cannot get away from me again, Little One. I respected your request for space even after you left St. Barth's without a word. I allowed Anton to handle the partnership negotiations so as not to upset you. But enough… is… enough," I growl as I grind my erection against her pussy lips.

Her eyes flutter closed from the intimate contact, and her D-cup chest heaves with her pants. Nipples strain against the material of her tank top.

I take advantage of her distraction to swipe her seam with my middle finger. Dampness meets my touch, and My Angel gasps.

"You cannot deny your attraction to me, Little One. So tell me, what made you cry red? Remember honesty, communication, trust," I command in my most dominant voice knowing her submissive nature will yield to me.

My years of being a Dom do not fail me. I read My Angel well.

She sags in the swing, and her grip on the silk lessens. Then, with her head tilted down, she peers up at me through her long eyelashes.

My cock jumps.

"We cannot be together," she breathes.

I lift my eyebrow and incline my head. Not enough.

She continues on a sigh, "She hasn't confirmed it, but I know you must be her Dom."

A cold band wraps around my lungs, sapping the air from them. Did Vicky tell her mother and Starr?!?! She's the only person we know in common to whom I'd be a Dom.

Fuck!

"—way she jumped on you says enough."

I missed the rest of Starr's answer. So I refocus.

"What do you mean?" I ask.

She recounts the scene outside of my villa. The band tightens when Starr's voice catches. Her angelic face falls, and she drops her gaze as she finishes.

"Vicky told me how upset she was after her Dom broke up with her before the retreat. That's why I invited her to get away for a while. Had I known you were her Dom, I never would have asked her. Hell, I don't know if I can do business with someone who's so heartless," Starr says with more conviction in her tone.

She glares at me, then pushes against my chest.

The swing arcs back, but returns with more force to press us closer. A frustrated growl slips from her lips, and she tries to wiggle away.

I grip her hips to still her. Then cup her chin to align our eyes.

"Starr, you cannot make a decision like that without allowing me to tell my side of the story,"—she protests, but I continue—"Vicky was my sub, but she broke the nondisclosure agreement we signed along with plotting to marry me. I will not go into details since I cannot. But know I am an honorable man who is far from heartless."

My Angel studies me intently while she considers my words.

I leave my facial expression open to allow her to find no guile. However, the first to speak loses ground. And I will not lose. My Angel is mine, even if she doesn't want to admit it. Yet.

She blinks away for a moment and nods her head. Decision made, she brings her gaze back to my unwavering one.

"You're right. I should have spoken with you about the... situation. But I really don't want any drama in my life after ending a six-month relationship recently," Starr says.

The idea of another man with My Angel makes me want

to claim her even more. But I can sense her hesitation. So rather than going ballistic, I ask what she wants.

Thankfully, she wants me—us. To explore our D/s relationship. But to take it slow.

Slow?

Damn, I'm a speed king. How the hell am I going to downshift?

I'll figure it out later. For now, I agree with her terms, and my cock weeps with joy.

My Angel must sense the change in my demeanor. She shivers and brings her plump lower lip between her teeth. Her sorrel-colored eyes sparkle with a carnal fire.

"Well, Sir. I apologize for my errant behavior. How can I make it up to you after these weeks? I must admit I missed your colossal cock greatly… BOB did not compare, Sir," she purrs.

The fuck?!?!?!

"Bob who, Naughty Girl?" I snarl.

Starr's giggle changes into a squeak when I turn the swing around and bend her at the waist. Her arms flounder as her hands reach for the floor. The angle hoists her ass in perfect alignment with the palm of my hand.

A swift smattering of spanks alternating from one butt cheek to the other has My Naughty Girl gasping and squirming to avoid her punishment. I wrap my arm around her waist and rain a sequence of left, right, sit bones, right, left smacks.

My Naughty Girl squeals and begs for forgiveness.

Undeterred and adamant she learns her lesson, I continue until she hangs limp and the thin strip covering her pussy blooms with a spot wet from her juices. The sight of it draws a groan from deep in my chest.

One hand grips her inner thigh while the fingers of my other hand peel the material away. Her clit appears, swollen with need surrounded by her soaked folds. A quick pinch to the sensitive bundle of nerves makes My Naughty Girl jolt with a strangled cry.

Both of us hiss when my thick fingers plunge inside her pussy, still rippling with aftershocks from her climax. Her inner muscles clench my digits, drenching them with her juices.

"Oh, how your pussy is soaked and ready for penetration, Naughty Girl. Do you deserve my 'colossal cock' or another spanking?" I demand.

The swing bobs with the movement of her nodding head.

THWACK! THWACK! THWACK!

I spank her clit with my fingers, then grind my palm against it.

"Words, Naughty Girl. I will have your words!" I bark.

She cries out yes and slaps her hands on the floor in emphasis.

"I have not been with anyone since you, Naughty Girl. Can I fuck you bareback, or do we need a condom?" I growl as I bend over her hanging body.

She mewls and cries, "No one since you, Sir!"

FUCK YES!!!

My fingers fly across my jeans to free my aching dick. My Prince Albert piercing balls wink in the light before I slam forward into her channel.

"Yes! Yes! Yes! Malcolm!" My Angel screams.

Her pussy clamps on my dick like a vice as I wring one orgasm after the other from her convulsing body. The swing jerks with my carnal possession of My Angel.

"Who... do... you... belong... to... Starr?" I growl as I spank that ass. "Tell me, or you will not cum for a week!"

She wails.

"Who?" I bark.

"Youuu!!!" Starr cries out on an extended moan.

"Do... not... forget..." I say between pistoning strokes. "Now, cum with me!"

Starr's body goes rigid as her pussy clamps onto my cock. When I reach around her hip and pinch her clit, she keens.

Her pussy throbs around my dick, drawing me deeper within her core.

"FUUUCK, STARR!!!" I roar as I throw my head back and unleash a torrent of cum inside her.

The grip on her hips will leave the impression of my fingers marking her as MINE.

"So, who the hell is Bob?"

We're sitting on the rooftop terrace of my penthouse in West Hollywood on the Sunset Strip. After Starr assured me her private studio is soundproof and no one could hear our raucous makeup sex, we hopped onto my Ducati Desmosedici.

She shifts on the double chaise lounge to face me. Her eyes light with mirth in the setting sun.

"Oh... BOB. He helps me when I'm in need. Never waivers and always gives me satisfaction. Particularly late at night when I can't get a certain rebel playboy Dom out of my mind," Starr says coyly.

I growl low in my throat, and she giggles.

"Down, boy! BOB is my current—"

With a warrior's whoop, I tackle Starr to her back and cover her with the full length of my body. The burgeoning erection presses into her mound.

"Bob cannot give you satisfaction like I can, Starr Knight," I cut her off in a guttural growl. "Admit it."

She laughs out loud and grabs the sides of my face.

"BOB stands for Battery Operated Boyfriend, Malcolm Steele!" Starr giggles, then gives me a mind-blowing kiss.

"Well, you do not need a battery operated one when you have the real thing, My Angel!"

Her laughter stops abruptly with a gasp.

I stare into her wide eyes as I still reel from her kiss. When she continues to stare at me, I replay my words in my head.

Holy shit!

I referred to myself as her boyfriend and called her by the nickname I gave her!!!

That kiss wasn't mind-blowing, it was mind-altering.

Baz thought he was messed up in the head…

"*I*mpressive."

My thought exactly whenever I come to the restaurants or Sky Bar at STEELE Rodeo Drive an iconic property at Wilshire Boulevard. The sleek, gray-glass, 70-story, mixed-use tower comprises a retail mall, office space, hotel with spa and restaurants, and an observation deck. The sun glints off the exterior as I crane my neck to gaze at the spire above.

Breathtaking!

But not as incredible as the weekend Malcolm and I spent together. Not only did we catch up where we ended in St. Barth's, we went beyond the edge—no pun intended.

Malcolm gave pleasure to me I never knew existed. From his attentiveness to my needs to his pushing my limits, opening me up to new carnal joys—and pain. The juxtaposition made me soar in subspace, a term I only read about and never thought I'd experience.

His insistence on caring for me afterwards made our connection even greater. He calls it aftercare; I call it sublime.

My body still hums from his erotic ministrations.

"Hey! You're not listening to me. Where's your head, Starr?" Adrienne asks as she prods me with her shoulder.

The action brings me back to the present, and I shake off my musings with a shudder of delight.

She rolls her eyes, knowing I was with Malcolm since she taught the rest of my classes. My best friend snorts at my Cheshire Cat grin.

"Yeah, impressive indeed!" I snicker as I waggle my eyebrows suggestively.

"Come on, Whipped Girl. We have business to attend. Not stand gaga at Steele's spire..." Adrienne laughs, looping her arm through mine.

The elevator doors open on thirty for STEELE International, Inc.'s executive floor. One of the three receptionists not busy with other visitors or on the telephone greets us as we walk through the waiting area. The modern decor features shades of gray from dove to platinum and white for the color palette. Luxurious accents of silk wall treatments, crystal light fixtures, and rich ebony wood floors complement the leather furniture, Lucite tables, and steel pieces. Original artwork with spotlights on them lines the walls. The sense of STEELE's power exudes from all angles.

My gaze flits past the receptionists' station to the panoramic view beyond the floor-to-ceiling windows. From this height, one can observe the Ferris wheel on the Santa Monica Pier to the west and the Pacific Ocean glittering in the distance.

"Ms. Knight, Ms. Anthony, welcome to STEELE Los Angeles."

I pivot to face the pretty brunette and smile.

She informs us Malcolm's assistant will be with us

shortly and asks if we care for a beverage. So LA she offers coffee, tea, bottled water, or a morning smoothie.

We decline and settle on the sofas along with my legal and marketing teams.

Today, we sign the contract for Starr Light Fitness & Wellness Beverly Hills' partnership with STEELE International. My dream of expanding to luxury resorts for retreats around the world and a location in the Caribbean comes true in moments!

It's not long before Miles appears and escorts us to a conference room. He introduces us to STEELE Entertainment Properties Division's legal and marketing teams already seated at the large, oval-shaped, ebony wood table. They rise from the black leather chairs and greet us warmly.

Just as we seat ourselves, the double glass doors open, and Malcolm and Anton enter.

My pulse quickens and my pussy floods with my arousal at the sight of My Dom. He's dressed immaculately in a lightweight wool charcoal gray with a hint of a check pattern suit and darker gray shirt with a silk stripped tie and black Oxfords. His lustrous ebony hair swept back to emphasize his chiseled jawline, no longer covered by the five o'clock shadow he sported over the weekend. Simply gorgeous.

A flicker of appreciation fills his eyes when his gaze sweeps over me from head to toe.

Not one to conform, I wear a sky blue suit—with shorts. The single-breasted jacket open to reveal a white silk shirt unbuttoned to hint at the lace camisole underneath. The cuffed shorts cover my upper thighs, displaying three-quarters of my toned legs ending in gray Manolo Blahnik stilettos. My body epitomizes my skill as a fitness professional focused on health and wellness. I use it to my advantage at all times. Even to entice Malcolm.

A slight smile plays at the corner of my mouth as he nods and extends his hand in salutation.

"Ms. Knight, welcome to STEELE International. You impressed us with your retreat greatly. We expect a conducive partnership with you," he says with a smug grin. "Shall we begin?"

"Thank you, Mr. Steele, Starr Light Fitness & Wellness agrees you make an excellent partner. You have proven you will always hold our needs as your utmost priority. I could not find a more capable partner," I respond with a firm grasp of his much larger hand.

Anton chuckles, but stops when Adrienne pins him with her intense stare.

Everyone settles around the table, and the STEELE legal team presents us with the contract. Since my team reviewed it before the meeting, we sign without delay.

My heart flutters as I beam at Adrienne. We're on our way to expanding SLFW!

Next Anton's development team presents the Jackson Hole at STEELE Resorts concept as members-only, high-end beach clubs for the jet set where SLFW will host retreats. Our fitness and wellness programs will offer more amenities for Jackson Hole and increase activities for guests and provide accommodations for retreat participants.

St. Barth's will serve as the center's first global location. They recommend others in Cabo San Lucas, Monte Carlo, and Koh Samui in Thailand, initially with others as demand requires.

The additional resorts surprise us. Adrienne turns to me with raised eyebrows, and I clap with glee. Malcolm and Anton smirk.

Fantastic!

The marketing teams present their plans, including timelines and recommendations for feedback. The ninety minutes pass quickly. In the end, I'm even more impressed by STEELE and their ability to generate revenue opportunities and their teams' skills.

We drink my favorite Krug Clos d'Ambonnay Champagne to celebrate our partnership.

Over my Waterford Crystal flute, I watch Malcolm. He must sense my stare and turns to face me. His eyes smolder for a moment, and I nod in recognition.

I'm ready to jump his bones. Now.

"Ladies and gentlemen, thank you. Now if you will excuse us, I have a matter to discuss with Ms. Knight," Malcolm says as he raises his flute for a final salute.

My insides melt.

The room hums with both teams jumping to action. Ever the Dom, Malcolm has them doing his bidding eagerly.

A giggle slips past my lips at the thought, but dies when Malcolm approaches and takes my elbow to lead me from the room.

He's silent as we walk, only acknowledging those we pass with a nod or a brief word. When we reach his office, he ushers me inside, locks the glass door, and blackens the glass walls. Cocooned in his soundproof lair, my heart rate increases and my eyes lower in submission.

His wicked chuckle makes me shiver.

"Congratulations, Little One. Our business partnership begins officially. We may be equals in the boardroom… But you remain my submissive behind closed doors. Understand?" My Dom states with authority.

"Yes, Sir," I respond as I lower to my knees and lean on my haunches with my hands laced behind my head, chin tilted downward, eyes to the floor.

"Excellent, Little One," My Dom croons as he steps forward and cups the nape of my neck to lift my gaze. "So beautiful. You please me tremendously."

My chest lifts on a deep inhale, ecstasy courses through me because I please My Dom.

The move draws his attention, and his fingers ghost over my exposed skin to slip inside my shirt. He hefts the weight of my heavy breast, then tweaks its turgid bud between his thumb and forefinger. As he rolls my nipple, My Dom leans over to brush his lips over mine as he murmurs naughty words of his plans for me. Plans that do not include Pilates or meditation.

He lifts me to my feet, and I tremble under his touch when his warm breath and wet tongue meet my nipple. He latches on and sucks. Hard.

My knees buckle as he moves between my breasts to lave, suck, and nip, devoting equal time to both. But I stumble on my stilettos when he steps back abruptly.

"Strip. Now." He growls.

My Dom folds his arms over his chest and watches me with hooded, lust-filled eyes as I remove my clothing without hesitation. Each piece drops to the floor until I'm exposed fully to his heated gaze.

As I stand naked before him clothed fully in his office only a door apart from others on the floor, I can't help but yearn for My Dom. No longer the Independent Woman, I've become his sub. And I do not regret my decision.

Malcolm walks around me. His gaze burns with longing. The light touch of his large palm on the small of my back makes me jump. He soothes me with his voice thrumming into my ear as he guides me to his desk.

Once there, he places my hands on the surface and glides his fingertip along my spine before he presses down to lower my torso to the top. My ass remains high in my stilettos, positioned for him perfectly. The most private parts of me on full display.

I drop my forehead to the cool leather and sigh when his

finger finds my damp slit. Then I jerk from pressure on my puckered hole.

"As I told you this weekend, I will claim each of your holes. Soon, I will fill your tight, virgin ass with my 'colossal cock.' So no need for shock at my touch," he smirks. "In fact, I have something for you, Little One. A gift."

I hear his footsteps retreat as Malcolm walks to the other side of his office. I chance a peek over my shoulder to find him removing an item from a closet. Unable to see it, I turn forward again and await my gift.

A cool, wet sensation slides from the top of my ass crack to land on my bottom hole. I shiver when I realize it's a lubricant. Oh dear.

My Dom smooths a generous amount of the substance over my hole as my legs quiver and my breath hitches. He spanks each butt cheek when I move away from his finger as he glides it inside.

"Oh no, Little One. You will hold position," he reprimands me.

The pressure increases until his first knuckle pushes past the tight rings of muscles. I groan and slap the desk.

Slowly he pumps his finger in and out, then adds a second one to scissor with the first. More murmurs of encouragement fill my ear as My Dom leans over me, his torso flat against mine.

The pain morphs to pleasure, and I squeeze my eyes shut, embarrassed to enjoy the foreign invasion.

"Very good, Little One. You like my thick fingers inside of your tight ass. I feel your pussy clench and smell your sweet arousal," Malcolm says with a throaty growl. "Now, for your gift."

Immediately, his fingers withdraw and cool stainless steel touches my bottom hole. He pushes it into my stretched back passage. With a pop, he seats it deep inside of me. The wide base rests between my butt cheeks.

I mewl.

Malcolm kneels behind me and covers my pussy lips with his mouth. He rims them with the tip of his tongue, then darts it in and out, picking up a steady rhythm. Soon his fingers join in. The erotic sound of my moans joins his rumbles of satisfaction.

The impending climax barrels towards me at full speed. I beg My Dom to allow me to cum as my pussy juices slide from my core to his hungry mouth.

He stands, and the sound of his zipper lowering makes me cry out in joy.

"Yeeesss!!!" I scream and slap my palms against the desk when he slams his engorged dick deep inside of me with its piercing scraping my sensitive tissue.

The added butt plug makes for a tight fit, and I squirm under the onslaught of his passionate, controlled thrusts. Malcolm pummels me. His groin pushes the plug deeper, and his seed-filled balls slap against my swollen clit.

It's all too much, and I keen as my orgasm rips through me. My back bows, and I grind against him, wanting to take him as deep inside of me as possible, and then even more.

"So fucking tight, Little One… Your greedy pussy wants more… I'll give you more!" Malcolm snarls as he slaps my ass.

His thrusts turn into a jackhammering as he pistons his hips to ramp up his domination of my body.

When wave after wave of orgasms follow, I can no longer focus and give in to the power of My Dom as he chases his release. My mind blanks and my legs go boneless.

Malcolm increases his hold on my hip and slips his other arm under me to wrap his fingers around my throat. Held in his grip, I rock with his movements and cry out in carnal bliss.

One last thrust lifts me to the balls of my feet, and he stills. His cock hardens further, then jerks as a torrent of his seed coats my womb.

We groan in unison as my pussy muscles milk every drop.

Malcolm collapses on top of me until our breath returns to normal. He nuzzles my neck, then kisses my sweat-soaked skin.

"How do you like your gift, Little One?" He asks against the shell of my ear as he slips from my core and taps the base of the butt plug with his fingertip.

I moan, then respond in a low throaty voice, "I love it, Sir. Thank you."

His dark chuckle reverberates through my body.

MALCOLM

"Oh, my goodness! This is amazing, Malcolm!"

After the last month of working on our new partnerships—business and pleasure—I have the urge to bring Starr further into my world. I want to experience more with her than just fucking or a D/s relationship. Crazy? Yeah. But when do I dodge the crazy?

Thus our trip to the Mayan city of Tulum in Mexico for cave diving at the Cenote Angelita.

It's the top site in the world for the extreme sport and one I enjoy the most for its challenging environment. With its cloudy layer resembling a magical veil separating the clear fresh water from the salt water below and a depth of 200 feet, one must hold an advance open water scuba diver certification. A surprise underwater river adds to its risk level.

The sandy bottom with tree branches and rocks lit by the sunlight as it filters through the fish-filled water can appear eerie or tranquil depending upon the person. For me, its mysterious environment intrigues me and tests my limits.

Fortunately, My Angel also loves a challenge and doesn't find the idea of diving in an underground hole squirm-worthy. She's bouncing on her feet as we wait in the dense tropical jungle to descend into the cave. She's excited to explore the famous sinkhole and its shadowy caverns.

The muscles in her long, toned legs flex and her D-cups jiggle in her triangle bikini top as she slips into her diving swimsuit. Her sorrel-colored eyes dazzle as she winks at me.

"I cannot wait to get down there! I've been to Ben's Cave in Grand Bahama since it's ideal for beginners who want to experience the world of cave diving"—Starr raises her hand to silence my reminder and lifts it to her heart in a pledge—"I promise not to stray from your side."

We had a long discussion about her interest in extreme sports. I agreed to invite her on some trips I take with the guys. Since she's athletic and remains calm under pressure with her breathing techniques, My Angel will make for a perfect mentee.

"Right! Do not under any circumstances stray from Malcolm or any of us. Remember the hand signals we discussed on the helicopter ride here," Lucien adds.

I have to control the caveman in me from snarling at his suggestion of my mate seeking protection from any other male.

"You'll do well, *malen'kiy*," Anton says as he high fives Starr.

Then, I let a growl rip out of my mouth at his *little one* reference. Asshole!

He and Borya chuckle at my possessive behavior while My Angel gapes at me. Even the guide and his team appear startled by my outburst. Like I give a fuck.

"Let's do this!" Lucien interjects as he claps his hands to diffuse the situation.

We spend the next forty minutes exploring Cenote Angelita's incredible submerged world. As promised, Starr stays at my side then only an arm's distance away when we swim along the misty underground river near the bottom of the water-filled pit. No need for the current to sweep her away.

The entire time Starr swivels her head left and right to take in the majesty of the sacred site. Through the face mask, her eyes flicker from one side of the limestone cavern to the other. She nods and points to the fish and formations in wide-eyed fascination.

I'm more intrigued by her than by the cenote.

Once we're topside, we pull out our mouthpieces, and Starr throws her head back to laugh.

"I want some more!" She says as her eyes twinkle gold in the sun's reflection from the water's surface.

The guys and I join in her laughter as we swim to the edge of the sinkhole. The guide and his team hoist us out, and we remove our scuba gear.

Starr leaps into my arms, wraps her limbs around me, and slants her lush mouth over mine.

I stagger back at the unexpected impact. But instinctively cup her ass and squeeze the round globes agreeably. My cock proves more entranced when it hardens against the tight scuba suit.

"Thank you, baby!" My Angel enthuses when we come up for air—literally.

I press my forehead against hers and tell her how happy I am she enjoyed the dive.

She slides down my body and kisses my lips before she shimmies out of her suit. Disappointment fills me when she pulls a long-sleeved t-shirt and track pants over her bikini. Then drops to the ground to put socks and hiking boots back on.

Soon we're changed and line up to head out. Starr slips her hand in mine and smiles up at me.

My Angel is a trooper who could not care less we have to trek through the humid, lush overgrowth to the clearing where the STEELE Tulum Hotel and Resort's Sikorsky S-92 Executive Helicopter awaits our return. She may be from a wealthy family, but her parents raised her down-to-earth as my mother insisted for my siblings and me. Plus being hippies, it accustoms the Knights to roughing it at outdoor festivals with rain, mud, and other uncomfortable situations.

"We take it you had a solid dive, *da*?" Borya asks when we're on board the helicopter.

Starr grins and nods, "Absolutely! It was an incredible experience. I'm ready for my next one!"

I beam at her reaction, then point out some sights, including the Mayan ruins as we soar overhead. The glittering water of the Caribbean Sea and the islands of Cozumel, Cuba, Caymans, and Jamaica appear on the horizon before us.

After the hike through the jungle, we're ready to hit the beach at the resort. Time for a dip, ceviche, and a pitcher of mojitos—My Angel's favorite cocktail.

When we land on the helipad, we race to the beach as we strip, then dive into the warm, sparkling water. Starr's melodic laughter fills the air along with a splash as I toss her into the waves. She resurfaces and pays me back with the sweep of her arm to arc water in my direction.

I wrestle her into my embrace, and she moans when she feels my erection against her belly. One swift move allows me to slide her bikini bottom to the side and impale her on my cock.

We groan as my girth stretches her tight pussy to bring our bodies as close as a man and woman can get. With the water up to my shoulders, I use my grip on her curvaceous hips to ride my rock-hard length. So aroused from my pent-up desire, I bring us over the edge to an epic climax.

The shudders from our sated lovemaking make ripples in the surrounding water.

Starr buries her face in my neck and cries out her pleasure against my heated skin. I press my mouth against her wet hair and groan in total carnal euphoria.

Fuck, she feels so good. This feels so good. I don't think I can ever get enough of my woman.

How crazy is that???

* * *

STARR TWIRLS in my arms as we dance at the resort's beachside club. Each night a local deejay or a live band performs for an authentic experience beneath the starry sky. The deep bass of the sultry music combined with the gathering of writhing bodies in the tropical heat makes erotic energy swirl around us.

My hands roam over her voluptuous body as the red slip of a dress skims the tops of her thighs. Her plump, brown nipples stand out in bas-relief, still swollen from my earlier suckling. The only thing she wears beneath the silky material is her butt plug gift.

Tonight I will claim her virgin puckered hole.

In the meantime, we join the other dancers as the rhythm pulsates through us—a prelude to the evening's hedonism.

"Sir, I don't know if I can continue to hold the plug inside of me. The sweat makes it slippery," Starr whispers in my ear.

Her warm breath—minty from the mojitos we drank

before we stepped onto the outdoor dance floor—tickles my skin.

I spank her butt cheek and appreciate the jiggle of her firm flesh.

"You will keep your gift deep inside until I remove it to fill your ass with an even better present… My cock. Understand, Naughty Girl?" I respond.

Starr closes her eyes and her lower lip trembles before she nods in the affirmative.

Another quick smack jars the butt plug, and she whimpers a verbal answer against my neck. Her arms tighten around me as she lifts to the balls of her feet in strappy fuck-me sandals.

I keep her on the dance floor for another twenty minutes before I take her hand and lead her to the path for our villa. We pass Borya grinding with a Mexican beauty, then Lucien with a blonde from Sweden. I scan the crowd to find Anton. He's at our VIP table whispering in the ear of the Cuban heiress to a tobacco company.

Knowing they set my boys for the night, I can enjoy My Angel. Time for my cave exploration…

STARR

"$\mathcal{H}$i, Starr. Long time no see. Hmmm… You're all tan. Where have you been, sweetie?"

I turn to the syrupy voice behind me to find Vicky in the doorway of my private studio.

The smile on her face doesn't reach her frosty blue eyes. She may be an actress, but she's having a tough time reigning in her emotions. With her tense posture and fingers fiddling the corner of her yoga mat, I sense her displeasure despite the forced smile.

"Oh, hi, Vicky. Good to see you, too, honey," I respond, returning her unnecessary term of endearment and ignoring her question.

I re-focus on the room's sound system to prepare for my next class. My class roster didn't include Vicky's name, so I guess she's a last-minute addition…

For the past month, I could avoid her since she was filming a movie in Toronto. Being on the other side of the continent proved the perfect barrier. Her scenes must have wrapped. So here she stands.

Hopefully Vicky doesn't have an inkling about my relationship with Malcolm. That would be a major disaster. I'm really not interested in her histrionics.

Not that I'd mention it. For one, Malcolm and I signed a nondisclosure agreement—in both our best interests. Another reason, it's none of her affair—no pun intended.

Once Malcolm explained the cause for their demise, I didn't harbor bad feelings for him, and I inclined no longer to feel sorry for Vicky.

I mean, who goes against an NDA and even worse plots to marry a multibillionaire. A giggle slips past my pursed lips when I remember the classic romantic comedy *How to Marry a Millionaire*. The screen sirens Marilyn Monroe, Betty Grable, and Lauren Bacall set up shop in a penthouse with the aim to snag wealthy men. The end cracks me up each time!

So, yeah, it's not farfetched for someone to plan on a big ole diamond ring from Malcolm Steele.

Except that's not my goal.

I'm thrilled with our time together thus far. But don't have the end goal of a walk down the aisle. He's still a playboy, no matter how many toe-curling orgasms he gives to me. I guess he wouldn't be able to give them to me if he didn't have the experience of being a playboy.

"So, where did you get your tan?"

Vicky's repeat question brings me back to the studio. She spreads her yoga mat in the front row opposite mine. Then turns her questioning gaze back to me.

Great. Talk about a dog with a bone.

"I visited some locations for more international retreats and an additional location for SLFW," I respond with enough truth I hope satisfies her curiosity.

I hate to lie. But will if necessary to protect what's mine. Plus, I don't trust Vicky exactly.

The marketing teams will release a joint statement to the

press next week now that we've had plenty of meetings to iron out all details and to complete the timeline. So it's no big deal to give Vicky a heads-up.

She eyes me for a moment, then grins.

"Congratulations, sweetie! You deserve it," Vicky says as she pulls me into a hug.

I pat her back, then sigh with relief inwardly when more voices sound behind us. One more squeeze, and I turn to the students arriving.

"Namaste, ladies and gentlemen," I say as I press my palms together at my breastbone and bow to the light in my students.

And thank God and every deity in every religion's pantheon for intervening Vicky's inquisition!

"HI, BABE. HOW WAS YOUR DAY?"

I'm seated on my cushion after meditation in the side garden of my home. Now's the time to tell Malcolm about Vicky while I have a clear head amongst the relaxing fragrance of the flower blossoms.

The class went smoothly. Some students stayed after for some hands-on adjustments and tips. Fortunately, Vicky left when I focused on the students and not her lingering on her mat. With a huff, she left my studio.

Crisis averted for now…

"You handled her well. She can be a gossip in general. But if she knows about us, I'm not sure how she'll react. However, I will protect you from any harm she may try to inflict on your or SLFW," Malcolm *The Enforcer* Steele declares vehemently.

A smile threatens to split my face. My body heats with warmth, not from lust. But from happiness he cares so much for me. His reaction makes me wonder how serious he is about us beyond our D/s relationship.

I've noticed Malcolm calls me babe or angel if we're not in a scene where I'm Little One or Naughty Girl.

Do I mind? No, not at all. It's a change from Quinn, and his concern for himself only. From Malcolm's focus on my sexual needs to my business goals to my protection, perhaps I could get used to being with him on a regular basis.

The thought warms me further.

"What did you conquer today, Mr. Steele?" I ask him.

His dove gray eyes glitter with mischief as I stare at my iPhone's screen. Malcolm is so damned sexy.

It's been a week since we last saw each other in person. FaceTime makes up for it. Well… Along with the explicit videos we share each night.

Fuck! I'm horny just thinking about them. That man's body, I swear!

Malcolm tells me about his latest acquisition of a floundering beach resort in Uruguay and his plans for a LEVELS Beverly Hills.

That perks my ears. The New York, Paris, and London locations appeared in my Google research on BDSM. I would love to become a member of the luxury clubs to live out my fantasies. Even better, as Malcolm's sub.

Lucien spotted an optimal location, and Malcolm plans a site visit in the coming weeks. Plus, we'll have a status update from our teams with Lucien for the first Jackson Hole retreat.

My alarm chimes.

"Oh, I have to get ready. I'll talk to you tomorrow," I tell Malcolm as I rise from my pillow.

He frowns and asks, "Get ready for what?"

Taken aback by his tone of voice, I bring the iPhone up

again to gauge his facial expression. His frown deepens when I scowl at him. Really???

"Girls' Night Out," I answer vaguely.

Malcolm narrows his eyes and tilts his head to the side.

"What does that mean?" He demands.

I put my hand on my hip and deepen my scowl.

"What do you mean by 'what does that mean?' I'm sure you've heard of the term?" I respond indignantly.

Is he seriously trying to control me outside of the bedroom??? I don't think so!

Malcolm takes a breath and wipes his hand over his face. Then pins me with his Dom stare.

Oh hell, no!

Before he can utter a word, I hold up my hand.

"Do not use your Dom-mind-control voice on me, Malcolm Steele! We are not in a scene, and this is my life to do as I choose. And I choose to enjoy a night out with my friends. Understand?" I retort, using his word for emphasis.

Malcolm stares at me for a solid fifteen seconds.

I refuse to give in. He will not control me. I am not into a total power exchange relationship. Not at all.

"Fine, Starr. As I said when we began our D/s relationship, the sub holds all the power, not the Dom. Enjoy your Girls' Night Out. I'll talk to you tomorrow," Malcolm responds with a stoic expression.

We end the call.

Somehow, I feel unsettled, as though I let him down. Hell, my stomach even hurts. As I walk inside the house to my bedroom, my mind replays the end of our conversation.

Maybe I was too harsh on Malcolm. He wasn't rude or anything.

Just as I consider begging off of my plans, my mobile rings.

"Hey, girl! I need your advice. Should I wear the black sequin romper or the fuchsia backless top and matching mini skirt? Claudia votes for the romper."

Adrienne's FaceTime call helps me to make up my mind. Girls' Night Out it is!!!

MALCOLM

"Lucien, you did it again, cuzz. This is the optimal location for LEVELS Beverly Hills. The view of the Hollywood Sign seals the deal for me. In the heart of luxury combined with an iconic landmark, we couldn't find a better spot for our hedonistic playground!"

I clap my partner in the pursuit of carnal pleasure on the back as we stand on the roof of the six-story former atelier. It once served as the workshop and later storefront for a famous costume designer to movie studios during the height of Hollywood glamour from the thirties through fifties.

The property remained in the family's possession, but they've since lost their fortune and failed to preserve the treasure. Lucien heard about it from a friend of theirs. We'll be able to purchase the building, its land, and its air rights for a fair price.

Just eyeballing the structure—interior and exterior—the renovation will require at least three months of construction and two weeks for the decor. Staffing will start immediately so we can vet the potential employees, have them sign the contract and NDA, and complete their training a month before the opening party.

Once we close on the property, we'll inform the current members for their referrals and we'll open the application to those we have on the wait list. Over the years, we learned it's best to boost the majority of our numbers from within with a smattering of those who come through the dance club or restaurant. Members and interests voice interest in a West Coast LEVELS, and now we can deliver.

"Like totally rad, dude!" Harris says in his surfer impersonation. "But seriously, this is spot on. Still within Beverly Hills with the added benefit of being on a street with less foot traffic. It will blend in amongst the surroundings and not call attention to its purpose—a hidden exclusive jewel."

We inform the real estate agent and the family's representative of our decision to move forward with the deal. Another glance at the Hollywood Sign lit up in the distance, then we leave.

"Smart idea to tour the property at night for a sense of its full impact. But even better, since it's time to hit the lounge, gentlemen!" Lucien says when we settle in my Black Badge Rolls-Royce Cullinan.

When we arrive, the valet parks the SUV while the three of us stride inside past the line of hopefuls. It pays to know the owner.

Lucien shakes hands with the door security and hostesses on our way to the VIP section, where we settle at his banquet in the center. The decadent lounge features plush leather and velvet seating, two bars, a spacious outdoor patio, and an opulent benitoite fireplace—the rare crystal known as the official gem of California discovered by James Couch. Hence the lounge's name: Jackson's Couch.

Immediately, the server sets a selection of bottles from Jackson Corporation's labels on the low table and pours our selections. Another server places platters of finger foods including wild mushroom crostini, salmon caviar sushi bites, and skewered shrimp with ham. All derived from Lucien's creative mind to tantalize one's palette with the dishes' rich flavors and just salty enough to increase one's thirst for the expensive libations.

The hungry eyes that followed us as we crossed the sofas and oversized chairs hone in on us as we sit back and survey the room. Two members of the STEELE Quaternity and one of the three Jackson brothers draw attention.

The preening and fluffing precede their stroll over. Low-cut tops reveal all sizes of tits; sparkly mini dresses cover asses barely; mile-long legs end in fuck-me sandals. Brunettes, blondes, redheads; long or short; curly or straight; a veritable rainbow or stunning women flock to us.

Everyone wants to score a young, hot, multibillionaire…

My mind turns to My Angel.

So unlike any of these females. She's more stunning. But that's where the similarities end. My wealth didn't draw Starr to me. Her interest lies with the success of her company and how STEELE can help her achieve it.

Not to mention she fell into me from behind with no clue as to my identity. Her speechless reaction wasn't from recognition of me from the *Forbes* World's Billionaires List or gossip pages. It was an instantaneous attraction on the carnal level. We called to one another through our pheromones. And I must say my cock sprang to life when I dazzled My Angel.

Since then, not one other female has done it for me. So the women strutting in my direction are about to waste their time.

Harris on the other hand leans back with his arms on top of the banquet and his legs spread in invitation. A cocky grin plays on his face.

And right on cue, a buxom beauty with smooth caramel skin and a mane of curly hair saunters over to stand between his legs.

Harris' smoky gray eyes travel over her curves in the white silk, drape-necked mini dress. She leans over and whispers in his ear. His smirk widens, and he tilts his head to suggest the space next to him.

The woman's topaz-colored eyes glitter in triumph as she sits beside my youngest brother, crosses her shapely legs, and places a small hand on his muscular thigh. She offers Lucien and me a brilliant smile, then turns her attention to Harris.

Just as Lucien and I glance at one another and chuckle, a voice calls out.

"Lucien, honey! We didn't know you were in LA!"

We shift our gazes in the woman's direction to find two statuesque brunettes beaming at *The Sexy Chef*. The gold bangles on their arms clink as they run their fingers through their silky tresses. Dressed similarly in miniskirts and midriff-baring halter tops. The nipples of their enhanced tits strain against the thin fabric.

Their gazes dart between Lucien and me.

I turn my head and sip my Jackson Special Blend Scotch. Hopefully, they'll get the hint…

Not deterred, one of them squeezes between Lucien and me while her friend sits on his other side. The one with the green eyes asks if she can have something to drink, then takes my snifter. Her gaze locks on me as she flicks her little pink tongue out to lick the rim before she takes a taste.

"It fills my mouth with a burst, then goes down so smoothly… Delicious," she purrs. "I'm Missy. You look familiar. Are you an actor?"

Her hand not cradling my snifter slides up my thigh as she cocks her head to the side in concentration.

Just as I clamp my hand on top of hers to stop her from reaching my crotch, she grins and squeezes my leg.

"Sebastian Steele! Oh wow! So—"

I stand disgusted by her and how she just proved my point. The world knows Baz married Lola since it's all over the Internet. The monikers *Couple of the Century* and *SeLo* trend on Twitter and Instagram since they announced their engagement.

Again, these thirsty broads don't give a damn. And I don't have the inclination to correct the mistaken identity.

Instead, I stride to the outdoor patio to collect a fresh drink from the bar in that section. The cooler night air has fewer people buzzing around. A few couples snuggle around the fire pits and some singles linger at the bar.

A woman gives me the eye while I wait for the bartender to fix my drink. But I pretend to receive a text message and lean against the bar facing the opposite direction. I turn at the clink of the glass on the surface and stride away with my Scotch.

I take a moment for a taste before I head back in. My thoughts drift to My Angel. She had dinner with her parents so couldn't meet me for the walk-through. Nor did she invite me to meet them. It's been four months and neither of us has introduced the other to our parents.

The realization shouldn't bother me. I'm not the heads-over-heels type, but I also realize I wouldn't mind the connection Sebastian has with Lola and Roger has with Leonie. Of course, neither of my brothers had their women sign a D/s contact and an NDA…

Then again, I can't understand the visceral reaction I had to Starr going on her "Girls' Night Out" last month. When she didn't back down, I attributed my irritation to the Dom in me wanting control of his sub. Later it occurred to me what I really didn't want was some fucker flirting with My Angel or worse.

Mine!

"Hi, do you mind if I joined you?"

I glance down to see the redhead from the bar smiling at me as she inclines her head towards a chair for two beside one of the fire pits.

"Thank you—"

"Yes! He would mind as would I!"

My head swivels to my left.

Vicky! Fuck. Me.

She glares at the other woman. Icy daggers shoot from Vicky's eyes as she stares the redhead down. She closes her mouth agape in surprise, then silently pivots on her heels.

I watch as she retreats to the bar without a backwards glance.

The pressure of a hand on my forearm brings my focus back to Vicky. I shoot my dominant glare at her until she releases me from her hold.

I step around her. But Vicky reaches out to clutch my upper arm with both hands. Not wanting to make a scene since a few of the patrons on the patio watch out every move, I take Vicky by the elbow and lead her to a corner.

She leans into me and reaches up to put her arms around my neck.

"Sir! Please! I miss you so much!" Vicky whines.

I put my hands on either side of her waist and push her away. She clings to me like a little monkey and squirms in my grasp, wiggling her hips.

"Enough, Vicky!" I command through clenched teeth. "Remove your hands and stop with the 'Sir' bullshit. You only acted submissive to get a ring. And… you… failed. Let it go already."

She steps back and stares at the ground as she twists her

hands in front of her. A faint sob comes from her down-turned mouth. Peeking at me from beneath her thick eyelashes, Vicky gives me a beseeching look.

"Malcolm, I am truly sorry. It's not that I don't derive pleasure from your… ways. You're the best lover I've ever had. I promise I won't tell a soul. Above all, I truly miss you… Miss us! Please forgive me and give us another chance," Vicky begs pitifully.

I scan her face for any sign of guile. The last thing I want is for her to become vindictive and talk shit despite the NDA.

But again, not even a spasm from my cock. And certainly nothing from my heart. No, My Angel has me whipped.

I shake my head and raise my hand when Vicky opens her mouth to protest. The memory that she questioned Starr in her studio about her tan gives me pause. We don't think Vicky knows about us, but we can't be too careful.

So instead of leaving Vicky with tears in her eyes, I try to assuage her.

"Vicky, I forgive you, and I want you to understand my goal is not to hurt you. But our time is over. It is best for you to move on. Good night."

I move past her, but stop at her words. A chill races down my spine.

"Like you have, Sir?!?!" She shouts.

Instead of reacting, I continue to walk inside. Without breaking stride, I send a text message to my attorney to handle this situation. Apparently Vicky has not learned the meaning of a nondisclosure agreement, and he will have to remind her. Again.

Next I send a text to Harris and Lucien to tell them I'm out. They'll get Lucien's driver to pick them up whenever they're ready.

See, this is the shit that can happen on a night out…

I ignore other attempts from women as I weave through patrons gathered on the furniture and past those at the interior bar. I acknowledge a few acquaintances with a nod or a raised hand. But my goal is to get out posthaste.

Once outside, I ask for my keys from one valet. They left my Cullinan to the side for easy access. In a matter of moments, I settle behind the wheel.

A glance at the dashboard clock shows it's nine-thirty. Starr's dinner started at eight o'clock. Not wanting to waste time before I can see My Angel, I decide to wait outside of the gates to her mansion. It's been long enough since we last saw each other in person. One can do so many FaceTime fucks.

Not long after I park, headlights flash across my windshield. Their light fills me with a brightness at the thought I'll have My Angel in my arms, then beneath me shortly.

I flip my high beams and wave.

Starr's eyes widen behind her window before she recognizes me. I drive behind her silver Tesla and follow her car to park in front of the garage. She marches towards me.

My gaze glides from her eyes to her curls piled atop her head to the cream, long-sleeved knit dress to her gold metallic pumps. It's not until she smacks me in the chest with her handbag do I realize My Angel is not at all happy to see me.

I grasp her wrists and hold her still.

"It's me, angel. What? What's the matter?" I ask when she yanks away from me and swats my reaching hands away.

Starr folds her arms over her chest and scowls.

"The better question, what are you doing here, Malcolm?" She snaps.

Baffled, I stare back at her with my mouth open.

She shakes her head and folds her arms tighter around

her body as though she's protecting herself from me. Or worse, blocking me out.

"Well?" Starr asks as she cocks her head to the side and raises an elegantly arched eyebrow.

"I honestly do not know what happened. We agreed to meet after your dinner. So, you tell me why you pushed me away," I respond with my hands palms up in surrender.

Starr narrows her sorrel brown eyes as they glint in the light from the wrought-iron sconces on the garage. Again she shakes her head, then reaches inside of her handbag. Her fingers fly across the screen. She advances with her mobile held aloft.

I peer at the screen and see several photos of me.

Me with Vicky in my arms. Caught in a compromising embrace: my hands planted on her waist; her arms around my neck with her fingers tangled in my hair; connected at our groins as she wriggles against me.

FUCK!

My eyes dart to Starr's, and I swear they glint not with light but with tears.

Fucking Vicky Pain in my ass!

Someone took photos of us at Jackson's Couch and posted them to Instagram. Then the bloggers picked it up, followed by the gossip rags. Headlines scream: Another Steele Down the Aisle? Billionaire Daredevil Malcolm Steele's Latest Feat. In a matter of thirty minutes, we were trending.

The world never sees me with a woman other than one-offs with a model or socialite at an event. I prefer to keep my dalliances private. Hence the contracts and NDAs…

Now I'm blowing up the Internet with Vicky, of all people.

I shift my gaze to Starr, who stares back at me with a flushed face.

"Angel, baby, I wasn't holding Vicky. She approached me at the lounge unexpectedly. Then she tried to hug me after she begged for my forgiveness. I was pushing her away," I say.

When Starr's expression changes to skepticism, I add, "Trust me, Angel. I will never lie to you."

She continues to gaze into my soul, then glances away as though a battle rages inside her mind.

I wait for My Angel to speak. I won't push her now, but I won't give up either. After what seems like a decade, she faces me.

"I trust you, Malcolm. But you have to understand how it appears to me. Hell, to anyone who sees the photos," she responds as she throws her hands in the air and blows a breath. "Fine, let's go inside, it's chilly."

My breath rushes from my constricted lungs—I didn't even realize I was holding it. I say a silent prayer of thanks, then catch up to My Angel. Satisfied, I clasp her hand in mine and bring it to my lips before I pull her into my arms and carry her inside.

"I'll warm you up real quick, My Angel," I croon against her neck.

She shivers against me, then squeals when I latch on her neck and suck. Hard.

The caveman in me wants to leave a bright red mark on her chestnut-colored skin. If I could make it indelible, I would. A permanent tattoo to prove she's mine all mine.

My Angel directs me to her bedroom where I make it my sole purpose to pump her inner fire and make her mine.

STARR

"**O**h, this is just what I needed… Sun, sand, cocktails, and my girls."

Lola says as she sighs and leans back against the chaise lounge. She sips her Tipo Tinto R&R rum and raspberry with a sigh. Her mouth stained red from the iconic Mozambican specialty drink.

Leonie, Blair, Haley, Billie, and I laugh at her drama.

"Hold on! You just returned from your two-month long honeymoon full of sun, sand, cocktails, and a sexy as hell husband," Leonie starts. "How could you need more two months later?"

Lola swats the pillow away that Leonie tosses at her and sits up.

"Right!" Chorus Blair and Billie.

I shake my head. My curly, dark brown hair sways along my back as my dimples deepen with my smile.

"Lola, you crack me up! Even I, a staunch believer in self-care, can't imagine why you need a break this soon!"

With that, I throw my pillow and ding Lola on the stomach. She laughs and hugs the pillow to her chest.

"I agree! Give us a break already, Lola!" Haley adds as she rolls her sharp gray eyes behind her glasses.

"Well, so that you know, I've been extremely busy catching up on work I missed while on my honeymoon with my sexy as fuck husband. Now, I need you, Ms. Knight, to work your magic to clear my head and relax me. And boy do you have your work cut out for you, again!"

Lola throws the pillow back at me, and I catch it.

"Fine. Challenge accepted, Mrs. Steele!" I reply with a giggle.

Lola swoons clutching her ginormous engagement ring to her bosom. She's right, it's definitely like her idol Elizabeth Taylor's ice skating rink ring. The nearly 30 carats glimmer in the torchlight.

The ring is a Steele family heirloom Shelley most recently wore. Since Sebastian is the eldest son, he inherited it and will pass it to his eldest son in time.

Lucky girl!

My thoughts turn to her brother-in-law and My Dom. We've been in our relationship for five months, and it's fantastic. Well, aside from the Vicky Internet Scandal… Sometimes when he sleeps curled around me, I think if our D/s situation can be more. Now listening to Lola, I wonder if Malcolm and I will go further like Lola and Sebastian. Hell, even Roger seems to have won Leonie back.

"Leonie… Hello there… Leonie?"

"Girl! Snap out of it!"

"Oh, don't tease her…"

"See, I knew it! He's blown her mind and her back—"

"Okay, okay! I hear you already!" She cuts into the girls' chatter with a laugh.

All eyes are on her, varying from expressions of concern to smirks.

When I called to invite everyone to my second

international fitness retreat, we agreed to make it a Girls' Getaway, too. Time for us to reconnect with our minds, bodies, and friends. Over the seven days, we plan to do just that.

The retreat is at a luxury beachfront resort on Buenguerra Island off the coast of Mozambique in the channel between the country and the Indian Ocean. The island is a haven known for its pristine, white-sand beaches, peaceful vibe, and five-star resorts.

The property we're staying at is the most exclusive with only three cabanas, ten casinhas, and one large villa scattered across eleven acres of beachfront and lush tropical vegetation. The retreat participants and my staff along with the girls secured the entire resort. It's our private oasis.

Lola, Billie, Haley, Blair, and Leonie claimed the villa since it features five large bedrooms with sitting areas, living room, dining room, and kitchenette. The outdoor areas include a pool, deck area with thatched-roof cabana and chaise lounges, plus chaise lounges down by the ocean. It's stunning and tranquil.

I chose a casinhas since I'm working more so than relaxing. Plus, I need more space to meet with my team and for one-on-one sessions with guests. It's just through the palm trees on one of the sandy paths that crisscross the property.

"Spill. You've been mighty quiet about Roger and you..." Billie says as her green eyes flash.

"Right! I know I've been away and busy. But even so," Lola starts. "You can always call me. I am your BFF!"

"Oh, don't pressure her!" Blair says concerned.

"No pressure, but... Do tell!" I join in the laughter.

Leonie smiles at her closest friends. Then takes a sip of her Tipo Tinto R&R. When she sets it down on the side table, we stare at her expectantly.

"I'm in love with the man of my dreams!" She throws her head back and roar. "He's mine, all mine! And I'm all his!"

We holler and stomp our feet.

"Another brother taken so he can get off my back about my love life! Thank you, Leonie! Hooray!" Shouts Haley, pumping her fists into the air as she falls back onto her chaise lounge.

Lola jumps up and grabs Leonie's hands to pull her to stand. They do their happy shimmy dance around the chaises.

"Yeah, Girl! Strut your stuff!" I call out as I fan herself.

Billie jumps up and joins their parade. Soon we form a conga line and weave in and out of the furniture. Then we head out to the beach where we form a circle under the brilliant moonlight and star-filled sky. My girls and I continue to dance around as our laughter carries out over the silent, inky black water.

* * *

"Let us end our practice with three oms together. Inhale through your nose gently, hold it for a heartbeat. Then slowly release your breath back through your nose. Let us begin."

The next morning, I set aside my thoughts on Malcolm and focus on my yoga session.

My entrancing voice guides the students through the last part of the class. We started with breathwork for five minutes to prep us for a vigorous, forty-five-minute flow sequence. As I moved through the poses to demonstrate, my muscles craved the fast-paced tempo. It allowed my body to focus on the asanas and not wander. The ten-minute meditation grounded the students as much as me.

"Namaste. The light in me honors the light in you," I intone when we finish.

We bow to each other with palms pressed together at our heart centers. We remind ourselves of the good energy and intention we set forth in our practice. As we sit up and open our eyes, I beam with happiness. My love of helping others reach their best mental and physical potential shines from my sorrel brown eyes.

Students murmur words of gratitude, then wipe down their mats before they hang them on the wooden racks inside the beachside, open-air pavilion. Some students gather around to glean more advice. Two of my assistants offer adjustments for those who want more instruction.

I glance up and wave at my friends. They wave back before they walk down the steps to the sandy shore. Two other assistants wait to offer frothy shot glasses filled with refreshing juice made from local fruits. The delicious concoctions cool the students down and fill them with energy.

The tasty refreshments have ashwagandha in them. An Ayurvedic herb that many studies show increases energy and reduces stress and anxiety.

I can take my time with the students who remain since the next session for Pilates isn't for another two hours. Once I answer their questions, I stroll along the beach to my villa. The sun glistens on the water between the island and the Mozambique coast. The waves splashing on the sand call to me.

I decide to change into my bikini and go for a swim. It's a good idea and a great way to wash away the sweat from my yoga class. Mind made up,. I jog the rest of the way and yank my sports bra over my head as I rush into my bedroom. I ditch the skimpy yoga shorts and stride to the wardrobe. Snatching the first bathing suit I can reach, I step into the bottoms as I head to the door. Then slide them up over my hips. I don't worry about a top since we're on the secluded side of the island—no paparazzi to snap unwanted photos for Malcolm to go berserk about. I zip out the door, down to the beach, and dive into the first wave of the warm tropical Indian Ocean.

* * *

"How did you like the retreat?" I ask as the girls and I sit at the outdoor dining table surrounded by fragrant torches.

The other participants left yesterday morning. We stayed two extra days to spend some quality time together off of the mats. Yesterday we took a long hike through the verdant patchwork of forests on the island. Then had a rejuvenating swim in one of the crystal-clear freshwater lakes.

Now, we're eating a delectable dinner of flavorful local favorites prepared by a chef on the outdoor grill and cooktop. The aroma is mouthwatering. I sip my Tipo Tinto R&R and nibble on a flaky chamussa. The appetizer is just enough to keep us sated until he presents the main dishes.

"You did such a superb job, Starr! I can't wait for the next one," Billie answers as she clinks glasses with me.

"Indeed! I thought nothing could top your first one on Fijian Laucala Island last year. That private paradise is surreal," Lola chimes in.

"It was the best I've ever been on! Fantastic!" Haley says as she rises to give Starr a standing ovation.

"Sign me up for all of them! I feel incredible, thank you very much!" Leonie exclaims.

"Me, too!" Blair says as she raises her glass. "A toast… Here's to good friends, good loves, and good times!"

Everyone cheers and clinks glasses. Lola pauses and peers at me.

"What's the latest on your conversations with Malcolm?"

I choke on my Tipo Tinto.

Damn! Is Lola a mind reader or what?!

I wonder if she's prying because she knows something I don't or at least I haven't admitted to the girls yet. Unsure, I avoid Lola's probing gaze. I shift in my chair and pretend to straighten the napkin on my lap.

Lola is relentless.

"Well?" She demands.

I think back to the conversation Malcolm and I had the morning after they photographed him with Vicky. Although he was apologetic and made my body vibrate with climax after climax, he had to ruin the afterglow.

He told me snarkily, "That's what can happen during a night out, even a Girls' Night Out."

He couldn't let it go how it irritated him I went out with my girls the month before despite him not wanting me to go. I snapped back how I didn't end up in bed with any of the guys who flirted with me. Of course he blew his Alpha male top. We argued, and I called him an arrogant control freak.

That was a couple of weeks ago…

I clear my throat and return Lola's gaze.

Defiantly I lift my chin as I respond, "Malcolm Steele is an arrogant, self-focused cretin!"

Blair, Billie, and Leonie gape at my heated reaction. Haley covers her ears, not wanting to hear such things about her older brother.

They're astonished since I'm no longer the normally quiet calm, namaste, om, center your mind friend. Now I'm flustered completely. Their gazes dart between Lola and me in shock. The question, what the hell did Malcolm do to Starr files their faces.

Lola bursts out laughing. Her last sip of Tipo Tinto

comes out on a snort. She pulls back from the table, doubling over in glee. The sight is too comical. They can't help but join in—even me.

Once Lola gathers herself, wiping tears from the corners of her eyes, she straightens. She lifts her left hand and waggles her fingers. The ice skating rink on full blast.

"That's the same thing I said about his doppelgänger brother, Captain Caveman… Now look at me, my friend!"

My mouth falls open. I look just as stunned as the rest of the girls. But Lola just keeps giggling. She definitely knows something I'm clueless about. When they question her, Lola shakes her head and sips her drink, laughing to herself.

MALCOLM

"So, who's next of my boys to walk down the aisle? My guess is Roger. But after him, who do you think, darling?"

Sebastian chuckles. Harris and I gape at each other. Our mother Shelley smirks wickedly.

The Steele Matriarch—the true boss of our family—is a striking woman in her mid-fifties with shoulder-length, wavy black hair and expressive brown eyes. At only five feet, six inches, we tower over our mother. But her feisty New Yorker personality doesn't allow us or anyone to bully her.

Hence Harris and I know we have to give Shelley some kind of answer. We use telepathy to spar over who speaks first. But they don't call me *The Enforcer* for nothing.

"Mom… I'm only twenty-nine years old. I have my entire life ahead of me," Harris says in defeat, having caved to my unspoken command.

Her smirk deepens as she leans forward across the dining room table.

"'Only twenty-nine?' You say. I married your father

when I was twenty, and I had you and your sister—the youngest of my five children—at twenty-seven. So, who do you think, darling?" She finishes as she swings her gaze towards our father again.

Morgan smiles at her lovingly. He may be an Alpha Dom, but he melts for his wife and sub.

With his strong genes, all of his children resemble him with varying shades of gray eyes, wavy ebony hair, and height. His sons are splitting images of him standing well over six feet. While his daughter is a stunning female version at five feet, eight inches tall. Although at sixty-six years old and still fit, his thick ebony hair is more salt and pepper.

"Sweetheart, when I met you nothing and no one could prevent me from claiming you as mine. Sebastian felt the same with Lola. I agree Roger recognizes Leonie as his finally. When Malcolm and Harris meet their true loves, we can be certain age will not matter," our father responds as he holds her dainty, manicured hand between both of his sizable palms.

Well, damn.

I sit back in my chair and stare at our parents. We know it was love at first sight. But every time they express their enduring love for one another, it's the most beautiful thing I've ever seen.

Aside from My Angel…

My Angel who I pissed off after being a bit of a jerk about going out and what can happen. She was none too pleased with my comment. She told me so without holding back her disdain. Then proceeded to tell me she's busy with her upcoming fitness retreat and wouldn't have time to see me.

I returned to New York after a few more days in LA and

a stopover in Las Vegas for business. That was almost two weeks ago.

True to her word, Starr couldn't spare me but a few minutes a day before she flew off to Mozambique. She's there with her clients and her girls, including my brothers' true loves. They're extending their stay after the retreat participants leave for a Girls' Getaway.

My only consolation is them being on the small island of Buenguerra off the coast with few people aside from the hotel guests. It's doubtful My Angel will meet the man of her dreams with limited options available. At least I hope she doesn't, or I'll be fucked.

The hair on the back of my neck tingles. I glance up to find my mother watching me intently—Roger inherited her reach-into-your-soul stare. I swallow.

"Malcolm?" She asks with a raised eyebrow.

My eyes skitter to Sebastian for some help.

He sits back in his chair and steeples his fingers beneath his chin. His shoulders shake with held-back laughter, dove gray eyes sparkle.

I shift my gaze to Harris, and he offers a devious grin.

Fuckers.

My last hope to run interference, I glance at my father. His expression of answer your mother doesn't help me in any way. I sigh inwardly and drag my eyes to face my mother's inquisition.

She raises her eyebrow higher and cocks her head.

"Mom, you know how busy I am with STEELE and my sports. How can I have time for a serious relationship?" I ask.

Then my stomach churns.

How the hell can I deny my attraction for My Angel? And to my mother?

But I'm just not ready to admit out loud it's more than

satisfying my Dom and my sexual needs. Especially since we ended our last time together angrily.

Honestly, I've never been in a relationship where emotion outside of a BDSM scene plays a part. I'm out of my depth.

My mother stares, unblinking.

I squirm.

Fuck. Am I thirteen years old again or what?

"Fine. When you're ready to share your newfound love…" Shelley says mysteriously, then slices into her *Steak Fromage*.

I steal a glance at Baz.

He grins behind his glass of Petrus.

Fucker.

"OKAY, fess up, Malcolm. How's it going with Ms. Knight?"

Baz asks as he raises the Baccarat crystal snifter to his mouth and sips the Rémy Martin Louis XIII Cognac.

He, Harris, and I sit around the fire pit on the terrace off the living room of my penthouse in The STEELE Tower New York. We retired here after dinner at our parents' duplex on the top two floors. My kid brother and I needed a drink after our mother's probing.

Baz swirls the reddish-grayish-brown liquid, watching the flames from the fire brighten its color as they flicker behind the crystal glass. He lifts his gaze back to me and cocks his head questioningly.

We stare at one another. Once again holding out on who speaks first. This time I cave. I need Sebastian's advice.

"She's driving me crazy, bro," I say with a sigh.

Then lean forward and place my snifter on the ledge of the fire pit. I run my fingers through my hair. A tug snaps pain to my scalp. My senses sharpen. Focus returns. I need answers.

"You never had more than a one-night stand, maybe two nights with someone at a LEVELS before Lola. I've only had D/s contracted relationships. How the hell do you handle the emotions outside of the sex? What do you do when Lola defies you? And why the fuck do I want to tie Starr to my bed, claim her, and mark her for every male to see?!"

I finish with another yank on my hair. Then throw back the rest of my Rémy.

"Bro… You. Are. Fucked!!!" Harris chortles.

Baz snickers and leans forward to pin me with his gaze.

"As I remember, you and Harris called me a 'Lost Puppy' not too long ago… You even made goo-goo eyes and clutched your hearts. Your loud guffaws filled the jet's cabin," he says pointedly. "You know what I did? I cringed, but couldn't care less. You know why? *That's my girl,* I thought to myself. And guess what? Now Lola is. All. Mine."

He flicks his gaze to Harris and adds, "When Dad told you to cut your shit and suggested you settle down, the two of you zipped your lips. Harris, you checked your newfangled gadget. And you, my lovesick brother, preoccupied yourself with refilling your drink."

Baz gestures to my snifter and holds his empty one up.

"Now go get that expensive bottle you cherish and bring it out here. You're going to need it for the knowledge I'm about to impart to you," Baz finishes with a wicked chuckle.

Dutifully—and gratefully—I rise and do as he bid. It's going to be a long night.

LATER IN THE early hours of the morning, as the sun's rays brighten the star-filled sky, I lie in bed and replay a key point Sebastian made:

Yeah, I get where you're coming from. At first in the back of my mind a niggle reminded me I was a wimp for allowing more feelings where there should be none. I shook it off and moved forward.

It's exactly my situation. I'll just have to shake it off, too and let our relationship progress organically.

I close my eyes and take a cleansing breath before I contemplate Sebastian's lesson:

Apologize. Period. Then listen while Starr says whatever's on her mind. Apologize. Listen some more. Apologize. Again. And again. Until she has no more to say. Then let my body express my true feelings better than any words as I make love to My Angel.

With that in mind, I roll over to grab my mobile off of the nightstand. A quick check of the time shows it's 5 a.m. here and 11 a.m. in Mozambique. Starr will be teaching according to the retreat schedule. Perfect, I can leave a voicemail.

Hi, Angel. I apologize. Let's talk when you return. I miss you.

STARR

i, Angel. I apologize. Let's talk when you return. I miss you.

"You will wear my collar to show your status as a partnered sub—my sub—at all times. You will obey me in all sexual interactions unless you want all play to end with the use of your safeword, *tantric*. For a Dominant to place a collar on a submissive equals the pair's commitment to their D/s relationship. On some levels as important as a wedding ring to a marriage. Do you understand, Little One?"

A giggle would bubble out of my mouth at Malcolm's 180-degree change from his gentle voicemail a week ago to his authoritative statement now if it wasn't hanging open.

The sight of the beautiful, intricate platinum lacework covered in tiny sparkly diamonds leaves me speechless. So delicate it looks as though it could break in his sizable hands as he lifts it in front of me and puts it around my neck. The soft click of the closure makes me blink and lift my gaze from the collar to his intense gray eyes in the mirror's reflection.

I trace my fingertips lightly over the exquisite crafts-

140

manship, then place them atop his hands resting on my shoulders. My heart slams against my rib cage at the enormity of the situation. Am I ready for such a commitment? With Malcolm Steele, no less?

"Yes, Sir," I whisper.

"I custom ordered this piece for you. I want to capture your beauty, elegance, fragility, and strength. Never have I given my collar to any sub, Little One. Do you understand the significance?" My Dom says as we continue to stare at one another in the mirror.

"Yes, Sir," I respond.

My Dom turns me to face him and lifts my chin with his forefinger. His eyes pierce mine as he seeks confirmation.

"Do you have any other words for me, Little One?" He asks after a moment.

I bite my lower lip and shift my gaze. My mind runs through different scenarios: what happens if we break up; how will people react to my collar, particularly Vicky; how will this commitment change me, us. Hell, it's been six months, but is it too much too soon?

The silence looms between us as my thoughts run amok.

Malcolm waits patiently without a word or reactions. In fact, he appears to hold his breath.

Is he as nervous as me?

My gaze returns to his, and it's my turn to study him.

His gorgeous face has a hint of concern despite his attempt to remain neutral. It's in the pinch around his eyes and the tension in his jaw.

I go so far as to guess he's nervous I'll turn him down, even though he closed the collar securely around my neck. The part about the marriage comparison has me anxious. I've read in my Google searches the importance of a collar, so I don't take Malcolm's gesture lightly. Add in he's given none of his many subs a collar makes it an even bigger deal.

My insides warm. Malcolm Steele wants me enough to collar me, and with one designed specifically for me? Well, hot damn!

He opens his mouth to speak.

But I place my fingertips against them and shake my head. I slip my arms around his neck and meld our bodies together. I need the connection with him, to feel his heat and to gain his strength.

On an exhale, I let go of the negativity and inhale the positive direction we're taking as a couple. With my lips pressed to his, I murmur words of consent and understanding. With confidence, I agree to being Malcolm Steele's submissive to his dominant.

WE REACH a set of heavy wooden double doors with two large, iron circular pulls opened by a man and a woman scantily clad in black leather strips and collars. They incline their heads at My Dom as he leads me by the delicate platinum chain clipped to my collar's ring past them. My jaw drops again.

The Cellar—LEVELS New York's BDSM dungeon—looms ahead of us.

My eyes scan the expansive, grand hall, austere in design. A multi-beamed high ceiling; cobblestone floors; brick walls; lighting that resembles flickering torches in brackets on the walls and in metal stands scattered around the room; an assortment of what looks like Medieval torture devices placed in clusters. My gaze skitters from one area to another. An older man cuffed to one of the several St. Andrew's Crosses, his head thrown back in pure ecstasy. His engorged dick eagerly sucked by a younger man on his knees. A woman in a swing, her thighs glistening with her pussy juices and stretched wide to accommodate the large man standing between them, aligning her core to his massive cock. Several men and women attached to hooks hanging from the ceiling in varied positions being whipped by Doms and Dommes with canes, floggers, and paddles extending from their hands. Still others lead naked subs by leashes while they crawl on their hands and knees to one of the partitioned rooms for a bit of privacy. Here and there voyeurs stand watching, mesmerized by the decadent sexual activities.

The sight has my throbbing pussy so wet I can feel my juices slipping down to coat my trembling inner thighs. The aroma of my arousal wafts around me to fill my nose and to join with all the other sex-induced scents. I shift on my feet, embarrassed by my immediate reaction to the scenes before me. My first time at a LEVELS club does not disappoint.

A gentle tug to my collar alerts me to My Dom's forward movement. I trail behind him, taking in our surroundings discreetly.

Several pairs of eyes peer at me from head to toe.

I push my shoulders back and lift my ample chest as I strut behind My Dom in my Lola's Coterie playsuit. Yes, darlings. Stare at my banging body as triple strands of black strips with tiny rose gold studs cross over cone-shaped pasties to caress my bountiful breasts. Two additional sets of strips wind from my back and up from my sheer-thong-covered crotch to connect at two rose gold rings on either side of my narrow waist. My long legs end in black suede, sky-high stilettos. I'm bound.

Many of those eyes stay riveted on my diamond collar as it flashes its brilliance in the golden torchlight, bared by my upswept curls. Numerous women gape openly as their eyes bounce from my neck to My Dom's face. Surprise colors their cheeks red. Jealousy darkens their eyes to green.

I smirk at the realization they must be prior acquaintances…

"Well Steele, looks like you met your match… finally?"

I peek around My Dom to encounter a devastatingly handsome man with sapphire blue eyes, jet-black hair, and a cleft chin. He smirks at My Dom, then flicks his gaze to me with a devilish grin.

Heat spreads over my exposed skin.

"Keep your eyes in their sockets, Reilly," My Dom snarls.

The stunning man raises his hands, palms outward in surrender. The smile vanishes from his face.

"Whoa, Steele. No disrespect. You and I have shared before…" He responds no longer undressing me further with his jewel eyes.

"True. But note my collar adorns my submissive's neck, Reilly. She is a dazzling beauty. But you cannot miss my obvious claim," My Dom responds, then nods his head as he leads me away.

I dare not glance back even though my skin prickles with goosebumps. Without a doubt, Reilly still watches me. Instead, I add an extra sway to my hips and strut along, pleased by My Dom's possessive behavior.

He circulates in the room, proud to show me off to those present. Occasionally, we stop and he introduces me to other members, many well-known in business or celebrity circles. No one appears uncomfortable at being seen in a BDSM dungeon. Many have partners or subs. Others voyeurs, satisfied to observe and not partake in the bacchanalia.

The hedonistic atmosphere with the melodic thrum of sensual music and satisfied cries as the backdrop to intense sexual play attracts people with kinks who want to indulge in a safe, VIP environment. The air heavy with the scent of perfume, cologne, and sex entices everyone.

By the time My Dom holds back the blood-red velvet curtain to reveal an intimate alcove, I'm impressed suitably with my observations of LEVELS and cannot wait to partake.

"This way, Little One," My Dom's deep baritone voice glides over my skin like a caress as he scans my body while I pass him. He licks his lips appreciatively.

Those on my face press together as my lower lips ripple with need. I. Want. Him. Now.

"Ah, ah, ah," he chastises as he drapes my collar's chain over my shoulders, then places his hands on top of them from behind with downward pressure. "On your hands and knees, ass high, head low. Crawl to the spanking bench over there."

Without a second thought, I lower to position gracefully. The cold cobblestones bite at my knees, but I maintain my form, eager to please My Dom. A growl from behind encourages me to add an extra oomph to my movements. A pat to my bouncing ass rewards my efforts.

"Good girl, Little One. You please me with your natural poise," he croons. "A true submissive."

An ease from years of experience allows him to position then strap me to the blood-red leather padded bench quickly. Once he secures my ankles in the suede-lined leather restraints, My Dom strides to my head and squats to encase my wrists. As he rises to his full height, the massive bulge in his custom-tailored trousers align with my vision.

Yes, please!

He chuckles wickedly in response to my tongue darting out to lick my lips hungrily.

"Would you like a taste, Naughty Girl?" He asks as he strokes the tented front of his pants.

His dick twitches, and I moan.

In a blur of movement, he unbuckles his belt, pops open

the button, and drags the zipper down. His pants and black silk boxer briefs drop from his narrow hips to pool at his Oxfords-shod feet. Goliath springs free.

Did I say, yes? I mean, hell to the yes, yes, yes!!!

Greedily, I stick my tongue out like a snake to savor the air full of his musky, masculine odor. I whine at the sight of his thick fingers wrapping around his length. He covers his dick and strokes it from root to mushroom tip. His Prince Albert piercing's balls jewelry glint in the low light.

"Do you deserve to suck my cock, Naughty Girl?" He asks as he tugs his turgid staff. Veins run along its surface. Velvet covered steel.

"Yes, Sir… I promise to be good," I purr.

My Dom taps his bulbous cock head against my lips. One thrust, and he's at the back of my throat, heading south.

Gag reflex kicks in, but I fight it off with a deep breath through my nose. I offer a silent prayer of thanks for my many hours of pranayama practice.

"Ah, yes, Naughty Girl, your promise holds true," My Dom grunts as he falls into a rhythm.

His hips snap back and forth—in deep and fast; out slow to the tip. The girth stretches my mouth as he glides over my willing tongue. Soon my jaw aches and drool spills from the corners onto the bench.

"You will suck me, Naughty Girl. Every. Single. Inch," he hisses. "Suck. Me. Well."

His hands grip the back of my head to hold me still as he plunders my throat. One last thrust, and his dick hardens further as it swells with his semen. Copious amounts spill down my throat in spurts as My Dom fills my belly.

I moan around his girth. My pussy creams.

His grunts and groans end as his body shudders from his toe-curling release. My Dom strokes my scalp to soothe the pain from his tugs on my hair.

So fucking worth it!

He reaches down to pull his briefs and trousers back in place. Then strides around to my rear.

I tremble in anticipation.

Pressure to the soaked gusset of my thong makes me yelp.

"All of this wetness from you blowing me, Little One?" He asks as he rubs his nose against the silk. On an inhale he continues, "Mmm mmm such a delectable aroma. Shall I have a taste, too?"

My whimpered response makes him chuckle. Then I yelp again from the pressure of my thong being ripped from my pussy. A glance over my shoulder reveals the tattered material on the floor and My Dom's face between my butt cheeks.

I buck against his mouth as he laps at my seam.

THWACK. THWACK. THWACK.

Oh. Oh. FUCK!!!

My mind takes a moment to catch up to the pain that replaces the pleasure. My globes jiggle under a flogger as its blood-red suede fringes smack my exposed ass. I grip the legs of the spanking bench as I jerk from the unexpected spanking.

"What was your first lesson in BDSM play, Naughty Girl," My Dom thunders between strikes.

I gulp and wrack my brain for the answer. My delayed response results in another volley of well-aimed smacks to the most sensitive areas on my butt and thighs.

FUCK!!!

"Hold my position no matter what unless I want to safe-word," I cry out in anguish as I still my body despite the flogger's fury.

My Dom is mad at me…

Immediately he drops the offensive implement, drops to

his knees, and laps at my inner thighs where my juices pour from my throbbing pussy. Grunts and growls fill the alcove as he feasts on my essence.

When my legs tremble from holding back my orgasm, My Dom returns to my punishment. His renewed efforts force me back from the edge even as they bring me closer to the orgasm of life.

I clench my eyes shut and my fists around the legs of the bench as I try to rein in my impending release.

"Aaaahhh…. Sssir… I… I… PLEASE!!!" I beg when the sensation gets to be too much.

The flogger hits the floor with a clatter again. My Dom grips my hips and slams home. He's so deep I can feel the balls of his piercing brush my cervix.

We groan in unison.

"Yeeesss, Sir!!!" I scream. My cries join those of the other members in the throes of erotic ecstasy.

"Who do you belong to, My Angel?!?!?!"

So caught up in the waves of my orgasm, I miss Malcolm calling me by my name. But I respond in kind unconsciously, already too far gone to analyze his slip in name choice.

"You, Malcolm… Only… You!!!" I wail as I lose myself to the bliss of subspace.

STARR

"You look beautiful, Angel. A breath of fresh air on this spring evening. But I have one more thing to add."

I spin around to face Malcolm.

The voluminous, ruffled midi skirt of my silk-organza midi dress floats around my bare calves. Its pattern features painterly camellias that symbolize eternal love and beauty, perfect for the season. The dress stresses my curves with a ruched sash to nip in at the waist and boning on the sides of the gathered bodice to support the strapless neckline. A pair of flesh-tone mules and a Bottega Veneta clutch with my curls in a loose topknot and natural makeup finish my look.

Tonight we have dinner with Malcolm's parents for the first time since we started our D/s relationship. Tomorrow morning we fly with them to France for Leonie's graduation from the Paris American Academy.

I adore Morgan and Shelley, having spent time with them for Lola and Sebastian's wedding. But that was as Lola's close friend, not their son's submissive… My armpits tingle at the thought. I pray they don't realize my collar is a *collar*. Perhaps they'll assume it's a choker necklace as others who have complimented me on it.

Well, all except for Vicky.

Her jaw hit the ground when she saw my day wear collar —platinum mesh with a diamond-pavé letter S in the center. Another student bumped into her from behind when Vicky stopped dead in her tracks upon entering my private studio. Her eyes widened in surprise, then narrowed into angry slits in seconds. She stormed from the room knocking past the other students leaving a wake of shocked faces and gasps.

Vicky's reaction confirmed my suspicions of her being aware of my relationship with Malcolm. Hell, the S could represent my initial, but not to Vicky. She'd dropped hints over the last couple of months. Prodding for my where-abouts when I took time off to go with Malcolm and the guys for a few of their extreme sports trips. Vicky never said it outright, and I never validated her assumption.

Fortunately, she's off filming in London for the next few weeks.

Good riddance to bad rubbish!

I smile at Malcolm.

He's so striking in his bespoke single-breasted three-button linen suit and chocolate brown suede, tasseled loafers. His tousled ebony hair hangs longer to curl around his ears—the perfect length to tug as he eats me out. Freshly shaved skin replaces the five o'clock shadow from earlier.

I reach up and caress the softness along his jaw, and Malcolm smiles then turns his head to kiss my palm. His dove gray eyes shine as he takes my left wrist in his fingers.

Cool metal wraps around it.

"Oh!" I declare.

A bracelet that matches my collar coils around my wrist. The diamond-covered platinum lace sparkles. I touch it gently, then bring my fingertips to my collar as I glance up from beneath my eyelashes at My Dom.

"Thank you, Sir," I whisper. "It's spectacular."

He nuzzles my neck above his collar and kisses the sensitive area.

"You are more than welcome, Little One," My Dom murmurs. "It is our one-month anniversary, and you have been an exceptionally good girl."

I tilt my head to give him more access to my neck and whimper when he nips it as he smacks my ass.

"Temptress, I know what you are up to pressing your lush body against me. We must go now," My Dom says with one more swat.

I pout, but follow him to his penthouse's elevator with a grin. There's always later…

"STARR! What a surprise! Malcolm didn't tell us you were coming."

I smile at Shelley's excitement as she pulls me into her warm embrace. Not concerned with the other patrons at the bar for Daniel, she claps her hands after she hugs Malcolm, too. Her eyes dance with glee as she gazes at us.

"Good to see you with Malcolm, Starr. However, now I owe my wife a spa trip," Morgan says genially as he kisses my cheeks.

"Yes! You see, my husband didn't believe me when I told him I saw sparks between the two of you at Sebastian and Lola's wedding. Mother's intuition. Mmm hmmm…" Shelley adds with a chuckle as she taps her neck.

I blush and risk a glance at Malcolm, wondering if he noticed her reference to my diamond-covered evening collar. But he beams at his parents, completely unaffected.

He places his hand on the small of my back and guides

me after his parents to our table. After Malcolm helps me into my chair, he sits and pulls my hand into his, resting on his muscular thigh. His thumb brushes over my bracelet as he chats with his parents.

We enjoy a lovely dinner with lively discussions on our travels, wellness, and STEELE Foundation. Shelley runs their family's philanthropic foundation that builds and manages attractive, affordable housing for urban, lower-income families. The name is a play on the house foundation, being strong and supportive like steel. She asks me to offer a custom fitness retreat for the annual gala's silent auction.

By the time the evening ends, I no longer feel anxious about their thoughts on me being their son's sub. During the meal, I notice the exchanges between Morgan and Shelley and surmise he's an Alpha Dom, and she's his sub.

Their love and ability to have a marriage that incorporates D/s makes me wonder about Malcolm and me. Perhaps I shouldn't fear how much I love BDSM and falling for my Dom lover.

Later in bed, Malcolm takes all of my fears away when he makes love to me until the sun rises and then in the shower. After we head to Manhattan's West 30th Street Heliport before boarding Morgan's Gulfstream G650 private jet at Meridian Teterboro, the deluxe FBO in New Jersey.

Sebastian and Harris grin like the Cheshire Cat when I follow Shelley aboard the jet.

No sooner than the pilot clears us to move about the cabins, Lola and Haley pull me to the rear to question me about Malcolm and of course my day wear collar. Although Lola is Baz's sub, she doesn't wear one of her collars at all times as Malcolm requires of me. Always the Rebel!

"So I see… I told you in Mozambique. Didn't I? Never doubt me, my friend!" Lola laughs as she claps her hands.

"Feel better now?" Haley asks with concern since I was none too pleased with her brother two months ago.

I grin wider than Baz and Harris combined as I nod vigorously.

We giggle like schoolgirls as I fill them in on the details —during some Haley covers her ears and hums. Shelley joins us, and we spend the rest of the flight talking.

When we land at Le Bourget Airport outside of Paris, we separate into chauffeured Mercedes-Benz G-Wagens. Lola, Sebastian, Shelley, and Morgan head to The STEELE Tower Paris for their respective penthouses. Malcolm, Haley, Harris, and I go to STEELE Place Vendôme where we'll stay in their three largest suites.

Malcolm and I spend the afternoon being tourists. The driver takes us to our favorite spots from the top of the Eiffel Tower to the Mona Lisa at the Louvre to Notre-Dame. By the time we return to our suite, we collapse from all the walking and stomachs full of pastries and *glace* from Berthillon, the famous ice cream shop near the Cathedral.

"Wake up, Little One. We must go now."

I raise my arms above my head and arch my back as I stretch languorously. The silk sheet slips from my naked breasts.

My Dom lowers his head and laps at my right nipple. Then brings his lips to lick at my mouth voraciously. He nips my lower lip and tugs it as he rises. It pops from his teeth, and I whimper.

"Up. Dress in the lingerie hanging in the walk-in closet. Then met me in the salon," he commands before he strides fully clothed from the bedroom.

My heart races as I jump from the bed.

A black silk corset with voluminous, long past-the-fingertips, flared sleeves that feature French lace cut-outs at the mid arms and cuffs displayed on a satin padded hanger greets me. Next to it hangs a black sheer tulle and leavers lace panels balconette bra with matching briefs. Black suede fuck-me pumps sit below the gorgeous Lola's Coterie set.

"Sir, kindly bind me in," I purr as I sashay seductively towards My Dom.

His eyes darken to obsidian as they rake over my sexily clad body.

I pivot in front of him.

Calloused pads of his fingers ghost over my skin as he collects the strings and tightens the corset. Then he smacks my ass, covered by sheer tulle.

I gasp and spin around.

He chuckles wickedly and drapes a floor-length, hooded black silk cape over my shoulders. He bows the ties at my throat, mid-section, and mid-thigh. My Dom takes my hand in his and leads me from the salon.

"*Bienvenue à* LEVELS Paris."

The buxom blonde says throatily as My Dom and I approach the greeter station.

This LEVELS in the 7th Arrondissement Palais-Bourbon Le Faubourg inhabits the former Parisian home of a pampered courtesan to a French king. The magnificent *maison* on a tree-lined street sits behind duplicates of the original double carriage doors and features a spacious interior courtyard. They host grand soirees during the warm-weather months under the stars and strings of fairy lights.

The layout—the same as the other two locations—spreads across seven levels. As with each club, the Sky Lounge offers a view of a nearby landmark. With Paris, it's the grand Eiffel Tower resplendent in lights at night. The beauty and history of the property takes my breath away.

I feel like a pampered courtesan in my corset and lingerie. Of course, My Dom made the best selection for tonight's scene. How apropos. Not to mention the jewelry and the trousseau of Lola's Coterie lingerie and loungewear he's purchased for me over the last seven months.

Spoiled much? Abso-fucking-lutely!!! And I love it!

My Dom unfastens my cape and passes it to the greeter who gives him a claim ticket he pockets in his trousers. Then he dons the gold enamel bracelet to signal he's a part-nered Dom, clips the platinum chain to my collar's ring, and leads me the doors for Peepshow.

We pass the seating alcoves, primary stage, mini-stages, and performance rooms. He stops at the bar and requests a mocktail. Once the bartender serves My Dom his drink—the faux Scotch shimmers like amber in the low lighting—he tugs my chain and strides to an alcove across from the primary stage.

He sits and tosses a pillow on the floor, then beckons for me to kneel facing away from him between his spread legs. The clink of ice against crystal sounds behind me as he sips his drink. Idly, he toys with my chain.

The lights dim, and a spotlight appears on the stage. A hush descends on those gathered. A tall, lean Dom steps into the center of the light. He bows to the crowd and his sandy blond hair brushes across his face. When he stands, he holds his hand out. A beautiful Chinese woman glides across the stage. Her silky curtain of waist-length hair shines like lacquer.

She places her dainty hand in his sizable one, and he draws her to him with her back pressed to his front. Completely naked except for the colorful dragon tattoo that winds from her ankle around her calf, thigh, and hip to end with its mouth open at her bare mound. The erotic exotic imagery is a work of art.

Her Dom whispers in her ear, and she trembles. Her pert breasts judder and her porcelain décolletage flushes crimson.

So entranced by the sight of the pair, I startle when My Dom brushes his icy wet lips against the heated flesh where my neck meets my shoulder. He trails open-mouthed kisses along my shoulder as he cups my breasts. His fingers rub my peaked nipples through the filmy material.

I sigh and lean back against him, tilting my head to the side.

The Dom onstage cuffs his sub to the wooden St Andrew's Cross. He checks her comfort, then moves to the table laden with BDSM implements. He chooses a peacock feather and a studded glove before he returns to his wide-eyed sub.

"Ah, a sensory demonstration. Perfect," My Dom croons devilishly against the delicate shell of my ear.

He unclasps the front closure of my bra and tweaks my nipples until they're fully aroused. A rustling precipitates a sharp bite, then another.

"Oh! Fuck!" I hiss. Then gasp when I peek down to find diamonds pavé in platinum clamps dangling from my heavy breasts.

A tug to the connecting chain, and I realize My Dom attached the nipple clamps to my collar.

Fuck!!!

"Excellent, Little One. Do you enjoy your new jewelry?" He murmurs as he tugs again with one hand and places the other over my throat to tip my head back to his shoulder.

Before I can respond, he covers my gaping mouth with his and kisses me until my toes curl in my stilettos.

A strangled cry of pleasure from the stage draws My

Dom's attention. He turns my head back in the demonstration's direction.

The sub writhes on the Cross, flexing her fists with her mouth open as she begs her Dom to allow her climax. He's on his knees before her, pinching her clit with the studded glove while he licks her swollen pussy.

Her wails rise above those of the members who like My Dom seek their pleasure induced by hers.

My Dom rends my briefs from my body. I cry out from the pinch of the silk against my skin before it gives way. His hand slides between my thighs to pinch my clit.

I'm soaked. His fingers slip in my wetness as they dart in and out of my pussy while his thumb pad rubs my clit in a circular motion.

A strangled cry falls from my lips when another bite grips my body. I glance down to find another clamp. This time on my clit with a chain connecting it to the others at a circle below my breasts. Another tug and another wail, followed by a wicked chuckle at my ear.

"Stand, Little One. Show your jewelry to me," My Dom commands with a tug.

I rise—not as poised as usual—and turn to face him.

Shadows play over his fine face, but his eyes glow with carnal lust.

"Beautiful," he breathes.

He leans forward and cups my ass. His full lips wrap around my distended clit. He suckles it while he squeezes my fleshy globes.

My legs quiver. But I try to hold position even though my knees jiggle like jelly, not firm enough to keep me upright. I want to melt into an orgasmic puddle at his feet.

"Aaahhh… Mmmmmm… Sir, please!" I beg just as the sub onstage screams from her long-awaited climax.

Spurred on by her wails, My Dom doubles his ministrations. He adds a finger to my pussy and moves it around until he rubs my G-spot.

My legs bow.

Quickly he removes the digit and presses it to my puckered hole.

My legs give way like the muscles in my rear passage.

He puts one of my thighs over his shoulder and braces me with a hand on my opposite hip. He preoccupies his other hand with thrusting in my bottom hole.

Fingers from the hand on my hip tug my chain, and I wail. The finger in my ass slides out and reaches up to free my nipples, then down to release my clit.

Stars dance before my eyes as the blood rushes to the sensitive areas just as My Dom impales me on his turgid length. The thick invasion pushes me over the edge, and I cum, screaming his name over and over.

His grunts and groans fill the surrounding air along with the scent of our sex. He holds my hips still and thrusts up into my tight pussy faster and faster. A final brutal stroke, and Malcolm roars his thick, hot release deep inside of my pussy. My name like a prayer of gratitude on his lips.

He pulls my torso against his powerful chest, binding us together tighter than the stays of my corset while we drift in a state of sheer rhapsody.

"I want you. I crave you."

Malcolm's hoarse whisper—barely audible—floats to my ears, still ringing from the pleasure we shared.

I bury my face in the side of his neck and sigh, too consumed by him to respond with words. My body speaks for me.

And it says, *"I love you, Malcolm Steele."*

MALCOLM

*I*t's been two weeks since Leonie's graduation dinner scare. The situation shocked everyone, and we closed ranks as the Steele clan does to protect its family members. I remained in Paris with my parents and siblings to offer support to Roger and Leonie. However, Starr returned to Beverly Hills after a week. It disappointed her to leave, but she had business to attend to in person. Whereas I worked from STEELE Paris.

Now, I can't wait to see My Angel. And to show her off at the opening gala for LEVELS Beverly Hills.

Our nights at the Paris club brought us closer, along with my collar around her neck. She trusts me and commits herself to me as I do with her—for us.

I never thought I would find someone I want to be with longer than a contract stated. Before My Angel left, we discussed how we no longer need a contract since we're officially a couple. I'm not ready to put a ring on it like my brothers. But with My Angel, I want more.

The STEELE Rodeo Drive's Sikorsky helicopter dropped Sebastian, Lola, Harris, Haley, and me atop the roof of The STEELE Tower Los Angeles. They're staying at the hotel's Penthouse Suites while they're in LA for the club's opening.

I had one of the hotel's drivers take me to my Sunset Strip penthouse where My Angel waits for me. The gleam in her sorrel brown eyes let me know I made the right decision to give the entry codes to her. Another step in our official status.

In return, My Angel told me she'll have a set of keys and a gate opener ready for me. Although I already told Harris to up the security on her mansion while he's here. Who uses keys anymore? I'll let her know, then soothe her protests if necessary with a spanking…

"Lucy? I'm home!" I call out à la Desi Arnaz when I step into the foyer of my penthouse.

No answer. Not a sound.

With a frown, I check my mobile to reread the text message My Angel sent to me earlier.

See you soon, Sir…

Okay. So where is she?

I shoot off the question. Immediately the three dots appear as she types her response.

Meet me on the rooftop…

A grin spreads across my face at her reference to the Sophie B. Hawkins song. I race to the stairs and take them three at a time. A week is way too long!

I skid to a stop.

Fuck. Me.

My Angel sits on her haunches kneeling on a white pillow with her palms up on her thighs spread to present her shiny wet pussy to me. The swollen nubbin of her clit protrudes from her folds. Her chestnut-colored skin shimmers gold in the warm sun from the rich chocolate oil coating her body. I sniff the air and scent tiare blossom, white frangipani, ylang-ylang, and vanilla. My beauty transports me to the islands of Tahiti.

What a treat…

As I stalk towards My Angel, her D-cup chest rises and falls with her excited breaths. My pulse quickens. Erotic energy crackles between us.

I place the tip of my index finger beneath her chin. When our eyes meet, her pupils dilate and her mouth parts on a sigh. I want to ravish her.

Upward pressure from my finger brings her to her feet. Gracefully, My Angel rises to stand in all her naked glory before me. Only my collar touches her skin.

My cock punches against my tracksuit pants.

"Hello, Sir—"

I move my fingers to her lips and shake my head. No D/s now. I plan to make love to My Angel. My mouth slants over hers as I devour her with the fervor of a starved man lost on a tropical island—hungry for her taste and company.

My Angel moans into my mouth and melts her body against mine as she grips my tracksuit jacket in her fists. Just as needy as me.

One hand goes to the back of her neck to hold her in place while the other plunders her pussy. Her wet sheath welcomes me and clenches on my fingers as she undulates her hips. I finger fuck her until she cums with a strangled moan I capture in my mouth. I want her ready for me.

A tug to the drawstring of my pants, and they drop to the floor. I cup My Angel's ass, hoist her up, and impale her with my diamond-hard cock, just as long-lasting as the gems in her collar.

We groan—connected as one, finally.

I give her a moment to acclimate to my girth while I continue to claim her mouth voraciously. The temptress' tongue mates with mine. So fucking good.

My grip on her lush globes tightens as I bend my knees. With a grunt, I snap my hips upward, driving my cock to the end of her channel. Fully seated to my cum-laden balls, I piston in and out of her tight pussy.

My Angel arches her back as she pulls from my mouth to scream my name to the open sky above. Her ample tits press under my chin, and I lower my mouth to suckle her beaded, brown nipples.

"MALCOLM!!! Oh… My… GOD!!!" She cries.

Her pussy quivers around my pounding dick. The orgasm takes her breath away as she gulps for air.

No mercy.

I shift my hands to wrap my long fingers around her hips and ass to still her writhing body.

"Fuck, Starr!!! So tight… So wet… So gooood!!!"

My shout joins hers as I lose myself in her wet heat. Sweat drips down my spine along with the tingle of my impending release. Once again, I latch onto her pebbled nipple, sucking greedily.

Starr keens and shudders with another orgasm. Her nails dig into my shoulders as she seeks purchase before she spirals into carnal bliss. Pleas for me to cum fall from her full lips.

"I'm not ready, yet. One more orgasm. Give it to me!!!" I demand.

She bucks and grinds on my cock. Another scream rips from her mouth as her pussy clamps down.

The vise-like grip pulls my orgasm from the top of my head and the tips of my toes to meet at my balls. I blow my load deep inside of my mate as a primal roar streams from my mouth.

My legs give out, and I lower us to the floor. The after-shocks of our lovemaking buzz through us.

I close my eyes and bury my face in her fragrant neck,

damp from her sweat. A vision of a tropical, white sand beach and an over-the-water bungalow in the distance with the sound of My Angel's laughter as I chase her appears.

The sense of complete satisfaction overwhelms me. The words—*I love you, My Angel*—beg to be said aloud.

Soon I quiet my heart and soul as I tighten our embrace. *Soon.*

* * *

My Angel shines like a brilliant star in a universe of lesser celestial bodies.

Glittery Swarovski crystals form various star shapes on her sheer, floor-length gown with train. Material drapes over one shoulder while another swath falls off her other shoulder from the sweetheart neckline. The corset top amplifies her bountiful breasts and cinches her tiny waist. A slit up to her hip exposes her long, toned leg and one of the strappy sky-high sandals. Filmy high-cut briefs cover her mound and grace the curves of her ass cheeks. Simply stunning.

To further dazzle the members gathered for LEVELS Beverly Hills' opening gala, I gave her pear-shaped diamond earrings, a stone at her ear and one dangling below. The giant gems sparkle along with her evening collar and matching bracelet.

My Angel must sense my stare as she swings her gaze to me and smiles radiantly, taking my breath away. She's chatting with Lola, Adrienne, her sister Claudia, and Lydie, who flew in with her brothers Lucien, Lachlan, and Laurent for the party.

I return My Angel's smile with a wink.

Earlier she told me I reminded her of a dashing movie star from the 1950s in my bespoke white-tie tuxedo and patent leather Oxfords with grosgrain shoelaces. It was her idea to theme the gala after Old Hollywood Legends with women in elegant gowns and men in the highest formal wear. The members love it and decked themselves all out in their finest attire and jewels.

I scan the clusters of members and guests—potential members—on the rooftop Sky Lounge. Baz and the head of a studio talk next to the plexiglass covered pool turned dance floor. Anton and Borya stand by the bar appearing to eye Adrienne and Claudia. Harris dances with a Brazilian supermodel while Laurent cozies up with a socialite from Palm Beach. We don't allow our baby sister anywhere near the clubs. She went to dinner with friends.

"What the fuck?!"

Lucien's furious declaration draws me back from my musings. He's no longer sipping the signature drink for the gala crafted from Jackson labels. Instead, he's glaring over my shoulder.

I pivot to follow his gaze.

Fuck me!!!

How the hell did Vicky get in?!?! I made sure she wasn't on the guest list. We even accounted for the plus ones by their names and background checks.

She teeters towards Starr, who has her back to the offensive gatecrasher. Judging by Vicky's faltering steps and the sloshing cocktail glass in her hand, she's drunk. But she's on an obvious mission to fuck with my woman.

As I move in their direction, I hear Lucien on his mobile with the head of security. They'll handle the vixen, but not before I get to her.

"—think you are? You steal my Dom—"

Vicky's accusation cuts off when I grab her elbow and pull her away from a shocked Starr. The stink of liquor assaults my nostrils as Vicky leans into me and breaths against my ear.

"There you are, Sir… I miss you so much," she slurs as she drops her glass.

Two members of the security team and the head approach me. I pass her off to them. But she doubles back and attempts to throw her arms around my neck. I duck her unwanted advances and glare at her.

In my most dominant voice, I command her to stop making a spectacle of herself since several members watch her antics and to leave quietly.

Vicky sputters as she gears up for a tirade.

The security members flank her and take her by the arms. They lift her from the floor and carry her from the rooftop. She kicks and yells obscenities, but they ignore her. Ever the professionals, they complete the task efficiently. Less than five minutes, and she's outta here!

I smooth my waistcoat and tug my French cuffs, then turn to face the audience.

Baz, Harris, Lucien, Lachlan, Laurent, Anton, and Borya stand before me placating the onlookers. Waitstaff brings forth more trays of cocktails and hors d'oeuvres. The band jumps into a lively jazz tune. With no more to see and plenty of distractions, the members and guests return to the evening's festivities unfazed.

My eyes scan the crowd for my only concern—My Angel.

She still stands with her girls, protected by their positions around her. Starr's stoic expression sends chills down my spine.

This is not how I planned our night.

Damn Vicky Reynolds… My attorneys will deal with her and request a restraining order for Starr and me. I don't give a damn if she's a client of the fitness center and retreats. Vicky Reynolds done, and out of our lives for good.

Lola gives me the once-over, and Lydie purses her lips. Adrienne and Claudia glance at Starr for her reaction. As do I…

When I tower over her, prepared to apologize, she reaches up to cup my cheek and beams with glittering eyes.

"Mr. Steele, dance with me… Sir."

And with My Angel's request, our world spins on its axis, properly aligned once again.

"Thanks, bro, we appreciate it. Get home safe."

I give Harris a pound and put my arm around his shoulder for a hug. Then step back for Starr to tell him goodbye or, as she says, *see you again.* As he hops into the G-Wagen, I put my hand on her hip and draw her into my side.

Since the LEVELS Beverly Hills opening gala, the world's gone crazy.

Gossip rags and social media trolls blew up the Vicky situation into the *Fiasco of the Century.* They ran stories and posts—even created fucking hashtags—to depict My Angel as a pain slut who frequents seedy BDSM dungeons and uses Starr Light Fitness & Wellness Beverly Hills as a cover. Of course, all details provided by a credible source close to My Angel. Even worse, they left me out of the narrative, and instead had her with a different dominant every night. Nor was LEVELS mentioned.

All fingers point to Vicky.

She had it in for Starr since she guessed Starr as my new sub, then saw her collar. The sight of Starr at the gala proved Vicky's assumption. Add in my dismal of her as my sub and thwarting her advances—not to mention ignoring the many text messages, voicemails, visits to my penthouses and to STEELE—made her flip.

Undoubtedly, Vicky is the "credible source." My legal team took over. This is shit show is my fault, and I will handle it. I take My Angel as my responsibility very seriously. She is mine to pleasure and to protect.

Therefore, Harris and the Technology team worked on Starr's new security system for her mansion and SLFW. I assigned four of STEELE International's security team members to work in pairs with her at all times, including driving her in one of the corporate G-Wagens. She didn't take kindly to the idea at first.

Then the hang-up or heavy-breathing calls started, along with salacious DMs to her social media accounts. Haley stepped in with the Cyber Security side to investigate. That is, after she reamed me for allowing Vicky to get out of control and threaten Starr.

Now, she agrees with the added security.

The news traveled down the grapevine…

My mobile blew up with calls from Sebastian, with Lola in the background on a rant. I calmed both of them down after I laid out the steps taken to protect Starr and to put an end to Vicky's shenanigans.

Roger called to suggest Starr travels with Leonie while she's doing a whirlwind marketing and photoshoot tour for Lola's Coterie before her pregnancy shows. The trip will get Starr out of LA and away from the fiasco. Starr as her yoga instructor and doula can continue Leonie and Roger's sessions in person instead of virtually. By the time the global three-week trip ends, the shit will have blown over and Vicky handled.

My Angel was hesitant at first because she didn't want to run away from the situation, rather to face it. She said she owes it to her clients, even though the fiasco caused ripples with some more narrow-minded ones. But after she spoke with Adrienne, My Angel realized it's best.

My parents called when the news reached their branch of the vine. We explained the situation, and they offered their full support. Later, my father called me separately to confirm I know how to handle a D/s relationship…

Which brings us to tonight. My Angel and I have cocktails and dinner with her parents at Spire 70, the open-air bar on the roof of STEELE Rodeo Drive with dinner at Restaurant 69 below. Not the optimal circumstances, I want to meet my girlfriend's family for the first time. But they need to see for themselves I'm serious about their daughter, not Starr assuaging them.

A squeeze to my waist wakes me from my train wreck of thoughts.

I glance down to a quizzical expression on My Angel's beautiful heart-shaped face. Not wanting to worry her any further, I lean over and kiss the tip of her nose then buss her neck. Her warm giggles unwind the cold, negative coil from around my heart.

"You were so far away, you didn't hear me speaking to you," she says as she strokes my cheek.

I kiss her palm and respond, "I'll never be far from you, My Angel."

Her face softens and unshed tears shine in her eyes. She bows her head, and I feel her chest expand on an inhale. She's reigning in her emotions with a calming breath. But I want her emotions.

My index finger lifts her chin.

We stare at one another, and I convey my love for her without words. The corners of her mouth curl up with a hint of a smile. I arch my eyebrow in a demand for more.

My Angel unleashes a megawatt grin as she wraps her arms around my waist and buries her face in my chest.

"Never hide from me, My Angel," I murmur against her silky curls.

She nods and squeezes me tighter.

"Every time I come here, the panoramic view takes my breath away. So expansive!"

My Angel says as she gazes past the glass surround that separates patrons at the Spire 70 rooftop bar from the pavement seventy stories below.

The setting sun glints off her halter neck, crochet jumpsuit embellished with light-catching gold sequins layered over silk-georgette. Its artfully twisted bodice features cutouts at the waist and the back and suspends from a braided rope at the neck encrusted with Swarovski crystals. The wide, floor-length legs move with the breeze as we walk towards the table reserved for us.

Of course, the diamonds in her evening collar sparkle even in the sunset.

I want to make a good impression on her parents. So I chose the best bar and restaurant in Beverly Hills: STEELE Rodeo Drive's Spire 70 and the 3 Michelin star Restaurant 69. Peace and Sun may be hippies, but they're wealthy free spirits who enjoy the finer things in life.

Along with the best table, I had the mixologist craft cocktails with organic ingredients and liquors ethically and sustainably sourced. For dinner I asked the chef to create a twenty-course tasting menu to not only showcase her culinary artistry elaborately, but to take advantage of fresh seasonal ingredients. It'll also give us three hours to spend together without being obvious.

My Angel stops short in front of me, and her body

stiffens under my hand on the small of her back. She stares at a couple near our table. The man raises his head and does a double take. The woman with him shifts in her seat to follow his surprised gaze.

With a sigh, My Angel moves forward. The man stands as we approach; his eyes dart between her and me.

"Starr. How are you?" He asks, his chocolate browns narrow on me.

What the fuck?! Who is this guy?!

Then I get it. He must think I'm one of her dominants, so colorfully depicted by the gossips. A protective growl rumbles in my chest.

MINE!!!

"Hello, Quinn. Well, thank you," My Angel responds and turns to me. "Malcolm, this is Quinn Peters. Quinn, this is Malcolm Steele—"

"Her boyfriend," I interject as I place a possessive hand on My Angel's hip.

Quinn's eyes dart to my hold. His chest puffs out, and he glares at me.

"I'm Courtney Rhodes. Quinn's fiancée."

The petite-Starr lookalike extends her hand to me.

I glance down, then shake her dainty hand.

"Malcolm Steele, and this is Starr Knight," I respond.

The women exchange greetings while Quinn and I size up the other.

"Starr, sweetheart?"

"Quinn, you're joining our dinner?"

The four of us turn.

A couple who can only be My Angel's parents stand behind us. The distinguished older man stands an inch taller and analyzes me with his obsidian eyes. Starr obviously inherited her father's height and her mother's stunning beauty. Three inches shorter than My Angel and a mirror image.

I won't have to wonder what Starr will look like twenty-five years from now. My eyes widen at the long-term thought.

"Mom, Dad, hi," My Angel responds as she embraces her parents. "No, Quinn happens to be here with his fiancée, Courtney Rhodes. This is Malcolm Steele, my boyfriend."

My Angel holds her hand out to draw me from the Quinn face-off into her family's circle. I smile and grasp her outstretched palm.

"Mrs. Knight, Mr. Knight, it's a pleasure to meet you at last," I tell them as I extend my other hand.

They smile and return my greeting and tell me to call them Peace and Sun. I gesture to our table—fortunately two away from Quinn. Her father turns to him and nods before he joins us as we walk away.

"So, Malcolm, our daughter tells us you handled this mess. How so?" Her father asks, not very peacefully.

I appreciate and respect his concern as I would ask the exact thing for my daughter. His attorney's mind absorbs what I recount and questions me ruthlessly. No wonder Starr says he's known as a great white shark in the courtroom. Sun watches and cross-examines me.

Fifteen minutes later, after My Angel intervenes. I'm grateful for the environmentally friendly drink in my hand…

Even more so when Peters stops by the table to bid goodnight to my woman and to her parents. He gives me a cursory nod, and I give him a chin lift. The thought of another man inside of my woman makes me grind my back molars. Mine!

Shortly thereafter, we move downstairs to the restaurant. As expected, the chef impresses My Angel's parents by presenting each of the courses personally and by offering insights. The sommelier matches the wine pairings perfectly. They make up for the blip with Peters.

"Malcolm, this is extraordinary!" Sun exclaims as she swirls her wine glass of Château Lafite Rothschild Pauillac.

Peace nods and adds, "Indeed. Excellent choice of dishes and wines, Malcolm."

My Angel tilts her head to grin at me and squeezes my hand beneath the table. I lean over and press my lips against her full mouth. She sighs softly.

The rest of dinner continues with engaging conversation about their causes, Starr's upcoming trip, and vacations. We even have a lively discussion on the impact of real estate development on the environment. I gain major cool points when I point out STEELE has been eco-friendly for the last decade with improvements each year. We have an entire department devoted to staying abreast of the latest technology and laws. They're pleased, and we move on to other topics.

By the time dessert and the after-dinner drinks arrive, everyone is enjoying each other's company.

"THAT WENT WELL! Thank you for a lovely evening, baby."

My Angel wraps her arms around my neck once we're settled in the back of my Black Badge Rolls-Royce Cullinan.

Her parents just pulled off from the valet stand in their BMW i8 convertible. Again, the hippie in them calls for their careers as environmental law attorneys while their love of luxury calls for a two-hundred-thousand-dollar electric car.

"You think so, Angel?" I ask as I scoop her onto my lap to bask in her elated glow.

She nods her head and kisses me.

When we come up for air, she nuzzles her head under my neck and sighs.

"And Peters?" I ask.

She stiffens, then inhales and relaxes with an exhale.

"My ex-boyfriend. Funny, he was there tonight. If I didn't know better, I'd think he arranged it on purpose since I haven't answered his calls after the Vicky thing—"

"What do you mean 'his calls?!' What the fuck is he calling you for anyway?!" I snarl.

The caveman in me wants to hunt down Peters and beat his ass with my club. Contacting my mate?! Fuck no! MINE!!!

Starr sits up to pin me with an annoyed look, then rolls her eyes as she purses her lips.

"Calm down, Mr. Steele… He was just concerned about me and the bad press since he knows how important my image is to me," she says, then continues. "That's all, obviously, since he has a fiancée."

I snort.

"Let him 'concern' himself with his fiancée. It is for me to have concern for you, Little One," I respond in my most commanding Dom voice.

My submissive lover shivers in my arms and bows her head.

I pat her ass and add darkly, "I will remind you of my responsibilities to you all night long, Little One."

Hours later, My Angel slumbers as I spoon my larger body around her exhausted form. Suffice it to say she learned her lesson threefold and then some more…

<h1 style="text-align:center">STARR</h1>

"Oh, Chérie! I sooo love being with you for our sessions! I mean, virtual is great and all. But I miss your live energy and hands-on adjustments. How perfect we met every morning at your studio. What a treat!"

Leonie says as she stretches on her yoga mat like the lion she's named after.

"Yes, Starr, fantastic as usual!" Roger grins as he rises to his feet in one fluid motion. He reaches down to help his fiancée up, then hugs her close.

Leonie melts against him and sighs contentedly.

It's been a week since they flew in for the start of her whirlwind Pre-The Twins Modeling and Marketing Push for Lola's Coterie. No pun, I giggle to myself as I think of Leonie. As her doula I shouldn't tease her, but she thinks it's funny, too.

Tonight we'll have dinner at STEELE Rodeo Drive's steak restaurant to satisfy Leonie's craving, then fly to Las Vegas for the second leg of the trip. Malcolm, Lola, Sebastian, Billie, Blair, and Luc Montaigne will join us. Luc flew in from Paris to take part in the trip since he's Lola's mentor and the multibillionaire investor in Lola's Coterie. Blair's happy he's here because the two can spend time together as she's in New York more often than in Paris where he's based.

As I move about my private studio at SLFW to put away the props from Leonie's and Roger's session, I thank her for insisting we meet here. Originally, I planned for them to come to my home studio—just as well-appointed—to avoid any traces of the Vicky fiasco at the center.

By now the members who were "offended by such behavior" canceled their memberships and private standing appointments. But murmurs from those who stayed— whether positive or negative—still echo off the locker room walls.

Leonie's fierce and now maternal behavior stood firm. She would not allow *"idiotes"* to ruin her close friend or her yoga sessions with me. Roger agreed and came ready to handle any wayward comments or stares. Some days Malcolm came, too. He stayed in LA to go with us to Las Vegas, then New York City, where he'll stay for meetings.

I turn to let Leonie and Roger know I'm ready to head out and see him holding her with one arm and his other hand on her still flat belly. They gaze lovingly at each other. Lost to the outside world. I duck my head and preoccupy myself with folding a stack of blankets until Leonie calls to me.

We leave my studio and walk past members as they bustle about the center for class, the boutique, or the café. They nod in greeting, and I smile assuredly.

"Starr, chérie, you are the absolute best! We adore you!" Leonie exclaims loud enough for those near and far to hear.

"Most definitely! We prefer no other!" Roger adds with even more gusto.

My smile widens, and I loop my arms through theirs as we head to the spa.

"HONEY, you are lit up like the Christmas tree at Rockefeller Center!"

Billie teases Leonie since she wears her new suite of rich, pure yellow and white diamonds set in a necklace, bracelets, ring, and hair comb.

"Ho, ho, ho! Well call me Santa!" Roger chuckles as he kisses Leonie's radiant hand.

"Thank you, Santa Baby," she purrs.

"See… That's what got you preggie in the first place!" Lola exclaims.

"Oh, don't tease them. They're so cute!" I chime in, smiling so wide my dimples flash.

We're gathered at the steak restaurant in STEELE Rodeo Drive for dinner on our last night. Billie flew in from Las Vegas for the week. Blair sits leaning into Luc, who's been super attentive the whole night.

"They're my rockstar yoga couple!" I add with a wink.

Since Leonie misses hands-on sessions, I promised them I'd fly with them to Paris after Dubai next month and stay for a week. Anita Green—a yoga instructor with a flourishing practice I know from our fitness world—can help. She's also the wife of Roger's luxury gym business partner, the former world heavyweight champion Norman Green. While we catch up, I'm going to ask Anita to partner with me on Leonie's sessions. Since her pregnancy is progressing, I want a teacher in the room with her. Roger and Leonie think it's a great idea.

"Okay. Besides, it'll help with the authenticity of the new maternity lingerie collection… Surprise!"

Lola's announcement appears to catch Leonie off guard, just as Lola hoped based on her gleeful expression.

"What do you mean?" Leonie asks excitedly.

Lola claps her hands and shimmies in her seat. Her hazel eyes shine.

"I want you to collaborate with me on a sexy maternity lingerie and loungewear collection! We can design the pieces together as you go through the stages. Plus shoot campaigns with you and Roger all along!"

She pauses and gazes at Leonie steadily. Suddenly serious.

"As long as Dr. Berger gives his approval. We will not overtax you," Lola adds.

It's Leonie's turn to clap and shimmy in her seat.

"How exciting! I already have some ideas! Like a bra with removable cups to allow The Twins to feed—"

"Hey! That's enough!" Roger cuts her off, growling at the mention of her breasts in front of other men.

"Cue the scene—Caveman Roger drags Leonie by the ponytail back to his den…" Lola jokes.

"And you are next, Lola," Dom Sebastian interjects.

Malcolm cocks his eyebrow at me, and I squirm in my seat, my face flushed with arousal.

Luc turns to Blair and asks, "Do you have anything to add, Blair?"

She blushes bright red from her hairline to her ample bosom.

"No, Sir!"

Billie chokes on her glass of Marcassin Estate Chardonnay. Then stares gobsmacked at Blair.

Lola's shocked eyes snap to Leonie and me, and we burst out laughing.

Dom Luc! Who would have thought? I guess their relationship is definitely doing well after all. To hell with long distance…

* * *

"THE BRIGHT LIGHTS of Las Vegas always give me a thrill! I love the partying, dining, and the cheers when people hit it big… The baccarat table is calling my name, baby!"

I exclaim as I lean closer to the window, my excitement palpable.

"It never gets old for me. Even after years of living here. I love Vegas!" Billie adds as she peers out of her window. Her Savannah, Georgia accent still prevalent. Forever a Southern Belle.

We finished the last business in Beverly Hills and now jet to Sin City for Lola's Coterie Las Vegas. The campaign for the latest collection exclusive to the boutique needs to get done earlier than expected. Thanks to The Twins—Leonie and Roger's future bundles of joy!

Billie, Malcolm and I flew with the parents-to-be aboard Roger's G650 private jet. Luc opted to fly with Blair on Sebastian's plane.

Leonie glances out of her window to take in the view of the world-famous Las Vegas Strip.

"You're so right, Starr! It's just so flashy with the neon lights in stark relief to the darkness of the night desert beyond," she says.

As the jet flies into McCarran International Airport, the lights are like beacons luring travelers to the revelry of the "What Happens in Vegas, Stays in Vegas" city.

Having grown up on the West Coast, Las Vegas is my go-to city for decadence. Leonie always speaks of Monte Carlo and Macau as her choices for gambling. Yet, as much as I enjoy those cities, I'm still drawn to Vegas.

"Really, Little One? Las Vegas gives you *thrills*?" Malcolm murmurs in my ear, his breath warm on the sensitive shell.

I shudder and turn away from the sparkling vision. My hooded gaze takes in the much more tempting visage of My Dom. My lips curl into a seductive smile as I scan his handsome face.

He hasn't shaved. So the five o'clock shadow adds to his sex appeal. The longer length of his hair softens his sharp cheekbones as the tips brush against his strong jawline. Gorgeous.

"Your *thrill* with Las Vegas lets me know I am not fulfilling your desires adequately. As your Dom, my duty is to heighten your desires. So you will appreciate the pleasures of release, no orgasms for the rest of tonight, Little One..." he murmurs in my ear with a wicked chuckle.

I shiver from his warm breath tickling my skin and the subsequent jolt of electricity that zings my pussy. Uh oh.

Soon we're headed to STEELE Las Vegas in Malcolm's Black Badge Rolls-Royce Cullinan, driven by a hotel chauffeur. The two five-diamond resort and casino properties in the middle of the action on the Strip are magnificent. Each soaring tower features the signature STEELE gray glass. They shimmer from the neon lights' reflection on their surfaces.

The valet opens the doors on the passenger side while the driver opens the other for us. Malcolm takes my hand just as Leonie and Roger hop out of their SUV. We stride through the ornate, but tasteful main lobby towards the private reception foyer for the twelve Bridge Penthouses.

They're designed to attract high rollers and the über-wealthy clientele. The penthouses act as a bridge to connect the two properties with the mall between them from the ground level to the third floor. Malcolm and I will stay in his penthouse that's on one of the top six floors. While Billie stays in another; Roger and Leonie in his; Sebastian and Lola in theirs, and Luc and Blair in a fifth.

As we pass through the lobby, various staff members greet Malcolm by name. A few of the woman watch the girls and me.

I smirk and peek up at him through my eyelashes. He brushes his lips against my forehead. Yeah, sweeties… He's very much mine.

Cameras flash to our left, and we turn to the source. What appears to be a soon-to-be-bride and her gaggle of girlfriends recognize Leonie. No doubt the images will show up on Instagram and Twitter shortly.

Used to the commotion her presence causes, she smiles and winks. Roger keeps his typical intense stare straight ahead, even increasing his speed.

I shudder and not in ecstasy, rather relieved the pseudo-paparazzi aren't targeting me. Malcolm was right, I need to get out of LA and away from probing eyes. Let things cool off and restore my peace of mind.

We reach the etched-glass, double doors for the doorman to allow us entry to the separate foyer of the Bridge Penthouses. Beyond are three reception and two concierge desks, four sitting areas, and a bank of three private elevators, each accesses two of the Bridge Pent-houses in this tower.

"Hey, we just arrived. I can't wait to hit the casino floor!" Lola says as she shimmies, her hazel eyes lighting up like the Strip.

"Where are Luc and Blair?" Leonie asks, glancing around the expansive room.

"Their penthouse is in the other tower. Billie and Malcolm and Starr are in two here," Sebastian responds.

Hmmmmm, more privacy for him and Blair, not in sight of the rest of our party…

Lola must think the same, because she titters as she shakes her head.

The receptionist brings a card key to Billie. Malcolm, Roger, and Sebastian's penthouses have entry plates coded to their palm prints. So we have no need for keys.

The porters take our bags via the service elevator as we ride up in the guest ones for each of our penthouses. We agree to meet in the foyer in an hour.

"Now what was it you said about *thrills*, Little One?"

Malcolm's deep Dom baritone makes me shiver as he pulls my back to his front. He bends his knees so his thick length nestles against my ass.

"Does my ten-inch long, thick-as-steel, velvet-covered cock not make you squeal in delight?" He rasps in my ear.

"Yes… Yes, Sir!" I mewl as I grind against him. "More than anything in the world…"

My Dom pulls the hem of my linen halter neck midi dress up to slip his hand underneath it.

"The bouquet of your arousal mimics the colorful patchwork of delicate roses printed on your dress," My Dom says as his fingers slide along the damp gusset of my silk thong.

The delicate material poses no barrier to his wandering fingers. His other hand slips the bow out of the slim ties at the neckline to cup one of my full breasts. The v-neck bodice exposes my bosom to provide ample room for him to explore.

"Ooohhh, Sir…" I moan as he flicks my pebbled nipple with his fingertip.

When two of his thick digits press past my slippery pussy folds, I moan and increase my grinding on his impressive erection with my ass.

My Dom's arousal mimics mine for some erotic foreplay.

Oh, fuck…

"So tight… So wet… So sweet…" My Dom says as he

slips his fingers out of my channel to suck them clean of my juices in his mouth.

The sound of his slurps intensifies my desire for him. I want more!

"Sir," I plead, arching my back to bring my breasts closer to his mouth.

He plucks my nipple as my breast fills his hand even more. Then returns to his fingers fucking my dripping core.

The juices slide down to coat my inner thighs, and I beg for release. The pressure builds as I ride his fingers, humping my bare mons against his palm to start my orgasm.

WHAP... WHAP... WHAP

"Aaarghhh!" I screech as My Dom spanks my aching pussy lips. The last strike hits my swollen clit, and I jolt, half ready to cum and half ready to flee. "Owww!"

"What did I tell you only an hour ago, Little One?" He growls.

"No... orgasms... for... the... rest... of... tonight, Naught Girl," he repeats in my ear huskily.

Each word marked by a smack to emphasize his jaw-dropping reminder.

Aaaah fuuuck!

The doors ping as they open onto the foyer of the penthouse. Disappointed and aroused painfully, I lean on My Dom as he leads us through the doors.

"Sir, please!" I beg woefully. "My reference wasn't to the way you make my body sing! What I meant was the gambling and decadence of Vegas!"

He grins wickedly and strides to one wall of windows without a backwards glance.

I want to drop to my knees and plead my case as I envelop his cock in my mouth with hopes he puts it in my empty pussy. Instead, I walk behind him, rubbing my thighs together for a frisson of relief.

When he senses my staggered stride, he tugs me along by the hand to keep up. He tsks at me disappointedly.

"Do you want to make it three days, Naughty Girl? Or have you forgotten I provide your pleasure?" My Dom throws over his shoulder.

Vigorously, I shake my head. Heavens, no!

At the windows, once again, he stands behind me and holds me in his powerful embrace. I sigh at the feel of being in my man's arms and at the sight of the Strip shining brightly all around us.

We stand in silence for a moment, absorbed in our separate thoughts. Malcolm brushes his lips across the top of my head and reminds me it's time to get ready for dinner and fun at the casino.

"Well, Mr. Steele, if I cannot cum, neither can you!" I quip as I sashay ahead of him to the bedroom. Then squeal when he slaps my ass.

"We shall see, Naughty Girl. We shall see," he smirks again.

* * *

THE FOUR DAYS in Las Vegas lead to our New York City leg of the whirlwind three-week trip.

We'll spend the next five days in the city. Then go out to the Steele Southampton Village waterfront family compound for the remaining four.

Billie stayed in Vegas while we flew a red-eye flight plan to arrive this morning. Today, after Leonie's session, I'm going to visit some friends at their studio and teach a couple of classes while Malcolm has meetings. At fifteen weeks, Leonie needs to rest as I notice her stamina decreasing because of the activity. So it's the best time for me to go.

"Remember to breathe with intention, Leonie. Inhale to reach; exhale to return. Your breath will guide you through the postures," I intone as I lead her through our session.

Roger surprised her with a custom yoga studio in at their penthouse in The STEELE Tower. He asked me to help him outfit it with every yoga-related item imaginable. Mats thick enough to protect her knees; straps to extend her reach as her belly grows; wool blankets to keep her warm during Savasana. Not to mention the candles, meditation pillows, and a *Puja* space.

I love it! She declared when we walked in.

We finish the opening sequence and move on to the standing asanas. As we flow through each pose, I instruct Leonie to allow her mind to focus on the movement and her breathing. The breath sets the way.

"Hi, ready for me?" Roger asks as he joins us for yoga *nidra*.

I smile and nod to the mat, bolsters, and blanket I set up for him next to Leonie's space.

"*Bien* sûr, *Mon Cœur*," she replies, holding her hand out to him.

Roger smiles at us and takes Leonie's hand as he lowers himself to a cross-legged position with ease. Once seated, he kisses her cheek. Then turns to me expectantly.

"Namaste, Enlightened One," he says, placing his palms together at his heart center and bowing his head to me.

"Namaste, Sassy Student," I say as I return the gesture.

We laugh good-naturedly.

I help the future parents to get into comfortable positions as they lie supine on the mats. I place the bolsters under their knees and necks. Then, like babies, I swaddle them in the blankets, ensuring they're covered fully. Before I step away, I place lavender-scented pillows over their eyes. I dim the lights and allow the candles to glow around the studio.

My soothing voice guides Leonie and Roger through the session from consciousness to a state of semi-consciousness. The mental countdowns and memories I ask them to invoke keep them from falling into a slumber. Not like Leonie's first few sessions where her snores woke her up!

The forty-five minutes pass peacefully. I use the sound of chimes to bring the pair back to full awareness. I ask them to recall how far they could count and the recollections from the past. It's amazing how their practice has improved.

Fully rested with the equivalent of three hours' sleep, Leonie tells me she feels rejuvenated. She and Roger head to their bedroom while I take the family's private elevator up one flight to Malcolm's penthouse on the fifty-third floor.

Situated high above the Manhattan streets, it's on the fifty-second floor of The Steele Tower skyscraper. Through the gray-tinted, floor-to-ceiling windows, the city stretches out with unobstructed views. The prime location at the southwest corner of Fifty-seventh Street and Fifth Avenue is in the heart of Billionaires' Row.

Central Park to the north, the Hudson River to the west, the East River opposite, and the rest of Manhattan to the south from Midtown to Battery Park. On a beautiful, cloudless day like this morning, the vista draws you to gaze out of the windows for hours.

But not this morning. I have an hour to get to my friends' yoga studio in the Flat Iron District. It's *the* neighborhood for fitness lovers with its many high-end gyms, sportswear stores, juice bars, and luxurious spas. I'll stop by my favorite athletic clothing boutique, Sweaty Betty, for some new leggings and tank tops before I head back uptown.

After a quick shower, I change into a pair of white biker short shorts and matching scoop-neck, midriff-bearing tank top. It's my go-to outfit for a hot yoga class. The sweat-wicking and quick-drying material works wonders!

I slip a pair of comfy joggers over the shorts and pull on a matching hoodie. Perfect to change into after I shower again. A quick head flip and I pile my long curls atop in a messy bun. Then slide my feet into a pair of sneakers and grab my gym tote.

Just as I put my mobile in the front pocket, it vibrates and dings with a text message in Malcolm's ringtone. Without breaking stride, I check the screen.

Hey, Angel, I have a last-minute business dinner tonight. Are you free to join me? I booked your favorite restaurant, Momofuku Ko...

My heart skips a beat, and my mouth waters. I hope the chef has Black Bass Dashi, Cherry Blossom and Mushroom Salad on the tasting menu tonight. I lick my lips and grin. How can I say no to his enticement?

Absolutely! What time should I be ready?

Right away the three dots appear, a sign of his forthcoming response.

Great, thanks Angel! 7:30 dinner is at 8

I reply with a kiss emoji and step into the elevator. Well, this requires a trip to SoHo for a cute outfit after Sweaty Betty! How I love New York!

* * *

"THESE SHOTS ARE INCREDIBLE!" Lola says as she peers over the photographer's shoulder.

We're in Dubai, the last stop on the five-city global trip. Luc returned to Paris after New York for meetings. The rest of us spent three of the seven days allotted to the United Arab Emirates' boutiques in Abu Dhabi.

Leonie suggested they contrast the city's sea of desert with the turquoise waters of Dubai, The Empty Quarter Desert in Abu Dhabi serves as the first backdrop. The Bedouin noblemen see the world's largest sand desert as a vast ocean to travel across on their journeys.

They paid homage to the local history with a twist. Leonie portrayed a desert princess who captivated a desert traveler, Roger. Their steamy affair took place over the course of three nights in a lavish tent.

Lola outdid herself with the collection exclusive to her Lola's Coterie Abu Dhabi boutique. The vibrant colors, sumptuous materials, and sophisticated lines make for extraordinary pieces. Of course Malcolm ordered a few sets of the lingerie and loungewear for my growing trousseau...

As a surprise, he was able to change his meetings to videoconference so he could join us. I think he just can't get enough of me!

Unlike the other days when he and I spent time together away from everyone else, today we're aboard the six-hundred-foot megayacht. They're using it for the Dubai photoshoot. It's lavish and belongs to one of the royal family members. The impressive boat parallels the view. Spread out beyond the dazzling water with glittering ripples that reach across to the shore is the city's varied skyline.

Architectural marvels grow out of the surrounding desert. The contrast of the modern glass towers—some in unusual shapes—to the nature around it is remarkable. It provides the perfect scenery for the Dubai boutique's collection.

Lola incorporated the gorgeous blues and greens of the water with the earth tones of the sand for the color palette.

Glittery Swarovski crystals embellish the bras, panties, slips, and evening wear pieces to mirror the glass structures.

This time Roger and Leonie play the roles of dashing billionaire mogul and paparazzi-hounded celebrity. Their holiday is fraught with dodging photographers with high-powered lenses while on their megayacht to being chased through the streets after a night out.

Not much different from reality my reality…

"*Oui!* It's as though we're experiencing our everyday lives!" Leonie giggles as she looks over the photographer's other shoulder at the photos.

Roger grunts and adds, "Right. Well, if it gets as extreme as this storyline, you're getting security."

Leonie opens her mouth to respond. But Sebastian cuts in, holding up his hand to stop her.

"I agree with Roger completely. You are carrying the next generation of Steeles. And as the eldest of this line, it is my responsibility to protective everyone. Period."

Malcolm leans over and whispers in my ear, "And you thought I was overly protective…"

Now I know how Lola must feel when Sebastian enacts his Alpha Dom. He's so commanding, I'm about to say, *yes Sir* to him, too!

Leonie turns to Lola, and she shrugs. Outnumbered and understanding their concern, Leonie nods in agreement.

"Words, Pretty Kitty. I will have your words," Roger demands.

"*Oui,*" she answers.

Roger, Sebastian, and Malcolm reply excellent in unison, and Lola smiles as she wraps her arm around Leonie's waist.

"Get used to it, Hot Mama. There's nothing that will stop these cavemen from taking care of their loved ones."

I can't deny they're more than right on this one…

. . .

WHEN THE CAMPAIGN IS COMPLETE, we stay in Dubai while Lola and Leonie round out this city's trip with marketing efforts. Malcolm had meetings he couldn't reschedule. So he flew to Brussels a few days ago.

The girls host private viewing parties for the city's VIPs and dinners at STEELE Dubai. They take part in interviews with local fashion magazines and lifestyle television shows. Social media takeovers increase followers for the business and their personal accounts. The results satisfy the public relations and marketing teams.

Thankfully, we're on our way back to Paris. Roger and Leonie sleep in the bedroom of his private jet while I stretch out on the sofa converted into an additional bed. Sebastian, Lola, and Blair head to New York City on his jet.

It exhausts everyone after the month of non-stop travel. But it was well worth it. The early shots are incredible, as predicted. The sales team expects great numbers in revenue and an increase in brand awareness.

But I told Leonie it's time for a hiatus when we arrive in Paris. She giggled when I added, *time to rest up, Haute Maman!*

"This is a fantastic facility right smack in the heart of Paris! Who would have thought a gym in a gem of a building in a prime area of a top arrondissement?!"

I exclaim once we finish the tour of Norman Green's Elite Training Facility Paris.

Anita beams with pride at my compliment of her husband's luxury gym. She nods her head as her jet black curls bob around her heart-shaped, honey-colored face.

"I know! Can you believe we're still in the city's bustling business district? The location proves the ideal spot to attract high-powered titans of finance, real estate, media, and other industries as members. The waiting list for membership stands at four months long," she says.

She tells me how the idea came about over four years ago when Roger met Norman in Las Vegas at a party at STEELE LV after his final KO match. He told Roger he promised his girlfriend, now wife, Anita he would stop with that fight. He was at the top of his game with no more to prove. Norman said it's better to leave on high than get carted away low.

Roger offered him the opportunity to open his chains of branded gyms through STEELE's Entertainment Properties Division. One for underprivileged youth and another as exclusive elite training facilities for the über-wealthy and star athletes.

Born and raised in Harlem to upper middle-class parents, Norman understands the importance of giving back to the community. A mentor taught him boxing after school and his career took off. As a celebrity athlete, he understands the need for specialized training and the demands on the body. He didn't hesitate and agreed to the deal. A perk for Roger is he became his first client.

When Roger moved to Paris, he and Anita came with him and opened locations in the city, London, and Madrid. The States has several besides the New York City flagship including Las Vegas, Los Angeles, Austin, Chicago, and Miami.

Morgan, Sebastian, and Malcolm are pleased with the profitable revenue stream. Especially since the membership and assorted fees of the elite facilities pay for the community ones. Norman can continue in the sports world and add even more to his multimillions. It's a win-win business partnership for all.

Then Anita expanded upon it after she finished culinary school at Le Cordon Bleu and started a meal plan delivery service. Norman added her customized plans to the paid offerings of the elite facilities and complimentary healthy snacks to the youth. She also took over the food services in both chains. They're a dynamic couple who raise the bar in the fitness industry.

In addition, she teaches classes and private sessions here in her eponymous full-service yoga studio—each Facility location includes one. We ended the tour in her private room. I admire the quiet-energy vibe.

"My man knows his stuff! He knows a good thing when he sees it—including me!" Leonie laughs.

Anita and I join in as we settle on the mats spread out on the bamboo floor.

We spend the next hour going over Leonie's health history, current level of activity, and goals, then we develop a practice plan. I take Leonie through a session I designed for her to give Anita a chance to observe Leonie's skill and comfort levels. It pleases me to see Anita take notes throughout our conversation and Leonie's session.

"If you don't mind... I'd love to join in on your yoga *nidra*," she says at the end of Leonie's asanas portion of her session.

She laughs and responds, "*Absolument!* It's my favorite part. No offense, Starr *chérie*! It's just so relaxing and *Haute Maman* needs her rest. Just doing as you say!"

The studio fills with our giggles, then quiets while I tuck them into warm blankets and place lavender-scented pillows over their closed eyes. A smile plays on my lips as I take a seat and begin their relaxation process.

Once the time ends and we recount their journey, we head to the locker room for quick showers. The spa for body treatments and massages comes up next on our Girls' Healthy Day. I'm looking forward to the body polish and a deep tissue massage with Anita's proprietary blend of essential oils for rejuvenation. My body needs recovery, too!

Afterwards, we meet upstairs on the rooftop for lunch. It's a clear sunny day. So the staff withdrew the retractable glass roof into its casing. The sounds of car horns, people's voices, and sirens drift up the six stories to remind us we're in the city and not drifting in bliss.

I don't mind it. With a sigh, I lift my face to the sky, enjoying the sun on my freshly scrubbed and moisturized skin.

"Well, hello there, ladies!"

We turn to see Norman striding over to our table.

He's six feet, five inches, solid two hundred-fifty pounds of muscle who moves with the grace of a gazelle and the speed of a cheetah. His extraordinary physique proves he can go a tenth year and knockout his ninth opponent with ease.

Norman is a fine chocolate bear of a man, but Malcolm has my heart.

Anita grins at her husband as he bends over to kiss her cheek. At five feet, three inches, he towers over the petite beauty seated in her chair. Her tawny brown eyes shine with love.

"Norm, honey, meet my friend, Starr Knight. She's the yogi from Beverly Hills I spoke with you about who teaches Leonie virtually. Starr, meet my husband Norman," Anita says.

"Nice to meet you, Starr," Norman replies as he shakes my hand in his sizable one. "Hey, Leonie, how are you feeling, little mama?"

Leonie giggles and pats her babies bump with motherly affection.

"The three of us are doing wonderful, Norm! Thanks for asking," she responds.

"Your facility is impressive, Norman—"

"Call me Norm, like my friends," he interrupts with a warm smile.

I nod and tell him how much I enjoyed myself and will visit his location in Los Angeles when I return home. He tells me he'll add me to the VIP VIP member list so I can access all locations. Then he leaves us to our meal.

We turn our attention to our delicious salads with grilled salmon or chicken made from fresh, locally sourced ingredients. Anita crafted the tasty dressing from her recipe. She tells us more about the meal plan side of her business and her goal to expand it to other wellness companies. I agree SLFW will partner with her, and she squeals with excitement.

"That's great, thanks so much!" She claps. "We can draft the contract before you leave. Then you can show it to your legal team when you return to Beverly Hills."

"Sounds good! Supporting one another is the yogi way!" I tease.

Leonie nods and lifts her glass of iced lemon ginger tea to add, "Here's to our friendship, health, and success!"

Anita and I lift our glasses of citrus-infused water to join in her toast.

"Hi, Angel, how was your week in Paris?"

I cuddle deeper under my blankets in the President's Suite at STEELE Place Vendôme and pull my iPad closer to me. Malcolm's handsome face fills the screen.

"It was great, baby. Leonie is happy with the plan for Anita to teach her. Anita and I worked out a partnership with her meal plan and food service company to run SLFW's café and offer food delivery for members. I did some shopping, naturally…" I laugh. "Tell me, how's London?"

He pauses, then bites his suckable lower lip between his front teeth.

"What?" I ask, curious as to the cause for his hesitancy.

Malcolm's lip pops out, and he sighs.

"I have to stay longer than expected, so I can't give you a ride to New York City as we planned. But it would be better if you flew over here and stayed until I leave. I miss you," he responds gruffly.

Now it's my turn to pause.

My mind goes over my schedule for the upcoming week: some business meetings, privates, and classes; a friend's housewarming party; Sunday dinner with my parents. Adrienne can arrange for teacher coverage; I'll send a gift; they'll understand—especially since they've grown to like Malcolm. Hell, I rarely take a vacation. I deserve some time to myself after years of growing my company!

My delay proves too much for him.

"I'll make it worth your while," he adds with a seductive smirk.

"Well, in that case…" I purr.

MALCOLM

I pace back and forth impatiently for the STEELE London Sikorsky S-92 Executive helicopter to land on The Tower's roof. A glance at my precise Patek Philippe watch shows the helicopter is two minutes late. Where the hell is My Angel?

Wind whips my hair as the sound of the helicopter's blades fill the air surrounding me. I lift my hand to shade my eyes, then sigh in relief when I see My Angel waving from the window above. With a grin that lights my heart, I wave back.

I don't wait for the pilot to stop the blades. Instead, I duck my head and rush forward to the door. Just as the helicopter settles, I reach for the door's handle. Before I can open it the flight attendant pulls the exterior door open.

"Good afternoon, Mr. Steele," he says with a slight nod of his head.

"Good afternoon," I respond, biting back the urge to push him aside and enter the cabin.

Not necessary at all.

"Hi, baby! I missed you!" Starr cries as she leaps into my

arms and wraps her long legs around my waist. Her inner thighs tighten, and my cock hardens.

"I missed you, too," I growl into her mouth as I take her lips in a savage kiss.

Without missing a step, I pivot and walk back towards the interior door. No need to put on a further show for STEELE staff, I chuckle to myself. And a show it will be. Guaranteed.

My hands grip her lush ass over the tailored pants she wears. Damn. Why didn't she wear a skirt, I wonder when I get us inside of the empty stairwell and kick the door shut.

My Angel's slim fingers tangle in my thick, ebony hair to pull at my scalp. The zap of pain makes my balls draw up tight. Her soft coos as I dominate her tongue sets me on fire.

I need to be inside of her. Now.

As though hearing my demand, My Angel unwinds her legs and stands to open her pants. She only gets one leg out before I'm on her again.

Her back slams against the concrete wall, and an oomph bursts forth from her parted lips. Undeterred, she tugs at the hem of my shirt as I wrestle my cock free from the now tight confines of my trousers. Not waiting to check—but knowing she's dripping—I align my weeping mushroom head to her pussy and ram it home. Deep.

We groan as one as our bodies merge in our carnal connection.

We share no dirty talk or words of love. We fuck hard and raw. Starved for the other.

My balls swell with my seed, ready to fill my woman's womb. One more passion-driven thrust combined with My Angel's quivering pussy walls, and I blow my load on a groan. I swallow her scream as her orgasm detonates with mine.

I lean my damp forehead against hers while we catch our

breath. My semi-flaccid cock remains inside of her channel, happy to never leave her tight, wet heat.

"Well, I guess you really missed me after all… Now, when are you going to make it worth my while?" My Angel quips breathlessly.

I chuckle and nip her neck.

I'm a fucking goner. Worse than Sebastian and Roger. Damn…

"—THE expansion plans for the Kuala Lumpur property are on track for an early completion date by three months. The technology team will install their equipment two weeks ahead of occupancy to allow for full system testing…"

I'm in the weekly status meeting with my Entertainment Properties Division, but my mind drifts back to the night My Angel and I had at LEVELS London. My cock stirs at the reminder. I shift in my plush leather chair for a more comfortable position. Then I almost laugh out loud when I recall My Angel whimpering as she couldn't hold her position on the Sybian Saddle.

I kept her on the masturbation device for twenty minutes as punishment for her smart-ass remark after I blew her mind in the stairwell.

Sweat dripped between her jiggling, D-cup tits as I increased the speed. The short, but extra-thick dildo I attached to the saddle kept her full and sopping wet the entire time. After the first five minutes and she realized I wasn't letting her off, tears ran down her reddened cheeks.

I sat back in a chair and stroked my engorged cock as I watched her go from ecstasy to pain to relief and back again with a flick of the remote control. She never knew what to expect. But her body loved it.

Flushed face; pointed nipples; quivering belly; trembling thighs; juices flowing; hands fisted, bound behind her back.

Yeah. My Naughty Girl loved every minute of it.

When I took her off of the Sybian and fucked her ass until it gaped for me, she climaxed four times in a row screaming my name.

I held my release back until she was writhing, blubbering, and mindless. Then I let loose.

My balls ache for release now. Surreptitiously, I adjust my junk beneath the conference room table. Then I glance at my watch and the meeting's agenda. Three more presentations; forty-five minutes more.

Fuck.

"Hi, baby! How was your day?"

My face splits with a broad grin when I spy my woman sitting in one of three salons of the STEELE Kensington's Presidential Suite. Unlike Sebastian, I don't bother with a mansion in London. I'd rather stay at one of the Presidential Suites of a STEELE hotel or resort when I travel for business or for pleasure.

"Long and hard. Sounds familiar?" I smirk.

Her contagious laughter tinkles around us. I join in as I swoop her off of the sofa and into my arms. I kiss her silly until she moans and grinds her bare pussy against my eight-pack abs.

As I decreed after she arrived: no panties and no bra shall come between her body and mine and only dresses worn.

No barrier keeps my fingers from entering her always-wet-for-me core. A second digit follows the first as they flex and curl to stroke her G-spot and prepare her for my entry.

"Malcolm, ohhhhh... Right there... Oh fuck... There, there, THERE!" My Angel explodes.

I allow her to ride out her orgasm on my fingers, knowing I'll have her cum a few more times before I seek my release.

She whimpers in my arms.

I slip my dripping fingers from her pussy and put them in her mouth. She licks them clean while she stares into my hooded eyes boldly.

The Temptress.

I stand her up and pull the coral-colored strapless cashmere maxi dress from her body—another of my favorites from the Lola's Coterie Collection. It brings me much joy to buy her lingerie and loungewear. Even more joy to rip it off.

My Angel stands naked before me. Her mouthwatering body ripe for my taking. It's like a magnet for my dick as it tents my trousers.

I shrug out of my suit jacket and vest, then remove my silk tie. When she reaches to help me, I put up a finger to stop her and shake my head. She will watch me undress and appreciate my body as much as I salivate over hers.

My striptease continues with the unbuttoning of my custom-tailored dress shirt. Slowly, I open it to reveal my hard chest and happy trail of dark hair leading to my erect cock. I tug the shirt hem from my pants and toss it to the ground.

Never do I remove my eyes from her face. But her heated gaze drifts to my bulging crotch.

Bingo.

I glide my hand over my taut abs to reach the buckle of my belt and the button on my trousers, then unzip them. They fall to my feet in a puddle. One step, two steps and I stand in my black boxer briefs and shoes only. My hand strokes my turgid length through the soft material and tug on the silver balls of my Prince Albert piercing.

I hiss.

My Angel licks her full lips.

My cock weeps.

I rest my hand on my bulge until her eyes come back to mine. Now that I have her attention, I put my thumbs in the waistband of my boxer briefs and pull them down. Then I toe out of my shoes and yank my socks off.

My Angel's nostrils flare as she inhales deeply. Undoubtedly she can smell my pheromones and her feminine wiles yearn to mount my dick.

She will. Soon.

My cock stands out straight towards her, dripping with pre-cum.

Her fingers twitch to touch me.

I beckon with my finger.

She drops to her hands and knees and crawls to me. Ass high, head low. Just as I taught my little sub.

When she reaches me, she kisses each of my feet and sits back on her haunches, hands clasping opposite elbows behind her back, eyes downcast to await my next silent command.

I fist my cock at its thick base and tap the tip on her wet lips.

She opens.

In my cock goes to the back of her throat with one thrust of my hips.

She gags. Tears fill her eyes. She whirls her tongue around and sucks.

I hiss. My head goes back, and my eyes roll to the ceiling as my toes curl.

Fuck. Me.

My Temptress works my cock like her favorite ice pop,

slurping up the juices, never letting them fall from her mouth.

I cum on a roar as I grip her head and piston my hips, driving my dick down her relaxed throat.

After I can see again, I lower my gaze to hers.

Tears stain her cheeks.

I kneel before her and lick them.

"Good girl," I praise her.

She mewls.

My day is complete.

STARR and I wait for the FaceTime call from Roger and Leonie, where they'll add in my siblings and sister-in-law. We're all impatient to know The Twins' gender since Leonie had her eighteen-week scan today. She and Roger wanted to wait until we were all gathered on the call or at a restaurant in Paris.

Our parents flew over yesterday afternoon, eager to hear the news in person. They and Leonie's parents Guy and Josy Beaulieu wanted to go to the doctor. But the couple decided to have dinner instead for their big announcement.

"Well??? What are The Twins?" Lola demands.

"Boys!!" Leonie cries. "See for yourselves!"

Dutifully, Roger passes out copies of images from the ultrasound to those gathered. While Leonie holds up one for the FaceTime group.

"Holy cow! You can see their faces and everything!" Harris exclaims peering closely from his iPhone.

Haley claps and adds, "They're absolutely incredible! Roger, they look like you!"

We laugh at the folly of her comment since they don't have true distinguishable traits yet.

"Fantastic, bro! We see what you made," I say, giving Roger a virtual high five.

Starr grins, "Can't wait to see you, little munchkins!"

"Mini Steeles in the oven!" Sebastian laughs, then glances between Leonie and Roger. "In all seriousness, we're so happy for you both. Congratulations, Mommy and Daddy!"

Leonie and Roger thank us all and prop the iPad on the table where we can see them.

Once it's quieted down, he turns to Leonie.

"My love, this is a day I want you to always remember"—he takes a flat black leather case out of the breast pocket of his suit jacket—"this is for you."

Leonie peeks up at him, then presses the sapphire-studded closure. She kisses his lips.

He removes the platinum necklace and place it around her neck. The three large, pear-shaped sapphires styled like her *toi et moi* ring settle against her heart. The intense, velvety, deep royal blue colored stones are the rarest and most valuable—just like the three males in her life.

"Oh, Roger, this is beautiful. *Merci, Mon Cœur*," Leonie says as she fingers the sapphires sliding along the chain. "All three of my boys close to my heart."

Tears fill her eyes as she cups his face and kisses him. Then she wraps her arms around Roger to bury her face against his neck.

He rubs her back soothingly.

"The heavenly blue of sapphires signifies the epitome of celestial hope and faith. Believed to bring divine insight, prosperity, and safe keeping according to the ancient and medieval world." Guy says from his worldly knowledge. Everyone comments on his words and the gift's beauty.

The wait staff enter with bottles of Taittinger Comtes de Champagne Blanc de Blancs. They bring Leonie iced lemon green tea in a flute. I hand Starr a flute and take one I poured before the call started.

Her laughter bubbles like the champagne when she spies her cocktail.

"*À votre santé!*" She says standing with her hand on her babies bump as she leans into Roger's side.

"Cheers!" We follow, raising our crystal flutes in the air with hers.

Lola has meetings in Paris. So she and Haley arrange to go together to see Leonie "live and direct." Harris tells us he'll create the best baby monitoring system ever with all the high-tech bells and whistles available. Starr says she's only a plane ride away from her doula duties. We chat some more. Then Roger ends the video call so they can eat.

I turn to Starr and pull her into my lap to kiss the top of her curls. I rest my lips against their silkiness as I ponder what it would be like to have a baby with My Angel.

MALCOLM

"*B*ro, this shit is fucking insane! I almost knocked the teeth out of some paparazzo on our way in."

Roger looks up to see me striding into his STEELE Paris office, followed by Harris. Sebastian is in a meeting in his offices down the hall.

He, Lola, and our parents have been here for the last two weeks to support Leonie and Roger. Harris, Haley, and I arrived this morning. We'll work from our offices here, too. However, Haley will work remotely from *Le Beaulieu Manoir* —Leonie's family's ancestral home with her parents. She wants to stay close to her sisters, Lola and Leonie.

Le Manoir offers the most secure residence for Roger and Leonie while the media goes wild over the pretrial. It's on the westernmost part of the outskirts of Paris in Neuilly-Auteuil-Passy. The majestic property features manicured park-like grounds, stables, tennis court, swimming pool and cabana, and a palatial French Rococo mansion. A part of the 16th arrondissement, it's in the wealthiest neighborhood.

They built the hamlet between the thirteenth and seventeenth centuries. Later, during the reign of Louis XV, it became a fashionable country retreat for French elites. The Beaulieu's twenty acres of land border Bois de Boulogne with parts of the acreage awarded to their ancestors by the monarch.

Roger smiles, thankful for our love and support. It's typical of the Steele clan to drop it all to rally behind one of us. This time, it's for my younger brother.

Fuck!

It's been a nightmare. More negative media coverage. More comments from "sources close to" blah blah blah. More absolute bullshit.

My experience isn't the worse of it.

Roger took my advice and followed my lead with Starr's security. He implemented a detail for Leonie when a reporter harassed her after leaving a baby boutique with our mothers. Eric Vogel—their driver—had to intervene and knocked the reporter to the ground for pushing her in his eagerness to get a shot of her in distress.

Like I did at Starr's mansion, Guy hired additional security for the *Manoir*. Some paparazzi scaled the wall to get photos of them on the grounds and in the mansion. Fucking drones circle overhead at all times of the day and the night. Federico Fellini said it best in his interview with *Time*: "Paparazzo… suggests to me a buzzing insect, hovering, darting, stinging." How apropos. It's an invasion of the worse kind.

Roger even upped the ante at STEELE Paris. Obviously to no avail based on my encounter.

He calls the vice president of security to update him and to request additional precautions. When he rings off, he nods at us and goes to the drinks cabinet for some waters.

"It's a pain in the ass. These fuckers are like sharks with one drop of blood in the vast ocean," he says as he tosses bottles in our direction.

We stretch out on the sofa and club chairs while he fills us in on the latest developments. Just listening makes my blood boil with rage. *The Enforcer* in me wants to handle it. My way. These fuckers know no bounds, again like with My Angel. Particularly since Leonie is visibly pregnant. They don't give a fuck.

"Man, I'll look into some type of tech to help—"

The ringing of Roger's mobile interrupts Harris' comments. Roger strides to his desk to retrieve it.

"Hi, babe. What's up?" He asks.

He physically sags with relief, as though it's good news and not something dreadful.

"Yes, they're here, and they wanted to surprise you. Surprise!" He laughs genuinely.

"It's good to see you smiling, bro," I say when he ends the call.

His gaze shifts from his mobile he was staring at with a goofy grin to me.

I smile just as wide and tip my water bottle to Roger in salute.

He returns my gesture and ambles over to talk some more with us.

"You know what time it is, don't you?" I ask, leaning forward and rubbing my hands together as I stare at Roger.

A smile quirks the corners of his mouth as the water bottle pauses midair. He cocks his head to the side and raises his eyebrow. An expression of *oh boy, here it comes from The Rebel* flashes across his face.

I chuckle wickedly, knowing I have Roger hooked. And Harris, if his sitting straighter in his club chair, serves as a sign of his interest.

"Guys' Night Out! Tonight. The Jackson boys are in town along with Borya, and of course Luc. Call your buddy Joel Bailey. We'll meet at Jackson Smoke&Scotch Lounge

Paris. Nine o'clock," I declare. "And I will not take no for an answer."

Harris whoops and punches the air.

"Yeah, baby! Count me in!" He exclaims.

The smile on Roger's face spreads to a full-on Cheshire Cat's grin. His slate gray eyes shine. With a nod, he brings the bottle to his mouth and chugs the water.

Harris eggs him on as though it's a shot of tequila—or more appropriately, Scotch.

I chuckle and wink before I finish my bottle.

The cure to the blues: family and friends.

"Here's to Guys' Night Out and the support of my boys!"

Roger lifts his Baccarat crystal snifter of Jackson Reserve Scotch in a toast.

We're in one of the glass-enclosed tasting rooms at Jackson Smoke&Scotch a new lounge Lucien opened nine months ago on Rue Saint-Honoré.

The legendary Place Vendôme/St. Honoré area is the place to see and be seen. Where money is no object for the people it attracts. Old society, fashionistas, and celebrities frequent the nearby high-chic spots to shop, drink, and dine.

It's the latest addition to Jackson Corporation's luxury establishments created by *The Sexy Chef,* as legions of his female followers dubbed Lucien. They slated locations in London, New York, and Los Angeles for over the next few months. Another hot property for the Jacksons to add to their list.

I rarely smoke, but tonight I take a long draw on my Jackson Cuban cigar and settle back in my leather club chair. The tasting notes of the spicy, earthy, and woody flavors linger on my palate. They blend well with the smoky, dark berries flavor of the Jackson Reserve Scotch. Its trademark bite drags along the back of my tasting.

My mind drifts back to our first night at the Lounge with Sebastian, Roger, Joel, and Lucien. Baz teased me about my encounter with My Angel at his wedding.

"Damn, it must be in the water!"

"Hell, as long as it's not in my Jackson Reserve, I'm good. Let those three keep the water!"

"I'll drink to that, bro!"

Everyone laughs at Lucien's and my banter.

"Funny, you were chasing after Starr Knight at my wedding," *Sebastian says as he blows out smoke from his Jackson Cuban Cigar.*

All heads swing to me, curious to know who sparked the interest of the Dom playboy enough for me to give chase. It's the reverse—I can't keep women from their pursuit of me. My face flushes and I take a swig of my Scotch.

"Fuck off, Baz," *I mumble an answer with the snifter at my lips.*

"Pardon... Say again? We didn't hear you, Lover Boy, er, play-boy..." *Sebastian teases me relentlessly as only an older brother can.*

Now recovered, I cradle the Baccarat crystal snifter in my palms as I smirk at Baz. His gray eyes flash with devilment.

"I don't know what you're talking about," *I scoff.* *"You must have been floating in the clouds, struck by Cupid's arrow." I respond as I make goo-goo eyes and bat my eyelashes coyly at Sebastian.*

We crack up, Baz included. His cheeks even redden with embarrassment. Poor guy. I got my big brother down pat.

"Say what you want, Hettie and I have a good thing going... As it is. No signs of marriage on our horizon," Joel states with a decisive nod between puffs of his cigar. "I'm way too young to commit for the rest of my life."

Lucien and I clink glasses with Joel, adding robust cheers and here, here.

Roger shakes his head and chuckles. Now that he's back with Leonie, he's as bad as Baz.

"Laugh all you want. I was just like you. Probably worse," Sebastian starts, eyeing each of his hecklers. "It'll happen to you, too. And I'm going to be the one yucking it up."

Lucien's, Joel's, and my eyes widen at Sebastian's proclamation. Then we burst out in hysterical laughter. Lucien wipes his eyes while Joel doubles over. Sebastian and Roger can't help but to join us...

Now let's go to the scoreboard: Sebastian married... Check... Joel married... Check... Roger engaged... Check... Malcolm head over fucking heels in love with none other than said Starr Knight... Check Check Check!

I chuckle and sip my Scotch.

"Private jokes, bro?"

Laurent's question pulls me from my reverie.

I glance at the youngest Jackson, who's four years my junior. Like me, he's the rebel of their clan, the one who marches to his own tune. And doesn't give a fuck. After Lucien, he's my favorite cousin.

"Just recalling how I was adamant not acknowledge my attraction to Starr Knight—you know Lola's yogi friend from her wedding—when the guys gathered her nine months ago. Now, I claim her and have to admit I'm in the same goo-goo world as Baz and Roger were then and still are today," I respond with a chuckle.

Laurent nods his head and smirks, "Yeah, I remember her, the brown-eyed beauty with the banging—"

I growl at him, and he raises his hands as he laughs.

"Whoa, cuzz! No disrespect to you or your woman," Laurent says. "She must be someone really special for you to go all caveman on me. However, I don't blame you, she is fine as fu—"

This time I chuck the pillow from my club chair at his head. He ducks and laughs uproariously. His emerald green eyes flash with mischief.

Instead, the pillow hits Borya on his back, and the former MMA champion spins ready to beat his opponent.

"*Kakogo cherta?!*" He growls *what the hell* in his native language as his glacial blue eyes spit icy daggers.

It's my turn to put my hands palms up in surrender.

"Pardon, bro! I meant that for mouthy Laurent," I chuckle.

Borya flicks his glare to him and says sternly, "Stop fucking around, *rebenok!*"

Laurent may not be a *kid*, but he's suitably chastened by the massive Russian.

Everyone laughs, then goes back to their discussions on sports, business, and typical guy talk.

Lucien and I update them on the latest with Jackson Hole at STEELE's construction. Then I tell them about Starr's SLFW Resort grand opening at STEELE St. Barth's coming up. Baz lets us know about an idea he has for a new retail opportunity that extends our brick-and-mortar offerings. Lachlan found an old recipe for one of the first Scotches Jackson Corporations's founder had hidden. Luc's Banque Montaigne just bought another, so he's added more to his billions. Our businesses thrive.

"Excuse us, gentlemen, but would you mind sharing with us what has your undivided attention?"

All talk ceases as every head turns toward the sultry, Spanish-accented voice. A stunning brunette with olive-colored skin and sable eyes smirks at us. Three other women stand in the doorway with her—another Spanish beauty and two blonde bombshells. Their faces flushed from the Scotch in their glasses or from the lust in their eyes.

Each takes her time gazing at one then the others of us. The women take our pause as an invitation to step inside of the room. One blonde sidles up to Sebastian. But he raises his left hand and wiggles his finger with the unmistakable platinum wedding band. Joel does the same when a brunette approaches him. Roger backs away with a firm shake of his head, his intense stare offers no chance of the affirmative.

When the initial brunette sashays to sit on the arm of my chair, I rise and shake my head no, too. Then gesture for her to sit, since Laurent has a gleam in his eyes for the stunner. She inclines her head and settles in my vacated seat.

I join Baz, Roger, Luc, and Joel at the bar.

"No thanks, I have my own brown-eyed beauty," I tell them with a laugh. "Besides, she'd have my balls if I flirted with another. Even though My Angel isn't here, I know what I do. And that I cannot do to her."

Baz grins and slaps me on the back.

"If I recall correctly, it was within these hallowed walls I told you what would happen when you teased me about Lola… *'Laugh all you want. I was just like you. Probably worse. It'll happen to you, too. And I'm going to be the one yucking it up.'* So…" Baz doubles over with laughter. His dove gray eyes fill with tears as he cracks up.

The fucker was right after all.

STARR

"*O*h, Leonie! Cheer up! Think how much nicer your wedding will be once this shit is over! You don't want to reminisce and have a cloud of negativity shrouding your big day, do you?"

She glances over at Lola and raises her eyebrow.

It's a few weeks later and we're on a Girls' Getaway to Arachon, France. The trip is in lieu of Roger and Leonie's wedding. All thanks to Delia Shaw, an intern at STEELE Paris and former classmate of Leonie's at the Paris American Academy, and her bullshit sexual assault and harassment lawsuit against Roger.

"Hey! I'm not taking sides. But Roger *The Responsible* is right," Lola adds. "That's the best solution. Now you can wear your choice of gowns without a big ole belly bump!"

She balls up her Hermès beach blanket and puts it under her tunic. Then grabs Leonie's and includes it to make her pseudo-bump larger.

Leonie rolls her eyes and walks faster towards the chaise lounges. But can't help laughing when Lola waddles past her, pretending to walk down the aisle.

"I hate you, Lola Steele!" Leonie calls after her best friend.

Lola puts her hands on her lower back and exaggerates her movements even more than before. Her snorts of laughter trail behind her.

"Some BFF, huh?" I ask Leonie.

She shifts her gaze from Lola to me as I loop my arm through hers. Despite my attempt to maintain a serious expression, my sorrel-brown eyes twinkle with mirth. When Lola sumo squats to sit on her chaise and the towels fall to the sand, I can't help but to burst out laughing. My dimples deepen in my face.

Although Leonie must think I'm acting the devil now…

"Oh, don't tease her—so badly," Billie chimes in as she cracks up.

Haley nods, "Well, you know Roger, he'll do what he thinks is best no matter what. However… I most definitely agree with his decision. For once, one of my overbearing older brothers is correct."

Anita, Bair, and Hettie Fuchs—the fiancée of Roger's friend Joel—stand firm with Leonie's fiancé, too.

Reality set in. She'd rather have her fairytale wedding than a blight on their big day.

Plus Roger arranged this Girls' Getaway to make up for the delay. A chance for Leonie to get her mind off of the pretrial madness and hang out with her closest friends for a fun time.

"Ha, ha, ha, Loser Girl!" Leonie says as she lowers herself down onto the chaise lounge next to Lola's.

"Remember to engage your pelvic floor, Leonie," says Anita.

Leonie nods, then puts her legs up and giggles to herself.

"I can't believe I've never been here before after all these years of living in France. It's spectacular!" Hettie exclaims.

Roger didn't want Leonie to go too far—no more than an hour's flight time from Paris. So her father suggested the seaside resort town of Arcachon on the southwest coast of France, known as the *Côte D'Argent* or the Silver Coast. Off the Atlantic Ocean, the luxury spot is south of Bordeaux's Haut Medoc vineyards and famous for its delicious oysters and seafood.

The stunning unspoiled sandy beaches, like the one we're on, make the change in wedding plans worthwhile. The magnificent villa we rented sits on the seafront and is only a brief ride to this beach.

Roger insisted Eric and a STEELE driver along with Leonie's security detail escort us. They drove from Paris in Roger's and Sebastian's Cullinans ahead of us. Then met our group at the heliport. Roger refuses to take any chances with The Twins and Leonie's safety because of harassment caused by the pretrial.

We arrived last night and just chilled at the villa. It's a marvelous architectural piece of history. The slate tile roof and stone facade with pale blue trim are ornate. With three floors and a large parcel of land on the seafront, it's a sizable property. Each of us has a suite of rooms with private baths.

After changing into Lola's Coterie loungewear, we met in the eat-in kitchen for a simple dinner prepared by the chef. She made several platters of freshly caught seafood, herb chicken, and roasted vegetables. We ate the tasty dishes buffet style around the table.

Later we stretched out in the media room and watched a movie while we stuffed ourselves with the variety of pastries the chef made from scratch. The rest of us enjoyed aperitifs while Leonie had her iced lemon ginger tea. We spent more time chatting than we did watching the latest chick flick. The drama in our lives proved more entertaining than the anything the characters faced!

This morning we headed to the beach. I chose a leopard print triangle bikini. It's sexy and fierce. A white mid-thigh length caftan, flip-flops, and a woven Kenya bag round out my outfit. I lift my glamour girl shades to peer at Leonie.

"Girl! Don't let Lola's antics get to you! If you didn't turn to the side or face us, we would never know you had a giant beachball for a stomach!" I say laughing.

"Nice compliment… I guess!" Leonie says as she tosses a pillow at me.

I lay my colorful Hermès beach towel over my chaise lounge then sit back to take in the view of the white sandy beach and deep blue-green Atlantic Ocean. The air is crisp with the saltwater scent as seagulls call out to each other. The sun is warm on my skin. Its warmth is a luxurious sensation after being in clothes for so long. I tilt my head back against the chaise lounge and close my eyes as I absorb my surroundings.

Peace and serenity.

"Great idea! Let's have a five-minute meditation session," Anita says when she spies my hands formed in a mudra on my thighs.

"Yes! Wonderful way to embrace all of this natural beauty," I respond.

Opening my eyes, I find everyone gathered around, settling on to the two chaises on either side of me. I smile and make room for Anita to sit at the foot of my chaise. We face each other cross-legged.

She leads us through a guided meditation that reflects on our connection with nature. Her melodic voice enchants us as we're led on the mind-body-surroundings journey. She ends with a chant and namaste.

When I reopen my eyes, my thoughts are clear, and I feel lighter. So far, so good.

"Tomorrow morning we should come down and do a

flow class on the beach. I'd love to start my day with a sunrise session," Billie suggests.

I nod, "I have a new sequence I'd love to share with you. Leonie, I can modify it for you. Although I must say, your strength shows in your movements. You can probably teach it!"

She laughs and thanks me for my words of encouragement, but declines.

"I'm not ready for prime time! I'll leave the teaching to you and Anita, *merci!*"

"Well, I'm all for morning yoga tomorrow. But right now, I'm getting in that glistening water!" Haley announces as she stands and takes off her Missoni tunic.

"Me, too! I can't wait to dive in," Hettie adds as she takes off her Norma Kamali sarong-style midi skirt. "I won't say last one in is a rotten egg because you smell nice, Leonie!"

Everyone laughs, agreeing she would be the last one in the water. Lola helps Leonie to her feet and links her arm through hers as they walk to the water's edge en masse.

The security team keeps a distance. But stay near since the beach is busy with other visitors, vendors with trinkets, and waitstaff. They're discreet in swim trunks and t-shirts. Only their clear earpieces hint at their purpose.

Leonie acknowledges them with a slight nod.

When we reach the water, the girls dive and jump in and Leonie wades in right behind us. The buoyancy makes me feel even lighter than the mediation session.

"The water is perfect! I'm so glad your father recommended Arcachon. Who knew France had Caribbean-style beaches!" Blair says as she floats over to me.

"We used to come often when I was younger. A simple trip my parents enjoyed since you get the beaches, the wine region, sailing lakes, and pine forests. The variety of activities kept us busy. The visits increased my interest in architecture with the historic homes of Ville d'Hiver," Leonie responds, smiling at the memories.

"I know it's early. But I can really go for some more of those oysters. They were delish last night!" Anita says. "They made me miss Norman!"

She adds with a wink.

"Why are you grinning like the Cheshire Cat?" Billie asks as she raises her elegantly arched eyebrow at Leonie.

She laughs out loud at being so busted for private jokes.

"Oh, let me guess… That fine ass man of yours and oysters?" Billie says grinning.

"Maybe, maybe not!" Leonie responds, then ducks away, averting her face.

"That's a definite maybe!!" Yells Billie at her retreating form.

We giggle and taunt the blushing Leonie.

We spend the rest of the time enjoying the sun, sand, and surf for a relaxing day at the beach. When we return, I check in with Adrienne on Starr Light Fitness & Wellness happenings, then send a text message to my man while the girls go about their business. Lola, Blair, and Billie get in some work for the boutiques. I told Anita I'd record Instagram videos for our thousands of followers for a crossover challenge. Haley geeks out on her computer where she's working on some top-secret project she's cagey about when asked. Hettie works on some legal cases for her clients. We're Independent Women who work hard and play harder!

"LEAD the way to the baccarat table, *merci*!"

I reply when the general manager for the Casino D'Arcachon greets us and asks for our favorite games. My eyes twinkle in glee as I clap my hands in anticipation of a night of gaming.

We decided to glam it up big time tonight in all red outfits. I chose a cutout crystal-embellished crepe mini dress that reveals a sparkly sequin and crystal-embellished bra cup. Lola flaunts her toned legs in a smock exaggerated pussy-bow hammered silk mini dress with ruffled shoulders and elasticized cuffs on the breezy sleeves. Haley goes for the sparkle with a crystal and paillette-embellished tulle mini dress. Blair picks a new piece from Lola's Coterie evening wear collection, a contoured lace-up satin mini dress with contrasting lace-up detail and underwire cups. Billie's elegant outfit of a strapless filigree-like appliqué crystal-embellished mini dress. Hettie goes for a 90s style in a slinky, open-back chain-mail mini dress. Anita does a take on the classic tuxedo with a crystal-embellished satin-trimmed halter-neck mini dress. Leonie rocked her babies bump in a stretchy, one-sleeve ruched mini dress with an asymmetric skirt detailed and adjustable drawstrings on the shoulder and hem. We're all flowy hair, tan skin, and high strappy heels!

"*Absolument mademoiselles!* Please follow me," he says with a chuckle at my enthusiasm.

We walk through the 19th-century Château Deganne, where the casino is located. The impressive Neo-Renaissance-style mansion on the edge of the beach harkens to the grand times the area experienced. It's elegance similar to the Casino de Monte-Carlo reminds me of a James Bond from the time.

"I'm going to try my hand at blackjack," Hettie announces when we pass the table.

Anita nods, "Oh, me, too! I love pushing as far as possible without going over twenty-one."

Blair and Billie join them as the rest of us set up at the baccarat table.

A crowd gathers around our table to cheer me on my

winning streak. Our laughter rings out above the excited din of the rooms.

"Come on, baby, let's make that money!" I laugh.

"This is such a blast! Who would have thought this little gem of a town would have a casino?" Haley giggles as she picks up her winnings from another bet. "This may become a regular spot for me!"

Lola and Leonie nod in agreement.

"STEELE should open a property here or take over this casino. I'm sure Malcolm would take it to the next level," Lola whispers so only we can hear.

I'm too absorbed in the game to pay them any attention —even if it is about my man. My laughter when I win yet another round makes them laugh, too.

"Girls, I'm on a roll! You better put your money down and get in on this streak!" I turn to my friends and say with a wink.

"Hey, I'm all in on this one!" Leonie answers, putting her chips on the table. "What's the saying, 'Mama needs a new pair of shoes,' right?"

They laugh as she rubs her belly in emphasis.

"*Oui, mademoiselle.* But your shoes seem more than good to me."

She glances over her shoulder, then tilts her head back to meet the eyes of the stranger. He's around Roger's height, handsome with aqua blue eyes, and a smooth baritone voice. His smile widens when their gazes meet.

Is he flirting with her? I wonder as I pause my game to face the attractive stranger.

"*Merci, monsieur.* How kind of you. My fiancé would agree," she says as she rubs her belly with her left hand, the giant stone shooting sparks in the light.

The stranger glances down and nods slightly.

"Lucky man, your fiancé," he replies. "Well, I shall leave you to enjoy your evening."

He bows and strides away just as Leonie's security detail moves into position behind him, ready to handle the situation.

Lola bursts out laughing, "Okay, MILF Alert! Roger better be careful!"

I nod in agreement.

"He needed to go. I don't want any bad vibes around my game!" I add with a scowl.

We crack up and get back to baccarat.

After a late dinner at the casino, we call it and head to the SUVs. The night is full of wins and losses, but all fun.

* * *

"Girl hush, don't give the surprise away, Billie!"

Blair says when we hear Leonie walking towards the villa's living room entrance.

Roger called Lola to tell her he was coming down to surprise Leonie since today is the original date of their wedding. He also told her it's the one-year anniversary of Leonie and him being back together.

It the last night of our Girls' Getaway, and we were supposed to go out to dinner at this great restaurant the house butler recommended. We know Leonie was feeling down today, and now we're puttering around in pajamas while throw her off. She'll never guess the truth!

"Hey, why aren't you guys dressed yet?" she asks as she walks into the living room to find us lounging about with the television on and eating ice cream.

"Oh, don't you look lovely!" Lola says sitting up. "Can you do me a favor and hand me my tote from the foyer?"

Leonie frowns and cocks her head questioningly.

Lola raises her hand to stop her from speaking.

"Come on, Leonie. You're already standing, and it's just around the corner. Please?!" She says with puppy eyes.

Leonie rolls hers and about-faces, grumbling to herself.

She probably thinks now we haven't even dressed, and we're going to be later than expected—considering she's ten minutes late as it is.

We jump from our seats to peek into the foyer where Roger waits for the love of his life. Leonie gasps when she sees him and starts to tremble. He embraces her, and she melts against him. With sighs of happiness for our dear friend, we turn away to give them privacy for such an intimate moment.

Ah, pure love. The Girls' Getaway just got even better! No need to think of the nasty pretrial. Only love.

MALCOLM

"*R*oger! Why did you sexually assault Delia Shaw?"

"No means no!"

"Roger Steele! *Honte à toi!*"

"Leonie! How can you marry a monster?"

"Leonie! This way!"

Fuck!

This is a damn media circus combined with a protest that's beyond fucked up. And this is only day one of the pretrial…

Albert Perry—STEELE Paris' General Counsel—and his legal team take the lead up the steps of the pretrial court-house. Their mood is no nonsense and all business. They set the tone for us.

Sebastian and Roger flank Leonie, holding her arms as they move through the crowd held back by their security detail and the police. Despite how nasty the crowd behaves, she keeps her head high and her back straight. Leonie is no shrinking violet who simpers in the face of opposition. She's a fierce *Lion.*

The rest of our family and friends follow them. All Steeles; Starr; Guy and Josy; Lachlan and Lucien; Luc; Joel and Hettie; Blair and Billie; Norman and Anita came out in a full force of support. Françoise Faucher—Roger's longtime assistant—along with several other STEELE staff members join us in solidarity. Their presence is a comfort for my younger brother and Leonie.

No one speaks while we proceed to the courtroom. The halls are full of people who turn in our direction as we pass. Our pace doesn't slow. We want to get in and settled quickly.

A flash goes off to our left. Followed by more as the media within the building take notice of our group.

More catcalls fill the already tense air.

It pisses me off. These people have zero knowledge of the facts. Yet they judge and condemn my brother. The state of the world today assumes the man is guilty automatically. Some may be. But Roger is not. The immediate castigation of him angers me.

Starr must sense my inner turmoil. She squeezes my hand as she peeks up at me with concern in her gorgeous sorrel-colored eyes.

I nod and squeeze her hand in acknowledgment of her support. What would I do without her?

She's been a total trooper the past couple of weeks. She's helped Leonie as her doula to lessen her stress with the upcoming birth of The Twins. Along with continuing to do meditation and yoga *nidra* with Leonie and Roger to ease their nerves. All on top of My Angel's other work with her company and the upcoming grand opening. She's even put off going to St. Barth's for a site visit to spend time with a close friend. That's my woman—selfless and loving of others.

Finally, we reach the doors to the courtroom. More police officers stand guard to maintain control and to prevent overcrowding. They allow us to pass with nods.

Upon entering, we see the lying bitch Delia Shaw at the claimant's table. She shifts in her seat to glance at some asshole guy next to her. Then faces us when he indicates with the tilt of his chin our entrance.

For a brief moment, the real Delia shines through with a sneer directed at Leonie. The fleeting expression reveals her cocksure attitude and devious intent. In a blink, it's gone, replaced by a chaste, eyes downcast countenance. Then she widens her eyes and covers her mouth on a sob before she turns away slowly. The guy standing behind Delia pats her shoulder comfortingly and whispers in her ear.

If I hadn't seen her glare at Leonie, Delia's performance would have been believable—and the Academy Award for Best Actress goes to…

Sebastian huffs in response to Delia's dramatic behavior.

I agree and growl under my breath.

My Angel squeezes my hand again, and I relax at her reminder to keep my cool. She made me promise this morning while we were getting dressed. Ever seeing the bigger picture, My Angel reminded me Roger didn't need any interference that would sway the judge's decision.

Now, I nod again.

After I help her into her seat on the bench between behind my parents and Leonie's mother and father, Roger joins Perry and the legal team at the defendant's table and faces forward. Not a glance at the liar.

Game on.

At the call to order, the din of voices quiets and everyone

stands. When the judge enters the courtroom, the solemnity of the situation hits me in the chest like a Mack truck.

This woman can cause my younger brother to go to an abysmal French jail for years all over her lies. This is beyond fucked up.

The proceedings start with an opening statement presented by Judge Favre as a summary of the claim and the parties involved. The magistrate outlines the timeline for the proceedings. He plans to convene eight times after today on alternating days over the next month. Today will give both sides the opportunity to make opening statements. With the investigation set to begin next week.

Delia's legal team presents their opening statement. They drone on to paint me as a sex maniac who preyed on Ms. Shaw—an innocent, trusting university student who earned her position as an intern. Her only mistake was being in the division run by a monster…

Her appearance would support her claim of purity with a navy blue conservative skirt suit, severe bun, and no makeup. Her curves no longer on display and her vivacious personality hidden behind a sorrowful persona.

It's hard to get a read on the judge. He sits stoically on his bench. Periodically during the claimant's statement, his eyes flick to me with an analytical stare.

Perry rises from his seat.

He presents Roger's statement in a succinct, factual manner. Unlike the claimant's attorney, Perry completes his opening remarks in less than fifteen minutes. Even the judge seems to appreciate the brevity of Perry's words as Judge Favre's face relaxes a fraction.

He thanks both sides for their opening statements. Then he reminds everyone we will re-convene next week. He rises from his bench and exits the courtroom as we stand.

We wait until Perry and his team gather their paperwork before we leave.

In a show of support, Leonie kisses Roger on the lips in full view of everyone. The sound of cameras clicking fills the room. She knows how to play the game, too.

We make our way back out to the waiting cars. Sebastian and Roger flank Leonie again as we move through the crowd. More insults and questions come at us from all directions. Fuckers.

At last we get inside the four Mercedes-Benz Sprinters and pull away from the courthouse in formation. Perry suggested we lease the souped-up vans instead of driving our personal vehicles since strangers would view the license plates. We certainly don't want stalkers finding our homes. The damn drones and paparazzi are bad enough. We take a roundabout way back to the *Manoir* to avoid being followed.

We wait until we reach the *Manoir* and sit in the living room before we discuss the investigation. Perry gives his feedback along with his team. They pulled a report on the judge and found him to be stern and only interested in facts, not emotions. The statement made by Delia's legal team was full of emotion. While Perry's was all facts. He says it's a score for Roger.

Our father and Roger ask more questions. But there's not much to go on at this point. The real action will occur next week. Perry suggests we enjoy the weekend, rest, and return ready for the tough part. He and the team leave, declining an offer to join us for an early dinner. Françoise also leaves and offers words of encouragement before they go.

The rest of the group heads to the dining hall—the larger eating area that harkens back to *Le Manoir Beaulieu*'s days of entertaining royalty in the larger space. The staff serves the meal prepared by their chef. Josy cooks on the weekends when she gives them the days off.

We dine on the scrumptious dishes and wines from their ancient cellar. No one discusses the proceedings. We opt to have a normal conversation with Harris teasing Haley about some mysterious project she's working on, and Hettie recounting Joel's time at their cake tasting with his allergic reaction to almond paste. Norman regales us with stories from his most renown matches, and Anita tells how he's a softy for their daughter Antonia. It amounts to a good time with loved ones.

* * *

"Yes, Sir!"

My Sweet Sub's cry of anguish as I stroke her clit engorged from my suckling makes me want to skip the demo and fuck her now.

We took Perry up on his recommendation to enjoy the weekend. But our idea of rest probably isn't what he had in mind... It's LEVELS Paris.

Tonight is Demo Night, where members experienced in various acts of BDSM offer to show their skills to others. Masters of play including sensory deprivation, edge, electrostimulation, flogging, and my favorite—suspension bondage and submission.

Shibari—my preferred method I learned under the tutelage of a Japanese Master—requires the utmost skill on the Dom's side and trust from the sub. Since the sub is partially or fully suspended in the air by their body parts, suspension bondage is intense, and it comes with significant risks. A Dom must use great care and maintain an absolute focus on the sub's responses to understand and to heed them. Years of training during which I was a sub to a Japanese Domme taught me the beautiful art of rope play.

I would bare any other sub completely to the eyes of the LEVELS members during our demonstration. And I—not one to shy from anything—would show my face.

But not tonight and never with My Sweet Sub.

Not one individual will ever glimpse Starr Knight naked. For. My. Eyes. Only.

With her eyes covered by a white silk blindfold, she lies supine on the table beside the white silk ropes. I chose them to contrast with her skin tone nicely and to remind her of my body wrapped around hers. I bound her heavy breasts with more of the soft material to form a narrow bandeau top and a strip of silk covers her smooth pussy.

I move the scrap of material back in place before I rise to my full height.

Completely clothed in a black long-sleeved shirt open to reveal my muscular torso, custom-fit black leather pants, and black leather boots, I'm the opposite of My Sweet Sub. Her black on my white. A full mask to maintain my anonymity finishes my outfit.

Now that she's primed and at ease, I help her to a kneeling position where her lush ass rests on her haunches and she grasps opposite elbows behind her back. I rub my hands along the tops of her thighs—just as silky as my ropes —letting my thumbs glide inward to soothe her. Then ask if she's ready. My Sweet Sub takes in an excited breath, then whispers yes against my lips as she nods her head. I nip her plump lower lip, and she yelps.

Playtime!

I turn to the members gathered around the primary stage in the Cellar and bow to signal the start of our demonstration. Through the holes in the mask, I see their excited faces, eager for the show. I smirk and face My Sweet Sub.

I skim the silk rope bundle over her heated skin. The cool touch of the sumptuous material causes another fluttery inhalation. I waste no time in unwinding the coil and setting to work binding My Sweet Sub.

An erotic pattern develops as I loop the silks around her arms to pull them closer to her back and make her chest rise so her ample tits jut out. Rope around her long, delicate neck exposed by her curls slicked into a topknot, then down between the valley of her tits to bind above and below the mounds. Encased in the white silks, her nipples peak and I can't help but to lean down to suckle them.

"Aaahhh, Sir…" My Sweet Sub moans.

I nip her and growl, "Silence, Naughty Pet!"

We agreed she would remain quiet since she's very vocal when we fuck. No need to risk her slipping in ecstasy and saying my name, revealing my identity and thus hers since the media photographed us together often. The global media spotlight cast on Roger has widened to the rest of the Steeles and those around us by association. We appear more than we prefer in the tabloids and news these days.

My Naughty Pet bites her lower lip and bows her head.

I leave a substantial length of rope to the side and help her lie back with her knees bent, feet flat on the table. Then I pick up two additional coils. A few loops around each thigh and calf pull them flush to the corresponding body part. I leave another substantial length of rope on her left thigh. The binding done, I squeeze her knees to signal we're ready for the next stage: suspension.

Once again, I ask My Sweet Sub if she's fine with phase two. This time I place a trial of open-mouthed kisses along her flat belly up to her luscious mouth. She moans a yes as I press my lips to hers.

I turn to our rapt audience, the hush in the room louder than the usual sensual cacophony of moans, groans, and cries of pleasure and pain in the BDSM dungeon. Even more members gathered while I focused on My Sweet Sub. Not one person present in the Cellar glances away from us.

With a nod, I pivot and stride to the metal ring suspended above the stage. For the third time, I check the ring, the chain, and the lever to ensure their sturdiness. Satisfied, I return to My Sweet Sub and push the table beneath the ring.

Then I attach the extra length of the two coils to the ring and another piece from her left thigh to both lengths to form a triangle. Only her right leg is free from the ring. Before I push the table away, I recheck the knots and go to the lever to hoist My Sweet Sub into the air.

My Angel hovers above the table, captured in my silks. Beautiful.

The ginormous bulge in my constrictive leather pants demands release. I stroke my length. Soon.

Striding across the stage, I move the table swiftly, then stand behind My Angel and do a Vanna White move with my hands to reveal her to the audience.

They clap, impressed by her nubile form. With her long limbs flexible and sculpted by years of yoga and Pilates, My Angel is an incredible sight to behold. She is a work of art. My work of art.

Mine!

With that thought in mind, it's time for her reward. I move to stand by her bent legs and grasp her bound thighs. She moans in anticipation.

Yes, My Sweet Sub, time to fuck you as you fly.

In a blur, my zipper opens and my cock springs free, already aimed at her sopping wet pussy as illustrated by the wet patch on the strip of silk. I swipe it aside and slide my girth into her ready channel.

Fuck yes!

My Sweet Sub arches her back at the carnal invasion of her body. Her mouth hangs open as she swings sideways on the ring rope attached on the left half of her body. Like a pendulum, she keeps coming back to sheath my cock in her tight, wet heat.

The rippling of her inner walls lets me know she's close to climax. Now after eight months, I trained My Sweet Sub, and she knows not to cum unless I give her permission.

And permission I am ready to give to her, along with my seed.

I redouble my efforts and grip her ass to keep her steady. My hips snap to jackhammer inside of her again and again until she's wailing with each brutal thrust. When her pussy clamps down on my dick, I'm gone.

"Cum for me, Little Pet! Cum for me. Now!" I command.

A shudder wracks through her body, and a keening sound comes from the depth of her soul.

"Oh, fuck… Fuck… Fuck… MALCOLM!!!" My Sweet Sub screams as her climax sends her over the edge to the erotic bliss of subspace.

Well, I guess she blew over cover now…

"Oh, baby! This is incredible! I can't believe how much work they did since I saw the last status video! Thank you so much!!"

My Angel's eyes glitter like the Caribbean Sea as the sunlight dapples its turquoise surface.

We're in St. Barth's for the first site visit of her new Starr Light Fitness & Wellness Resort at STEELE St. Barth's. We came for the topping off ceremony. In construction, it's the Viking practice of topping off a building with an evergreen tree on the peak to celebrate the completion of the major structural components of a building.

In SLFW's case, we put a palm tree on the roof and toast with My Angel's favorite Krug Clos d'Ambonnay Champagne. The construction crew completed the two-story building's foundation, outer walls, interior walls, and roof. Phase two of the project focuses on the interior systems and the exterior finish. The last phase for the interior design and external landscaping appears on schedule in three months. The grand opening celebration will occur a week after a soft opening.

"Yes, Starr! How fantastic is the view of the Caribbean!" Adrienne exclaims as she shields her eyes from the bright sun.

Her comment draws Anton's attention. He can't keep his eyes off of the green-eyed feline beauty.

"*Da*, and what a spectacular view," he growls thickening his Russian accent.

Adrienne may not respond with words to his call, but she shivers visibly and gulps the champagne in her crystal flute.

My Angel chuckles and wraps her arm around my waist as she reaches up to kiss my cheek.

"I can just picture Beach Barre out front on the warm sand. Or, or Moonlight Yoga on the roof deck! I love it!" She says.

My heart slams against my chest. Fuck! I thought she was about to say the L-word about me. I stiffen, then relax when I realize I'm not averse to it after all. Not now. Even though I haven't spoken the words, the last few times we made love or spent time together, I attempted to express them with my actions. Hey, like they say, actions speak louder than words and all that.

She must have felt my knee-jerk reaction because she moves away from me. But I slip my arms around her from behind and clink my flute to hers.

"I'm glad you love it or me if that's what you meant," I tease, brushing my lips against the shell of her ear before I nip the lobe.

A little pleasure and pain to lighten the mood.

"So arrogant, Mr. Steele," My Angel replies. "Huh… Putting words in my mouth."

"I have more than words to put in that sweet little mouth of yours, My Angel," I smirk.

Just as I hoped, she giggles and pushes me off of her.

Disappointed from the loss of her curvy body, but thankful she's not pissed, I'll take it.

We spend another hour in discussions with the project manager and his crew. My Angel and Adrienne ask questions, and they satisfy their concerns with sound answers. Anton speaks with them to complete the timeline, then we head back to the main resort for lunch.

It's only a six-minute walk or two minutes in a property golf cart. We wanted guests to have easy access to the center. Its prime beachfront location will serve My Angel's business well.

She and Adrienne walk ahead of Anton and me as they chat about the new location.

My Angel looks cute and feminine in what she calls a playsuit. The shorts length suits the Caribbean heat and the red floral-print reminds me of tropical flowers. But it's the vision of her long, toned, sun-kissed legs squeezing my ears that makes me grin.

Her curly pony hair bounces with each step, beckoning for me to wrap it around my fist and use it like a pair of reins while I ride her all night long. Moonlight Yoga won't be the only thing pumping on the rooftop deck. We'll have to christen each room for prosperity. Now that's the Malcolm *The Rebel* Steele version of a topping off ceremony!

"Don't you look sexy, My Angel."

She spins around and the layers on the linen and silk mini skirt she wears flares out, showing off her long, flawless legs. When she faces me, my eyes travel up her body to the white cotton cropped tank top. It molds to her luscious tits.

I marvel at the way her nipples plump up under my

hooded gaze. I lick my lips, and she bites hers. I feel her teeth on the tip of my cock.

"Thank you, baby," she says with an extra sassy twirl. "You look hunkalicious yourself."

The wink she gives me makes my cock twitch. It's need for her increases constantly. Damn.

But it's the sight of my collar around her neck that gets the blood flowing to my groin in earnest. My Sweet Sub wore her day wear version. The diamond-pavé letter S in its platinum mesh center brings out the caveman in me. S for Steele equals mine, all mine.

If we hadn't agreed to dinner with Anton, Adrienne, the project manager, and his wife, I would drag My Sweet Sub by her curly ponytail to bed and never let her leave it. Rawr!

She must sense my growing desire for her, and she smirks.

"This way, Mr. Steele, duty calls now, playtime later. That is, if you are a very good boy and deserving of a treat..." My Angel teases, looping her arm through mine and heading for the villa's front door.

"Watch yourself, My Naughty Girl, or playtime will become punishment time," I rejoin with a carefully placed swat to her sits bones.

My Naughty Girl yelps and skips from the unexpected smack.

I chuckle wickedly as we exit the villa.

We hop into the golf cart and drive to the resort's beachfront restaurant. Anton waves us over to the bar where he stands next to Adrienne. The hulking, blond Russian dwarfs the green-eyed, buttery pecan-colored skin beauty as she sits on a bar stool.

"Hi, there! You should have one of these cocktails. The bartender made it for me especially," she says, casting a sultry smile at the mixologist.

I chuckle when Anton's fists clench and his nostrils flare. Oh boy…

My Angel giggles and reaches for the glass the bartender places in front of her. Then rolls her eyes when I growl in her ear possessively.

Mine!

Fortunately for the mixologist, the project manager and his wife appear and distract Anton and me from explaining how close to dangerous ground he treads.

Instead, the hostess leads us to our table by the beachside railing.

I help My Angel into her chair and take the seat beside her. We order a tantalizing seafood tower for our appetizer and an array of mouther-watering meat and chicken entrées. Conversation flows freely as we chat about everything from island life to the benefits of coconut oil to the best restaurants on the closest islands.

The project manager regales us with stories of him catching a great white shark by mistake when he went night fishing. He has us cracking up when he describes it landing on the shore and him running out of his sandals when he recognized the apex predator.

His wife chimes in with how her husband left out the part where he swore the shark flew out of the water with its mouth wide open, ready to devour him, and he ran screaming. Like a baby, she adds for emphasis as she laughs hysterically.

My Angel's carefree giggles and her shining eyes make my heart soar with affection. She makes it harder and harder for me to deny the level of my attraction to her. And I'm not sure if I want to ignore it any longer. Even if I admit it to myself only.

I lean over and kiss her cheek, not giving a damn it's PDA in front of a STEELE staff member.

MINE!

Later that night, I show My Angel just how deep my emotions for her go as I make slow and deliberate love to her. I worship every part of her delicious body. From the tips of her toes I suck to the kisses I place on the backs of her knees to the special attention I pay to her supple breasts. By the time my mouth covers hers for a soul-stirring, passionate kiss, she trembles beneath me and widens her legs as an invitation to fill her with my aching cock.

I slide into her with ease as her hot, soaking channel envelops my turgid length. My thrusts alternate between slow and deep and shallow and fast until she writhes as she cums over and over. I draw the maximum orgasms from her I know her body can handle before I seek my release.

As her core quivers from her last climax, I propel my cock forward, aiming to fill her womb with my seed until it spills from her pussy to trail between her thighs and the crack of her ass. I plan to mark My Angel as I claim her all night long.

* * *

"How's it going, bro?"

My Angel is in the office of the beachfront villa at the resort working with Adrienne on plans for SLFW Resorts, so I place a call to Roger. The pretrial is still happening and not being there to support him is working on me. But as he told me when I said I had to go for business, STEELE needs us as much from us as our family members. He said with the rest of the clan in Paris along with Leonie's parents and Luc, they have plenty of support.

Starr and I will return after she heads to Beverly Hills and I go to New York City to handle some in-person work. Even though she's Leonie's doula, she told Starr to focus on her business first, there's plenty of time before Leonie gives birth.

"As to be expected. She said, he said, blah, blah, blah. Let's give it a rest for now. Tell me about Starr's venture," Roger responds wearily.

Fuck, my brother really doesn't need any bullshit with Leonie ready to pop and her concerns for a healthy delivery. Fucking Delia Shaw!

I fill him in on the status and he offers some valuable advice. He says it's good to focus on STEELE and not the pretrial. Then he hits me with an unexpected question.

"Have you told Starr you love her, yet, *Rebel*?" He asks.

From the tone of his voice, I can tell he has an intense expression on his face. Roger has always been the responsible one of the siblings—Roger *The Responsible* Steele. As the middle child, he worries about the rest of us as much as Baz does as the eldest.

I take a moment to consider his question and how best to answer it. True, I have feelings for My Angel unlike any other woman before her. True, she makes me behave as I never have in the past.

But I sense she's holding back from me, and it bothers me more than I want to admit. I know she still has reservations about how quickly she's picked up on being a submissive and on balancing her Independent Woman. Even as free-spirited as she is—and not falling in line with convention—My Angel still struggles to give in to a D/s relationship completely.

And I've let it evolve into a vanilla relationship of boyfriend-girlfriend to help her ease into things. But I want it all with her, the BDSM and the vanilla rolled into one.

Fuck, who would have thought?

So I don't know how to answer Roger truly.

I do feel deeply for Starr. But I hold off on saying those

three words. If I'm honest with myself, it's because I fear she doesn't love me as deeply as I've fallen for her. I use my bravado to hide my fear. So far, it works. Just like earlier when I teased Starr to keep her from getting upset. How much longer will that work?

"Who says I love her?" I ask, falling back on my rebel playboy bravado with a chuckle. "We're just in the here and now, bro. Not all of us are ready to run down the aisle to the love of our life!"

A noise behind me makes me shift in my chaise lounge on the deck. I see My Angel in the doorway behind me. A fleeting expression ghosts across her face, but it's too fast for me to decipher it.

My stomach drops.

Fuck! I sure as hell hope she didn't hear my callous remark about loving her and marriage. That would be a major blunder. Damn.

Then she smiles.

I can't tell if it reaches her eyes because they're covered with giant sunglasses.

With a hope for the best, I smile back and hold my hand out to her.

She sashays over and sits between my legs with her back resting against my torso. I twine our legs and place my hands on her lower belly. She stiffens a bit, but relaxes with a sigh when I kiss the side of her neck where it meets her shoulder.

I chat with Roger a bit more—after changing the subject—then end the call.

"How'd your plans go?" I ask to test the waters.

Starr nods and tells me some of their ideas.

We talk through them, and I make suggestions. Then she asks me about Roger and Leonie. I fill her in, and she says she'll go back to Paris after she handles some affairs at home. After a while, we fall silent.

The sound of the water lapping on the shore and the seagulls' cries lull us into a nap. When I awake, Starr is gone. For a moment I panic, thinking she heard me after all and left me. Fuck!

When I rush from the chaise lounge calling her name, I spot her on the beach.

She's practicing her asanas.

I watch her for a while, marveling at her poise and strength. The way she can contort her body with ease amazes me. She's so flexible.

That's how I need to be—allow myself to just go with the flow. Not try to fight the norm for a change. No more need to prove how I can stand apart and do things my way,

I wouldn't mind the relationships Baz and Roger have with their women. The loves of their lives. My mind plays scenarios for My Angel and me: love, happiness, marriage, children, BDSM…

Why can't I have it all?

Haven't I always gotten what I wanted? And I want my brown-eyed beauty. Forever.

My Angel finishes her practice with a bow of her lovely head. When she stands and faces the villa, she notices me on the deck watching her. She pauses and appears to gather herself. Then she lifts her angelic face and waves at me.

I stand and walk down the steps to the seawall to embrace my love. My future. My Angel.

I can't believe what Malcolm said to Roger! Just as I came to terms with this whole D/s thing—me, an Independent Woman with a successful business and satisfying life.

While I laid next to Malcolm in bed at his private suite in LEVELS Paris after his—I mean our—demonstration with the ropes, I thought if I could do that for him, I must love this man. Hell, I mean I let him tie me up with ropes with nothing but bits of cloth covering my tits and pussy, hang me from the ceiling by said ropes, then fuck me delirious while I screamed his name all in front of a crowd in a damn BDSM dungeon!!! Without a doubt, the world now knows who we are and my addiction to submission!!!

Even the extreme sports we did—water jetpacking, cliff diving, zorbing, and OMG BASE jumping—excited me. He turned me on to the idea of thrill seeking and to cutting loose for real. Being an actual free spirit...

I've put up with mad shit from Vicky Reynolds: public embarrassment, gossip, and fucking with my business! And for what? For what?!?!

ARGH!!!

Really, Starr??? You lose all cool points for falling for a man who gives ZERO fucks about you!

Does he?

Yeah, dummy... Didn't you hear what he told his own flesh and blood?!?!?! He has no reason to lie to his own brother... "Your Dom... Man" sure as hell didn't sound as though he were joking!!! For fuck's sake he was LAUGHING. ABOUT. YOU!!!

True, so true.

Now look at me! This man has me not only talking to myself, but responding for a full-on conversation!

My wise great-grandfather used to say, "It's all right to talk to yourself, but just don't answer. Then you worry!"

Okay, so I'm very, very, I mean very worried right now...

I couldn't let Malcolm know I heard his words. Instead, I pasted a smile on my face for the rest of the three days we stayed. Even when he made lo—I mean fucked me or held me close to him. Not only was I in shock, but I had to save face and handle my business—even if he didn't know I love him.

* * *

"LEONIE, HONEY, YOUR MIND WANDERS."

Softly, I speak when I notice her fidgeting during her evening yoga *nidra* session.

When I did a video call to check on my friend after I returned from St. Barth's, she appeared so glum. Not at all like the sparkly Leonie or the fierce *Maman*.

She recounted her OB-GYN's words to her, *"Leonie, you have a noticeable increase in your blood pressure. It's not from your pregnancy, as you have no other signs. It's stress related. How are you holding up with the investigation?"*

I flew to Paris a few days later. All thoughts of arrogant Malcolm Steele set aside. My focus shifts from wallowing in self-pity—and a quart of Häagen-Daz Belgian Chocolate ice cream—to Leonie, The Twins, and Roger. Time to step up my doula duties.

Now, I sit beside her on the chaise lounge Roger added to her yoga studio at *Le Beaulieu Manoir*. It's easier for her to settle on her side on the piece of furniture than to lower herself to the ground at nearly thirty-six weeks pregnant.

He cares so much for his fiancée. Unlike his brother for me…

I give my head a firm shake to dislodge the negative thought. Focus, Starr!

Leonie opens her eyes, and a tear slips from a corner. A pitiful sob follows.

Sensing she doesn't need words, I gather her into my arms and rock her gently. I think of positive thoughts: Roger and STEELE International cleared of any charges; the healthy birth of The Twins; her upcoming wedding to the love of her life.

Put in the Universe what you want; ask and you shall receive; give thanks. Every tenet I can think of to surround Leonie with peace and tranquility, positive vibes.

After a few minutes, she sniffles and raises her head. A small smile of gratitude blooms on her tear-stained face. She nods, and I help her sit up with the pillows behind her back.

"*Merci, chérie.* You are such a comfort, Starr," Leonie says, now smiling fully.

"You're more than welcome, my dear friend," I respond with a grin.

As I rise to get a tissue for her, her next words stop me in my tracks.

"What's happened between you and Malcolm, *chérie*?" She asks quietly.

Caught off guard by her question and by my visceral reaction to his name spoken aloud for the first time in days, I shudder.

"Starr?" Leonie asks.

I scoop up the tissue box and walk back to her, avoiding her amber eyes.

"I don't know what you mean," I hedge. Surely he hasn't mentioned I've not responded to his voicemails and text messages.

Yeah! What does he care?! Pipes up my inner warrior.

I have to stop myself from telling her to shut it. No need to freak Leonie out as I hold a conversation with myself…

"He told Roger you're avoiding his calls," Leonie responds, watching me closely.

I shrug, going for denial.

"No, not at all!" I exclaim brightly. "I've just been so busy with work. You know the grand opening of the Resort's first location at STEELE St. Barth's happens soon."

Leonie nods, but I can tell she doesn't quite believe me. So I launch into the things I'm doing and plans for the new center along with others. Better to expound on the truth than to lie.

Re-directed, Leonie lets my non-answer go, and we stick to safer topics.

Besides, the last day of the pretrial happens tomorrow.

She needs to relax tonight since she's insisting upon going to the courthouse to support her fiancé. The purpose of our evening yoga *nidra* is to ease the day's troubles from her mind and prepare it for a night of peaceful slumber.

After a while, Roger enters the studio to collect his wife. He bids me good night, and I return to my guest suite.

Hopefully, I'll have peaceful dreams, too.

* * *

"Leonie, come sit here, sweetheart."

I stop speaking with Lola and shift my gaze at Shelley's words to the door where Leonie enters the pretrial courtroom with her parents, Guy and Josy.

"*Merci, Maman Aussi,*" she answers as she double kisses Shelley's cheeks in greeting.

Leonie takes a seat between her parents and Morgan and Shelley, then waves at her family and friends. Lola, Sebastian, and the rest of the Steele clan, the Jacksons, Joel and Hettie, Norman and Anita, Luc, Blair, Billie, Françoise, and some STEELE employees gather in support.

Moments later, the bailiff calls the court to order, and the judge enters the room.

I close my eyes and send a silent prayer to God and every deity in every religion's pantheon for Roger and STEELE cleared of these false claims.

Delia Shaw just wants attention and money. None of what she said holds an ounce of truth. It's absolutely terrible!

I choose to ignore the liar and keep my eyes stay riveted on Judge Favre as he reads his summation of the case.

He's so slow.

Mentally, I push him to read faster. Just give us the answer already!

"Because of the testimony provided by both the plaintiff and the defendant, the evidence brought forth, and of my careful deliberation, I determine Roger Steele and STEELE International, Inc. should—"

"*AAAH... MON DIEU!!*"

"Qu'est-ce que—"

"Oh, Mon Trésor!!"

"Leonie!! What's wrong?!" I cry at her scream.

Pandemonium breaks out.

I jump up and rush to her side just as Roger springs over the divider.

We reach Leonie at the same time.

Her water broke, and she's having contractions.

Sebastian shouts orders, and everyone moves.

He and Roger carry Leonie between them while their other brothers, male friends, and security detail clear a path for them. Lola leads the way for us to exit out the back of the courthouse. Then we hurry into one of the Mercedes-Benz Sprinters Roger leased to transport everyone during the pretrial.

Meanwhile, I call Leonie's OB-GYN, Dr. Pierre Berger. I confirm he's on his way to the hospital as the five of us speed off. I do my best to keep Leonie relatively calm during the ride.

Once at the hospital, Dr. Berger arrives with his team. An anesthesiologist, two pediatricians—one for each Twin —two labor and delivery nurses, an OB tech, and a nursery nurse follow him into Leonie's suite.

They prep her for pre-labor—in twin pregnancies, it can take up to thirteen hours for her body to be ready for the actual delivery. He expects the first Twin within two hours after and the second Twin less than twenty minutes later.

Leonie appears less fearful now that she's in the hospital's safety and under the doctor's care. Her golden caramel complexion flushed rosy from the sensations overtaking her body. Her feline amber eyes glower, while French curses spilled from her lush lips.

Lola and I fuss over Leonie. I put her long mahogany

waves—once pulled in a sleek ponytail—in one thick braid down her back.

Roger and Sebastian hover around her bed. Soon the rest of their family and friends arrive. Josy and Shelley hurry to her side, hustling Roger and Sebastian out of their way. Haley joins us at the foot of Leonie's bed as she massages her feet and calves to comfort her.

Surrounded by the most important women in her life, Leonie braves the birth of their twins.

Despite her snarls, cursing at Roger in French, and swatting him away when he attempts to comfort her, she gives birth to two healthy, identical boys. Rodolphe Beaulieu Steele and Gaspard Beaulieu Steele enter our world. With gray eyes and black hair, the Steele family traits continue.

Later that night, I return to my guest room next to Leonie's suite at the hospital. I'm so happy for my friend and grateful for her successful birth and new little family. She and Roger are beside themselves with joy!

So engrossed in my doula duties, I didn't have time to think about arrogant Malcolm Steele. Since I spent all of my time at Leonie's side, he and I didn't interact. Until moments ago.

"Hi, Angel," he said tentatively. "Crazy day, huh?"

Trapped in the hallway heading back from the nurse's station, I couldn't avoid him. So I nod and try to go around his massive frame.

He sidesteps to block my path again.

We do a shuffling dance that Haley interrupted inadvertently. As soon as she asked Malcolm a question, I dodged the entire scene and fled to my room. I could feel Malcolm's penetrative stare on my back, but I rushed on.

Now I shoot a quick text to Roger and Leonie to let them know to call my room since I'm turning my mobile off. Already Malcolm is blowing it up with messages. With a sigh, I shut it down.

Unfortunately, shutting my mind down proves more difficult. Dreams of mini Malcolms play on repeat: swaddled in blankets held in my arms; smiling up at me as I breastfeed them; coos as I talk to them. All the while, his magnetic presence hovers on my periphery. Watching his sons, me.

* * *

"THE NEXT GENERATION of Steeles is born! May they carry on our clan name and STEELE and Beaulieu forever!"

Declares Morgan as he holds his day-old grandsons proudly.

"*Oui, Mon Trésor* extends her family's line with males, one for Beaulieu and one for STEELE!" Guy adds proudly as he plucks Gaspard from Morgan's arm.

Leonie shakes her head and smiles.

Roger slips his hand in hers and dips his head to kiss her lips.

She whimpers and buries her face in his neck as she sobs.

"Let's give them some privacy—" Lola suggests.

With fresh resolve, Leonie faces us.

"*Non, non,* stay. Don't mind my blubbering," she says as she dabs her face with Roger's handkerchief. "You do not understand just how much I love and appreciate you. It's been a trying time. But new life brings great joy."

Her mother goes over to the bed and clasps their hands before she kisses them.

"*Mon Trésor,* never make excuses for your emotions! Your body is going through a lot"—she turns to Shelley and gestures for her to join them—"I may have had only one baby, but I know how you're feeling. Shelley, who's had five, will agree."

Roger's mother smirks and strokes Leonie's cheek.

"Yes! And you thought you had some choice words for Roger. Well, let me tell you, I laid Morgan out each and every time!"

The room fills with our laughter, Morgan's chuckles loudest of us all.

"I agree! Norman may have been the champ in the ring. But I won by a TKO when he dared to utter one word while I was in labor," Anita says from the sofa.

Norman feigns the impact of a crushing blow and collapses against the armrest. The same king of the boxing ring who plays dress up and has a tea party with his toddler daughter.

Again, the tough guys are always the softies at heart.

I feel Malcolm's stare from across the room. I can't help but to meet his gaze.

His forlorn face almost breaks my resolve. Noticing my lingering look, his eyes brighten, and he starts toward me.

Quickly, I avert my eyes and chat with Anita. Out of the corner of my eye, I see Malcolm slouch back against the wall with a frown marring his handsome face.

Good. Leave. Her. Alone! My inner warrior growls.

Funny how it's her I want to kick out of my life.

"WHAT TIME IS IT? Have you heard anything, yet? I'm worried sick—"

Leonie stops speaking when she sees Roger standing in the hospital suite's doorway. Her eyes widen and her mouth forms a perfect O before she claps her hands over it.

"Hello, my love," he says gruffly as he steps into the room. "It's over."

Leonie gasps and closes her eyes as she falls back against the pillows. Her body shudders as her sobs increase in her hands.

Roger glances at Josy and me, barely. His sole focus is Leonie as he rushes to her side and pulls her into his arms, kissing her face as he murmurs words of love.

Josy smiles at her daughter- and son-in-law, then turns to me and nods at the door.

I nod back and follow her from the suite with a smile on my face.

"Oh!" I exclaim as I bump into a wall of muscle when I close the door behind me with a click.

My head tilts back to see Malcolm glowering at me.

Without a word, he takes me by the elbow and ushers me next door to my guest room. He cocks his eyebrow at me wordlessly demanding I unlock it for him.

I do.

Once inside, he grabs my face between his sizable hands and crushes my mouth with his in a possessive, toe-curling kiss. Malcolm doesn't let me catch my breath before he hoists me up and slams my back against the door.

Automatically, my legs wrap around his waist and lock at the ankles. My hands seek out his thick, silky hair.

He rips at my wrap dress, pulling the hem up to my waist. The sound of his zipper, then the feel of his Prince Albert piercing's balls jewelry against my pussy lips brings me back to reality.

I push him away.

My palms against his broad chest offer no help to dislodge me from his clutches. I squirm in his firm hold and try to get down.

Malcolm laps at my tongue with his as he continues to breach my core.

"RED!!!" I scream against his mouth.

At once he lets me go and steps back. His gray eyes darkened to obsidian with lust, now peer at me dazed and questioningly.

Despite my body's betrayal—flushed face, pebbled nipples, swollen clit, wet pussy—we can't, I can't. My eyes close and I take a deep cleansing breath to settle my racing heart. Then I smooth my dress before I bring my gaze back to Malcolm.

He scrubs his hand over his face and runs his fingers through his hair. He too takes a deep breath and shakes his head to clear it. The wild look leaves his eyes as he stares back at me.

I break the silence.

"Malcolm… I… You told me we could explore one another. That it will have no negative impact on our business. You swore to uphold your promise to me for our business to proceed, no matter the result of our 'interaction.' I hope you are a man of your word," I say and pause for his confirmation.

His mouth opens and closes, then opens again.

I hold up my hand and ask, "Yes or no?"

Malcolm cocks his head to the side and raises his eyebrow as he studies my face intently.

I hold my ground, lifting my chin to stare back at him.

His face shutters, and he grows taller, aloof.

"Yes," he responds.

A part of my heart cracks. I had hoped he'd argue. In his Dom voice tells me he won't let me do this to us. Then spank me until I saw the light. But no. No fight for me, for us.

Told you!! My inner warrior says gleefully.

I ignore her.

"Good. I no longer wish to pursue the D/s relationship with you. However, I intend to continue as planned with Starr Light Fitness & Wellness' partnership with STEELE International. Agreed?" I ask.

Without hesitation Malcolm responds coolly, "Agreed. Anton will continue as your contact. Goodbye, Starr."

"Goodbye, Malcolm."

Hi Starr. I'm on my way to LA and want to see you. Come by my place at 8 tonight. I'll be on the rooftop.

My heartbeat speeds up faster than Malcolm's Koenigsegg Agera RS as I read the text message from him.

It's been a month, and as we agreed, no contact between us.

At first I thought he may take part in the SLFW Resort meetings. But only Anton showed up. The most recent site visit without him was hard when I stood on the completed rooftop deck and remembered him teasing how he planned to christen it for prosperity before the other areas.

In the weeks that passed, I realized I should have given him a chance to explain himself rather than cut all association. When he didn't blow up my mobile or send flowers as he had in the past, I gave up on my wishes, hopes, and prayers for a reconciliation with Malcolm.

But this text message—albeit out of the blue—makes me tingle and in all the right places. Heart and pussy.

I'm not saying we'll jump back in bed together or restart our D/s relationship right away—although I do miss his domination. But I do want to hear what he has to say for himself.

Despite my I will do nothing but talk mindset, I go to the spa at SLFW to pamper myself. A body polish followed by a hot-stone massage, manicure and pedicure have me walking on air when I head home to change.

I opt for a simple white silk slip dress that brushes the tops of my knees and flaunts my curves and flesh-tone mules. I leave my hair out in a cascade of curls to the middle of my back. Before I leave, I dab on pink lip gloss and coat my eyelashes with waterproof mascara. Perfect to entice Malcolm with my shiny full lips and no chance of raccoon eyes should my gag reflex kick in. Just saying…

Girl… just stop, you mean! My inner warrior chides.

I snap her shut like the clasp on my Chanel clutch handbag and stride out the front door.

In no time, I arrive at Malcolm's West Hollywood penthouse. I park in his extra space, then head up on his private elevator. I smile to myself when the old code still works.

Ha! He trusts me. Probably because he expected we'd get back together.

Well, maybe we will, I giggle to myself as I fluff my curls and reapply my lip gloss while gazing at my reflection in the reflective surface of the elevator doors.

When they open, I glide off the elevator and pause in the entry foyer to inhale the scent of Malcolm's cologne, John Varvatos - Dark Rebel Rider. The name says it all. It's all about the biker, the man who doesn't give a damn, the man who's out to make his way no matter what. The orange, balsam, leather, and amber fill my nostrils. Fearless. Sleek. Unconventional. Just like my man, dark, masculine, and sexy! How I've missed his smell.

I walk through to the stairs that lead to the rooftop deck.

With a smile on my face, I climb my stairway to heaven. When I open the doors, I almost call out to him. Instead, I stare, a bit confused.

Ahead of me is a naked woman straddling a naked man on a chaise lounge. His back is to me. But she faces my direction. The sounds of her moans and his grunts, their skin slapping skin fill my ears.

My vision tunnels on them. Everything else fades out of view.

I step closer, my mind attempting to process what my eyes see before me and my ears pick up distinctly.

When we're only yards apart, the woman tosses her long blonde mane of wavy hair over her shoulder and pins me with her blue eyes. Her mouth a moment before contorted in a cry of ecstasy now morphs into a wicked smirk.

She leans back and her large breasts bounce from the man's brutal upward thrusts into her pussy. Then she leans forward—never taking her eyes from mine—and cups the man's face. Her red manicured fingernails poke through his ebony waves above the back of the chaise lounge.

"Oh, God, Malcolm, baby! You feel so fucking good! I missed you so much, too!" She cries out.

* * *

Malcolm & Starr's Story Continues: *Embrace My Desires*

STEELE
INTERNATIONAL. INC.
A BILLIONAIRES
ROMANCE SERIES

Embrace my
DESIRES

MALCOLM & STARR PART II

Charmaine Louise Shelton

I dedicate this novel to lovers who shoot for the sky and reach the stars. Follow your heart.

Fulfill Your Desires.

xoxo
Charmaine Louise

ABOUT EMBRACE MY DESIRES MALCOLM & STARR PART II

Malcolm

Come along with me—the second son; the rebel; the bad boy billionaire playboy of the family—as my brown-eyed beauty—laid-back LA girl who owns a luxury yoga and wellness center—and I embrace our true desires as our steamy love story continues.

Will my ex-psycho-playmate drag me back to my old ways? Or will My Earth Angel ground me for a second chance at our love?

Trip the light fantastic with us and see for yourself. If part one was enough for you, then it's been real.

Starr

All I can say is damn that man!

Join Malcolm on his journey of self-discovery and his quest for the ultimate thrill—Starr Knight—as they seek to rebuild their love in Bali, Mnemba Island, Monte Carlo, and wherever the sun takes this stellar pair in their sizzling second chance billionaire romance.

Their love story is a standalone romance trilogy in the series. Get a glimpse of their dynamism in other books.

Anthem: "Stop Dragging My Heart Around" Stevie Nicks featuring Tom Petty
https://www.youtube.com/watch?v=H5i7j0VhEHw

Playlist:
https://www.youtube.com/playlist?list=
PLXwYvn0e218DQDFhgWBlFO7mk8WakpGyA

Visit CharmaineLouiseBooks.com

MALCOLM

1 *Month Ago*

"I DON'T KNOW. She fucking ghosted me, bro... No, I have no idea what happened. One minute we're dancing at the STEELE St. Barth's beachfront club. The next, she's ignoring me. Not answering my calls, texts, emails. She even had her collars hand delivered by courier to my West Holly-wood penthouse. So yeah, you tell me, Sebastian."

My frustration with my wayward sub-cum-girlfriend hits its limit after weeks of her MIA action—or lack thereof...

Starr Knight, my beautiful woman with the face of an angel and the body of a sinner. When she smiles, dimples dot her sculpted cheekbones the color of warm chestnuts and her wide, sorrel brown eyes shine. I smirk at the memory of fisting her long, curly dark brown hair as I lose myself in Starr's sexy AF body—five feet, six inches, fit, curvy. Her submissive behavior—after eight months of being together—trained to match my Dom needs. Perfect. For. Me.

As a multibillionaire bachelor, women flock to me with the goal to gain a hunk of ice on their left ring finger. Visions of dollar signs float before their eyes, right along with my striking visage. Arrogant, maybe, but true.

Starr? No.

My Angel is a boss. Stanford University undergraduate degree in economics then continued on to the B-School for her MBA. She earned multiple fitness certifications, including her specialty in yoga. Followed her passion for health and wellness combined with helping others and opened Starr Light Fitness and Wellness Beverly Hills seven years ago at 25 years old.

Her initial goal achieved lead to a partnership with STEELE International, Inc. to expand into worldwide fitness retreats at luxury resorts and to add a second center location in the Caribbean. Beautiful, bodacious, smart as hell, and a self-made multimillionaire. Boom.

Fortunately for me, I head STEELE's Entertainment Properties Division as the president and First VP of the Board. I oversee our casinos, hotels, and resorts. My division generates the most revenue for my family's multigenerational, multibillion-dollar luxury real estate development and management company based out of The STEELE Tower in New York City.

SLFW falls within my milieu.

Another stroke of luck came in the form of Lola Lewis, now Steele. My sister-in-law met My Angel at her first international fitness retreat in Fiji on the private Laucala Island. Lola raved about her experience and how cool My Angel is as a yoga instructor. Then she acted as a matchmaker. Well, that is for a business partnership…

Lola insisted I contact My Angel to discuss the opportunity. I agreed. But it was at Lola's wedding to my older brother Sebastian that I first met My Angel when she bumped into me. My eyes fell onto her gorgeous face, and sparks flew when my fingers brushed her soft skin as I balanced her on those fuck-me sandals.

Unbeknownst to me, the angel at my feet who shocked me to my core was Starr Knight, Lola's yoga teacher and close friend. It wasn't until the morning after the wedding I learned they were the same—Starr Knight, My Angel. Then she proved elusive.

After using my wiles to orchestrate a trip to STEELE St. Barths' instead of a boring conference room for potential partnership discussions, our mutual interest in the other led to us being in a Dominant/submissive relationship for the past eight months. A relationship I thought was on the cusp of a permanent situation.

Unlike my previous D/s relationships I had based on contracts for no longer than three months, the one with My Angel morphed into much more.

Within a month of being together, I took her to dinner with my parents, Morgan and Shelley. The Steele Matriarch knew My Angel from Lola and Sebastian's wedding preparations, then caught my interest in her at the festivities, naturally. My mother didn't disguise her pleasure in My Angel being in our family as more than Lola's close friend.

My mother's expressive brown eyes lit up at the sight of My Angel approaching the restaurant's bar. She's a striking woman in her mid-fifties with shoulder-length, wavy black hair. Compared to my father from whom my siblings and I inherited various shades of his gray eyes, thick ebony hair, and six-foot-plus height. Except for our baby sister, Haley, who's two inches taller than our mother at five feet, eight inches.

She's the fraternal younger twin to Harris. Roger was the youngest until the twins were born—a double surprise for our parents. Then there's me with Sebastian as the eldest.

Each sibling works at STEELE International and has a board position: Sebastian recently took over the helm from our father as CEO and Chairman of the Board while he remains president of the Retail Properties Division; Roger, president of the Residential Properties Division and Second VP; Harris and Haley, fraternal twins, co-founders of the subsidiary STEELE Technology and Cyber Security and Members. Each of us head divisions best suited to our knowledge and interests.

I'm the most appropriate sibling to take on the Entertainment Properties Division. My wild ways of pushing the envelope and my love of the challenge extreme sports triggers prepared me for the role to lead our division focused on pleasure and thrills.

I thought cave diving and heli-skiing pumped my adrenaline. But the pleasure and thrills My Angel gives to me beats them all. And I can't get enough.

It was on to the next level when we had dinner with her parents after being together for two months.

In their city, but on my ground at Spire 70 and Restaurant 69 in STEELE Rodeo Drive. Despite the initial annoyance of meeting Quinn Peters—her ex-boyfriend—unexpectedly My Angel and I had a good time with Peace and Sun.

Yeah, her father Peace Knight and mother Sun Knight—Jordan and Belinda originally.

They're brilliant environmental law attorneys who take on the most challenging cases against big businesses and win billions. The law firm—Knight & Knight LLP—her parents founded years ago after they met at a music festival while at Stanford Law School ranks in the top five of the United States. With offices in LA, Seattle, Denver, Chicago, Houston, New Orleans, Miami, New York City to represent cases in the top environmentally focused cities. They may be hippies, but they're sharks in the courtroom.

Needless to say, I succeeded in making a good impression on her parents.

Now, the big question: is Starr still My Angel?

My head spins as I rattle off the last few weeks of no contact with My Angel to Sebastian. I need Baz's advice as a fellow Alpha Dom for whom Lola is his sub and wife.

I know it's selfish of me, so absorbed in my life while Roger faces a crazy ass pretrial for sexual assault and harassment and STEELE International is the co-defendant. The baseless case brought forth by Delia Shaw, an intern at STEELE Paris and former classmate of Leonie at the Paris American Academy. Leonie *The Lion* Beaulieu gorgeous megamodel and then girlfriend of Roger, now fiancée and mother of his twin boys. He refused to pay Delia Shaw any attention, and now this bullshit.

Just as the pretrial judge was announcing his determination, Leonie cried out in the courtroom. Her water broke. The stress of the media frenzy and pretrial caused her to go into labor early.

Morgan, Shelley, Leonie's parents, Lola, Sebastian, and the rest of the Steele clan, the Jacksons, Joel Bailey and Hettie Fuchs, Norman and Anita Green, Luc Montaigne, Blair Thomas, Billie Chandler, Françoise Faucher, and some STEELE employees who gathered in support left the courtroom en masse.

Hours later, after Leonie gave birth, I caught up with My Angel, finally. She was so engrossed in her doula duties she didn't notice I followed her down the hallway as she headed back from the nurse's station. We hadn't spoken since the slight nod she gave to me when she entered the courtroom. Then she spent all of her time in the hospital at Leonie's side, so we didn't interact until the hallway encounter.

And what a dismal encounter…

"Hi, Angel," I say tentatively. "Crazy day, huh?"

She couldn't avoid me. So she nods and tries to go around my massive, six-foot-four-inch frame. I tower over her by ten inches.

I sidestep to block her path again.

We do a shuffling dance that Haley interrupts inadvertently. As soon as she asks me a question, My Angel dodges the entire scene and flees to her guest room next to Leonie's suite.

As she hurries away, I watch her retreating back. Once Haley finishes, I call My Angel's mobile and send text messages eager to speak with her. No. Fucking. Answer.

I finish my sad story and glance over at Baz.

He doesn't show any judgement on his face that mine resembles. At only two years apart, I'm his absolute doppelgänger: same six feet, four inches in height; gray eyes; black hair; clean shaven or 5 o'clock shadow covers a firm jaw. People often confuse us or think we're twins.

It used to drive me crazy as a teenager. I strove for my own identity, hating being in Baz's shadow. It resulted in my rebel ways for years. Now we're good, and I see Baz as a confidante and not as a competitor. Still similar driven and dominant playboys—well, not anymore.

Baz gave up his one fuck and done ways after he met Lola. I gave up the sub contracts after I met My Angel. Call us reformists…

"I get how frustrated you must be, given how Lola iced me out of her life so abruptly. Did you do or say anything that may have upset Starr? Even if you don't think it bothered her?" Baz asks as he frowns.

A moment passes while I consider the last few times My

Angel and I were together. Nothing untoward comes to mind. Hell, I was planning our next trip!

"No, bro, nothing. Not a damn thing," I respond as I stroke my five o'clock shadow thoughtfully.

Baz nods, then pulls out his mobile. After a finger presses on the screen, he lifts it to his ear.

"Hey, babe. Are you near Starr? Okay. Question, what's she saying about Malcolm?" His gaze remains on my questioning face while Lola speaks. Then he ends the call with an *I love you, too*.

Lucky fuck.

"Well, Starr has mentioned nothing to Lola. And she doubts Starr said anything to Leonie or she would have told Lola," Baz starts, then runs his fingers through his hair. "Either Starr doesn't want to interfere with Roger and Leonie's moment, or Starr isn't ready to disclose anything to them yet."

I nod in agreement.

"So, just leave it for now. Give her a couple of days once she's not as busy with Leonie"—he claps me on the back, and angles us toward the door of the waiting room —"Go to your President's Suite at STEELE Place Vendôme, shower, and eat a good meal. Then come back to the hospital refreshed. You need to clear your head, bro."

I take his advice and head out after I check in on the new parents. My heart swells with love when I see them holding Rodolphe and Gaspard. Could that be My Angel and me one day?

* * *

"The next generation of Steeles is born! May they carry on our clan name and STEELE and Beaulieu forever!"

Declares our father as he holds his day-old grandsons proudly.

"*Oui, Mon Trésor* extends her family's line with males, one for Beaulieu and one for STEELE!" Guy—Leonie's father—adds proudly as he plucks Gaspard from Morgan's arm.

The rest of the conversation fades into the background as I lean against the wall, watching My Angel across the room. Fuck if I don't feel like a lost puppy hoping to be reunited with its loving owner.

When at last she raises her gaze to mine, my heart thuds in my chest. At last!

Then it crashes to the ground, cracked.

She averts her eyes and chats with Anita—the wife of Norman Green, the former world heavyweight champion, STEELE's partner in his eponymous chain of luxury fitness facilities, and Roger's personal trainer.

My feet no longer propel me towards My Angel. Instead, I slouch back against the wall with a frown marring my face. Okay, this shit will not fly for much longer. Enough.

I am far from one who bows in defeat when I want something. No matter the challenge, I stand firm and get what I want. And I want my brown-eyed Angel back in my arms and writhing beneath the sting of my palm and the pounding of my ten-inch cock.

* * *

"Oh!" My Angel exclaims as she bumps into me when she closes the door behind her to Leonie's suite at the hospital with a click.

Her head tilts back to see me glowering at her. It's been two days since Leonie gave birth and one since our hallway encounter. Yesterday I resolved to put an end to this limbo.

Without a word, I take My Angel by the elbow and usher her next door to her guest room. I cock my eyebrow at her wordlessly, demanding she unlock it for us to enter. This intervention requires privacy.

She does.

Once inside, I grab her heart-shaped face between my sizable hands and crush her mouth with mine in a possessive, toe-curling kiss. I don't let My Angel catch her breath before I hoist her up and slam her back against the door.

Automatically, her long, toned legs wrap around my waist and lock at the ankles. Her hands dive into my hair, tugging at my scalp.

The pressure of her warm pussy against the front of my shirt coupled with the pain from her frantic tugs makes my cock jump to life. It's been too long since I buried it balls deep in her tight, wet core.

With a growl, I rip at her wrap dress, pulling the hem up to her waist. The sound of my zipper, then the feel of my Prince Albert piercing's balls jewelry against her pussy lips drive me to the brink. Only to be jerked back from the edge of carnal bliss.

My Angel pushes me away.

Her palms against my broad chest offer no help to dislodge her from my firm hold. She squirms in my arms and tries to get down.

I lap at her tongue with mine as I continue to breach her pussy.

"RED!!!"

My Angel's scream against my mouth jolts me—her safeword.

Fuck. Me.

At once I let her go and step back. My gray eyes darkened to obsidian with lust, now peer at her dazed and questioningly.

Despite her body's betrayal—flushed face, pebbled nipples, swollen clit, wet pussy—she wants me to stop. My Angel closes her eyes and takes a deep cleansing breath. Then she smooths her dress before she brings her gaze back to mine.

Meanwhile, my heart continues to race.

I scrub my hand over my heated face and run my fingers through my mussed hair. Now I tug in frustration. I too take a deep breath and shake my head to clear it. The wild look leaves my eyes as I stare back at My Angel.

She breaks the silence.

"Malcolm... I... You told me we could explore one another. That it will have no negative impact on our business. You swore to uphold your promise to me for our business to proceed, no matter the result of our 'interaction.' I hope you are a man of your word," she says and pauses for my confirmation.

My mouth opens and closes, then opens again as I remember my words to her so many months ago. I try to formulate an answer. One that will get us beyond this line of questioning.

She holds up her hand and asks, "Yes or no?"

I cock my head to the side and raise my eyebrow as I study her face intently.

My Angel holds her ground, lifting her chin to stare back at me. Her sorrel brown eyes defiant, no longer filled with passion or submission. Or us.

My face shutters, and I grow taller, aloof. So be it. Malcolm *The Enforcer* Steele begs no one.

"Yes," I respond blandly.

"Good. I no longer wish to pursue the D/s relationship with you. However, I intend to continue as planned with Starr Light Fitness & Wellness' partnership with STEELE International. Agreed?" She asks.

Without hesitation, I respond coolly, "Agreed. Anton will continue as your contact. Goodbye, Starr."

"Goodbye, Malcolm."

That answers my question: Starr Knight is no longer My Angel.

STARR

resent

*"O*ʜ, *God, Malcolm, baby! You feel so fucking good! I missed you so much, too!" She cries out.*

A month later, and icy fingers still grip my broken heart in a vice.

That hussy Vicky Reynolds!

I should have known better than to trust Malcolm and his former or current or whatever sub. She's a Hollywood royalty actress who tends to name-drop her great-grandfather the founder of a movie studio, her father a major producer, and her mother a screen siren.

After over two years of her being my client, to me she was like a little sister. Albeit a petite, blonde-haired, blue-eyed sister from another mother. Four years younger than my thirty-two, her acting career and travels make her worldly. But she appeared to look up to me. Often asked my advice. It could have been the yogi tenets I shared in my dharma talks.

That is, until I started my D/s relationship with Malcolm. Vicky used to tell me about her escapades with her Dom, but never mentioned his name.

Her erotic tales made me want the same experience. I would fantasize about being submissive to a sexy, powerful Dominant. After I bumped into Malcolm at Lola's wedding, it was his visage that appeared on my faceless dream Dom.

My pussy clenches at the vision and at the memories of his calloused palm spanking my tender ass and his massive cock tunneling into my virgin bottom hole. And he made me want even more. Submission. Pleasure. Pain. Love?

Damn that man for making me want him!

Vicky picked up on my relationship with my new Dom at SLFW's demo fitness retreat at STEELE St. Barth's. Unfortunately, she caught My Dom with me in an intimate embrace on the path to the villa I was staying in.

I did not know the Dom who dumped her was none other than Malcolm Steele.

Vicky showed up to Malcolm's high-profile members-only luxury BDSM and dance club LEVELS Beverly Hills opening night gala drunk off of her ass. She accused me of stealing her Dom in front of the guests.

Afterwards, she made my life miserable with the media, gossip blogs, and paparazzi hounding me. It reached the point where Malcolm provided a security detail for me and upped the systems at my Benedict Canyon Drive mansion and at SLFW.

If that wasn't enough, Vicky went so far as to tamper with my business. That was the last straw!

I canceled her membership and banned her from the center. Some members sided with her and left while others stayed loyal to me. It's one thing to talk shit about me, but not to fuck with my company and the good it provides for our clients. No ma'am!

Thankfully, Malcolm took full responsibility and protected me from the worse of the scandal.

We made it past that unpleasant blip in our relationship. But this? Him inviting me over to talk, and he's fucking Vicky like a stallion? No way, no how will Malcolm and I ever rekindle our relationship. The End!

"Hey! You're not even listening to me, Starr!"

Adrienne Anthony's accusatory voice cuts into my reverie. My CMO and General Manager of SLFW Beverly Hills and best friend of nine years scowls at me.

We met at Stanford Graduate School of Business. Everyone referred to us as Night & Day since we contrasted in our appearances and attitudes. From our long, curly hair with Adrienne's light brown and mine dark brown to her green feline eyes and my sorrel brown angelic eyes to her buttery pecan-colored skin and mine the color of warm chestnuts. I have dimples to her sharp cheekbones. But we're both five feet, six inches with curvy fit bodies from our years of yoga, Pilates, and strength training as certified teachers and students.

Again alike with our hippie vibes, independent nature, and outgoing bubbly personalities. We're loyal and open to a fault. Resourceful and trustworthy round out our traits.

Where Adrienne has a tattoo of a peacock wrapped around her foot up her ankle to symbolize success, I have shooting stars on the back of my neck for wishes.

We hit it off immediately at Stanford and work well together with SLFW.

Our first location outside of Beverly Hills has its grand opening celebration in two weeks, seven days after the soft opening with VIPs and health and wellness editors and bloggers. Starr Light Fitness & Wellness Resorts at STEELE

St. Barth's will open its doors for the world. And I cannot wait!

St. Barth's will serve as the center's first global location. Malcolm's team recommends more centers at STEELE properties in Cabo San Lucas, Monte Carlo, and Koh Samui in Thailand, initially with others as demand requires.

The Jackson Hole at STEELE Resorts is Lucien Jackson's latest concept of members-only, high-end beach clubs for the jet set where SLFW will host retreats. Our fitness and wellness programs will offer more amenities for Jackson Hole and increase activities for guests and provide accommodations for retreat participants.

LEVELS—with locations in New York, Paris, London, and now Beverly Hills—is another one of many business partnerships that STEELE has with Jackson Corporation. World-renown for their award-winning eateries, choice cigars, and distinguished liquors and wines, their products pair well within STEELE's casinos, hotels, resorts, and residential and retail properties.

The Steele family's cousins—if not by blood—the Jackson clan has several business ventures with them. Shelley Steele is best friends with Lucie, the Jackson matriarch. They spent most of their adult lives together forming a closer bond than they have with their blood siblings and relatives. Not sharing DNA doesn't keep their families from being a close-knit group.

And SLFW benefits from their partnership, too.

At least, the business partnership survived the arrogant Malcolm Steele...

"Oh! Pardon! I'm listening now," I respond to Adrienne as the thoughts of my ex recede like the waves from the shoreline before Adrienne and me.

We're up on the rooftop terrace of SLFW Resorts St. Barth's sitting on chaise lounges facing the Caribbean Sea.

The breeze off of the turquoise water wraps around me as I straighten my legs from lotus position and inhale deeply. Salty air fills my lungs, and the warm sun soaks into my toasted skin. It's early morning, so no one is out. So peaceful.

As much as I'd rather practice my latest class asana flow on the warm powdery sand, work calls. I turn my attention to my bestie.

Adrienne smiles knowingly. She doesn't take pity on my tryst with the playboy billionaire. She's too caught up with Anton Alexeyev—Malcolm's Vice President of Development and college friend. The giant six-foot-six-inch, blond-haired, glacial-eyed Russian has Adrienne in his sights. Her erotic tales with the Alpha Dom rival mine!

"Glad to hear you're with me…" Adrienne quips with a smirk, her green eyes sparkle with mirth.

We discuss the upcoming soft opening: two-day retreat activities, guests, media, staff, and the STEELE team's responsibilities. Having worked together for so many years, Adrienne and I finish our agenda quickly.

We head down to the beach for phase two of our meeting. I take her through my new flow class followed by a meditation focused on nature and the body. Afterwards, Adrienne practices her Beach Barre class with a couple of the SLFW teachers who now live on site and me. I don't blame some of the girls for requesting a relocation from Beverly Hills to St. Barth's. I'm tempted to stay after being here for a week!

Later we have lunch on the patio in front of the center. The delicious menu crafted by Anita. Besides her fitness certifications, she completed culinary school at Le Cordon Bleu and started a meal plan delivery service. Norman added her customized plans to the paid offerings of the elite facilities and complimentary healthy snacks to the youth.

She also took over the food services in both chains of his gyms.

When I was in Paris five months ago, she told me more about the meal plan side of her business and her goal to expand it to other wellness companies. I agreed SLFW would partner with her and couldn't be happier.

The flaky local fish and steamed vegetables over cauliflower rice melts on my tongue. The flavors burst across my taste buds in a profusion of tantalizing spices. Even the fruit punch dazzles my palate. Delicious.

I look forward to Anita's arrival so I can rave in person! Without a doubt, the guests will love her food selections, too.

As we finish our meal, one teacher shifts the conversation to the fun she had last night at the resort's beachfront dance club. Everyone laughs as she recounts the sexy as sin men who flirted with her and another teacher shamelessly.

My mind drifts once again to my sexy as sin Dom turned boyfriend. I recall the nights we danced to the sensuous island music as we melded our bodies together. Then the dancing we continued between the sheets. My empty pussy throbs with need.

Damn that man!

MALCOLM

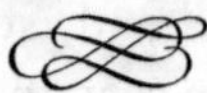

"This chalet hasn't sold yet. It's the largest with five stories, twelve bedrooms, sixteen bathrooms, four fireplaces, an oversized ski room, and the usual entertainment rooms including a sixteen-person cinema room, game room, gym, and wine-tasting cellar. The indoor-outdoor heated pool pavilion with spa is an added bonus. Staff quarters are above the six-vehicle garage."

I nod my head as the project manager rattles off the details of the luxury chalet. As always, the spectacular view of Verbier and the Swiss Alps through the floor-to-ceiling windows captures my attention.

Roger and I have business in the chichi ski town.

After a month of being with Leonie, Rodolphe, and Gaspard, they only left *Le Beaulieu Manoir*—Leonie's ancestral home—to attend their friends Joel and Hettie's wedding. He couldn't put off the final walk-through of STEELE Residential Properties Division's latest Swiss project.

I oversaw the STEELE Verbier Hotel & Resort's grand opening during last year's ski season. It's been a success from day one. Roger planned his division's completion of the by-application-only compound of ten state-of-the-art chalets and private clubhouse to take occupancy for this year's season.

Verbs, as the in-the-know jet-set call it, is a town in the Swiss Alps. A part of the Valais canton in the southwest of Switzerland, France borders Verbier to the west with Italy to the south. It's the most exclusive ski destination in the world and one of my favorite for heli-skiing off-piste.

It's the winter version of Monaco, with the difference being people who go to Monaco want to watch or be watched. Whereas Verbier has an understated style where wealth is glamorous, stylish and tasteful. People are here for the reasons one goes to a ski resort—the superb skiing. Not to mention the phenomenal bars and restaurants; the après-ski is perfect for party lovers. Verbier is a glamorous winter playground.

The luxury chalets occupy the area south of the Médran lift. They're slightly away from town along Rue de Médran, where the extra space means they are rarely overlooked and have a private, exclusive vibe. The residential compound is opposite to the STEELE Verbier that's closer to the heart of the village square. The concept is for the STEELE Verbier Chalets to access the resort for its five-star amenities. The most important include the luxury thermal bath spa and the three Jackson Corporation restaurants headed by our cousin Lucien the *Sexy Chef* as he's known by his millions of followers.

I'm surprised this chalet is still on the market. The decor is modern Alpine chic with traditional materials of timber and stone complemented by the high-quality fixtures and fittings and custom furniture. Combined with the view, it's an incredible property.

"Well, damn. Maybe I'll buy it."

Roger says as he glances over at me and raises his eyebrow questioningly.

"Why not? We all ski and could use a place here to hang out," I reply with a shrug.

We're all close. And close enough to hang out together regularly. We even spend lots of time with our parents going on vacations, the holidays, birthdays. What can I say? The Steeles enjoy each other's company.

Roger's thought leads to a brilliant idea.

"I'll buy the chalet and gift it to Leonie for Christmas. She loves to ski, and winter is her favorite season," he says with a broad, goofy smile.

"We can have our wedding at *Le Beaulieu Manoir* as planned two days before Christmas Eve. The next day we come to Verbier to celebrate the holiday and New Year's Eve with our families, then our honeymoon alone. Leonie and I didn't want to travel too much with The Twins since they will be with us. Perfect!" He adds now grinning like the Cheshire Cat.

"I'll buy it," Roger says with finality as he glances from me to the project manager.

I cock my head to consider his pronouncement. Then I nod.

"Sounds good to me, bro," I respond. "Leonie will love it. Man, what a way to celebrate, new babies, new wife, new beginning. I'm happy for you, brother."

He smiles at me. We're only a year apart, so I've never lorded over him with an age difference. Harris and Haley get ribbed the most for being the youngest, especially Haley for being the only girl. Her declaration that we're not her father never gets old.

"Thanks. Sebastian, me... Now it's your turn..." Roger says, waggling his eyebrows.

He's on a roll with his love matches—Luc and Blair, now he's focused on Starr and me.

I thought no one was aware of my feelings for the brown-eyed beauty. But I made it clear at Baz and Lola's wedding Starr was on my radar, as evidenced by my mother's comments and Roger's smirk. Neither Starr nor I have said much recently. But Roger must think that ends now.

"How's Starr by the way?" He asks.

Uh no…

I dodge the answer and pull out my mobile.

"Listen, I have a conference call with my team in five minutes I have to take, then some work at the resort. I'll meet you for dinner later," I say over my shoulder as I high-tail it out of the chalet.

A nod to the project manager, who hides his laugh with a cough at my fast exit, and I'm out the door.

"HELLO, you look like you could use a friend, Mr. Steele."

A glance to my right reveals a statuesque platinum-haired stunner. Her obsidian eyes—a sharp contrast to the paleness of her waist-length silky tresses and porcelain skin —level on mine. She all but purrs as she brushes her hand along my muscular thigh, then leans in to press her surgically enhanced tits against my side.

"How would you like to join me by the fireside with your drink?" She whispers in my ear, her Swedish accent thickening.

I shudder, not from interest but from irritation at her bold behavior when her palm grazes my groin.

"My, my, you're a big boy, aren't you?" She breathes lustily.

In a flash, my hand grasps her wrist and removes the

wandering digits from my flaccid cock. A scowl covers my face. I shake my head, then angle my body away from her.

The thought of canoodling with another woman makes my stomach roil. Fuck.

"You—"

"Hey, bro! My bad for keeping you waiting."

I turn back around to find Roger standing behind the handsy woman.

She tosses the curtain of hair over her shoulder to peer at him. Her eyes widen to see another Steele brother within reach. She had her sights set on one ultimate prize and found two.

Just like many others, she's more than willing to have a one-night tryst with one of the STEELE Quaternity, as the media has labeled my brothers and me. They've dubbed us the most sought-after of the world's eligible multibillion-aires. Our near-limitless wealth, power, and good looks attract women like bees to honey. They clamor for a taste, even one night.

Behind her dark lust-filled eyes, her mind goes into overdrive thinking of how to snag Roger and me. The tip of her little pink tongue pokes out to glide along her glossed full lips. A sultry smile spreads across them as she sizes us up, glancing at us from head to toe.

"Well, aren't I the lucky one tonight?" She purrs as she reaches for Roger's arm.

He steps aside deftly and raises his hands to ward off her grasp.

"Neither of us are available," Roger adds with a firm shake of his head. "Pardon, my brother and I have dinner plans. Good night."

I take my cue and hop off of the barstool. Without a second glance, I walk past the woman and follow Roger to the maître d's station at STEELE Verbier's STEAKhouse restaurant. It's run by Lucien through one of their many Jackson Corporation partnerships. A reservation at the three Michelin star restaurant is the most sought-after in this part of Switzerland. The host leads us into the dining room to a prime table with unobstructed views of the slopes lit for night skiing.

He places menus in front of us that offer the expected fare typical of steakhouse cuisine of choice cuts of beef, chicken, lobster, and the fish of the day with favorable sauces and sides. Lucien complements the tantalizing dishes with an award-winning wine list and delicious desserts.

As to be expected, the client care is impeccable. So, I don't flinch when the server quietly appears at my side and places a napkin-covered basket with an assortment of warm, fresh-baked breads on the table. I glance up to see a twenty-something woman who is model-perfect and polished with coffee-colored hair pulled in a neat, low ponytail, minimal makeup, and bright hazel eyes. Her all-black uniform of a long-sleeved shirt, knee-length skirt, butcher apron, and sensible heels is spotless—the de rigueur fashion for restaurant employees.

"Welcome to STEAKhouse, sirs. My name is Denise, and I'll be your server this evening. May I take your drink orders? We have some lovely specials tonight. May I share them with you?"

Roger and I give her our drink and meal selections, then catch up on STEELE business. His Residential opening still on track and exceeds revenue expectations. With the hotel and resort still booked years in advance, the one-year anniversary party RSVP list includes the über-wealthy, royals, and celebrities. Baz sent emails to each of us commending our divisions' performances in Verbier.

As we finish our entrées, Roger pulls out his mobile. He grins and hands it to me.

It's a text message from Leonie. The sounds of babies ah-gooing along with their mother singing a lullaby to them in French floats from the speakers. The adorable scene plays on the screen. I can't help but to chuckle.

Too cute!

I hand the mobile back to Roger. When he doesn't let go, I glance up at him.

He pins me with his intense, gray-eyed stare and quirks his eyebrow at me.

Oh boy, here we go. I should have known I couldn't keep the situation with Starr known to my parents and Baz only…

"Could be you, you know," Roger says pointedly as he pockets his mobile and stands.

The server automatically places the bill on the Steele family account, so no need to waste time signing the check.

Roger strides from the dining room to the floor-to-ceiling stone, double-sided fireplace in the lounge. We settle on leather club chairs before the roaring flames. The scent of the pine kindling fills my nostrils. Another server approaches to take our after-dinner drink orders.

I sip my Rémy Martin digestif as I watch Roger over the Baccarat crystal snifter. Might as well let him ask. It's been a month since Starr ended us. Perhaps he can enlighten me as to the cause of her abrupt change of heart.

"So?" He asks with no room for dodging an answer.

I incline my head and nod. Then tell him the latest. Just like Baz, Roger listens intently without interruption, his gaze unwavering.

He agrees it's best I don't attend the grand opening celebration for Starr Light Fitness & Wellness Resorts at STEELE St. Barth's out of respect for Starr's wishes. Leonie told him the possibility of me making a scene or of me making her feel uncomfortable if I showed concerned Starr.

Now the grapevine news continues…

But I appreciate my family's involvement since their chatter provides a clue to Starr's mindset. Sure, I told her goodbye. However, that doesn't stop me from wanting her, needing her. Or wanting a video of her singing to our babies.

"Starr!! This is spectacular!"

"Yes! I'm so proud of you!"

"Absolutely amazing!"

I smile at Haley, Billie, and Lola. Along with Leonie, Blair, Anita, Adrienne, and her younger sister Claudia, my girls flew in to SLFW Resorts at STEELE St. Barth's early. I want them to experience the center before the guests and media arrive tomorrow for the soft opening, then stay for the party.

"*Félicitations!*" Leonie chimes in as she hugs me. "Your dream came true, *chérie!*"

"And in a big way! A brand-new center designed to your specifications on a beautiful resort property," Anita adds, then grins. "Not to mention your sexy boyfriend!"

The smile slides off my face. From such a high to a terrible low...

Anita's brown eyes widen as they dart from me to the other girls. Lola, Leonie, and Haley quirk their mouths and lower their gazes. Billie and Blair stare back, unaware of Anita's unintentional flub.

"Sorry, honey! I didn't realize!" She recovers quickly. "No matter, you did it and I'm beyond happy for you!"

We hug, and I return her smile.

"No worries. Remember, we must embrace the good and the bad. They have equal purpose in our lives," I respond despite the crack in my heart reopening like a chasm.

Adrienne told me Anton confirmed Malcolm won't attend the soft or the grand openings.

I pretended not to be bothered, but it hurt. All along I envisioned us together celebrating my triumph. With a sigh, I turn my attention back to those who love and support me, thankful for their presence in my live.

"Well, let's get started with our morning yoga session, ladies!" I say as I clap my hands and gesture for them to sit on their mats.

They scuttle to their seats, and we spend the next hour and a half absorbed in our pranayama, asana, and meditation practices.

Fortunately, my disappointment in Malcolm floats away on the warm sea breeze.

"Tell me, how do you really feel?"

Billie says in her Southern Belle accent. Her Granny Smith apple green eyes search my face as we sit on the patio of my beachfront villa sipping mojitos later in the evening.

She and Blair are Lola's administrative assistants. With Billie based in Las Vegas, we've grown close over the last couple of years. We meet up in Vegas or Beverly Hills at least once a month. Hitting the baccarat tables at STEELE Las Vegas as frequently as the massage tables at SLFW.

With her wavy, medium-blonde balayage hair and pecan-colored skin, everyone says she's Tyra's doppelgänger. Billie is curvy like the megamodel, but a petite version at five feet, four inches.

"I miss him. I won't deny it. Hell, I can't deny it. The thought of Malcolm makes me want what we had," I respond sadly.

Billie takes a sip of her cocktail and stares out at the setting sun hovering on the horizon of the Caribbean Sea.

The streaks of fiery red, orange, and gold dapple the surface. A few seagulls soar above the waves, seeking their dinner. Their cries fill the salt-scented air.

"Well, what happened? You seemed happy—both of you," Billie says as she shifts on her chaise lounge to face me again.

I hadn't told Lola or Leonie about overhearing Malcolm speaking to Roger the last time Malcolm and I were at STEELE St. Barth's over two months ago.

"Who says I love her?" he asked with an arrogant chuckle. "We're just in the here and now, bro. Not all of us are ready to run down the aisle to the love of our life!"

I gasped at his callous words, and my stomach dropped as I stood in the doorway behind him. The noise made him shift in his chaise lounge on the deck. A fleeting expression of shock ghosted across my face, but it was too fast for Malcolm to decipher it.

From his expression, he appeared just as shocked as me.

I pulled on the strength of my inner Independent Woman warrior. Then I smiled. She gave me just enough oomph to move my lips, but not enough for the smile to reach my eyes. Fortunately, they're covered with giant glamour girl shades, so he couldn't tell.

Malcolm smiled back and held his hand out to me.

I took it and pretended all was fine for the next three days.

And definitely didn't tell them about discovering Malcolm fucking Vicky on the rooftop terrace of his Sunset Boulevard penthouse...

After I recount that sad tale, Billie nods thoughtfully.

"I can understand why you haven't told Leonie and Lola. We're girls and all, but Malcolm is the brother of their men. But don't discount the loyalty Leonie and Lola have to you, too," Billie says.

"Loyalty to you for what?"

Billie and I startle at the unexpected question coming from the path beside the villa.

Lola appears with Leonie and the rest of the girls.

"Well?" Leonie adds to Lola's question.

Billie rises and pours the mojito in the pitcher into the other glasses on the table before us. Once everyone has a glass, she lifts hers and inclines her head towards me.

"Here's to girl power and the support we give to each other," Billie says, then continues in a great impersonation of Bette Davis' voice. "Now, fasten your seat belts, it's gonna be a bumpy ride."

I take my cue and tell my girls everything.

* * *

"Congratulations, Starr, sweetheart. You accomplished your dream. I'm happy for you."

I smile up at my ex-boyfriend Quinn, who's taller than me by six inches. His chocolate brown eyes sparkle in his just as chocolatey face.

My parents introduced us years ago since he's an attorney at their law firm. They thought we'd have a lot in common.

I finally gave in to his dinner requests, then to spending time with him. Finally, we started seeing each other. The sex began shortly thereafter. Not at all what I expected or wanted.

After six months, I decided I needed more, and Quinn couldn't give it to me. I broke up with him.

But before I flew down for the soft opening, he reached out to me, wanting to talk. I agreed to meet him for dinner. We spent the evening being honest about our prior relationship and where we stood now.

Quinn admitted he was wrong and had gotten engaged to someone who resembles me because he wanted more with me. He ended the engagement and courted me instead.

I told him I was not in the headspace to date or to rekindle our relationship. Not one to bounce from one pillar to the next, I prefer time between relationships. Time to get back to me.

"Thank you, Quinn," I respond.

Then smooth my hands over my vintage Versace outfit. The saffron yellow corset top with a sweetheart neckline and lacing in the front accentuates my perky D-cups. The matching ankle-length skirt with a full leg slit held closed with more lacing on my left hip drapes across my lower body. Strappy yellow sandals elongate my toned legs. Red lipstick is the extent of makeup and my long curls spill down my back.

My body is my best advertisement for SLFW. I flaunt it for the grand opening celebration—and any chance I get!

Quinn's eyes burn into my skin as his gaze follows the path of my hands.

I ignore his lustful heat and move away to mingle with the other guests and the media.

My parents beam as we pose for the cameras. Quinn slips into the frame, and his hand locks onto my left hip possessively. The pressure from his fingertips on my bare skin makes me flinch. He takes my reaction as an invitation and pulls me closer to his side.

Not wanting to ruin the photos, I stay in place.

"Starr, we need you over here. Kindly come with me now."

I thank God and every deity in every religion's pantheon for Adrienne.

Deftly, I extricate myself from Quinn's clutches and follow her. As I pass Anton, he quirks his eyebrow at me. I widen my eyes and shrug questioningly but keep moving. His icy glacial stare pierces my back.

Great, I can only imagine the report he'll make to his boy…

Then I pass Borya Alexeyev and Lucien.

Oh, it just gets better.

Lucien inclines his head and raises his flute of Krug Clos d'Ambonnay Champagne—my favorite and despite it all, Malcolm arranged cases for the celebration.

Borya scowls at me—the brooding Russian cousin of Anton and a close friend of Malcolm.

I suppress an eye roll and keep strutting.

"You have every brute here imaginable!" Adrienne exclaims as we weave through the throngs of guests. "He who shall not be named may not have deigned us with his presence, but he made certain his cronies attended. Or should I say spies?!"

Her bright green feline eyes flash and narrow.

Adrienne looks fabulous in a coral Swarovski crystal embellished mini slip dress with sky-high strappy sandals. Her long, curly brown hair pulled up into her version of a messy bun—perfectly coiffed. Simple, clear lip gloss coats her full lips.

I have to wonder if she's not dressing to impress another certain Russian more than advertising SLFW's benefits…

"I know right!" I respond after I greet a VIP new member of the Resorts' center.

Malcolm assured me residents of St. Barth's would apply

for membership. With over fifty on file from day one of the list opening, I have to give him his credit. He knows his market.

No matter how much I try to keep him out of my mind tonight, I. Just. Cannot.

Damn that man!

"Hey there, Ms. International!"

I turn to find Norman and Anita approaching.

My friends came all out to support me, *The Champ* included. Guests went gaga and angled to get selfies with him. He posed and signed autographs with a smile graciously.

"Ha! You know it!" I giggle.

"I agree. Well done, Starr!"

Sebastian and Lola emerge from the crowd with Leonie and Roger.

Billie, Blair, and Claudia join us.

I glance around our circle and smile ruefully. It's a happy, but bittersweet moment. But I am grateful for my success and my supportive friends and family.

"You. Are. Mine. Naughty. Girl!"

Comes his snarl as he roughly yanks me from the arms of my would-be playmate for the evening.

I nearly stumble in my feather mules as the caveman, gray-eyed stranger pulls me close, my back to his firm chest. I tense as his massive cock thickens and lengthens against my round bottom. His possessive behavior triggers my core. My juices immediately gush from my pussy and drip down my clenched thighs.

I peer up and over my shoulder at this dominant man. His upper lip curls, his nostrils flare, his eyes the color of molten platinum shoot poisonous darts at the Dom who was preparing me for a scene.

My unknown cockblocker wants to take me as his very own.

As I decide whether I want him more than the Dom who first drew my attention, he puts his hands up, palms out in surrender.

My mouth gapes at his retreating back.

Suddenly, I'm hoisted onto the stranger's shoulder in a fireman's carry as though I weigh next to nothing. He swiftly strides to one of the darker areas of the BDSM dungeon. I kick my legs and pummel his back—my small fists ineffectively hit a wall of steel and earn me four swift spanks on my exposed rear. A lightning bolt shoots through my pussy, liquifying more of my juices to pool on the shoulder of his bespoke suit jacket.

A gasp pops from my mouth as he sits on a red velvet sofa in the alcove and drapes me over his hard, muscular thighs. My belly presses against his engorged cock that twitches when our bodies collide.

He makes quick work of lifting my silk negligee and snatching the matching thong down to bind my knees. My bare ass and throbbing pussy exposed to his view. He runs his hands over my lush curves gently—quite a contrast to his previous brutish behavior. I shiver under his delicate touch; his calloused hands caress my soft skin.

"Holy mackerel!" I yell as the first slap of his rough palm against my ass shocks me from the gentle lull.

I reach my hands behind me in an attempt to block his painful blows.

The caveman grabs my wrists in one sizable hand and presses them against my lower back. His other hand never misses a beat and continues to punish me—left, right, left, crease of my ass and thigh, right, left.

I squirm on his lap pitifully as the pain blooms across sore ass.

"You are mine. No one else will ever touch you again, Naughty Girl," he growls.

He punctuates each word with a hard spank, drawing heat and pumping blood to the surface of my bare, jiggling ass.

An unexpected shift in his movements brings two of his thick fingers to my seam—I'm soaking wet for him.

"Is this all for me?" He asks seductively.

His voice deepens with lust as he slides his fingers in and out of my pussy, fucking me, the wet sounds loud in my ears.

As if I were a puppet on a string, I widen my legs to allow him better access to my slippery pussy, but refuse to respond.

My lack of a verbal answer results in another volley of spanks—left, right, left, crease of my ass and thigh, right, left.

"Yes, Sir!" I scream as I wriggle on his lap, attempting to get out of his reach and to close my legs.

"Open!" He demands.

Instantly, my thighs part. My traitorous body takes over from my logical brain.

"So, sweet, Naughty Girl," he rumbles.

The sound of the caveman lapping his fingers with the flat of his tongue to clean off my erotic essence makes me gush even more than before.

A wicked chuckle slips from his full lips as he smirks at my carnal reaction.

He bends to press his lips against the delicate shell of my ear to whisper, "You like being mine and receiving the sting of my palm on your luscious ass, do you not, Naughty Girl?

How would you like to have my colossal cock in your little, virgin ass?"

I cry out and shudder, aching to have his thick cock in all three of my holes. I can't deny I want this caveman to take me in every single one roughly, bent over and fucked by him like a feral animal…

"Ohhh… Malcolm!"

The sound of my hoarse voice screaming aloud rips me from my dream. I bolt upright in the bed sweating, breathing heavily, wildly looking around for the LEVELS members, the Cellar, and My Dom… Malcolm.

I flop back down against the pillows, noticing the sheets tangle around my body in disarray. Not the arms of my former Dom-cum-boyfriend holding me in his warm embrace as I dreamed. The realization sinks in my mind past the veil of my sexy fantasy that I'm not in Beverly Hills at all. Rather, I'm in the villa at STEELE St. Barth's after the party.

With a groan, I roll over and leave the stifling confines of the empty bed. I rip the damp, silk tank top and sleep shorts from my hot, drenched body that's still reeling from a sleep-induced orgasm. Then head to the en suite bathroom for a cold shower.

The first tendrils of the sun's morning rays breach the dark blue sky.

I might as well join the morning yoga class on the beach and release the last of the sexual tension from my humming body.

Damn that man!

MALCOLM

"Cut it out, Harris! Pass the cranberry sauce to me already!"

Haley growls, frustrated with her twin's antics as he teases her relentlessly. Her gray eyes flash like a stroke of lightning as she glares at him.

"Harris Steele! That is enough, young man. Stop taunting your sister and give her the platter at once," our father commands in full-on Alpha Dom mode.

Immediately Harris complies—albeit grudgingly, with a smirk on his face—and hands Haley's favorite Thanksgiving side dish to her.

"Jerk," she mutters under her breath as she snatches it from him.

He in turn mimics her response wordlessly lest our father hear his new gibe. I hide my laugh with a cough and shake my head at Harris. He smirks until our father pins him with a steely stare.

Then I can't help myself, and I laugh out loud.

Those two will never stop. It's their usual behavior at any of our family gatherings. When we were younger, Haley would sometimes leave the dining room in tears. Our parents would chastise Harris and send him to his room.

Now it's our first Thanksgiving as a family with Leonie, Rodolphe, Gaspard, Guy, and Josy. Even Luc joins us. My gaze travels around the dining room table of my parents' new penthouse on the twenty-eighth floor at The STEELE Tower Paris designed by Leonie. Everyone smiles and appears peaceful. The atmosphere is one of gratefulness and happiness.

Our family has a lot to be thankful for: the pretrial judge declared Roger innocent and STEELE International clear of all charges; The Twins were born; my division's revenue outpacing last year. All is right in the Steele World.

Well.. almost.

I lost my mind when Anton gave me a recap of the SLFW Resorts' grand opening celebration.

All was routine and went as expected until he recounted seeing Starr kissing that fucker Peters—her supposed ex-boyfriend. The last we saw him, he was engaged to some Starr lookalike. I should have known he wasn't over her then.

It was bad enough the photos of Peters holding her possessively in the event photos made my blood boil. I damn near crushed my mobile when the Google alerts linked to a gazillion social media and blog sites showing the laughing, lovey-dovey couple.

Nothing prepared me for Starr to move on to another man so soon after she and I ended our relationship. Starr really didn't seem the type to jump around so easily.

Now I know better.

I wish I could just say fuck it and move on, too. But in the six weeks we've been apart I haven't been able to scene with anyone despite going to LEVELS New York. Each night—and morning for that matter—my palm meets my aching cock, and I spill my jizz down the shower drain.

What a sad schmo I've become.

Fuck. Me.

"Leonie, you did such an incredible job with the redesign of our penthouse!" My mother declares as she raises her glass of Chateau Lafite Rothschild. "*Merci ma fille aussi!*"

"Well done, Leonie!"

"It's marvelous!"

"Cheers!"

Congratulatory comments draw me back to the room. My thoughts of Starr disperse as I refocus on my family.

"It was an honor. Thank you for entrusting me with your home," Leonie responds humbly.

Luc shifts in his seat to face her and asks, "When do you expect to return to your new career, *chérie*? We know how important interior design is to you."

Leonie glances at Roger, then turns to Luc.

"Roger and I haven't spoken about it yet. But I was thinking once Rodolphe and Gaspard reach six months, I could return to STEELE's Interior Design Team part-time as a project designer."

She glances at Roger from beneath her eyelashes and smiles.

He returns her smile and kisses her hand.

"Whatever you want, my love. We have Nanny Grace to help us. Plus, you can even design a nursery for The Twins next to your office if you want to keep them close," he says.

"Oh, *merci, Mon Cœur!*" She squeals as she pulls his mouth to hers and plants a kiss on his lips.

We rib them for their PDA. Me included even though I wish I cuddled Starr in my arms for our family gathering…

"Well, that means you have to make time for your Lola's Coterie campaigns, too! And we need to work on more designs for the pre- and post-natal collections. They've been a colossal hit!"

"*Oui, oui! Absolument!* I cannot wait. I have some new sketches for you, *Chérie*," Leonie says giggling as Roger continues to plant kisses on her cheek.

"*Très bon*! That's splendid news," Luc says. "Excellent idea, Roger. Leonie, you should consider a specialization in interior design for children. What I've seen of three of the… What is it? Nine? Nurseries for The Twins, they're incredibly well done. You could design nurseries, playrooms, bedrooms—"

"Ooh, and playhouses that match the families' mansions!" Haley adds. "I've read they're extremely popular with chichi parents."

Luc's thoughts are never far from revenue-generating ideas. Haley, the nerd, more than likely read about the mini mansions during one of her many Internet searches.

"That's an area STEELE International doesn't cover. The focus has always been on the main properties and amenities. Perhaps you'd like to lead your own division?" Sebastian asks.

With a nod to our brother he adds, "If Roger is game, we can set it in motion as a subset of his division."

"That would add another offering to our clients, and we would include it in future projects. Another revenue stream," Morgan adds, ever the CEO even while retired.

Leonie looks at Roger, her amber eyes glow with excitement.

He scowls, then chuckles.

"How can I deny my love anything? Not to mention the CEO and Steele Patriarch… Thanks, Luc, for an excellent idea!" Roger proclaims as he raises his glass of Chateau Lafite Rothschild. "Here's to Leonie's new division!"

"Hear, hear!"

"*Félicitations!*"

"Cheers!"

Leonie claps her hands and turns to Roger with a grin to kiss him again.

Roger grins like the Cheshire Cat.

Lucky fucker.

"How did you like Thanksgiving dinner, Josy?" Shelley asks as we sip Rémy Martin digestifs in the library.

Josy gestures to my mother with her Baccarat snifter, "It was delicious, *merci!* Guy and I spent Thanksgiving with Lola at her Parisian penthouse on many occasions. She would cook a delectable multi-course meal. Luc would bring scrumptious pastries, and I would bring my double-chocolate soufflés for dessert."

She turns to Leonie and quirks her elegantly arched eyebrow at her daughter.

"Leonie, however, brought the wine since she doesn't cook despite my best efforts to teach her our Tunisian family's recipes."

Lola scoffs, "That's a wasted effort, *Maman* Josy! I've told you so for years!"

Leonie's golden caramel cheeks flush red, and she shakes her head.

"Don't tease her, *Mon Amour*. She takes after her Beaulieu side with her love for beautiful things," Guy responds as he winks at Leonie.

Daddy's Little Girl blows him a kiss in thanks.

"Well speaking of food, Nanny Grace just sent a text to me. The Twins are ringing their dinner bell! So pardon me," Leonie says.

Roger rises with her, but she pushes him back to his seat gently.

"Stay, *Chéri*, Nanny will help me," Leonie says as she smiles lovingly at me while she runs her fingers through his hair, massaging his scalp.

I clap my hands, and everyone glances at me in surprise.

"Do bring my nephews back. I haven't spent enough time with them," I say. "I don't want them to forget their favorite uncle!"

Sebastian sputters on his sip of cognac.

"Hell no! I'm their favorite uncle. So bring them to me!" He exclaims.

Harris and Luc join in, all proclaiming their place in The Twins' lives.

Leonie laughs, and her eyes twinkle.

"Simmer down, boys! You're all their favorite!"

Roger chuckles as she leaves the library.

"Well, don't get me started on their favorite aunt!" Lola adds.

"Yeah… Me!" Haley cuts in, lifting her snifter in salute.

Everyone laughs good-naturedly.

"Since Leonie is out of earshot, I'll tell you some stories about her as a child," Josy says gleefully.

We listen and laugh some more until Leonie returns with The Twins.

Roger goes to Nanny Grace and takes Gaspard from her arms with a word of thanks. Then he kisses his rosy cheeks as he coos happily.

"That's it. Hand him over, bro," I hustle over and pluck Gaspard from his arms just as Sebastian scoops Rodolphe from Leonie.

Roger rolls his eyes at our antics and shakes his head.

"Hey, you could have your own, you know…" he ribs us.

Baz smirks and inclines his head towards Lola.

"Yeah, no need to tell me. Have that conversation with your sister-in-law," he retorts.

Lola gives Roger the stink eye, and he opts to not comment. Instead, he cocks his head at me.

"So what's your excuse, lover boy? How're things with—"

"You mean the sexy AF yoga teacher? Because if you're not interested, I'll step in without hesitation!" Harris says.

The hairs on the back of my neck bristle. A growl erupts from my chest. The Alpha Dom in me rears his possessive head as I glare at our youngest brother.

Harris snickers and pulls out his mobile, typing on the screen.

"Oh, hi Starr… Yes, Happy Thanksgiving to you, too… I wanted to wish you a wonderful holiday and ask how the new surveillance system is going… Mmm… Right… Okay, great! I'm looking forward to the retreat, too. Thanks for inviting me… See you soon."

Silence descends on the library, making the sound of my ragged breathing loud.

10… 9… 8…

"You. Little. SHIT!" I explode. Steam pours from my ears as I flare my nostrils.

Roger reaches for Gaspard. But I pull away and turn my glare on him.

"I know what I'm doing with a baby! Lest you forget, I used to wipe the snot from your nose," I snap before I pin Harris with another heated stare.

"You'll pay for that when you least expect it, little brother. And lest you forget, I'm. Not. Haley," I snarl viciously.

Harris' smirk falters since he knows I'm *The Enforcer* amongst us.

"Ha! Good! Get 'em for me too, Malcolm!" Haley shouts, punching the air in victory.

I wink at her and respond with a dark chuckle, "Will do, Baby Girl, will do."

"One day you'll learn, little bro," Sebastian laughs. Then leans over to Gaspard and adds, "Just ignore your *Oncle* Malcolm's foul mouth…"

Oh, damn…

Now I glance at Leonie, chagrined.

"Sorry, sis. It won't happen again," I promise.

Leonie's laughter morphs into snorts as tears fill her eyes. She shakes her head and waves her hands in front of her flushed face.

"No worries, *mon frère*! They don't understand words yet, just emotions," she tells me as she pats my shoulder. "But, Harris, boy oh boy, I feel bad for you!"

LATER WE GO UP to Roger and Leonie's redesigned triplex penthouse for a tour.

Leonie did another excellent job with combining my parents' former penthouse below my duplex to create one large home for their growing family. It's on the top three floors, thirty through thirty-two.

Located in the Front de Seine district of Beaugrenelle in the *quinzième*, the property, like The STEELE Tower New York, is mixed-use with commercial and residential space plus the largest mall in Paris. The views of the Seine and of the Eiffel Tower are incredible, especially now at night when the spectacular light display flits across the monumental iron structure.

"Nicely done, Leonie," Luc says when we return to the main living room on the first floor. "*La Tour Eiffel* resembles a sparkling Christmas tree!"

"My favorite room is your Pilates and yoga studio," Lola gushes. "I need one! Then I can get a good workout at home."

Sebastian snorts and whispers in her ear.

Lola blushes scarlet red, but her hazel eyes spark with desire. Playfully, she swipes at Baz. He chuckles, wrapping his arms around her waist and pulling her back to his front. He places his hands possessively on her lower belly as he nuzzles her neck.

Leonie slips her hand into Roger's and smiles up at him knowingly.

I guess it won't be long before Baz and Lola have a baby of their own.

And my sad story continues…

"This is the most high-end karaoke place I've ever been to before! It feels more like a nightclub for dancing than for getting on a stage drunk reading from the teleprompter! I'm glad I listened to you and came out after all."

My gaze goes around the well-appointed interior of the multilevel club in West Hollywood. The sleek decor of black leather, chrome, and gray velvet with glass touches breathes luxury. They covered one wall in floor-to-ceiling mirrors with rows of top-shelf liquor shining like jewels in their crystal bottles. Sofas and club chairs on two levels like an arena face the stage. A female DJ with diamond-covered Beats by Dr. Dre headphones stands behind her Plexiglas booth spinning the latest tunes and the all-time favorites for karaoke lovers.

Then there are the fabulous glitterati attending the club's grand opening night. The current box-office blockbuster action hero and his sexy guy friends; *Los Angeles Confidential* magazine's cover girl for November with her tech mogul husband; the heiress to a private jet company and her entourage. All decked out in their finest attire.

And so am I.

A red, long-sleeved, sheer mock turtleneck with glossy ruby red leather motorcycle pants custom made to hug my curves taper to cover the backs of my cinnamon-hued stilettos. My curls blown straight, brush the top of my ass and sway with each step. Subtle shades of smoky red highlight my eyes while the rest of my makeup remains in nude tones.

Yeah, I want to look fierce since we're at the newest addition to Malcolm's portfolio: STEELE Karaoke Club West Hollywood.

Adrienne confirmed my former lover won't be in attendance since he's still in Paris with his family for Thanksgiving, according to Anton. So along with Claudia, we came for a much-needed night of fun—karaoke, my favorite!

"I'll never steer you wrong, girl!" Adrienne says as she dances to the song being performed. "This club is amazing!"

I nod and raise my tall glass of mojito in salute. Then pick up the song scheduler to cue my choice. It's time for me to enter the contest. First prize, a week's stay at STEELE Cabo San Lucas. Who'd pass up the opportunity to visit stunning Palmilla Beach?

"Ready to go up? You're the last of us, bring it home, Starr!" Claudia says as I take a sip of my mojito and stand.

"You know it!" I respond, slapping high five with her.

I leave our VIP cluster and strut to the stage. My heart pumps with excitement the closer I get to the stage. Then it drops when I join the queue of performers.

Malcolm Steele!

He's here after all and with a group of people including two women clinging to him as he laughs at something one of them said in his ear. His handsome face lights up, and he turns to the woman on his left to whisper something in her ear.

Really?!

Well, I've got something for you, you arrogant…

When my time comes, I ask the coordinator to change my song selection. Let's see how he laughs now.

Game on!

I take to the stage like I'm Annie Lennox herself. The sound of a motorcycle revving as it blares from the surround-sound speakers catches the audience's attention. All heads turn to the stage, to me standing like a diva gripping the mic like my lover.

I belt out the words to "Would I Lie to You" and stalk the stage with such emotion, it's not long into the song people clap and cheer. I refuse to direct my soulful rendition in *his* direction. Instead, I play to the action hero and his friends seated at the edge of the stage.

When I beckon to the movie star, he jumps up and helps me down from the stage. I sashay around serenading him as he plays along. The audience goes wild with stomps and wolf whistles when my performance ends and the actor kneels before me, bowing down.

The emcee names my group the winners, and everyone cheers even louder.

I kiss the sexy actor on the cheek, and he swings me in the air before setting me back onstage to collect my trophy.

Adrienne and Claudia join me, and we thank the audience. I chance a look at Malcolm only to find he's gone.

Couldn't stand the heat? Good riddance, Mr. Steele!

"I'm going to the ladies' room to freshen up," I tell my girls as we exit the stage.

It's not until I stand before the mirror I let the hurt sink in.

How could Malcolm just move on so easily? And with two women?!

Hell, I knew he was a playboy. But I didn't expect him to forget me so soon. It's been almost two months. I'm the one who should have moved on weeks ago! Quinn's still in hot pursuit. Maybe I should give him a booty call. BOB just isn't doing it. A battery-operated boyfriend doesn't compare to a full-blooded dick...

I shake my head and reapply my lipstick, then leave the ladies' room.

"Oh!" I exclaim as I bump into a wall of muscle when I step through the door.

My head tilts back. A red-faced Malcolm scowls down at me. I frown back and jut out my chin in defiance.

Fuck you, Mr. Steele!

Without a word, he grabs my elbow and forces me along the hallway.

I pull back, but he's having none of it. When I punch his side, he lifts me over his shoulder and stalks further down the corridor.

He slaps his palm on the wall; I hear a lock disengage. Once inside the room, he kicks the door closed, re-locks it, and puts me on my feet.

I clutch the front of his black cashmere sweater to steady myself as the blood rushes from my head. Then jerk back at the sensation of his heaving chest under my hands.

"What the hell, Malcolm?!" I yell as I pivot to open the door.

He slams his palms on either side of my head and presses his firm body against my back, boxing me in. His heavy breathing sends chills down my spine—and makes my nipples tighten and my pussy clench with need.

I push back against him to get space. But he refuses to budge.

"Get the fuck off of me, Malcolm!" I screech, slapping my palms on the door in frustration.

He continues to breathe and not answer me. The massive bulge in his trousers lets me know what's on his mind.

Oh. Hell. No!

"Get… the… fuck… off… of… me… I said, Malcolm!!!" I repeat yelling again.

Someone has to hear me, I guess.

His sizable hands cover my smaller ones, and his fingers intertwine with mine, locking us together. He leans his forehead against the back of my head, and he inhales deeply.

My body continues to respond to his nearness and need. I can't help it. He's trained me to crave him, to cum on command, to submit to his dominance. To love him.

Damn this man!

We stay melded together. Malcolm bent at the knees to angle his groin to cradle my ass. My body caught between his and the office door. The urge to flee dissipates, the fight in me gone.

I press my forehead against the door and inhale deeply.

"Why, My Angel?" Malcolm whispers in my hair.

The fact he doesn't consider his callous words to Roger about love and marriage not enough for me to end our relationship makes my body tense once again. How could he be so hard-hearted? To me?

I resolve not to let him hurt me any further. With a sigh, I straighten and unwind my fingers from his. He's proven twice now I'm not enough woman for him. He desires others more.

"Talk to me, My Angel," Malcolm says softly in a voice full of raw emotion.

"Malcolm, you know very well I'm not *your angel*. Listen, I don't want to argue with you. Especially since Leonie and

Roger's wedding is next month, and we're partnered in the bridal party. I will not upset my friend during a special time of her life," I respond and push back again. "Please, just let me go."

When he doesn't move and seeks my fingers, a small cry falls from my lips. I can't hold back the tears much longer.

"Red," I whisper my safeword hoarsely, lowering my head in defeat.

Malcolm squeezes my fingers, but steps back, respecting my limit.

I unlock the door and open it, then pause facing the hallway.

"Some people cherish love and marriage, even if you do not, Malcolm."

"Hey, hey, hey! The gang's all here and ready to celebrate the blushing bride-to-be!"

I say, then blow my party whistle upon entering the living room to Leonie's wing of *Le Beaulieu Manoir*.

Billie and I with her boyfriend Patrick Rockett flew to Paris for Roger and Leonie's wedding on his private jet. Her Scottish billionaire beau and the CEO of Rockett Construction Company—the competitor to STEELE International, Inc.—went to their suite at STEELE Place Vendôme while we continued to *Le Manoir*. When they first started dating, Lola had to calm Sebastian down when she reminded him Billie signed an ironclad nondisclosure agreement and she swore her allegiance to Lola.

Leonie, her mother Josy, Shelley, Lola, Blair, Anita, and Hettie gather in the East Wing. Leonie, Roger, and The Twins stay here while their STEELE Tower Paris triplex penthouse reconstruction completes. They took over her former bedroom suite.

The rest of the wing comprises several bedrooms and bathrooms, kitchenette with eating area, library, art studio, media room, and living room. In essence, it's a house within a house and was all hers before Leonie bought her duplex in the *seizième*. It's where she stays when she visits her parents.

"Let's get this party started right! Let's get this party started quickly! Time to set it off!" Billie chimes in as she dances into the living room.

"Hey, *chéries!*" Leonie squeals as she jumps up from the navy blue velvet sofa and rushes to embrace us. "I'm so glad everyone made it!"

"Is it too early to break open the Taittinger Comtes de Champagne Blanc de Blancs? Since Leonie is marrying her very own Double-O agent in a couple of days!" Lola asks, giggling as she pretends to pop a bottle open.

"It's five o'clock somewhere in the world!" Blair cosigns, tapping her gold Cartier Panthère watch.

Leonie is a huge James Bond fan. In *Casino Royale*, 007 requests the decadent libation and makes history. Now, it's her preferred champers.

Everyone laughs at their antics.

"Now, now… Time to review the wedding activities schedule," Josy says.

"Yes, work before play, ladies," Shelley adds.

Leonie and Lola giggle at the drill sergeants. We remember how in control Shelley was for Lola and Sebastian's nuptials. Somehow no one expected Josy being just as commanding!

We settle down instantly.

An hour later, we finish just in time for The Twins' feeding. Leonie excuses herself when Nanny Grace rings her mobile. Josy and Shelley go to help Leonie.

While she's gone, we catch up on our lives since we last saw one another a month ago at SLFW Resorts. After Billie fills us in on her latest escapades with the bonnie Scotsman at LEVELS Beverly Hills, she turns to Blair.

"So, Miss Secretive, what's new on your front? I'm still surprised Monsieur Montaigne let you loose to attend Starr's celebration!" Billie quips.

Blair blushes, turning her porcelain skin crimson. As always, she dodges the question and swings her chestnut brown colored hair over her face.

I keep my mouth shut, not wanting to draw any unwanted attention to myself. Instead, I rise and walk to the window. The majestic property features manicured park-like grounds, stables, tennis court, swimming pool and cabana, and a palatial French Rococo mansion. A part of the 16th arrondissement, it's in the wealthiest neighborhood.

The picturesque view extends past *Le Manoir's* twenty acres of land to Bois de Boulogne. I can visualize a young Leonie riding her horse on the trails. Now her sons will grow up in its splendor.

Wistfully, I turn back to the room. My gaze meets Shelley's as she re-enters the living room. She smiles and heads towards me.

"It's such a magnificent mansion. I can't keep my eyes off of the landscaping either," she says as she loops her arm through mine.

After a moment of gazing at the grounds, Shelley speaks again.

"Everything wrapped prettily isn't always what it seems. Sometimes we have to search deeper—past the facade—to get to its depths. If we give up and don't dig deep enough, we miss out on the gem inside."

She squeezes my arm and smiles when I glance at her. Obviously she's referring to Malcolm. But I don't know what to say. So I nod respectfully.

"OMG! Look at my handsome nephews!"

Shelley and I turn at Haley's words to find Leonie and

Josy carrying the three-month-old twins into the living room.

We gather around the babies, oohing and aahing at the adorable duo. They've grown so much and resemble their father even more than before.

As we take turns holding Rodolphe and Gaspard, my mind drifts back to the dreams I had of mini Malcolms swaddled in blankets held in my arms; smiling up at me as I breastfeed them; coos as I talk to them. All the while, his magnetic presence hovers on my periphery. Watching his sons, me.

By the time we leave for the rehearsal and the dinner, my ovaries ache.

"Hello, Starr."

My heart flips.

Malcolm stands behind me, dressed in a bespoke three-piece charcoal striped suit. The ruby red silk tie and pocket square pop against the bright white dress shirt. His tousled hair—longer than usual—brushes the collar. The two-day stubble surrounds his lush lips that curl up at the corners in a hint of a smile. His dove gray eyes sparkle in the fairy lights of the Chapel of *Le Beaulieu Manoir*. But his eyes lack their usual luster.

We're lining up to practice for the ceremony. With everyone milling about, I didn't notice his arrival. But as I inhale deeply to calm my nerves, I smell his John Varvatos - Dark Rebel Rider cologne. The orange, balsam, leather, and amber fill my nostrils, promising long nights of rough fucking.

I'm wet instantly.

Damn this man!

"Hello, Malcolm," I respond, hoping he doesn't notice my arousal.

"You look beautiful—"

"How have you bee—"

We laugh awkwardly as we speak over each other. Then again, when we repeat the same slipup.

"You first," he says, bowing his ebony head graciously with his typical smirk.

I nod and start to speak. But this time it's the wedding planner who interrupts our reunion.

Malcolm gestures with his hand for me to proceed ahead of him to the front of the pairs. Roger stands at the altar with Sebastian as his best man. So Malcolm and I take the lead for the processional, followed by Haley and Lucien, Blair and Luc, and Billie and Harris.

"You look beautiful, Starr."

Malcolm's words whispered in my ear along with his warm breath tickling its delicate shell make me blush and preen.

My hands smooth across the stretch-knit of my one-shoulder midi dress—ruby in keeping with Leonie's Christmas theme. The shoulder ruffle leads to a figure-skimming fit. Heeled sandals bring the top of my head with my hair in an elegant chignon close to his lips.

"Thank you, Malcolm," I murmur as I take his proffered arm.

What I really want is for him to lower the gold zipper on the back of my dress, slam me against the wall—Chapel or not—and fuck me senseless...

The rehearsal goes well and doesn't last long. We travel in Mercedes-Benz Sprinters to the rooftop ballroom at STEELE Montaigne. Funny enough, the city named the street for Luc's family.

In the *huitième* arrondissement the five-star hotel has

extraordinary views of the Champs-Élysées, Arc de Triomphe, and the Place de la Concorde, not to mention the Seine. At night, with the lights of Paris shining brightly, prove a spectacular venue for the rehearsal dinner.

When we arrive, dozens of guests—the rest of the Jacksons clan, STEELE associates, high society, friends—mingle during the cocktail hour. Leonie's Winter Wonderland Wedding theme continues at the ballroom with shades of cranberry, gold, champagne, and ivory. If this is any sign of the actual ceremony, we're in for a sumptuous fairytale!

With the amount of people, I don't spend any more time with Malcolm. The way he tended to me during the rehearsal reminded me of our time together, especially during aftercare or spooned together sated from our lovemaking.

The exuberant sound of his laughter carries over the band's background music and the murmurs of guests' conversations.

I peek over my shoulder and spy him sitting with his boys—Anton, Borya, Lucien—and others. They're talking animatedly, gesticulating, and egging each other on. Malcolm tosses his head back and roars with laughter.

A chuckle falls from my lips as I watch from across the room.

As if sensing my presence, Malcolm glances around until his eyes meet mine. His narrow as he finds the source. Pinned by his possessive wolf-like gaze, I bite my bottom lip and lower my eyes submissively.

Hell, I might as well roll over and show him my belly.

Before I can go through with the silly thought, Anita hands me a flute of Champagne. Coming back to my senses, I turn away from temptation and gulp down the bubbly.

"Well, I guess you needed that, huh?" Anita teases as she

lifts her hand to snag full flute from a passing server's tray. "Here, have another!"

I giggle, feeling the effects of the Champagne and nod.

"Yes, well, I need something to get me through the next two days!" I respond, saluting her with my crystal glass.

This time it's our laughter that floats through the air.

I ignore the sensation of Malcolm's eyes on me for the rest of the evening. His magnetism is strong, but I'm stronger.

My Independent Woman roars in agreement.

* * *

"You were putting them back last night at our Girls' Night In, Little Miss Moderation…"

I attempt a smile at Lola, then winch. The next French Martini I see, I'm going to run from it!

While the guys went to Roger's bachelor party, we played karaoke and games at *Le Manoir*. Leonie stuck with water since she's breastfeeding. She'll pump today and indulge for her wedding.

We had an amazing time chilling out. But the cocktails packed a punch.

Fortunately, Roger transformed the living room of the East Wing into a mini spa so Leonie and her girls could get pampered before the wedding. He arranged for her favorite day spa in Paris to set up multiple stations and rooms for our treatments.

She and her mother have facials done in an area separated by an antique, hand-painted Chinese partition. While Lola, Shelley, Haley, Blair, Billie, Anita, Hettie, and I have five-star massages, scrubs, and waxings. We'll all end up together in the manicure and pedicure chairs.

We started the day with a vigorous yoga flow led by

Anita, followed by meditation with me. So this is a much-needed respite. So relaxing and rejuvenating!

"Remind me all day and night," I moan.

Once we're done, we troop into the living room to find Leonie laughing.

"What's so funny, love bunny?"

Billie's silly question evokes more snorts from Leonie. She sits up from the facial table and fans herself. Cucumbers roll off her eyes and plop onto her lap.

"Ha! She's hysterical! Leonie is losing it, folks!" Lola says, bouncing on her feet and clapping her hands.

Everyone laughs, even the aestheticians, albeit discreetly.

Shelley walks over and plucks the cucumbers from Leonie's lap and says, "Oh, let her be. It wasn't so long ago you were in the same position, Mrs. Sebastian Steele."

Then with a wink, she adds, "Although I can understand why… My sons are fine catches!"

She glances at me, and her smile broadens.

I, however, bite my lower lip and suddenly find interest in the nail polish selection.

Shelley snickers.

"I remember how nervous I was before I walked down the aisle to Joel," Hettie starts. "It terrified me he'd get cold feet and duck out of the church!"

We laugh.

"Up and at 'em! We've got a schedule to maintain," Leonie's mother says as she slips off her table and joins the others at the mani/pedi chairs.

Lola and Leonie glance at each other and bust out laughing.

As our nails finish drying, one servant enters the living room-cum-spa with a beautifully wrapped box in her hands.

Leonie thanks her before she lifts the top. Inside is a flat blue velvet box. She presses the sapphire cabochon closure, and the lid lifts to reveal an exquisite suite of diamonds set in clusters of pear-shaped stones in various sizes: a pair of earrings; a bib necklace; a bracelet. They glitter as the light bounces off their flawless surfaces.

"Whoa! Someone pass my shades to me, stat!" Exclaims Blair as she shields her eyes from the brilliance of the diamonds.

Haley claps and adds, "My brother knows how to treat a lady!"

"Shelley, *chérie*, you are right. Your sons are fine catches!" Leonie's mother says.

We head to the solarium in the East Wing that faces the Bois de Boulogne for the bridesmaids' luncheon. To go along with the spa theme, the menu comprises green salads, grilled herb-crusted salmon, roast chicken, and citrus-infused water. We prefer to eat light before putting on our gowns.

Leonie giggles to herself.

"There she goes, again," Lola says gleefully as she twirls her finger in a circle by her temple. "Looney Tunes alert!"

I can't blame Leonie. She and Lola married the men of their dreams. One day, I hope to do the same.

MALCOLM

"*Some people cherish love and marriage, even if you do not.*"

Starr's words continue to haunt me even a month later and while I'm at Roger's bachelor party—or Bro Bonding, as our cousin Laurent calls it.

After our encounter at STEELE Karaoke West Hollywood, I realize I hurt Starr. No matter how hard I try, I can't figure out what I did to drive her away. The reference to love and marriage makes me wonder if she wants a ring. Since I've given her collars only, she's given up on us.

I resolved to find out before the wedding, but Starr ignored my calls and messages. I stopped trying since we'd see each other for the festivities.

And boy, did we…

Starr was smoking hot in her red dress last night. The material cluing to her luscious curves and reminded me of what I've missed. The gold zipper was like a beacon begging me to lower it and slide my hands inside to cup her round ass and bare pussy. My lips ached to plant a trail of open-mouthed kisses along the shooting stars tattooed on her exposed neck then shoulder before I turned her and suckled her plump brown nipples. Hard.

Hard. Exactly what happened when I laid eyes on Starr. My cock awoke from its slumber—a beast hungry for the succulent morsel of its mate.

And I wasn't the only one aroused by our reunion.

Starr shuffled on her feet, obviously rubbing the apex of her thighs to manipulate her swollen clit. Her chest heaved when she inhaled, and my lust-filled eyes followed the lift of her full tits happily.

I wanted to bury my face between the pillowy mounds. Then lave and lick her beaded nipples until she climaxed a dozen times. Her soft coos in my ears, and her sweat-slicked skin warm against my tongue.

Fuck. Me.

I shift in my club chair, just fantasizing about the moment.

Starr thought she could avoid me the rest of the night after I spied her watching me with desire written all over her gorgeous heart-shaped face.

I allowed her to flit around the ballroom of the rehearsal dinner, sipping Champagne and engaging in conversation with other men. She sensed my possessive stare and chose to ignore it. Fine. For now.

However, I dodged single—and some married—female guests who thought they could wrangle a ride in the sack with the rebel of the Steele family. No thanks. I have my hands full with roping in Starr again. Besides, she'd flip if I so much as glanced in their direction, and she definitely would never speak to me for life.

The promise I made to respect her limits and not pursue her before or during the wedding will remain intact. Once Roger and Leonie finish their eternal vows, game. Fucking. On.

For now, I'll focus on my brother and his happiness.

We're at Jackson Smoke&Scotch Lounge Paris—what's quickly become our favorite spot to unwind with the boys as we partake of their top-shelf Scotch offerings. I rarely smoke their fine Cuban cigars, but tonight is a special occasion and all of us join in.

I take a long draw on it and settle back in my leather club chair. The tasting notes of the spicy, earthy, and woody flavors linger on my palate. They blend well with the smoky, dark berries flavor of the Jackson Reserve Scotch. Its trademark bite drags along the back of my tasting.

Much like my delectable and tantalizing Starr. As Pam Grier says in *Foxy Brown*, "the darker the berry, the sweeter the fruit, honey." And Starr is all that, and then some, even if she no longer wants us together.

Joel raises his Baccarat crystal snifter in a toast.

"Well my friend, this time tomorrow you'll be a happily married man and join the likes of Sebastian, Norman, and me in the bliss of wedlock. Here's to you and your beautiful bride-to-be!"

"Damn, man! Get a grip on yourself with that goofy ass smile on your face!"

Busted, Roger laughs along with Joel and Norman, Luc, our brothers, our cousins Lachlan, Lucien, and Laurent guffaw.

"Who would have thought from one meeting over two years ago would bring us to two Steele men capturing the hearts of my mentees and friends?"—Luc shakes his head and his navy blue eyes sparkle with mischief—"Roger, *oui*. But Sebastian… mmm mmm. A surprise!"

Harris, Lachlan, Roger, and I chuckle remembering how jealous Baz was of the Silver Fox's relationship with Lola.

Luc may be in his early fifties. But as Leonie and Lola pegged his nickname, he can go toe-to-toe with any of us for a woman's affection. Hell, he may even win! An Alpha Dom at six feet, four inches with salt and pepper hair, a clean-shaven face that highlights the cleft in his chin. He could pass for a movie star. Not to mention being a billionaire duke, the last of his noble line.

We laugh some more when Baz bristles.

Only after he put his ring on Lola did he loosen up a smidgen on Luc. Obviously, it's still a touchy topic…

"Ha! Just fucking with you, Steele," he chuckles. "I trust you and your brother will do well by Lola and Leonie. That is, if you know what is best for you."

He pauses to pin both of them with a don't-fuck-with-them stare, then raises his glass for a toast.

"*À la tienne, mes amis!*" He proclaims with a smirk.

The rest of the night we rib each other and reminisce about our time growing up. Damn, who would have thought we'd end up with two Steele brothers down so close in time? And if I have my way, another falls in line… Soon.

I ARRIVE BACK at my suite in STEELE Place Vendôme, a slight sway to my step. Fuck, I drank more than I thought. The need to distract myself from images of Starr drove me to take the shot challenge Laurent put forth.

That fucker can drink like a fish!

As I walk into the room and my eyes light on the empty bed, I know what needs to happen next… Let my fantasies free.

I toe off my Gucci loafers and strip out of my cashmere sweater and trousers, tossing the garments to the ground with my boxer briefs. I pad to the bathroom.

The light bounces off of the white marble as I flick the switch. While I shield my eyes from the opulence, I make my way to the oversized glass-enclosed shower.

As I duck under the spray from multiple shower heads, I let my eyes close and tilt my head back. The warm water sluices down my rock-hard body as I brace my palms on the marble wall. The ache in my cock—and surprisingly in my heart—increases. I drop my head and groan aloud.

Fuck, I miss My Angel.

My thoughts drift to her—my celestial beauty—so bright and out of reach.

I groan as my cock lengthens, and the girth thickens. The Prince Albert piercing makes my tip super sensitive. The platinum piercing glints in the light.

The wings of my tattoo ripple as my back flexes. The mantle lays heavy.

Only when I'm buried balls deep in My Angel's tight, wet heat do I feel free completely. She welcomes me into her willing body and becomes one with me. No burden is too heavy when I'm wrapped in her warm embrace.

I groan again when I think about how much time we've wasted. Days… Weeks… Months. Damn.

Flashbacks play across my mind's eye.

Her bodacious curves in the coral-colored long-sleeved dress at Baz and Lola's wedding.

Starr in a tiny bikini on the beach when we met officially in St. Barth's.

My collar of intricate platinum lacework covered in tiny sparkly diamonds on her long neck.

Her sorrel brown eyes shining as she giggles at my lame joke.

That red fuck-me dress…

My hand slips from the steam slick wall and slides down between my eight-pack abs, the well-defined ridges taut beneath my calloused fingertips. The texture of the trail of hair leading from below my navel to my groin contrasts with my bare skin.

I suck in a ragged breath as my fantasy begins...

My Angel sub naked on her knees before me with her mouth open wide, eager to receive my engorged ten inches. Her eyes—darkened with lust—stare back up at me as she pokes her little pink tongue out.

My hand grips the base of my dick and taps the reddened tip against the flat of her tongue. A pearl of pre-cum drops onto it.

She moans and sways as she closes her soft mouth around my dick. Her eyelids droop as she takes my swollen length down her throat. Her gag reflex spasms sending a zing to my seed-heavy balls.

I squeeze my eyes tight, not wanting to lose the vision before I'm ready to blow my load.

After a moment, I regain control and my fantasy continues...

"Just like that, take it deep, Little One," I praise her, pulling on my Dom. "I want to see tears meet the drool on your chin before I give you my seed to swallow."

My hand dives into her wet curls. I grip the back of her head as I snap my hips forward until the tip of her nose meets my happy trail.

She sputters and gags. Her widened eyes fly back up to gaze into mine as she panics.

"Breathe through your nose. Understand, Little One?" I command.

She nods, then winces from my grip on her scalp.

When her breathing evens out, I pull back until my tip leaves her mouth with a pop. A string of saliva runs from her lips to my cock. Tears flow down her reddened cheeks. She stares at me as she licks her swollen lips.

Fucking beautiful.

"Some more please, Sir."

I nearly bust my nuts.

Instead, I drop my forehead to the slick wall and brace myself on my forearms for what promises to be a leg wobbling experience.

My Angel sub does not disappoint.

One hand massages my sac and the other grips and tugs my turgid dick. The rhythm she sets alternates between gentle and painful, keeping a delicate balance that has me close in moments.

"Fuuuck... Angel... Shit, that feels so good," I growl as my palms slap the wall. She has me slipping between Dom and boyfriend.

A pinch to my tip sends me rocking onto the balls of my feet, driving my hips forward to pump against her hand. My Angel sub senses how close I am to release, so she speeds up her pace.

"ANGEL" I roar as my dick jumps in her hand and ropes of creamy cum splash onto the wall.

My hips move on their own since my brain exploded with my cock. She snakes her fingers that were massaging my balls around my hip and slips one into my ass. Her fingertip strokes my prostrate, and my cock hardens again.

"FUCK!!!" I roar, surprised by the erotic invasion. Then I ride out another mind-blowing, spine-tingling orgasm.

My body slumps, and I join My Angel sub on the wet marble floor as the shower water rains down on us. I pull her onto my lap and bury my face in her neck, still breathing heavy. The feeling of her fingers running through my hair soothes my racing heart.

"I love you, My Angel," I murmur, no longer in my fantasy.

The love is real, and I will deny it no longer.

MALCOLM

"*R*oger, I'm so proud of you. Shrewd business executive, worthy father, soon to be a loving husband. You did it, bro! Congratulations!"

"Yeah, well, as long as Leonie doesn't leave him standing at the altar looking like a love-lost puppy!"

"Shut the fuck up, Harris!"

He laughs and grabs his big brother in a bear hug that lifts him a few inches from the floor.

"You know I love you, man!" Harris chuckles. "I just can't help myself!"

"Obviously! But I love you, too!" Roger replies, mussing Harris' hair.

"Aw damn, dude! Cut it out already!" He groans as he rushes to the mirror to fix his ebony waves.

Along with Roger and Harris, Baz, Lucien, Luc, and I gather in a tent beside the Chapel awaiting our time to enter for the nuptials.

We rode in one of the Sprinters from STEELE Place Vendôme earlier, already dressed in our bespoke tuxedos. Suited and booted in white-tie attire for Roger's big day.

He attempts to maintain his cool Alpha male demeanor. But we see straight through it. He's nervous as fuck!

"You are already on my list, Little Harris. Keep messing around, and you will be on Roger *The Responsible*'s ugly side," I warn our kid brother with a smirk.

"Exactly!" Roger adds, pointing his index and middle finger at his eyes, then at Harris. "I see you, bro…"

Baz chuckles and flips his fingers through Harris' hair as he turns from the mirror. He huffs and fixes his artfully tousled locks again.

"Roger, you make Leonie thrilled, *mon ami!*" Luc says.

"Gentlemen, it is time for you to take your places in the Chapel."

We face the tent entrance at the sound of the wedding planner's voice.

"All right, Roger. Time to rock and roll!" Lucien says as he claps Roger on his shoulder.

I grin as a smile filled with love spreads across Roger's face. He takes a deep breath, adjusts his diamond and platinum cuff links—a gift from his bride-to-be—and strides to his future.

Enchantress.

Words fly from my head. But that's the only one to describe the sight of My Angel.

The bridal party stands in the anteroom of the Chapel, alight with tiny lights and covered in flowers as the background. She looks like a celestial being. My fantasy come to the Earth.

Her strapless dress has layers of silk chiffon with a neckline of a confectioner's sugar swirl of the silk. An intricate appliqué of gold, champagne, and touches of cranberry attaches at her waist and crosses her body from one hip up to cover the opposite breast.

I want to unwrap my early Christmas present. Right. Now.

"Hello, Starr," I say instead as I approach her.

"Hello, Malcolm," she responds a bit tense.

To rib her, I repeat my words from before.

"You look beautiful, Starr," I whisper in her ear. Then smirk when she trembles slightly.

"Thank you," My Angel murmurs.

I hold out my arm, and she slips her hand under and around my elbow. Locking her forearm to my side, I turn to face the wrought-iron gates at the entrance to the Chapel's primary space.

Thousands of fairy lights twine with the dark greens leaves and red berries of holly around the gates, the columns, and up the walls to the ceiling bathing the Chapel in a soft, golden glow. An abundance of wreaths and flowers ranging in hue from deep cranberry and burgundy to champagne and ivory fills the Chapel. The sweet, hot spiciness of cinnamon mixed with the floral scents waft through the air. The space is at once elegant and festive.

Leonie and her father Guy arrive behind us. The bridal party turns to face them, and everyone smiles as we shower the beautiful bride with our praises. Then the music changes for the start of the procession. The Trans-Siberian Orchestra perform their "Christmas Canon." The strains of the violins swirl around the Chapel.

The wedding planner cues us to proceed.

I glance down at My Angel, and she tilts her head back to gaze at me. Tears shine in her sorrel brown eyes. I ache to kiss her eyelids but smile at her instead. With a nod, we march down the aisle.

While we walk, I wonder what it would be like if this

were our wedding day. I know My Angel will make a stunning bride. But is she ready for more?

We settle in place and await Leonie and Guy. Roger's hands twitch as though he wants to race up the aisle to claim his bride before she reaches him.

"Slow down, bro. She's yours forever."

Sebastian stills him. But nothing can hold back the beaming smile on Roger's face when Leonie comes into view.

She resembles a princess bride floating towards her prince on an ethereal carpet of fragrant white rose, camellia, and gardenia petals. Through Leonie's veil, we can see her brilliant smile rivals the diamonds in her ears and on chest. Their eyes lock, and the grin that spreads from one ear to the other threatens to split Roger's face.

After the couple exchanges their vows, the officiant pronounces them husband and wife.

Roger kisses Mrs. Roger Steele until she's breathless.

The bridal party whoops while the guests stand and clap.

Lola places Leonie's bouquet in her hand and straightens her long veil and the hem of her gown as the pair turn to the guests. Roger grasps Leonie's hand, and they scoop The Twins from their grandparents. As a family, they stroll down the aisle to the cheers of family and friends.

Baz and Lola leave the altar next.

I stride to My Angel and extend my arm. She peeks at me from beneath her wet eyelashes, damp with tears. This time I brush my thumb beneath her eyes and bring my fingers to my lips. She ducks her head and loops her arm through mine.

We follow the newlyweds down the aisle and to the closed door of the separate room off of the Chapel's anteroom. My Angel disengages herself from my arm and dabs her eyes with a handkerchief.

Lola knocks at the door, and Roger calls out to come in.

"Yeah, yeah, yeah... Time for pictures in this Winter Wonderland Chapel, Love Birds!" Lola teases as her hazel eyes sparkle with mischief. "The guests head back to the *Manoir's Grand Hall*. The wedding planner said to hang out in here until they're all gone."

My Angel laughs, "Lola, you are no good!"

I stand close to My Angel with my front inches from her back. My focus remains on her the entire time we're in the room.

Hell, I can't take another moment without My Angel. I don't know what it's about weddings. But it's hard to evade love when it swirls around you. The very atmosphere charged with the electricity of two people deeply in love.

I chuckle at myself, waxing poetic.

My Angel faces me, and for a moment we're lost in our own world.

Leonie cracks up about something, drawing everyone's attention to her and Roger.

The wedding planner enters and ushers us into the primary space. Hairstylists and makeup artists touch up the girls' before we pose for the cameras.

The Twins steal the show. The photographers and videographers came prepared with colorful fuzzy balls suspended from sticks to keep Rodolphe and Gaspard looking toward the cameras. They reach for them and track the balls as an assistant moves them through the air. Pros just like their *Maman*—the world-renown megamodel.

A photographer and a videographer captured the guys in candid and posed shots. The girls did the same. So we spend little time on the group photos.

When we exit the Chapel, everyone laughs at the golden coach led by four horses with a driver and two footmen waiting to take us back to the mansion. Their liveries just as formal as our white-tie attire, harkens to days of the centuries past.

The beauty of the snow-covered lawns and twinkling trees remind me of being inside of a snow globe for a wintry fairy-tale. The stars glitter in the ink-black sky and the air is crisp. Sound muffled by the falling snow. It's fantastical.

While Roger and Leonie climb into their carriage, the bridal party boards the Sprinters for *Le Beaulieu Manoir*'s *Grand Hall*. The girls take one of the luxury mini coaches. My Angel thinks she can evade me. Not happening.

When we arrive at the *Grand Hall*, the bridal party gathers at the closed double doors and partner up again for our introduction to the guests inside.

I skim my hand along My Angel's flank to rest at her lower back. A shudder runs through her.

Gotcha!

Baz and Lola enter the massive room, dancing to the music. The rest of us strut in laughing and clapping. I hold My Angel's hand in the air and wave them around. She squeezes my hand back as she shimmies.

My cock jumps.

We take our seats at two tables below the dais where the high table waits for Roger and Leonie. Set on the other side of the dais, our and Leonie's parents sit at tables with their closest friends. Our Uncle Connor and Aunt Lucie Jackson —parents of Lachlan, Lydie, Lucien, and Laurent—join them as the women have been best friends since before either married their billionaires.

Everyone turns their attention to the double doors when the music pauses.

"Ladies and gentlemen, presenting Mr. and Mrs. Roger Steele and their sons Master Rodolphe Beaulieu Steele and Master Gaspard Beaulieu Steele!"

The room breaks out in applause for the couple and The Twins. They make their way to our parents' tables and hand their sons to them before they have their first dance. When the song ends and they dance with our parents, the rest of us join in.

"Starr, will you dance with me?" I ask as I rise and extend my hand to her.

She nods and takes my hand.

I pull her close and whisper in her ear, "Words, Angel. I will have your words."

It's a risk, but I'm going full throttle.

I'm rewarded with another shudder and her sweet words, "Yes, Sir."

My world rights itself. I want to fist pump and holler but hold back. I am an in-control Alpha Dom, after all.

The feel of My Angel in my arms is so right. Her body melds to mine as I hold her close. The alluring scent of her perfume's sandalwood, jasmine, and vanilla notes makes me want to bury my face in her neck and suck on her tender flesh. The urge to mark My Angel grows stronger.

My cock rouses and presses against her flat belly.

A small gasp falls from between her lips when she feels my desire for her. Instead of pulling away, she lays her head against my chest.

Fucking perfect!

Céline Dion finishes the song, and we return to our seats. I have to shake my leg surreptitiously to adjust my burgeoning erection.

My Angel giggles, then stops when I peer down with a raised eyebrow at her. She coughs and averts her gaze.

Between courses of our meal, I circulate amongst the guests and dance with Haley, who seems forlorn whenever Lachlan comes near.

Baz already told that fucker to back up off of our baby

sister. We don't give a damn if he claims nothing is going on between them. Haley acts like a sad puppy around him.

From the time we were kids growing up together, Baz and Lachlan were best friends. Haley would trail after them from the time she could walk. Then she stopped as a teenager. Now she's flustered with him.

I've already warned Baz if I have to step in, it'll be a problem. Hell, I love Lachlan like a brother, but he better not fuck with my baby sister. He's an Alpha Dom like me and a big-time Global All Access member at LEVELS, so I know his proclivities…

Purposefully I don't interact with My Angel. I want her on the edge, wondering when I'll follow through on my dick poking her. I can tell my strategy works whenever I catch her watching me with a burning hunger in her eyes.

After Leonie gives a touching speech to her new husband, Sebastian takes the mic followed by each of the siblings. Then we listen to our family and friends regale Roger and Leonie with fond memories and best wishes.

They cut the cake and toss Leonie's bouquet and garter.

Funny enough, My Angel catches the flowers. She giggles and waves the bouquet over her head. The girls tease her, and she avoids my gaze again.

When Roger prepares to toss the garter, I position myself in the center of the bachelors' group behind his turned back.

"All right now! Who will be the lucky guy to catch the garter and match up with the lovely Starr Knight?!" He challenges those gathered.

I brace myself.

"Watch out, sucker! This is all mine!"

Harris makes a grab for the garter; he'll never learn.

With my three inches on him, I snatch it mid-air.

"Take that. Take that. Take that!" I say à la Puffy and stalk towards my prize, swinging the garter on my index finger.

We lock eyes.

I pull My Angel into my embrace, dip her into a deep arc, and capture her mouth in a mind-blowing kiss. I bring her back on her feet, and she peers at me dazedly while I grin wider than Roger.

"Time to go, My Angel," I murmur against her luscious lips.

"Yes, Sir," she whispers, then nips my lower lip.

I growl.

My cock thickens down my inner thigh.

We leave the dance floor with her tucked against my side and her head on my shoulder.

Everyone whoops and hollers—Harris the loudest with wolf whistles.

Gotcha, My Angel! Love takes all.

STARR

The buildings and monuments of the City of Light blur by as Malcolm navigates the Parisian streets in his sleek, black on red Aston Martin DB7 Vantage expertly. Funny how he parked it on *Le Manoir*'s driveway. Pretty convenient...

Where we're going, I'm not sure. To his hotel suite at STEELE Place Vendôme or to his private suite at LEVELS Paris? Either destination would suit me just fine.

I squeeze my thighs together as my arousal increases in anticipation of his carnal touch—fingers, lips, tongue. My pussy clenches at the thought. Best to stare out of the tinted window to prevent a puddle of my juices from forming on his plush leather seat.

How much further?

An unbidden sigh escapes my lips.

Malcolm's heavy hand placed on my thigh makes me jump and gape at him.

Dammit! I feel like a jittery virginal bride.

"Relax, My Angel. We'll be there soon," he says as his gaze shifts from the street to me briefly.

The rumble of Malcolm's deep baritone voice heightens my desire for him. I return to watch the city fly by, still uncertain of our destination.

When the obelisk of the Place de la Concorde appears before us—lit up in the night sky like a beacon—I know we're headed for the hotel. In a matter of minutes, we'll be at his suite.

Thank God and every deity in every religion's pantheon! I almost shimmy in my seat.

We pull up to the hotel's grand entrance, and a doorman helps me from the low sports car. A hair-raising growl draws my attention from smiling in gratitude at the man.

Malcolm curls his lip in a snarl as he glares at the doorman, pointedly moving his eyes from the man to my leg, exposed by the slit in my gown.

Apparently Malcolm doesn't appreciate the doorman staring at what he believes is his. The Possessive Caveman returns.

He flicks his wrist to wave the man off and takes my arm.

"*Pardonnez-moi, Monsieur Steele,*" he stutters, now realizing Malcolm's identity. "*Je veux dire aucun manque de respect, monsieur.*"

Malcolm gives a cursory nod to the doorman's apology of no disrespect. French being one language in which he's fluent. But he doesn't slow down as he bustles me through the hotel's glass and wrought-iron doors held open by another doorman. He too nods to Malcolm as a sign of respect to a Steele.

I smile as I move as briskly as possible in my heels and gown.

More staff greet Malcolm before we reach etched-glass, double doors where yet another doorman allows us entry to a separate foyer. Beyond sit three reception and two concierge desks, four sitting areas, and a bank of three private elevators. Malcolm ushers me into one and places a keycard on a plaque for access to the most exclusive suites.

He stares at the floor numbers as though counting the minutes, equally eager to arrive at his rooms. The warmth of his palm on my lower back grounds me.

The entire time, I can't keep my eyes off of Malcolm. He looks fine in his elegant white tie. So very debonair. He shaved the growth from his chiseled jaw and trimmed his hair. Whether rugged or polished, Malcolm Steele is sex AF.

No sooner do the doors open than Malcolm guides me through them and down the hall. Our steps muffled by the silk carpet quicken the closer we get to the double doors at the end of the corridor. Soft music plays over hidden speakers as the rustle of my gown hints at my speed.

"After you, My Angel," Malcolm purrs as he holds the right door open.

I sashay past him, putting an extra sway in my hips. All the more to entice my... Dom, boyfriend, post-wedding-love-haze hookup?

Not clear on the status of our situation, I shrug inwardly. *Just go with the flow, Starr,* I admonish myself. Interesting how my inner warrior remains silent. Either she wants to reunite with Malcolm or is just horny; I'm grateful for her compliance.

"Would you care for a glass of Champagne? I noticed you enjoyed it at the rehearsal dinner," Malcolm says as he appears at my side.

For a moment I'm transfixed by the magnificent view of the Tuileries Gardens, Place du Carrousel, and the Louvre beyond. Lights placed strategically to exhibit the former royal residence to its finest. The other day Anita and I had pastries and tea at Angelina Paris—the legendary 1903 tearoom near the gardens.

"Oh, yes, thank you"—I start as I turn with an arched eyebrow to face him—"I didn't realize you were watching me so closely, Mr. Steele. What else did you spy?"

Malcolm chuckles wickedly and clasps my chin between his thumb and index finger, holding my head in place. He stares into my eyes intently.

"Oh, so much more, My Angel. Such as you flirting with a few of the male guests and letting them dance with you, giggling when they whispered in your ear. Not very nice. I believe your transgressions are rather punishable. Do you not agree?"

Huh! He did not go there with accusing me of flirting when he was fucking Vicky Reynolds! I had planned to leave it in the past and see what the future held. But no, Sir!

"*Flirting*, you say? Well, then what is *your* punishment for *fucking*?" I narrow my eyes to glare at him as I jerk my chin from his grasp, then explode. "And is it double for your tryst being with Vicky Reynolds after you tricked me in to going to your rooftop to WITNESS YOU FUCKING HER?!?!"

Malcolm pales and staggers back. His gray eyes bulge, and his mouth drops open. Then he squints his eyes and cocks his head, never taking his eyes from mine. He stalks back to tower over me.

"What are you talking about, Starr?" He asks in a deadly tone.

I blink and step back to put some space between his hulking frame and my smaller one.

He has none of it and moves within inches of me again. The heat radiates off of his body in waves.

"Starr?" He questions; his deep baritone sending a shudder down my spine.

"You heard me, Malcolm!" I retort, recovering from his threatening posture quickly. "Do not attempt to scare me, either, *Enforcer*! You're the one who's wrong here. Not... me!!!"

I deliver the last words with pokes to his solid chest, not that they budge him in any way. But they make me feel stronger. I refuse to cower before him.

"I heard you, but I do not know what you speak about. Give me details, when, where?" Malcolm demands.

Now it's my turn to stagger back, eyes wide, mouth agape.

He doesn't know what I'm talking about? How the hell is that possible?!

I yank my mobile from my clutch and unlock it. My fingers tap with fury on the screen—fury at him, or Vicky, or me, I'm uncertain. Then I shove the mobile in his face.

"Here! See your text for yourself, Malcolm!" I screech.

He takes the mobile from me and reads the text message, once, twice.

It's imprinted on my brain: *Hi Starr. I'm on my way to LA and want to see you. Come by my place at 8 tonight. I'll be on the rooftop.*

Malcolm with an eerie calm hands the mobile back to me.

"I presume you used the code I gave to you to enter my penthouse?" He asks quietly.

When I nod, he continues.

"What did you see when you arrived at the rooftop?" He questions as he stares into the depths of my soul with turbulent gray eyes.

I recount the horrible night...

I walk through to the stairs that lead to the rooftop deck. With a smile on my face, I climb my stairway to heaven. When I open the doors, I almost call out to him. Instead, I stare, a bit confused.

Ahead of me is a naked woman straddling a naked man on a chaise lounge. His back is to me. But she faces my direction. The sounds of her moans and his grunts, their skin slapping skin fill my ears.

My vision tunnels on them. Everything else fades out of view.

I step closer, my mind attempting to process what my eyes see before me and my ears pick up distinctly.

When we're only yards apart, the woman tosses her long blonde mane of wavy hair over her shoulder and pins me with her blue eyes. Her mouth a moment before contorted in a cry of ecstasy now morphs into a wicked smirk.

She leans back and her large breasts bounce from the man's brutal upward thrusts into her pussy. Then she leans forward— never taking her eyes from mine—and cups the man's face. Her red manicured fingernails poke through his ebony waves above the back of the chaise lounge.

"Oh, God, Malcolm, baby! You feel so fucking good! I missed you so much, too!" She cries out.

Blindly, I back away and rush through the door and stumble down the stairs to the elevator, then to my car to careen out of the parking garage...

A deafening roar fills the rooms surrounding us.

I jump as Malcolm detonates. WTF?!?!?!

He storms around the salon ranting and raving, pulling at his hair, and ripping the white tie from his neck.

I stand stock still, shocked by his unusual behavior.

Suddenly he stops, whips his mobile from his trousers pocket, and jabs at the screen.

"Nightingale! Do... it... NOW!!!" Malcolm barks when his call connects.

He keeps his back to me as he places his mobile on the coffee table and slides his hands into his trouser pockets. Then he faces me.

The placid expression on Malcolm's face hides the whirlwind from moments before. His still-wild eyes bore into me as he scans my face. He holds his hand out to me.

My eyes dart over his face to gauge his mindset. In my heart, I know Malcolm would never harm me or anyone. Well, those who don't deserve it, that is...

I keep my eyes on his wild ones while I walk to him and place my hand in his.

A calm settles over Malcolm. His features soften, and his body relaxes, releasing the fury. He squeezes my hand and lifts it to his lips to kiss it gently. Then he leads me to the sofa. He cradles me on his lap and buries his face in my neck. His warm breath tickles my skin.

"I was in Verbier with Roger. I do not know who pretended to be me. But I guarantee you I will find out. The matter is being taken care of as we speak," Malcolm says as he cups my face. "I wondered why you shut us down—"

With a shake of my head, I place my fingertips on his lips. He needs to know all of it. We need to clear the past to make way for our future. A future I know I want with this man.

"I overheard your conversation with Roger in St. Barth's, Malcolm," I start, then continue when he frowns. "When you were on the deck of the villa, you told him you didn't love me, and we were just a thing for now, not ready for marriage."

He moves his lips to speak, but I cut him off again.

"I love you, Malcolm Steele, even if you don't love me. It's impossible to deny my feelings for you any longer. I miss you... us and hope you feel the same. Perhaps not love, yet... But much more than a fuck," I finish as I shrug, resigned to love a man I hope will love me someday.

In a flurry of movement, Malcolm has me over his knees, my head hanging, and my gown bunched around my waist. He slides my G-string down to bind my legs.

THWACK.   THWACK.   THWACK.   THWACK. THWACK.

I buck beneath his punishing blows as he spanks my ass, one cheek after the other, followed by the tops of my thighs and sit bones.

The swift smattering of spanks has me gasping and squirming on his lap, his massive erection pokes my hip. When I squirm almost free, he wraps his arm around my waist and puts his leg over my thighs to rain a sequence of left, right, sit bones, right, left smacks.

I squeal and beg for his forgiveness—and for his dick inside of my sopping wet pussy. My safeword never comes to mind.

Obviously not caring to succumb to my pleas, Malcolm continues until I hang limp, and wetness from my juices coats his trousers. The sight of it draws a groan from deep in his chest.

Malcolm lifts me to straddle his thighs—the cool air swirls around my reddened ass and swollen pussy. He cups my face and kisses me until I feel nothing but erotic elation coursing through every cell of my being.

His chest heaves as much as mine while our tongues tangle. He demands dominance, and I willingly give it to him with a mewl for more.

Malcolm complies readily.

I nearly cum from the sound of his zipper lowering and the rustle of his shirt and boxer briefs moving to free his ginormous cock. A moan slips from my mouth when the cool platinum balls from his Prince Albert piercing brush against my heated pussy lips. His engorged tip seeks the entrance to my core.

My knees widen to spread my thighs, giving him better access.

His dick breaches my folds. One thrust of his hips, and I'm impaled on his incredible girth. The platinum balls graze my G-spot, then press against my womb.

"Aaaahhhh, baby…"

"Fuck yes… So tight, My Angel… Still mine!"

Once my core adjusts to his size, Malcolm grips my hips, fingers digging into my flesh. He lifts me to his tip, then flexes his thighs to snap up and bring me down at the same time.

Shooting stars dance before my closed eyelids as I grip his shoulders to brace myself. So fucking good…

Malcolm sets a controlled tempo of slow and deep stokes. His eyes never leave mine after he commands me to open them and to not look away. His hooded gaze burns with passion.

I'm mesmerized.

He continues his thrusts but refuses my cries for release. His commands of *not yet* set my thighs aquiver and my breath to come in pants.

Malcolm bands his arms around my waist and hoists me into the air with ease to settle me onto my back. His knees brace on the sofa cushions as he leans up to remove his jacket and open the vest and shirt. His mussed hair falls into his eyes as he places his hands on either side of my head to loom over me.

Did I say sexy AF, or what?

His hips go berserk as he pistons in and out of my greedy little pussy, my thighs tight around his hips. Squelching joins his grunts and my moans. He rides me like a thoroughbred stallion, taking his mare in heat.

My fingernails dig into his biceps as I hold on for dear life.

"Cum… for… me… NOW!" Malcolm demands.

The pent-up orgasm rips through me from the top of my head up from the tips of my toes. My back arcs off of the sofa as I throw my head back, my mouth open wide in a silent scream. The muscles of my pussy spasm. My juices gush as Malcolm tweaks my engorged clit.

Another orgasm followed by another has my mind floating in erotic bliss. The sensation of Malcolm's dick expanding then jerking as his hot seed spurts in copious amounts to paint my pussy walls and to fill my womb sends another orgasm through me.

A carnal roar rips from his mouth as he yells through his climax to the ceiling.

The air is rich with the scent of our arousal and the mingling of our perfume and cologne with our natural musk. I inhale deeply and close my eyes to savor this moment.

Sill hard within me, Malcolm lowers his head to my heaving chest. We remain locked in our embrace until our breathing returns to normal.

I brush my fingers through his hair, wanting skin-on-skin contact beyond the intimacy of our groins.

Malcolm lifts his sated gaze to mine.

"Only you, My Angel. No one since, and no one after. I am yours and you are mine," he declares as he holds my chin in his fingers. "I will allow no one to hurt you. Only I will give you pain and know that pleasure will always follow."

I nod, then correct myself and respond with words.

Malcolm caresses my lips with the pad of his thumb.

"I love you, My Angel."

With a contented sigh, I nuzzle against his neck. I guess that answers my question about what he is to me—Malcolm Steele is mine, all mine.

And I am *his* Angel.

MALCOLM

*A*s the sun rises and Paris awakes, I lie in bed and stare at My Angel who sleeps so peacefully. Her lips curl up at the corners when I brush my knuckles along her soft cheek. A soft sigh escapes her mouth at my feather-light kiss.

"You're mine again, Starr Knight—My Angel," I murmur. My eyes never leave her gorgeous face. "I love you."

A smile spreads across my face, pleased to admit the words aloud with ease. At last.

"GOOD MORNING AT LAST, Mr. and Mrs. Roger Steele! So nice of you to join us..."

The cabin explodes with a ruckus of wolf whistles, stomps, and laughter as Roger and Leonie board one of STEELE's Gulfstream G700 private jets. They had us waiting on the tarmac at Le Bourget Airport for twenty minutes. Leonie may be notoriously late, but I have my suspicions for the newlyweds' tardiness.

We're bound for Verbier to celebrate Christmas through

New Year's Day as a family—the Steeles, Beaulieus, and My Angel. Then Roger and Leonie will remain for their honeymoon with The Twins as he planned.

The ultra-plush G700 easily accommodates both our families and staff. The spacious interior boasts the tallest, widest, and longest cabin of all private jets. Its size suits the Steele men and Leonie's father, whose large frames range from six feet, one inches to six feet, four inches.

"Leonie, I'm surprised you were on time to your wedding!"

Lola cracks up at her clever remark.

"Leave the newlyweds alone," Morgan says as he chuckles. "We added a buffer to the flight plan. So, we have plenty of time to spare."

Roger and Leonie thank him and head for Rodolphe and Gaspard. Haley and My Angel hold them playing with colorful rings on their laps. They're seated on the sofa across from where I sit at the table near the center of the large jet.

Roger murmurs in Leonie's ear as he nods towards Starr. Leonie's amber eyes shine as she grins, her gaze darts between My Angel and me.

I ignore their whispers.

"*Bonjour, mes beaux fils*," Leonie coos, as she lifts Rodolphe from My Angel. "And to you too, *mon amie*. Nice to see you spending Christmas with us."

Leonie's eyebrows waggle as she purses her lips.

My Angel attempts to hold in a laugh unsuccessfully. Her kissable dimples deepen as a flush reddens her smooth chestnut complexion.

"Well, the more the merrier. Right, Malcolm?" Roger adds as he scoops Gaspard in his arms.

I roll my eyes and stretch my long legs in front of me with a huff. Fucker.

Roger and Leonie take the fifth living area behind us. They settle The Twins in their car seats, one next to each of them at the dining table.

Everyone has space to enjoy the luxury of a custom-built seventy-five-million-dollar aircraft.

My Angel reaches across the aisle to squeeze my arm and winks.

I bring her hand to my mouth to kiss it. My eyes drift to the diamond-pavé letter S in its platinum mesh center gleams in the sunlight from the oval windows. My collar rests securely on her neck once again. Where it belongs and will forever stay.

We stare at one another and smile as only couples who are in tune can communicate without even speaking. Smiles that say, nothing can bother our love.

Haley smirks.

"Yeah, I gave Haley and Lola my AMEX Centurion Card to buy everything Leonie will need for our winter honeymoon —ski gear, après-ski, clubbing. Plus an entire wardrobe to leave here. Based on the walk-in dressing room, they splurged... Shelley and Josy bought everything for The Twins. So that will preoccupy them for a while," Roger says, shaking his head.

Women and clothes. Good grief.

Although I must admit I take great selfish pleasure in buying lingerie for My Angel, particularly from Lola's Coterie. My sister-in-law's luxury lingerie, loungewear, and evening wear company makes the most delightful little pieces. Wait until My Angel sees her closet in our room.

As soon as we arrive and walk into the great room with its magnificent Christmas tree, Leonie's mother declares we'll spend every Christmas and New Year's here. "One big happy family," Shelley claps in agreement.

Roger gives us the grand tour of their new residence Leonie named *Chalet de la Joie* since the home will bring everyone such joy to spend family holidays here.

The girls head to the primary bedroom and nursery.

The rest of our family migrate to different areas of the chalet. Our parents choose babysitting duties, or as they say, "important bonding time with their grandsons." So their nanny retired to her suite of rooms above the garage.

My brothers and I stand in the garage to check out the new snow toys he ordered. We take the snowmobiles out before we meet back up for an early dinner with a meal prepared by one chef from STEELE Verbier.

When we return, I shoot a text message to My Angel to ask her whereabouts in the massive house. Moments later, I stride into our room with my hair disheveled from the cap and my olive-toned cheeks reddened by the icy mountain air. My eyes dance when I see her stretched out in a red silk and lace teddy with matching G-string on the furry rug in front of a roaring fire.

In no time, I strip and prowl over to her. Stalking my prey.

My Angel squeals when I burrow my face between her thighs to nip at their apex. The stubble on my cheeks rasps her sensitive skin.

I slide the string aside and plunge my tongue and two middle fingers inside her wet pussy. The walls flutter as she squirms from the stretching of her inner muscles so quickly. Unceasing licks and suckling on her clit along with my fingers stroking her G-spot send My Angel spiraling over the edge.

Once.

Twice.

Three times.

A trial of open-mouthed kisses leads me to her succulent brown nipples. I take my time to pay homage to her full tits until she climaxes again. I grip her hips and flip her onto her knees—ass high, head low—and sink my turgid length balls deep into her still-quivering pussy.

Then ride My Angel until she screams and begs for no more. I thank the architect for soundproofing the bedroom suites.

* * *

"LAST ONE DOWN!" I yell as I—like Roger before me—race past Leonie towards the finish.

It's Christmas Eve morning and we're out en masse for an early morning run. My Angel—who I just zipped past—the entire Steele clan, and Beaulieus make our way from the top of the mountain piste to the base lodge. It's a popular time to come out, so other skiers bob and weave around us.

I laugh at My Angel and Leonie muttering and tuck to bullet my way down the piste. My movements unrestricted by my white and green Bogner ski suit. I bob my head covered by a green helmet and mirrored googles over my eyes.

"That was incredible!" My Angel exclaims when she reaches the base lodge.

One by one, everyone arrives. Our ski butlers help us remove our equipment and hand us our heated après-ski hats, sunglasses, and footwear.

My Angel loops arms with her friend, and they follow our group inside for a hearty breakfast on the deck kept warm by heat lamps. As we walk through the great room of the lodge, we wave at friends who happen to be on holiday in Verbier, too. It's a popular destination for the low-key of the chichi crowd.

"So what's the plan for the rest of the day?" Harris asks as he piles his plate high with eggs, bacon, sausages, and toast from the table laden with delicious food and steaming beverages.

We turn to Roger *The Responsible*—always prepared. He claps his hands like a group excursions guide. Leonie giggles at a private joke.

"Yes, my darling wife, we will have loads of fun! We'll go for another run, then return to the chalet. Shower and change to stroll through the village with The Twins. Take in the sights and do gift buying for those who are always last minute…"

Roger raises an eyebrow at Harris, who shrugs.

"That may be true. However, I always have the best presents. This year, you'll get coal in your stocking if you keep it up, big bro," he retorts as he takes another giant bite of his food.

Everyone laughs and digs in.

"It's just so beautiful here! Usually, we go to Aspen."

My Angel says as we meander through Verbier Village for its bustling Christmas market.

The cloves and spices of mulled wine mix with baked goods like bredele, semi-sweet cakes, pretzels, and macarons to scent the crisp air. Carolers dressed in costumes stroll through the aisles singing cheerfully and ringing bells. Vendors fill their stalls with handcrafted music boxes and toys, knit sweaters, scarves, and gloves, and candles and ornaments.

"The festive atmosphere fills me with such joy!" She continues with a sparkling smile.

I lean over and kiss her lush lips, then pull the bottom one with my teeth.

"I'm glad you like it, My Angel. Verbier has the best off-piste trails, so more expert skiers choose the town. The après-ski partying is just as attractive as the slopes. We'll take advantage of both."

She grins up at me as she squeezes my arm.

"Let's find the others, then get back to the chalet. I have plans for you and that syrup you bought..." I tell her with a smirk.

We catch up with Roger, Leonie, The Twins, Sebastian—similarly laden with shopping bags—and Lola who's squatting in front of the stroller. My Angel replaces her as she chats with Rodolphe and Gaspard.

Roger and Sebastian laugh out loud. I smirk.

AFTER RETURNING FROM THE MARKET, we add our new gifts to the already vast number beneath and around the tree's base. The colorful boxes of all shapes and sizes fill the space. Harris winks at us and adds more.

We're gathered in the great room with a blazing fire in the sizable stone hearth. Mariah Carey's "All I Want for Christmas Is You" plays in the background from my favorite Christmas playlist. The classic songs of Nat King Cole, Johnny Mathis, Céline Dion, Gladys Knight and the Pips, Frank Sinatra, and of course the Trans-Siberian Orchestra.

The chef prepared steaming mugs of delicious hot chocolate and mulled wine for us to enjoy with the tasty morsels we bought.

In keeping with the French tradition, we unwrap two presents each on Christmas Eve and the rest tomorrow before we partake of le *Réveillon de Noël* for the Christmas meal. The dishes include Beluga caviar, foie gras, oysters, lobster, scallops, fresh truffles, roast goose, venison, and cheeses. We end with the paramount French Christmas dessert *la bûche de Noël*—the Yule log. All the while, a selection of wines and champagne please our palates.

To incorporate a Steele clan tradition, we move to the cinema room to watch *It's a Wonderful Life*. I settle My Angel between my thighs on the suede chaise lounge with popcorn to enjoy the film.

"What do you want from Santa this year, Little One?" I growl in her ear.

She shivers and whispers, "Only you, Sir."

I chuckle wickedly.

Yeah, it's a brilliant start to the holidays. Like Josy, I look forward to making Verbier our traditional gathering spot, especially with My Angel on my lap.

* * *

STARR

Lola, Leonie, Haley, and I finished a few runs and kick back on chaises at the base lodge deck sipping hot cocoa.

Malcolm and his brothers skied off-piste on Chassoure, as the locals call it, or Tortin to everyone else. It's one of the most challenging runs in Verbier and well-known in the ski world. The terrain and the level of difficulty concerned me, so I bowed out of going with him. But for his safety, he assured me they would take precautions with a trail guide, and each of them set with high-tech tracking devices and satellite phones.

In fact, all of us wear the gadgets and carry the mobiles whenever we're on the mountain slopes.

Still, I told Malcolm we just reunited, and I don't want to lose him again!

He promised me they'd be perfectly safe and would meet

us back at the chalet later. After a mind-blowing kiss, he spanked my ass and strode from our room. Always My Dom…

But damn if juices didn't saturate my pussy and my nipples pebble. Yeah, I can't wait for my virile caveman to return.

Leonie's loud singing draws me from my musings.

We're on a Girls' Day Out of good friends, laughter, and plain ole silliness!

"What's going on?" I ask as I lean forward from her chaise.

Lola hesitates for only a moment. A giant smile breaks out on her face, and the gold flecks in her hazel eyes glitter more than the bright sun. She launches into the details of her conversation about having a baby with Sebastian. Afterwards, she stares at Haley and me pointedly.

"So, who's next? Hmmm? Lachlan… Malcolm… Do not consider for one second we haven't noticed signs and sexual tension between you guys!" Lola says, waggling her perfectly shaped eyebrows. "Don't even try to deny it."

"Yeah! Sparks were zipping amongst you at my wedding from the rehearsal dinner through the reception," Leonie adds, tossing her mahogany mane, daring us to dispute the obvious.

Shy Haley flushes crimson while I glance away, flustered.

Lola and Leonie rag on us some more, but all in good fun. We make a bet on who will come back next Christmas with whom. Included in the lineup are Luc and Blair and Billie and Patrick. Both couples showed their affection for one another openly during the nuptials.

"Well, Starr's already in this year and Malcolm is not one to bring women around at all," Lola says. "In over two years, I've never seen him with anyone seriously. But you had him disconcerted the morning after my wedding."

Leonie agrees.

"I know. But I'm not sure if I'm ready to get involved with anyone, and I've been putting him off for quite some time now," I admit. With a sigh, I tell them about our difficulties and how we seem to be better for now. I'm staying positive and letting fate take us where we're meant to be.

They offer words of advice and encouragement.

"And you, miss?" Leonie asks.

"Right... What's your story, morning glory?" Lola chimes in as we turn to Haley.

Normally she would push her glasses up her nose, but she's taken to wearing contact lenses recently. She says it's better for her peripheral vision. So instead, she pushes her mirrored Ray-Ban Aviators to rest better on the bridge.

Not one of Haley's big brothers would appreciate Lachlan getting involved with their baby sister. Particularly Sebastian since he and Lachlan are best friends and Baz knows he's an Alpha Dom. Malcolm told me the idea of his little sister being a sub to Lachlan makes him want to finish him, cousin or not.

Even though they refer to the Jackson siblings as their cousins, there's no blood relationship—only their mothers being BFFs for decades. So technically, the boys should stay out of it—if an it exists truly.

The girls and I think Haley and Lachlan make a cute couple—shy, curvy Haley and movie-star-looks, dominating Lachlan.

"What's so funny, Leonie?" Haley asks self-consciously.

Leonie waves her hand and responds, "Thinking about your overbearing brothers. Better you than me!"

Haley shakes her head and purses her lips. She fills us in on her latest escapades with Cary Grant lookalike Lachlan.

"Speak of the devils... Look who shows up now. I

thought they were meeting us at the chalet," Lola says, nodding towards the entrance.

As Haley finishes, and we were ready to dive deep with an analysis and strategic plan, the boys walk out onto the deck.

Every woman's head turns to gawk at them—young and old alike.

They're like a pack of Alpha males whose high testosterone levels call to every women's womb with an aching need to be pounded and filled by them. The STEELE Quaternity live and in full effect.

I'm overcome by the urge to jump up and yell, "Malcolm Steele is mine!" So I guess I'm more ready than I thought.

All of us but Haley salivate at the sight of them. She groans and throws her head back against her chaise in annoyance at the interruption of her relationship advice session.

"Give me a fucking break already," she mutters.

Malcolm tilts my head back and takes my mouth in a possessive kiss.

Yup, he's got me good! My Dom-cum-boyfriend sexy AF Malcolm Steele.

* * *

MALCOLM

"Dude, you need to open a LEVELS Verbier. Ski in, ski out style! A little action on the slopes and in the playrooms."

Harris says as we take shots of Oval Vodka.

We hit all the hot spots leading up to New Year's Eve since we'll celebrate it at the chalet. The other night we went to Farm Club Verbier, the dance and nightclub famous since the early 70s. It's maintained its popularity for decades, symbolized by its glamorous vibe and great reputation. It's like the Studio 54 of Verbier—if the walls could talk.

My Angel and I made the bathroom walls talk—or rather scream—when I pounded into her, braced against the vanity. Her sequin mini dress rode up her toned thighs as they gripped my hips. She threw her head back, calling my name on repeat. Ah, such sweet music to my ears.

Tonight it's Public Verbier, the swanky spot and counterpart to Public London.

"You know, that's not a bad idea," Sebastian adds, slamming his glass down with a smile next to the Swarovski crystal bottle of vodka. "Of all the clubs we've partied at, none can compare to LEVELS. Bring the heat to the Alps!"

"Yeah, spoken like a true Alpha Dom," Roger chuckles.

Baz's laughter rings out. He's been in an exceptional mood.

"I can see that being a profitable possibility. Surprising how a tech geek can think beyond code," I rib Harris good-naturedly.

Yet, he's still an Alpha male, who like the rest of his brothers seeks release within the LEVELS clubs.

I continue thoughtfully, "We can take over one property near the hotel and close by the other clubs for accessibility. I'll run it by Lucien tomorrow, thanks."

We fist bump, and everyone downs another round of shots.

Our server appears with an assortment of finger foods including Russian pancakes with Beluga caviar, marinated mushrooms, and cheddar olives. The leggy blonde bends over the table to reach for my plate, nearly spilling her ample tits out her top.

Nope, not gonna happen. I ignore her and carry on my conversation with Baz.

She lingers to throw a meaningful glance Harris' way. Then leaves satisfied he made plans with her.

"Obviously you're doing all right without the play-rooms," Roger says, smirking.

Harris sits back and plants his feet wide on the floor, spreading his arms along the back of the booth.

With a smug expression he responds, "You could say so. I'll have some not so little action tonight."

I lift my shot glass in a toast, "Here's to ski in and ski out, my brothers!"

"Hear, hear!"

"Abso-fucking-lutely!"

"You can say that again, bro!"

We raise our glasses and toss back the vodka shots.

Leonie slides up behind Roger and whispers in his ear. With her off of the dance floor makes me glance around for My Angel. They must finish shaking their asses.

"Come bump and grind with me, Sir."

I grin as my cock twitches at My Little One's seductive purr in my ear.

Time to take our club sexcapades to the dance floor or bathroom…

* * *

STARR

"What did you and Sebastian get up to today?"

Lola, Leonie, Haley, and I stretch out in the chalet's spa sauna before our deep-tissue massages start. Ninety-minute of pure decadence.

As a treat, Malcolm arranged for a Girls' Spa Day with masseuses and aestheticians from the hotel's facility to pamper us prior to our New Year's Eve dinner and party. He said we were good girls and deserved special goodies.

Haley and Leonie rolled their eyes at the "good girls" part. But Lola and I grinned from ear-to-ear. My Dom-cum-boyfriend is so sweet!

I'm grateful for the treats. Between Malcolm's marathon lovemaking—"to compensate for lost time"—and the rigors of skiing, tobogganing, and ice skating, my muscles need a rubdown.

"Oh, a little bit of this and a little bit of that," she hedges.

I shake my head, causing long, curly tendrils to escape my messy topknot. As I tuck them back in to the Scünci, I laugh.

"What kind of evasive answer is that?" I ask. "What exactly does that entail?"

Lola giggles and waggles her eyebrows.

"Well, if you'd prefer all the details... Sebastian bound my arms and legs to the four bedposts with red silk cords—"

"Uh, no, thank you!"

"TMI!"

"Girl! Not all of those details! Please!"

Lola's giggles turn into snorts as she doubles over, cracking up. Her hazel eyes twinkle with mischief when she lifts her gaze. The petite firecracker strikes with her sex tales again.

"Okay, okay! I mean, you did ask for it!" She starts. "After a morning of multiple orgasms, we went ice skating. Boy, when I tell you my legs were wobbly—"

Haley throws a towel at Lola's head and she ducks, laughing hysterically.

"Lola!! I do not care to hear of my brother's sex life!" Haley shouts. "And that goes for the two of you, too. Not interested in the least."

Leonie and I exchange looks, then throw towels at her. Lola grabs the one Haley threw and tosses it back at her. We end up laughing and exchanging our tales for the day, minus the sex scenes.

A gentle knock on the sauna's door draws our attention. A masseuse reminds us it's time, so we troop out to rinse off.

Aside from the sauna and showers, the spa accommodates a steam room, plunge pools for hot and cold therapies, a tranquility lounge, and four of each manicure stations, pedicure chairs, and treatment rooms. We settle in the rooms for our sessions.

The rejuvenating massages put us in even higher spirits when we reemerge. They added a body polish treatment, so our skin glows and feels like satin. The warm oil soothed my achy body and added to the softness.

The aestheticians help us into the pedicure chairs first. We gab some more while they set to our feet and hands. The start of a new year excites everyone. We're ready to leave all the drama behind and to begin anew!

"So, who's the bonnie Scotsman with Haley?"

I ask Leonie and nod towards the other side of the wine cellar.

She glances at me before she turns to the cuddled-up couple.

"Well, don't you look fabulous, darling!" Leonie tells me.

I feel super sexy in a slinky metallic lamé brown and gold wrap-effect mini dress. My long, toned legs end in brown sky-high sandals with gold serpentine metal straps wrapped around my ankles. The long curls of my chocolate-colored hair frame my heart-shaped face, the dimples pop as I giggle.

"You remind me of Christie Doll, Barbie's friend!" Leonie laughs.

"Why thank you! We're hot babes, huh?" I respond.

"Very hot indeed."

Leonie and I startle at the unexpected gruff voice of Malcolm. He chuckles and strokes the five o'clock stubble on his chin. His eyes rove up and down my body as I shift from one foot to the other.

He ignites a passion deep inside of me with one word or a glance.

Leonie laughs and pats his shoulder as she makes a fast exit. Our erotic energy pulsating between us, too hot for her to handle.

We're enjoying pre-dinner cocktails with our families and friends, including some we meet up with on holiday. The bartender and sommelier for STEELE Verbier crafted a selection of drinks and wines for our dinner and party.

"Is your shiny new gift still in place, Little One?" My Dom asks with a raised eyebrow.

"Yes, Sir," I answer as I flex my ass muscles around the platinum butt plug with its sapphire—for its faithfulness and sincerity—embedded base.

"Excellent, Little One. You will receive another gift if you are a good girl," he murmurs in my ear as he pats my butt cheek.

A shudder passes through me and threatens to undo the plug. I gasp and squeeze tight.

My Dom smirks, "Good girl. Do not allow your gift to slip out. I want your ass ready for my ten inches at the *stroke* of midnight."

THE DJ from Farm Club spins a range of music perfect for everyone.

We party it up in the disco next to the wine cellar. The set up works well with people moving seamlessly from the bar to the dance floor or the banquettes along the walls. A gigantic screen shows scenes of countries around the world celebrating the start of the New Year with Sydney, Australia first.

Malcolm twirls me, then pulls me close. He buries his nose in my hair as I drape my arms over his shoulder. We move as one, allowing the past to fade away with each move we make.

A piercing whistle blasts, and we turn to see Sebastian on a raised platform with one arm around Lola and the other beckoning to Leonie and Roger. Then Sebastian raises his champagne flute.

"Before midnight strikes, I want to congratulate my brother on his new bride and darling Twins, my new sister and nephews. We love you all. Steeles for life!"

Everyone claps and stomps with more wolf whistles.

Roger picks Leonie up and swings her around before dipping her and kissing her silly.

The DJ calls for more champagne with five minutes to go.

Earlier, Harris angled the exterior cameras toward Verbier Village and relayed the footage to the screen. Now, he switches the feed, and the live view appears for the countdown clock and fireworks display.

As the lights dim for the countdown, My Dom guides me from the disco and to one of the many rooms on this level of the supersized chalet.

"Ready to make our own New Year's fireworks, Little One?" He rumbles, his eyes hooded with carnal need.

I spin to face away from him, wiggle my ass, and toss my hair to glance over my shoulder then purr, "Yes, Sir… Happy New Year…"

STARR

"Baby, you're my best Dom boyfriend!"

My other gift for being a good girl is a surprise trip to Laucala Island, the private retreat in Fiji.

We flew from Verbier to New York City for a walk down Fifth Avenue to see the Christmas lights and the Rockefeller Center tree. Gazing down from Malcolm's penthouse terrace on the fifty-third floor of The STEELE Tower to the giant crystal snowflake star above Fifty-seventh Street and Fifth Avenue was a highlight.

After two days of ice skating at Rock Center, store window gazing, and making love, Malcolm had us back on his private jet.

I thought headed to Beverly Hills when we landed at LAX. But no, it was a fuel stopover. He refused to tell me our destination even when I threatened to deny him access to my body.

Well, my sore ass and pussy say otherwise. My Dom's spanks and strokes won me over to his way of thinking in no time…

"You mean your *only* Best Dom Boyfriend," Malcolm growls, eyeing me briefly.

I lean over to kiss his cheek as he drives the golf cart along the frangipani-lined path to our cliffside villa. Then inhale the luscious floral scent as I shift in my seat to take in the island's extraordinary view.

The sparkling, cyan-colored South Pacific Ocean reaches the horizon. The hues range from the darkest to the lightest blues and greens so varied in depth captivate me. Nearby verdant islands with rings of coral rise from the ocean.

Gulls and terns hover over the waves while shadows of fish schools appear below the crystal-clear surface. The birds swoop in and out of the water to catch their meals.

Malcolm removed the canvas roof before we hopped into the golf cart. I tilt my head back to gaze at the cloudless, blue sky. The sun beams down on us. My bare shoulders and arms appreciate its warmth. Such a welcome 180-degree change from the cold of Switzerland and New York!

"Glad to be back, My Angel?" Malcolm asks.

I grin from ear to ear.

"Absolutely! It's divine! Have you ever been here?" I ask. When he shakes his head, I continue. "Oh! You'll love it. I can't wait to show you the rain forest and the white sandy beaches!"

I prattle on until we stop in front of the villa.

When I was here for my retreat two years ago, I stayed at a beachfront villa. It was spectacular. But this villa and its views are breathtaking!

A butler, chef, and maid greet us as we step from the golf cart. The butler gives us a tour while the maid unpacks our belongings. The chef explains he stocked the refrigerator and prepared a light meal for our arrival. Back at the entrance, they smile and leave us. The staff is present at our call only, so we can enjoy complete privacy.

"What shall we do first, Sir?" I purr glancing up at My Dom through my eyelashes.

"That swing facing the ocean appears the best place to begin our holiday," he responds. His hooded gaze travels from my pink-painted toes up my bare legs, past my strapless romper to linger on my lips. "Strip."

Without hesitation, I rip my clothes and sandals off. My hands grasp my elbows behind my back, and my feet widen. With my head bowed, my long curls skim the bottoms of my heaving breasts. Eager to play on the swing, my breath quickens.

My Dom tsks as he sweeps my hair behind my back and braids it.

"Never cover your tantalizing tits from my sight, Little One," he chides me. "Understand?"

An unexpected whack to my ass makes me jump and gasp. My mind distracted by the scent of his cologne and the sensation of his thick fingers in my hair delayed my answer.

"Y-y-yes, Sir!" I yelp rising to my toes from the impact of his palm on my butt cheek.

My Dom chuckles wickedly, "Come."

I follow him back through the villa to the rear terrace overlooking the Pacific Ocean. Its natural splendor extends for miles. I sigh, content to be miles from the bustle of our lives.

My Dom takes my hand and helps me to sit on the cushion of the rope swing. It hangs from a palm tree surrounded by more frangipani shrubs. The white flowers symbolize Fiji and remind me of my previous tropical vacation each time I smell them.

To position me to his specifications, My Dom places my

hands on either side of the swing at shoulder height with my fingers wrapped around the ropes. Next he pushes me back gently as he tells me to put my butt on the edge.

I take a deep breath when he steps back and undresses.

Each garment comes off with slow, precise movements. Saliva fills my mouth at the sight of his sculpted chest and the feathered line of dark hair from below his belly button to his trimmed pubic hair. I have to swallow as his massive dick springs free from his shorts and boxer briefs. The platinum balls glint in the sunlight.

A shiver runs through me at the memory of them rubbing my inner walls just right each and every time. My pussy creams.

My Dom notices and chuckles again. His eight-pack abs ripple.

Damn!

He stands before me and grips the base of his cock. Slow, long strokes followed by a tug draw a pearl of pre-cum from his swollen tip. He uses the pad of his thumb to smooth the delicacy around his piercing.

How I'd rather it were my tongue.

To show My Dom, I poke the tip between my lips and curve it up to brush against the top one. A moan escapes.

My Dom's eyes narrow as a growl rumbles from his chest—now rising and falling in sync with mine.

"Want a lick, Naughty Girl?" He asks in tone sultrier than the humid air surrounding us.

"Yes, please, Sir," I reply with an eager nod and full-on lip lick.

He stalks closer and places his hands on either side of my hips to steady the swing. I entwine my legs with his muscular ones and bend at the waist.

My mouth engulfs his dick from tip to mid-shaft. Yum…

He groans at the dual sensation of my hot, wet mouth

and my small fist around the rest of his girth. My other hand kneads his heavy balls.

"You will suck me, Naughty Girl. Every. Single. Inch," My Dom grinds out. "Suck. Me. Well."

I hum in pleasure.

My tongue performs acrobatics on his shaft. Swoops, circles, laves, twirls. All to bring him erotic ecstasy.

His cock swells and pulsates.

"Enough," My Dom commands as he grips my braid, and his dick pops from my mouth. "Give me your pussy, Little One. I want your slick heat wrapped around my cock. Now."

I pout because giving him head gives me power. I love to see My Dom with jelly knees when he spills his seed down my throat.

But I comply because nothing compares to the feel of his dick filling my weeping pussy to capacity. I lean back again, then unwrap my legs from his and spread them wide. The heady scent of my arousal mingles with the frangipani.

"Fuck, you're beautiful, My Angel," Malcolm says slipping into boyfriend mode.

He dips his head to place his nose against my dripping folds and inhales with a groan. When he stands, he grips the swing and aligns his erection with my gaping hole. The swing jerks forward to impale me on his dick.

"FUCK!!!" We cry in unison.

Once my inner walls adjust to his length and girth, Malcolm pushes the swing backwards. I arc through the air, then close my eyes as the pendulum reverses.

He rolls his hips against me, filling me with his cock to the root.

"So good, My Angel," Malcolm says in my ear gruffly.

We continue our adult playtime until I'm panting from

multiple toe-curling orgasms and a sheen of sweat glistens on our skin.

"Give me one more, Little One," My Dom returns to make demands of my body.

A demand I give in to happily.

A final arc brings me home, and an all-encompassing orgasm overtakes me. My pussy spasms around My Dom's massive ten inches and showers it with my juices. They run down the crack of my ass to pool beneath me on the already-soaked cushion.

"MALCOLM!!!" I wail as my body convulses.

Now it's his turn.

He lifts my limp body from the swing. Automatically, I drape my arms over his shoulders and wrap my legs around his hips. His fingers dig into the fleshiest parts of my ass, and he pistons his hips.

Malcolm's feral caveman grunts and growls punctuate each deep thrust.

Another climax rocks my world, and I scream his name.

He responds with my name—a howl to the sky—as his dick expands, then jerks his seed inside of my wrecked pussy. Malcolm lowers to his knees. He continues slow strokes in and out of me as he suckles my nipples until our minds return from our carnal trance.

"Welcome to paradise, My Angel," Malcolm murmurs as he lays his head against my breast.

* * *

WE STRETCH out in the sunken tub on our villa's veranda to soak our sore muscles—nothing beats aftercare with My Dom lover. Five days of hiking through the rain forest, scuba diving, and the pleasurable rigors of marathon lovemaking fade away. And each one makes me love this man even more.

Malcolm is so attentive and loving. The words *I love you, My Angel* flow from his mouth with ease. From the moment we reconnected in Verbier, he's made it his mission to make up for the time we spent apart.

I relish in every second of it. Just like now.

It feels fantastic to lean back against Malcolm's solid chest and allow the fragrant essential oils—amplified by the warmth of the water—lull us into a peaceful state. The sounds of the ocean waves lapping against the rocky cliff mesmerizes us.

"Ready to return to reality tomorrow?" He asks.

I sigh and shake my head.

The soapy sponge he smooths up from my lower belly to the hollow between my breasts as he bathes me makes me wish we never have to leave.

Malcolm chuckles and nuzzles my neck, pulling me tighter in his embrace.

"I'd rather stay too. But duty calls for both of us," he says wistfully.

Water sloshes onto the stones as I turn to straddle his powerful thighs. I cup his face with my palms and press my forehead and nose against his. We share each other's breath for a peaceful moment.

"Fine. But promise me we'll come back," I tell him.

He grips my hips and lifts before lowering me onto his throbbing cock. When his groin meets my ass, he sighs.

"I promise, My Angel."

MALCOLM

"All rise... This court is now in session. The Honorable Judge Dixon presiding."

From my peripheral vision, I see Vicky stand with her legal team. She smooths the skirt of her conservative navy blue suit, then adjusts the headband holding back her blonde hair.

When My Angel, her parents, Sebastian, Harris, Haley, and I arrived with my legal team, Vicky glanced over her shoulder at us. Fire filled her cornflower blue eyes as she glared at my hand interlocked with Starr's then at me.

Now Vicky pulls on her acting skills for the performance of an innocent young woman.

Fuck that. I have to suppress the snarl in my chest. Keep it together, Steele. This shit will be over soon enough.

At the call to order, the hum of voices and sounds of shuffled papers quiet. Everyone stands for Judge Susan Dixon's entrance.

Part two of Nightingale begins. Game on.

The hearing starts with an opening statement presented

by Judge Dixon as a summary of the trespassing claim and the parties involved.

I'm suing the hell out of Victoria Anne Reynolds. For the last time, this bird is going to learn to not fuck with My Angel and me. She damn near ruined my chance for happiness.

Obviously it wasn't me she was fucking on my penthouse rooftop terrace. The security footage revealed the mystery man as Dante Rossi, the new concierge for my apartment building—a STEELE International residential property. Who happens to resemble me in hair color and body build.

Vicky seduced him for access to my penthouse for her grand scheme of hurting My Angel and ending us. Vicky led Rossi to believe she was interested in him. Starstruck, he fell for it. After a couple of weeks, she persuaded him to show her the nighttime view of Sunset Strip from my terrace.

Gullible, he used the passcode security keeps for emergencies to enter my penthouse's private elevator. Once on the rooftop, Vicky instigated sex on the chaise lounge angled with his back to the access door. She put on an Oscar-worthy performance when My Angel stepped onto the terrace as depicted in the security camera's lens.

The expression of raw pain on her face nearly undid me. My Angel looked as though someone ripped her beating heart from her chest and squeezed it before her eyes. The anguish was so intense she stumbled down the stairs and to the elevator. She sped through the garage and out to the street. Her sobs still echo in my ears. Damn that bird!

I clench my fists on my thighs as the judge finishes.

Engelbert Douglass—my lead attorney—presents my case. He plays the security footage from the time Vicky entered the garage to the time My Angel drove away. Afterwards, he calls Rossi to the witness stand where he spills his guts. Poor sucker.

The lead attorney for Vicky cross-exams Rossi. He doesn't waiver in his previous testimony. But he agrees he was wrong in giving Vicky access to my property. The attorney doesn't have much to smirch Rossi. As a STEELE employee—now former—he went through an extensive background check and proved spotless. The attorney ends his questioning.

Next Douglass calls My Angel to the stand to testify.

I want to grab her in my embrace to shield her from Vicky's bullshit. Pride wells in my chest when My Angel strides to the stand confidently. I also can't help but appreciate the sway of her hips in her dress and how her heels lift her lush ass just so…

Once she's settled in the chair, she flicks her gaze to Vicky, then to Douglass.

"Ms. Knight, kindly share for Judge Dixon what led you to Mr. Steele's penthouse rooftop terrace on the night in question," Douglass says.

My Angel maintains her composure as she recounts from the text message through Vicky's words during the sex to her return to the garage. Her nostrils flare when she glances back at Vicky as she finishes her testimony.

Douglass provides the judge and the opposing counsel with copies of her cell phone records. Then yields the floor to Vicky's attorney.

He attempts to discredit My Angel. But being the daughter of brilliant legal eagles, she avoids any pitfall he puts before her. I can sense their pride in her as they sit behind my table. When it's apparent her testimony is irrefutable, the attorney ends his cross-examination, albeit begrudgingly.

When he returns to his seat beside Vicky, she whispers

to him fervently. He shakes his head, and she gesticulates as she raises her voice. He tries to calm her, but she's not hearing it.

"Get your client under control, counselor," Judge Dixon warns with her eyebrow arched in reproach. "I am prepared to issue my summary judgement."

"Apologies, your Hon—"

"Wait one minute! Malcolm Steele is a liar! He's trying to ruin my fucking life! My film deals ended... Clothing contracts canceled... He beat me... He... He tied me up—"

Bam! Bam! Bam!

"Silence your client, counselor! Now!" Commands Judge Dixon as she slams her gavel with a frown.

"Order in the court! Order in the court!" The bailiff demands.

The room explodes with Vicky's wild rantings of BDSM, torture, lies, bullshit. Her madness pisses the judge off, and she calls for counsel in her chambers.

Two other members of Vicky's legal team escort her still screaming from the courtroom. Once they leave, the room is silent.

I shift in my seat to face My Angel and the others. Her sorrel brown eyes dance as she grins. Baz smirks and nods his head. I sigh, relieved she's not mad at me.

"Well, Ms. Reynolds was entertaining..." Harris snorts. "I wouldn't pay to see her though."

Haley giggles at her twin's dry wit.

"I know Judge Dixon. She's fair and will not allow that woman's unsubstantiated claims to interfere with her judge-ment. They're irrelevant to this hearing," Peace says while Sun nods in agreement.

"Not at all," she says.

My eyes never leave My Angel, and she reaches over the

railing for my hand. I smile and clasp her dainty hand between my larger ones.

"You did well, My Angel. How are you?" I ask.

Her grin broadens.

"Fine! I just can't wait to smudge everyone when we leave that woman's toxic presence!" My Angel quips.

Everyone laughs, and the tense moment passes.

Douglass returns to the table. Vicky's team agreed to a monetary settlement with me and extended the original three-year civil harassment orders to five years. To ensure she doesn't have time to fuck with us, Judge Dixon added options for five additional years to protect My Angel and me. The seven figures will go to STEELE Foundation.

Our mother Shelley runs our family's foundation that builds and manages attractive, affordable housing for urban, lower-income families. The name is a play on the house foundation, being strong and supportive like steel. Appropriate since Vicky broke into my home she'll pay for others' homes.

When a subdued Vicky and her legal team return, Judge Dixon re-enters the courtroom.

She announces her summary judgement as Douglass informed us and ends the hearing with one more strike of her gavel.

I can sense Vicky's glacial glare from across the aisle. A glance at her face makes a cold band of iron squeeze my heart. Such blatant hate surprises me. A shiver races down my spine.

A hand pressed into mine draws me from the chilly abyss of Vicky's blue orbs. I look down into My Angel's warm gaze and shake off the morose gloom that permeates my soul.

"Let's go, baby," she smiles as she tugs my hand.

I ignore Vicky's ire and leave the courtroom, fingers locked with My Angel's again.

Peace and Sun and my legal team head for their respective offices. The rest of us go to my penthouse.

"Thank fuck that's over with quickly. We've had enough with the courtroom drama between you and Roger. Give it rest for a while, will you?" Sebastian sighs as he sips his Jackson Reserve Scotch.

"Hear, hear!" Harris agrees, raising his Baccarat crystal snifter. "Moving on, fellas!"

I nod and take a sip from my glass, then hug My Angel closer to my side on the sofa. She rests her head on my shoulder, and I kiss her curly top.

"Not that I want to hear about your sex life—never! But her accusations concern me. Especially given the situation with Roger and that other hussy. We don't need another he-said-she-said situation to arise later," Haley says.

"I have videos of our sexual encounters and her signed contract for her consent, including the taping," I respond. "That's standard for any sub relationship I've had. No chance for misinterpretation."

My Angel stiffens in my arms and leans back to look at me.

"You record us, too?" She asks with wide eyes. "I don't recall—"

I place my finger on her lips and shake my head.

"You're the only one I have never recorded. Well, except for—"

My Angel claps her hands over my mouth, shaking her head vigorously. She looks at my siblings, horrified I'll disclose our private activities.

Baz chuckles while Haley sings with her fingers in her ears.

"Bro… Messy Malcolm!" Harris guffaws.

* * *

It's been a month since the hearing—Nightingale Part II—and no disturbances from Vicky.

Nightingale Part I...

Ruin her acting career: video surfaced of her disparaging remarks on her co-stars, crews, industry heavy hitters led to every top agent, producer, director refusing to hire her.

Destroy her paid endorsements: documentation of her lies and manipulative behavior goes against the clean-reputation clause of her contracts.

End her sexual partnerships: her medical record of STI treatments circulated on the Internet.

They don't call me *The Enforcer* for nothing. I handle bullshit my way. Just like I did for Roger that gold digger Delia Fucking Shaw.

I returned to New York City a week after the hearing. Working from STEELE Los Angeles makes it easy for the bicoastal relationship with My Angel. Although I'm encouraging her to open Starr Light Fitness & Wellness New York.

She's hesitant to take on more than one at a time since Cabo San Lucas is under construction and St. Barth's just opened its doors—doing extremely well, in fact. With Monte Carlo on the list next, she wonders if New York should come before it.

I say, hell yeah!

The expansion to Jackson Hole at STEELE Resorts for her international retreats also proves popular. Not only her regular clients attend, but wellness buffs from around the world bringing new guests to our resorts. Those who happen to be at the properties for their holidays tend to join the classes since they receive the schedule at check-in.

The new revenue stream impresses STEELE CEO Sebastian. He's given the green light for any future SLFW projects. My Entertainment Properties Division continues to surpass expectations.

My Angel laughs that the media coverage from the Vicky situation boosted SLFW and her social media followers and e-newsletter subscribers.

I follow her channels to watch the yoga videos she posts. Damn if she's not the most flexible little thing!

A knock at my office door causes me to shift in my chair to adjust my burgeoning erection. Then I call for the person to enter.

Anton strides in for our weekly meeting with a shit-eating grin on his face.

"Adrienne is still in town, I take it?" My question makes him smirk even harder.

"*Da, moy drug,*" he responds. "Unfortunately, my little *khlopushka* leaves tomorrow."

I clap my friend on the back before I sit at the conference table.

"And your woman? All good?" Anton asks as he pulls out his chair.

Now it's my turn for a shit-eating grin.

"Ha! That good, huh? Well, I'm happy for you, my friend! Don't let her get away like you did before…" He chuckles as he shakes his head. "We took care of that *cyka*. Now enjoy a real woman!"

Nah, not this time, I chuckle to myself with a shake of my head. My Angel is going nowhere. I've got her on lock!

STARR

"**G**ood morning… I guess. Why are the lights off? Some new welcoming of clients I'm not aware of?"

I joke to one greeter as I stride through the entrance to Starr Light Fitness & Wellness Beverly Hills.

Clients mill about the darkened interior, sitting at tables near the café, browsing in the boutique, and on line for check in at the front desk. It's time for the first group classes and private sessions to start in fifteen minutes.

Everything appears normal, but no lights.

Adrienne stands beside the front desk. As I approach her, she glances up from a tablet with her mobile to her ear, a frown on her face.

Okay, now I'm concerned.

What the heck happened? I wonder, glancing around the lobby.

Now I notice no sound of the blenders for smoothies or the piped-in music. It's not just dark, the center is silent. WTF???

A client walks over to me with a quizzical expression.

Not wanting to seem worried, I smile at her.

"Good morning, Gail. How's your husband doing?" I ask pleasantly.

We take great care to familiarize ourselves with SLFW's clients—their names and the life happenings they share willingly. They appreciate the human connection and don't feel as though they're only dollar signs to me or to my staff. SLFW clients pay a sizable amount of money each year on the annual membership dues, semi-privates, duets, privates, and retreats. Not to mention the ancillary services including the spa, boutique, café, kids' club, and the valet. SLFW values our clients.

"Good morning, Starr. He's doing much better, thanks for asking! Your suggestion of turmeric tea—"

"When can we go inside the Pilates studio? I want to get my preferred tower!"

Inwardly, I sigh. Not every member is laid back. Some Type A personalities—ultra competitive, demanding, impatient—exist, even in SLFW's mellow environment. They come for the amazing bodies our yoga, Pilates, Barre, and strength training sessions develop. The infamous Yoga Butt...

I excuse myself from Gail and turn to Ms. Tower with a smile.

"Good morning, Shelby. I've only arrived. Let me check the status," I respond, then nod as I continue to Adrienne.

Just as I reach her, the lights turn on, and everyone claps. Immediately, the front desk staff check in the clients and the café blenders whir.

"Hey, girl. A mix-up with the electricity company. They thought I canceled our service. Everything's back in order. Crazy, huh?" She says as we walk towards our offices.

We nod and smile at clients along the way. They return our greetings as they go to the studios. I giggle when I notice Shelby rush past everyone. Good grief. Take it easy, girl!

"Ah, Shelby…" Adrienne laughs outright.

"*Buenos días!*" Says Márcia Souza, my administrative assistant and a yoga substitute teacher. "Thank goodness the power is back on! A flashlight would not work…"

The Brazilian petite spitfire follows Adrienne and me into my office and shuts the door.

"I know, right! Simple error on the electric company's part. It's fixed now," Adrienne says as she sits across from my desk.

Márcia joins her in the other chair while I take my seat and plug my MacBook Pro into its docking station on my desk.

"Tell me what's going on today," I say as my monitor screen flicks on.

We settle into our morning routine: the day's agenda; administrative tasks; client and staff concerns; upcoming events; the expansion status. More teachers clamor for a transfer to St. Barth's and Cabo San Lucas. Even Monte Carlo has a wait list, and its construction not scheduled for months!

We set the international retreat schedule for two every other month. I'll lead one while one of our top teachers leads the other. They rotate based on the fitness focus of yoga or Pilates; Barre and strength training occurs with both types. Based on the location, we'll include additional activities for wine tasting, cooking, hiking, painting, or whatever the place is known for. Clients book the retreats as soon as we promote them.

I'm beyond pleased with the success of our STEELE International partnership. Their team from Malcolm to Anton to the directors and their staff have been phenomenal. Malcolm says we impressed Sebastian, and he's given the okay for more SLFW Resorts. Whoohoo!

"So when do you leave for the retreat in Monte Carlo?" Adrienne asks as she we sync our calendars.

I swipe through to next month on my app, then give her the date for two weeks from now.

I'm looking forward to it since I'll have time to see Leonie and The Twins while I'm in Europe. I miss the little munchkins. It's their six-month birthday party. Unbelievable how time flies so quickly. Leonie and Roger return from their two-month honeymoon, so we'll gather at the family's newly renovated triplex in Paris.

Adrienne, Márcia, and I finish our meeting. I go to my studio for my first private session. My day won't end until four this afternoon with my last group class. Then I'll have a massage at the spa before an early dinner with my publicist and a fitness magazine editor.

As I enter one of the group yoga class studios, my heart swells with gratitude. From the continued success of my company to my friends to the love of my life, the Universe shines its blessings on me.

The smile that spreads across my face is genuine as I sit in lotus position before my students. I place my palms together at heart center and bow my head.

"Let us start our practice with the Anusara chant, Niralambaya Upanishad…

Om Namah Shivaya Gurave
  Satchidananda Murtaye
  Nishpranchaya Shantaye
  Niralambaya Tejase

My heart opens to the power and source of grace that takes form as truth, knowledge, bliss. Always present, boundless peace. Shining source, limitless and free."

* * *

"*Joyeux Anniversaire!*"

"Happy Birthday!"

Josy, Guy, the Steeles, Luc, and I celebrate The Twins' six-month birthday the day after Leonie and Roger returned from Verbier.

Yesterday, Malcolm flew in from New York City with his parents and his siblings to update Roger on another legal claim involving that woman, Delia Shaw. Ninety minutes ago, I flew up from The Jackson Hole at STEELE Monte Carlo after SLFW's retreat. Malcolm met me at the airport, and we fooled around like a pair of hormone-crazed teens in the back of his Black Badge Rolls-Royce Cullinan.

After a quick shower, we joined the family in Leonie and Roger's new triplex penthouse. We're gathered around the dining room table with Rodolphe and Gaspard sitting in their high chairs. They're bedazzled by the flickering candles on the identical cakes before them.

As everyone sings, The Twins bounce and wave their arms in amusement. Each has one little tooth that gleams in the light. I laugh when I recall Leonie's stories about all their drooling and tears. Now The Twins have their first tooth each!

I still can't believe it's been half a year already.

Roger and Leonie bend over to blow out the candles. When they lean in to kiss The Twins' chubby cheeks, Gaspard says, "Dada, dada!"

Leonie's eyes fly to Roger, who looks stunned.

"Dada, dada."

Everyone looks over to Rodolphe, and he waves his arms, repeating the words.

Roger has tears in his eyes as he lifts first Gaspard, then

Rodolphe into his arms. He kisses their cheeks and holds them close.

Leonie wraps her arms around the three of them. Roger buries his face in her hair. It's an unexpected, momentous occasion that overwhelms the first-time parents.

The room is silent save The Twins and their baby sounds.

"Well, Dada, don't get all sappy on us!" Harris chuckles and smacks his lips. "I'm ready for some cake, bro!"

Everyone laughs at the jokester.

While Roger continues to hold The Twins and chats with Sebastian, Lola helps Leonie cut the Gateau St. Honoré cakes. She shares it's made by Josy from the recipe tips their Verbier chef shared. The Twins' birthday gave Josy the perfect excuse to try her recent version.

I glance up to see Josy nervously watching Lola and Leonie cut into the flaky confections. Her mother looks relieved after Harris takes a bite and raves about the delicious factor being off the charts.

I take a bite of my piece and swoon at the delicious flavor. It's incredible!

Then I turn to Lola with a question that's been burning in the back of my mind since we had dinner last month at Spago Beverly Hills with Billie and Blair. A mystery man—Simon Blanchett—had his eyes on Lola from the moment we sat at our table until he left from speaking to her. She waved us off with assurances nothing was amiss when we asked her about the sexy Frenchman.

But I want the deets.

"So, how was your business dinner with Simon Blanchett?" I ask when we're away from the others.

Lola blushes and darts her hazel eyes in Sebastian's direction.

As I thought, something's there. I won't pry, but we've

grown close enough to share our lives. I arch my eyebrow and cock my head to the side questioningly.

Lola clears her throat and brings her gaze back to me. Her eyes fill with guilt, then sadness.

"He was a lover for a brief time years ago. I ended things when he wanted more than I was ready to give. It took him a while to give up. Then I met Baz," she says, then sips her Champagne. "Simon owns Blanchett Retail Enterprises, SAS, the largest online luxury retailer in the world. At dinner he asked me—rather Lola's Coterie—to partner with his company."

I smile and congratulate her. But she shakes her head sadly.

"Baz is jealous, you know, Captain Caveman. No different from Malcolm… Baz and I are supposed to be working on a baby. But I want to hold off until—"

"Time to open the presents!" Haley exclaims.

Lola shakes her head, and I nod. Now's not the time.

We spend the next half an hour opening presents. With The Twins' development in mind, the gifts include stacking toys with different-sized rings and multi-colored cubes; cars, trains, and balls that roll, light up, and make music to encourage crawling; roly-poly toys; sturdy toys that encourage pulling up to standing; to keep them entertained, colorful board books.

Harris and Haley—the Dynamic Duo—give them some gadgets claiming one is never too young for technology.

Luc bought them their first stock portfolios. The men were more impressed and had a lengthy discussion about the growth potential.

Afterwards, we go to the cinema room with aperitifs.

Haley surprises Roger and Leonie with a compilation movie of our first family Christmas and New Year's. No one even realized she was taking footage while we were together. Some scenes from us skiing, the angle straight on as though we were still on the piste; making s'mores at the outside firepit; The Twins first snowfall; the New Year's Eve fireworks in the village.

She has it set to some of Leonie's favorite Christmas songs, including "Christmas Canon" and Andrea Bocelli and Céline Dion's "The Prayer."

She gives Haley an enormous hug as tears well in her amber eyes.

Haley impresses everyone, and we request copies. Always prepared, she hands out artfully packaged copies to each of us.

Then everyone departs since we have a busy workday tomorrow. Lola to her atelier with Leonie; the Steele siblings to their Paris offices; Luc to his Banquet Montaigne; me to guest teach at Norman Green's Elite Training Facility.

Morgan, Shelley, Lola, and Sebastian take the family's private elevator to their respective penthouses on the two floors below Roger and Leonie. Their residences occupy the top floors, twenty-eight through thirty-two.

The Tower is in the Front de Seine district of Beau-grenelle in the *quinzième*. Like its New York City counter-part, it's mixed-use with commercial and residential space plus the largest mall in Paris. The views of the Seine and of the Eiffel Tower are incredible, especially at night when the spectacular light display flits across the monumental iron structure.

Malcolm, Harris, Haley, and I return to our suites at the STEELE Place Vendôme. Guy and Josy leave for their fami-ly's ancestral home, *Le Beaulieu Manoir*. Their driver will take Luc to his mansion first as both live in the posh *seizième* arrondissement.

"Good night, Haley and Harris!" I say as we part ways at the elevators once we're back at the hotel.

"Sleep tight!" They chorus, then laugh.

"See you tomorrow at the office," Malcolm tells them as he takes my hand and leads me down the hall at a hurried pace.

"Slow down, bro! I promised I wouldn't steal Starr from you!" Harris chortles.

Malcolm growls and flips him the bird while Haley and I laugh.

Once inside our darkened suite, Malcolm whirls me around to face the wall of windows and slaps my ass to push me along.

"Strip. There. Now," My Dom commands in a husky voice.

I hesitate, concerned someone may see my naked body from the street to the Tuileries Gardens beyond. Warm breath on the shell of my ear and hands gripping my hips startle me.

"You do not trust your Dom, Little One?" Malcolm murmurs in my ear as he grinds his impressive erection between my butt cheeks.

A shudder travels along my spine, and I close my eyes with a whimper, leaning into his muscular embrace.

"I trust you, Sir," I reply breathlessly. "I'm just nervous someone will see me."

He nips my ear lobe and growls.

"No one but I will ever see your naked beauty, Little One," My Dom corrects me.

I jolt with a yelp from the pain caused to my sensitive flesh.

"The windows—as in all STEELE properties—have treatments. No one can see in, while those inside can see out," he says. "Now, go do as I told you, Naughty Girl."

My ass jiggles from another harder smack. I hasten into position and remove my silk wrap dress and lace Lola's Coterie lingerie. When I lean over to unwrap the strings from sandals, My Dom stops me with an ah, ah, ah. I bite my lip and rise—feet planted wide apart; arms behind back grasped at opposite elbows; head bowed slightly with eyes downcast.

The lights of Paris shine against the ink black sky before me.

My ears strain to hear any movement from My Dom. The silk Aubusson rugs hide his footsteps. Tinkling of ice in a crystal glass makes me aware he's at the bar on the side wall of the salon. Liquid splashes in to the snifter, undoubtedly his favorite Jackson Reserve Scotch. The ice clinks. He must take a sip of the smooth, amber liquid. Another clink, then silence.

Time passes—a minute, five, one hundred???

My only thought: I must maintain position.

Then the opening strains of Edith Piaf's "Hymne A L'Amour" whispers from the surround sound speakers.

The heat of My Dom's naked body reaches into my soul as he stands behind me suddenly. His head dips to brush his lips along the column of my throat.

As I tremble from his touch, I tilt my head to the side to give him more access. My pulse beats beneath his full mouth rapidly. Fire licks at my skin when his fingers feather down my flat belly to slip inside my soaked pussy and to stroke my swollen clit.

My Dom finger fucks me through two mind-blowing climaxes. On jelly knees, I lean against his sculpted chest. His arm bands around my waist to hold me close. The musky scent of my arousal wafts beneath my nose when he lifts his fingers to my slack mouth.

"Clean them," he demands huskily.

Without hesitation, I swirl the tip of my tongue around his thick digits, then lave them with its flat surface. Our groans mingle from the erotic act. His velvet covered-steel cock thumps against my ass as he bends his knees to align his groin to my crack.

He dips the mushroom head into my pussy, thrusting slow and long, fully coating his dick with my natural lubricant.

"Spread your ass cheeks for me, Little One," My Dom commands while he places his palm between my shoulder blades to bend me forward. "Remember your safewords are green to continue, yellow for a moment, and red to stop all play at once."

I comply and grip my ass, baring my most private hole to him. Then I rest the side of my face against the cool surface of the window. Another shudder runs through me when his tip—balls piercing and all—pushes past my rings of muscle. Instinctively, I clench my ass—he's huge and stretches my tight hole to the max. But I loosen on a mewl when My Dom spanks the tops of my thighs.

"Open for me, Naughty Girl! Who do you belong to?" He grunts as he presses another inch inside.

I stutter, "You, Sir… Ohhh…"

Fully seated within my forbidden hole, I bow to his dominant possession of my body. The submissive in me rolls over to bare her belly under My Dom's sexual thrall.

With no safeword—only throaty moans—falling from my parted lips, he offers no mercy as he pounds my ass fervently. My cries of carnal pleasure spur him to rise onto his toes and lift my hips to take me even more voracious.

"Mine. Mine. Mine." My Dom chants with each toe-curling thrust.

"Please, Sir! Please let me cum!" I beg, clamping the muscles of my hollow pussy.

"No!" He responds with a slap to my butt cheek for emphasis, then increases his brutal pace.

I squeeze my eyes shut and pant through my open mouth. The glass fogs from my heated breaths, and my hands slide along its surface, slick from the sweat on my palms. The lights of Paris blur before my hooded eyes when I open them unseeingly.

"Sir! Please!" I wail as my legs tremble, unable to hold back my orgasm any longer.

"Yes! Now!" My Dom shouts with one last snap of his powerful hips and a pinch to my distended clit.

My mind blanks as the climax of life overrides my systems.

The last cognizant thought: Ms. Piaf is correct; my body quivers under My Dom's attentive hands. I sigh in contentment, his name a whispered breath across my lips.

STARR

"*H*ow I love my job!"

Haley professes as we stretch out on chaise lounges on the white sand of Palmilla Beach.

We're on a construction site visit of Starr Light Fitness & Wellness Resorts at STEELE Cabo San Lucas.

The beach features a one-mile-long stretch of gorgeous, soft golden desert sands and blue-green swimmable waters. The five-diamond SCSL is the only resort with direct access. It's nestled near the southern tip of Palmilla Beach and commands stunning views over the turquoise water. Guests enjoy complimentary activities including snorkeling, stand-up paddleboarding, and kayaking at SCSL's very own Pelican Beach.

SLFW Resorts sits back from the shoreline behind lush foliage of palm trees and hibiscus bushes. Close to the primary hotel, the center has beachfront footage for our activities without interfering with guests of the hotel. The structure mimics the Spanish-style property with white stucco walls, red tile roof, arches, and blue accents. A rooftop terrace takes advantage of the panoramic view—

miles of turquoise water dotted by mounds of earth breaking its surface.

Haley joined me as co-head of STEELE Technology and Cyber Security to oversee the installation of the center's systems.

Malcolm told me the twins are the youngest of the Steele clan and a double surprise for their parents, who had not planned on having more children. Then a twofer to boot. Roger—who's three years older—had been the baby of the family until Harris and Haley popped up. Harris is older by mere minutes.

Although fraternal, they share a similar love of technology, with Haley being a hacker and Harris a coder. Their brothers tease them for being nerds, but they're wizzes at what they do, which led to the approval for them to create their subsidiary. As co-heads, they're responsible for all of STEELE and external clients from around the globe, including Jackson Corporation. They're super smart and their brothers have grown to depend upon them, even if Haley and Harris are the babies now.

Haley is a shy beauty who—like Harris—matches the rest of the Steeles with jet black hair. Hers hangs mid-back in a silky curtain. Their signature gray eyes in her are soulful, set in her heart-shaped face with cheeks that display dimples when she smiles or laughs.

Like she does now.

"Harris wanted your project, but he lost out. My paper beat his rock. I always tell him brawny doesn't always win!" Haley giggles.

Their antics crack me up. If they weren't so smart, people would think they're crazy to do business based on a random game of chance!

"I'm glad you won, too! Now we can hang out when the

workday ends and sip mojitos!" I declare as I clink my glass with hers.

We sip our cocktails as we catch up on our lives. Haley has been pretty mum about some important project she's working on. I can only gather it involves Roger. She said she'll let everyone know soon.

"How do you feel about your collar?" She asks as she fingers her bare neck.

I choke on my drink.

Malcolm would go ballistic if he knew Haley was asking me about BDSM. Especially a collar, which means she must be interested in submission. Her big brother would end any guy who tried to spank her. Hypocritical much?

I don't let the fact Malcolm does to me exactly what he doesn't want someone to do to Haley bother me. He's her protective big brother—albeit his thirty-four to her thirty years. It's not that he's thinks BDSM is bad for her, he just wouldn't want her with a Dom who's inexperienced and could hurt her.

That's why I'm surprised he and his brothers are anti-Lachlan for Haley.

"Why do you ask?" I respond while I consider my response. A bit of deflection may give me time to plan my answer.

Haley sighs and stares towards the horizon.

"I want to be dominated," she responds.

Oh dear.

Well, she's my friend, and I will be honest with her. Besides, Haley needs a woman's perspective and not her fire-breathing brothers acting as naysayers.

"Lola told me how you helped her after she broke up with Baz. She says you offered really excellent advice"—Haley shifts in her chaise lounge to gaze at me—"I'm torn between Lachlan and Callum—you know the Scottish duke I was with in Verbier. They're both dominants. But I…"

She tells me about her desires, heartache, and determination to live her life without her brothers controlling it. We laugh when she says they can't control her, but she'd welcome it from her prospective Doms.

I tell Haley it's the giving up of control to a man who is powerful, cares for me, and focuses on my needs. His dominance doesn't supersede my Independent Woman. Rather, she allows him to take over in the bedroom, not in the boardroom—or any other area of my life. His possessive caveman provides us with great pleasure.

Haley understands when I tell her I wear Malcolm's collar not just as a symbol of our D/s relationship but as a sign of our commitment to one another. The collar may not be a wedding band, but it declares our connection to those in the lifestyle. I'm his and Malcolm is mine.

"See! I knew you'd help me figure things out," Haley exclaims with a grin. "You do not know what it's like having four brothers and two male cousins in my business! Of course I exclude Lachlan from our Jackson cousins."

She raises her freshly topped off mojito to mine.

"Here's to my sisters. First Lola, then Leonie, now you! At least Baz, Roger, and Malcolm are worth something. Harris… Well…" Haley giggles, then tips her cocktail to her smiling lips.

My heart swells from her including me with her sisters-in-law. I love her brother very much. But we were only together for eight months before we broke up. Now it's five months since we reunited. I need to give us some more time before I'm ready for SIL level.

What's the rush?

* * *

"HEY, babe. How's your site visit going? I hate I couldn't come with you."

I smile at Malcolm, whose handsome face fills my iPad screen during our nightly FaceTime call. His dove gray eyes dim with disappointment.

"That's okay, my love. Everything looks great," I respond, then tell him about the status, including the call I received from Adrienne the other night.

The fire department showed up to SLFW Beverly Hills during our peak evening time—sirens blaring and trucks lining the street. The captain told the general manager on duty they received a call about a three-alarm fire.

Despite the GM telling the captain nothing was amiss, he insisted upon evacuating the premises and doing a thorough search. The hullabaloo upset and scared our clients.

Two hours later, the crew left. No evidence of a fire. At. All.

Adrienne told me other weird things had happened, and I told her I thought the same.

My gut pointed to Vicky as the most likely culprit. But it turns out she's in Europe, as confirmed by Haley.

Malcolm takes it in as he frowns.

I sense he's ruminating about it, so I change the subject and ask him his opinion on other matters.

Fortunately, Malcolm lets the bad vibes of Vicky fade.

His thoughtful recommendations help to iron out some unexpected issues, and he promises to speak with the project manager the next day.

"And how did things go with Haley? She told me the systems cleared their checks," Malcolm says.

My hand flutters to touch my collar unconsciously. I stifle a gasp when I realize my tell.

Malcolm raises his eyebrow and cocks his head to the side.

I lick my lips and clear my throat.

"Perfect!" I answer brightly. "She's brilliant! Did she tell you she beat Harris at Rock, Paper, Scissors to handle my project?"

My voice rises as I chatter on.

"Naughty Girl, what are you hiding?"

My head snaps up at My Dom's commanding tone.

Fuck!

I swallow, then blank my face. No way will I betray Haley's confidence.

I fudge a bit instead.

"Oh, Sir… You're so good at reading me. I told her how much I miss you," I purr while batting my eyelashes.

A smirk grows on My Dom's face.

"Is that so, Little One?" He rumbles as he shifts on his bed to tug at the placket of his silk pajama bottoms.

Distracted him! Yes!!!

I want to whoop, but I keep my cool. Besides, it's not a lie. A couple of weeks have passed since we saw each other in Paris. Video sex and text message games only go but so far as satisfaction…

"Oh absolutely, Sir," I respond honestly.

My Dom smirks wider.

"I'm in Paris again next week. Shall we plan for an in-person playtime at LEVELS Beverly Hills when I return? You have been such a good girl, you deserve an award, Little One," he purrs seductively.

The vibrations ripple over my skin. Now it's my turn to shift on my bed.

The sheer teddy reveals my peaked nipples clearly. Judging by My Dom's dilated pupils, he sees them too. A lick to his full lips confirms my guess.

I bounce a bit under the guise of sitting on my haunches to tease him with the visual of my fleshy mounds jiggling. His passion-filled groan rewards my efforts.

"I'm sorry, Sir. Are you all right?" I tease as I lean into the iPad's camera.

My breasts fill the screen, and he growls outright.

"Are you teasing me, Naughty Girl? Must our reunion start with you trussed up on the St. Andrew's Cross while I flog your juicy brown nipples and tits?" My Dom queries.

My response is a shiver that causes my breasts to bounce even more—this time not purposefully. I still cannot control my reactions to him.

I suck in a heated breath, then sigh as I sit back on my heels, head bowed.

"If that would please you, Sir," I answer, knowing it would please me even more.

He chuckles wickedly, and I steal a direct glance to his face.

My Dom's cheeks infused with blood heated from his lust make his darkened eyes stand out as they roam over my body.

Is it my fault the strap of my teddy slipped below my left breast?

No, but it's My Dom's fault when I cum screaming his name with my fingers plunging in and out of my soaked, greedy, little pussy...

MALCOLM

"**Y**eah, baby! You got it, Starr! Fly, baby, fly!!" I yell through the megaphone as I stand on the superyacht's aft deck.

My Angel zips by with her feet strapped in special boots that use a propulsion mechanism from the jet ski guiding her flyboarding experience. It's her second time doing the extreme sport and the first session of our trip. She's become good at it in a short time because of her strong core muscles developed from years of Pilates.

A grin and thumbs-up serve as My Angel's response.

I grin even more than she does as I watch her plump ass in a yellow string bikini bottom when she passes the boat. A life jacket covers her lush tits. I'd have to gouge out the eyes of the crew should a tit pop out of her bandeau bikini top from the jostling of the powerful propulsion. Mine!

We've known each other for two years now. Sure, we split for a couple of months after we started dating, but now we're back together. Seven months. A long ass time for someone like me. A devout playboy with only contracted subs for a few months each before My Angel. Well, aside from Vicky who lasted longer since I didn't see her but for two or three times a month given she lives in California and I'm in New York.

Somehow the distance doesn't make a difference with My Angel. I see her more often—at least every other week. Whether I work out of STEELE LA or my offices at STEELE Las Vegas Resort & Casino, my work gets done and I'm near My Angel. Both of my priorities get my utmost attention. Although I'm still encouraging her to open a center in New York City. Then we can spend even more time together. My woman, my family, and STEELE International in one city. Why not have it all?

That's exactly why I surprised her with a getaway to Bali. I intend to dazzle My Angel with private excursions to the religious sites, the volcanic mountains, and secluded beaches. We'll do more adventures: free diving, wakeboarding, and my favor paragliding over the scenic lands.

The four-hundred-ten-foot superyacht I rented allows us a chance to explore Bali and the surrounding Indonesian islands while we cruise the Indian Ocean. Nights spent in each other's arms as we make love or play. Over the next five days, My Angel will be so awed, she'll only have one word for me, *yes*.

* * *

"HOLD ON, bro. Tell me that again."

Baz and I sit at the conference table in his office at The STEELE Tower after our weekly one-on-one meeting. His face registers shock.

Yeah, me too.

It's our last night in Bali, right before sunset. I scoop My Angel out of the tender and carry her over the water lapping on the shoreline of the secluded beach.

She giggles and kicks her shapely legs as she hugs my neck. The filmy material of the coral-colored maxi dress she wears flutters around us.

Even when my bare feet touch the sun-warmed sand, I continue to carry My Angel. I don't want to let her out of my embrace.

I inhale the seductive scent of gardenias from her coconut oil lotion and bury my face in her curly hair. She's just so soft and sweet, but all woman. My woman. It makes my cock punch the front of my drawstring linen pants.

My Angel squirms in my arms, trying to get down.

I tighten my hold.

"Malcolm! I can walk now. I won't get wet," she insists, unwinding her arms from my neck to brace her palms against my chest.

Her thumbs dip under my linen shirt and brush my pecs as she pushes at me.

"I know you can walk, My Angel. But I want to carry you. Shall I command you stay still, Little One?" I respond with my eyebrow lifted. My Dom transitions from boyfriend seamlessly.

Her mouth drops open, then closes as her eyes widen and narrow. Torn between her submissive tendencies and her I am Woman Hear Me Roar. She doesn't have to choose since we reach the table set on the beach for our dinner.

"Good evening, Ms. Knight, Mr. Steele."

The greetings from the chef and the server distract My Angel.

She swivels her head towards them. Her eyes widen again, and her mouth forms a perfect O. The romantic setting renders her speechless.

A white gauzy canopy with its four posts covered in white hibiscus, frangipani, and orchards floats above the table like a fragrant cloud. The tropical scent of the flowers mingles with the aromas from the tantalizing dishes on the white linen tabletop. Our chairs have more gauzy material drapes over them, with a bow in the back and a floral bouquet at its center. Bamboo torches around the perimeter and white tapers on the table will provide lighting once the sun sets on the horizon.

After dinner, we'll move to the sunbed covered in white sumptuous bedding beneath a gauzy canopy. A bonfire to the side and more bamboo torches situated nearby, ready to be lit. Krug Clos d'Ambonnay Champagne and two crystal flutes chill in a bucket nestled in the sand.

"Oh, Malcolm," My Angel breathes, still staring in awe at the setup.

I take another inhale of her natural fragrance enhanced by the gardenias, then place her on her feet. Cupping her face in my hands, I kiss her softly. The tip of my tongue swipes across the seam of her mouth asking entry. On a sigh, My Angel opens to me. I swoop in and coax her tongue to dance with mine.

She sways.

My hands glide down her neck and flanks to hold her slim waist, bracing her for our soul-stirring kiss. Her gentle moans undo me.

I drop to one knee, then reach into my pants pocket to withdraw the little navy-blue velvet box. My thumb presses the sapphire cabochon closure to reveal the oval-shaped, twenty-eight carat diamond and platinum engagement ring—a Steele family heirloom. It glitters in the setting sun's orange and fuchsia rays.

I look up at My Angel; the words marry me on my lips.

Her alarmed expression takes me aback.

WTF?

"What's wrong? Are you okay?" I question.

My Angel blinks, then takes a deep breath. When she reopens her sorrel brown eyes, they shine with tears.

Okay. Now a crying fiancée I can handle. A smile spreads

across my face as I remove the ring and take her left hand in mine.

"Wait!"

Her startled cry jolts me. Then her hand burns mine as she yanks her finger from my grasp.

WTF???

"I mean... I... I don't want to marry you!" Starr cries out as she backs away from me. Her palms held out in front of her as though warding me off.

Now my mouth drops open. In fact, my jaw hits the sand beneath my knee. I stand to my full six-feet-four-inches with a scowl on my face.

Oh, hell no. Did she just say what I thought she said? Is she running away from me?? What the everlasting fuck!

"Damn, bro. I don't know what to tell you."

Baz shakes his head in pity. Even he can't get his head around the unbelievable situation.

Yeah, My Angel told me no.

I meet the one woman who makes me want to settle down, and she tells me no. No.

No.

"But why? What reason did she give for turning you down?" Baz asks. "I thought the two of you were doing well. Trips together. Family gatherings. The holidays together... You spend more time on the West Coast than you do at any of your other offices worldwide. Damn... How long have you been together?"

Baz babbles on as he tries to make sense of her rejection.

"Well, to be honest, Starr admitted she was 'saying no for now.' Since we broke up so easily and haven't been together for long, she wants to wait. She went on about the Universe and things aligning when they should. You know go-with-the-flow Starr..."

Baz nods, then spins his chair to stare out of the floor-to-ceiling windows thoughtfully.

I leave him with his thinking while I check my mobile for emails and text messages. Then chuckle when I read a message from My Angel.

Hi, my love. You came across my mind, so I want to check in. Are you okay?

"What's got you beaming?" Baz asks.

My fingers fly over my Virtue's screen as I type my response.

Hi, My Angel. Just telling Baz how you broke my heart. But otherwise, all's good...

There's a long pause.

Fuck! I shouldn't have teased her.

"Starr just texted me because I came across her mind. But I think I upset her with my resp—"

My sentence cuts off when my mobile vibrates with an incoming text. I brace myself.

The message opens to a video clip close-up of My Angel using a red lipstick to draw a letter S over her heart in the hollow between her bare voluptuous tits.

My mouth salivates.

The camera moves up to her gorgeous face, and a smile plays on her full lips as she speaks softly.

You have my heart, my love. I can never break yours without breaking mine. I love you, Malcolm Steele.

And just like that, my heart solidifies with her love.

She got away from me once; she turned down my marriage proposal. But I'm a patient man who always gets what he wants.

My collar.

My Red S.

My ring.

With a Cheshire Cat grin on my face, I glance up at Baz. His platinum gray eyes shine like the band on my ring. Like Starr, I view it as a sign.

In the end, I will put my ring on My Angel's finger. The brown-eyed beauty will be all MINE.

MALCOLM

"I haven't been to the Hamptons in so long. I forgot how the Atlantic Ocean has different shades of blue around Long Island. Your family's compound sits on the best beach!"

Haley grins at my exclamation as we stroll along their private expanse of golden sand. I close my eyes and inhale deeply. The briny scent of the ocean fills my lungs. The calls of seagulls ring out.

Steele Southampton Village is their beachfront property on ten acres off a private road. Its incredible surroundings include native trees, grassy areas, and closer to the ocean sandy dunes. A security guard in a gatehouse to allow access through the oversized wooden gates set between stone pillars with wrought iron lanterns. A long driveway of pressed oil and natural stone leads to the primary mansion and branches off to driveways for three more mansions—one for each of the elder siblings.

Malcolm's home is a modern contemporary three-story mansion. The exterior features vertically placed gray weathered shingles, oversized panes of floor-to-ceiling windows, and multiple balconies with white metal railings. A luxurious all-white interior with pops of color from the art and accent pieces has five en suite bedrooms have breathtaking ocean views. The adjacent outdoor entertaining space surrounds a waterside gunite pool with spa, outdoor showers, and outdoor kitchen. A shingle-lined pathway with white metal railings leads from the entertainment patio over the grass-covered dunes to the sandy beach. It's a spectacular home.

Of course being the rebel of the family, Malcolm's mansion is opposite of the others. Their three-story residences with robin egg blue or sea green shutters against gray weathered shingles where blossoms fill the windowsills flower boxes epitomize classic Hamptons-style.

I love Malcolm's home the most! So different and stands out from the crowd, just like us.

Yesterday evening he picked me up from the Southampton Village Heliport in his Black Badge Rolls-Royce Cullinan. We had a delicious dinner with fresh oysters and lobsters with truffle sauce at one of Lucien's restaurants on Main Street before we went to Malcolm's home. Where I ate him covered in whipped cream and strawberries for dessert.

It's been a month, and it relieved me he wasn't angry with me or didn't end our relationship after my negative reaction to his proposal.

Honestly, I love Malcolm, but at this point I'd rather let us continue as we are without a commitment beyond his collaring me. We need more time as a couple before we marry for life.

Sure, it disappointed him, but he understood my concerns and agreed not to pressure me.

I suppose the daily deliveries of frangipani, orchids, and hibiscus bouquets wrapped in white gauze and silk bows, handwritten declarations of love and our future together, and aphrodisiac delicacies of figs, chocolates, and pomegranates don't count as pressure…

A grin spreads across my face as I giggle at the memories of our last FaceTime tryst. We played strip poker during which he divested me of my new Lola's Coterie cashmere kimono, tank top, and matching boy shorts, not to mention the lace lingerie beneath it.

Malcolm didn't win all the rounds. I got him down to his black silk boxers and one sock. Besides, I wasn't keen on winning. My goal was to tempt him with my body. After treatments at SLFW Beverly Hills' spa, my skin shone golden and not one stray strand of hair found—buffed perfection!

As the victorious one, he controlled the scene using some delicacies he had delivered that morning. By the time Malcolm finished, my sweat-soaked body trembled with ecstasy while my mango-coated fingers plunged in and out of my spasming pussy. I cried out his name until my voice was hoarse.

If anything, my *no* answer spurred him to up his game with not only romantic gifts, but with intense, passionate lovemaking. Be it in person or virtual. This Labor Day weekend promises to be amazing!

"Well, I'm so glad you came early! I can update you on my Lachlan-Callum drama while we set up for tonight's sunset dinner on the beach—a traditional New England Clambake. It's my favorite part of the weekend. I cannot wait, yummy tummy!"

Haley laughs as we turn around to head back to the beach area in front of Morgan and Shelley's home. She loops her arm through mine and fills me in on the latest with her love life.

"Good of you to join us, Haley…" Harris says as he slaps

his gloved hands free of sand from the wood for the bonfire. "Care to help us?"

"Do not worry, Haley. I'll help Harris," Callum responds in his sexy Scottish accent.

She grins and thanks him with a chaste kiss to his cheek.

Malcolm and Harris exchange glances. Sebastian hired his guy to conduct an extensive background check on Callum Graham, Duke of Montrose, as soon as they met him while we were in Verbier for Christmas. Nothing in it caused concern. They're happier Haley is with Callum and not with Lachlan.

We finish with the setup for the clambake, then the siblings drive to the heliport to pick up Lola, Sebastian, Blair, Leonie, Roger, The Twins, and Nanny Grace. Billie will fly in with Patrick on his helicopter later this afternoon and stay at his beachfront property. Leonie's parents and Luc should have landed by now at the private airport for the Hamptons. They flew in from Paris on Luc's jet.

The day turns into evening, and we go to the beach for a seafood feast with the backdrop of a spectacular sunset. The perfectly steamed clams, lobsters, potatoes, and corn on the cob topped with melted butter and paired with local beer and white wine make for a scrumptious meal. Dessert options include warm blueberry and apple pies with vanilla ice cream. Afterwards, we sit around the bonfire chatting.

"Don't forget beach yoga at seven tomorrow morning!" I call out to Leonie as she and Roger leave the beach with The Twins.

I lean back, huddled up with Malcolm and sigh happily.

"And don't you get too comfortable, My Angel. I have plans for you tonight," he rumbles in my ear.

"Bring it, baby," I whisper against his smirking lips, then rise to my feet and extend my hand to him.

* * *

"WHAT A GORGEOUS START to the day! I'm so glad the summer weather continued into September."

"It could stay summer year-round as far as I'm concerned."

Lola, Leonie, Haley, Billie, and Blair spread their yoga mats out on the sand at the beach in front of Shelley and Morgan's house. Originally, I wanted us to gather for a sunrise meditation at six-thirty, but after the long night they convinced me to start later—if only by half an hour.

After a reflective guided meditation, I plan to take them through a vigorous flow that builds up to the challenging peak pose of Scorpion Handstand with a dharma talk during Savasana.

"Let us begin. Come to a comfortable sitting position with your palms face up on your knees, fingers in Gyan Mudra. Center your mind…"

In practicing asanas, the point isn't to twist oneself into a pretzel and the more you can bend, the better. Rather, the focus on the breath and releasing the mind to move the body.

I love to push my students' abilities to focus, and Scorpion Handstand requires lots of it.

During Savasana they settle onto their backs with their eyes closed and their minds open, I speak to the girls about surrender. My submission to Malcolm's Alpha Dom dances at the edges of my mind.

Just as we stand to take a dip in the ocean, here they come…

"Rats, did we miss the yoga?" Patrick jokes in his thick Scottish accent as he strides towards his lover.

It turns out he and Callum know each other, and it surprised them to find the other with us.

Last night at the clambake, Billie teased how she and Haley are into bangers and mash. The visual of the double entendre made her blush and Callum sputter his ale.

"Of course it's over since I left you snoring almost two hours ago!" Billie replies, her Granny Smith apple green eyes sparkling in the bright sunlight.

Patrick towers over her by eleven inches. He scoops Billie into his arms and carries her off to the water as she giggles.

"How about we put you in that position with your pussy in the air? Then I'll come up behind you, grab your thighs, and fuck you until you see stars in the daytime."

A gasp slips past my lips as my pussy flutters and my nipples tighten beneath my orange cropped tankini.

"Namaste!" I call to the others as Malcolm flips me over his shoulder and jogs up the dune.

* * *

THE NEXT FEW days are so relaxing. We do more yoga, lounge around the pool, swim in the ocean, or hang out on the entertainment level of the primary house to bowl, play in the arcade, or watch movies.

It's good to unwind with everyone since it's the first time we've all been together in a few weeks.

Malcolm's laughter comes easily, and he jokes with his siblings. They along with Patrick and Callum played a rowdy game of touch football on the beach.

Between drooling over the gleaming muscles, the girls and I cheered them on. Morgan, Shelley, Guy, Josy, Luc, and The Twins watched from the sidelines.

Patrick and Callum told them American football sucks and isn't even football since the ball stays in the players' hands more often than not. They insisted on a round of rugby—"the real man's sport."

We couldn't care less as long as the guys remained sweaty.

JUST AS GOOD as they look shirtless, they look incredible dressed for social events. The STEELE Quaternity along with Patrick and Callum stand out amongst the guests gathered for the annual STEELE White Party.

The giant side lawn of Morgan and Shelley's house, aglow with thousands of fairy lights and lanterns, has two sumptuous pavilions, one for dinner and the other for dessert and dancing. Beyond it, on the beach, several bonfires burn. Waitstaff mill about with trays of champagne and wines or hors d'oeuvres. To one side a band plays lively music piped through speakers, also out on the sand.

Guests mingle, sipping drinks in the different areas, all dressed in the theme.

It's already bustling since it's the party of the season and everyone wants a ticket for a chance to see and be seen amongst the world's elite. Not to mention raising funds for STEELE Foundation.

My gaze scans the room as I stand beside Malcolm. I catch sight of Haley and Lachlan talking off to the side. It appears serious, so I'll greet her later.

The Jacksons, who also have a compound nearby, came over for the party. Laurent, the playboy, flirts shamelessly with three female guests. Lydie—Lola's former rival for Sebastian's affections—who seems to have a new boyfriend laughs with some industry titans. Lucien, whose Southampton restaurant caters the event, holds court in the dining pavilion for last-minute preparations.

"You're the most beautiful woman here, My Angel. Your eyes sparkle brighter than your earrings."

Malcolm's compliment rouses me from my musings.

My fingertips graze one of the dangling diamond drops that match the beautiful, intricate platinum lacework covered in tiny sparkly diamonds of my collar. The earrings complete the set with the bracelet he gave to me for our one-month anniversary.

"Thank you, Sir," I purr.

The gong rings to announce dinner.

We follow the guests to the dining pavilion and take our seats. The Steele clan disperses across the room, sitting at tables with guests to make everyone feel welcome and included.

Malcolm helps me into my chair. Once he's seated, he introduces me as his girlfriend to our dinner companions. Malcolm reaches into my lap to hold my hand in his and place it on is thigh.

I smile at him. As I turn my gaze to my dinner partner, I catch a snippet the hushed conversation on his other side.

"—came to meet Malcolm Steele! Only him and Harris are left, Daddy!"

I bristle. WTF?!

The twenty-something's father glances at me, then averts his gaze quickly. He whispers in her ear, and she throws a glare in my direction before she shifts her attention to the man on her other side.

A squeeze to my hand distracts me.

I put a smile on my face and turn to my man.

Malcolm brings our entwined hands to his mouth and kisses my knuckles. His dove gray eyes twinkle.

In my periphery, the wannabe huffs.

Yes honey, Malcolm Steele is mine.

After appetizers, Shelley makes her speech, and the

emcee keeps the party going through dinner and on to the dessert and dancing. A DJ famous for his skills on the turntables spins popular music that gets the guests on their feet.

The fireworks display from a barge offshore lights up the inky night sky with vivid sparklers, crowns, glitter, and crosettes. We cheer with each round, delighted by the glitziness.

"I'd like to thank you properly for your lavish gifts, Sir. Do you approve of us returning to your home now?"

For the rest of the night and well into the early morning, we make our own fireworks.

* * *

"YOU HAVE TO GET A MICROCHIP. It's not up for debate, Starr."

Malcolm decrees.

It's been two weeks since we left Southampton Village for Beverly Hills. We stayed an extra week after they kidnapped The Twins to support Leonie and Roger. Fortunately, the boys had a microchip connected to an app Harris created. The state troopers found them quickly and unharmed. It was still a terrifying ordeal.

All the Steeles have microchips for just those circumstances.

Now Malcolm insists I have one too.

I'm not partial to a foreign object implanted underneath my skin. So we've been debating me getting the tracking device.

My stubbornness kicks in at his declaration.

Who does he think he is? He can't just tell you what to do?!

My inner warrior goes off on a rant.

I'm about to voice her words when Malcolm stops me.

"Babe, I can't lose you."

His voice cracks.

Surprised at this vulnerability in my strong Alpha Dom, I shut my mouth and stare at him.

The anguish in his eyes is heart-wrenching.

Since The Twins' kidnapping and the injuries Leonie and Lola sustained, Malcolm has been fierce and super protective of them. The Steele clan with the Beaulieus closed ranks. He and Sebastian led their combined families like a force to be reckoned with.

To see a chink in *The Enforcer*'s armor makes me give in.

He only wants to protect me too. Include me in his precious nest of loved ones.

Why not allow him to take care of me in this way? I tell my inner warrior, who agrees wholeheartedly, softened by Malcolm's vulnerability.

I reach up to cup his face in my hands. When he lowers his head, I cover his mouth with mine. I pour my love into our kiss, and he responds just as ardently.

Malcolm lifts me from the ground, and I wrap my legs around his waist. My tunic raises up my thighs to bunch at my waist. My hot bare pussy rubs on his eight-pack abs through his t-shirt.

His caveman takes over with a feral growl. One arm bands under my ass while the other reaches between us to loosen the drawstring on his lounge pants. The bulbous head of his massive dick prods at my pussy folds. A snap of his hips drives his length deep inside of my slick core.

We groan when our bodies connect as close as a man and woman can. Lips locked; groins fused.

Malcolm's need to protect me rushes to the forefront, and he pours it out with each upward thrust. We ride out his urgent desire until we're a panting, sweaty mass collapsed on the living room floor of his Sunset Strip penthouse.

Once I catch my breath, I gaze up from resting my head on his muscular chest.

Despite the release, Malcolm's eyes still burn with vehemence. He opens his mouth, but I place my fingers against his lips and shake my head. He raises an eyebrow to protest.

"Okay," I interject. "I'll get the microchip."

Malcolm beams and slants his mouth over mine.

"Thank you, My Angel," he says as he rises with me in his arms.

Once he places me on the sofa, he pulls a briefcase from beside the coffee table and opens it on top. A syringe nestled in a foam surround appears. Malcolm puts his mobile on speaker and smiles at me reassuringly.

"Hey, bro. Walk me through the process for implanting the microchip," he says.

"Hi, Starr! Our boy persuaded you to join the Steele side?" Harris' voice comes through the speaker.

Before I can answer, Malcolm grasps my chin between his thumb and idea finger, bringing my gaze to his burning one.

"Almost, bro, almost."

MALCOLM

"**W**hat's going on in that head of yours, Steele?!"

The smirking face of Quinn Fucking Peters flies out of my head. Borya *The War Defender* Alexeyev—my personal trainer, former MMA champion, and Anton's cousin—delivers a roundhouse kick to my right flank.

Damn… that shit hurts likes a motherfucker.

When I was younger, my fighting was chaotic. Now with the proper training from Borya, I control my fighting with the MMA fights I take part in regularly to blow off steam.

Harris nicknamed me *The Enforcer* from my lethal fighting skills and for my no-nonsense, take-care-of-it attitude.

So while Baz is the leader and Roger the responsible one, I've become the guy everyone comes to get shit done… Or corrected.

Right now, I want to use my skills on Peters. The only reason I'm holding back is because of My Angel. I refuse to allow anyone—including myself—to ruin the opening of her

Starr Light Fitness & Wellness Resorts at STEELE Cabo San Lucas.

Borya, Anton, Lucien, and I arrived yesterday afternoon two days ahead of the opening celebration. The STEELE teams along with My Angel, Adrienne, and SLFW's staff have been on site this past week for the soft opening.

When My Angel posted to her Instagram account photos leading up to the event, my head spun.

Apparently that fucker Peters came with Peace and Sun on their private jet the day before. He weaseled his way into some photos My Angel posted. He positioned himself next to her for every. Single. One.

I didn't mention my irritation to her because she was already frantic over the shipment delay of some important custom items. A mix-up caused the delivery to SLFW Beverly Hills instead. Anton called in some favors and had the factory complete a rush order with expedited shipping.

Adrienne swore she provided the company with the correct delivery address and showed the confirmation email. The owner said he received a phone call to change the delivery but couldn't recall to whom he spoke. Another unexplained occurrence for them I think is Vicky, but no proof.

Haley has a person on her Cyber Security team investigating all the instances. If they even hint at a connection to Vicky, she'll answer to me.

In the meantime, I have to deal with Peters and his bull-shit. He better quit sniffing around my woman. Or he'll regret it.

Last night, I kept My Angel in our villa, reminding her who she belongs to—ME!

"Get—"

Whack!

"Your—"

Bam Bam!

"Shit—"

Whack!

"Together!"

Bam Bam!

Before Borya's next series of blows can hit me, I quickly crouch low and use my leg to sweep him off of his feet. The giant Russian lands on his ass with an oomph.

"What were you saying, asshole?" I growl as I crack my neck from side to side.

"Da, mal'chik!"

Borya punches his fists together as he effortlessly back-flips to land on his feet.

"Da, that's more like it, Steele. Be here or go jerk off. No room on this mat for *zhopas* with the smell of *kiska* on their breath! Meow. Meow."

Sufficiently chastised and pissed that I'm letting Quinn Fucking Peters mess with my head, I refocus.

I fake a charge at Borya, then at the last second turn and back kick him, the momentum throwing him off balance and causing him to stumble forward. I follow the kick with a few, well-placed punches then taunt him as I bounce on my toes backwards, fists in the air, "Take that, sucker!"

Norman throws his head back and laughs.

"Neither of you are ready for me. So hurry up pussy-footing around and give way for the Champ!" He says giving the speed bag a last punch.

"Exactly!" Lucien chimes in from the weight bench.

Anton chuckles between crunches on the floor.

We're in the gym for the primary hotel getting a workout in this morning. My Angel went to her center earlier for classes, so I met my boys here.

"Norman Green! I'm a huge fan of yours!"

Our heads swivel to the glass double doors to find Peters

grinning at the Champ. The fucker strides over with his hand extended for a shake.

Norman—unaware of my ire with Peters—grips his hand firmly and smiles.

"In the flesh, man," he responds.

"Starr didn't mention you'd be here. She told me some names the other night—"

His words end in a gurgle.

With a growl, I launch myself at him and slam my forearm against his throat as my elbow and palm make contact.

His back hits the wall, and I lift him the four inches to my eye level.

"Keep my woman's name out of your mouth, or I will rip your fucking face off. Be thankful I do not want to upset her, otherwise I would kick your ass all over this gym. In fact, I give you thirty minutes to pack your shit and get the fuck off of my property. Security will escort you to your room and remove you from the premises. Move. Now."

I tell him in a deadly tone, eyes blazing molten platinum. Then remove my arm from his neck to let his body crumple to the ground in a heap.

I stride to my mobile and dial the head of hotel security while I keep my narrowed eyes locked on Peters panting on the floor. This fucker went too damn far talking too much shit.

"Forget her name and that you ever knew her. Oh, and do not think I give a damn you are an attorney. Any legal action you take, and I will bury you," I promise him as he struggles to his feet.

Security arrives within moments, and Quinn Fucking Peters exits My Angel's life for good.

"Well, I see *The Enforcer* is up to his old tricks…" Sebastian chuckles as he walks into the gym past Peters and the two security team members.

Harris slaps his forehead and adds, "Damn! I missed all the fun."

* * *

"Congratulations, Starr. Another successful center launched. Your partnership with STEELE International is a coup! Here's to an even brighter future with our family."

Morgan beams at My Angel as he lifts his crystal flute filled with mimosa in a toast.

I grin broadly at my father's not-so-subtle hint at her being a part of our family. Everyone knows I plan to make her mine in every way.

The opening celebration exceeded expectations: more guests than the St. Barth's center; a wait list three months long; extensive media hype with excellent reviews; on track to cover the center's costs within five months. It impressed Morgan and Baz as former and current CEOs, respectively.

"Yes! Hear, hear!"

"Wonderful, Starr! We're so proud of you!"

"Girl Power rules!"

A congratulatory chorus rings out.

My family—except for Roger and Leonie—My Angel's parents, Anita, Norman, Billie, Patrick, Blair, Luc, Anton, Borya, Lucien, Adrienne, and Claudia gather for brunch at the resort's beachfront restaurant. Lucien's three Michelin star eatery known for its blending of Mexican traditional dishes with contemporary cuisine. It's the perfect backdrop for our families and friends to meet for the first time.

Tonight My Angel and I will dine with our parents. Of course my mother can't wait. I'm sure she thinks I'm going to propose. I learned my lesson; I'll wait a little longer.

When I'm guaranteed a yes response, I'll pop the question again…

"Thank you so much, everyone! I'm so grateful for your support!"

My Angel's effusive response brings me back to the conversation.

"I have to thank Lola for paying it forward when we met three years ago," My Angel says as she raises her flute and inclines her head to my SIL.

"You saved me and Baz. So you deserve all your success and happiness with a Steele!" Lola responds with a wink.

My Angel's cheeks sun kissed to copper blush red as she peeks at me.

I lean over and brush my lips over her temple. She smells so good. I take a deep inhale of her fragrant skin and sit back.

She sighs and rests her head against my shoulder.

Automatically my arm wraps around My Angel, and I hold her nestled against my side.

My gaze lands on her mother, who smiles back. I grin in acknowledgment of her approval and hug My Angel tighter.

Once again, my mind drifts.

"Are you satisfied with your expansion so far?" I ask My Angel as I wrap my arms around her from behind.

Her round ass presses against my upper thighs as I draw her closer to me with my palms on her lower belly.

We just returned to our villa after the party ended and stand before the open terrace doors facing the beach. The full moon shines down on the inky surface of the Pacific Ocean while multitudes of stars twinkle in the night sky above. The sounds of the waves crashing on the shore create a seductive rhythm.

My Angel raises her arms over her head to run her fingers in my hair, then twine them behind at the nape of my neck.

The movement juts her ample D-cups in her ocean blue back-

less maxi dress. The lustrous, fluid silk-satin skims her bodacious curves. While the hip-high slit shows off her long leg and the glittery crystal straps frame her toned back.

I slide my hands along her flanks, then slip them inside her dress to cup her tits. My thumb and index fingers pinch and tug her plump nipples into peaks. I dip my head to skim my lips down the column of her neck to nip the sensitive juncture at her shoulder.

"Oooh... Yes... So satisfied..." My Angel moans as she pulls my hair, prickling my scalp.

I chuckle wickedly. My mouth sucks on her sensitive skin, and she cries out. Once my mark raises on her neck, I kiss it softly.

"Are you satisfied with the expansion or with my mouth and hands on your sinful body, My Angel?" I ask her.

She purrs and gyrates her hips.

My cock thickens and lengthens in response to the pressure.

I step back and press my palm between her shoulder blades to bend her forward.

Knowing what's coming, My Angel widens her stance and braces her hands on her thighs. Her curly hair falls like a curtain on either side of her head.

Thwack. Thwack. Thwack. Thwack.

She yelps but holds her position.

My nostrils flare at the sight of her ass jiggling beneath the soft material of her dress. A few more spanks have her rising on her toes and a wet spot forming where her bare pussy rests against the silk-satin. Her arousal fills the surrounding air.

"Oh, Malcolm," she moans as she wiggles her hips.

A spank to her pussy has her yowling.

With a quickness, I flip her dress over her head and unzip my trousers to free my cock dripping with pre-cum.

"Hold your ankles, Little One," I command on one breath, then thrust in the next as I mount her like a stallion taking a mare in heat.

"Oh... Ohhh!" She cries out at my forceful entry to her tight, wet pussy.

A pattern of a fast thrust followed by a slow drag with shifts in my stance to vary my angle has her panting in moments. The difficulty to hold back her orgasm causes My Angel to beg for release.

I deny her.

Again.

And again.

Until her legs tremble and her pussy walls quiver.

I pull out, spin her around, and lift her leg to place her calf on my shoulder. Gripping her hips, I bend my knees and drive up into her throbbing, soaked pussy. The balls of my Prince Albert piercing brush her engorged clit, then stroke her G-spot until they rest deep against her womb.

"Oh, my—"

My Angel's groan catches in her throat when I draw her nipple into my hot, wet mouth to suckle. Hard. I latch on to her tit as my hips continue to piston.

Her head lolls from side to side. One last plea falls from her parted lips.

"Malcolm," My Angel pants.

"Who... do... you... belong... to... Starr?" I growl with each upward thrust.

"Aaaahhhh..." She replies as her pussy pulsates around my cock.

I smack her ass to make her focus and not cum.

"Words!" I demand.

She yowls, then cries out my name over and over.

"Then cum for me. Now!"

No sooner do the words leave my mouth than My Angel explodes.

Her greedy pussy clenches hard on my dick.

White sparks flash before my eyes. I increase my tempo while *my cock expands painfully. My head falls back as a roar rips from me along with copious amounts of my seed. The release is so intense, my knees buck.*

I carry her up the stairs to the bathroom of our bedroom suite and settle her on the pouf. My clothes drop to the marble floor as I stride to the shower. The spray jets from the rain shower. I return to my sated, sleepy Angel and lift her in my arms.

After I bathe and dry us, I place her under the cool sheets and slide in behind her, aligning our bodies—her back to my front. My eyes drift close.

"Malcolm, what happened to Quinn?" She murmurs.

Ah, no.

I shift to my elbow and cup her chin to turn her head towards me.

"I will tolerate no one attempting to come between us. He's gone from your life, Starr. And I will not hear his name from your mouth, especially not in our bed," I tell her.

Her eyes widen, and she bites the corner of her mouth.

I prepare to argue my point, but My Angel surprises me.

She shifts to face me and wraps her arms around my neck, burying her face. She inhales deeply, then sighs.

"Thank you, my love. He was becoming too much," My Angel responds.

I stiffen. WTF?!

"Malcolm, baby, no need to do anything more. He's done. Okay?" She breathes.

My molars grind, but I give in with a roll of my eyes. This woman makes me do things I never thought I would do. Ever.

Just as now when Billie asks if I'll take My Angel's prenatal yoga class since I lost the bet Patrick would lose the drinking contest we had two nights ago. I should have known the Scott would drink me under the table.

My Angel giggles and claps her hands.

"Oh, I cannot wait for this one! The women in the class

will have a proper laugh at this brawny man doing Kegels!" She says gleefully.

I zerbert her neck, and she giggles hysterically.

"The makings of a beautiful partnership!" Harris quips.

Everyone joins in our laughter.

Absolutely! I chuckle as I kiss My Angel breathless.

"Understand Starr is my only child and means everything to her mother and to me. Our family unit is inseparable. Starr shares every aspect of her life with my wife and with me. She made us aware of the situation with Vicky Reynolds and her declination of your proposal, along with the lifestyle she's chosen with you. My daughter is an intelligent, grown woman who thinks for herself. However, Starr is still mine to protect by any means necessary. I am no Quinn Peters. You were together for eight months; broke up for two; back together for ten. Now what are your intentions with my daughter, Steele?"

Peace's sharp obsidian eyes pierce me as we stand in the garden of his and Sun's Bel Air mansion.She and Starr are in the kitchen with the chef finishing our early Thanksgiving dinner.

My Angel and I want to spend time with both of our families for the holiday. I extended an invitation for Peace and Sun to join the Steele clan in Capri, then Verbier for Christmas. But My Angel felt it's too soon for a blending of our families. I kept my disagreement to myself—no pressure, for now.

I consider my response carefully.

Of course, My Angel has a close relationship with her parents. She's made that clear many times. I value and cherish my family, so I appreciate their connection. Besides, I'd have our children do the same.

Vicky Fucking Reynolds. No words.

My Angel's no, still rubs me wrong, but I respect her decision. My actions since reinforce my love for her and desire to build a life with her.

Interesting, she revealed our D/s lifestyle, and her father hasn't killed me… But as he said, My Angel thinks for herself and chooses to be my sub.

I wouldn't expect anything less from Peace whose Alpha male protectiveness of his daughter equals mine.

Apparently Peters ran like a wuss to Peace. Fucking loser. Peace must agree with me since he's said nothing in a month. But as I said: I give zero fucks because I. Will. End. Peters.

What are my intentions?

"Peace, I respect Starr, Sun, and you—your family dynamic. I love your daughter with every fiber of my being. I value her and the life I want to build with her. Starr may have said no once. But I am a patient man determined to prove my worthiness. I ask for your permission for her hand in marriage now. So when Starr is ready, we will have your blessing."

My Angel's father scans my face as he considers my heart-felt words.

"I appreciate your candidness and your respect. Starr loves you and in time will say yes." His gaze goes beyond my shoulder and his lips curl up in a smile that makes his obsidian eyes shine like liquid ebony.

Then Peace narrows his eyes at me and extends his hand.

"You have my blessing. But… Do. Not. Fuck. Up. Steele," he says, emphasizing his words with a firm handshake.

"Daddy! Don't break Malcolm's hand!"

My Angel's exclamation returns the smile to her father's mouth.

He deadpans, "Well, if he can't handle a handshake, how will he handle me whooping his ass if he hurts you?"

My Angel and Sun gasp as their matching sorrel brown eyes widen.

Peace chuckles and slaps me on the shoulder.

"Come, let us enjoy our early Thanksgiving dinner."

* * *

"WHAT A GORGEOUS VIEW of Southern Italy and the Mediterranean Sea from up here!"

Malcolm and I ride in the Sikorsky S-92 Executive Helicopter with Morgan, Shelley, Sebastian, Lola, Harris, and Haley en route to Roger and Leonie's Villa dei Fiori in Capri for Thanksgiving.

After Malcolm and I flew from LAX on his Gulfstream G650 to meet up with his family in New York City, we joined them on STEELE's Gulfstream G700. The $65 million expansive private jet accommodates nineteen passengers and the ten-hour flight to Naples.

"The Med is my favorite place. Morgan and I either stay at our Villa Sogno in Positano or yachting aboard *Serendipity*. I've heard great things about Roger and Leonie's villa. I can't wait to see it!" Shelley says.

Everyone agrees, and I turn to glance out of the window.

Moments later, the Sikorsky touches down on the helipad at the rear of the villa. Leonie and Roger stand holding The Twins, waving at us.

Morgan and Shelley alight from the back of the helicopter first, followed by Sebastian and Lola. Malcolm and I, then Harris and Haley disembark next. We wave and troop over.

"Hey, Little Pumpkins! Did you miss your favorite auntie?" Lola asks as Sebastian scoops Gaspard out of Roger's arms.

"And your very favorite uncle?" He adds giving Malcolm and Harris the side eye with a grin.

We make our way around to the terrace where Guy and Josy sit. They flew in this morning. Everyone exchanges greetings before Leonie and Roger show us to our sumptuous bedroom suites.

Villa dei Fiori has fast become one of their most cherished homes. It's where they had their babymoon when Leonie was nineteen weeks pregnant and they'd been back together for nine months. She fell in love with Lucien's former home the moment she set eyes on it. So, of course, Roger bought it for her.

The salmon-colored stucco exterior with white trim around the windows, columns, and roof lines blend beautifully with the lush greenery and stunning sea views from all sides. The sea-edge gardens, bountiful with camellias, magnolias, and palm trees prove as captivating as the impressive views of Mount Vesuvius, the Peninsula of Sorrento, the entire Gulf of Naples, and Anacapri. Its private swimming pool set in the side garden's grass and its exclusive sea access with a second plunge pool below makes it a unique property.

Malcolm and I, the siblings, and Guy and Josy take advantage and stay on different occasions. Since Morgan and Shelley have Villa Sogno across the Tyrrhenian Sea and their megayacht, this is their first visit.

While Roger shows them around, Malcolm and I settle in our plush suite. Then we head outside.

We find Leonie, The Twins, and Haley seated on blankets in the grass near the lunch table. They gathered here before we have lunch alfresco in the seaside garden. Just as we sit down, Roger strides over.

"How was your flight?" He asks me since Malcolm and I traveled the farthest from Beverly Hills.

I smile and my dimples pop.

"It was long and hard, but comfy on Malcolm's jet," I respond, winking at him.

He smirks and adds, "Yes, and rather palatable."

Leonie bursts out laughing, then starts to snort uncontrollably.

"What's so funny?"

We glance up to find Sebastian and Lola behind us.

"Oh, just the rigors and demands of travel," I deadpan.

Malcolm sits back on his hands, all smug with a cocky grin on his face. The Alpha Dom took his carnal tastes to the skies for fifteen hours.

Sebastian snickers and Roger snorts.

"No comment..." Haley says, rolling her eyes, disgusted as usual with hearing about her brothers' sex lives, even as innuendos.

She glances down at her mobile and smiles. Then types a response at lightning speed. When she raises her head, her cheeks flush, and her eyes shine. No longer wearing her glasses makes the dove gray orbs more expressive. Happy Haley, hmmm interesting.

"What's up, Baby Girl?" Roger asks, knowing the nickname drives her crazy.

Still in la-la land, Haley startles, then responds rushed, "Oh, uh... Callum's over in Sorrento."

When she doesn't continue, Roger prods her. He wants

to take Haley to dinner. So Roger tells her he can come here if they want. He's more than welcome. They agree, and Roger arranges for the helicopter to pick him up in an hour.

Leonie and Roger's parents appear. We gather around the table for a delicious lunch of flavorful local dishes prepared by the chef and served by the staff with wines from the villa's prized cellar.

Malcolm rubs my thigh under the table while we chat with everyone.

Shortly after we finish eating, Callum touches down. Haley goes to greet him, and some time later they join us for Limoncello Gin Collins on the lawn furniture. Her lips appear swollen, and his eyes gleam.

Mmhmmm.

"How are things with you, Callum?" Morgan asks as he sips his digestif. "I read in the *Financial Times* renewable energy is on the rise for another year in a row for Scotland."

They get into a discussion on Callum's family's business, Graham Energy, Oil & Gas Company, based in Aberdeen, Scotland. His father still leads the company as CEO, but he's in the process of grooming Callum for the role in five years. His younger brother and sister hold positions, too.

The conversation flows easily with everyone's participation.

The siblings grew up discussing business to prepare for joining their family's legacy while I worked to create SLFW. All of us volunteer in some way to help others, so we're a well-rounded group. All of our perspectives add to the conversation.

As we continue to chat, Malcolm reaches over and pulls me onto his lap. Content to relax in his arms, I snuggle against him and drift off, exhausted from the travel.

* * *

"Let's begin with some breathwork."

Each morning I start our day with yoga in the sunroom facing the sea. Aside from the girls, the guys join us. My influence runs deep.

Even though we welcomed the guys to yoga, we're kicking them out so we can have some much-needed Girls' Time. We have a lot to catch up on and only two days left before we go our separate ways until Christmas.

After a peaceful Savasana and light sharing namaste, we kick Malcolm, Sebastian, Roger, Harris, and Callum out of the sunroom.

Malcolm swats my ass on his way out and growls in my ear, "Do not think you are the boss of me, Little One."

I stifle a yelp as I hop onto the balls of my feet.

Malcolm chuckles.

"So, spill with Callum and Lachlan, Haley," I say as soon as I shut the door behind them.

Haley turns scarlet and reaches to push her glasses up the bridge of her nose. It's her nervous tell she can't stop even after wearing contact lenses for the last couple of years.

"What do you mean?" She asks, not realizing we know she's bluffing.

We giggle at her gaffe.

"Oh, don't play the innocent, Ms. Kiss Me Until My Lips Swell Steele!" Leonie laughs.

On a breathy sigh, Haley fills us in on the last couple of months since she saw Lachlan at the Labor Day fundraiser. The drama of her love triangle with one man who's her brother's best friend and one man who's had his eye on her since Harvard Business School proves more intriguing than any telenovela I've seen!

"Well then, what about you, Ms. Comfy on Malcolm's Jet Knight?" Lola adds.

Now it's my turn to blush. My chestnut-colored skin adds a crimson hue to my cheeks.

Haley smirks.

"Fine! He's a monster!" I laugh as I hold my hands two feet apart in front of me.

We fall onto our mats, snorting as Haley sings at the top of her lungs with her fingers in her ears.

Once we catch our breath, I fill my girls in on how Malcolm fills me and not just with his "monster" dick. I admit he proposed, and I said no. They empathize with my need to go with the flow—especially Leonie, my fellow free spirit. Lola repeats it'll only be a matter of time before I head down the aisle. Haley agrees, crossing her fingers.

By the time I finish my tales, Shelley and Josy come in the sunroom to invite us on a shopping trip to Capri town between the Piazzetta and Via Camerelle. It's one of the most fashionable centers in the world, with high-end boutiques and jewelry stores.

Less than an hour later, we're strolling along the streets, popping in and out of the boutiques filled with designer pieces and handcrafted items by local artisans.

Most of the people in the shops and on the streets recognize Leonie. She takes it in stride when they ask for her autograph or a selfie. Our security detail keeps any overzealous fans at bay—precautions Sebastian and Roger implemented after the Labor Day situation.

My shopping spree is complete when I order two pairs of bespoke Canfora Sandals, my favorite, purchase some hand-painted silk scarves, including three ties for Malcolm, and perfume that reminds me of the island's natural scent.

"Lola, honey, the sun did you some good. You're glowing."

Lola glances up into Shelley's smiling face.

"Yes, the fresh sea air and warm sun make a tremendous

difference," she grins. "Plus, your son makes sure I eat properly and rest."

Shelley throws her head back and laughs. Her brown eyes shine with mirth.

"I'm sure he does! My boys better treat their women well. Right, Starr and Leonie?" Shelley adds with a wink at the girls.

We giggle and nod our agreement.

Maman Josy cups Leonie's face and says, "And you treat those boys well, *non?*"

"*Oui, Maman, absolument!*" Leonie smiles lovingly at her mom.

I sigh and think about having children with Malcolm. But Leonie's cry stops my musings.

"*Chérie!* What's the matter?!" Leonie cries as she rubs Lola's back.

Shelley answers, "She's fine, just a bit overwhelmed. Let's head back to your villa, shall we?"

Leonie agrees and takes Lola's arm while Shelley holds the other. Josy, Haley, and I gather around them, and we make our way back to the Mercedes-Benz G-Wagens. The security detail follows, then drives us to the villa.

We'll gather for Thanksgiving dinner tonight.

"THIS IS FANTASTIC! I agree we should have an opulent Edwardian-themed-*Gigi* party!"

Leonie and Roger finished giving everyone a tour of the vintage steam yacht he bought for her. She named it *Gigi* after her favorite film.

Lola tells everyone how she can't wait to plan the soiree.

She and Leonie do their happy shimmy dance, then continue on to the bow where we'll have cocktails before Thanksgiving dinner begins.

The last few days have been full of swimming at the private beach or in the pool and excursions to the Blue Grotto, Monte Solaro, and Villa di Tiberio. The Blue Grotto thrilled The Twins when their laughter echoed inside of the water-filled cavern.

Leonie wanted to save *Gigi* for last as the highlight and setting for our Thanksgiving dinner as we cruise around Capri for three hours. They time it for cocktails at sunset and dinner by torchlight—electric since they don't want to risk damage to the boat.

We dress in semi-formal attire with the guys in suits and the women in dresses. The Twins wear shirt and shorts one-piece sets with socks that mimic shoes and outdo us all.

Once we're gathered at the bow with drinks in hand, Morgan leads us in expressing his thanks over the past year. Each of us takes a turn ending with Roger. It's obvious he's already emotional after Leonie's heartfelt words of gratitude for their lives together and most of all for the safety of their sons.

On the end of her touching speech and tears, he holds her close in his arms and address us.

"Thanks can never express the depth of my feelings for all of you and others who are not present. Your love and support from the start of that fiasco to the joy of our wedding with the addition of my in-laws and the wonderful holidays we shared to the return of our sons mean more than you can imagine. Mom, Dad, all of our lives you raised us to be a close-knit clan. This past year proves you succeeded. I love you all beyond measure."

Roger lifts his glass and proclaims, "Now let us enjoy this Thanksgiving dinner and here's to many, many more!"

"Hear, hear!!"

"Bravo, Roger! We love you, too!!"

"Happy Thanksgiving, everyone!!"

Malcolm nuzzles my neck and whispers, "Happy Thanksgiving, My Angel. I love you with all my heart. Next year, we'll have an early dinner with my family and spend the weekend with yours. Unless, of course, we're all together…"

I turn to Malcolm and caress his cheek with my palm, the five o'clock shadow prickles my palm.

"We should all be together, my love," I respond with a smile.

The Cheshire Grin that breaks out on his face makes my heart swell. Yeah, I can see us having babies and so much more.

"Hey, hey, hey! The gang's all here!! Merry Christmas Eve!"

Roger and Leonie laugh as Harris makes his way through the front door after Lola and Sebastian, arms laden with gifts. They tease he looks like a young Santa Claus.

He rejoins with, "A sexy AF one, no doubt! And no last-minute presents for me, Roger dear! Let's see if you get coal in your stocking this year..."

Malcolm and I enter behind him, and the girls hug while Malcolm and Roger bro hug.

"Good to see you, man!" Roger tells him.

"Still looking goofy, bro!" Malcolm teases.

Haley walks in looking glum, and Roger pulls her into a bear hug, lifting her off her feet.

As per Lola's intel, Haley was going through some relationship issues, so he tries to cheer his baby sister up posthaste. Malcolm told me *Duke* Callum will rue the day if he hurts their little sister: *I'll duke his ass.*

"You better have brought your, A game or I'm going to leave you in the powder tomorrow morning for our

Christmas Day run!" Roger teases Haley. "Don't blame me when your googles get covered in snow!"

She rolls her eyes and retorts, "Even on my worse day, I can outrace you, Roger!"

Guy and Josy enter carrying The Twins. They cared for Rodolphe and Gaspard while Roger and Leonie enjoyed their first wedding anniversary.

They scoop The Twins up and hold them close. These past few days are the longest they've been apart from them. They laugh at their parents' overzealous kisses and pat their faces with their chubby hands.

I smile to myself at their cuteness. Then I wonder what it would be like to have babies with Malcolm and where they'd stay: Bel Air with my parents or New York City with Shelley and Morgan.

Come to think about it where would we live in general? I've never lived anywhere besides California other than a semester abroad in Oxford, England to study economics at Pembroke College at the University of Oxford.

The idea of living in the concrete jungle of Manhattan doesn't appeal to me. Despite Malcolm's urging to open an SLFW in the Flat Iron District. It's *the* neighborhood for fitness lovers with its many high-end gyms, sportswear stores, juice bars, and luxurious spas.

But his home in Southampton Village more than makes up for the lack of open space near water. Perhaps we could live there instead of The STEELE Tower. That's a consideration and compromise. Then I'd open a center out there—

"Where are you, My Angel?"

Malcolm's rumbling baritone rouses me from my thoughts. His lips brush against the shell of my ear, and I tremble.

Damn this man gets me every time!

I peek at him from beneath my long eyelashes.

"The Twins are so cute. I can't help but wonder what my children will be like," I murmur, baiting him.

Malcolm growls under his breath, "You mean *our* children. No other man will plant his seed inside of your womb, Starr Knight!"

I swallow my yelp when he smacks my ass.

"We'll work on them later…" he adds quietly as Morgan and Shelley pass us to greet Roger and Leonie warmly.

"This tree is even bigger than last year's," his mother says, smiling as she takes a glass of hot mulled wine. "I love the new decorations!"

After we place presents beneath the Christmas tree, everyone makes their way to their suites while Leonie and Roger tend to The Twins. Malcolm grasps my hand and tugs me towards the stairs.

"How many? I think two is good, maybe three," Malcolm says from the bathroom as he unpacks his kit.

I walk back out of the closet to slip my arms around him from behind. My hands stroke his eight-pack abs beneath his red cashmere turtleneck sweater. My man is ripped!

"How many what?" I ask peeping at his handsome reflection in the vanity mirror.

Malcolm's dove gray eyes twinkle as the corners of his mouth lift.

"Babies!" He exclaims as he spins and places his palms on my lower belly. "*My* babies inside of *my* woman!"

He nuzzles his face between the valley of my breasts and mumbles, his words muffled by the cashmere.

"What???" I ask giggling when his teeth nip through my sweater. "Hey!"

Malcolm lifts his gaze to mine while he continues to mouth my breasts now against my skin.

"Breastfeed… I want your milk, Hot Mama…" he says between licks.

I roll my eyes and cup the back of his head, then moan when he pushes my bra aside to suckle my aroused nipple.

"You'll have to share with *our* babies, Malcolm Steele!" I admonish.

He chuckles before he pulls back with a pop. My wet nipple glistens from his attentive ministrations.

"But of course. But I get first dibs!" He teases.

I adjust my breasts since we don't have much time before dinner starts.

"Well, you'll eat le *Réveillon de Noël* now!" I say as I swat his wandering hands away from the waistband of my leggings.

With a wicked chuckle, Malcolm promises later, and we head back downstairs to the dining room where Josy chats with the chef she favored last Christmas about tonight's dinner. It's like the holiday before, in honor of the French tradition of le *Réveillon de Noël* for the Christmas meal.

We relish in each other's company as we dine on fine dishes and excellent wines. The conversation flows easily.

Once we're gathered in the great room and exchanged our first gifts as our tradition for Christmas Eve, Roger stands and pulls Leonie to her feet with him. The two female Bichon Frise puppies Roger gifted Leonie and The Twins scamper around their feet, playing with a toy.

"Well everyone, Leonie and I have some news to share with you," Roger gazes from one smiling face to the other before his eyes turn to his wife's gorgeous face.

"We're twenty weeks pregnant with a baby girl!!" Leonie announces, grinning like the Cheshire Cat.

Everyone whoops and hollers.

"Congratulations!!"

"*Oh, Mon Dieu!*"

"Awesome news, Roger and Leonie!!"

"*Fantastique, Mon Trésor!*"

Malcolm nudges me and raises his eyebrow as he mouths our turn.

Before I can answer, Sebastian clears his throat and stands, too.

"Roger and Leonie, Lola and I are so thrilled for you! Once again you'll make us an aunt and an uncle—the most favorites, of course," he pauses to pull Lola into his side. "And we will make you an aunt and uncle, too. The most favorite is up to the others."

At first everyone smiles and nods. Then the room erupts when they realize what Sebastian mean about them expecting a baby, too.

"We're twenty weeks, too!" Lola gushes as she rubs her belly covered by an oversized sweater. "Can you believe it, BFF?!"

"Oh, Lola, Sebastian! We're so happy for you, too!!" Leonie exclaims as she hugs a beaming Lola and they start to cry, overcome with hormonal emotions.

Malcolm bro hugs his brothers while I embrace Leonie and Lola. We squeal with Haley, Josy, and Shelley.

The doorbell chimes, and Shelley waves Roger off as she heads to the entryway to answer. Everyone is present, so we're not sure who it could be.

Roger glances down at Leonie, and she shrugs her shoulders.

Everyone turns to the entry, wondering who has arrived at this late hour.

Shelley returns to the great room with Lachlan behind her. She glances at Haley questioningly, then at Sebastian worriedly.

Lachlan strides right in and stops in front of Haley, clasping her hands in his. Without his emerald green eyes leaving her dove gray ones, he addresses Morgan and Baz.

"No disrespect, Uncle Morgan. We're like brothers,

Sebastian. But Haley is mine, and I won't go another day without her for anyone."

Silence descends on the great room. Talk about the other shoe drops, rather the third…

"What the fuck, Lachlan?!" Sebastian growls as he advances on his best friend. "What do you mean Haley is yours?"

Lola puts both of her hands on Sebastian's arm to hold him back.

"Baz, babe, let them be. It's Haley's decision, not yours," Lola says calmly.

"*Oui*, give them some privacy," Leonie adds, then turns to Haley and Lachlan. "Haley, go to the library. No one will disturb you, *Chérie*."

"Leonie—" Roger pins her with his intense stare.

"*Non!* Enough of the big brother meddling! Let Haley live her life," Leonie demands, her fierce feline gaze sparking golden amber.

Haley nods, and she leaves the great room with Lachlan in tow.

Malcolm, Roger, Harris, and Sebastian glare after them. I swear I hear Harris growl. He's the most easygoing of them, but he's extremely protective of his twin.

"Now, Sebastian, Lola, boy or girl?" Josy asks, clapping her hands to diffuse the situation. "We must know how to prepare, *non?*"

Lola jumps right in and tugs Sebastian to the sofa.

"We're having a… baby… BOY!!" She shouts as she shimmies in her seat beside me.

Her exuberance melts the arctic chill from the air in the room. No one can resist her joy, especially her husband.

He wraps him arm around her shoulders and leans over to kiss her temple. Then he faces their family.

"Yes, a son! A healthy baby boy! See for yourselves,"

Sebastian says as he stands to pass out color copies of the ultrasound images he had in an envelope.

"Fantastic! You're right, Josy, we have so much to prepare!" Shelley gushes. "June will be here before you know it."

"A girl and a boy at the same time! Busy, busy, busy!" Sebastian laughs.

While I chat with Lola and Leonie, I subconsciously place a hand on my lower belly. Then giggle when Leonie arches her elegant eyebrow as her feline gaze that never misses a trick shifts between my hand and Lola.

They join in my laughter, and we hug each other.

"Well, My Angel, when will we make our announcement?"

Malcolm strokes my bare lower belly as he spoons behind me in our bed later that night.

I place my hand over his and turn my head sideways to speak.

"The em comes before the cee, you know," I respond softly.

Malcolm rises to an elbow and stares down at me.

I shift into a seated position and meet his questioning gaze. My fingers twist the sheet in my lap as I consider my next words.

"Starr and Malcolm, sitting in a tree, K-I-S-S-I-N-G. First come love, then comes marriage. Then comes Starr with a baby carriage." I whisper as I shake my head.

I'm still not quite ready to walk down the aisle. Nor do I want a baby before I get married. I may be carefree, but I am traditional.

Malcolm opens his mouth to respond, but I silence him with my raised hand.

"I'm all for babies—in our future. So let's just leave it there for now, my love," I request.

Malcolm nods without commenting, a wistful expression marring his handsome face. He understands it's best not to push me.

Instead he makes sweet love to me, pouring all of his emotions into it. My body quivers with need and succumbs to his carnal intensity over and over again.

Other than our passionate cries and the joining of our bodies, we remain silent allowing our actions to speak for us.

Afterwards, I lie with my head resting on his heaving, sweat-slick chest. The rhythm of his heart lulls me to sleep.

My last thought before my sated slumber overtakes me: we have plenty of time.

STARR

"*I* know you'll be busy with your pregnancy, your work with Lola's Coterie and STEELE, and your volunteering with the girls. But… I'd love if you'd design my nurseries… Please, bestie?"

Lola, Leonie, Haley, Blair, Billie, and I sit in my chill room on the first floor of my New York City penthouse while The Twins play with their Bichon Frise puppies and toys on a blanket. The boys including Morgan, Luc, Patrick, and Lachlan went to the STEELE box at Madison Square Garden for the Knicks versus the Los Angeles Lakers basketball game.

The girls and I take advantage of some time alone. It's been a month since we left Verbs and the first time we've all been together.

As the Head of STEELE Children and Young Adults Division and since she did a fantastic job with Lola's Sutton Place penthouse, Leonie would be perfect to help her BFF.

The Twins' nurseries—nine in total, no less—are spectacular and suit each of Leonie and Roger's and their grandparents' residences. They need eight: their and Morgan and

Shelley's New York City penthouses; their and their Southampton Village beach houses; our and their Paris penthouses; Josy and Guy's Paris mansion; their London mansion.

It's a Herculean task. Lola gives Leonie puppy dog eyes.

"Of course, *Chérie*! I was hoping you'd ask!" She says clapping her hands as her amber eyes twinkle in delight.

Leonie has always had an eye for design. The combination of being the world-renowned megamodel *The Lion* for almost nineteen years and as the daughter of an old, wealthy Parisian merchant family that travels seeking antiques, antiquities, and fabrics instilled in her a love for the aesthetics. Transitioning into interior design was her dream for years.

"*Merci! Merci beaucoup, mon amie!*" Lola thanks her with a huge sideways hug to avoid bumping their bellies. "We must start with the nurseries here and in Southampton Village. The ones in Paris and London can wait since we won't travel abroad until after the summer season."

Since Baby Boy is due in June, Sebastian and Lola decided to stay out in The Hamptons after they're born. Time away from the city during the sultry New York summer proves just the solution. Who wouldn't prefer to be on the beach?

The smart parents-to-be are on the same wavelength as me. The Hamptons are much better as a residence.

Shelley already told the couple she and Morgan will stay out there and not go to Positano for the summer. So Sebastian and Lola will have plenty of support.

"Do you want to remain true to your interiors or go with unique designs? Have you decided which rooms you want to convert? Oh, and Shelley showed me some incredible heirloom pieces from their family we can incorporate like we did for The Twins. Not to mention antiques from mine and pieces from the collections of Beaulieu Enterprises. I know just the ones…"

We jump right in on ideas. Leonie sketches on a pad Lola pulls from her secretary desk as her creative juices flow from her head to her fingers. In no time at all she has several options from themed to traditional, down to the layouts and the color palettes.

We love them!

"Do you think Nanny Grace would make a blanket for Baby Boy? Rodolphe and Gaspard's are beautiful," Haley says. "They'll treasure them forever."

Nanny Grace hand-crocheted two navy blue cashmere blankets. Everyone admired the fine stitchwork of the intricate design. The center panels have entwined B and S for Beaulieu and Steele, surrounded by a twelve-inch border of swirls and whorls. She made matching beanies and booties to complete the sets.

Lola claps her hands together and lace her fingers as she bounces on the sofa.

"Ooooh! That would be phenomenal! Will you ask her for me, Leonie?" She says. "I'd love to combine Baby Boy's initials."

"Have you chosen a name, yet?" I ask.

Lola shares their decision to wait until the day he's born to pick based on which feels best once we set eyes on Baby Boy with us, and we understand.

"Being that you and Lola are due at the same time, I spoke with Anita since she's a doula now. She can help you, Leonie, while I help Lola. It's better for you both with me in the States and Anita in Paris. We can give you the attention you need without concern for distance," I say.

Lola smiles at me. She asked me to be her doula. She did not know when she asked Leonie was expecting too and would want to have me help her again.

Of course, Lola's easygoing BFF took it in stride. Leonie rarely allows situations to become problems. She figured she'd make do with a referral from Dr. Berger, her OB-GYN.

"Starr offers the perfect solution!" Leonie exclaims as she hugs me too.

Anita became Leonie's yoga instructor once she was further along in her pregnancy, and I wanted her to have hands-on attention not possible through our Skype sessions. Over the years, Anita and Leonie, then with the other girls, became close. She's now a part of our clique.

"Wonderful, *Chérie*! I remember when Anita completed her doula training. She'll be perfect, *merci*!" Leonie gushes. "I'll send a text message to her now."

"While we're on the topic of baby plans… Leonie, Sebastian and I want to meet with Nanny Grace's agency for selecting a nanny and a nurse," Lola says. "Baz and I figure you can speak with the owners since they're based in Paris before we meet with their New York City office."

Grace Hart is one of their stellar nannies who's also a trained nurse. The überwealthy and celebrities use her agency to hire their nannies, nurses, and governesses. Their training is top-notch in everything from changing a diaper to language lessons to disarming a would-be kidnapper. Even though Sebastian has a security detail for his wife, it's good for the nanny to have training.

"*Absolument!* Nanny Grace is the best! Roger and I will call them tomorrow morning Paris time. Perhaps we can video conference into the call the head of this office," Leonie responds.

The house intercom rings, and Lola answers it to Shelley on the line. The spa day with her best friend and the Jackson Matriarch Lucie ended early. Shelley asks what we're up to, and Lola tells her to come down since we're talking baby plans.

When she arrives, we fill her in on the latest. She's just as excited as we are about the developments.

"More grandchildren to spoil," she laughs, clapping her hands. "I cannot wait!"

She turns to me and beams as she winks.

My cheeks heat, and I glance down at my hands in my lap. The baby bug has bitten everyone, and they want Malcolm and me on deck.

Not just yet, I say to myself. Even if my womb begs to be filled by Malcolm's virile seed...

"EXCUSE ME, everyone. May I have your attention? I have an announcement to make."

With a nod, Lola stands and smiles at Blair.

We're in the private East Room of Per Se, Lola's favorite restaurant in New York City.

As we walked in, my gaze went to the stunning views of the Manhattan skyline and Central Park clear across Columbus Circle to Fifth Avenue. The other side of the East Room is a glass panel that overlooks the restaurant's main dining room. But prior to our arrival, the staff closed the silk drapes for privacy.

"Years ago I thought I was Wonder Woman and could do every aspect of Lola's Coterie by myself. From the design to the marketing to the management of the Paris flagship and the London boutique. My wise mentor told me to focus on the creative design side and let an assistant handle the day-to-day tasks. In came Blair and she blew me away with her efficiency, dependability, and cleverness when balancing the activities that didn't need my constant or immediate attention."

Then she turns to Billie seated beside Patrick and smiles.

"I learned from my experience with Blair to find someone I can rely on to handle my business affairs long distance for Lola's Coterie Las Vegas. Thanks to Baz's director of STEELE's West Coast retail properties, I met Billie. I needed someone who could handle the contractors, staff, and clients who like me could charm the best of them but can turn into a spitfire when necessary."

Everyone laughs when Lola waggles her eyebrows.

"Over the years, you've proven yourselves to be incredible in your jobs, but also wonderful friends. With Baby Boy on the way, I realize once again, I cannot do it all"—she raises her glass of iced lemon ginger tea—"So this decision was a no-brainer. Blair I would like to offer you the position of my chief marketing officer and Billie my chief operating officer!"

Blair and Billie gasp while the others stand and clap, then raise their glasses in a toast.

"So deserved, *Chéries!*"

"Whoohoo! Congratulations!"

"*Félicitations!*"

"Cheers!"

After a few moments, Lola quiets everyone down and turns back to Blair and Billie.

"Do you accept?" She asks. "I mean, just don't leave a preggie lady hanging, no pressure!"

Billie jumps up and gives her a hug, and Blair does the same. They agree wholeheartedly. And the servers appear with chilled bottles of Dom Pérignon Rosé Vintage 2005—another of Lola's favorites—and a variety of desserts.

"We'll drink for you, Leonie and Lola!" Malcolm teases.

Lachlan adds, "We know it's your favorite bubbly, Lola!"

"Awww… Don't tease my sisters. Although I must say you are missing out, ladies!" Harris chuckles.

Leonie laughs, and Roger pops Harris on the back of his head good-naturedly.

We spend the rest of the time chatting and enjoying one another. The boys rehash the basketball game, including the "incredible last second three-pointer by LeBron *King* James." Billie jokes about her date with another basketball super-star. But Patrick whispers in her ear, and her eyes widen as she turns bright pink. He sits back and smirks.

I giggle knowing Patrick being an Alpha Dom must have told her just how he feels about her date with another man. Malcolm squeezes my thigh under the table, and I can't help but snort. Then cover my mouth with my linen napkin to hide my laughter.

Malcolm silences me with words said in my ear. His warm breath tickles my neck as he leans over. His lips trail along the side of my neck, making my nipples pucker against the silk of my wrap dress and my pussy clench with need. My mind was already on lascivious thoughts. He just drove me closer to the edge.

"You had better never mention being with another man with me around—or not, Little One," My Dom warns.

It cracks me up further to realize how each of my friends —who despite being Independent Women—find themselves attracted to Alpha males, Doms or not. Sometimes when you're in control of your business, career, life… it's a relief to turn over control to your lover. No need to think, just feel as Malcolm tells me.

"Well, Sir, since you asked… A vision of my wrists bound by red silks to the corners of your bed with my ankles in the spreader bar in your private suite at LEVELS New York. My legs thrown over your shoulders as you lie between my trembling thighs, thrusting your tongue and fingers into my dripping, tight pussy. I scream your name—hoarse from my previous carnal cries—as you wring a fourth orgasm from my wrecked pussy. My pussy juices coat your mouth and chin as you rise to your knees. Your tongue darts out to lap it up, then grip your massive dick to align it with my dripping slit. With a ravenous cry, plunge into my depths and take me mercilessly until I cum again and again. Head thrown back, eyes shut, a roar rips from your throat as you blow your load deep inside my pussy. It squeezes every drop from your cock."

I lift my lowered gaze to his and smile in triumph when I see his pupils blown and his mouth slack.

Malcolm flares his nostrils and smirks, "Well Naughty Girl, let us go to LEVELS to make your vision our reality."

My grin widens, "Yes, Sir. Thank you, Sir."

"MASQUERADE NIGHT at LEVELS New York, how perfect. How does a scene in the Cellar sound to you, Little One? You bound in my white silk Shibari ropes trussed up from the ceiling above the primary stage for a bit of breath play? After which—if you are a good girl—we will retire to my private suite for your aftercare before we bring your fantasy to life. The choice as always is yours, Little One."

My pussy creams and my nipples tighten against the silk of my wrap dress when My Dom gazes at me with hooded eyes as we ride in the back of his chauffeured Bentley Mulsanne. As promised, he's taking me to his club for an after-dinner treat...

And what a treat he proposes!

"The scene sounds marvelous, Sir. And I promise to be a very, very good girl deserving of my fantasy brought to life," I respond huskily as my fingertips brush against my evening collar.

"Excellent! I will have one of the staff bring masks to the car. No one gets to know it is you or see what is for my eyes only, Little One," My Dom says with a gleam in his dove gray eyes.

I have to suppress an eye roll. The possessive caveman!

"I will keep my shirt on so no one will recognize my tattoo," he adds as he types a text message on his mobile.

When we arrive, a handsome man brings masks to us a pair of flesh-tone silk thongs packaged in a tiny box. My Dom tells me to put them on. Then the staff member escorts us into the renovated warehouse in a prime spot of the Meatpacking District. The building is six stories and has a brick facade with oversized windows treated to block outsiders from seeing through the panes of glass since the interior is not visible.

Two men in custom-tailored black suits stand outside. A queue that extends around the corner of people in expensive attire patiently await admittance to the Dance Club. Not surprising given LEVELS is for the über-wealthy and influential, too refined to behave boorishly. The hopeful patrons are not rambunctious as one would ordinarily see waiting outside a Manhattan nightclub.

The flagship location has seven levels: 7th Sky Lounge that offers a stunning, 360-degree view of Manhattan and across the Hudson River to New Jersey's shoreline, a bar, restaurant by day dance club by night, a coverable pool that's open during the warmer months, and a glass-retractable roof; 6th and 5th multilevel dance club with two bars and a lounge for food and drinks; 4th Level 4 Restaurant and bar open for breakfast, lunch, and dinner; 3rd has twelve private suites for members to continue their pleasure apart from the BDSM levels; 2nd Peepshow for BDSM with seating alcoves, primary stage, mini-stages, performance rooms, and a bar that serves non-alcoholic mocktails; below ground the Cellar a BDSM dungeon with mocktails bar.

Tonight, My Dom leads me by the hand through

Peepshow and down the stairs to the erotic pleasures offered by the Cellar...

I shiver in anticipation when we step through the double doors. My eyes scan the expansive, grand hall, austere in design.

A multi-beamed high ceiling; cobblestone floors; brick walls; lighting that resembles flickering torches in brackets on the walls and in metal stands scattered around the room; an assortment of what looks like Medieval torture devices placed in clusters. My gaze bounces from one area to another. An older man cuffed to one of the several St. Andrew's Crosses, his head thrown back in pure ecstasy. His engorged dick eagerly sucked by a younger man on his knees. A woman in a swing, her thighs glistening with her pussy juices and stretched wide to accommodate the large man standing between them aligning her core to his massive cock. Several men and women attached to hooks hanging from the ceiling in varied positions being whipped by Doms and Dommes with canes, floggers, and paddles extending from their hands. Still others lead naked subs by leashes while they crawl on their hands and knees to one of the partitioned rooms for a bit of privacy. Here and there voyeurs stand watching, mesmerized by the decadent, sexual activities.

The sight has my throbbing pussy so wet that I can feel my juices coating my inner thighs. The aroma of my arousal rising to fill my nose and to join with all the other scents. I shift subconsciously on my feet. I'll never get over the initial sight of the BDSM dungeon, no matter how many times My Dom brings me.

"Come along, Little One."

The warm breath of My Dom against my ear rouses me from my thoughts. With a *yes, sir,* I follow him to the primary stage. Where miraculously his kit awaits us beside a table. He did more than request masks...

"Strip while I prepare our scene," My Dom commands.

I comply then stand in my black lace balconette bra by Lola's Coterie—his favorite style.

He smirks in appreciation before he lifts me onto the table. With knowledge gained from years under the guidance of a Japanese Master, My Dom begins the complex task of binding me in his Shibari ropes.

This is one of my favorite forms of play. The sensation of the silk rope bound in an erotic pattern against my skin to hold me immobile allows me to let all stress, problems, life shit, fade away. I give in to complete submission under the trustworthy hands of My Dom. Pure bliss.

In moments, he has me hovering face down above the table, captured in his silks—arms bound behind my back; breasts jutting forward; knees spread and bent with thighs pressed to calves. Only my head and feet move freely.

"Are you fine to proceed, Little One?" My Dom asks for my permission to take our scene to the next level.

"Yes, Sir," I respond with a shudder as his lips skim the side of my neck.

He pushes the table away, and I sway in the air. A soft push to my hip, and I spin in a circle to display My Dom's beautiful art of rope play.

Murmurs of appreciation come from the members who gather around the stage.

Once the circle completes, My Dom grips my hip with one hand while his other unzips his pants to unleash his beast of a cock.

Eyes already closed from the thrall being bound has my submissive mind, I moan in anticipation.

My sopping wet pussy as illustrated by the wet patch on the thong calls to his primal need to mount his mate. He swipes it aside and slides his girth into my ready channel that begs for him to stuff it full.

"Fuck me!" My Dom grunts when he's balls deep inside of me.

My mouth hangs open as I swing on the ring rope attached to the middle of my body. Like a pendulum, My Dom keeps me coming back to impale my pussy on his erect cock.

The rippling of my inner walls precedes my climax. But I will not give in until My Dom allows it. When I'm at the point of begging, he gives me the command.

"Cum for me, Little Pet! Cum for me. Now!" He roars as he lets loose a torrent of his seed inside of me.

My pussy implodes, and my mind floats in subspace as I hear a faint:

"Good girl. You deserve your fantasy…"

MALCOLM

"Well, I must say, Lola did a good thing when she recommended you reach out to her friend Starr Knight, Malcolm. The partnership with Jackson Hole at STEELE Resorts for her fitness retreats pleases Father. And of course Lucien and me. Father says it was an excellent decision—CEO worthy!"

Lydie's emerald green eyes glow as she speaks.

As always, my cousin hyper focuses on gaining Uncle Connor's approval of her as the next head of Jackson Corporation. He prefers Lachlan as the eldest male child, despite Lydie being the *eldest* and her passion for running their family's business. Not to mention she's proven herself repeatedly over the years from internships through her current role as their overall Vice President.

While Lachlan is their Vice President of Liquor. He loves his sister too much to battle her for the role. Instead, he's a reluctant heir apparent who's happy to take a back seat and let Lydie shine.

Her and Lucien's idea of Jackson Hole beach clubs serve as a prime example. They approached Baz with it just over three years ago. Now it's another profitable STEELE-Jackson partnership. My Angel's fitness retreats add another level to the clubs' offerings. An impressive addition to the revenue over a short period. People look and feel better in their skimpy bikinis and trunks when they're in shape. Getting their summer bodies ready, Lydie says. I agree.

"We should add more retreats to the calendar or develop a theme around the location's holidays or make them a permanent feature—"

"Whoa," I cut in with my hands raised palms out in surrender. "Let's have this conversation when Starr arrives. We can discuss your ideas at dinner tonight or tomorrow as we do a construction site visit for Starr Light Fitness and Wellness Resorts at STEELE Monte Carlo."

Lydie throws her head back and laughs heartily.

Her silky, dark brown hair flows down her back to her narrow waist that flares to her curvy hips and long legs. The cut of her silk blouse accentuates her full tits as they jiggle with her laughter. She's definitely a banger, so I can understand Lola's concern when she started dating Baz.

Combine Lydie's beauty with her smarts and her confidence, and she makes most women nervous around their men. Besides the fact she was crushing secretly on Baz for years hoping to appease her father by blending our families and companies through marriage... I shake my head recalling the drama.

"Okay, okay, I'll reel in my exuberance, Malcolm!" Lydie says as she continues to chuckle. "It'll be good to see Starr. The last time I was in Beverly Hills, I had a few sessions with her. She's phenomenal!"

I beam with pride for my woman. Everyone loves her, but not as much as me!

"I've had plenty of yoga teachers, but Starr is the best by

far…" Lucien quips with his emerald eyes dancing with devilry.

His play on words makes a vicious growl rise from the depths of my chest. MINE!

Lucien snickers.

"Oh my, Malcolm. Aren't you the possessive one all of a sudden?" Lydie says joining in her brother's laughter. "I never thought I'd see the day the rebel bad boy would hand in his playboy Dom card!"

I roll my eyes and sit back on the sofa. Instead of knocking Lucien onto his arrogant ass, I jab a brass stud in the tufted leather.

Lydie and Lucien continue to crack up at my expense while they recall some of my bawdier moments through the years. I recount some of Lucien's for good measure before we get back to business.

The vibration of my mobile interrupts our discussion.

As I remove it from my trousers pocket, I notice Haley's name appear on the screen. I excuse myself from the sitting area of my office to move to my desk before I accept the call.

"Hey, Lil' Sis, what's up?" I ask as I stretch my long legs beneath the desk.

"Hey is for horses, Malcolm…" She responds dryly. "I'm still working on the psycho sub reconnaissance, nothing concrete as of now. But I found an interesting bit of information…"

Haley fills me in after I remind her ex-psycho-sub, and I promise on our family to hold tight until she has irrefutable proof. She knows I'm about to go ballistic.

"As Starr says, 'take a deep cleansing breath' before you explode, Malcolm. Do it for Starr," Haley cajoles.

I squeeze my eyes shut on an inhalation through my

nose, pause, then exhale through my mouth slowly as I envision the anger leaving my body. Another inhalation brings in fresh air with thoughts of Starr smiling at me with her sorrel brown eyes sparkling. The process calms me. For now.

"Fine. But as soon as you have solid intel, call me no matter the time," I tell Haley.

She agrees, and we end our call.

Before I rejoin Lydie and Lucien, I vow to exact revenge upon that *psycho sub* then take another deep cleansing breath to rid myself of the negativity.

"All good, cuzz?" Lucien asks, no longer gleeful when I sit down on the sofa again.

His concerned expression lets me know the breath didn't clear my face…

"Yeah, no worries," I respond. "Let's finish before Starr lands."

Lydie eyes me for a moment, then nods as she picks up her laptop. Lucien turns to his notes. We end our meeting shortly thereafter.

When my eyes land on My Angel, I relax finally. No breathwork needed.

Well, except for the air I capture as I kiss her breathless, held aloft in my embrace.

Fuck, I miss my woman!

A month is way too long a period to pass before she's in my arms. Between our businesses—my travels to Latin America and her retreat in Bali—claiming our attention and being on opposite ends of the planet, we haven't had a moment to connect in person. FaceTime goes but so far.

"Wow! You missed me that much, huh?" My Angel giggles once I put her back on her feet. "Maybe I'll host two retreats next month! Absence makes the heart grow fonder and all!"

I narrow my eyes at her and growl in her ear, "I do not think so, Naughty Girl!"

Her giggles make my heart soar. She loops her arm through mine, and we stride to the Black Badge Rolls-Royce Cullinan driven by one of STEELE Monte Carlo's drivers.

"How was your flight?" I ask as I pull My Angel onto my lap on the back seat.

She drapes her arms over my shoulders and grins.

"Wonderful! I love the new bedding. Not only was I floating in the clouds, I slept on them!" My Angel laughs.

I shake my head, "More than you love me?"

Fuck if I don't sound like a wuss. I used to tease Baz and Roger when they swooned over Lola and Leonie. Now, I'm exactly like my pussy-whipped, lovestruck brothers. Good grief.

My Angel smirks and ruffles her fingers through my hair.

"No need to worry, little boy, I love you too," she says.

I thrust my hips up to bump her lush ass with my burgeoning erection.

"Who is a 'little boy,' Naughty Girl?" I rejoin with a growl.

Her pupils dilate and her chestnut-colored cheeks flush with desire. When her the tip of her tongue swipes across her plump lips, I lose my control.

My mouth slants over hers as I claim her in a dominating, passionate kiss. My tongue sweeps the seam of her mouth, demanding admission.

Her lips part on a pleading mewl.

I enter with gusto. My tongue licks inside her warm mouth from side to side, top to bottom, before it seeks hers. It wants to prove it's in charge of our reunion kiss.

My Angel writhes on my lap. Her movements insistent. She wants me as much, if not more than I want her.

Her moans fill the enclosed section of the luxury SUV. No better music to be heard.

I pour every aching second we've spent apart into our kiss. My wicked tongue battles for dominance while dancing with hers. I grunt.

The little minx nipped my tongue!

Without missing a beat, I flip her over onto her belly, across my muscular thighs, pull her yoga pants down to bunch at her knees, and smack that ass.

THWACK. THWACK. THWACK.

She squeals and jolts with each connection my palm makes with her fast-glowing-red ass.

"Malcolm!" My Angel wails under my unrelenting blows.

But for the scent of her musky arousal and the dampness on my palm as it makes contact with her pussy, one would think the spanking displeased My Angel. Ah, no.

The more I punish her, the wetter she becomes. Her pussy juices flow below her butt crease and along her legs to puddle on my lap.

My cock weeps.

"Ooohhh fuuuck… Sir… Yes… Yes.. Yeeesss!" My Angel screams in ecstasy, her head tosses side to side and her eyes squeeze shut.

The rough pads of my fingers rub against her G-spot as the thick digits plunge in and out of her soaking wet, tight pussy.

"It appears as though you missed me and love my erotic touch, Naughty Girl," I growl in her ear.

She groans and rides my fingers as I continue to fuck her just how she likes it.

Her inner walls contract, squeezing my four fingers to

the point of pain. One more stroke, and she'll explode in orgasmic bliss. Her mouth opens ahead of her climax.

THWACK. THWACK. THWACK.

My Angel screams in frustration, then shock as I withdraw my fingers from her pussy and spank the swollen folds.

"You will not cum until tonight or tomorrow depending upon your behavior for the rest of today, Naughty Girl," I purr in her ear.

Her fists clench tighter than her empty pussy. She throws me a dirty look and grinds her molars.

"Ah, ah, ah… One word and it will be three days of edging you for hours before you cum," I warn her.

One last glare, and My Angel collapses with a sigh onto my lap dejectedly.

I pat her reddened ass before I rearrange her silk G-string and pull her pants back up. Another pat, and I sit her beside me.

Just in time since the Cullinan stops in front of STEELE Monte Carlo. The valet opens the door.

My Angel throws one last glare over her shoulder at me before she takes his proffered hand to exit the SUV.

I chuckle. Still so naughty. I love it.

"STARR, so good to see you! I adore your outfit! The mushroom color looks great against your tan. Where have you been?"

Lydie gushes as she hugs My Angel.

We arrived at the bar of the seafood restaurant run by Lucien on Avenue des Spélugues, close to the hotel. Lucien stepped into the kitchen to survey his domain while Lydie waited for My Angel and me.

I agree with Lydie, My Angel dazzles.

The fluid, semilustrous silk brings an understated elegance to her camisole and track cargo pants. The draped neckline and delicate chain straps embellished with lustrous pearls add to the luxurious appeal. While the strappy sandals and clutch won't allow one to mistake the evening outfit for the gym.

I only care she swept her long, curly hair in to a bun atop her head so my collar shows on her swan-like neck.

Perfect. And mine!

"Thank you, Lydie! So good to see you too! I was in Bali for a retreat. When will you join one? The next is in Sri Lanka," My Angel replies as she returns my cousin's hug.

They chatter on while I place our drink orders, then sip my Jackson Special Blend Scotch. My eyes rove the room, forever vigilant.

The glitterati celebrities, royals, and the überwealthy congregate as they people watch as much as they enjoy the top-shelf liquor and the fine cuisine. I nod and raise my glass in greeting to a few of them who catch my eye. Every Steele is instantly recognizable. But keep my gaze moving as I'm not here tonight for small talk—it's family time.

"Damn cuzz, you cost me a stack!" Lucien says as he claps me on the shoulder from behind. "I bet Lydie you'd cop out on us since you haven't seen your woman in a while. But here you stand with a drink in hand, as calm and cool as ever. Thanks a lot..."

He taps his crystal snifter to mine and rolls his eyes.

"You know me, Mr. In Control. As tempting as my woman is for me, I can handle my carnal urges"—I cock my head at him and smirk—"One Alpha Dom to another, you could learn a thing or two from me, cuzz..."

We laugh as he fake punches me for my audacity.

"Come on, you barbarians. Let's get to our table. I'm

starved!" Lydie says, shaking her head at our less-than-adult behavior.

"*Little boys* will be *little boys*," My Angel adds referring to her earlier comment saucily.

She hops off of her bar stool and flashes her sorrel brown eyes in my direction.

The girls loop arms and saunter into the dining room without a backwards glance. My Angel's grip-worthy hips sway in the soft silk of her pants as she walks away from me. Talk about making it clap…

I growl under my breath. The minx won't cum for days, I vow.

"Man, you are whipped as fuck!"

Lucien's chuckle makes me give him the stink eye before I follow My Angel's blazing path across the room.

* * *

"THIS IS ABSOLUTELY STUNNING, Malcolm! Look at the sparkling waters of the atoll! I cannot wait to go scuba diving!"

My Angel's cries of delight fill my headset as we hover in a helicopter over Mnemba Island off the coast of Unguja, the largest island of the Zanzibar Archipelago.

The beautiful tropical private island of Tanzania off the coast of East Africa makes for a barefoot beach paradise. Its seclusion proves the perfect setting for my Valentine's Day surprise to celebrate a year of us being back together.

We can relax and unwind in the exclusivity of our stretch of beachfront, where our banda peeps out onto unblemished sands from the dappled shade of the casuarina pine forest. The villa is situated to overlook the Mnemba atoll. As My Angel suspects, it's a scuba diver's delight. From snorkeling, swimming, and kayaking to massages in the beach, to doing nothing at all—plus sex on the beach—that's my plan for our holiday.

"I'm glad you like my surprise," I respond through the mic attached to my headset. "Wait until you see the villa's outdoor bath."

My Angel faces me with a breathtaking smile.

Gorgeous. And all mine!

Once we land, I jump off of the helicopter and swing My Angel into my arms to carry her to the villa. She laughs and wraps her arms around my shoulders as she cranes her neck to take in the island's splendor.

"Incredible," she whispers as she stares at the fragrant flowers, the lizards that scurry into the foliage as we pass, and the white-washed villa.

A grin spreads across my face at her happiness.

"How long can we stay? I never want to leave!" She exclaims as she kicks her legs and throws her head back in jubilation.

I laugh and hold her tighter in my arms.

"Five days, but who knows. If you're a good girl, maybe longer," I tease.

My Angel turns puppy eyes at me and pleads, "Oh, I'll be so very, very good, my love."

We barely make it to the bedroom before I ravish her.

"This is simply amazing, my love. Thank you so much."

My Angel sighs as she leans back against my chest in the warm water of the outdoor infinity edge bath.

I agree the view is unlike any other I've seen—and I've traveled to all parts of the world.

The white powdery sand of the beach leads into the turquoise waters of the Indian Ocean as it stretches before us. We're nestled amongst the pine trees as we soak right in the heart of nature. Planks made from native trees and softened by the weather surround the bath. The staff spread flower petals on the planks and tossed some into the water to fill the air with their floral bouquet.

I kiss the side of her head, pressing my lips against her damp curls. A deep inhalation allows the fragrance of the flowers, pine trees, and My Angel to soothe my senses. Then I sigh with equal contentment.

"You're beyond welcome, My Angel," I murmur.

I hand to her a crystal flute filled with her favorite—Krug Clos d'Ambonnay Champagne—and take one for myself.

"Happy Valentine's Day and here's to gratitude for one year of togetherness," I add in a toast.

"Happy Valentine's Day and here's to many more years of togetherness," My Angel replies as she shifts in my arms to face me.

Her heart-shaped face has an open expression of such love my heart stutters in my chest.

Wuss and all, I love my woman with every fiber of my being. I capture her mouth with mine and proceed to prove my everlasting love and devotion with my body and my soul.

MALCOLM

"Go Baz! Go! Don't lose them, bro! No one wants to listen to them gloat!"

Harris shouts over the crashing waves of the Atlantic Ocean as he trims the jib sheet of the new sailboat we're racing against Roger's team.

We're on a Guys' Getaway before Sebastian and Roger become dads for the first and second times in just over a month. Along with Roger, Lachlan, Lucien, Laurent, Borya, and Baz's close friends Scott and Porter join us for the four-day getaway. The destination of choice is Bougainvillea Cay in the Exumas, Bahamas, Caribbean. The guys wanted to have time to try out the new toys I ordered for the private island retreat Baz bought for Lola a few months ago.

The racing yachts are on top of the list. So now it's the United States against The Others. Baz, Harris, Scott, Borya, and I make up the US. Roger, Lachlan, Lucien, Laurent, and Porter—based in Paris, Aberdeen, and Dubai—comprise our opponents.

"Scott, adjust the mainsheet! Let's go, let's go!" Baz shout as he mans the helm.

Exhilaration runs through me as we take to the open water at the top speed of fifteen knots. The balmy weather —clear of any rain—provides the best backdrop for being on the ocean. Salty spray flies back and lands on my face. I laugh as I lick it from my lips, not daring to move my hands from the wheel.

"Yeah, baby!! We're gaining on them!!" I whoop. "Let's get it, boys!"

Lucien chances a quick glance as we come abreast with their sailboat. Lachlan shouts orders for Porter and Lucien. They rush to adjust their sheets for optimum performance.

Aside from being Alpha males, we're a super competitive group. Not one of us likes to lose. So it's balls to the walls on both yachts.

We round the regatta buoy for the return stretch with The Others ahead. But we're on their asses! Damn near our bow to their stern.

As we overtake them, Porter gives us the finger and Borya yells back curses in Russian. Both crews hustle to reach the finish line. The winner's buoy beckons to us.

With a burst of wind in our sails, we pass the marker less than a minute ahead of Roger's sailboat. The US crew hollers in victory as we head for shore.

"Yeah, yeah, yeah. Whoop it up all you want. Congratulations already…" Lachlan says as he claps Baz on the back when he steps onto the dock.

"Tomorrow it's the JetSki relay, so let's see who's bragging then!" Laurent adds as he grabs Harris in a headlock.

At thirty-one, they're the two youngest boys of the Steele and Jackson clans. Laurent's bottle-green eyes sparkle with mirth as he noogies Harris in the back of his head. Evenly matched in muscle although Laurent at six feet, three inches has two inches on Harris, they wrestle as they've always done—two wolf cubs angling for dominance.

They're close, like Baz and Lachlan. Although I'm still not that keen on him and Haley, I've let it go to avoid a distance between my baby sister and me. Not to mention sparking Starr's ire. Not worth it.

However, should Lachlan misstep, I'll beat his ass senseless. And he knows it.

"Fuck off, Laurent! Sore loser," Harris retorts as he flips him off the dock and into the water.

Everyone laughs. Then Borya hauls Laurent from the water.

"*Davay rybka*," Borya rumbles as he pulls the little fish back onto the dock. "We'll do a training tomorrow so you can learn to defend yourself!"

Again, we crack up. While Laurent rolls his eyes and shakes his head, slinging water over us.

"Time for celebratory drinks, boys!" Baz chuckles as he strides back to the villa. "The winners will even pay!"

"Aw hell, dude! Pay what? We're at your place!" Porter responds.

Baz chuckles and nod, "True!"

WE SHOWER and change into swim trunks. Then lounge on the beach drinking local favorite Kalik beers. In the outdoor kitchen, the chef grills vegetables, fresh fish, lobster, and steaks to go along with the pigeon peas and rice.

The sun dances on the waves as they lap onto the beach before us. Other yachts dot the horizon, taking advantage of the glorious weather. The Exumas live up to their name as one of the best yachting areas in the world.

"Okay, Pops, how do you feel?" Lucien asks as Baz as he lifts his bottle to his mouth.

A goofy grin spreads across my brother's face.

"Oh brother, man. He's grinning like the Cheshire Cat.

Sebastian the Alpha Dom playboy turned faithful married man, soon-to-be father will complete his transition to domesticated chap," laughs Porter. "I can't bloody believe it!"

"Well, my friend, believe it. And I'm thankful for it!" Baz responds as he tips his bottle in Porter's direction. "I pray you'll find a woman who will make an honest man out of you. Although I don't know how lucky she'll be. Bless the poor lass!"

Porter throws his head back and guffaws.

"What about you, Daddy of Three? What're your thoughts on fatherhood?" Laurent asks.

Roger grins wider than Baz did. His usually intense stare softens whenever he thinks of Leonie, The Twins, and now Baby Daphne.

"Enjoy every day with your children. Cherish each moment. They grow up in the blink of an eye," he answers, leaning forward with his elbows on his knees as he glances at each of us. "Don't waste a second of your time with them. And just as important with the woman who gave them to you."

"Amen, brother," Baz says as he strides over to him and taps his bottle to Roger's beer. "And I will add, take the advice of those who have gone through it. Roger has been an invaluable resource for me. Thanks, bro."

Roger grins and inclines his head.

"You're more than welcome, brother. Based on the way you've cared for all of us from childhood to now, you'll be an incredible father," he says sincerely.

Harris and I along with Lachlan, Lucien, and Laurent nod in agreement.

Now it's Baz's turn to bow his head.

Then he takes a swig of Kalik.

We sense he has to give himself some time to control his emotions before he responds. So we give him a moment. A brief, but comfortable, silence descends on our group. The sizzle of the food on the grill amplifies. The aroma tantalizing.

With a nod, Baz rises.

"Thank you, my brother. Now, let us eat. Team The Others will need their strength for tomorrow's challenge!" He quips.

Boisterous claps, whistles, and denials fill the air.

* * *

"The perfect way to end our retreat: pumping music, fine liquor, and most of all hot babes! Here's to Harris for the fantastic idea!"

Laurent says with a flourish as he raises his crystal snifter of Jackson Reserve Scotch in salute.

"Hear, hear."

"*Za nashu druzjbu!*"

"Yes, Borya, to our friendship!"

After two more days of testosterone-filled macho challenges, we had a tiebreaker this afternoon for the best water jetpack acrobatics. I—the biggest daredevil of us all—won. So the US beat The Others with flying colors, literally.

To celebrate and to cap off our Guys' Getaway, we came to STEELE Exumas Hotel and Resort for dinner at the restaurant run by Lucien. Afterwards, the singles—Harris, Lucien, Laurent, Porter, Borya—wanted to party at the resort's nightclub.

Everyone agrees to go.

Harris makes out with a leggy brunette in a micro dress damn near showing her ass cheeks. Borya sandwiched between two fashion models bumps and grinds on the center platform of the dance floor. Lucien has Miss

Bahamas in a corner on his lap with his hand between her legs devouring her mouth.

While they flirt with the more than interested female guests, those of us in relationships hang out in our VIP section partaking in a rum tasting. Lachlan gained cool points when he declined an offer to dance from a Bahamian beauty with long curly hair and doe-shaped eyes in her sepia-colored face. Instead, he stayed seated at one booth in our area.

"You should have seen Scott's face when—"

"Excuse me, aren't you Sebastian Steele?"

A stunning ash blonde woman interrupts our conversation to approach Baz. She stares at him with large turquoise blue eyes before she scans him from his head to his lap, her gaze lingering on his groin.

Oh brother, here we go… I tune her out and talk to Lachlan about his new blend of Scotch.

After a bit of banter, a member of the security team strides to our section and asks the woman to return to her table. She takes the hint and throws a nasty glare at Baz before she leaves with no further comments.

"Good grief. That was the worse pickup line ever," Scott laughs.

"And equally ridiculous reaction," Lachlan adds with an eye roll as he sips his rum.

Roger and I agree and return to our tasting.

These women are thirsty as fuck! My mind drifts to Starr. I cannot wait to get to Beverly Hills to her, my soul mate love.

* * *

"BABE, WHAT'S THE MATTER?!"

My urgent demand results from seeing My Angel sitting in her bed crying.

I just flew in from Bougainvillea Cay, not wanting to miss the chance to see her before I have to fly tomorrow night to New York City for meetings the next day. I thank the time difference for getting a few hours with my woman.

I used my access code to enter her Benedict Canyon Drive mansion, then made my way to her bedroom. She looks distraught. Red-rimmed eyes and a puffy face greet me.

What the fuck?!?!?!

"Talk to me or I'll lose it," I say as I close the distance between us and cradle her on my lap.

The warmth of her body through her silk camisole and sleep shorts coupled with her alluring scent of coconut and frangipani tempt my cock.

Down, boy. Not now.

Between hiccups and more tears, My Angel tells me a third of her clients canceled their memberships after a breach in SLFW's database exposed their personal information to the dark web.

I growl and reach into my jeans pocket for my mobile. Angrily, I jam the screen to call Haley.

"Starr tells me—"

"We're on it! She called me a couple of hours ago—"

"Why didn't anyone think to call ME?!?!?!" I roar.

My Angel jumps, and Haley gasps.

Fuck! Now I've upset them. I'm just so fucking pissed because I just know it's that scheming bitch Vicky Reynolds! I'm going to—

"Listen, Malcolm, I do not have time for your Alpha Dom bullshit right now. I have work to do. Tell Starr I will have an update shortly," Haley retorts then ends the call.

I drop my head, ashamed of yelling at her and My Angel.

Then type a quick apology text message to which Haley responds with an eye roll emoji. Typical little sister.

"Angel, I apologize for yelling. It pisses me off—"

She places her fingertips against my lips and shakes her head. She shifts on my lap to straddle my thighs, then leans back to the mattress to bring my body over hers.

"I need you, Malcolm," she whispers. "Make it all go away. All the craziness: the blackout, the delivery mix-up, the schedule confusion…"

My Angel rattles off a string of odd occurrences, but I cut her off with a searing kiss.

Eager to meld our bodies together, I strip us of our garments. Then slip between My Angel's welcoming thighs, notching my ready cock to her warm, wet pussy. I nuzzle her neck to inhale her sweet scent and palm one of her D-cup breasts with my sizable hand.

"Oh, Malcolm!" Starr groans asks in a voice husky from her tears as I drive my cock balls deep in one brutal thrust.

"Yes, babe, give it to me. Give me all of your pain. I'll make you feel so much better," I respond, as possessive of my mate as ever.

No one gets to make My Angel cry. No. One.

I lower my mouth to latch onto a plump brown nipple and suckle. My hips continue to piston with long, fast strokes to get her over the edge quickly. She needs me to ride her hard, and I oblige.

Rolling my hips, I deepen my thrusts. The Prince Albert twin balls stroke her G-spot and her cervix.

She tosses her head and digs her fingernails into my back. My Angel meets each of my thrusts with one of hers as we rock as one.

I flex the muscles of my back and make the tattoo wings beat. The mantle is heavy with the weight of protecting My Angel. I will do whatever it takes to remove the pain from her. Until she slumbers peacefully in my arms, I give My Angel just what she needs.

While I watch her rest, I consider my options to deal with Vicky Fucking Reynolds one last time. Haley better get me that solid intel pronto. Or I'll take matters into my own hands.

STARR

"*T*hese onesies are just too cute! Look at the little giraffes doing cartwheels!"

I giggle as I hold the tiny outfit up. It's just so nice to be away from Beverly Hills for a while and not having to deal with the drama. Thank goodness for Lola's pregnancy and my doula duties!

"I love it!" Shelley exclaims. "And get a load of this one with teddy bears!"

At forty weeks pregnant, Lola wants to complete the finishing touches before Baby Boy's arrival. We're in nursery one at her and Sebastian's duplex penthouse at The STEELE Tower. They kept one close to their bedroom, so it's two doors down.

After the summer, Baby Boy will move into his suite of rooms that includes nursery two, a bathroom, sitting room, playroom, and a room for Nanny Janice Smart when she's at the penthouse. They moved her into an apartment on the thirtieth floor so she can be always near.

The parents-to-be chose Nanny Janice since she's trained appropriately as a nurse and has a master's degree in early childhood education. She can dress a scrape, teach early academics and social, motor, and adaptive skills, and disarm assailants. She's a total Wonder Woman!

Nanny Janice never married and is a mature woman in her late forties. Equally important, she has zero interest in Sebastian. I laughed when Lola told me that benefit—not that I blame her. I'd have a major problem with a nanny-gate situation. Vicky was enough of a problem…

Also checked off her list is the completion of the nurseries here, Southampton Village, and Paris in our and Morgan and Shelley's and Guy and Josy's residences. Surprisingly, the London nursery only needs the furniture delivered. Leonie worked her magic and finished ahead of schedule.

Each nursery reflects Lola and Sebastian's homes: the color palettes, and whether traditional, Parisian elegance, or beach chic interior design style. She told me her favorite is the Southampton Village with its calming greens, blues, and tans. The bleached wood and hand-painted tiles keep with the nautical theme.

The girls and I surprised Lola and Leonie with a dual virtual baby shower a week ago. It was so much fun to play the games and to open the many presents while we interacted on the giant screens in our respective media rooms.

Blair, Billie, Shelley, and I decorated Lola's while Josy, Haley, Anita and Hettie Bailey—a friend of Leonie's from Paris married to Roger's good friend Joel—did Leonie's room. They decorated hers in shades of pink and cream and mine in blues and grays.

Lucien had their favorite dishes from his restaurants in both cities for their lunches. The only downside for Lola was not having *Maman* Josy's delectable desserts! Instead, Sylvia Weinstock the Cake Queen who made her wedding confectionery delight crafted a gorgeous and delicious cake in the shape of a cradle. It was an edible piece of art.

Instead of the baby showers being limited to women, we included the guys. Anita and Norman's daughter Antonia and Joel and Hettie's toddler son came, too. Rodolphe and Gaspard, almost two years old, helped to hand presents to Leonie.

The whole affair turned into a fun fete we enjoyed for hours.

Since that time, Lola has had the urge to nest. Hence reorganizing the gifts they received from the shower along with others delivered in the last few days from her friends, fashion colleagues, and business associates. She even reordered Baby Boy's supplies in his bathroom!

I agree with Dr. Rice: it's instinct to use the burst of energy she's gotten to prepare for the baby's arrival. It's no different from mama birds, cats, and other humans—male included.

Lola straightens up to glance at the onsies Shelley and I hold.

"Oh, those came from Anna Wintour. A baby boutique in Londo—"

Her words get cut off as she doubles over with a cry. She whimpers and clutches her belly as she collapses.

But instead of hitting the floor, two sets of hands hold her up.

"We have you, Lola, sweetheart!" Shelley exclaims.

"Deep breaths, Lola," I tell her in a calm manner. "Focus on your breath."

We maneuver her to the glider, and she sits gingerly. The bracelet on her wrist beeps, and my mobile vibrates. A second later, her mobile rings.

Sebastian.

Harris—the tech wiz—created a monitor to track vitals,

particularly for erratic or elevated heart rates that deviate from the norm. Plus, it has a fall detection and a GPS tracker for location of the wearer. He gave one to Lola and one to Leonie. The app connects to the monitor, then alerts Sebastian, Roger, Harris, Anita, the OB-GYNs, and me.

Shelley answers Lola's mobile while I check her vitals.

"Lola! What's happening?!" Sebastian asks over the speakerphone.

A pitiful moan spills from her lips as she grimaces.

I rub her back and murmur for her to breathe.

"I'm on my way up!!" Sebastian shouts and disconnects the call.

"Where do you feel pain, Lola?" I ask, followed by more questions about her pre-labor.

Meanwhile, Shelley answers a call from Dr. Rice's nurse. Shelley and I relay Lola's answers to the nurse, and she advises we come to the hospital even though Lola's water hasn't broken since her due date is tomorrow. Dr. Rice will meet us there.

"Okay, Lola, sweetheart. We'll help you to stand," Shelley says.

I clasp her arm and brace to lift her.

Just as we stand Lola on her feet, Malcolm and Sebastian rush in the nursery room's door. Sebastian takes one glimpse at Lola and barks for his mother to call their driver Eddie to bring the car around. He and Malcolm carry Lola between them.

I grab her hospital bag and follow them out the door.

"Hold on, babe, we got you!" Sebastian says as we hurry down the hallway to their private elevator. "Just breath like Starr taught you."

"Yeah, Little Sis. Don't worry, just focus!" Malcolm adds with a nod. "You and Baby Boy are all good!"

I smile at his words, so like mine. I've rubbed off on him.

Shelley talks to Harris, who called because of the alert on his mobile. Lola grimaces, then glances around, embarrassed.

I raise my eyebrows and cock my head to the side at Lola. My silent question hangs between us.

She glances down at her lap, then at me with wide eyes as we descend in the elevator. She's wearing a white off the shoulder loose tunic and black leggings.

Ah, her water must have broken. I nod in understanding and turn to Malcolm.

"Honey, before you put Lola on the car's seat, let me place a towel down," I say as I rub his back.

Malcolm nods, and Sebastian's gaze shifts from Lola to me to Malcolm.

"Did your water break?" Sebastian asks softly.

Lola flushes bright red and nods.

"It's okay, babe. That's good! Baby Boy is on his way!" Sebastian says with a smile full of love.

WHEN WE FIRST ARRIVED AT the hospital, the nurses settled Lola in her suite at New York's best hospital, renowned for its OB-GYN department, of which Dr. Rice is the head. Moments later, he arrived with his team. An anesthesiologist, a pediatrician, labor and delivery nurses, an OB tech, and a nursery nurse followed him into her suite.

I reviewed my role as Lola's doula and her expectations before they went to work in prepping her for the first stage of pregnancy, pre-labor.

Dr. Rice explained in first-time pregnancies, it can take six to eight hours for my body to be ready for the actual delivery. Once her cervix dilates to ten centimeters, he expected the second stage to be as short as 20 minutes or as long as a few hours.

Seven hours later and Lola screams at Sebastian so badly, he's struck speechless. Poor man.

"Let's have the labor nurse check your cervix. Since the contractions are coming closer together and occur for ninety seconds, you may be ready," I suggest as I massage Lola's calves.

Shelley agrees, and I step out.

"Oh! Babe, how's she doing?"

"Is everything all right, Starr?"

Malcolm and Morgan wait in the anteroom of Lola's suite. They ask about her as the door shuts.

Since she and Leonie are due around the same day, the family split between New York City and Paris. Haley and Harris flew to Leonie as support for her and Roger three days ago.

I give them a brief update as I head to the nurses' station. The labor nurse and I return to the suite.

"Let's have a peek, Mrs. Steele," she says.

Lola nods, and I help her lean back against the pillows while the nurse peeks under the sheet.

"Well, well, well, Mrs. Steele, your cervix dilated to ten centimeters. I'll get Dr. Rice now," she says with a warm smile and a gentle pat to her knee.

"Oh, thank you, Lord!!!" Lola cries.

Sebastian takes her hand in his and smiles as he says, "Babe, you're doing so well. Soon it'll be over, and we'll have our Baby Bo—"

He yowls.

"FUUUCK!!!!!" Lola bellows, followed by a string of curses.

The labor nurse chuckles as she leaves for Dr. Rice and the rest of the obstetrics team.

"Mr. Steele, would you like me to have a look at your hand?" She asks over her shoulder.

"No, thank you. That's all right," he grunts as he rubs his hand.

Shelley rises from the sofa and reaches for Sebastian's hand.

"Sweetheart, it's not the best idea to hold a woman's hand when she's in labor," she laughs as she massages his hand with her fingertips. "Ask your father and brother. I'm sure I broke one or two of your father's fingers over the years!"

Sebastian groans, "Lesson learned, Mom, thanks."

"Sounds as though you're ready for me, Mrs. Steele!" Dr. Rice booms as he enters the suite. "Let's have a look."

He takes a seat on the stool at Lola's feet and lifts the sheet.

"All right, Mrs. Steele, we're in the second stage of labor. The time to push is now," he says with a fatherly smile.

"Thank the good Lord!!!" Lola cries.

Shelley places a kiss on Lola's sweat-soaked, flushed forehead and murmurs words that bring a smile to Lola's face. Shelley gives the rest of us a nod before she leaves the suite.

My attention stays on Lola as I dab her face with a cool cloth. For a moment, my thoughts drift to me being the one on the delivery bed. My mouth curls up in a smile, and a wistful sigh escapes my lips. I'll leave it to the Universe.

"He's crowning. Get ready to push, Mrs. Steele," Dr. Rice raises his eyes to mine and nods. "All right, now! Push!"

"AAARRGGGHHH!!!" Lola growls as she bears down.

"Breathe with it, Lola. Breathe," I say as I stand to Lola's right, just in her line of sight. "Focus on your breath."

"That's it, my love. You're doing well," Sebastian murmurs as he strokes Lola's hair that I put into one long braid down her back.

"SHUT UP STEEEELE!!!" Lola growls as she slaps his

hand away from her with a kyber crystal-powered super laser stare from the Death Star. It's strong enough to destroy an entire planet. Or a Steele.

Sebastian opens his mouth, then thinks better of it speaking and closes it. He glances at me.

I shake my head, biting my lip as I suppress a giggle. Poor man.

More contractions, more choice words, more killer looks, more pushing, and their Baby Boy makes his debut.

"Mr. Steele, you may cut the umbilical cord now."

Dr. Rice hands a pair of sterile scissors to Sebastian with a broad smile and a nod of encouragement.

I have to avert my gaze from Lola and Sebastian's private moment as their love-filled gazes meet after nine hours of intense labor.

Once Sebastian does the honor, the pediatrician, Dr. Samantha Woods, takes the newborn off to the side in order to care for him.

I comfort Lola.

"You did it, Hot Mama," I whisper as the team works on her.

She nods, resting her head against the pillows. A tired smile appears on her face.

"Thank you so much, Starr," Lola murmurs as her eyelids close.

The labor and deliver may have tired her, but she's radiant. I'm so happy for my friend.

Then Lola reopens her eyes as if just remembering something.

"Baz? What's taking so long? Is he okay?" She asks in a soft voice filled with concern.

"He's perfect, my love. See for yourself," he responds as he strides over to her and places their son on her chest.

Lola's face lights up with such love and joy when she

stares at their Baby Boy. Tears stream down her cheeks. Her fingers tentatively touch his soft jet-black hair, and his eyes open slowly.

Gray eyes and black hair. The Steele family traits continue.

Lola peers up at Sebastian and smiles angelically.

"Your son, my love," she whispers. "He looks like you, like a true Steele. Are you pleased, Baz?"

Sebastian nods, overwhelmed, and buries his face in her damp hair.

Discretely, I take a few more photos for their album, then leave the new family to bond.

"Well???"

"Are we grandparents again?"

"How's Baby Boy?"

A grin threatens to split my face in two as I clap happily at Malcolm, Shelley, and Morgan.

"Baby Boy is in excellent health! All ten fingers and toes! He weighs 7.8 pounds. An acceptable size for a male newborn. Congratulations!" I exclaim, bouncing on my feet.

Malcolm swoops me in his arms and spins in a circle as he shouts with joy.

Morgan grabs Shelley in a bear hug and kisses her.

"Lola is doing well, and Sebastian survived!" I say with a laugh once Malcolm sets me on my feet, still tucked into his side.

Shelley walks over and hugs me.

"You're so very good, Starr sweetheart! First Leonie, now Lola. I want you next!" Shelley declares as she arches an elegant eyebrow at Malcolm.

"Shelley, honey," Morgan says sternly.

She purses her lips, then squeezes me again.

"You're good for my son, too," Shelley whispers before she releases me.

My gaze goes to Malcolm, and he smirks.

A vibration from my pocket draws my attention to my mobile. Anita.

"Hey! How's Leonie?" I ask when I accept the call.

I put it on speaker as Anita tells us Leonie gave birth to Daphne Beaulieu Steele right on time.

More cheers fill the anteroom of Lola's suite.

We spend the next hour chatting while we wait for Sebastian to give us the all clear to join them.

Shelley can't contain her eagerness and calls.

Sebastian and Lola have been so focused on enjoying these first few moments with Baby Boy they forgot to communicate with us. They ask for a minute before we enter the room.

As soon as we walk in, Shelley makes a beeline for Lola and Baby Boy. She coos softly as she strokes his little leg.

"How are you, Lola, sweetie?" Shelley asks. "You look so happy. But you need to rest. We won't stay for long."

Morgan agrees, "No, we won't keep you, dear. Only a quick peek. You need your rest."

"Congratulations, Little Sis, bro! You did it," Malcolm says as he fist bumps with Sebastian. "Now, what do we call Baby Boy officially?"

Sebastian grins like the Cheshire Cat as he wraps his arm around Lola's shoulders while he pats their son's back. Lola turns him around to rest against her big boobs so he can face everyone. Sebastian hands his mobile to Malcolm for him to take the video.

"Dad, Mom, Malcolm, Starr, Roger, Leonie, Harris, Haley, meet Slade Steele!" Sebastian announces, beaming.

"Slade! I love his name!" I exclaim as I clap my hands. "It means valley."

"It sounds badass!" Malcolm grins, his eyes twinkle with mischief.

Morgan grips Sebastian's shoulder and smiles. "Well done, son, daughter! A strong name for the next generation of Steeles. Your brother- and sister-in-law had Daphne, a beautiful baby girl. Today is a great day for our family!"

"Four and counting!" Shelley says pointedly.

Everyone turns to me, and I feel my cheeks heat.

But my womb tingles.

MALCOLM

"Ihave irrefutable proof Vicky Reynolds sabotaged Starr and Starr Light Fitness & Wellness Beverly Hills, Resorts, and SLFW's international retreats at Jackson Hole at STEELE Resorts. That psycho sub cannot writhe her way out of this intel!"

Haley's triumphant declaration settles on us gathered around the conference table.

We're in Sebastian's office at STEELE International Inc. along with Starr, Morgan, Roger, Harris, Anton, Adrienne, and my attorney Engelbert. Haley called me to schedule this early morning meeting and insisted Starr and Adrienne attend. I flew them to New York City on a STEELE jet, and they came straight to the office.

The room erupts.

"What the fuck?!?!?!"

"That bitch!!!"

"Are you fucking kidding me right now?!?!?!"

"Gotcha!!!"

"Shady AF!!!"

I swivel my chair to face My Angel.

She sits speechless. Her eyes shine with unshed tears as a myriad of expressions cross her flushed face. Then she closes her eyes and breathes deeply. Her lips move in silent words—undoubtedly one of her prayers of gratitude.

"Let's get that hoe!" She exclaims as her eyes pop open and flash with anger. "What do we do next?"

I grab her heart-shaped face and level our eyes.

"Finish that bitch," I respond.

My father coughs.

All heads turn to him at the head of the table opposite Baz.

"Haley, run through the details," he says, then adds. "In language we understand."

She nods and presses the button to lower the big screen to project a presentation from her laptop. In four-color, bold as day, she outlines every move Vicky made over the last year. Photos, itineraries, emails, phone records, text messages, names and details on associates, and more. She used software Harris developed to track Vicky. Then Haley compiled a complete dossier.

I sit back in shock, completely clueless Haley started her surveillance before I asked her. Damn, my little sister beats the FBI, CIA, Interpol, and any other espionage organization. Case in point as to us nicknaming her and Harris the Dynamic Duo.

"Well, all righty then, smarty pants. I'm so glad you're on our side!" Sebastian quips.

Roger nods and adds, "Absolutely! Look how she saved the cases with Delia Shaw."

"Haley, Harris, thank you so very much. I am ever so grateful for you and your work. We had an inkling it was Vicky, but now you've cemented it as fact. I want her to pay. What are the next steps?" My Angel says.

Anton gives me the look, and I nod subtly. He excuses

himself, but winks at Adrienne as he stands. She stiffens and purses her lips. With a chuckle, Anton leaves the office.

Engelbert leans forward and thanks the Dynamic Duo before he goes into his recommendations. He reminds everyone the civil harassment orders still hold, so Vicky has them as a strike against her. The best course of action involves a meeting with Judge Susan Dixon, who presided over the case. Engelbert will meet with her at her earliest availability.

I make it clear civil harassment orders will not suffice. Vicky inflicted monetary and psychological harm. Like My Angel, I agree Vicky must pay.

An incoming text message from Anton lets me know my version of her paying is in play as we speak. No more pussy-footing around with Vicky anymore. Time to deep-six the bitch.

"Make sure you handle the situation completely, we don't want another slim opening like Delia Shaw took advantage of."

Roger's comment draws me back from my response to Anton. My brother continues as he speaks on his experience with a nutty bird and the legal system—albeit in Paris, then New York City.

As Steele's we're used to frivolous lawsuits sprouting from disgruntled exes, vindictive employees, and randoms. From my father to Haley, we've had our fair share of legal situations. The most absurd being a former assistant of my mother accusing her of throwing a hot cup of tea in her face. The woman had an adverse reaction to Botox and didn't want to admit it. Everyone wants a piece of the Steele billions…

"Not a crack will we leave for that weasel to slip through," I assure everyone while I squeeze My Angel's hand.

She nods and covers her mouth to hide a yawn.

"Malcolm, take Starr upstairs. A red-eye flight is never restful, even on a private jet," my father says. "Adrienne, are you staying in one of the guest apartments?"

Her buttery pecan-colored cheeks flush. Then she lifts her gaze to respond, "No, I'm staying at Anton's apartment."

My Angel stifles a giggle.

I maintain a blank expression. I'm no snitch.

We part ways with a promise for dinner later with Harris and Haley. My father, Baz, and Roger will return to STEELE Southampton Village. They're still out on the Island with my mother, Lola, Slade, Leonie, The Twins, and Daphne.

I thank my father and brothers for coming into the city for the meeting. They brush it off with a reminder: Steeles stick together.

My father pulls me aside as we head to the elevator.

"I taught you and your brothers better. Take care of your woman. Let no one harm her, Malcolm," he says with a raised eyebrow.

He's an Alpha Dom and knows my past with subs and Vicky being one of them. So he doesn't judge me. Instead, he reminds me of the importance to keep every aspect in check.

Vicky became a loose cannon despite an ironclad nondisclosure agreement, warnings, civil harassment orders, and her ruined career. My father expects this shit to end right here, right now.

I agree.

* * *

"WHEN WILL YOU LEARN, *NARUSHITEL' spokoystviya*? You fail to heed warnings. Why?"

The thickly accented, giant Russian paces in front of the *troublemaker* firing off questions.

"What will it take to make you stop your nonsense?" He asks, then pauses before a table covered with a selection of implements. "You enjoy pain. But not the kind I enjoy, *narushitel' spokoystviya.*"

Vicky's cries increase tenfold behind her gag as he lifts a long, serrated blade in the air. The dim light from the single bulb in the ceiling casts an ominous shadow across the dank, underground bunker. Dirt floors, rough-hewn stone walls, timbered ceiling.

He puts the knife down in favor of a medical-grade bone cutter.

The whirring sound fills the air as Vicky's garbled pleas intensify, and she rocks the wooden straight-back chair she's bound to by her wrists and her ankles. Her bare tits bobble with her useless efforts. She's going nowhere.

"Such a pretty little girl you are, *narushitel' spokoystviya.* A pity you chose to ruin an innocent woman and her business. All for your selfish vendetta against a man who treated you well and ended things with you nicely."

He pivots to face Vicky with a pair of pliers held aloft.

"You were given chances he so graciously afforded you. I am not that kind of man. No chances, only lessons. Very. Precise. Lessons."

The pliers snap together with each word spoken.

"Let us see if we can change your mind and end your quest. Shall we, *narushitel' spokoystviya?*"

Vicky screams past her gag, and liquid gushes to puddle beneath her chair.

The six-foot-nine-inch Russian towers over her. With the tips of the pliers, he swipes a sweat-soaked strand of blonde hair from her eyes, displaced by Vicky's thrashing to break free.

A menacing growl erupts from him.

"*Dostatochno!*" He roars.

The situation proves *enough* for Vicky. She faints.

I stride into the bunker from the outer room, where I watched the scene unfold on the monitor. Not a scene my ex-psycho-sub's pussy weeps for; but she did weep.

Good.

It was easy to lure Vicky here under the pretense of making up with her. She's still so focused on being the next Mrs. Steele, she didn't hesitate when I asked her to meet me. She just didn't figure I'd tie her to a chair after she stripped and leave her with a scary as fuck mountain of a Russian…

The malodorous scent of sweat, piss, and fear hit me as I cross the threshold. I inhale deeply. Ambrosia.

The giant Russian nods at me, and we converse in his native language fluently. We agree Vicky may be ready to sign the new agreement at this stage. If not, he'll continue to terrify her with the threat of pain until she complies.

It's not a raw deal. Vicky must agree to move to South Africa—far from any STEELE or SLFW property—immediately; end her acting career—already in shambles from Operation Nightingale—officially; never contact Starr, myself, or any of our connections directly or indirectly. Hell, it could be worse.

I grab the smelling salts and pop them open under Vicky's nose. The pungent odor wakes her posthaste.

Her red-rimmed eyes widen in her puffy face when she sees me standing in front of her. Then she starts to beg me through the gag.

The glare I shoot her makes Vicky flinch.

"You have two choices: sign this agreement and leave or stay here with him. What say you?" I snarl as I yank the gag from her cracked lips.

The Enforcer in me brokers no empathy for this psycho sub.

Vicky sobs and blubbers on about being sorry and never hurting me again.

Only me.

Well, damn.

After this scare tactic, she still disregards My Angel.

"You do realize you're sitting in that chair because you fucked with Starr—my girlfriend?" I growl in frustration.

Vicky stares at me wide-eyed.

When I cock my eyebrow, and the Russian snaps the pliers, she nods emphatically.

"Words!" I thunder.

She jolts and responds, "Y-y-yesss, Sir!"

I swipe my hand through the air.

"I am not your 'Sir,' and you know that!" I growl. "Sign it or stay!"

Vicky's mouth gapes at the face of my unprecedented anger. Then she agrees to sign. After she reads the document and confirms she understands every detail, she signs.

"Get dressed in the clothing in the corner. He will escort you to your home and to a jet. You leave now," I tell her, then stride to the door.

"Or I will ship you off my motherland. I have friends who will find good use for you there or wherever they deem fit for a *narushitel' spokoystviya*," the Russian threatens as he cuts her ankles loose with a hunting knife.

Vicky jumps from the chair with a whimper and rushes to the darkened corner like a frightened rabbit.

Good, I smirk as I leave the bunker.

I'll have to pay the Russian actor a bonus.

MALCOLM

"Hey, guys. I hate to bother you during your baby leaves. If we could have avoided it, we would have done so. But Dad said it's best to run the situation by you."

I say over videoconference from my office at STEELE International's Asian headquarters in Tokyo to those gathered at Sebastian's beach house office at Steele Southampton Village. The trip is my latest to oversee our most recent division combined project.

The plan requires Retail, Entertainment, Residential, and Children and Young Adults. Even Lola's input matters since her lingerie boutique will serve as an anchor for the mall—her largest location to date because of the popularity of her lingerie in Japan. Harris and Haley join for their take on technology and cyber security. So the gang's all here, as Harris loves to say.

"Fine, tell us the net net of the situation," Baz responds as he sits back in his chair at the conference table. The shift from beach bum to multibillion-dollar global company billionaire seamless.

Lola sits across from him with her tablet at the ready. She has a determined expression on her face. Her shift was as seamless as his.

"We can also incorporate the children's clubhouse within the adults' and require a form of recognition to enter the section. The added security would ease my worries for The Twins and Daphne. Don't you agree, *Chérie*?" Leonie suggests as she turns to Lola.

She nods and leans forward, "I most certainly do agree, Leonie. Now, with the mind of a mother, I understand their concerns. The security wouldn't have to be imposing and scare the children. But obvious enough for those who shouldn't be there and warn them off."

Roger and Baz glance at each other over the screen and grin. Their wives—the mothers of their children—have become not only an integral part of their personal lives, but of STEELE. They prove their worthiness of heading a division, as with Leonie, and holding seats on the board, as with both of them.

I beam and sit back in my chair as I clap my hands and chuckle.

"Well, ladies, your points provide another perspective and solutions we can use to solve that part of the problem. Do you agree, Haley and Harris?" I ask.

The Dynamic Duo nod and go into tech lingo that's above my pay grade! Their knowledge of their industry astounds all of us each time we listen to them. They expound upon Lola and Leonie's recommendations.

After another hour, we call it a wrap.

I take a moment before I start my next task.

This has been a peaceful month since the final phase of Operation Nightingale. Vicky left that night for Johannesburg on a chartered jet accompanied by a member of my security team. No disturbances reported during the flight or when he escorted her to the apartment I paid for two months in cash. She has the funds to build a new life for herself far the fuck away from My Angel and me.

No drama means my full focus on business.

First, I'll finish my business in Tokyo, then make stops in Singapore, Hong Kong, Beijing, and Kuala Lumpur. I plan to make the most of the Tokyo trip with visits to cities in the area before I return to the United States. Afterwards, I'll stop by Beverly Hills for business and pleasure. My Angel will return with me to Southampton Village for Labor Day.

Harris leaves for site visits in South America. Several of our retail and hotel properties require a review of their infrastructure. He and his team will meet with the leadership and the staff for concerns and feedback before Harris makes changes. Afterwards, he'll fly here.

Haley is over the Pond in the United Kingdom. She's working on a project out of our London headquarters. Some new idea she has for cyber security. Although I believe Lachlan the bigger factor in the choice of her location. Haley can work anywhere in the world with her gadgets. However, London is closer to Aberdeen, Scotland than her base in New York City. How convenient? As though she can fool her big brother…

Roger and Leonie won't leave Monte Carlo until it's time for them, along with Guy, Josy, and Luc to fly here. Roger doesn't want Daphne to fly such a long distance now. She and Slade will celebrate their three-month birthdays when everyone arrives.

So, I bid everyone safe travels and end the video call.

To witness how well my brothers fare with their wives and their children makes me want the same. My mind drifts to My Angel.

We're at a good place, but I still want more. It's been a year since I proposed, and my patience is waning on putting my ring on her finger. I'll let her have the next month with our planned Labor Day festivities and all. But after I return from my Guys' Getaway, it's on.

Mine!

* * *

"WELL, well, well, My Angel, don't you look stunning this evening."

A wolfish glint to fills gray eyes as I walk down the stairs of my beach house at Steele Southampton Village.

We're headed to the village for Date Night with Sebastian, Lola, Roger, Leonie, Anita, and Norman. We arrived earlier for Labor Day next week.

It's the first time we've been together since Lola and Leonie gave birth almost three months ago. They wanted to take My Angel and Anita out to thank them for being their doulas. However, Baz overheard their conversation and invited himself and the boys saying he and Roger are just as grateful.

Anita and Norman will stay through the Labor Day festivities and STEELE Foundation fundraiser. They're offering great silent auction items with custom VIP fitness training sessions with them for a year. The way they whipped Leonie into shape postnatal every person at the event will want to win the bid.

My Angel and Borya put Lola on a mommy makeover regimen—My Angel and her names for things. She says the intense kickboxing, strength training, and conditioning workouts with Borya trim the extra pounds and tighten muscles. Meanwhile, the vigorous yoga and Pilates sessions with her increase mind-body connection, flexibility, and core strengthening.

Hell, she's even put me on her client list. It went from

occasional sessions to regular ones in person or via Skype when we're apart. I don't mind it since my fighting improved from the added flexibility and use of my muscles at a deeper level with Pilates. Even better are My Angel's hands-on adjustments. Nothing beats her delicate hands on my flexing biceps and her tits at my mouth level in Trikonasana.

"Why are you leering at me, Mr. Steele?"

My Angel's question brings me back from my lust-filled thoughts to realize I'm licking my lips.

I chuckle and wrap my arms around her, then bury my face in her neck. Damn she smells good, like a tropical vacation all coconuts and frangipani. My cock tents my trousers to poke against her lower belly.

She shimmies her hips in her seashell and starfish printed dress. The thin-pleated jersey material skims her curves with a scoop neckline showing the tops of her ample D-cups. A ruffle hem mimics the ocean's waves dancing around her calves that lead to fuck-me mules.

I smirk down at her.

"Playing with fire are you, Naughty Girl?" I ask as I finger my collar around her neck.

My Angel sub smirks back and purrs, "Is it a punishable offense, Sir?"

My palm taps that ass, and she yelps.

"Does that answer your question, Naughty Girl?" I rejoin.

She licks her plump lower lip, then bites it.

My nostrils flare.

Mine, all mine. Hot damn!

We kiss until my mobile pings with a text message. My Angel growls at the disruption, and I smack her ass before I respond to Baz. Roger and Leonie picked him and Lola up, so we need to get going.

We take my Mercedes-Benz G-Wagen and head to the village.

When we arrive at the restaurant, everyone waits for us at the bar. Anita and Norman are staying at STEELE's version of a bed-and-breakfast just outside of town. It's a luxury property with excellent amenities similar to the offerings found at our large resorts.

We move to banquets at the bar for cocktails while we catch up before we move to our table in the dining room. The Champ tells us about some of his encounters with celebrity clients—without divulging names—that crack us up. Then Leonie adds her handsy times with some of the fashion industries most prominent designers and CEOS of conglomerates. Roger however will hear none of it and growls his dissatisfaction.

Laughter ensues, and we decide it's time to move to our table. As we make our way through the bar and dining room, other patrons follow our progress. Some greet us and others—particularly the women—ogle the guys.

I lift My Angel's hand to my lips and kiss it. Make no mistake, my heart belongs to Starr Knight. We may be the only couple of our group unwed, but not for long. I'll wear a platinum band on my left ring finger that *should* deter women like the ones here who can't seem to control their desire for a Steele man.

With a chuckle at their boldness, I help My Angel into her chair.

Once we're settled at the table, we order our dinner and wine.

Lola turns to Leonie and nods. They raise their glasses to My Angel and Anita.

"Starr and Anita, thank you for helping me through our pregnancies, from the breathing exercises to the Kegels to the last push. Without your support and friendship, our pregnancies would have been a lot more complicated," Lola says.

"Oh, so what we're chopped liver?" Sebastian asks as he nods at Roger.

Leonie laughs and responds, "Of course you and Roger are invaluable, Sebastian! *Merci beaucoup, mon frère!*"

Everyone laughs.

"Well, you're more than welcome," Anita says. "You have a beautiful, loving family, and I'm glad to have had a part in it."

"Absolutely!" My Angel replies. "Bringing a baby into this world is a blessing and a joy. Here's to your health!"

We raise our glasses in a toast.

"Hear, hear!"

"Thank you so much!"

"Well said!"

"Here's to family and friends who are as close as our blood relatives!"

The rest of dinner we relish each other's company and delicious dishes. We end the evening with promises to meet in the morning for beach yoga and breakfast. The guys plan for golf and lunch. Then we'll meet for dinner at Shelley and Morgan's residence.

We say our farewells until the morning and hop into our SUVs. Anita and Norman decide to stroll back to the bed-and-breakfast to work off some crème brûlée dessert.

Once we arrive back at the compound, Roger drops Baz and Lola off while My Angel and I continue to my beach-front home.

"Sweet dreams!" Leonie calls out as they drive away.

My Angel and I wave.

"I know something sweeter than dreams, My Angel," I growl hungrily. "And I'm going to eat it up all night long."

STARR

"**O**h… Ohhh… Malcolm!!!"

My knees knock against my lover's ears as my back arcs off of the bed and my eyes roll with shudders from my colossal, toe-curling climax. I pull on the red silk cords binding me to the headboard.

I want to touch him. Push on the back of his just as silky head of ebony hair to engulf his face within my pussy.

"FUUUCK!!!" I scream hoarsely as another orgasm overtakes me.

Malcolm Steele is an extraordinary lover…

His tongue continues to lick at my pussy as he laps up my abundant juices with feral growls and grunts. My swollen folds prove no barrier for his carnal invasion. The erotic sounds of his feasting and the heady scent of my arousal surrounds us as we lie in his bed at Steele Southampton Village.

Malcolm shifts my thighs to his wide shoulders and parts my pussy lips with his thumbs to dive in deeper. His nose presses into my core.

It's a wonder he can breathe.

I stare down my torso to the top of his head. His hair—tousled from my thighs—moves as Malcolm bobs with the rhythm of his talented mouth.

He must sense my heated stare as he lifts his eyes—pupils blown with lust—to mine.

"You taste like manna, a goddess," Malcolm groans between laps, smacking his lips.

I tug at the silk cords and raise my eyebrows.

He shakes his head with a smirk and returns to his meal ardently.

With a frustrated growl, I collapse onto the soft sheets, damp with our sweat commingled from hours of hedonistic delight.

Malcolm chuckles wickedly, blowing warm air into my pussy. When he pinches my engorged clit, I explode into a million pieces. Bright lights flash behind my eyelids, and my hearing fades.

"Oh... My... Go—"

A slick, thick finger once plunging into my depths makes its way to my back passage. The calloused pad rims my puckered hole in lazy circles, then presses against its center.

Even after all our ass play, my cheeks clench to bar Malcolm's naughty entry. Momentarily distracted from the pleasure of him gorging on my pussy, I squirm.

Thwack. Thwack. Thwack.

I yelp and lift my hips off of the mattress. Only to be held down firmly by his hand on my lower belly.

"Do not deny me access to my holes. Your mouth, pussy, and ass are mine, Naughty Girl," My Dom chastises me.

The indignation in his voice would make me laugh, but the stinging pain from him spanking my sensitive pussy stops me.

"Open!" My Dom commands.

Like the obedient sub I am, my butt cheeks relax and my ass muscles loosen as he pushes his finger past my rim—correction, *his* rim.

The burning sensation gives way to intense erotic pleasure with each inch My Dom takes. My bottom hole stretches to accommodate two, then three of his thick digits. He's prepping me for his massive ten inches.

Ten inches in my little hole.

Fuck. Me.

I close my eyes and smile, relishing the taboo act.

"Ready for me, Little Girl?" Malcolm asks as he sits back on his haunches with a smirk. "It appears you look forward to my giant cock in *my* tiny hole."

With hooded eyes I nod, overwhelmed by the multitude of orgasms. I need My Dom inside of me, filling me completely.

In one swift move, he flips me onto my knees by the spreader bar at my ankles. The silk cords on my wrists shift into the new position easily. My forehead drops to my forearms. I sigh, ready for more.

A few well-placed swats to my ass and to the backs of my thighs remind me I didn't vocalize my response.

"Y-yes, Sir!" I squeak.

My Dom grunts.

He squats behind me with his inner thighs bracketing my hips.

I visualize him gripping the base of his big, beautiful dick with a bead of pre-cum shining at its flared tip. A shudder races down my spine so hard my ass jiggles.

My Dom chuckles.

We groan as one when he plunges his massive girth to the root in my sopping-wet pussy. The natural lubrication will ease his passage into my bottom—now top—hole.

"Always so tight and so wet for me, Little One," he groans between rapid, controlled strokes.

Primed, My Dom grips my butt cheeks and parts them to give him an unobstructed entry. The platinum balls of his piercing stroke my inner walls as he breaches the rings of muscle.

The burn returns.

His skill follows it with bliss as he reaches around my hip to tug on my distended clit.

"Tell me. What do you want, Little One?" He asks in a voice gruff with desire.

My Dom's damp torso presses against my back as he murmurs in my ear. Melded as one, he rides me while I buck beneath him, caught up in his carnal embrace.

"You, Sir!" I mewl. "Deep… Hard… Please!"

His wicked chuckle serves as the only warning before his hips let loose.

The muscles in his thighs flex against my hips as he pumps in and out of my ass. My fingers grip the sheets as I pant with each thrust.

"Feel every ridge, every vein and inch of my cock, Little One. It is all yours, as you are mine!" My Dom rumbles as he strokes my ass covetously.

Suddenly my pussy is no longer empty. An impressive dildo slips between my folds, filling my greedy core.

"Yessss!" I hiss as my hips match his pumps eagerly.

With each glide of his dick and the dildo, my body notches up from my impending climax. I squeeze my ass and pussy muscles.

"Cum for me. Cum on my enormous cock and your toy, Greedy Girl. Now!" My Dom commands.

Accustomed to respond on his demand, my back bows and my toes curl as I slap the bed with my palms. The orgasm that rips through me makes my skin tingle and my nipples harden to points on my heaving breasts.

An incoherent string of words ending in a wail pours from my parted lips as my climax peaks. But for My Dom's steel grip on my hips, I would collapse to the bed, spent and sated.

He drives on, chasing his release with savage grunts and growls.

Once again, my body responds to his caveman call. I cum. Explosive.

My Dom roars as his dick expands and jerks while copious amounts of his seed fill my back hole. He strokes through his release as my muscles milk every drop.

With a sigh, he wraps his arm around my waist and lowers us to the mattress spooned together.

"Aren't you glad you skipped beach yoga this morning?" Malcolm murmurs in my ear huskily.

I think I nod then float in a state of sheer euphoria.

Ah… subspace….

* * *

"Happy Birthday, Daphne and Slade!"

"*Joyeux Anniversaire!*"

The Steeles and Beaulieu, Luc and Blair, Billie and Patrick, Anita and Norman along with Borya, Anton, Lachlan, Lucien and the other Jacksons gather on the deck of Morgan and Shelley's beachfront mansion. Today we celebrate the babies' three-month birthdays.

Their party will kick off the Labor Day festivities with the family beach bonfire and seafood feast tomorrow night and the STEELE Foundation fundraiser the next evening. Malcolm and I will stay out here through the rest of the week, then return to New York City and Beverly Hills, respectively.

My parents fly in tomorrow morning to attend the festivities and to spend the week. It's the first time they'll meet everyone officially. Almost a year passed since Malcolm extended an invitation to my family to join us I Verbier for Christmas and I told him it was too soon to blend families. Now here we are and I'm so nervous!

I shake off the negativity and say a prayer of gratitude before I turn my attention back to Daphne and Slade.

I cannot believe how quickly time passed, and they grew so big. They're absolutely adorable in their matching sailor onesies. Daphne with the French flag and Slade with the Stars and Stripes on their caps. I cannot with Leonie and Lola!

One table has a scrumptious buffet from Lucien's restaurant and delicious birthday cakes made by Leonie's mother. The other table overflows with presents.

"Nanny Janice and I spoke about the developmental stage Daphne and Slade are in now. So I ordered a few things," their grandmother says as she bites her lower lip and raises her eyebrows above twinkling brown eyes.

Shelley is about to burst with excitement.

Everyone busts out laughing. She just can't help herself when it comes to her grandchildren.

"Well, if I'm fully honest, Nanny Janice, Nanny Grace, and I spoke about The Twins' stage, too. So they have some goodies too," Shelley continues with a giggle as she claps her hands.

Josy's amber eyes shine so like Leonie's as she admits she's done the same thing for all four grandchildren.

We discuss the merits of brightly hued toys that captivate babies because of the high-contrast patterns and bright colors, infant play gyms, mobiles, and anything else three-month-old babies can swipe at. Along with the benefits of pretend play for two-year-old toddlers' learning and development.

By the end of the evening, my womb—hell, even my inner warrior—beg to grow a baby of my own. Like Shelley said after Slade was born, it's time for me to be next. My womb more than tingles at the thought.

A smile plays on my lips as I recall my dream after The Twins were born. Images of mini Malcolms played on repeat: swaddled in blankets held in my arms; smiling up at me as I breastfeed them; coos as I talk to them. All the while, his magnetic presence hovered on my periphery. Watching his sons, me.

"What has you grinning, Starr?"

Billie's Southern accent rouses me from my daydream. Her Granny Smith apple green eyes search my face as we sit on the chairs by the firepit sipping mojitos.

My gaze shifts to Malcolm talking with the boys across the deck. He's breathtakingly handsome. I wonder if our children would take after him.

He must sense my stare and raises his head to look in my direction. When our eyes connect, he beams and winks at me.

My heart flutters in my chest. My man.

I grin and blow a kiss to him.

He catches it and brings it to his lips before returning the kiss.

The guys must rib him because he shrugs and smirks. They return to their conversation, and I face Billie.

"Ah, I get it. All the baby hoopla. Girl, I know how you feel," she says wistfully as her gaze drifts to Patrick standing next to Norman.

Her man senses her too and mimics Malcolm's kiss with

a wink of his own. More ribbing followed by wolf whistles, and they troop over.

Malcolm scoops me up from my chair and sits down on it with me placed on his lap. Patrick does the same to Billie, who squeaks when he nips her neck.

"Miss me, babe?" Malcolm murmurs in my ear as he trials open-mouthed kisses down to my collarbone.

I shimmy on his burgeoning dick wishing it were inside of me pumping his seed into my womb.

He growls and swats my butt cheek.

"Antsy there, Starr?" Patrick rumbles with a Scottish lilt.

He and Billie make a pair with their strong accents, I giggle.

Malcolm however, growls at Patrick who lifts his hands palms forward in the surrender as he throws his head back to laugh heartily.

"No worries, mate. I have enough to handle with my Billie!" He quips.

"You know it!" She giggles.

The boys talk about their preference for the most thrilling of extreme sports while Billie and I shoot the breeze.

Haley and Lachlan join us, and we enjoy each other's company until Patrick carts Billie away to his beachfront mansion. Her laughter floats through the night air.

"Ready to make our exit, My Angel?" Malcolm asks.

I nod, and we bid the others a good night.

Malcolm growls at Haley's suggestion of beach yoga, and everyone laughs. Instead, we promise to meet up for breakfast around ten—no sooner, Malcolm adds with a smirk.

Lachlan agrees, which gets him a glare from Malcolm.

No need to remind him of his baby sister's love life…

"On that note, good night!" Malcolm says as he grabs my hand and tugs me along behind him.

We give his and Leonie's parents hugs as we head to the side path leading to the driveway.

"I cannot wait to meet your parents tomorrow, Starr!" Shelley says before she pulls me into her embrace. Then she whispers in my ear, "Now, don't forget what I told you about your turn when Slade was born, Starr honey…"

My throat catches with emotion. So I nod and attempt a smile.

Shelley gives me an extra squeeze, then hugs Malcolm.

He too nods when she says something in his ear and grins.

They turn to me resembling Cheshire Cats.

I can't help but laugh. Then grab Malcolm's arm and wave.

When we arrive back at his residence, he dips to put me over his shoulder in a fireman's carry. I squeal and clutch his ass. Each cheek a solid muscle flexes beneath my palms as he takes the stairs two at a time.

"Come on, My Angel. I have plans for you!" Malcolm says as he swats my ass playfully.

My pussy clenches as juices flood my core. The thin cotton of my halter neck maxi dress does nothing to stop my nipples from puckering and rubbing against his linen button-front shirt.

I moan from the contact and the ache escalating within me.

"I've got you, My Angel. I know exactly what you need," my lover promises.

All tension drains from me as I give him control. I trust him implicitly. Let go and let Malcolm is my mantra.

Once inside his bedroom, he places me on my feet beside the king-size bed. The maid turned down the bedding so only fresh linens greet us. Just in time for Malcolm's 'plan.'

He reaches around to tug the string of my halter.

The soft fabric ghosts down my body exposing my heavy breasts, flat belly, and curvy hips as my maxi dress flutters to the floor to pool at my feet. I take his proffered hand to step out of the fabric and my flip-flops.

A sexy rumble comes from Malcolm's chest as he gazes at me from head to toe. His hands reach out to smooth along my skin from my shoulders to my flanks then to my hips. He tilts his head to the side and captures my mouth with his.

We moan in unison.

My hands lift to run my fingers through his wavy hair as I mold my naked body to his fully clothed one. No longer does my maxi dress pose as a barrier. My sensitive nipples scrape against the raw linen of his shirt, causing an erotic frisson to run through me.

I mewl.

Malcolm growls.

Without breaking our passionate kiss, he rips his shirt off. Buttons fly in every direction to clatter to the hardwood floor. The sound of his zipper is music to my ears. His erect cock springs free to bob against my belly as his pants fall past his hips—commando all the way.

Yes!!!

He scoops me up and tosses me onto the bed.

I bounce and my breasts wobble from the impact. My legs spread wide, and my arms stretch out in welcome. I crook my finger at him.

Malcolm throws his head back and howls.

Then he pounces.

I purr and scratch at his back as he strokes my wet folds with the mushroom head of his dick, coating it with my essence.

He plunges deep within my needy pussy.

YESSS!!!

I match his thrusts with frantic ones of my own as our lovemaking reaches a crescendo. His dominance overtakes me.

"I'll put my baby in your belly, My Angel. I'll mark you from the inside with my seed and out with my rings and collars. You. Are. Mine!"

Malcolm Steele forces my body into total surrender. But it is now I can no longer deny he's taken my heart too.

"**I** appreciate you making the introduction, Peace. We're always on the lookout for well-respected, global, luxury real estate developers who align with our core values. Few care about the environment. Their sole focus on the bottom line blinds them to their impact on our planet. STEELE International impresses my board. We'd like to schedule a sit-down to discuss our forthcoming ventures."

The head of an international consortium that owns vast tracts of land worldwide says to me once we place our lunch orders at the Bel Air country club's restaurant.

Peace invited me to join him and his clients for a golf foursome at his club.

The only foursomes I used to enjoy were the kind I partook in at one of my LEVELS clubs. Now those days are more than over since Starr captured my heart—and cock...

Her father told me they are interested in developing some of their land in Northwest Canada for a high-end, green hotel, resort, and casino. Peace thought STEELE would make an excellent partner for them because of our recent addition of an environmentally focused development team within my division.

After over three years of being with My Angel—almost two as a couple—she's rubbed off on me in more ways than one. Her environmental beliefs and causes spurred me to review STEELE's initiatives a year and a half ago. The study found we could implement new processes in our development or existing properties not only in my Entertainment Division, but across Retail, Residential, and Children and Young Adults.

Baz gave the green light—no pun intended—to make the necessary changes nine months ago. Since then, our division-combined project in Tokyo won global acclaim for its level achieved in green building. Two additional projects received positive reviews while they're in the early stages of development. As a result, STEELE has received more requests for proposals from property owners interested in our development and management services.

Peace's client may think other developers only focus on the net net, but STEELE still appreciates a profitable revenue stream. And adding a green team to our company added lots of green to our coffers! Cha-ching!

So I put on an empathetic expression and nod in agreement with the consortium's head.

"I absolutely agree. We dedicate STEELE to lessening our impact on the Earth for generations to come. We only have one planet, and STEELE values it," I respond about the Earth sincerely.

From my periphery, Peace sits back in his chair and nods, impressed by my answer.

My Angel taught me well.

Lunch continues with more business discussions

followed by sports and the upcoming holidays. Before we leave, I exchange business cards with the consortium representatives. Our administrative assistants will schedule a meeting for next week. Peace and I walk with them to the club's front entrance.

When they head to their cars, I turn to him.

"Labor Day went well with our families meeting for the first time officially. So I'm glad you and Sun will join us in the Exumas on Bougainvillea Cay for Thanksgiving," I say as we walk towards our cars. "Especially since I plan to propose to Starr."

I stop to gauge his reaction.

Peace gave me The Talk almost a year ago, asking my intentions for his daughter and his only child.

As I told him then, I am a patient man determined to prove my worthiness to his daughter. The ensuing period was a courtship filled with romantic gestures, support, and most of all love. Now I'm certain I fulfilled my goal and will propose again. This time My Angel will say yes.

Her father—an inch taller than me and just as fit as I am—pierces me with his intense obsidian gaze.

Fuck! He's worse than Roger *The Responsible*!

But I don't blame Peace. I will treat a man dating my daughter the very same way—if I allow her to date at all…

Peace nods, then claps me on the shoulder. He smiles as brightly as My Angel.

"Excellent, Malcolm! Exactly what I expected to hear from you. I believe you'll get your yes this time," he says. "Sun and I look forward to spending Thanksgiving with family."

Hell, yeah!!!

My heart bursts with happiness. I offer a silent prayer of gratitude and shake my future father-in-law's hand.

"Oh and remind Starr we'll see the two of you for Sunday brunch as per the norm," Peace adds before he strides to his BMW i8 convertible. "Her mother and I also believe in family traditions."

I confirm our attendance as I hold back a chuckle.

The hippie in him calls for his career as an environmental law attorney while his love of luxury calls for a two-hundred-thousand-dollar electric car.

Here's to saving our planet and to living well on it!

"I'M GOING to turn in early tonight. I have a private yoga session to teach at six tomorrow morning. So no hanky-panky, Mr. Steele!"

My Angel shimmies out of my embrace as we lie on the sofa in her media room. Some romantic comedy movie she insisted we watch just ended—thank fuck!

"What if I say I can get you off in under five min—"

The ding of a text message disrupts my lascivious counteroffer.

My Angel giggles and sashays towards the door, wiggling her fingers as a good night wave.

A glance at my mobile's screen shows Anton's name.

Great, thanks a billion, man…

Hate to bother you this late... But I just remembered a part of the deal and had to go in to the office. Meet me there???

With a grumble I respond yes and an eyeball emoji—so Haley right now.

I roll off the sofa and stalk to the foot of the stairs.

"Babe! I have to go in to the office. I'll be back later. Get your rest. For now!" I yell up towards the second floor.

As I head to the mudroom to access the garage, I think about where we should live once we're engaged. I finally convinced My Angel to open a Star Light Fitness & Wellness Resorts at STEELE Southampton Village. She didn't want to enter the oversaturated Manhattan fitness scene. Her preference for incorporating her center with the bed-and-breakfast-style resort suits a more intimate setting.

So my bet is on us based in New York City with my penthouse at The STEELE Tower and with my beach house at the compound. Rather ours, not mine, I think gleefully.

I even whistle as I put my helmet on my head and swing my leg over my Ducati Desmosedici. The two-hundred-plus-thousand-dollar engine purrs as I start it up. Much like my woman when she stretches, sated from a multitude of climaxes.

My cock twitches.

Later, I scold my unquenchable libido.

It's after eleven, so the night is quiet as I ride my motorcycle along Benedict Canyon Drive in Beverly Hills. The secluded residential enclave has some of the most magnificent sprawling estates in Los Angeles. Celebrities, moguls, and royalty own properties nestled in the natural habitat of the canyon.

Between the gates and walls, nature thrives. Trees and the underbrush make homes for birds, snakes, coyotes, mule deer, bobcats, and the kings—mountain lions. The switch from people populated to animal ruled is seamless.

My Angel loves the area because of its closeness to nature yet offers a superb setting for her environmentally friendly mansion. Like Dad, like daughter, I chuckle.

"You fool! You think you can get away with what you did?!"

An irate voice cuts through the tranquil night.

What the fuck?!?!?!

I turn my head to the right but see nothing.

"No! No, you cannot!"

A glance to the left reveals nothing.

"Now, how do you feel trapped?!?!?!"

The disembodied voice screeches.

A bright spotlight hits me face on.

Blinded, I throw my left hand up to block the light.

My front wheel jerks to the left. I pull it to what I assume is center again but overcompensate. The tire hits gravel on the side of the road. Pebbles and dirt fly up.

Fuck!

I correct the wheel and stop, then swivel my head to find the source of the voice and the spotlight.

There!

A fucking drone hovers beside me.

Hysterical laughter emanates from it.

What the everlasting fuck?!?!?!

The drone bobs and weaves around me.

I will not freak out anymore. Instead, I straighten on my seat and center my mind. Whomever it is will cut this shit out at some point. Then I'll get the fuck out of here.

The drone flies away.

Now!

I rev the motorcycle's engine and U-turn; the gravel sprays up behind my back wheel. A metallic sound suggests some of the debris hit the drone.

The fucker isn't gone after all.

And it has no problem keeping up with me speeding back towards My Angel's mansion.

The drone swoops in low and out fast as I continue to ride and duck my head. All the while the crazed voice goes on about me being an asshole.

"You don't get to ruin me, Malcolm Steele!"

Now, I know.

It's Vicky Fucking Reynolds.

And she's trying to drive me off of the road and into the brush off the side.

Not happening!

I change gears and race ahead.

The drone appears to my right.

I take my glove off and sling it at the drone. It crashes to the asphalt.

Yes!!!

"Direct hit, you fucker," I yell over my shoulder as I watch it bounce.

With a relieved chuckle, I face forward.

A different spotlight hits me, and I lose control of my motorcycle at this speed. My brakes squeal in protest as my back tire fishtails. More gravel spews around the road as my Ducati and I careen off of the side.

Everything slows.

Then I tumble to the Earth—the planet we must protect. It offers me no comfort as immense pain wracks my broken and twisted body. I roll to a stop, face up, unable to move.

How much time passes, I have no clue. Only coughs as blood fills my lungs break the silence of the canyon floor that surrounds me.

As I lie on my back and the cold seeps through my body, I am grateful the clear night sky—so full of twinkling stars —fills my vision. My Starr, My Angel, is with me to the end.

I try to raise my hand to touch her beautiful, smiling face floating before me, but my arm feels like lead. A tear trickles past my temple and collects in my ear. I'll never touch my love again.

A low growl of a mountain lion comes from my left. Its feral stench wafts to my nose. The king is near.

Fuck. Me.

As the soft crunch of dry grass under its pads increases,
my last thought is of her, Starr Knight—My Angel.
I love you, My Angel, whispers my failing mind.
With a shudder, I give in to the incredible pain.
My world fades to black…

* * *

Malcolm & Starr's Story Continues: *Cherish My Desires*

Cherish my DESIRES

MALCOLM & STARR PART III

Charmaine Louise Shelton

I dedicate this novel to my readers! It's been a year since I started writing. This is the final book in the STEELE International, Inc. Series that started my career as an author. I thank you for your support and kind words of encouragement! Here's to many more Sexy Fantasies starring with a crossover series dancing in my head waiting for their stories to unfold!

Fulfill Your Desires.

xoxo
Charmaine Louise

ABOUT CHERISH MY DESIRES MALCOLM & STARR PART III

Malcolm

This is the conclusion of a rebel, bad boy billionaire and my laid-back LA girl, brown-eyed beauty's steamy love story. It's been one hell of a trip that almost saw the last of me—the last of us.

Will I make the most of my resurrection? Or will I screw up... Again?

Starr

That man has put me through all sorts of changes—Shibari; stalker ex; mountain lion... Now, he pulls this stunt on top of everything we've faced. With an unexpected pregnancy? Oh hell, no! Where's my mala?

Take the leap with Malcolm as he learns the true meaning of unconditional love with his Starr from Beverly Hills to

Laucala Island to the Exumas in their too-hot-for-words second chance billionaire romance.

Their love story is a standalone romance trilogy in the series. Get a glimpse of their dynamism in other books.

Anthem: "Leather and Lace" Stevie Nicks and Don Henley
https://www.youtube.com/watch?v=Ob4cgakHwsQ

Playlist:
https://www.youtube.com/playlist?list=PLXwYvn0e218AaAPcbS9RFC_N-z5VLXJjX

Visit CharmaineLouiseBooks.com

"I'm going to turn in early tonight. I have a private yoga session to teach at six tomorrow morning. So no hanky-panky, Mr. Steele!"

I shimmy out of my lover's embrace as we lie on the sofa in the media room of my Benedict Canyon Drive mansion. We just finished watching the rom-com movie my girls were raving about. It lived up to the hype, even if the male lead isn't as sexy as my man. Well, then again few men can compare to Malcolm Sexy AF Steele!

His gray eyes zing me, set my nether regions afire with carnal lust. The full lips and angular jaw coupled with his thick, tousled ebony hair I love to run my fingers through then pull the silky strands. All six feet, four inches of pure muscle developed from years of MMA fighting and extreme sports. Either clean shaven or a 5 o'clock shadow covers his firm jaw. The dominating sex god with wings tattooed across his powerful back and a Prince Albert's piercing on his ten-inch dick captured my heart despite our crazy love triangle start.

Vicky Reynolds Malcolm's ex-psycho-sub who

happened to be my client unbeknownst to me. The same client who sought to ruin my company Starr Light Fitness & Wellness Beverly Hills in her zealous desire to reclaim her Dom—now my Dom—and get that ring. Vicky the Hollywood royalty actress who tends to name-drop her great-grandfather the founder of a movie studio, her father a major producer, and her mother a screen siren. Crazy woman!

"What if I say I can get you off in under five min—"

The ding of a text message from my lover's mobile disrupts his lascivious counteroffer and pulls me from my musings.

Not tonight, Vicky. You won't get in the middle of me and my man! I giggle to myself then sashay toward the door, wiggling my fingers to wave good night to Malcolm. But to be sure I escape his amorous demands, I rush through the house and up to my bedroom. The way we go at it, I'd never sleep and my client would not appreciate me yawning throughout her session.

"Babe! I have to go into the office. I'll be back later. Get your rest. For now!" Malcolm yells up from the foot of the stairs to me on the second floor.

Momentarily saved by the proverbial bell!

Minutes later I hear Malcolm's Ducati Desmosedici motorcycle rev its way out of the garage and down the driveway. Yeah, a two-hundred-plus-thousand-dollar motorcycle. My man is a badass rebel multibillionaire—and an Alpha Dom to boot!

Malcolm *The Enforcer* Steele.

The second son; the rebel; the bad boy multibillionaire playboy of the Steele family, as in STEELE International, Inc. His family's multigenerational, multibillion-dollar luxury real estate development and management company based out of The STEELE Tower in New York City.

Malcolm is the President of STEELE's Entertainment Properties Division and the First VP of the Board. He oversees their casinos, hotels, and resorts and generates the most revenue of all divisions.

That's how we met, through our partnership negotiations for SLFW Beverly Hills to expand to a location in the Caribbean and in to international fitness retreats at luxury resorts.

I followed my hippies turned into super successful environmental law attorneys parents'—Peace and Sun Knight, aka Jordan and Belinda—footsteps to their alma mater, Stanford University. Undergrad I received a degree in economics, then continued on to the B-School. Not exactly the Law School, so I couldn't join their law firm Knight & Knight LLP with eight offices around the country. I wanted to forge my path.

Health and wellness became my focus after my first trip to Rishikesh as a teenager. It helped me to regroup from the taunts of the It Girls of Beverly Hills Junior High School. Then stayed with me through adulthood.

I wanted to combine my love of wellness with helping others. So I opened my center nine years ago at 25 as my initial goal with Adrienne Anthony my CMO and General Manager of my SLFW Beverly Hills.

We met at Stanford Graduate School of Business. Everyone referred to us as Night & Day since we contrasted in our appearances and attitudes. From our long, curly hair with Adrienne's light brown and mine dark brown to her green feline eyes and my sorrel brown angelic eyes to her buttery pecan-colored skin and mine the color of warm chestnuts. I have dimples to her sharp cheekbones. But we're both five feet, six inches with curvy fit bodies from our years of yoga, Pilates, and strength training as certified teachers and students.

Again alike with our hippie vibes, independent nature, and outgoing bubbly personalities. We're loyal and open to a fault. Resourceful and trustworthy round out our traits. Where Adrienne has a tattoo of a peacock wrapped around her foot up her ankle to symbolize success, I have shooting stars on the back of my neck for wishes.

My close friend Lola Lewis when we met then Steele, paid it forward when she made the connection for me to STEELE through Malcolm since my center falls under his Entertainment Division's purview. Lola attended my first international retreat on the private Laucala Island in Fiji and loved it. Especially since the yoga and meditation recalibrated the petite spitfire and owner of Lola's Coterie—the luxury lingerie and evening wear brand—after she broke up with her then boyfriend, Alpha Dom Sebastian Steele, the eldest of the five siblings. Malcolm is Baz's doppelgänger. At thirty-six and only two years younger than Sebastian, people often confuse the brothers or think they're twins.

Each sibling shares the same Steele genetic traits and works at STEELE International and has a board position: Sebastian took over the helm from their father Morgan as CEO and Chairman of the Board while Sebastian remains president of the Retail Properties Division; Roger, president of the Residential Properties Division and Second VP; Harris and Haley, fraternal twins, co-founders of the subsidiary STEELE Technology and Cyber Security and Members. Each of them head divisions best suited to their knowledge and interests. While their mother Shelley runs their STEELE Foundation, their family's philanthropic foundation that builds and manages attractive, affordable housing for urban, lower-income families. The name is a play on the house foundation, being strong and supportive like steel.

Malcolm and I have known each other for over three

years and been together for twenty-one months after we broke up because of a misunderstanding with Vicky. Seeing your boyfriend fucking another woman after he invites you over to his penthouse would end any relationship. But of course it was a ploy by Vicky. The man she was fucking on Malcolm's Sunset Strip penthouse roof deck was the concierge and not my man… It cost us time together, but we're back together. Thank God and every deity in every religion's pantheon!

For whatever reason Vicky moved to Johannesburg and has disappeared from our lives since Haley found out Vicky was behind the mysterious occurrences at SLFW that disrupted my business. Again, thank God and every deity in every religion's pantheon! Although I believe in my heart of hearts, her abrupt relocation is Malcolm's doing—not that I care, since Vicky is outta here!

I laugh out loud as I take a shower.

Since Malcolm had to go into the office unexpectedly, I settle in bed and read my book to wait up for him. Undoubtedly he'll be back soon. Nothing could be that time-consuming at this late hour.

"HEY, My Angel. Wake up, babe. I'm back. Did you get your rest? I have plans for you…"

Malcolm murmurs as he strokes my soft cheek with his calloused pad of his thumb.

My open book slides from where it slipped to my chest to land on the bed as I roll towards Malcolm's warm embrace. I sigh and stretch languorously, certain his mouth will land on my peaked brown nipples. A throaty moan slips from my parted lips. Back bows and arms reach overhead. I spread my thighs wantonly.

Fingertips skim along the insides of my bare arms from

my crossed wrists to the outer curve of my D-cup breasts. A thumb flicks over my silk-covered nipple, then with an index finger pinches the bud hard like a clamp.

I tremble in erotic delight.

Malcolm's tousled ebony hair tickles the sensitive skin of my inner arm as he leans over to take my other nipple into his warm, wet mouth. A hand and a mouth tease me.

A mewl escapes from my lips.

"Wake up, babe," Malcolm murmurs against my skin as his mouth slides down my belly to cover my mons.

My hips raise from the mattress when his lips close on my swollen clit.

He slips his arms beneath and around my legs, then places his palms against my inner thighs to spread me wider. His broad shoulders keep my legs separated as he settles in to feast upon my sweet nectar. Lips, tongue, and teeth partake ravenously.

Unable to move my legs and trained to keep my arms above my head in a submissive position, I toss my head side to side as the carnal pleasure and pain rolls through me.

"Wake up, babe," Malcolm murmurs as he slides his cold body over my heated one.

His ten-inch dick rests limp at the entrance to my welcoming core.

Caught up in the echoing sensations of his mouth on my breasts and pussy, I writhe beneath him, lips parted in a silent plea for more.

An icy chill blasts through my bedroom.

My writhing changes to a shiver.

"Wake up, babe," Malcolm murmurs, his cool breath hangs between our faces. "I need you."

I open my eyes, a seductive purr at the back of my throat.

Malcolm's once handsome face floats above me.

His skin no longer olive toned, but gray, like his soulless eyes sunken in their sockets; his mouth agape in agony. Blood drips from the back of his head to land in droplets on my cheek.

His face contorts in pain.

On a stuttering breath he murmurs, "I love you, My Angel…"

"MALCOLM!!!" I gasp.

STARR

"*M*ALCOLM!!!"

Sweat drenches my skin as I jolt awake screaming his name, terrified by the nightmarish vision. Disoriented, I shudder as I wrap my arms around myself, gasping for air. My tear-filled eyes sweep around my bedroom frantically. Then settle on the bed beside me.

Empty!

With a cry I jump from the bed, snatching the tangled, damp sheets off of my body.

"Malcolm?!?!?!" I cry, racing to my en suite bathroom.

Empty!

"Malcolm?!?!?!" I yell as I rush through my bedroom doors into the hallway.

From the top of the stairs, I scream his name again.

Silence.

Panicking, I pivot and run back to my bedroom. My hands shake as I unlock my iPhone to call Malcolm's mobile.

It rings to voicemail.

I call his office number.

It rings to voicemail.

The clock shows thirty minutes passed since he left. I must have been more tired than I thought and fallen asleep instead of reading my book.

Where is he?!?!?!

Then it hits me. Malcolm's microchip!

With the back of my hand, I swipe tears from my cheeks. Then I open the app Harris created to track all the Steeles and me—thanks to Delia Shaw's madness with kidnapping The Twins.

I click Malcolm's profile.

His vitals pop up on the screen.

Yellow, not green.

"NOOOOOOOOOOOOO!!!" I scream.

Should the person's vitals change from green to yellow or to red, Harris programmed the app to dial the local police and medics and provide the GPS coordinates automatically. Thankfully, help should arrive shortly.

The GPS view shows Malcolm somewhere along Benedict Canyon Drive, close to my home.

I pray to God and to every deity in every religion's pantheon for Malcolm to hold on.

"I'm coming, baby. Don't you dare leave me!!!" I say, praying my words reach him as his message reached me in that horrific vision.

As I run to the mudroom, my iPhone rings. A glance at the screen shows Harris' name. I answer as I slip my bare feet into my Hunter rubber Wellington boots. I disregard the fact I'm only clothed in silk sleep shorts that cover my ass barely and a camisole.

"Oh, Harris!" I wail as I fling the mud room door open to the garage. "I'm going to him—"

"Starr!!! Where are you?!?!?" Harris shouts.

"Home! Malcolm got a text from Anton to meet him at

the office! Malcolm left thirty minutes ago on his motorcycle! I'm driving to the location now!" I respond, speeding down my driveway.

My mobile connects to the Tesla Model X Long Range as Harris' voice booms through the speakers.

"Hurry, Starr!!! Hurry. FUCK!!!!" He yells. "Don't hang up! Stay with me, and I'll guide you to the location. I see your blip and his on my screen. The live feed is loading now."

I floor the pedal as I hit Benedict Canyon Drive. Only moments pass before Harris tells me to stop and to get out. My headlights reveal debris from some electronic thing, gravel strewn across the side of the road, and tire marks.

"Go down the incline!" Harris directs now on speaker. "WHAT THE FUCK?!?!?!"

With the flashlight from my iPhone, I rush headlong down the steep ravine, following the path created by Malcolm's Ducati. Just as I reach the canyon floor, the sound of scuffling reaches me. I scan the area, but don't see Malcolm.

The flashlight picks up a trail of blood leading to movement in the grass.

I blink and look again.

No fucking way…

A mountain lion has Malcolm by the leg, dragging him deeper into the underbrush.

My stomach drops.

"STARR!!!! A LION!!! DON'T GO—"

I trip over a large branch in my haste to rush forward and drop my iPhone. Harris' voice still yells over the speaker.

The movement stops.

Adrenaline races through my body as I leap up, grab the

branch, and charge the mountain lion. An almighty roar rips from my mouth, louder than the lion's hair-raising growl.

"LEAVE HIM ALONE!!!" I scream, swinging the branch like a giant club before me. "GET AWAY FROM HIM!!!"

The mountain lion crouches, ready to pounce on me. It has no desire to share its meal.

I brace myself in a warrior's stance, ready to defend my man and myself.

"BRING IT YOU FUC—"

A shot rings out just as the mountain lion springs in the air.

With a surprised screech, it crumples to the ground.

Shouts from behind me filter through my mind. So preoccupied with protecting what's mine, I didn't notice the police and the medics yelling at me.

I ignore their commands to wait and run to Malcolm. As I drop to my knees beside him, the branch falls to the ground.

"MALCOLM!!!" I scream.

Tears pour from my eyes once again.

He's still and his hand cold to the touch.

From my years of anatomy studies, I know better than to move him. He may have a spinal injury from the crash. God forbid.

"NOOOOOOOOOOOO!!!" I wail, as a police officer lifts me to my feet.

A flurry of activity precedes the air ambulance's arrival. They place Malcolm—strapped to a board with a neck brace and an oxygen mask on his face—inside. The door shuts. Police officers tell me they'll take me to Cedars-Sinai Spine Center.

Wrapped in a blanket, I huddle in the back of the cruiser. The adrenaline rush leaves me shivering and dazed. The police officers' words of comfort wasted. All I know is Malcolm doesn't look good. At all.

"Ms. Knight?"

I startle at the sound of my name. I fell asleep again. A glance up shows a woman—dressed in a business suit and not scrubs—stands before me in the waiting room.

"Malcolm?!" I cry. "Is he okay?!?!?!"

Her mouth twitches, not quite a smile or a grimace.

"The doctors are still with him. I do not have an update for you," she responds. "I'm the CEO of Cedars-Sinai Spine Center. Morgan Steele wanted me to touch base with you and to give you a staff mobile. Mr. Steele will call momentarily. Should you need anything, do not hesitate to call me."

I nod mutely and thank her as I take the mobile and her business card. Then watch her leave.

My stomach roils.

When I arrived, a nurse insisted I shower in the staff locker-room and change into a set of clean scrubs. She explained I can't help Malcolm if I'm not at my best. Afterwards she gave me a cup of chamomile tea and a blanket, then led me to a private waiting room. Before she left, she told me the Steele family is in route to the hospital.

I feel a bit better, but still achy from my fall. Only Malcolm concerns me. It's been hours, and no word. A tear spills down my cheek as I hug the mobile to my chest like a lifeline. With my parents on an eco retreat in Belize, I can't reach them. Awake again, I feel so alone.

The ring of the mobile brings me back to the room.

"Morgan!" I cry.

"Starr, honey, thank you for saving our son!" he exclaims as his voice cracks with raw emotion. "We landed at LAX and will be there soon."

In the background, I hear Shelley.

"What do you need, Starr?" He asks for her.

"Only Malcolm," I cry pitifully.

There's a pause as Morgan girds himself.

"I know… I know," he murmurs as Shelley wails.

"MR. AND MRS. STEELE?"

A chorus of yeses fills the waiting room as the doctor enters with two others.

Morgan and Shelley, Sebastian and Lola, Roger and Leonie respond in unison as they rise from their chairs.

Haley, Harris, and I stand with them, eager to hear any news after hours of silence.

Morgan steps forward—the patriarch and Alpha Dom of all his sons.

"Morgan Steele. How is my son?" He asks.

The doctor gestures for everyone to sit.

Shelley screams.

Or is that me?

Arms catch me as my world fades to black.

"—FINE. Make sure she stays hydrated. Her temperature is a bit higher than normal, so monitor it. Ah, there you are, Ms. Knight."

One of the other doctors smiles at me as I open my eyes.

Heat floods my face when I notice everyone around me with concerned expressions. I make to sit up, but Lola's hand on my arm stops me. I glance at her, and she shakes her head.

"I… I'm so sorry to interrupt—"

"Nonsense! You have been through a lot of stress, Starr," Morgan chides. "How do you feel?"

"Fine, thank you. But, Malcolm? Please?" I answer.

Our gazes shift back to the doctor.

"I apologize for scaring you. Mr. Steele is being monitored in the ICU. The surgery went as expected," the doctor pauses. "He's had extensive damage to his spine and the back of his skull, not to mention the mauling of his calf. He came in unresponsive and remains in a coma—"

Shelley's heart-wrenching wail sends a chill through me.

Lola sobs and pulls me close.

I'm too numb to react.

The doctor continues, but his words blend incoherently for me.

Malcolm. Unresponsive. In a coma.

"How long until he wakes?"

Sebastian's question breaks through my haze.

I sit forward, praying for good news.

The doctor shakes his head as he replies, "We cannot predict when someone in Mr. Steele's condition will awake or if he will—"

This time I howl in anguish for my mate.

My stomach roils again. I jump from my seat and rush to the corner where a trash can stands. The tea and remnants of our dinner erupt from my mouth.

"*Chérie, oh chérie!*" Leonie croons as she kneels beside me and rubs my back.

Lola joins her and whispers, "Breathe, Starr. Remember your deep cleansing breaths, honey."

No yogic pranayama or sutras can ease the pain of my broken heart.

Malcolm, oh, my Malcolm!

"I still can't believe what you did. Charging a full-grown mountain lion with a measly stick? Total badass Starr!"

Harris as always uses his jokester ways to make light of the situation—even a situation as dire as my love being in a coma.

In response, the corners of my mouth turn up slightly. If any other time, I would laugh at the absurdity of me facing off with a hungry, wild beast over its next meal. Now, not so much.

A month has passed since Malcolm's life-altering accident. And no change.

Even with the Steele billions of dollars, we can only do but so much to help my love. As the doctor said that fateful night, only time will tell the outcome of Malcolm's condition.

The Steeles will have none of it.

Not a clan to sit back and allow life to lead the way, Morgan held a strategy session only hours later. He invoked his substantial influence to take over a section of the hospital and to gather the best doctors, researchers, and physical therapists from around the world for a video conference. Within a relatively short period, they devised a plan and designed a custom facility dedicated to Malcolm and his recovery. The following day, they descended upon Cedars-Sinai Spine Center, ready to heal my love.

Malcolm's medical team wasn't the only ones to make a major move unexpectedly.

Morgan and Shelley took up permanent residence in the President's Suite at STEELE Beverly Hills. Roger, Leonie, The Twins, Daphne, and Nanny Grace moved in to a long-term mansion rental next to my home—*"to be near you, chérie"* as Leonie said. Harris moved into Malcolm's Sunset Strip penthouse.

After two weeks of staying at the hotel, Sebastian, Lola, and Haley returned to New York City. Since Lola is pregnant with their twins and needs to see her OB-GYN on a regular basis, they didn't move permanently.

The siblings divided STEELE International responsibilities too.

Sebastian claimed the East Coast since he needs to be in New York City as CEO and head of his Retail Division. Roger took over Malcolm's Entertainment Division and the West Coast operations in addition to his Residential Division. Haley chose the East for her and Harris' Technology and Cyber Security.

The other half of the Dynamic Duo remained in LA. Besides his STEELE duties, Harris is working with the police on the case since they recovered a drone from the scene of Malcolm's accident. Harris has shared little information with us, but I know he and Haley are wizzes and will solve any problem.

And like his family, I devote myself to my man. After my initial hysteria, I drew upon my inner strength, inner warrior, and absolute love for Malcolm to gain the power to never leave his side. While I may not have a medical degree, I intend to nurse him back to optimal health. The powers of prayer and intention are strong.

Adrienne—BFF that she is—stepped in to handle SLFW Beverly Hills and Resorts along with the retreats until further notice. She keeps me up to date with weekly meetings here at the hospital, but I trust her to run my company in my absence. Márcia Souza—the Brazilian petite spitfire also known as my administrative assistant and a yoga substitute teacher—helps Adrienne and updates me regularly. My team amazes me, and I am grateful for them.

With a sigh, I think of my one regret: I told Malcolm no when he asked me to marry him over a year ago. Often as I sit at his bedside reading to him, my mind wanders to thoughts of *what if?*

What if I said yes?

We may have been in our penthouse at The STEELE Tower, and he would have taken the private elevator to his offices.

We may have been in our beachfront mansion at Steele Southampton Village, and he would have taken our Sikorsky S-92 Executive Helicopter from the Island to Manhattan.

We may have been paragliding above the magnificent cliffs of Miraflores overlooking the Costa Verde, and he would have been unavailable.

A tear trickles down my cheek, and I try to blink more away as I turn my head from Harris.

"Ah, Sis, I'm so sorry. You know me, just trying to make you smile. Instead like a dummy, I made you cry—" Harris' words cut off as his voice cracks on a sob of his own.

Yet he manages to hug me close in his powerful embrace.

His hard body and build so like his brother's give me a moment of respite.

Then I recall Harris' use of "Sis" as a term of endearment, and it makes me cry harder since that's what he calls his sisters-in-law, Lola and Leonie. He views me—like they all do—as Malcolm's.

And I could have been if I weren't so *as the Universe takes me.*

Fool!

"Come on, honey, have some chicken noodle soup. You'll feel better."

My mother's suggestion as she smooths her hand along my back brings me out of my pity party.

I nod and loosen my grip on Harris.

Then I smile at my mother. We look exactly alike. Sorrel brown eyes full of love as she peers at me. Smooth chestnut-colored skin glows from healthy eating and regular exercise. Long, curly, dark brown hair pulled up in a topknot. Dimples highlight her sculpted cheekbones when she returns my smile. She's a beautiful woman in her late fifties.

"Yes, eat. You look a bit wan," Shelley adds in concern. "Remember your health is important, Starr sweetheart."

Again I nod. If Malcolm's mother can show strength and grace, I can too.

The Moms settle me at the dining table in the waiting room turned living room with comfy chairs, sofas big enough to sleep on if not in one bedroom, and desks for work.

When I lift the cloche covering the soup, the smell makes my mouth water. And not in a good way…

I rush to the trash can and empty my stomach contents. In the back of my mind, I wonder why I can't seem to hold food down. But I chalk it up to the stress.

"Starr, I will not hear another excuse. You will see your

doctor today," my mother states in her no-nonsense-attorney voice.

With a feeble nod, I agree.

A call to my PCP's office, and I'm scheduled for later in the afternoon. Fortunately, it's during Malcolm's second physical therapy session of the day. Those are the only times I leave his side for an extended period.

"Good morning, Mr. Steele has finished his PT. You're free to join him in his suite," one of his private nurses tells us from the doorway.

"Oh, no, you won't!" My mother says, placing her hand on my shoulder as I rise from the table. "Eat the crackers and drink the tea before you return to Malcolm."

Shelley agrees, then goes with Morgan to their son.

Harris steps out to get some fresh air.

Alone, Sun turns to me.

"Starr, honey, Shelley is correct. You don't seem well"—my mother raises her hand to stop me from speaking—"You worry your father and me. Tell me, how are you doing really?"

Through more tears, I confess to Sun my fears, regrets, and my wishes. My parents and I are extremely close, so I share everything with them.

They didn't judge me when I told them I'm in the BDSM lifestyle and share a D/s relationship with Malcolm. Being hippies who keep fluid minds, they understand my desire to give up my control to a powerful and experienced Dom in a power exchange. Through their interactions with Malcolm, they respect my choice of him. Even my father admits he likes Malcolm.

My mother understands my heartache at not being his wife and my guilt at not giving him the one thing he ever asked of me after wearing his collar. Now I may never marry the love of my life.

"Starr, sweetheart, always remember my favorite yogic piece of advice," Sun starts. "Be equally thankful for what you perceive to be good and for what you perceive as bad. It all happens for a reason. Either way, you don't let it disturb your inner peace. Strive for tranquility no matter the outer circumstances."

Fresh tears fill my eyes as I clutch at my mother. Deep inhalations of the calming floral notes of her signature perfume relax me as they have since I was a child. The peace her scent instills in me dries the tears from my eyes and the pain from my heart.

I vow to be strong for Malcolm and for me. We may not know now why the accident happened, but we will get on the other side of this situation. Our love will thrive forever.

"THE DOCTOR WILL SEE you in a moment, Ms. Knight. Kindly have a seat in the waiting room."

I smile at the receptionist for my PCP, then sit. Another waiting room…

Fortunately, the wait isn't long. The nurse calls me shortly after I arrive and ushers me into the examination room. She checks my vitals and notes my temperature is slightly higher than normal. She takes my urine sample and leaves the room, saying the doctor will be in.

I answer some emails from Márcia while I wait. Then I glance up when the door opens, and the doctor walks in with the nurse.

"Ms. Knight, you mentioned nausea, super tender breasts and nipples, food aversions, and fatigue during the last few weeks. Do you have any idea why?" My doctor asks.

I have to hold back an eye roll. Isn't that why I'm here? To find out what's bothering me???

"Yes, doctor," I respond instead.

She smiles and says, "Well, I think your gynecologist is better suited to your needs. Or I can refer you to an OB-GYN."

I stare blankly at her. Maybe I'm more tired than I thought. What is she getting at?

"Ms. Knight, congratulations! You're pregnant!" She says, now grinning broadly.

I sit back on the exam table in shock.

When the doctor suggests I make an appointment with my OB-GYN, the puzzle pieces started to fall into place. After her bombshell announcement, the pieces fit snuggly. After she assures me there's no mistake, I call my gynecologist who happens to be an OB-GYN. Dr. Leticia Sánchez has an appointment in half an hour.

My mind still works to process the information even after Dr. Sánchez confirms my PCP's diagnosis. Diagnosis?! Ha! Life-changing pronouncement.

How the heck did I—a doula who's helped women with their pregnancies—miss my own symptoms?!?!

I was so focused on Malcolm; I lost sight of myself.

Malcolm!

My heart pounds as I think how fucked up this whole situation is for us. He's made hints and overt comments about having babies with me. I've felt the tug of my ovaries being around The Twins, Daphne, and Slade. Now Lola's expectant twins.

Lola!

She's 14 weeks, and I'm 16. We'll be pregnant together! Give birth days apart! Who will be our doulas?!?!

By the time I return to Cedars-Sinai Spine Center, I'm a jumble of emotions. Damn hormones!

There's only one person I want to see, need to see. My love, my Malcolm.

Quickly, I slip past the door to the living room. A peek

through the window of Malcolm's bedroom of his suite reveals a nurse taking his temperature. I nod at her as I enter and close the curtain.

With a smile, she leaves us.

I have to swallow around the lump in my throat as I stare at my love.

Malcolm lies in bed motionless save for the rise and fall of his chest powered by a machine. He's still unresponsive to his surroundings. Regular massages and grooming keep his skin with a touch of color and his hair and facial hair well kempt. One would assume he was asleep. But unlike a deep sleep, any stimulation cannot awaken Malcolm, including pain. Nor hear my stifled sob.

I take a deep cleansing breath to clear my mind of what I perceive to be negative, to give way to the flow of positivity. I'm pregnant with his babies. Twins.

As I stand beside his bed, I take my love's hand in mine. I bring it to my lips for a soft kiss, then place his palm on my lower belly. The belly I thought was growing because of the cortisol running rampant in my system. No, it's our babies trying to tell their Mommy they need me too. And their father.

"Malcolm, my love. Guess what? Your wish came true. You put your baby in my belly. Two babies, in fact! Here, my love, see for yourself! Two little blips. Two Mini Malcolms! You marked me from the inside with your seed and out with your collars. Now you have to put your rings on my finger, my love I. Am. Yours. We need you, Malcolm Steele. Come back to your little family. I won't tell anyone because I want us to tell everyone together. Okay, my love? I love you so much."

Determined to be strong for all of us, I blink the tears away as I place his limp hand back on the bed.

Then I settle into my chair for my constant vigil.

STARR

"*M*s. Knight, today we'll do the twenty-week anatomy scan to gauge the development of your twins. We can also determine your babies' sex, if you like. The ultrasound takes about thirty to forty-five minutes. If you watch the monitor, I'll point out some details. Would you like that?"

The sonographer smiles at me encouragingly as she applies the gel to my melon-sized belly.

With their watchful eyes, my mother and Shelley noticed the roundness of my usually flat stomach and added my symptoms to deduce I was pregnant a week ago.

"Starr, sweetheart, what do you have to tell me?" My mother asks as I walk past her to sit at a desk in the hospital living room.

Shelley and Morgan read to Malcolm in his suite. Roger and Harris have meetings at STEELE Los Angeles. While Leonie visits a project site for her STEELE Children and Young Adults Division. Sebastian formed it almost two years ago for her to incorporate for residential nurseries, bedrooms, playrooms, and playhouses and for hospitality kids clubs and play areas. As the head of the division. She reports to Roger and to Malcolm, respectively.

I gaze over my shoulder at my mother as my hand unconsciously lands on my belly. When I notice the natural reflex, my hand drops to my side.

Damn! Did she notice?

"What do you mean, Mom?" I ask, busying my hands with my booting up laptop.

When my question silence meets my question, I risk a glance in her direction.

Sun sits with her head tilted to the side, a perfectly arched eyebrow raised, and her full lips pursed. Her expression of doubt confirms my suspicions.

Flowy shirts and baggy joggers do not fool my sharp-eyed mother in the least. Damn!

My hand resettles on my babies bump as tears threaten to fall.

Damn hormones!

In fact, damn this whole fucked up situation!

My shoulders shake as my mother wraps her arms around me.

"Oh, Mom!" I sob. "Only Malcolm knows, but does he hear me???"

She rocks me and whispers words of love and support. Her soothing presence draws the confession out of me in a rush of blubbered words. She holds her comments until I finish on a hiccup.

"I'm trying to be strong for Malcolm, our babies, and for me. But it's so hard. I miss him so much! I'm scared out of my mind he won't wake up. Oh, Mom!" I end.

Sun dips the linen napkin from my half-eaten lunch into the glass of ice water, then dabs it on my flushed face.

"Hush, child of mine. You and my grandchildren will be fine. We come from a long line of courageous women capable of thriving despite the circumstances," my mother says as she cups my face.

Then she continues, "As for Malcolm, he has the absolute best care. Our prayers and thoughts surround him in the light of healing and love. He is young and strong. Continue your vigil. I believe he hears you and senses your presence. The babies will give him even more to fight for. You'll see. He loves you beyond any doubt."

I nod and take a deep cleansing breath.

"Now, show me my grandchildren," my mother says with a grin. "Your father will be overjoyed! He's at court, so we can tell him when he comes by later."

I grab my portfolio, and she takes my hand to lead me to a sofa. At last, I can caress my babies bump outside of Malcolm's suite. Surprised, I rub my hand over a spot one of Mini Malcolms kicked, and I laugh.

"Oh, Mom! Feel this!" I exclaim.

"Starr?"

So engrossed in the scans from today and the first of weeks ago, we don't hear Shelley and Morgan enter the living room.

A clearly distraught Shelley stands a few feet away. Normally a striking woman in her late fifties, her expressive brown eyes swollen and red from tears, stare at me. Her shoulder-length, wavy black hair pulled back in a messy bun appears greasy. Worry lines form between her elegant eyebrows. Shelley's feisty New Yorker personality takes a backseat to weariness. She's a shell of the shopgirl who captured Morgan Steele's heart when he visited one of his family's retail properties years ago.

Understandable since it's been weeks her second son lies unresponsive in a coma. She and Morgan just returned from visiting Malcolm, and she sags against her husband for support.

Their gazes shift between my belly and the ultrasound images in my mother's hands.

A glimmer of hope fills Morgan's platinum gray eyes as they widen in wonder. His sons get their handsomeness from their father. My heart constricts seeing Malcolm in his features.

Unsure of how they'll react to the news, I offer a smile to the Steele Matriarch and Patriarch.

"I'm nineteen weeks pregnant with Malcolm's twins," I say confidently.

Shelley faints.

When Morgan rouses her, she grabs me and cries. My tears join hers along with my mother, and even Morgan sobs.

When our eyes no longer fill with tears, Shelley sits back and clutches my hands.

"If anything happens to my son, you carry his babies... all that would be left of him on this Earth... Please... Please let us be a part of your and their lives, Starr... I know Malcolm would want us to care for you and for them," Shelley says as her voice cracks with pain.

Too overcome by the thought of anything happening to Malcolm, I can nod and squeeze her hands only.

Now, as I lie on the exam table, Shelley squeezes my hand. I turn my head from the monitor to her.

"Oh, Starr, will you find out their sex? I'm sure Malcolm would love to hear. What a wonderful present," she says softly.

In the week since I told her out about my pregnancy, Shelley transformed. She and Morgan went to their President's Suite after my announcement. The next afternoon, they returned refreshed. Shelley told me she had a spa overhaul from head to toe and booked one for me in an hour. *"No more moping around being sad! We have to be strong for Malcolm's babies—and you of course, Starr, honey!"*

Morgan assured me even though I am a brilliant, Independent young woman with mighty, wealthy parents, he and Shelley guarantee Malcolm's babies and I will want for nothing. Morgan then presented me with a document outlining the trust funds he created for Mini Malcolms and a document for palimony retroactive by nineteen weeks for me.

Despite my protests, Morgan and Shelley insisted and had my parents as backup. Outnumbered, I gave in, and my heart swelled with love for them.

As it does now.

"Yes, Shelley, let's find out," I respond, as I return her squeeze.

My mother smiles and kisses my other hand.

Flanked by The Moms, we watch the monitor as the sonographer points out different parts of Mini Malcolms. When she pronounces both twins are healthy with one a female and the other a male, The Moms and I burst into tears.

This time tears of joy!

"Well???"

"Don't keep us in suspense, Starr!!!"

"Come on, Hot Mama! Fess up already!"

I can't help but to giggle as my father, Morgan, Roger, Leonie, and Harris gathered in the hospital living room and Sebastian, Lola, and Haley via video conference demand to know Mini Malcolms' sex.

"Okay, okay!" I laugh with my hands up, palms out in surrender.

I glance at my mother and at Shelley on either side of me, then face the group.

"Malcolm and I are pregnant with... a girl and... a boy!!!" I announce, holding my babies bump and grinning like a Cheshire Cat.

Whoops and hollers fill the air. Harris wolf whistles while Leonie throws her arms around me.

"I'm so happy for Malcolm and you, *chérie!*" *The Lion* says as her amber eyes glow with happiness. "Lola and I sent a trousseau from my Lola's Coterie maternity lingerie and loungewear collection to your home. I have a few pieces here for you, too! It never hurts to feel sexy, *non?*"

"Yes! Welcome to the Sexy Mama Club, Starr!" Lola says, blowing kisses from the flat screen TV. "Now Baz's and my twin girls will have another girl their age! The grandkids will be even, four girls—Daphne, yours, my two—and four boys—Rodolphe, Gaspard, Slade, yours!"

Roger pulls me in for a hug and says, "Congratulations, Starr! Malcolm will be so happy to have one of each!"

My father and Morgan embrace me while The Moms pass out crystal flutes of Champagne.

"None for you, preggies!" Haley teases as she lifts her flute with Sebastian. "We'll have enough for the two of you!"

We spend more time chatting about nurseries—Leonie to the rescue!—expectations, and most effective practices. Everyone tries their best to keep the mood festive since it's Christmas Eve. As the French tradition Leonie—the half Tunisian, half Parisian megamodel turned interior designer —reminds us it's time to open presents.

After a while, I excuse myself and go to Malcolm's suite. Time to celebrate the news with my man and to give him his presents—two framed scans of each twin.

"Merry Christmas Eve, my love," I whisper as I kiss his soft lips. "Our Mini Malcolms are a healthy girl and a healthy boy! And guess what? Lola and Sebastian are having girls! Can you believe it? Wake up soon, my love. I can't wait for you to see your presents. We love you, Malcolm."

MALCOLM

"—*C*hange in his lips mean? Where—"

My mind dredges through mud worse than the quicksand I stumbled in near the Amazon River. None of my limbs move despite my brain's demands. Not even my eyelids open.

What the fuck is wrong with me?!?!?!

The voice fades in and out as I try to make sense of this world I'm trapped in.

Pain shoots through my heavy head; a dull pounding beats in my ears; blackness alternates with a spark of light beyond my sealed eyes.

"Mr. Steele? Can you hear—"

Yes! I scream, but the word rattles in the back of my throat. My thick, dry tongue sticks to the roof of my mouth. I try to cough, swallow, but nothing happens.

"—Malcolm! Can you hear me?"

My Angel?

What is she doing here? In fact, where the hell am I?

Her anguished cry cuts through the mud, pushing the

viscous goo to the edges of my mind as I try to make sense of my surroundings. If only briefly.

Another flash of pain wipes my response from my mouth. Bile fills it. The acid burns.

Fuck. Me.

"—Ms. Knight, please—"

"I'm not imagining things! I caught the corner of his mouth move!"

My Angel's distress triggers my protective instinct. With a Herculean effort, I part my lips. Even to my ears, the hiss sounds nothing like the word *stop*. But it's enough to get someone's attention.

"Mr. Steele? We heard you. Just a moment. Let me get the doctors."

The unfamiliar voice says more to My Angel, but I can't decipher their words.

Another attempt to open my eyes or to speak makes my head hurt. Instead, a groan slips past my lips.

"Malcolm, baby. It's me, Starr. Don't try to move anything, baby, please. Just wait for the doctors."

My Angel's plea gives me pause.

Doctors?

My brain scrambles with the additional information. Like a short circuit, the word triggers a rush of disjointed memories.

Watching a movie with My Angel.

The crunch of leaves.

Stars.

The revving of a motorcycle.

Vicky Reynolds.

A mountain lion!

My eyes fly open at the horror.

Pain slices through my skull. Light blinds me. More voices.

My eyes close.

"Fuuuck!!!" I groan.

Immediately darkness descends. Urgent whispering. A door opens.

"Malcolm!"

Mom?

"Oh, Shelley! He's awake!" My Angel exclaims.

"Mrs. Steele, Ms. Knight, please stay back."

I lift my head, but it's still too heavy. Again the words don't form properly, only an incoherent jumble of sounds falls from my parched lips.

"Mr. Steele, this is Dr. Stevens. We closed the shade to block the sunlight from your room. You can open your eyes now."

I focus all of my effort on my eyelids. Open dammit!

Still darkness.

"Excellent, Mr. Steele. I'm going to use my penlight to check your responsiveness. Don't attempt to speak yet," Dr. Stevens says.

My eyebrows pinch together.

What the hell is he getting at? I can't see a damn thing.

A spot of light appears before me, then gets closer. My sluggish eyelids blink to block the unwanted brightness. The light alternates between my eyes a few times.

"You're doing very well, Mr. Steele. Blink once for yes and twice for no. Do you understand?" Dr. Stevens asks.

My eyelids close and open for an affirmative response.

A gasp nearby draws my attention. I turn my head, but pain shoots from the back of my skull to between my eyes like a scalpel sliced my head in two. A garbled cry escapes my mouth, and I close my eyes to shut out the excruciating pain.

"Keep your head still for now, Mr. Steele. We'll give you

medication to ease the discomfort," Dr. Stevens says as I pick up movement from my left.

I blink once, then my world fades to black once again.

* * *

WHISPERING VOICES AWAKEN ME. It takes a moment to reorient myself as my eyes open to a dimly lit room. I shift my gaze left and right, but I can't distinguish shapes, only a brightness. What the fuck?!

"Malcolm, my love, you're awake."

My Angel.

My lips move, but my tongue still sticks to the roof of my mouth. A straw touches my lips.

"Drink some water, sweetheart."

Mom.

I take a few sips and swallow past the cotton stuck in my throat.

"Excellent son, very good."

Dad?

Another memory flash puts the pieces of the puzzle together.

I didn't die in the canyon. I'm in a hospital.

Thank fuck!!!

MY ELATION at being alive lasts as long as it takes for the doctors to tell me I was in a coma for two months and paralyzed from the waist down. They say it's an improvement since the paralysis was from the neck down when I arrived. The doctors gave me a bit of encouragement when they told me being awake is the next step in my recovery and to give my body time to heal.

But on top of that fucked up shit, I'm blind as a bat. Well, at least they think it may be a temporary affliction because of the impact of my fall.

Yeah, my fall somehow caused by Vicky Fucking Reynolds. That vindictive broad. I should have hired a real hitman to off her ass and not an actor to scare the shit out of her. Obviously my plan didn't work.

Harris and the police plan to meet with me tomorrow morning. The doctors don't want me to deal with but so much in one day. The less stress the better.

I agree wholeheartedly.

The only bright spot is Starr, My Angel who grounds me always. From what I could tell, she was in the room while the doctors delivered the bad news. But now she sits beside me. Alone at last.

However, my mind races faster than my heart, as I wonder whether she thinks less of me now. My Angel risked her life to save mine. She fought a damn mountain lion. Talk about love…

But does she still want me? Half a man? She's stayed by my side for two months knowing my situation, so that's a positive. But I can't determine her state of mind since I can't see her face…

Fuck!!!

A squeeze to my hand stops my brooding.

"Hi, my love," My Angel whispers as her soft lips brush my knuckles.

"Hi, Angel," I respond, disheartened.

"I missed you so much," she says as her voice catches.

I may not be able to peer at her, but I can perceive her distress. It makes my heart ache even more. How the hell can I comfort her when I want to cry like a baby?

This shit is so fucked up.

* * *

"It's time to finish that bitch once and for all!!!"

I can sense my little sister's vehemence without being able to put eyes on her. A vision of Haley leaning forward with silver sparks flashing from her dove gray eyes as she slams her palms on the conference table appears in my mind's eye. Along with Baz and Lola, Haley is on his Gulfstream G650 en route to LAX.

The police and my attorney, Engelbert Douglass, left moments ago after I gave my statement of the night's events.

As it turns out, Harris used the drone I knocked to the ground with my glove to track the owner through the drone's serial number. Some tech nerd who stalked Vicky in the past exchanged jail time when he agreed to follow me for her. The conniving broad dropped her charges against him to use his cyber skills and drones. He sang like a canary when the police arrested him for his involvement in my accident.

Now with my statement confirming her voice and words over the drone's audio feed, they'll extradite Vicky from South Africa and begin her legal case. She won't get out of this so easily with a first-degree attempted murder charge.

But Haley has other plans.

"Don't look at me like that! I mean it, Baz! These females are going crazy for my brothers. First Roger, now Malcolm. Uh uh, no!" She interjects.

"Haley, we will handle this situation through the proper channels. Do you understand?" Our father's commanding tone stops any further discussion as Haley mumbles her concession despite the fire still burning in her molten platinum eyes.

Besides Morgan, my mother, Starr, Roger, Leonie, and Harris sit in my room. The direction of their voices clues me in to their locations. As though I still have my vision, my head turns towards them whenever they speak.

The brightness of the light increased. So the doctors have me wearing some shields to protect my "sensitive eyes" from the glare. Last night My Angel told me she refused to let them keep me in the dark with the shades drawn: "You need sun in your life, no different from before."

My concern for her no longer wanting me lessened as we spent the night talking. She held my hand and chatted on until we fell asleep, exhausted after the long day—a barrage of tests for me. It hurt like hell when I couldn't wrap my body around hers and hold her tight to me. Instead, My Angel kissed my lips and slept in another bed. Out of my reach.

I fucking hated my life right then.

Now it's not much better.

I'm with Haley. Finish that bitch!

But what the hell can I do about it?

I'm a bedridden, former enforcer who can't even see to dial a phone number to make the call.

Fuck. My. Life.

And *fuck* you Vicky Fucking Reynolds!

* * *

"Angel? Angel, is that you?"

I whisper the words, afraid the vision before me is a mirage—a trick of my weary mind.

A couple of weeks passed—or so they tell me since I can't see worth a damn—and instead of just light, I glimpse a shape beyond the shields. A figure in the form of My Angel with her back to me. I recognize her long, curly hair atop her head as she does a yoga pose. That is, if my eyes don't deceive me. I remove the shields for a better look.

The figure gasps and whips around, then grabs what appears to be a high chair to steady herself.

"Malcolm?! You see me?" My Angel asks, shocked.

No denying the soft lilt of her voice. It's My Angel, and I can see her!

YES! YES! YES!

I don't realize I shouted out loud until a nurse rushes into my room.

"Mr. Steele, are you all right?" She asks as she hurries to my bedside.

The concern on her face is clear, just as clear as the tears shining in My Angel's sorrel brown eyes wide with surprise.

"I can see you! Angel! I can see you, baby!" I shout and sit forward with my arms open.

She covers her mouth and comes into my embrace. As soon as she settles on the bed, I bury my face in her neck. My tears mingle with the dampness of her warm skin from her yoga session. I inhale her coconut and frangipani perfume.

Heaven on Earth! My Angel!

"Oh, Malcolm!" She sobs as she pulls back to look into my eyes. "Oh, Malcolm, my love! Thank you, thank you!"

The door bursts open before I can say more. My mother and father rush in, followed by the doctors. After a moment for my parents to see me for themselves, the doctors ask everyone to take a seat. I watch my father usher my mother with her arms around My Angel to a sofa.

The doctors perform more tests and pronounce my vision returned in full. Another improvement in my healing process.

Thank fuck!

Unfortunately, no change in my lower half. Still unresponsive to their pokes or whatever they do since I can't *feel* anything…

The medical team leaves with assurances to step-up my

treatments since I have my vision back. They can add alternative methods to the routine.

Good. I'm sick of this shit already.

"Malcolm, sweetheart! You're doing so well!" Shelley says, as she approaches my bed.

My father adds, "We are so proud of you, son!"

But I only have eyes for My Angel.

My gaze travels from her curly bun to her gorgeous heart-shaped face down to her tits. Wow, they're bigger than before. Or am I seeing things? No matter, I'm a T&A man, anyway. When my gaze lands on her belly, I cock my head to the side in wonder. Maybe my vision isn't fully restored. Her normally flat stomach appears distended. I shake my head and close my eyes, then reopen them to double-check.

"Did you gain weight?" I blurt out.

In my periphery, my mother and father glance at each other, then leave the room without a word.

My Angel bites her lower lip and averts her eyes as she puts her hands on her swollen belly.

What an asshole thing to say!

"Babe, I'm sorry—"

"I'm pregnant—"

We speak at the same time, and I think my hearing may have gone just as my vision returned. I cock my head again and lower my gaze to her stomach.

She moves forward and takes my hand to place it on her belly.

"Malcolm, I'm pregnant with twins"—she reaches to the nightstand and holds picture frames in her hands—"Your baby girl and baby boy. They're twenty-four weeks now."

As she speaks, my hand jumps. My wide eyes lift to hers, and she giggles.

"One of them says hello to their daddy. That was a kick or a punch," she says. "Here, another one."

My jaw drops as my brain re-circuits to comprehend her words.

My Angel is pregnant with my babies?!?!?!

Fuck. Me.

MALCOLM

"Trust funds and monthly palimony guarantee Mini Malcolms and Starr well taken care of. Even though Starr insisted our actions were unnecessary. Your mother and I implemented them while you were in a coma. We want to ensure you do not need to concern yourself with your family's well-being. We want you to just focus on your health, son."

My father's words register barely as I sit stewing in a wheelchair. A wheelchair.

Another month and shit in progress.

Fuck. My. Life.

What started as optimism has swiftly plummeted to doubt.

Doubt I'll ever walk again.

Doubt I'll ever make love to My Angel again.

Doubt I'll ever take care of my babies or make children again.

Doubt I'll ever be a real man again.

Instead, a sense of self-loathing suffocates me. Each failure in my physical therapy sessions results in another layer of disgust wrapping around me like gauze on a mummy. I might as well join the dead with the lack of worth I now represent.

Everyone from the doctors to my family tries to encourage me. Hell, they even arranged for a shrink to meet with me twice a week. As fucking if. I kicked his ass out of my room the minute he started with his gobbledygook. Not impressed.

What I need is to get the fuck out of here. I can't think straight with all the constant, unwanted attention. In the back of my mind, I know my family means well. But I haven't had a moment alone to process my predicament.

Despite her best efforts to comfort me, My Angel even grates on my nerves.

I'm tired of her New Age hippie words of enlightenment. There's but so much deep breathing, meditation, and dharma talks I can take. I'm not that man anymore.

With an inward sigh, I recall our first argument—one of many in the past couple of weeks.

"Time for your morning meditation, my love!"

Starr's melodic teacher's voice fills my room.

I squeeze my eyes shut and slow my breathing, hoping she won't notice I was awake. I just do not have the energy to deal with this right now.

It was a hell of a night with the usual horrible dreams plaguing my mind. Each night they're different but with the same theme—I can't walk. Helpless.

Last night was the trapped in an unending corridor of a hospital with a snarling creature just beyond my vision stalking me. I fall out of my wheelchair and use my forearms to crawl along on my stomach, legs trailing limp behind. Sweat drenches my skin, causing the pajama top to stick to my back. The salty fluid burns my eyes as it drips from my forehead. Not one of the doors I heave myself up to reach the doorknob opens. I fall back down to the floor and continue my quest. Escape.

Just thinking about the nightmare makes my torso shudder.

"Are you all right, Malcolm?" Starr asks as she places her small palm on my not-so-muscular-anymore chest.

"No!" I yell as my eyes snap open to glare at her. "No, I am not all right, Starr! I am a fucking mess. Okay?!"

Her soft gasp and stricken face do little to assuage my anger. An anger that I keep simmering beneath a placid surface, hidden from my family and the medical team. Only the psychiatrist caught the full force of my fury. Now Starr is at the receiving end.

Tears fill her eyes. She averts her gaze to my bed. Her attention goes to straightening the covers on my legs.

The legs I cannot feel.

"Stop!" I snarl.

Starr brings one hand to her heart and the other to her swollen belly. A sob escapes her parted lips as she backs away from my bed.

"I—I'm so sorry, Malcolm," she says softly without gazing at me. "I don't mean to upset you—"

"Enough. Just go. I need to rest," I interject as I turn my head towards the window, not wanting her to see my tears.

A moment passes before Starr leaves me alone. Alone, to drown in a pool of self-pity.

Good.

I slam my fists into the mattress with my eyes squeezed shut, tears spilling out, and my mouth open in a silent, anguish-filled scream.

More tears creep from the corners of my eyes to puddle in my ears. A roar fills them, making my head pulse. The weight of it all is unbearable.

I cannot take much more.

Now as I half listen to my father, I wonder if Starr will even stay since she and our babies are more than financially stable thanks to my parents' foresight. Or their belief I would have succumbed to my injuries and never awoken from the coma...

After each fight—all one-sided—I tell her to go. But Starr always returns, undeterred by my histrionics. Dark circles rim her eyes and a bit of her free spirit drains. Yet she the glow of impending motherhood surrounds her like a protective shield. Nothing can take away from her innate beauty. Not even the pain I cause her.

Damn, I'm a miserable asshole.

"Malcolm."

My father's commanding tone drags me from my thoughts.

I shake my head to clear it from the jumble and lift my gaze to his stoic face.

He scrutinizes me for a moment. Sharp gray eyes bore into my very soul. One could hear his brain analyzing the situation, trying to make sense of his wayward second son.

I tumble back in time to my rebel teen years. Many a day did I stand before Morgan Steele to face his disappointment at my misbehavior. Never one to follow the rules, it was an everyday occurrence.

Sebastian took the role of eldest sibling seriously and made it his mission to watch over the rest of us as the leader. Roger *The Responsible* middle child served as the mediator with his intense stare and need for order. The unexpected twins Harris and Haley—the youngest jokester son and the baby girl—had everyone fawning all over them.

Me? I was the second son; the rebel; the bad boy billionaire playboy of the family. Even before I had my own billions. The one with the back tattoo from shoulder to shoulder around to my pecs of wings to symbolize freedom from family constraints and the flying as I sped along on my motocross bikes. Later, the Prince Albert piercing to give optimal pleasure to the many women I bedded.

My parents could have recorded the scoldings they gave to me and set them to auto play. Not that it mattered.

Now I'm a grown ass man, not here for chiding.

"Yes, Dad?" I ask with a stubborn lift to my chin as I meet the Alpha Dom's gaze.

Only the slight narrowing of his eyes provides any sign of his annoyance with me.

Too damn bad.

I'm the one who's suffering. Sitting immobile in a fucking wheelchair. No end in sight based on the dismal progress I've made since I awoke.

My father schools his features then responds, "Malcolm, we cannot fathom what you must go through. Nor will we make light of your feelings. However, keep in mind you have a responsibility to yourself and to Starr and to your babies. Get your head in the game, son. Do all you can to improve your situation. It may not be ideal in your mind, but it is the situation you must deal with. We are Steeles, and we let nothing stop us. Do you understand, Malcolm?"

I take a deep inhalation and a slow exhalation to calm myself—damn if Starr's New Age technique comes to the forefront.

"Listen, Dad. I'm trying here. A stalker ex almost killed me; a mountain lion almost ate me. In a coma; temporarily blinded; paralyzed from the waist down; my girlfriend is pregnant with twins. It's a whole lot to 'deal with' and not that easy, you know," I respond truculently. "Give me a break already."

He opens his mouth to speak, but I hold my hand up. I'm not that teenager anymore.

"I appreciate what you and Mom did for Starr and for the babies. For me with this custom facility and best-in-the-world medical team. Thank you. But I need some space. Some time to myself," I say. "Please."

Without hesitation, my father nods and responds, "I understand, son. Know that we love you and want the best for you. I'll speak with our family and the doctors. However, you must continue with your healing plan. Nonnegotiable, Malcolm. Do I have your word?"

I nod; he raises his eyebrow.

"Yes, Dad," I respond, knowing how Starr must feel when I demand a verbal response during our playtime.

"Very well, son," he says.

He embraces me, then strides out of the door.

A relieved sigh slips from my mouth as I navigate the wheelchair to the window. If I can't walk outside, I might as well stare at the bustling streets of Beverly Grove. The six lanes of traffic forming South San Vicente Boulevard stretches before me. Fortunately, the treated windows block the noise. Although I would welcome the distraction of honking horns and sirens.

How much time passes, I'm not sure. But the soft cough behind me makes me glance up. Reflected at me is the vision of My Angel.

Her sorrel brown eyes meet my stormy gray ones questioningly.

"Excuse me, Malcolm. I don't mean to disturb you. I will respect your request for time apart from us. But before I go, I want to let you know I love you with all of my heart, body, and soul, and I will be here when you are ready," Starr says in a voice tinged with sadness.

Her passionate words knock the wind from my lungs. I jerk with the force of it, and my head snaps to my chin and back. An incoherent grunt pops out of my mouth.

My Angel takes my visceral reaction as her dismissal and

hurries from the room as best as she can at twenty-eight weeks pregnant with twins.

Just as the door clicks shut, I find my voice.

But it's too late. Starr left. Only the aroma of her coconut and frangipani perfume wafts around me.

Once again, I take a deep inhalation to imprint her tantalizing scent on my brain. Then a slow exhalation, saddened by the loss of the last vestiges of my love.

I am alone.

STARR

"How are you doing, *chérie?*"

The concern in Leonie's feline amber gaze causes tears to fill my eyes. I shift to face the antique dresser she added to Mini Malcolms' nursery in my home—one of the five she designed—to avoid her noticing my pain.

More like gut-wrenching pain from being abandoned while pregnant by the one man I love and trust more than any other before him. The man with whom I want to spend the rest of my life. The man who captured my heart.

How could Malcolm do this to me? His Angel.

If anyone told me he and I would end up separated by not only miles but blocks put up by his mind, I would have laughed and told them not my Malcolm. Not my love.

Yet here I stand two weeks after he requested space from his family, thirty-weeks pregnant preparing for the arrival of our babies without their father.

Sure, I understand and respect Malcolm's need for some time to acclimate to a life vastly different from the one he had before being paralyzed. Cave diving; paragliding; kitesurfing; hell just walking down the damn street. At this time, not possible. And it must cause him a lot more pain than my sense of abandonment.

But my heart aches still.

So many nights I spent in his hospital room wishing he could hold me in his arms and ease some of the pangs of pregnancy. Rub my back; massage my calves; soothe the pulsing ache at the apex of my thighs. I know women I've helped as a doula spoke often of their increased sexual desires, but I never expected to be this needy. And BOB while watching the sex and dungeon videos Malcolm and I made do not cut it in the least. No Battery Operated Boyfriend can make up for the girth and length of Malcolm's ten inches of velvet covered steel wielded with such skill. Nor the two-dimensional image of him, even in all its glory on the giant screen in my media room. My greedy pussy clenches at the reminder.

Damn that man for being so self-involved!

What about me and my needs—including the horny ones, huh?

How does he expect me to go through pregnancy, birth, and raise twins by myself?!

Every day we're apart it's a constant struggle for me to continue being empathetic. And the raging hormones don't help my emotional rollercoaster. Not even my daily—now twice a day—meditation sessions help me refocus.

I'm nearing my wits' end.

If it weren't for my parents, my girls—Adrienne, Lola, Leonie, Anita, Billie, Blair—and of course the Steeles, I don't know what I'd do. But as my mother told me, *we come from a long line of courageous women capable of thriving despite the circumstances.* This too shall pass, and I will come out stronger for it.

And my babies will only know love and joy. They will

never know their father didn't spend time with me while I carried them. I just pray he'll be at their birth.

Each day I record our pregnancy progress so Malcolm won't miss one moment of Mini Malcolms' development—or the beauty of my body he's missing! After I shower and rub nourishing oil on my damp skin, I stand naked before the full-length mirror in my dressing room to record front, profile, and back views. Then I take still shots and place printouts along with the official ultrasound scans in the journal I write my musings in throughout the day.

What started as a way to document our babies since Malcolm was in a coma now is a means to provide him with the experience secondhand. His being absent is his choice.

So how am I doing? Not so great, to say the least…

"Oh, honey, don't worry. We're here for you," Billie says in her Southern Belle drawl when a sob slips from my trembling lips. "And for your little broccoli bunches!"

I can't help but to giggle through the sadness at her reference to the size of Mini Malcolms. Each time I see my OB-GYN, Billie wants an update so she can tease me. It's become our running joke.

As she wraps her arms around my shoulders, her Granny Smith apple green eyes twinkle with mirth. With her wavy, medium-blonde balayage hair and pecan-colored skin, Billie reminds me of Tyra Banks' doppelgänger. Billie is curvy like the megamodel, but a petite version at five feet, four inches.

Her joking is just what I need to drag me from the funky mood. I say a silent prayer of thanks she's spending more time at Lola's Coterie Beverly Hills than in her base at the boutique in STEELE Las Vegas' luxury mall. Since meeting her as Lola's West Coast assistant, Billie and I have become fast friends. When Lola promoted Billie to COO, we celebrated with a weekend getaway to Napa Valley.

I wish I had a glass… no, make that a bottle of wine now.

I rub my broccoli-filled belly and giggle. Well, maybe not *right* now.

"I know, and we thank you," I respond as I hug Billie in return. "You do not know how mind-blowing this whole situation has been. I wish that woman never messed with Malcolm and caused the accident. But I am grateful for your support. All of you. It means so much to me and helps make it a bit better."

"That's what friends are for, Starr!" Anita chimes in with a smile on her honey brown face beaming at me from where she sits cross-legged on the floor folding onesies. "We'll always have your back."

Indeed.

Last week she moved into my guest house. As my doula, Anita wanted to be close to me during the last weeks of my pregnancy—not all the way in Paris. She's a yoga instructor with a flourishing practice I know from our fitness world and my partner for the cafés in my SLFW Beverly Hills and Resorts. She's also the wife of Roger's luxury gym business partner, the former world heavyweight champion Norman Green. He relocated with her and will train out of his Beverly Hills facility. It's also nice to have their young daughters here for Mommy practice.

Along with Daphne at nine months and The Twins Rodolphe and Gaspard at two years old, I'm getting lessons in newborns, toddlers, and pre-schoolers. Whew!

On the babies' front, I'm covered. However, a man, not so much.

Roger and Harris try to make up for Malcolm's absence. They bring foods I crave, surprise me with goodies for Mini Malcolms, and put together their mobiles and custom baby monitors. Harris—the self-proclaimed *Bad Boy Bachelor For Life*—even offers to go with me to my doctor appointments. I pass on the visits, but love him for the thought.

Instead, The Moms go with me. They helped me to select a nanny with a nursing background who can assist me with twins. Patience Beck came highly recommended from the agency Leonie, then Lola used. One the überwealthy and celebrities use to hire their nannies, nurses, and governesses. Their training is top-notch in everything from changing a diaper to language lessons to disarming a would-be kidnapper. Although Morgan arranged a security detail at the ready since The Twins' kidnapping put everyone on high alert.

Nanny Patience presented as the best candidate—even aside from her name. Besides being appropriately trained and smart. She fits in with my personality, has the stamina to handle twins, and is a widowed, early fifties, mature woman. Zero interest in my man adds to her pros column. She'll be on call twenty-four, seven and live in the two bedroom, two bath apartment above the garage.

"However, I don't appreciate you leaving me to handle Anton Alexeyev," Adrienne huffs as she rolls her feline green eyes. "That man takes advantage of Malcolm and you being out of the loop to pester me all day!"

We laugh at her melodrama.

I know without a doubt the striking Russian giant weakens her resolve to fall hard for a man. Who can blame her with him resembling sexy AF Dolph Lundgren as the Russian boxer in *Rocky IV* with shoulder-length hair and glacial blue eyes?

As Malcolm's friend from Harvard University undergrad and B-School turned Vice President, Development for Entertainment Properties Division, Anton oversaw the partnership between STEELE International and SLFW. Adrienne unknowingly charmed him with her beauty, brains, and fluency in his native language. Not to mention disinterest in him makes her the perfect conquest for the

Alpha Dom. She's been mum about their relationship so far...

"Girl, like you don't love it!" I tease Adrienne with my own exaggerated eye roll. "We see you!"

She snorts and returns her attention to organizing the walk-in closet.

"Well, I'm just glad Starr likes Mini Malcolms' nurseries. My favorite is the one at Steele Southampton Village. There's something about the tranquility of a beach to soothe babies," Leonie says as she fluffs the pillow in one glider.

"I don't just like them, I love them!" I exclaim. "You did an awesome job with each nursery matching it to the mansion's decor yet giving them a unique feel. My parents love theirs too, as do Shelley and Morgan. I can't thank you enough, Leonie."

A twinge of sadness pokes at the tenuous edges of my happiness. The thought of Malcolm not being pleased with me changing rooms in his penthouse at The STEELE Tower in New York City and at his Hampton's beachfront mansion makes my stomach flip. Leonie started work on them as soon as I found out I was pregnant, while Malcolm was still in a coma. Now he's awake.

Shelley and Morgan assure me Malcolm won't mind despite his current standoffish behavior.

It pains me to think he would demand their removal considering they're for his babies. But with the way he's acting, who knows?

I give my head a firm shake to dislodge the gut-wrenching thought. No time for negativity, Starr Knight! I admonish myself.

Now there's a positive thought... Starr Steele.

Perhaps if I ask Malcolm to marry me, he'll see I love him unconditionally.

Whether or not he can walk, our love supersedes any

setback. Together we can overcome the blocks he's set in his mind. I won't let him lock himself away from me, his babies, or his loved ones. No more than I left the blinds drawn in his hospital room.

Malcolm needs the light and the love of those closest to him, despite his pushback.

I refuse to give up on us, on our little family. I'll give him another two weeks. After, I'll propose to the man I love—then, now, and forevermore.

My heart lifts, and a smile of pure joy spreads across my face.

"Honey, you are the epitome of a glowing Mommy-to-be!" Billie says.

Leonie claps her hands and adds, "Oh, *chérie*! You are simply stunning!"

Adrienne and Anita express their agreement with grins of their own.

I smile and rub my babies bump.

It's not my glow alone; it's Malcolm and our love that shines so brightly.

Soon we'll be together again.

"Thanks, bro. I appreciate you helping me out with my office. I need to do some work or I'll go crazy sitting around here all day long. It's time I focus on my work for STEELE."

Harris pauses at my words as he connects the monitor to the new computer he set up in the living room area of my suite at Cedars-Sinai. He turns a steely stare in my direction. The chill radiating from his gray eyes sends a shudder down my spine.

What's eating his ass?!

When I ask, Harris narrows his eyes into points as he glares at me. The space between his eyebrows furrow and his nostrils flare. He takes a deep breath.

"Really? It's time for you to focus on your work for STEELE?! What the fuck, *bro*?! How about you focus on your pregnant girlfriend?! Who do you think needs you more? Starr or STEELE? I'll help you out... It damn sure ain't STEELE!" Harris rails at me.

No sign of the jokester younger brother in sight. He's spitting mad with eyes blazing shards of platinum into me.

Well, damn.

"Listen, Harris. I do not need—"

"You do not need? You do not need?! Fuck you, Malcolm! You see those scars from fangs on your calf? Starr risked her life to save your sorry ass when a damn mountain lion was dragging you away to devour you. I saw the crazy sight with my own eyes, and it nearly gave me a heart attack! She stayed by your side every damn day and night. And this is how you treat her?! Damn, even if Starr wasn't pregnant—with your twins by the way—she doesn't deserve the cold shoulder you're giving her. How the hell can you justify icing her out of your life like this? You dumb fuck!" Harris continues, not slowing for air in his tirade.

Each time I open my mouth, it sets him off. All I can do is sit here and take his shit.

Like I want to be away from Starr?!

No, I don't! But what the fuck am I going to be able to do for her? And for our babies?! Riddle me that, little brother?! Little brother who's never been in a serious relationship a day in his thirty-two-year life!

"Fuck off, Harris!!!" I roar.

He shuts his mouth, but glares at me before he shakes his head with a look of pure disgust.

"No! *You* fuck off, Malcolm and get your shit together," Harris bites out. "I'm only helping you because Dad said so. Otherwise, I'd leave your sorry ass to wallow in your pool of self-pity. So. Shut. The. Fuck. Up. and let me finish so I can go see how your pregnant girlfriend is doing. Without you, loser."

Well, damn.

I sit stunned silent in the wake of Harris' fury. I can only watch as he finishes hooking up the computer. My mind reels. No one has spoken to me as he has since Baz and I had our arguments as teens. And even then, Baz didn't admonish me to the level Harris has.

Maybe I am being a total dick to Starr.

But she doesn't need a paralyzed man in her life. What the fuck can I do for her or for our babies other than give them money? And my parents took care of that issue with the trust funds and palimony.

Starr needs to just move on without me. Live her best life. Not to be saddled down with a gimp like me.

My mind drifts back to the disappointing conversation I had with my lead doctor this morning.

"It's been five months since the accident; the last three with me awake from the coma. I follow all of your team's directions; complete my physical therapy and strength training; hell, I even meet with the psychiatrist twice a week. Yet no new progress. Tell me your honest, medical opinion: will I ever walk again, doctor?" I ask.

Dr. Stevens stares at me for what seems an eternity before he responds.

"Mr. Steele, as I said when you woke, we cannot give you a definitive answer or a timeline. We can only adjust your treatment plan according to the progress you make using the best research and therapies available. It is a process you must trust," he says.

Now it's my turn to stare at him.

"So you're saying I may never walk again?" I press for a more concrete answer.

He shakes his head.

"Equal odds for you to experience a full recovery or for you to remain at your current state. I assure you we do our best for you, Mr. Steele."

The last fragile thread of hope snaps. I free fall. This time the thrill of the extreme sport disappears.

"Stay positive, Mr. Steele. That can be the most effective course

to maintain," Dr. Stevens *says before he leaves me sitting in my wheelchair despondent.*

"—And if you think Mom and Dad or any of the others are happy with your stupid behavior, think again, fucker."

Harris' declaration jars me from the disappointing memory. Then the door slams with enough force, the artwork on the walls shake as he storms out of my suite.

So lost in my thoughts, I hadn't realized he finished installing the computer. The login screen blinks silently with the STEELE International, Inc. logo awaiting my credentials.

Starr or STEELE?

Right now, it's still STEELE.

With a sigh, I type in the required information and set to work.

This is what I need right now. No one understands what I've been through or the hell I face every. Single. Damn. Day.

* * *

"It's good to have you back, Mr. Steele. We'll be sure to add you to all status updates and communications going forward. Should you need anything, just let us know. Good day!"

I smile at the screen before ending the video conference call with my Entertainment Properties Division. I gave myself a week to get up to speed on the various projects and this week marks my full return as the head.

Roger didn't argue with me about resuming my role from him. He only gave me shit about Starr. Again.

I wish they would back the fuck off already. If Starr's not complaining, why do my siblings need to berate me constantly? Hell, even Lola read me for filth a few days ago.

Fuck!

I shrug it off and lift my gaze to Anton.

The giant Russian pins me with his glacial stare.

"I am glad to see you back at work. But doing shit for your woman? Not glad, *zhopa*," he tsks with an aggrieved shake of his head.

I raise my arms in the air and glare at the ceiling in a silent plea for strength to deal with more bullshit. My blood heats in my veins. I'm sick of being treated poorly.

With a roar I respond, "Not you too, Anton. ENOUGH!"

I wheel around the desk and make quick work of the distance between us to face him head on. Our eyes on level since he's remains seated at a table allows me to square off with him.

Sure I may be in my wheelchair and legless, but my upper-body strength returns with each personal training session. I point my index finger in his face and snarl.

"Get the fuck off my back, *zhopa*! You do not know what the fuck you are talking about. And I damn sure do not need your judgement of my personal life! Either you are here to work or get the fuck out!" I say in a menacingly low growl.

Anton raises his eyebrow and slowly shifts his gaze between my finger in his face and my blazing eyes.

"You better get off the painkillers, Steele. Do not tempt me to beat your *zhopa* right here, right now. You damn sure need someone to knock some sense into you," he responds with his Russian accent thickening in his anger. "We have work to finish. Then I will take my leave of you. I am a man who handles his responsibilities."

My head explodes.

"Fuck. You—"

A polite cough from the doorway interrupts my rebuttal. I swing around to see who stands at the door.

Forget Anton… Fuck. Me.

It's Starr.

STARR

Today is the day. I will ask Malcolm Steele to step into the light of our love forever. I will ask him to marry me.

My heart flutters as I walk off of the elevator at the hospital. I nod to the nursing staff at their station, not wanting to stop and chat as I would normally. There's no need to check in the living room since Shelley told me she and Morgan were taking a spa day.

It'll be just Malcolm and me—no disruptions. Or witnesses if he tells me no, like I told him so many months ago…

With a deep cleansing breath, I shake my head and roll my shoulders back to rid myself of such negative thoughts. Get thee behind me!

As I near Malcolm's suite door, I hear shouts from within.

For a moment I consider leaving. I don't need him in a foul mood when I'm about to risk a proposal. Then I decide the risk of losing him proves greater than a hit to my ego. I take one more breath and knock on the door.

Malcolm's raised voice prevents him from hearing me.

He really shouldn't get himself so worked up. Nothing is worth elevated blood pressure in his medical condition.

I open the door and survey the room.

An enraged Malcolm points at Anton, who has a deceptively calm appearance. Knowing the Russian, I can tell he's pissed too.

I cough to bring their attention from ripping each other's head off to focus on my presence.

Their heads whip in my direction.

The fire in Malcolm's eyes resembles molten platinum.

A shudder trips down my spine. I clutch my babies bump protectively. I'm not at all concerned Malcolm would harm me. But he looks ferocious.

Our eyes lock—mine wide, his wild.

"Malcolm?" I judder.

"*Dorogoy*, come in. I was just about to take my leave," Anton says with a bright smile as he rises from his chair and gathers his things.

Malcolm's nostrils flare and he bites out, "Starr is not your *sweetheart!*"

Oh, dear. Perhaps I should rethink my proposal now, after all…

Anton ignores Malcolm and double kisses me before he exits the suite without a backwards glance at his best friend.

My eyes shoot up at the growl from Malcolm. I take in his flushed face and heaving chest. I don't know what they argued about, but it has Malcolm out of sorts.

"Would you like some cool water?" I ask as I move further into the suite. "I'm a bit parched myself."

I add the last part to not isolate him. So I proceed to the mini refrigerator and remove two bottles of Fiji Water. I smile to myself. The brand has become our favorite since our trips to the island chain. Then I go to his side.

Malcolm sits silent as I pass a bottle to him. His eyes study my face.

His intense gaze makes me blush.

"Well, I missed you too, Mr. Steele," I joke to lighten the mood. "I'll bring a framed photo the next time I come, and you can stare at it all day!"

After I sit in the chair Anton vacated, I take a much-needed sip from the frosty bottle. Then clear my throat and set our bottles on the table.

"Malcolm, I know you said you needed some space. But I

want to ask you a very important question," I say as I take his hands in mine.

Once again his eyes search my face, and I keep my expression open, hoping to share my unconditional love for him through it.

I take one final cleansing breath before I begin:

"Malcolm Steele, you mean more than the world to me. In fact, you are my sun and my moon—my everything. I love you beyond mere words. Over three years ago, you captivated me as I sat on the beach in St. Barth's while watching you kitesurf. Throughout that time, you taught me to embrace my desires by trusting you with my heart, body, and soul. Our love is unconditional. Nothing can tear us apart—no psycho sub or hungry mountain lion. I am yours and you are mine. Together we have our Mini Malcolms as proof of our love. I ask you to bind me to you forever, not just with your Shibari ropes, but with your commitment to me, to us, to our babies. Malcolm Steele, will you marry me, your Angel?"

Silence descends on the suite. Not even Malcolm's breath sounds from his parted lips as his mouth hangs open. Whether his reaction is a good shock or a horrible one, I cannot decipher as I continue to hold on to his now sweat-dampened hands.

Malcolm stares at me as his eyes darken. Then he drops his gaze to our hands clutched on his thighs. A strangled noise comes from the back of his throat. He pulls his hands from mine and wheels his chair backwards—away from me.

"I cannot even feel our hands on my lap," Malcolm whispers, again wild-eyed.

I sit frozen as he pivots the wheelchair to turn his back to me.

His shoulders droop, then shake.

His chin drops to his chest, and he brings a fist to his

mouth.

A gut-wrenching sob tears from his lips as his body convulses with each anguished cry.

I jump to my feet and go to Malcolm as fast as my body allows at thirty-two-weeks pregnant. My heart breaks and tears fill my eyes when I see my powerful Alpha Dom boyfriend so broken. Not once since he woke up did Malcolm display this level of pain and sadness. I knew he was hurting, but not to this extent.

"Malcolm, oh, Malcolm, my love," I start as I frame his face in my hands. "It's okay, baby. Just let it out. I'm here for you. Always."

I cradle his head to my babies bump and rock him as I hum while praying to soothe him and to give him strength. He wraps his arms around my back and clings to me while his sobs reach a peak.

We stay as one for a long while until Malcolm gathers himself and pulls back.

I wipe my tearstained face and lean over to kiss his full lips.

He turns away from me. Again.

"No," Malcolm whispers.

I stare at his profile blankly. *No?*

"I am a broken, angry, and bitter man, Starr, and I vowed to protect you. Even if that means protecting you from me," Malcolm says in a more firm voice as he stares at the wall. "Go, Starr. I can do nothing for you like I am. The babies will bear the Steele name. I will make certain they and you are financially secure for life. But I can do no more."

Without sparing me a single glance, Malcolm wheels himself away from me one final time. The bedroom door of his suite shuts with a resounding click in the silent room.

The pieces of my broken heart turn to dust, and my tears wither away.

STARR

"**I** do not give a damn what you say, Starr Knight! By the time I finish with Malcolm Steele, he will not need to worry about being 'a broken, angry, and bitter man!' He will not have to worry about a damn thing!"

I imagine steam pouring from my father's nose, mouth, and ears as his pecan complexion reddens with his rage. His obsidian eyes flash with each step he takes as he storms around the living room in my parents' Bel Air mansion.

After Malcolm's harsh dismal, I was so upset I needed the comfort only my mother and my father could provide for me. I love my girls and their support, but I needed more. Much more.

I still don't know how I made it from Malcolm's suite, then outside to my new SUV.

Morgan and Shelley gifted the chauffeur-driven Black Badge Rolls-Royce Cullinan to me when my babies bump made it difficult to drive my Tesla. The future grandparents explained the SUV would prove a more convenient method of transportation to get around with the babies. They insisted Ernest Rowland—a member of STEELE

International's security team based in Los Angeles—join my detail and serve as my driver.

Even though I protested initially, I was thankful to have him waiting outside of the hospital. I was in no condition to drive. One look at my facial expression, and Ernest ushered me into the backseat. The comfort of its sumptuous interior with the scent of lavender wafting from the built-in diffuser wasn't enough to soothe me.

I asked Ernest to take me to my parents.

As we drove the thirty minutes along Sunset Boulevard, my mind replayed the scene on repeat, analyzing every detail and nuance. The expression of concern around Anton's eyes; the tic of Malcolm's cheek as he ground his molars; his eyes shifted from stormy gray to closed off while I opened my heart during the proposal.

By the time Ernest helped me from the Cullinan, nausea made me weak and my stomach roil. My parents weren't home yet, so he helped me to a sitting room and put my legs up on a sofa. He disappeared and returned with a cool glass of water. Then he offered to stay until my parents returned. I assured him I would be fine and told him to take the rest of the day and tomorrow off. With a sympathetic look, he left.

Tears welled in my eyes at his simple actions.

Ernest, my parents, Morgan, Shelley, my girls... Hell, even the man who held the elevator as I waddled towards it exhibits more care for me than my boyfriend and the father of our babies!

After I pulled the cashmere throw over me, I cried myself to sleep curled in a fetal position on the sofa. Rest evaded me as nightmares of being abandoned in the hospital room or alone giving birth plagued me.

I gave up on peaceful sleep.

Instead, I made my way to the kitchen for a cup of lemon

ginger tea. Leonie hooked Lola and now me on to the tasty beverage. Perfect for upset tummies.

As the water heated in the kettle, I rubbed my babies bump and murmured words of love to the only bright lights in my life. I vowed to give them my all and to stop pining over Malcolm. They need me more than he does, apparently. And they deserve a home full of warmth and love.

So as I learned from one of my favorite movies—*Like Water for Chocolate*—the power of emotions and cooking, I put a stop to my tears. I refused to have my sadness transferred to my babies. Their happiness supersedes my despair.

By the time my parents arrived from their law firm, I made up my mind. I will care for my babies to my fullest without Malcolm Steele. They will bear his name and receive his monthly child support in addition to the trust funds, as they deserve. However, I will no longer accept the monthly palimony. I only agreed to it since I believed Malcolm and I would marry.

Silly Starr no more!

So as my father steams—not at all peaceful like his adopted name—I await an opening to tell him again I can handle my life. I only ask for their support. And not the reckoning of Malcolm Steele...

"Starr, honey, let your father talk to Malcolm. And I mean *talk*, Jordan. I cannot believe he would behave in such a callous manner. He's been such a pleasure," my mother says, shifting her gaze from my father to me.

Whenever she reverts to his given name, Sun means business.

From my father's chastened expression, he understands. With a growl, he spins on his heel to stalk towards the liquor cabinet where he pours himself a double straight up of Michter's Bourbon. The ultra-premium Kentucky Bourbon is his liquor of choice. He tosses it back without a flinch and pours another. His piercing eyes go to my mother.

"Sun, would you care for a drink?" He asks gruffly.

"No, darling. One of us needs to maintain a clear head," she replies with an eye roll.

She returns her attention to me and pats my leg.

"Honey, men are funny creatures. When they hurt, they either withdraw or lash out. In Malcolm's case, he's done both"—she pauses to cup my cheek as a stray tear leaks from my eye—"Honestly, I'm surprised he hasn't broken before now. You have four weeks until Mini Malcolms' births. Time heals all, Starr."

Across the sitting room, my father snorts as he finishes his second Christofle rocks glass.

Our gazes lift to him.

He shakes his head and mutters to himself.

"You'll just talk to Malcolm. Right, Dad?" I ask.

With a sigh, he strides back over to where my mother and I sit on the sofa. He perches his six-foot-five-inch frame on the edge of the armrest and kisses my forehead, then my mother's lips.

"Starr, sweetheart, I cannot imagine what you are going through—or Steele for that matter. But I will repeat for you what I told him over a year ago and then the afternoon before his accident."

My father goes on to tell me—verbatim as the attorney he is—his conversation with Malcolm about our relationship.

"Understand Starr is my only child and means everything to her mother and to me. Our family unit is inseparable. Starr shares every aspect of her life with my wife and with me. She made us aware of the situation with Vicky Reynolds and her declination of your proposal, along with the lifestyle she's chosen with you. My daughter is an intelligent, grown woman who thinks for herself.

However, Starr is still mine to protect by any means necessary. I am no Quinn Peters. You were together for eight months; broke up for two; back together for ten. Now what are your intentions with my daughter, Steele?"

"Peace, I respect Starr, Sun, and you—your family dynamic. I love your daughter with every fiber of my being. I value her and the life I want to build with her. Starr may have said no once. But I am a patient man determined to prove my worthiness. I ask for your permission for her hand in marriage now. So when Starr is ready, we will have your blessing."

"I appreciate your candidness and your respect. Starr loves you and in time will say yes. You have my blessing. But... Do. Not. Fuck. Up. Steele."

Then Malcolm's conversation with my father about a second proposal.

"Labor Day went well with our families meeting for the first time officially. So I'm glad you and Sun will join us in the Exumas on Bougainvillea Cay for Thanksgiving. Especially since I plan to propose to Starr."

"Excellent, Malcolm! Exactly what I expected to hear from you. I believe you'll get your yes this time. Sun and I look forward to spending Thanksgiving with family."

My mouth falls open.

I did not know Malcolm planned on proposing to me again. I was just excited both of our families would join for the holiday. Spend time getting to know one another while enjoying the tranquility of Lola and Sebastian's private island in the Bahamas.

Damn that Vicky Reynolds for finally destroying our love!

Despite my recent pledge to not suffer sorrow, tears slip from my eyes as I sob uncontrollably. The heart I thought couldn't hurt anymore shatters.

What if the accident didn't happen?

Where would Malcolm and I be right now, five months later?

How happy would we be together instead of miserable apart?

I squeeze my eyes shut and swipe at the tears.

No more, Starr!

As my mother suggests, I will give Malcolm more time and take a coping mechanism from him.

Between now and our babies' expected birth date, I'll focus on my Starr Light Fitness & Wellness business. Ernest can drive me so I can spend at least four days at the center. It will keep me busy just as Malcolm returning to STEELE International must do for him by the looks of the office he set up and Anton being present with his laptop. With the nurseries finished and my home ready for the twins' arrival, I can turn my nesting to my original baby—SLFW Beverly Hills and my jewelry making. It's time for a new collection for the center's boutique and those at the SLFW Resorts.

Refocused, I smile at my loving parents to reassure them.

My mother stops fussing with the throw around me as my father returns with a fresh pot of lemon ginger tea. They gaze at me expectantly when I clear my throat.

"Mom, Dad, I love you so much and am grateful for your love and support," I start as I clasp their hands in mine. "Now that I know Malcolm planned to propose again, it gives me the strength to believe in our love again and to not let anything break us. I'll give him the time, as Mom said. Meanwhile, I'll get back to work on SLFW. Adrienne can use my help as a buffer for Anton!"

They laugh, knowing Anton's potent attraction to my bestie.

Just as then the chef enters to announce dinner is ready.

My stomach growls louder than my father from earlier since I haven't eaten in a while, too nervous about my proposal. Once again we laugh as I link my arms through theirs and head to the dining room.

* * *

"WHAT DO you think of this set, *chérie*? I love the sheer panels on the legs!"

I glance up from the rack of clothes to see *The Lion* modeling a new tank top and matching leggings. Never one to notice her impact on others, Leonie sashays on her legs for days around the boutique at SLFW Beverly Hills while clients gawk at her flawless beauty.

No makeup, wavy mahogany mane in a high ponytail, and barefoot one can't help but to admire Leonie. She stuns the crowd, whether on a Parisian catwalk, on a billboard in Times Square, or in workout gear. With her flat toned abs peeking out, no one would guess she's the mother of three children under the age of two years old.

I grin at my close friend.

"Fantastic! The gold highlights your caramel skin perfectly. Here, try this on next," I respond.

She flashes her billion-dollar smile and takes the hot pink leopard print catsuit, then ducks into the changing room.

"You know, I could play *Dress Up Leonie The Lion* all day, you know!" I tease. "No wonder they pay you the big bucks, girl."

Leonie's tinkling laughter fills the shop and carries to the lobby where clients waiting to check in or who sit at the café tables turn to the sound. She reemerges moments later, crawling on the floor like a big cat. Her feline features play to her nickname. She roars then leaps to her feet, clapping her hands while giggling.

"I couldn't help myself, *chérie*!" She exclaims. "I knew you'd laugh, and it's good to see you in high spirits at last!"

I nod and think how it's been a week since I declared only happiness in my life. During that time, I've enjoyed getting back to work full time after being by Malcolm's side for months. And as I thought, Adrienne was more than enthusiastic about my return!

"Absolutely! I flew in just to check on you for myself. I needed to see your face in person to make sure I didn't have to beat my dumb brother up," Haley adds.

I grin as she throws imaginary punches and bounces on the balls of her feet.

"Okay, Ms. Muhammad Ali!" Anita trills. "Malcolm better watch out, or he'll get stung by the Champ! He said he'll come out of retirement if Malcolm doesn't get himself together."

We laugh at her reference to Norman making Malcolm his ninth TKO.

"Well, get in line because my Dad is on deck raring to go at him!" I giggle.

"His brothers too!" Leonie says as she comes back out in her yellow terrycloth romper and Nikes. "Roger is beyond pissed. But, he insists Malcolm will come to his senses by the time the twins are born. So no worries, *chérie, non?*"

I nod and with a sweep of my arm along my body I respond, "*Oui!* I agree. Besides, he cannot deny all of this!"

Haley lets loose with a series of wolf whistles.

"Yeah, Starr! That's it, girl!" Anita claps. "A man will throw away a bone, but he'll keep the meat!"

That old adage has us cracking up so loudly everyone within hearing distance turns in our direction.

Red faced with tears of mirth spilling from our eyes, we make our way to the café for lunch. As I pass the shop girl, I ask her to wrap the girls' purchases up and to put the bags to my office.

Adrienne meets us halfway with a smirk on her face.

"Okay, what's the joke, ladies?" She asks, cocking her head to the side. "I could hear your cackles and snorts as I walked past the front desk."

Haley jumps into a fighting stance, and Anita faces off with her as they pretend to box. Anita mimics an exaggerated upper cut, and Haley crumples to the ground. Mrs. World Heavyweight Champ raises her fists in the air triumphantly as she prances around in a circle around her ninth TKO.

"I see!" Adrienne laughs. "Well, let's get you a steak to replenish your protein, Anita."

Steak has us cracking up all over again while Adrienne stares at us in wonder.

Leonie loops her arm through Adrienne and says, "We'll explain over our lunch of champions, *chérie.*"

As I follow them past the surprised clients, I say a silent prayer of gratitude for my girls.

Yes, Starr, this too shall pass, and you will come out stronger for it. I smile to myself, rubbing my and Malcolm's babies bump.

MALCOLM

"*D*on't fuss, sweetheart. You're perfectly fine. Are you certain you want to wheel yourself? No need to overexert yourself before we get to the courthouse."

My mother smooths the Full Windsor Knot of my platinum silk tie and adjusts my navy blue striped suit vest. She winks at me and smiles.

"No one is as handsome as my sons. Well, other than your father, and you look exactly like him!" She adds, fluttering her eyelashes.

My return smile resembles more of a grimace. I appreciate her attempt to lighten the mood. But I can't help wondering if my being in a wheelchair will make me appear weak in Vicky's eyes. I'd rather not witness a triumphant gleam in her eyes.

Once her Alpha Dom; now her victim.

How far I've fallen.

This will be the first time I see Vicky since three months before the accident.

When I had her naked, bound, and gagged in a dank, underground bunker with a menacing Russian who encouraged her not to fuck with my or Starr's lives. After I entered the room with its dirt floors, rough-hewn stone walls, timbered ceiling, I presented her with two options: sign an agreement and leave or stay there with him.

The Russian actor I hired scared the piss—literally—out of Vicky.

She chose the agreement.

Vicky moved to Johannesburg, South Africa—far from any STEELE or SLFW property—immediately; ended her acting career—already in shambles from Operation Nightingale—officially; never contact Starr, myself, or any of our connections directly or indirectly.

It wasn't a raw deal. Especially since she violated the five-year civil harassment orders. I could have pressed further charges.

In hindsight, I wish I had…

For this major infraction, the court ordered Vicky extradited from South Africa to stand trial for the accident that nearly killed me. The process was lengthy. But when she arrived two months ago, I wasn't ready to have her see me.

Fortunately, my medical team didn't approve of the added stress of a trial at that time. So Dr. Stevens informed my attorney. Judge Susan Dixon—who handled my other cases against Vicky—accepted their decision and moved the trial date.

Another stroke of luck was the tech nerd Vicky used to follow me and to direct the drones.

When confronted with the enormity of his involvement, he ratted Vicky out. Being a techie, he kept detailed accounts of every single one of their communications— written and visual. His court-appointed attorney—bogged down with other cases—offered no type of defense for him. The attorney recommended he plead guilty with a chance for a lesser charge and sentence based on his testimony against Vicky—the mastermind behind the accident.

Engelbert conferred with me and my family. He thought it best to go after Vicky the hardest. The techie would still serve plenty of time. But his limited resources wouldn't allow for any financial recompense.

Roger—who had a similar situation with his stalker and her sidekick—agreed with Engelbert. After further discussion, during which everyone voiced their opinions, we agreed as a whole. As Haley said, *"Deep-six, that bitch!"*

Now Haley's voice draws me from my musings.

"Malcolm, I'm with Mom. At least let me push you to the Sprinter. The press is out front, and our security team roped off the rear entrance to prevent a crazy paparazzo from sneaking in," Haley adds.

Again, I appreciate the help, but I'd rather not have my little sister push me, a man. It's bad enough a male nurse has to come with me to help me in and out of this damn wheelchair—carry me like some overgrown baby. At least he's dressed in a suit and not in his regular white uniform.

I open my mouth to decline her offer when Sebastian speaks.

"Thanks, Haley. But I'll take care of Malcolm. He's too big for you to handle, even in a chair," he says with a smirk.

And like that, our older brother naturally steps into his role of caring for his younger siblings. He nods at my grateful expression and steps behind my wheelchair.

I also appreciate him coming to the trial instead of staying in New York. Lola—at thirty-two-weeks pregnant with twin girls—can't fly so close to her due date. She has their nanny and her doula to help her, not to mention the rest of their staff.

Lola didn't want to hear my suggestion: Baz not come.

She reminded me I was already on very thin ice with her over Starr and to not push her buttons further.

Starr.

Despite me being a total jerk and her being thirty-four-weeks pregnant, she's meeting us at the courthouse with her parents. She's set to testify and refused to do it via video conference. Judge Dixon granted Starr the option to appear in person or via video since she's two weeks out from her due date.

When I found out about Starr testifying, I called to tell her to put the babies' and her health first. I need nothing happening to them on my account. I couldn't bear it. No more losses.

She kept the conversation brief and only on confirming her decision. Then she hung up.

And I thought I would have to end the call. Not that I can blame her.

It'll be awkward seeing Starr, too. We haven't seen each other since her proposal.

Just remembering hearing her gasp when I told her no proves painful. I knew then I couldn't look her in her sorrel brown eyes and took the coward's way out. Wuss that I am.

Again, how far I've fallen.

Baz steers me out of my suite and to the back entrance of Cedars-Sinai Spine Center. True to what Haley told me, Mercedes-Benz Sprinters sit right outside the door and STEELE security man the perimeter.

Thank fuck since the media went into a frenzy with news of a first-degree attempted murder of a member of the STEELE Quaternity by a Hollywood Royalty starlet in a jealous rage. Add on the love triangle involving BDSM and international tabloids had their newest fodder.

Yeah, the STEELE Quaternity... The media dub Sebastian, Roger, Harris, and me the moniker for being the most sought-after of the world's eligible billionaires. Well, that was prior to Lola and Leonie snagging Baz and Roger off the market. And boy, did the world go wild when that happened.

So for one of the two remaining to almost die at the hands of a famous actress, they clamored for details, exclusives, insider information, the works. The hospital had to dismiss an orderly and a nurse for sneaking a photographer onto my private floor and for recording me during my physical therapy session, respectively.

After tips from other staff members, my security detail intercepted the cameras and the iPhone before they could share the images and the video. What people will do for a buck…

Engelbert enlisted the power of STEELE's public relations department to counteract any negative press. They also implemented campaigns to present me most favorably. Highlights of my philanthropic work with STEELE Foundation. Multiple interviews with prominent individuals and businesses to support me as an upstanding business executive. The PR machine fills the networks and publications on a global scale daily.

It's easy going to the courthouse.

Until I spy the crowd of onlookers, international television crews, and photographers out front.

I have a flashback to Roger's court appearances. Not a pretty sight. Except this time no one is chanting, "Off with his cock!" This time I'm perceived as the victim, not the woman involved.

The drivers take us to the rear of the courthouse where once again the secured area hides no cameras. We pull up behind a Cullinan and disembark. When the nurse sets me in my wheelchair, the Cullinan's doors open and Peace steps out.

He shots me a scathing glare before he walks around the back and leans in to the other open door. Legs swing out and dainty hands reach for his more sizable ones. Followed by a head of curly dark brown hair appears.

Starr.

She scoots forward and into her father's arms. He steadies her before he wraps his arm around her lower back. She graces him with a beatific smile. He says something to her, and she laughs, cupping her much larger belly.

Damn!

A sensation I haven't felt in a long time burns within me. I recognize it barely—possessiveness.

That should be me Starr smiles at so lovingly, my caveman snarls.

Starr must sense my heated stare as she flicks her gaze in my direction.

Her father follows her gaze, then says something to her.

She nods and the light that only moments before filled her sorrel brown eyes dims.

Damn.

Suddenly my view of Starr gets obstructed by Haley and Leonie rushing to her side making a fuss. Anita and Norman exit a Mercedes-Benz G-Wagen and make their way to her, too.

The forward movement of my wheelchair jolts me. Baz pushes me to Starr.

Her gaze returns to mine, and we stare at one another.

"Thank you for—"

"You look good—"

We speak at the same time. Then shake our heads and start again.

"No, you look beautiful—"

"You're welcome—"

Again we talk at once.

This time Peace interjects.

"Judge Dixon hates when people are late to her courtroom. Let us get going. Starr needs to sit," he says in a clipped tone of voice.

My father agrees, and we proceed to the courtroom.

Surreptitiously, I glance at Starr. She is more than beautiful. She's stunning. A glow makes her normally gorgeous face even more angelic. The way she cradles her babies bump so protectively makes me want to wrap her in my arms and hold her close where no one can hurt her or the babies.

I snort to myself.

I fucking hurt her…

Damn!

We continue on inside the courthouse en masse. Anton along with my boys—his cousin and my MMA trainer Borya *The War Defender* Alexeyev and my cousin and business partner with LEVELS our BDSM Dance clubs Lucien *The Sexy Chef* Jackson—wait inside the entrance. Their presence for support and as character witnesses, especially since they've seen me with Vicky and know the type of person she is. They too greet Starr first before they turn to me.

Again a growl threatens to rip from between my curled lips at the sight of them putting their arms around her, even if they're only hugs. I. Do. Not. Like. It. At. All.

Baz gives me no time to process these unexpected emotions wreaking havoc with my mind. He presses on and doesn't stop until we're outside of the courtroom. Then he pauses and leans down to speak so only I can hear him.

"Malcolm, are you ready for this?" He asks.

Again, I have to give it up to him. Baz's protective behavior for his family shines through. He knew what I was feeling as we neared the double doors.

I nod and respond affirmatively.

He beckons for our security members to open the doors.

We enter, and all heads swivel in our direction. Countless eyes gawk at me, surprised I'm in a wheelchair.

I draw on my Alpha Dom to raise my chin higher and met their stares with a cool indifference. Yeah, I'm in a wheelchair, but don't think for one minute I'm some chump.

I am Malcolm *The Enforcer* Steele.

* * *

DAYS LATER, Judge Dixon had enough.

Vicky exploded at the sight of Starr pregnant. The actress could no longer adhere to the pretense of being an ingenue corrupted by a lascivious male who drove her to one moment of madness. She also went berserk when the techie took the stand against her and delivered damning testimony unrefuted by her lead attorney.

I never had a chance to recount the night since Harris pulled video footage from security cameras of the mansions along Benedict Canyon Drive into a complication. The entire scene unfolded in one agonizing clip from the moment I left Starr's garage to me being harassed by the drones to my Ducati Desmosedici motorcycle flying over the embankment.

The body-cam footage revealed Starr charging the mountain lion with a stick while the police officers shouted for her to stop. The moment the lion leaped in the air to attack her, my stomach dropped.

A chill snaked down my spine as I watched, transfixed by the replay. I think of a thousand different ways I could have handled the situation.

Stop and call the police.

Stop and smash the drone before the other one showed up.

Stay at home and make love to My Angel.

The last had me wishing I could still feel my cock...

Each day Starr arrived with her parents and waited to enter the courthouse until I arrived. Wanting to show a united front, she never wavered from supporting me.

Until I caught her grimacing, and I told her to go home and rest.

Starr put up a protest, but gave in when her mother, Anita, and Shelley told her it was best. She gave in grudgingly. But her parting shot to Vicky was a kiss to my lips that made my heart stutter and the ex-psycho-sub scream.

Since that day I wonder if it was all for show. But I don't allow the seed to plant itself too deeply in my mind. I still can't do anything for Starr or for the babies.

Still, I can't stop thinking about her, about us. And how differently things would stand had I handled the situation any other way.

The only good thing is Vicky Fucking Reynolds is out of our lives permanently.

Engelbert proved beyond a shadow of doubt Vicky demonstrated an intent to murder me, but failed. Judge Dixon—who made it clear she was none too pleased Vicky disregarded the civil harassment orders the judge issued—handed down the most severe punishment. Life in prison!

Take that. Take that. Take that!

The expression on Vicky's face was priceless. I wished I had a photo of it! Until then she held no regard for the legal system and obviously assumed she would get off scot-free.

Nope.

The bailiffs had to drag her from the courtroom, kicking and screaming obscenities at me, her attorney, then at Judge Dixon, when she dared to order Vicky to leave in silence.

She was so out of line the judge issued fines and mandatory anger management sessions.

Vicky's parents and friends hurried from the courtroom, avoiding all eyes and questions from the press. Their security team had to shield her entourage from microphones shoved in their faces for statements and cameras.

I sat back in my chair, relieved it was all over. A weight lifted off of my chest. Then my mind jumped to Starr.

The urge to swoop her into my arms and make love to her in celebration was intense. But not possible. One, I can't feel my cock. Two, her OB-GYN due to stress put her on bed rest and couldn't be at the courthouse.

What should have been elation for us being rid of the ex-psycho-sub was a bust. So completely fucked up.

Still, I called Starr and gave her the news. Then I asked if I could see her. She agreed.

"Thank you for being so supportive of me, Starr," I say sincerely.

Now it's my turn to sit beside her bed.

She rests in a chair by the window of her bedroom with her back against pillows and a cashmere throw on her lap. A delicate lace and satin peignoir in a soft pink sets off her luscious curves.

My mouth salivates at her now double-D size tits. I've always been a T&A man. But the fetish of adult lactation jumps to the forefront...

I have to shake my head to clear it. Not now, Steele.

"You're welcome, Malcolm," Starr responds quietly.

"I have to ask you something," I start, then continue when she nods her consent. "When you kissed me in the courtroom, was it for effect or because you meant it?"

Starr studies my face for a moment, then turns her head as tears shine in her eyes.

I give her some time to collect herself. When she doesn't answer, I place my hand over hers and squeeze.

"Starr?" I press.

She gasps at my touch and swings her head back to stare at our joined hands, then at my face.

I'm reminded of the day I first laid eyes on her at Baz and Lola's wedding. The face of an angel stares up at me. Her sorrel brown eyes widen in surprise as her lush mouth forms a perfect O. My cock may not twitch as it did then, but my heart and soul ache for her.

"I—I," My Angel closes her eyes and takes a deep breath as though clearing the stutter then begins again. "I kissed you because... because you seemed so alone, despite being surrounded by friends and family. I didn't want to leave you, but I needed to rest. So I kissed you to fill you with my strength as you've done for me in the past."

Her response hits me in the chest with enough force to shatter the block of ice surrounding my heart. The light of her love for me melts the remaining shards and cleanses my mind, body, and soul. The negativity I carried for months falls away, replaced by hope.

Now tears fill my eyes.

Without a word, My Angel slips her free hand behind my head and draws me to her breasts. The rhythm of her heart beating fast confirms her emotions are as high as mine. As she massages my scalp like she used to, I rub my thumb over her knuckles to deepen our connection.

Her babies bump sits so close to my face.

I realize I haven't touched it since she placed my hand on her belly months ago. My free hand slides over the round surface until my palm rests over her belly button.

A kick greets me.

I jolt and gape at My Angel.

A smile plays at the corners of her mouth, and her eyes sparkle with glee. She puts my hand back on the spot, then moves it around until another kick connects with my palm. We sit with both of our hands connected in a comfortable silence for a while.

"Can I come to their birth?" I ask in awe.

When My Angel doesn't answer, I lift my gaze from her belly to her face.

Tears of joy fill her eyes.

My heart clenches.

Through vision blurred by my tears, I cup the back of My Angel's head and draw her to me. My mouth crashes onto hers. Our teeth click and tongues twist as I engulf her with a kiss so full of emotion it's hard to breathe.

She matches my intensity.

When she moans into my mouth, all the barriers I erected to keep her away crumble into dust. I will let no one tear us apart again—not even myself.

This woman is mine all mine.

"*O*h, how adorable! I love the little pink bows on this onesie and the blue ties on this onesie. Oh and these, too! I can't wait to see Mini Malcolms in their new outfits! Thank you, Billie and Patrick!"

My heart soars as My Angel holds up the gifts from Billie and her lover Patrick Rockett—the CEO of Rockett Construction Company and STEELE International Inc.'s competitor. But that's another story.

Then my heart soars even higher when I think back to the last two weeks. Every day I visit with My Angel for hours. It's the total reverse as I sit by her side while she remains on bedrest as she did for me.

My Angel even made a joke about it, and it was easy for me to join in.

The best gift she gave to me was the journal along with videos she's taken since she found out about her pregnancy —our pregnancy. The daily snapshots and her thoughts help me make up for the time apart. When she gave it to me, I was so overwhelmed, emotions robbed me of the ability to speak. She cupped my face and kissed me softly in understanding.

Leonie gave me a tour of the nursery and presented the ones in my New York penthouse and my Southampton Village beachfront mansion. She arched an elegant eyebrow at me when I asked how they gained access and told me with a superior look to fuck off in French.

Roger pinned me with his intense stare and cussed me out, too.

But I held up my hands, palms out in surrender, and told them I was only curious, not at all angry. They're my babies, after all!

Once we passed that minor blip and we shared our feelings and concerns along with effusive apologies on my end, our transition back to a couple was smooth. I told My Angel I love her and she told me the same.

However, Peace, not so much.

He ripped me a new one, and I allowed it since he was absolutely correct. When he finished, I explained myself—something I do rarely. Peace's parting shot was for me to prove him wrong.

And I intend to wholeheartedly.

"You do not know how many baby boutiques Billie dragged me to until she found 'the cutest outfits.' So, I am beyond thrilled you love them!"

Patrick's Scottish rumble brings me back to the present.

We're in the garden of My Angel's mansion for virtual baby showers. Her girls surprised My Angel and Lola with the parties. The location of my sister-in-law's being on a terrace of her and Baz's penthouse in The STEELE Tower.

Instead of the baby showers being limited to women, they included the guys. Anita and Norman's daughters and Roger and Leonie's twins—Rodolphe and Gaspard—helped to hand presents to My Angel. While their baby sister, Daphne cooed on Roger's lap.

I'm sure Baz and Roger are no more pleased than I am to see Lachlan helping Haley hand Lola her gifts. Lucien's older brother, Baz's best friend, and the President of Liquor at Jackson Corporation is in New York instead of his home base in Aberdeen, Scotland. We love Lach to death, but our baby sister with an Alpha Dom? *Grrr.*

My mother, Sun, Leonie, Billie, Anita, and Adrienne decorated My Angel's garden while Haley and Blair did Lola's terrace. They decorated the garden in shades of pink and blue and the terrace in pink and cream.

Lucien provided My Angel and Lola's favorite dishes from his restaurants in both cities for their lunches. One of his pastry chefs crafted an incredible and delicious cake in the shape of a cradle. It was an edible piece of art.

Blair led us through silly games before the presents, all while we interacted on the giant screens Harris and Haley installed. So far the whole affair turned into a fun fete we've enjoyed for hours.

Luc Montaigne—Lola's mentor and the Parisian multi-billionaire head of his family's multigenerational Banque Montaigne empire—laughs.

"Well, Patrick, I know what you mean! Blair did the very same with me," Luc adds.

Both women laugh, as does My Angel.

Then she cries out.

Every head swivels in her direction.

She grimaces and drops the onesies in her lap as she grabs her babies bump with a second cry. She doubles over.

What. The Fuck?!?!?!

"Babe, what's wrong?!" I ask, panicked, as I reach for her hand.

She shakes her head and moans.

Everyone shouts and jumps up to rush to her side. Anita makes her way past Sun and my mother to crouch in front of My Angel.

"Starr, where do you feel the pain? And how strongly?" Anita asks, going into doula mode.

My Angel catches her breath and raises her head.

"My lower back has been bothering me all morning. A sharp pain in my lower belly and lower back just now. The pain radiates down my legs," she whimpers and clutches her belly with the hand not holding mine. "Ooooh…"

"Patrick, get the Sprinter. Leonie, get Starr's bag by the front door and put it in the van. Roger, Harris, lift Starr between you in a sitting position and put her in the van," Anita gives the orders calmly. Then adds, "Now!"

They rush to do her bidding.

"Norman, stay with the children and their nannies. Everyone else, get to Starr's suite at Cedars-Sinai. Her OB-GYN is Dr. Leticia Sánchez," Anita finishes as she follows my brothers and my woman into the mansion.

I roll my wheelchair after them, then watch as my family and friends scatter for their vehicles. The front door closes, and I'm forgotten completely.

"FUCK!!!" I roar as I bang my fists on the armrests.

Just as I said: I cannot do shit for Starr or the babies! Hell, I can't even get myself in a fucking car to drive to the hospital. She has to depend on any and everybody else! My heart plummets.

"DAMMIT!!!" I yell.

"What's going on?!" Norman barks as he rushes from the garden, holding hands with his daughter and Rodolphe.

He stops when he sees me. Sympathy floods his face.

Great.

"Oh, man," Norman mutters. "Hold on, let me call Anita."

"No! I'll—"

"Malcolm! Bro, let's go! Starr's calling for you," Roger shouts as he and Harris storm back through the front door.

I sigh with relief as Harris pushes me to the Sprinter.

"*Sois sage et surveille tes frère et sœur, Rodolphe!*" Roger calls over his shoulder to his eldest son to behave and watch his siblings.

My Angel lifts her distressed eyes up when we reach the van, then smiles wanly.

"Malcolm, thank God! I need you," she cries, holding her hand out to me.

And with those words and action, my heart soars anew.

"MAAALCOLM!!!!!!"

The breathing exercises Anita had Starr do early on during pre-labor go out the window twelve hours later. My Angel huffs and puffs like the wolf in *The Three Little Pigs*— although I would never tell her that now. She already snapped my head off for stroking her cheek.

We're in her private suite at the hospital.

Over the past couple of weeks, I had rooms next door to my suite converted into one for her and a delivery operation room. With twin births we don't want to risk not having access to all medical equipment and not having support available.

Plus, she can recover near me, and I can keep her and our babies close.

"Oh, my God!! How much more?!?!?!" My Angel bites out as she squeezes my hand so hard I fear my bones will break.

When I try to wiggle my fingers, she glares at me. Her sorrel brown eyes flash.

"You think that hurts, Malcolm Steele??? Well, let me—"

Her face contorts, and her body stiffens.

"Take a breath, Starr," Dr. Sánchez says, stifling a smile.

She peers between My Angel's legs to check the progress.

Fortunately, Dr. Sánchez is a woman. Otherwise, the caveman in me would gouge out the eyeballs of a male doctor.

"Okay, Starr, one more push. You can do it. The first baby is almost here," the doctor declares. "Push. Now!"

In what proves to be a Herculean effort, My Angel delivers Mini Malcolm I. Their piercing cries mingle in the tense air of the delivery room.

A new Steele enters our world.

My first child.

Tears fill my eyes as I gaze at mother and child—wait, daughter!

Our baby girl came first.

"Mr. Steele, you may cut her umbilical cord now."

Dr. Sánchez's words pull me from my ecstatic musings, and I glance at her. She holds out a pair of sterile scissors for me with a smile and a nod of encouragement.

Starr hums her approval.

Anita comes around to wheel me to the end of the table so I don't contaminate my hands on the wheelchair.

"Congratulations, Daddy Steele," she says with a grin.

My heart swells and my eyes well with tears. I blink them away as I take the scissors. Before I make the cut, my gaze goes to My Angel. So beautiful as she holds our baby girl to her breasts.

"Thank you, My Angel. I love you and our daughter," I say as she smiles.

"We love you, too, Daddy Steele," she replies.

The pediatrician lifts my baby girl from her mother. I wheel after the doctor as he carries my daughter off to the side in order to care for her. When he's done, he places her in my arms and announces she's a healthy 4.8 pounds.

I glance down at her red face. She's tiny, but my responsibility to her hits me like a breath-stealing blow from Borya. Her safekeeping ranks as my utmost priority, along with her soon-to-be-born brother and their mother. They are the fruit of my loins. I am their father.

"I HAVE HAD ENOUGH OF THIS SHIT! YOU DID THIS TO ME, MALCOLM STEELE! AAARGH!!!"

The seventeen minutes of familial bliss pass as the next stage of delivery has my son making his way into our world. Only our baby girl rests comfortably in a warm hospital crib nearby.

Anita dabs My Angel's face with a damp cloth and offers her more ice chips.

I sit like a lump praying the demon releases My Angel back to me before she slaps me like she did a moment ago.

I merely suggested she practice her deep cleansing breaths.

Her eyes rolled up in her head and her neck twisted to bring her face to face with me. I swear flames flew from her mouth as she cussed me out using language I didn't even know existed. And I speak four fluently.

Damn.

More contractions, more colorful words, more soul-stealing looks, more pushing, and our second twin makes his debut.

Mini Malcolm II—a healthy 5.2 pounds—joins his sister in a crib after I cut his umbilical cord, the pediatrician cared for him, and his mother breastfed him.

Mommy—My Angel once again—rests in her suite's bed as her gaze shifts between our babies and me. The nurse bathed her and rearranged the braid Anita had made. An expression of love and happiness makes My Angel glow like a celestial beauty.

I lift my mobile to take more photos of her. I already have a full album of Mini Malcolms throughout their birth and after. Their mother, not so many since she nearly broke my mobile when she swatted at it. She accused me of being too close and demanded to know who the hell wants photos of a sweaty woman in labor with two ginormous babies pushing through a quarter-size hole.

Now she smiles and beckons me to her side.

I wheel myself over and take her hand. I bring it to my lips for a kiss.

She cups my cheek.

"Thank you, Malcolm Steele. I love you; we love you," My Angel says softly.

A knock at the door interrupts us.

I roll my eyes, and she giggles.

"Come in," she calls out.

The door cracks, and Sun pops her head inside. Then my mother leans in. Both gaze at us questioningly.

"Come in, come in," I huff.

Then I chuckle when the whole gang bursts in the bedroom.

They gather around us, and Anita helps me to lift Mini Malcolms onto My Angel's breasts.

Sun coos softly as she strokes Mini Malcolm II's little leg. My mother rubs circles on the back of Mini Malcolm I.

"How are you, Starr, honey?" Sun asks. "You did it. But you need to rest. We promise not to stay too long."

My mother agrees, "No, we won't keep you, sweetheart. Only a quick peek. Then we'll leave you to rest."

"Congratulations, Little Sis, bro! Well done!" Roger says as he fist bumps with me and smiles at My Angel.

"Don't keep us in suspense any longer! What did you name Mini Malcolms, *chères*?" Leonie asks.

I peer at My Angel, place my hand over hers, and take a deep breath.

"Starr means the world to me. She completes me like no other. Now, with our daughter and our son, she gives me the moon and the sun to represent the other heavenly bodies in our universe. To keep with the Knight tradition of unique names, we'll name them after Greek gods: Selina for the moon and Elio for the sun. We present Selina Steele and Elio Steele," I respond.

My Angel cries out. This time not in pain of labor, but for joy.

"Oh, my love…" she says as tears slip down her flushed cheeks. "How perfect. Thank you."

My father grips my shoulder and smiles. "Well done, son, daughter! Powerful names for the next generation of Steeles. Today is a great day for our families!"

Peace holds his hand out to me.

I grip it firmly and look him square in the eye.

"Excellent, Malcolm. I'll be even more proud of you when you put your ring on my daughter's finger," he states.

"Absolutely," I respond confidently.

Then turn to My Angel and hold her hand again.

"Will you marry me, Starr Knight?" I ask.

"No."

Fuck me.

Not again.

STARR

"*I* still cannot get over how you told Malcolm no. Again! *Mon Dieu, chérie!*"

Leonie fans herself dramatically as she widens her feline amber eyes at me.

Yeah, everyone's mouths dropped to the floor when I said no to his second proposal.

I even surprised myself. I was thinking about it but hadn't expected to say it out loud. My mind was still loopy from having given birth to Selina and Elio.

However, I always believe everything happens for a reason, no matter how I may perceive the outcome.

And in this case it is for the best.

After everyone left, I explained my reasoning to Malcolm.

The sight of disbelief in Malcolm's eyes nearly changes my mind. His head snaps back, and his mouth gapes in shock. He blinks and shakes his head as if rousing himself from a dream—or a nightmare in this case.

"What?" He murmurs.

The Moms herd the group from the bedroom and out the main door of my suite. When the door clicks shut, I speak.

"Malcolm, I said no," I respond firmly.

He shudders and lets go of my hand.

I reach for his hand and hold it while I balance our babies on my breasts. A squeeze draws his stormy gray eyes back to mine.

"Why not?" He asks in the bedroom's silence.

"I, we—Selina, Elio, me, and you—need *you to get yourself together, get back to the man I know. The powerful Alpha Dom who takes control and lets nothing or anyone stop him in his pursuits," I start, then grip his hand tighter when he tries to pull away.*

"See. Just what you're doing now and have done since you awoke from the coma. You avoid instead of attack. Lash out in anger and cause pain instead of lash out in love and cause erotic pleasure," I say and press on when he opens his mouth.

"Yes, for the past couple of weeks, you've had a breakthrough. The trial ended not only favorably, but it ended Vicky Reynolds from your life giving you a new start, a reason to move forward. And I'm happy for you," I say and take a breath. "But you still have a way to go. And I don't mean with you walking or not. I love you as you are, period. You have to get back into your previous mindset of abundance and not lack."

I bring his hand to my lips and kiss his knuckles.

"The time apart from you taught me I had to put myself and our babies ahead of you if I were to be strong enough to care for them without you. And I intend to do just that. Our babies are my top priority, Malcolm. Your top priority right now needs to be you," I smile softly at him.

"I love you. So my no *doesn't mean no forever. Just not right now. You have work to do, Malcolm Steele. And I expect you to get at it if you want to be a part of my life again," I end.*

He takes a moment to absorb my words and to scan my face that I keep open and full of love.

"I'm so sorry I hurt you, My Angel. Never will I push you away again. You continue to love me and to believe in me. Know that I love you and believe in us enough to vow I will be the man you, Selina, and Elio need me to be," Malcolm says passionately.

"Thank you, my love," I say.

"But I have one ask: stay here for a week, then allow me to visit you and our babies at your mansion," he adds.

A Cheshire Cat smile spreads across my face as I nod.

"Words, Little One. I will have your words," Malcolm, my Alpha Dom, commands.

I bite my lower lip and peek at him through my eyelashes.

"Yes, Sir," I purr.

He smirks and kisses my hand.

"What did Sting say about freeing someone you love? Well, I had to give Malcolm a chance to find himself again before we can be one," I tell Leonie as I sip my iced lemon ginger tea.

We're in my garden catching up after she returned from Paris.

She, Roger, and their babies flew home to take care of some business. Anita, Norman, and their girls left Beverly Hills with them. Norman has some boxers who need him in Paris. So I thanked them for helping me and promised to visit as soon as I could travel with Mini Malcolms.

Their nickname stuck since every day they take on more of Malcolm's traits: ebony black hair, platinum gray eyes, and olives skin tone. Instead of waves like their father, their silky strands curl like mine. So even at only a month old, they resemble their Daddy.

And they couldn't satisfy him more.

Malcolm fusses over them whenever he's here. The gleam returns to his eyes each time he holds them against his chest. A permanent smile stretches across his face. It's as though they light him up from within.

My mother tells me it's the light from my star, Selina's moon, and Elio's sun that burns so brightly inside of Malcolm.

I just adore her views on life!

I made matching bracelets for Malcolm, our babies, and for me. Set in platinum to represent Malcolm with semi-precious stones for the rest of us. Moonstone promotes healing and balance and enhances one's intuition. Sunstone clears and cleanses all the chakras, restores joy, and nurtures the spirit. Starstone—the stone of ambition—resembles a starry night and promotes optimism and personal growth.

Malcolm was so impressed, he asked me to design a set of cuff links.

Since I'm on maternity leave from SLFW, I'm able to make them and other designs. My work with crystals always brings out *my* inner light.

"True. Roger says Malcolm asked his medical team to go back to review all of their research and his chart to come up with an alternative plan. He works hard at it every day. So, *your* plan is working!" Leonie exclaims.

I nod in agreement.

"Yes. Malcolm told me about his meeting with them. I'm so glad he's vested in himself truly now," I say. "He's not coming today because a new machine arrived he wants to exercise on. Already I see an increase in his muscle definition."

Leonie winks and says, "I'm sure you do, *chérie!*"

I throw my head back and laugh.

"Unfortunately, he's put the kibosh on any intimacy—Alpha Dom control, you know. But I'm sure you as a woman who's given birth to twins can appreciate me having no desire for a very well-endowed Steele man near me!" I laugh. "Although my hormones still rage…"

Leonie's laughter turns into snorts, and soon we're gasping for air.

"Okay, what's so funny?"

We turn around to find Haley strolling towards us.

She flew in with Leonie and Roger for some time with her West Coast niece and nephew. Since Lola had Sabrina and Stella two weeks ago, Morgan, Shelley, and Harris swapped cities with Haley.

I love how the Steele clan ensures all family members get time with each other.

Even to the point where Roger bought the mansion he and Leonie were renting, Morgan bought the one on the other side of mine, and Sebastian bought the one next to Morgan's. Not that any of the residences were for sale originally... They said they need a Steele West Coast compound.

Roger had his Residential Properties Division build a secured perimeter fence enclosing all four mansions. Each will maintain its entry gates with the addition of guard houses. Harris' Technology team arranged all security, even updating the system he installed in mine after Vicky's mess started. The Steeles are sticklers for security.

The Residential team is also working under Leonie's direction to redesign the homes to Shelley's, Lola's, and to her specifications. As a surprise for Malcolm, I asked Leonie to reconfigure my primary bedroom suite, along with other key areas to accommodate his accessibility needs. Thankfully, an elevator already existed. The projects should complete in a couple more months.

"Oh, *chérie*, just about the virility of your—"

"Ah, no!" Haley shouts as she plugs her ears with her fingers and sings aloud.

Our laughter kicks up again.

* * *

"Hi."

I glance up from breastfeeding Mini Malcolms in their nursery to see the man himself sitting in his wheelchair at the doorway.

He takes my breath away, and my hormones rage with need. A need only my Alpha Dom can satisfy. He hasn't shaved in a couple of days, so the five o'clock shadow skims along his sculpted cheekbones and chiseled jaw. Either the wind blew his hair, or he tousled it just the way it looks after my fingers tug at the strands while he eats me out.

Damn.

I shiver so hard my nipple pops from Elio's cherubic mouth and the milk dribbles from the turgid tip. My eyes jump back to Malcolm at the sound of a low growl.

My Alpha Dom licks his full lips and bites down on the lower one. His chest rises and falls beneath the black long-sleeved t-shirt, making his pecs stretch the fitted material. His biceps bulge and his bare forearms flex as he wheels himself further into the nursery.

Our eyes remain locked as he makes his way across the hardwood floor.

"Ms. Knight, the baths are ready for Selina and Elio—"

Nanny Patience must sense the sexual tension permeating the room. She stops mid-sentence and stares between Malcolm and me. She clears her throat.

"Since Mr. Steele has arrived, I'm sure he'd rather help you. Excuse me," she says hastily and leaves the nursery with a polite nod to Malcolm.

Without breaking our eye contact, Malcolm thanks her for her thoughtfulness.

When she's beyond earshot, his lips curl into a smirk and his eyes twinkle mischievously.

"Feeding without me, Naughty Girl? Well, it appears as

though my son has had his fill. Shall I relieve him?" My Alpha Dom asks.

My lips part, and my eyes widen at his innuendo.

He's never referred to drinking my breastmilk before.

I swallow and blink.

My Alpha Dom cocks his head to the side as he stops in front of me. His eyebrow lifts in question.

"I... Uh... Yes, Sir," I respond breathlessly.

A full smirk spreads across his handsome face. He takes Elio from my arms and puts him over his shoulder with the cloth. He burps his son with ease.

"The little bugger was full," he quips.

My nostrils flare on a deep inhalation. Calm down, Starr. I exhale and nod.

"Yes, and Selina finished. Would you care to burp her, too?" I ask in a level voice.

"Of course. I *am* here for Daddy Duty," he smirks.

I want to growl at his teasing. Instead, I take Elio, and Malcolm lifts his daughter to his shoulder.

I rise from the glider, purposefully leaning my bare breasts in Malcolm's face.

Two can play this game.

Now he gulps and warm air fans across my sensitive buds.

Damn.

"I'll start on Elio's bath. You can join us," I say over my shoulder.

I catch Malcolm's eyes on my ass before he lifts his heated gaze to my face. Now I'm glad I wore the zipper-front terrycloth romper my butt cheeks peek out from underneath.

I adjust my Lola's Coterie nursing bra and sway my hips slightly as I walk to the en suite bathroom.

He groans.
I giggle to myself. Gotcha, Malcolm Steele!
Who's in control now, Alpha Dom?
The sub, that's who!

MALCOLM

"*Aaaahhhh… Mm mmm… Oh fuck!!!*"

Wait, what the fuck?!?!?!

A red veil descends before my eyes as I envision another man fucking My Angel. Who does she have in her bed?! When did she start seeing someone else??? How can she do this to me, to us trying to rebuild our relationship?! And with my babies under the same roof!!!

Thankful for the new aerodynamic wheelchair that allows me to move quickly, I race down the hallway towards the partially open double doors to her primary bedroom suite. I make haste as I maneuver around the sitting room, spurred on by the sounds of her pleasure reaching a crescendo.

Fuck. Me.

When I reach her partially open bedroom door, I pause.

Maybe I should back off. Starr deserves a real man in her life. Sure I've proven I can care for our babies—change diapers; give baths; burp them. But I haven't taken care of Starr. I haven't been able to give her the erotic pain she craves as my sub and the carnal bliss as my woman.

Obviously *he* can.

Crestfallen, I change direction.

"Oh, God… MALCOLM!!! Malcolm… Ahhh, Malcolm… Malcolm…"

My head snaps up.

Me?

Starr calls my name in ecstasy?

"Mmmmmm…. Malcolm…"

Her last moan confirms My Angel is still mine all mine!!!

I do a silent whoop as I fist pump the air with both hands.

Thank fuck!

I spin around and nudge the door open.

In the dimly lit room, my vision tunnels on My Angel lying sated atop rumpled linens alone in her bed. Eyes closed, her head thrown back against the pillows as her bare breasts heave from the exertion. One hand kneads a heavy breast while the other hand rests between her toned thighs pressed together, trapping her fingers in her pussy. A soft whimper escapes her slack mouth.

The musky scents of her sex and of her coconut and frangipani perfume waft through the air to tease my nostrils.

Tantalizing!

Quietly, I roll to the side of her bed. I lean forward and skim my fingertips from her inner calf to her knee.

My Angel gasps and jumps to a crouch.

"Tsk… Tsk… Tsk, Naughty Girl," I chide her.

"M—M—Malcolm?" She asks shocked.

I cock my head and ask, "Who else do you expect in your bedroom stroking your leg, Naughty Girl?"

She swallows and sits with her legs tucked beneath her ass.

"Uh, no one else, Sir," she responds with wide eyes.

"I thought not. But your naughty behavior needs addressing," I say.

She blinks, then opens and shuts her mouth.

I crook my finger at her.

Her heavy tits sway as she crawls towards me, ass high, head low. She bites her full lower lip when she stops before me. My well-trained sub sits on her haunches with her eyes downcast, back straight, and palms face up on her spread thighs.

Divine.

If possible, the intensity level of my gaze would scorch her soft skin already flushed with her arousal. I take in her beauty from her tousled curls—now reaching her middle back—to her heart-shaped face, down to her mouthwatering tits, and to her just-as-appetizing pussy; her engorged clit visible between the plump, soaked folds.

Fuck. Me.

I lick my lips and hold my hands out to her.

Without hesitation, she places her dainty ones into my sizable hands.

When I tug her towards me, she rises to her knees and makes her way closer to the edge.

"Lie down, knees bent with your feet on the bed," I command huskily.

Fully spread before me, I reacquaint myself with My Angel's most intimate places. Several minutes pass as I test her ability to remain in position despite her need for release. And release she needs based upon the puddle forming below her ass cheeks as her pussy weeps for my erotic touch.

Unable to resist, I lean forward and bury my nose between her folds. The tip brushes her sensitive bundle of nerves.

She whimpers but holds still.

I inhale deeply, then slowly blow my warm breath over her pussy and puckered hole. As both holes clench with want, My Angel mewls and her hips shift.

A predatory smile spreads across my face.

WHAP. WHAP. WHAP.

She yowls and jerks away as my thick, calloused fingers spank her swollen pussy, causing more fire to erupt across her sensitive flesh.

"Ah, ah, ah, Naughty Girl. Take your punishment for pleasuring yourself without my permission," I command in my stern Alpha Dom voice.

She whimpers but settles back in to position.

I soothe the ache with gentle laps of my tongue.

Her whimpers morph into moans. Then her hips lift. Again.

A sharp pinch to her clit, and my Naughty Girl squeals.

My tongue wraps around the tiny bud, engorged from her arousal and sucks. Hard.

"Oooooh, Sir... Please let me cum, Sir!" My Naughty Girl cries out.

I deny her with a grunt as I continue to feast on her succulent pussy. She's as sweet as ambrosia. How I've missed her essence on my taste buds.

Eager for more, I wrap my arms around the backs of her thighs and lift them over my shoulders, then sit up straight. Only her head, upper back, and arms remain on the bed in an erotic Half Wheel Pose.

My super flexible yogi. Perfect.

I alternate my ministrations between erotic pain and pleasure to heighten my sub's desire. A steady stream of moans and sighs sings in my ears. Our carnal energy flows around us.

So enthralled by her, I nearly miss the signs of My Angel on the brink of coming apart for me. Only when her inner thighs squeeze the sides of my head do I return to the bedroom. The quivering of her pussy walls; hands fisting the sheets; shallow pants from her parted lips.

My Angel needs to cum.

With a deep thrust of my tongue and with the tip of my finger stroking her G-spot, I give her permission.

"Cum for me, Little One. Cum in my mouth. Now!" I command, as my lips brush her wet skin.

Her hands rip the silk sheets as she presses her pussy further onto my face. The muscles of her taut belly tighten as a keen rises from deep within her to erupt in a high-pitched wail. It goes on unstoppable as I coax more of her sweet essence down my throat.

While her climax abates, I lap at her folds lazily and suckle her clit softly. I hum my approval.

"Good Girl," I purr.

"Mmmmmm…. Malcolm…" she mumbles from the bliss of subspace.

Yeah. You know that's right!

After I gloat for bringing My Angel over the edge, I don't want to break our connection. I grasp her ass and lower her onto my lap.

Again I'm thankful for the new wheelchair. Sans arms, My Angel settles her legs on both sides of my hips unhampered. One hand glides up her sweat-damp back to grip the back of her neck while the other holds her hip, pinning her against my chest. I bury my face in her neck as my breathing slows.

"Oh, Malcolm!" She exclaims and leans back to stare at me.

I frown.

"Malcolm, baby, you're erect," she says in wonder.

What???

She grins at me and adds, "Your dick, it's hard."

Stunned, I loosen my grip, and she slides to her knees in front of me. Her hands reach for the drawstring of my sweatpants.

"Oh, Malcolm! This is marvelous, baby!" She exclaims as she pulls the bow like a present she can't wait to unwrap on Christmas morning. Her eyes dance in delight at my ten inches tenting my sweats.

Just as she reaches inside, I come to my senses.

"No!" I snap as I yank her hands away and roll backwards.

My Angel's face drops, and her hands drop to her lap.

The fierce expression on my face makes her eyes lower.

I didn't even feel my cock grow. Not. One. Inch.

Fuck. Me.

I'm torn between horror and excitement as I stare at the massive bulge. My cock has a mind of its own and obviously its own nervous system. My legs remain numb…

"I'm so sorry, Malcolm. I didn't mean to—"

A cry over the high-tech baby monitor Harris designed for the Steele Grandchildren interrupts My Angel.

Thank fuck for the small things in life!

I give a noncommittal grunt and pivot for the door.

"I'll see to Selina and Elio. I'd like to spend Father's Day morning with them as I planned," I say as I roll away.

A gasp behind me makes me pause.

"Oh, Malcolm! Happy Father's Day, my love!!!" My Angel says.

Arms wrap around my neck from behind before she swings around to land in my lap, planting kisses on my face.

I still can't feel my dick poking her round ass. But I can't deny her and kiss her back with fervor.

"I'm sorry I snapped at you, My Angel. I just don't feel—"

She places her fingertips against my mouth and shakes her head. Glossy curls bounce around her gorgeous face as she smiles.

"No need to apologize. Especially for that monster! I'm just glad he wants to play. When you're ready, that is, Sir," she says with a wink as she licks her lips.

Hot damn! That's my girl!

"Welcome to the Club of Fatherhood, Malcolm!"

"Yeah, bro! You are official!"

"Hear, hear!"

"Doubly, Malcolm!"

"*Félicitations!*"

I chuckle as my father, Baz, Roger, Peace, and Leonie's father Guy Beaulieu—the Parisian multibillionaire merchant—raise their Baccarat crystal snifters of Jackson Special Blend Scotch in a toast. I salute them with mine held high.

"Thank you, gentlemen! It pleases me beyond words to join your illustrious club!" I respond before I knock back a healthy swig.

My Angel and Leonie turned the garden into a men's club while Lola and Haley did the same on the deck of my parents' beachfront mansion at Steele Southampton Village.

Since Mini Malcolms can't fly yet—even on our private jet—we along with Roger and Leonie opted to stay in Beverly Hills at Steele West Coast. The rest of the clan escaped balmy New York City for the cooler Hamptons shore. They'll stay through Labor Day after The STEELE Foundation Annual Fundraiser. My Angel and I will join them for the event, since Selina and Elio will be four months old.

"Well, just don't get any bright ideas to add me to your club any time soon. No, thank you!" Harris quips, rolling his dove gray eyes.

"Ha! Your time is a coming, bro. Just you wait and see. That special someone will sneak up on you when you least expect her," Baz says from experience.

Roger and I nod in agreement.

My eyes drift to My Angel as she and Leonie sit on blankets surrounded by five of the eight Steele Grandchildren. The grandmothers—Sun and Leonie's mother Josy, the Tunisian beauty she resembles—sit beside them, playing with the little ones.

The sight infuses my soul with love.

I'm a lucky man.

A firm grip on my shoulder brings my attention back to the men around me and those on the giant screen. I glance up to meet Peace's gaze. Even without me sitting in the wheelchair, he has an inch on my six feet, four inches.

He smiles.

"I am proud of you, Malcolm. You've stepped up to your responsibilities admirably. I understand your new healing program shows improvement," he says.

For a minute, I think he's referring to my earlier erection since My Angel shares details of her life with her parents unashamedly. But then I know she wouldn't have told her father that not so little tidbit.

I return his smile and say, "Yes, the new regimen pleases me, and the results are impressive. As I said, I intend to take care of my family. They give me the strength to move forward."

"Excellent," Peace says with a nod.

After everyone eats and sits around relaxing, I go inside and make a call to Baz. He answers on the first ring.

"Hey, bro. What's up? Everything okay?" He asks, concern laces his voice.

"Yeah, thanks," I start. "But I have an ask of you."

"Whatever you need, you know I got your back, Malcolm," he responds without hesitation.

"Baz, if anything should ever happen to Starr or to me, promise you will take care of my children as your own," I ask my eldest sibling.

Silence descends on the call.

Then I hear Baz say something to Lola before shuffling comes over the line. A door slides open and closed.

"What's going on, Malcolm? Did the doctors tell you something you haven't shared with us?" He asks gravely.

I slap my forehead.

Damn! He must think I'm not much longer of this world. Hell, no! I'm here to stay with My Angel and my babies—with more to come if I get a say in the matter.

"No, bro! I'm perfectly fine. Trust me," I chuckle as I think about my first erection since before the accident. "Father's Day has me thinking. I want to be certain Selina and Elio are well taken care of. I know everyone would pitch in—including their maternal grandparents. But I know how you've always been our second dad. I may have given you shit as a teenager. But I've come to value you more than you could ever know, Sebastian."

My voice hitches, and I pause to collect myself.

Baz clears his throat, also caught up in our brotherly moment.

"Absolutely. And I ask the same of you for our little ones. We may have had our differences as kids, but you're my closest friend, Malcolm," he says. "I love you, bro."

And there you have it: Sebastian Steele, former Alpha Dom billionaire playboy turned husband, father, and softie!

"I love you, bro," I respond.

We're in the same boat. And neither of us would ever choose another. No matter how tricked out it may be. My Angel and Lola have us on lock.

MALCOLM

"*J*ust because you're in a *rolly chair,* you think I am going easy on you, Steele? *Net!* Don't be a *kiska!* Meow. Meow. Hands up. Now!"

As I combat a barrage of lethal punches and kicks from Borya, I second-guess my decision to switch from the doctor-appointed personal trainer to the former MMA world champion. He's merciless.

If I were in my full capacity, I could hold my own and sometimes overtake him. But now, not so much. However, I know it's the best move to get me back to peak performance.

After six months of being awake from my coma—nine in total since the accident—I'm more than ready for the next level. And I want it more than ever.

The ability to defend myself and my family—no matter my circumstances—runs high. Sure, we have a security detail, but I need to know I can step up. Well, *roll up...*

"Fuck you, Alexeyev! Is that the best you have or does retirement have you soft, *prisoska?*" I taunt the *sucker* as I block a vicious roundhouse kick to my head.

I follow the block with a punch to his inner thigh. Albeit I aimed for his balls, but he dodged the blow.

"Aha! So you want to play dirty, Steele? Bring it, *kiska*!" Borya growls.

I jerk my chin and smirk as I punch my fists together. Who's the *pussy* now?!

"Let's do this, *kiska*!" I sneer.

Thanks to my previous MMA training and my wonder chair, I successfully maneuver around the mat. Quick turns to one wheel allow me to pivot easily then use my other arm to fight. I even catch him with unexpected headbutts.

The first one causes the giant Russian to throw his head back and roar with laughter—or at least what he considers laughter, others barks.

"Well done, Steele! Sneaky fucker!" He guffaws.

Then comes at me like a freight train going downhill with no brakes.

Damn!

An hour later I'm sufficiently sore from the intense workout but amped. This is what I need to reach the next level. The strength training program designed by the medical PT helped me to regain my upper body muscles and to keep my lower half from atrophy. Borya makes me use my mind, needing to think fast to avoid being knocked the fuck out and the power of my muscles to thwart him. His sessions make for the perfect combination.

"What's your plan for the rest of the day? A catnap?" Borya smirks as we head to the steam room.

"Ha, ha, ha. Actually, no. I'm surprising My Angel with a Mother's Day brunch since Mini Malcolms arrived a few days after the traditional date. As hard as she worked to carry my babies, deliver them, then to care for them, she deserves Mother's Day every damn day," I respond.

"*My Angel* this. *My Angel* that. You are pussy whipped,

Steele," he smirks. "But Starr is an excellent woman. Better than you deserve. *She* deserves it all. Just do not fuck up again…"

Borya narrows his eyes at me and smashes his massive fists together.

I shake my head and grin like the Cheshire Cat.

"Nah, bro. That wimpy shit is done," I say as I pull my t-shirt over my head.

"Hey, don't look at me!" Borya says, aghast.

I throw my t-shirt at him and roll my eyes.

"I'm not stripping for you, dumbass! My new tat," I tell him as I point to my chest.

Right above my heart I added a tattoo of a star with My Angel written inside and a moon with Selina and a sun with Elio orbiting around it. I had the best tattoo artist in LA come to the hospital a few days ago. He created the design based on my vision: My Angel and our babies as my universe. I left space for more baby names, at least two…

"*Velikolepnyy!* Now you'd have to scour your skin to remove Starr from your life. And it'll hurt *you* like fuck that time!" Borya guffaws.

I join in and agree not only is my tattoo *magnificent*, so is my little family.

"Oh, Malcolm! What a wonderful surprise! Thank you, my love!"

My Angel smothers me in kisses when she walks into the solarium of her mansion to find it decorated for Mother's Day and me sitting with Mini Malcolms in their slings across my chest.

I enlisted the help of my mother, our family's party planner and drill sergeant—as Lola and Leonie learned during the planning of their weddings. Sun proved her high-powered attorney skills when she negotiated the contracts with the vendors. She even had Lucien nervous when he offered to provide the food and the dessert.

Now I cup My Angel's cheek, smiling at her delight.

So worth it!

"No, thank you for giving me the greatest gifts—our babies, Selina and Elio. I love you, Hot Mama," I respond with a grin.

My Angel giggles at me teasing her with the nickname Lola coined for Leonie when she was pregnant with Rodolphe and Gaspard. Now all three women are a part of the club.

My brothers and I are lucky AF.

"Okay, Sexy Daddy!" My Angel purrs as she nips my earlobe and tugs on it.

Fuck. Me.

Now she's rocked me with the Daddy kink along with adult lactation. If I could feel my cock, it would be hard as steel.

I shift Mini Malcolms to peek at my crotch. Yup, the anaconda wakes.

My Angel notices and licks her plump lips.

I smirk at her, then gesture to the table.

"Come, Naughty Girl. Let us eat," I command.

"Oh, yes, Sir. I'm famished, absolutely..." she purrs as her gaze darts to my lap.

Yeah. Fuck. Me.

I've created a sex-starved sub wrapped in a Hot Mama.

And I wouldn't have her any other way.

"Oooh! Are these dishes from Lucien's latest restaurant? I remember he mentioned a lobster frittata with golden Sevruga caviar. My mouth watered as he described it to me. Tell me this is it!" My Angel exclaims, clapping her hands.

Okay.

So when the hell did Lucien speak to my woman? And why did he make her mouth water?! My caveman demands an answer and a jab at *The Sexy Chef*.

My Angel giggles.

"What's so funny?" I snarl.

My question has her cackling and snorting as she fans her flushed face. Her dimples deepen as tears fill her eyes when I grunt incoherent words of irritation with my close friend. When I spear a slab of bacon with my fork and it shoots off the platter to the floor, My Angel loses her shit completely.

Try as I might to maintain a stoic expression, the frown on my face flips as chuckles burst from between my pursed lips.

"You! You're so funny, Malcolm!" She titters with glee. "He's *your* friend, not *my* lover."

I growl.

Then reach across the table to grip the back of her neck, then pull her to me. My mouth captures hers in a display of dominant possession. Her gasp gives me full access to plunder her mouth with my demanding tongue.

My Angel grabs the table's edge for balance and gives in to me. Mewls meet my growls. A nip to her bottom lip makes her cry out. A lick, and she sighs.

When I've proven my point, I release my hold on her neck, and she collapses to her chair, staring at me with hooded eyes.

"Mine!" I rumble.

She shivers and responds, "Yes, Sir. Only you."

With a satisfied smirk, I spear another piece of bacon and pop it into my mouth.

My Naughty Girl watches me chew while her little pink tongue pokes out to taste her lower lip swollen from my passionate kiss. Her sorrel brown eyes glow. The front of her silk maxi dress can't hide the peaks of her nipples. She is so aroused.

Good.

The denial will be even sweeter.

"Eat up. I have plans for you," I tell her.

Her eyes widen with carnal want.

"Yes, Sir!" she says eagerly as she picks up her fork and dives in to Lucien's lobster frittata.

The moan that slips from her lips as she takes a healthy bite gets cut short when I raise my eyebrow and cock my head at her. She swallows thickly and attempts to assuage me with a tiny smile.

I chuckle darkly. Oh, my Naughty Girl.

"I'M SORRY! Please, Sir! Forgive me!"

My poor Naughty Girl begs after multiple orgasms being denied. Her head hangs to her heaving chest pitifully.

Sweat drips from her forehead to between her luscious tits as she stands naked, blindfolded, and bound spread eagle to the posts at the foot of her bed. Rosy hued stripes tint the chestnut-colored skin of her heavy tits and her flat belly from the lashes of my suede flogger. Her pussy lips mimic the shade from the erotic caresses. Even her clit swelled as the tresses curled around the sensitive bud.

"Safeword?" I ask huskily.

I will push My Angel's limits beyond yellow. But I will never force her past red. Years as an Alpha Dom—and those I spent as a sub to learn both ends of the spectrum—provide me the experience to sense my sub's breaking point.

And My Angel is not there.

"No, Sir!" She responds.

Her head jerks up, as though horrified at the thought.

I smirk. Yeah, she wants to swing along the pendulum of erotic pain and pleasure some more.

I reach past her hip to pluck the Wartenberg wheel from the bed. Time for some sensory play.

A perk of being in the hospital with a spinal issue is access to the medical device used to test nerve reactions as it rolls systematically across the skin. The wheel has sharp pins evenly spaced and rotates with each stroke. One can't miss the sensation it causes under normal circumstances. It's heightened more on rosy stripes…

"ARGH!" My Angel yowls. "FUCK!!!"

"How pretty you look with my marks painting the canvas of your soft skin, Little One," I croon as I lean forward to lap at a welt on the underside of her tit re-sensitized from the Wartenberg wheel.

She hisses, then moans lustily when my mouth engulfs her tit, areole, and nipple at once.

I hum as her delicious milk drips down my throat.

The vibrations make her mewl.

Her nipple pops from my mouth, and her milk dribbles down my chin when she yanks back from the unexpected nip of the pins across her lower belly. She cries out.

Dutifully, I trail open-mouthed kisses from her tit, then down her belly to provide relief from the pain. I alternate the sensations until My Angel's legs quiver with her need for release.

I toss the toys to the floor and sit back in my wheelchair to survey her perfection.

"Cum for me, Little One," I murmur.

Instantly, she arches her back as she grips the white silks binding her wrists and throws her head back to let loose a wail as her climax overtakes her body. She convulses as it goes on and on, prolonged by the earlier denial.

Spent, she sags against her restraints.

I roll forward and untie her ankles, then pull the extra material hanging from her wrists to free the knots. I catch her as she collapses and hold her on my lap, pressed to my chest.

She curls into me and buries her face in my neck as I murmur words of love and stroke her back to soothe her. Lost in subspace, she sighs contentedly.

While she still flies, I roll to the side of the bed and carefully lay her on her side in a fetal position. Then I head to the bathroom for soft cloths dampened with water to cool her heated flesh and a tube of aloe vera gel to heal my marks.

No permanent damage to My Angel's flawless skin. My marks may fade by morning, but they're indelibly written on her psyche to remind her she's mine all mine.

"Hi, babe. How do you feel?"

I ask as she awakens from her sex-induced slumber.

My Angel does a feline stretch, then smiles up at me.

"Wonderful, Sir. Thank you," she purrs as she cuddles against my side as I rest against pillows on the headboard.

While she slept, I used the new overhead trapeze she had installed to help me in and out of the bed. The triangle bar hangs from the hook of a metal base attached to the floor behind the headboard. My Angel learned it has more than a medical purpose…

I give her a glass of cool water, and she gulps it gratefully. Then she finishes a second one, but declines a third with a shake of her head. Curls bounce around her face and shoulders.

I nuzzle the top of her head and kiss their silkiness. The citrus scent of her shampoo fills my senses.

"No more water; I'm about to pop now," she laughs as she rises from the bed.

I watch, entranced by the sway of her grip-worthy hips as she sashays to the bathroom.

"Malcolm!" She shouts.

What the fuck?!

I nearly fall out of the bed in my haste to reach her.

Seconds later, she rushes through the bathroom door. Her hands clasped between her tits.

"Malcolm! What is this?" She asks as she raises her hands to me.

Oh, that.

A smile broader than the Cheshire Cat spreads across my face.

"Your push present, of course," I respond triumphantly.

Her mouth drops open.

I crook my finger at her.

My Angel hurries to the bed and knees her way to me.

I kiss her lips until she's panting. Then I murmur against her them.

"The pink diamond pendant represents Selina, the blue for Elio. Their tear-drop shape represents the tears of joy you gave to me for having my babies. The diamond and platinum necklace represent the brightness of your star that lights my way, and the silver-white metal marks the three of you as Steeles. Mine."

I sit back and point to my chest, now bare.

My Angel studies my new tattoo, then brings her tear-filled eyes to mine.

"Oh, Malcolm. Thank you, my love," she whispers, over-whelmed.

"Oh, Lola! This is the best idea ever! I miss our Girls' Getaways. And to have this one on Laucala Island where you and I met at my first international fitness retreat. Can you believe it's been four and a half years?! We've come so far. All of us."

I'm so excited about the surprise trip Lola planned. We're aboard a STEELE Gulfstream G700 heading from LAX to the luxury private island.

The ultra-plush jet easily accommodates us plus Slade, Sabrina, Stella, Leonie, Rodolphe, Gaspard, Daphne, Haley, Anita, her girls, Billie, Blair, our nannies, and the flight crew. The spacious, custom-built interior boasts the tallest, widest, and longest cabin of all private jets. Its size suits our needs and allows us to fly internationally without having to stop for fuel. At seventy-five-million-dollars it better be the best aircraft ever made!

"Yeah, well, some of us didn't get married and pop out babies!" Blair laughs.

Haley slaps a high five with Blair and says, "Exactly! Although I wouldn't mind being married..."

We gape at her since she rarely speaks about her relationship—at least we believe there's one—with Lachlan. I've tried to get tidbits out of her, but she remains mum. More than likely, Haley fears the wrath of her big brothers and doesn't want to risk Lola, Leonie, and me slipping up accidentally.

Hell, I don't blame her with those cavemen.

"No! I will not divulge a word," Haley declares, then turns to Slade. "Not even to you, Sweet Babboo. Your daddy is the absolute worse of the whole bunch. I feel right sorry for Sabrina and Stella."

We laugh and agree. Sebastian still can't get over his best friend with his baby sister.

"Anytime you care to share, let me know. I won't spill the beans!" Billie drawls in her Southern accent. "I promise those Steele men won't get a peep out of me, honey!"

Haley blows her a kiss as thanks.

The ten hours fly by as we catch up and make plans for our adventure in paradise. Anita and I will do yoga, meditation, and Pilates sessions. Lola suggests a hike, since she enjoyed the ones we did during the retreat. Billie claimed mixologist and rightfully so as she makes the best cocktails. Haley offers to put suntan oil on everyone's backs since she plans to stay on the beach all day!

As soon as my sandaled feet hit the tarmac, I close my eyes and inhale the tropical scent of frangipani flowers—the source of my signature perfume. Warm rays of the sun heat my skin exposed in my halter-top maxi dress. The sense of peace that fills me invigorates my soul. It's so good to be back on an island that means so much to me.

"Come on, slowpoke! Let's get going!" Lola urges as she waves at me from beside one of the Mercedes-Benz G-Wagens.

Nanny Patience smiles at me as we hurry to another

SUV. We strap Selina and Elio into the backseat and climb in. The driver greets us after he finishes with our luggage.

We head from the airport in a caravan.

I shoot a text to Malcolm.

Hi, my love. We landed and are riding to the villa. Miss you already... xoxo

Immediately three dots appear as he writes his response.

Hi, My Angel. I'm glad you're safe. I miss you more. XOXOXO

I grin as I stare out of the window at the lush beauty of the island.

The sparkling, cyan-colored South Pacific Ocean reaches the horizon. The hues range from the darkest to the lightest blues and greens so varied in depth captivate me. Nearby verdant islands with rings of coral rise from the ocean.

Gulls and terns hover over the waves while shadows of fish schools appear below the crystal-clear surface. The birds swoop in and out of the water to catch their meals.

Soon the resort emerges, and the SUVs diverge to different paths leading to our villas. I opted to stay in the cliffside one Malcolm and I had when we were here over two years ago. It's spectacular, with breathtaking panoramic views of the ocean and the beaches below.

After the butler, chef, and maid greet us as we step from the SUV, I head inside. My priority to situate Selina and Elio. They were so easy for the entire flight: eating once and sleeping. Now they lie own their tummies surrounded by pillows on the bed watching while Nanny Patience and I put away their things. They laugh at the colorful toys I dangle in front of them. And I can't help but to join in their musical sounds.

My mobile rings with a call from Haley.

"Hey, almost ready? Remember to wear your new white

string bikini and to put Mini Malcolms in their white rompers and matching sun hats. I'll swing by to pick you up in ten minutes," she says before ending the call.

I giggle to myself.

Haley cannot wait to get to the beach.

As promised, she waits for us in an SUV moments later. She helps me to buckle the babies into their car seats, then we're off.

"I love your sarong. The white on white floral patterns remind me of frangipani," I tell Haley.

"Thanks! I bought it in Bali when Lachlan and—"

She stops abruptly and peers at me.

I grin at her unintended revelation.

"You were saying?" I tease.

Haley waves her hand and ruffles Elio's ebony curls.

"And don't you look handsome, sweetheart," she coos. "Selina, darling, you are gorgeous!"

I let her slipup go and watch the foliage give way to the white-sand beach and the vibrant Pacific Ocean beyond.

"Where's everyone else?" I ask as we carry Mini Malcolms across the powdery sand. "And what's that tarp for?"

"Oh, darn!" Haley exclaims loudly. "I forgot my bag in the SUV. Starr, can you get it for me? Here, I'll hold Elio and your bag for you."

"Oookay…" I reply and hand him and my bag to her before I pivot on my heel.

"My Angel."

I stop, surprised to hear Malcolm's voice behind me. I miss him so much that I'm hearing him?

"Babe."

I whirl around to find the man himself sitting in his wheelchair, where only moments before Haley stood. My wide eyes scan the beach. She's no longer in sight. Only the tarp between two poles flutters with the breeze.

"Malcolm? What are you doing here?" I ask as I close the distance between us.

"You said you missed me," he chuckles and holds out his arms. "Here I am."

I giggle and wrap my arms around his neck as I slip on to his lap.

"It's a Girls' Getaway, you know," I tell him teasingly. "And here you are."

"And here I am, My Angel," he replies as he nuzzles my neck with his nose. "I promised I'd bring you back here before we left the last time. And I keep my promises."

I grin and kiss his full lips.

"Thank you, my love," I murmur.

"You know they say three times the charm, right?" He asks, then continues when I nod. "Well… This island represents firsts for us. It's where you held your international retreat and where we reignited our love. But I hope it will bring me luck for our third try at this… Marry me, Starr Knight."

Tears of joy fill my eyes, and I nod vigorously.

"Words, Little One. I will have your words," Malcolm commands.

"Yes, Sir!" I exclaim before I cover his mouth with mine. "A thousand times, YES!!!"

Malcolm smirks and pats my ass for me to rise.

I stand before him and tilt my head in question when he grips my hips and moves me backwards.

Then he stands from the wheelchair, strides to me, and kneels.

I cry out in disbelief, "Malcolm! You can walk!"

"I'd walk a thousand miles for you, My Angel," he grins.

Malcolm removes a little navy blue velvet box out of his

white swim trunks pocket then opens it. A ginormous, flawless pear-cut diamond set in platinum glints in the sunlight.

My mouth drops open as he reaches for my left hand and places the stunning ring on my finger.

"It is a family heirloom given by one of my paternal great-grandfathers to the love of his life. They remained married for over sixty years. I chose it from the family's collection for that very reason. I want a long, happy life with you, My Angel," he explains its provenance reverently.

Tears stream down my face, overwhelmed by such love. It matches the diamonds of my push present—more happy tears.

He stands and wipes my face, even as his eyes glisten with unshed tears.

Suddenly the air fills with the opening chords for "By Your Side" followed by the soulful voice of Sade Adu.

I glance up to find the tarp gone to reveal the singer and her eponymous band with our family and our friends smiling at us dressed in all white beachwear.

Malcolm recreated his Bali proposal setting with a few additions.

The white gauzy canopy with its four posts covered in white hibiscus, frangipani, and orchards floats above the sand like a fragrant cloud where an officiant stands. Sebastian and Anton, with Lola and Adrienne holding Selina and Elio, flank the officiant.

Everyone else—my parents, the Steeles, the Jacksons, the Beaulieus, the Greens, Billie, Patrick, Blair, Luc, and Borya —stands beside canopy-covered round tables dressed in white linens and extravagant floral centerpieces. Chairs have more gauzy material drapes over them, with a bow in the back and a floral bouquet at its center. An aisle forms between them, lined with more flowers.

The tropical scent of the floral arrangements mingles

with the aromas from the tantalizing dishes on white-linen-covered banquet tables manned by servers. Magnums of Krug Clos d'Ambonnay Champagne chill in silver tubs nestled in the sand.

Bamboo torches around the perimeter and white tapers on the tables will provide lighting once the sun sets on the horizon. A bonfire to the side and more bamboo torches situated nearby, ready to be lit.

Further down the beach sits a white tent covered in gauzy material with white hibiscus, frangipani, and orchards entwined.

"For us later. I want to make love to my beautiful bride on the beach all. Night. Long."

Malcolm's husky whisper rouses me.

I turn to face him, surprised again.

"We're getting married now?" I ask.

"Absolutely! I will not waste another day without you as Mrs. Malcolm Steele," he growls in my ear, then nips the lobe.

I yelp just as my father touches my elbow.

"Starr, time to walk down the aisle, sweetheart," he says with a loving smile.

I glance around at Malcolm. But he's already striding to the ceremony canopy. Transfixed by the sight of his easy gait, my father has to nudge me to move. I take the beautiful bouquet of frangipani and Blue Sapphire orchids he hands to me and smile back at him.

We proceed down the aisle to the love of my life and our babies. Before he lets me go, my father pins Malcolm with an intense stare, then states he and my mother give this woman to be married to this man. He whispers, I love you, as he embraces me. I return the words with an extra squeeze to reassure him.

Lola takes my bouquet with a wink before I place my hands in Malcolm's outstretched palms.

We listen to the officiant, then recite our vows of everlasting love. Malcolm tears up, as do I when we each say I do.

But I squeal when Sebastian presses the clasp on a flat, blue velvet jewelry case. I thought my engagement ring was magnificent, but the enormous diamonds of the custom hand harness and an eternity band nearly blind me!

It's like Lola and Leonie's wedding jewelry.

The chain of diamonds connects to the eternity band on my middle finger by three pear-cut diamonds in a row that rest atop my hand attached to a diamond triple bracelet. My engagement ring sits on my ring finger. The harness is removable. So I can wear my band and ring together.

Malcolm slips the entire piece on me, and I gasp. My eyes fly to his, and he cocks his head as he raises his eyebrow.

"Three times the charm, remember? Now, you're marked as mine for all to see," he says with a smirk.

I lift my hand to admire the harness. Sparks fly from the flawless diamonds, making prisms on the white gauze covering the canopy.

I smirk and ask, "Where is your wedding band so I can claim you, Malcolm Steele?"

The gathering laughs, and he joins in.

Smiling, Sebastian hands a classic platinum band to me. I return his smile, then place the ring on Malcolm's finger. I hold his gaze and add, "*You're* my charm, my love."

The officiant pronounces us husband and wife.

Malcolm whoops and lifts me from the sand, then dips me into a deep arc. He captures my mouth in a mind-blowing kiss. When he brings me back on my feet, I peer at him dazedly while he grins.

"Mine all Mine, Mrs. Malcolm Steele!" He says triumphantly. "And I will cherish you forever more, My Angel."

My heart bursts with joy. Ecstatic to complete our bond after almost four years of knowing each other and over three as a couple.

Malcolm leans down to whisper in my ear, "But your neck is bare... We will take care of that tonight when I put your collar back on, Little One."

A shiver races down my spine, and I bite my lower lip in anticipation of my Alpha Dom-turned-boyfriend now husband collars me his sub-turned-girlfriend now wife.

We lift Selina and Elio into our arms and make our way down the aisle as a family. A Photographer and a videographer I didn't notice before snaps shots and films. They direct us to another area for photos after Malcolm and I sign the marriage documents. The bridal party and our parents join us, along with the rest of the Steele clan.

"Congratulations, sweetheart!" My mother says as she hugs me, then Malcolm. "My son!"

Malcolm returns her embrace with a broad smile.

"Thank you, Mama Sun!" He beams.

Shelley pulls me close and exclaims, "Oh, Starr, honey, we're so happy to have you as part of our family forever!"

Malcolm and I receive more well wishes while we finish the photo shoot.

Before we sit at our table, Malcolm leads me to the dance floor as Sade performs "Cherish the Day." I lose myself in his loving embrace as I bury my face against his powerful chest. His heart beats as fast as mine, quickened by our emotional moment. I lift my gaze to his, and we stare into each other's eyes until the last strands of music fade.

Malcolm kisses me softly, then takes my hand. We visit each table to speak with our guests, accepting their congratulatory remarks. Afterwards, we settle at our table with Lola, Sebastian, Adrienne, and Anton. Mini Malcolms sit nearby with the other children and their nannies.

The meal is delicious with local dishes using the flavors of the Fijian people. Lucien offers his approval of the fine fare and jokes how he'll have to open a restaurant featuring the specialties.

Following up on his teasing, Sebastian—the Best Man —rises.

"Friends and family, thank you for joining the Steele and the Knight families for the union of my bother Malcolm and my friend Starr. This day is a long time coming and marks the start of a wonderful life for them as a family with their adorable twins, Selina and Elio. Kindly raise your flutes in a toast to the newlyweds," he says.

Everyone drinks to our prosperity.

"Now, let me say this. Malcolm you are a rebel who has always done your own thing. And done it well I might add— even if unconventional, like your spectacular yet romantic bikini beach wedding. In Starr, you found your mate who shares your need to live as a free spirit on her own path. Thankfully, you are now one. *Namaste,* my brother and my sister," Sebastian ends with a bow.

Malcolm stands and pulls his older brother into a fierce hug. They murmur words only they can hear as Lola and I watch with tears in our eyes.

When they sit, she rises.

"Starr, on this very island, you put me back together again after I thought I could never love Sebastian Steele. You taught me a yogic piece of advice: *be equally thankful for what you perceive to be good and for what you perceive as bad. It all happens for a reason.* And today proves your point. Here we sit with the men we will love for all time despite any past missteps. Much love to you, my sister and my brother," Lola says as she raises her flute in a toast.

We hug and I thank her for her loving words. How right she is!

After we eat, Lola tells me to come with her.

We go to a tent where I change into a white bandeau top string bikini with a sarong. She hands a blue garter to me and giggles.

When we return to the gathering, a chair sits in the middle with Malcolm holding my bouquet beside it.

Ah, now I know why Lola giggled!

He crooks his finger at me, and I laugh as I make my way to my husband. He helps me to stand on it and hands my bouquet to me. I toss it over my shoulder to the single women.

Haley snatches it first and holds it high.

Malcolm helps me down to sit before he kneels and removes my garter with a flourish.

"Okay, boys! Who's next?" He calls out to the guys in front of us. "Catch!"

With ease, Lachlan grabs it from the air and twirls it around his finger.

Malcolm snarls, "Not you, Lachlan."

But I place my hand on his forearm. He glances down at me, and I give a shake of my head. He purses his lips but remains silent.

Lachlan takes Haley's hand and leads her to the chair.

We switch places with them.

When he touches Haley's leg, Malcolm issues a warning growl that Lachlan ignores. He slides the garter up Haley's leg and kisses her lips softly. Her face flushes prettily, and everyone claps—well, except for her brothers…

Staff changes the tables arrangement into an all-white lounge with the torches and the bonfire lit. Sade leave us for a DJ to spin. The night continues as we dance and party, sipping signature cocktails crafted by Billie.

As I'm shaking my grove thang to Zhané with my girls around me, firm hands grip my hips from behind and pull me flush against a rock-hard body.

Malcolm!

My pussy floods at the feel of his turgid length nestled between my ass cheeks.

He sways us to the beat as he nuzzles the sensitive juncture of my neck and shoulder. When the song blends into another, he nips my neck and murmurs for my ears only.

"Time to consummate our marriage, Mrs. Malcolm Steele."

MALCOLM

I stalk towards my wife as she's shaking her ass, dancing with her girls.

If My Angel thinks she can taunt me all this time by changing into one tiny bikini after the other all night, she has another think coming. Or she won't cum on her wedding night…

It's been ten long months since I had her moaning and writhing beneath me, balls deep in her sweet, tight pussy. My aching cock's been hard from the moment she sat on my lap. Thank fuck, I can feel it now. I can feel everything.

After four months of intense therapy, I surpassed the expected stages set by the medical team. Dr. Stevens warned me results from the new treatment plan could take at least six months, if not more, with no guarantees of success.

I told him I would overcome every obstacle and walk again a hell of a lot sooner than his timeline.

And I did.

Two weeks ago, I awoke to immense pain radiating down my spine and into my legs, to the tips of my toes. My screams drew nurses to my bedroom. I could barely speak as nausea overtook me. My body was on fire. Sweat coated my skin as though I ran the New York City marathon.

The night doctor arrived and explained my nerves were reconnecting to my brain. Those simultaneous actions were overloading my system with the unexpected onslaught of synapses firing. The new trial neurostimulation therapy worked, he proclaimed excitedly.

Dr. Stevens arrived and conducted tests. The results confirmed my spinal injury was ninety percent healed. He was just as excited as the other doctor since their research paid off. The success will make the medical journals, he said proudly.

I told him I was happy to be the guinea pig and thanked the team profusely.

The weeks since were full of more testing, extensive therapy, and no-holds-barred sessions with Borya. Aside from him, only Baz knew I could walk. Even when I visited Starr and our babies, I used the wheelchair. I trusted the medical team, but I didn't want my family upset if my progress reversed.

Immediately, I asked Lola to arrange a Girls' Getaway as a ruse for getting My Angel to Laucala for a surprise wedding. My sister-in-law was more than happy to set it up. Once again, I enlisted the help of my mother and of Sun with the wedding arrangements. The family and our friends arrived yesterday to ensure all was in order and no one missed the big day.

The expressions on my parents' faces when I stood on the tarmac to greet them were priceless. I had the photographer and videographer document it as they did with My Angel—unbeknownst to her. My mother cried so hard I had to console her. When she found out it was weeks, she swatted me like a misbehaving toddler. My father teared up and nearly crushed me in his embrace. Roger and Harris understood and pulled me into a group hug.

My ability to walk again thrilled Peace and Sun as much as my family. The wedding had My Angel's parents pleased, but my recovery drove them to tears, too.

Before the wedding, Lola couldn't believe I didn't tell her and let Baz know she was none too pleased with him keeping it a secret. He spanked her ass, and she composed herself with a huff. I had to hear it from Haley and Leonie, too. Looks from Lachlan and Roger silenced them. I eyed Lachlan, and he smirked. Fucker.

The ultimate reaction was my wife's expression of pure gratitude for my healing. Her sorrel brown eyes glistened with tears as she murmured a silent prayer to, as she says, "thank God and every deity in every religion's pantheon."

I thank them too for bestowing me with the love of my life. Even if she's giving me blue balls, at least I can feel them again.

Once I stand behind her, shimmying to the music, I grip her hips firmly and pull her back flush against my front.

My wife gasps at the sensation of my no-longer-to-be-denied dick nestled between her round ass cheeks.

Without a word, I take control of her movements to set a sensual rhythm while I nuzzle the column of her swan-like neck down to her shoulder. Once the next song begins, my teeth graze her skin.

"Time to consummate our marriage, Mrs. Malcolm Steele," I murmur against the shell of her ear.

She shudders, and my cock thumps her ass.

I nod to her girls who titter as I scoop my wife into my arms like the bride she is and carry her away from our still-partying guests.

They hoot and holler—Harris the loudest with wolf whistles—as we make our way down the beach to the tent she spotted earlier.

My Angel laughs and waves then kisses cheek.

"I love you, caveman of mine," she sighs against my neck.

"I love you too, woman of mine," I answer, brushing my lips over her curls.

The music fades and the light of the reception bonfire gives way to the tranquil sound of the ocean lapping on the sand of the moonlit beach. Thousands of stars twinkle above us—as bright as My Angel covered in her diamonds. Ahead of us, smaller torches flank the entrance to the tent.

We're kicking off our honeymoon, so it's not just any old tent. We're glamping in a luxury, temperature-controlled one. The floor covered in colorful handwoven silk rugs and oversized silk pillows; the walls lined with delicate silk drapes; a large, round bed strewn with sumptuous white silk bedding takes up most of the interior space; flowers and flickering pillar candles surround it with a magnum of her favorite Krug Clos d'Ambonnay Champagne on ice and crystal flutes on a side table; soft music blends with the sounds of nature; a fully functional bathroom in a separate tent adjoins the main one.

As we step beyond the netting covering the entry, My Angel's mouth drops at the romantic sight. She squeals and kisses me passionately, murmuring words of love. I return her kiss just as zealously. Then set her on her feet and turn to untie the tent flaps.

"Alone at last, Mrs. Malcolm Steele!" I say as I pull her into my arms for another kiss.

"Yes, Mr. Malcolm Steele," she purrs with hooded eyes after I let her up for air. "Now, what are you going to do to me... Sir?"

My nostrils flare as my lips curl up in a smirk, and my

eyes narrow on hers, dancing with mischief in the candlelight.

"I am putting another baby in your belly. In fact, two more for another set of twins. That is how much I am filling your womb with my seed, Mrs. Malcolm Steele," I growl low in my throat.

As expected, her pupils dilate, and she pants through parted lips. Her plump nipples strain against the one-shoulder bikini top, begging to be suckled. She shifts from one foot to the other as she rubs her thighs in earnest for some much-needed friction—friction only I will sate.

I spank my wife's ass cheeks in rapid succession.

"Still!" I command.

With stuttered breath, she complies.

I take her hand in mine and lead her to the vintage bathtub with fragrant flowers and essential oils in the warm water. More candles fill the bathroom with their sensuous glow and heady scent. A stack of white fluffy bath sheets rests on a table.

Once again, I kiss my wife until she whimpers in my mouth. Silently, I pull the ties of her bikini bottom to reveal her bare mons. I lick my lips, remembering her delicious juices on my tongue. My eyes drift up to the bikini top. Cupping her tits, I knead the lush flesh as I stroke her nipples with my the pads of my thumbs through the material. Not wanting to release my hold. I dip my head to nibble the string between my teeth. My lips brush her heated skin as I tug the tie slowly. I spin her around to face the tub and pull the last string on her top. It cascades to the floor atop her bottoms.

"Get in," I murmur in her ear.

She trembles from the caress of my warm breath. Then she takes my proffered hand and slides in to the water.

I kneel beside the tub and dampen the sponge, then

squeeze the water on to her chest. Rivulets form around her mounds and drip from her pointed buds. Another dip of the sponge glides it along her inner thighs. They quiver beneath the surface, sending ripples through the water. Wanting to heighten the sensations, I skirt around her most sensitive areas as I bathe my bride from head to toe.

Her blissful sighs and moans surround us.

When I stop my erotic ministrations, she opens her eyes and parts her lips with a coo relaxed against the tub. She raises her arms to me.

"Your turn, my love," she whispers.

Unable to deny her anything, I stand and strip out of my swim trunks. My erect ten-inch cock—red and veiny—points at her accusingly; its mushroom head drips pre-cum.

She kneels in the tub and swipes the evidence of my need for her with the tip of her tongue. She hums; I groan.

"Come," my wife demands.

I gaze down at her, confused she means for me to *cum*. But she shakes her head with a teasing smile and gestures for me to sit opposite her in the tub.

I smirk and comply.

Now I lose myself in the rhapsody of my bath. As if reminding me two can play that game, my wife touches every part of my body except for my hungry cock and heavy balls. Not having her patience, I wrap my arms around her and rise from the tub.

Thinking more clearly than me, she snags towels as we pass them.

I stand her beside the bed and dry her gently, then quickly take the other towel to myself. Patience at an end.

I toss her on to the bed, and she giggles as she bounces in the middle.

"Caveman!" My Angel teases as she swipes damp curls from her face.

I grunt as I drop to my hands and knees to prowl towards her.

She squeals when I grab her ankles and lift her legs onto my shoulders.

Open-mouthed kisses trail down her inner thighs until I reach their apex, glistening from evidence of *her need* in the glow from the candles. I blow warm air on to her seam; she whimpers.

"Shh… I know exactly what you need, My Angel. Let me give it to you," I murmur as I stare into her hooded eyes.

She bites her lower lip and nods. Then catches herself and responds verbally.

I chuckle as I lower myself between her thighs. My broad shoulders widen them to give me room to lie flat on the bed. I glance up the flat plane of her belly, over the rise of her tits to gaze into her eyes.

"Cum as much as you want, Mrs. Malcolm Steele," I tell her.

She lifts her hips and grips handfuls of my hair to urge me on.

I begin my meal with a nip to each leg and devour her until—after countless orgasms—she begs for me to stop while her legs tremble uncontrollably.

A kiss to each leg, and I plank my body over hers. Muscular arms and toes bear the weight as thighs and ass flex. My turgid length presses between us with the trail of hair leading to it tickling her lower belly; she squirms with need.

"Malcolm, baby, please… I need you inside of me," my wife cries as she digs her heels into my ass and her fingertips in my biceps.

"I will never deny you, My Angel," I rasp.

I lower to one forearm then reach between us to fist my ready cock and align it with her pussy. The tip brushes her soaked, swollen folds as it makes its way inside her greedy channel. My hands cradle her face as I roll my hips against her, filling my wife with my cock. I give her exactly what she needs.

We groan in unison as her tight pussy walls stretch to accommodate my ample girth, especially after months of being without.

She grips me with a stranglehold. Undoubtedly still vitalized even after giving birth from the Kegel exercises she loves so much. I hiss from the carnal pain.

Her cries for *harder and deeper* fuel me to shift from slow thrusts and drags to pistoning strokes. My heavy balls slap her ass with each brutal thrust. I change the angle to glide along her G-spot, making her scream with pleasure.

As My Angel's back bows, I latch onto her tit and suckle. Hard.

She wails and digs her nails in to my back as she meets me thrust for thrust.

Fuck yeah!

We hurtle unstoppable to simultaneous climaxes.

My thumb finds her puckered hole and presses against the ring of muscle as I plunder her pussy.

She howls in wild abandon as a last wave overtakes her spasming core.

I roar as my release follows hers.

As promised, I coat my wife's womb with copious amounts of my virile seed until it spills down her ass cheeks to pool beneath her. Mind blown, I collapse atop her. She welcomes my heavy weight, wrapping her arms and legs around me.

My wife soothes me with tender strokes to my sweaty back as she clutches the back of my head, holding me to her neck.

Once our breathing evens out, I roll on to my back and pull her to my chest.

Sated, we lie stargazing through the top of the tent, clear so the stars shine brightly above us.

I take Starr's left hand adorned with my rings and harness in mine and kiss her open palm. She turns her gorgeous face towards me. Her sorrel brown eyes gleam as she smiles with a palpable intensity, mirroring my absolute love for her.

"I love you, Mr. Malcolm Steele," she coos.

"I love you, Mrs. Malcolm Steele," I rasp.

Then I kiss my Lucky Starr.

* * *

THE MORNING SUN filters through the tent's roof to dazzle my wife curled beside me. I brush a curl from her cheek and smile when her lips—still swollen from my kisses and my cock—turn up at my touch. So beautiful. So mine.

Even more so now that my collar readorns her neck. I kept her original ones—for day and for evening. Since it's our wedding, I chose to put the evening one on her. Hand-crafted in an intricate platinum lacework covered in tiny sparkly diamonds. The sun glints off of it and the diamonds on her left hand as it rests on the pillow.

"Like what you see, Mr. Steele?"

Her laughter rouses me from my musings.

Then she squeals when I lift her from the bed, leave the tent, and stride to the water where I dive in. She splutters when we breach the service and pushes at my chest.

"Good morning, Mrs. Steele!" I chuckle as I float beside her.

"You're so lucky I'm still recuperating from your

exuberant lovemaking, or I'd 'good morning' you!" She huffs as she swipes water from her face.

I stand to tower over her and stroke my hard cock.

"Oh, so you're not up for some morning loving?" I taunt as I fist it.

My Angel attempts to hold back her smile but fails miserably. With a whoop, she throws herself at me and wraps her arms and legs around my torso.

I lift her hips and impale her on my cock. She rides me as the waves lap around us. We climax as one.

Back inside the tent, we bathe and dress for breakfast with our family and friends. A driver takes us to her parents' villa as I tease my wife in the backseat of the G-Wagen.

"So glad you can join us, Mr. and Mrs. Malcolm Steele!" Leonie teases when we walk on to the patio.

Laurent—the youngest Jackson and Harris' best friend—adds, "The newlyweds arrive! Cheers!"

Everyone greets us as we head to Selina and Elio, who sit between their grandmothers. We hug our twins close and kiss their cherub faces as they giggle.

Once we're settled at a table, I thank everyone for celebrating with us, then turn to my wife.

"Mrs. Malcolm Steele, for the next two months, we will remain on this special island for our honeymoon. However, you never have to wonder when we can return. We may at any given moment, as it is my wedding gift to you. Laucala Island is yours, my love," I say, lifting my mimosa in the air.

She gapes at me with wide eyes.

I laugh and lean over to cover her open mouth with mine in a loving kiss.

She regains herself and kisses me back with enthusiasm as she bounces on her chair.

"Thank you, my love! Thank you so much!" My wife's sorrel brown eyes sparkle.

I grin, knowing I will keep her this happy and more for the rest of our lives.

STARR

The warm rays of the tropical sun soak into my sweat-dampened skin as the sound of the water-fall mingles with my moans in an erotic symphony amongst the wild foliage of Laucala's rain forest. As I float face up to the cloudless cerulean blue sky—my arms bound behind my back and my knees bent with my ankles bound to my thighs —I cry out with each thrust of my husband's massive dick into my dripping pussy.

The jute rope drops from the palm tree above me to coil around my body like a snake capturing its prey. Each care-fully crafted knot strategically placed to hold me firmly proves my husband has mastered the art of Shibari.

He knows it's my favorite form of play since the compli-cated yet beautiful knots restrict my movement, swaddling me with a sense of security, allowing my mind to just. Let. Go. Submit to him fully.

Over the past two months, my Alpha Dom husband has taken control of my mind, body, and soul to send me into the euphoria of subspace over and over. Each time we've done a scene, he's brought me to greater heights, proving he hasn't lost his mastery of my body.

And I love him even more for it.

"Are… you… still… with… me… Little One?"

His throaty growl with snapping hips that punctuate each word bring me back from my musings.

"Yes… Sir…" I pant breathlessly.

"Look at me!" My Alpha Dom demands. "I want to see your eyes as I fuck another orgasm out of your greedy, little pussy."

As if on cue, my core clenches on his hard length, and I keen through my climax.

"Aaaaaahhhhh… Yeessss…" I wail as my body convulses, jerking the dangling rope.

He continues to arc me through the air, swinging me back and forth like a pendulum to impale me on his thick cock. Corded muscles flex from his neck to his broad chest down along his eight-pack abs. Sweat drops onto my belly as he stares down at me with molten platinum eyes.

When my Alpha Dom bends his knees to thrust up at me on the next return arc, his Prince Albert piercing jewelry balls scrap my G-spot and the bottom of my channel.

"Arrrrhhhh….. Ffffuuuuck!!!" I scream, throwing my head back as my eyes slam shut.

Too much.

Another climax rips down my spine to curl my fingers and my toes. My mind explodes with my pussy.

"Give it to me… Give it all to me!" He barks barbarically.

As I soar through subspace, my last sensation is of my husband's dick expanding, then jerking as he releases a torrent of his seed within the depths of my womb. In response, it spasms to coax every single drop from him. I shudder and feel no more.

. . .

"WELCOME BACK, MY ANGEL."

As my eyes flutter open, they alight on Malcolm's handsome face, so full of love. I lift my arms overhead and straighten my legs in a languorous stretch. It's then I notice I'm sitting on his lap across from the waterfall with the waves lapping at the tops of my breasts.

With a contented sigh, I wrap my arms around his neck and cover his mouth with mine.

Lazily, our tongues twine until he dominates the kiss. My breath hitches in the back of my throat as my husband nips at my bottom lip, then soothes it with a long, sensuous lick.

When he lets me up for air, I press my forehead to his and stare into his lust-filled eyes.

"You're insatiable, Mr. Steele," I purr.

He smirks, "And who's fault is that, Mrs. Malcolm Steele?"

In response, I circle my hips to drag my ass against his thick erection. It thumps.

"Mmmmm mmmm… What you do to me, wife," he groans and tightens his firm grip on my waist.

In one swift motion, he lifts me and lowers me onto his dick one inch at a time until my lips kiss his groin.

"Better, Mr. Steele?" I purr against his slack mouth.

He nods and kisses me as he guides my hips in the rhythm he prefers.

Our climaxes find us easily, and we rest on a colorful Hermès blanket, staring at the sky.

I roll over to face him and trail a fingernail down his powerful chest, bumping over his nipple.

"Ready for more, Mrs. Steele?" He rumbles.

I shake my head and sit up, gesturing around us.

"The island is so beautiful, and we've used so many areas of it for our playtime. I think others would enjoy its natural beauty and the privacy it affords for their playtime," I say.

Malcolm cocks an eyebrow at me and rises to an elbow. His flexing biceps distract me, and I stare, concentration broken. He tweaks my nipple.

"And?" He asks with a smirk.

I giggle and shake the carnal thought of jumping my husband's bones from my mind. For now.

"You and Lucien could convert the resort into LEVELS Laucala Island. BDSM on the Beach!" I say, grinning like the Cheshire Cat.

Before he can respond, I continue.

"And I can open Starr Light Fitness & Wellness Laucala Island to keep LEVELS LI members limber… However, we'll keep the other side of the island private for our family with the six villas. What say you, My Alpha Dom?"

He lays back down with his arms folded behind his head —again with the bulging biceps and now the pecs and abs to mesmerize me. He ponders my idea in silence for a few moments.

The next, I'm flat on my back with all those tantalizing muscles on point above me. I giggle and squeeze his arms.

"Excellent idea, Little One! Another first for our island… Introducing LEVELS Laucala Island, exclusive members-only BDSM resort!" He proclaims.

My laughter turns into moans as he makes me soar once more.

* * *

"Now, you have my permanent mark, Mrs. Malcolm Steele."

I grin at my husband then at my left hand where three number threes interlock across my left ring finger to symbolize three's the charm forever.

"Yes, Mr. Malcolm Steele, indeed I do. Again!" I quip.

Sebastian may think Malcolm the rebel for having our wedding on the beach in bathing suits. But I loved it and wouldn't have it any other way. Even when Malcolm told me we could have the wedding of my dreams anywhere in the world. No thanks. Our family-only, beachfront wedding was absolutely perfect!

Elio must find my joke amusing as he laughs and waves his hands in the air. Selina joins in with her brother, and we laugh. So freaking cute!

The tattoo artist—the best in Asia—Malcolm flew over asks me if I'm ready.

Malcolm cocks his eyebrow, and I pat his cheek.

"Be back shortly," I smirk with a wink.

When I return, Malcolm stops playing with his babies and faces me questioningly, arms crossed over his broad chest. I saunter over to him and lower the v-neck of my shirt.

His eyes light up at the sight of a small heart with the letters MSS in the hallow between my breasts.

"Malcolm and Starr Steele?" He asks.

"Yes, my love," I confirm.

He jumps up and swoops me into his arms as he kisses me. Then he sets me on my feet and growls possessively.

"Did he see your tits?"

I throw my head back and laugh.

My Caveman!

MALCOLM

"*D*amn, bro. If I knew I had to do manual labor in order to snag your Sunset Strip penthouse permanently, I would've bought another one. Give me a damn break already and hurry the fuck up!"

I chuckle and clock Harris upside the back of his head as he grumbles more under his breath.

We're in the new playroom I'm having installed in My Angel's—I mean our—Benedict Canyon Drive mansion. While we were on our honeymoon, my personal assistant and her PA organized the move of my stuff from my penthouse to here. This will serve as our West Coast residence while our beachfront mansion at Steele Southampton Village takes the place of my penthouse in The STEELE Tower as our East Coast residence. We'll use that home when we're in the city overnight. Otherwise, we'll take my Sikorsky S-92 Executive Helicopter to and from the compound.

When I tried to persuade My Angel to move in with me at my New York City penthouse while we were dating, she declined. She told me she's a beach girl and prefers the

Hamptons with access to the Atlantic Ocean. I couldn't even bribe her with an SLFW in the Flat Iron District—the Manhattan neighborhood renown for upscale fitness centers and retailers. She countered with SLFW Resorts at STEELE Southampton Village. She didn't want to enter the oversaturated Manhattan fitness scene. Her preference for incorporating her center with the bed-and-breakfast-style resort suits a more intimate setting. Fine by me.

Baz's words about *happy wife, happy life* come to my mind, and I chuckle.

"Really, Malcolm? You're standing there with a goofy AF grin on your gaga face with hearts circling your head while I'm holding this heavy cross?!"

Harris' reprimand yanks me from my pleasant little family thoughts to the playroom.

"Quit, your whining. I'm almost done," I smirk. "Didn't you say your one rep max bench press was 195? Maybe you need more time with Borya…"

Harris pulls his lips sideways and rolls his eyes while I finish mounting the St. Andrew's Cross to the wall. I had the rest of the heavy pieces installed, but the cross just arrived, and I want to surprise My Angel with a complete playroom tomorrow night.

Tonight we're going to LEVELS Beverly Hills for a party by a pair of my favorite members' collaring ceremony. We closed the Peepshow level for their private event. It promises to be a night of love and hedonistic bliss.

"Okay, what the fuck is this for, bro?"

I glance over my shoulder to find Harris holding a toy My Angel spotted when we made a stop in Hong Kong for some shopping on our way back from Laucala Island.

A pink glass dildo shaped to resemble an octopus' tentacle with a double row of suckers on top and ridges along its bottom, finished on one end with a loop for an easy grip. Perfect dipped into cool water or heated with my mouth. The stimulation it gave My Angel's channel drove her into sensory overload real quick.

"Put that down. Starr and I don't need your grimy paws on our toys," I scold him with a shake of my head.

Harris returns it to the drawer then leans on the chest with his arms folded across his chest.

"You and Baz with your Alpha Dom shit. Whatever happened to using what you got naturally to get what you want?" He asks as he pumps his hips.

I snort and throw the towel I was wiping my hands off with at him.

"You'll learn little, bro. Even Roger dips into the *other side* now and then…" I chuckle.

Although we're all Alpha Males and Global All Access Members of the four LEVELS clubs, he and Roger aren't Doms.

I grin when I recall helping Leonie to do a burlesque performance at LEVELS Paris as a wedding present for Roger. The next day, Lucien and I had hell to pay with him, despite the way his eyes lit up at the memory.

My Angel and I enjoy my clubs and make use of them regularly. But I like to have a playroom in my residence. Since Harris took over my Sunset Strip penthouse that has one in it, I had to design a new space here. And I cannot wait to play with my wife!

"You're still coming to the party tonight?" I ask Harris as we head downstairs to the entertainment floor.

I promised him a round of *Call of Duty: Black Ops Cold War* in exchange for his help.

"Me, miss a party? At LEVELS? Absolutely, I'll be there," he responds. Then goes on to tell me about a member he's had his eye on the past few times he's been at the club.

Before we get into the game, I shoot a text to My Angel

to let her know I'm in the game room. She's with Leonie for a spa day while the nannies watch the babies. It's great everyone bought a house out here and created a new Steele compound.

"Oh, come on already, whipped boy..." Harris grumbles as he tosses the controller at me.

"Game on, bro!" I say, settling in for some fun time with my youngest brother.

Yeah. Family first.

"CONGRATULATIONS ON YOUR MARRIAGE, Mr. Steele, Mrs. Steele."

My wife smiles and thanks the LEVELS Beverly Hills greeter while I tighten my grip on Mrs. Steele's hip.

It feels damn good to hear those outside of our clan refer to My Angel as Mrs. Steele. I grin to myself.

After our wedding, the press release went out to announce our marriage and Selina and Elio to the world. Our family prefers to remain low key in the media—despite the hoopla around my accident and the trial—other than business-related activities. But marriages, births, and deaths warrant press releases.

We make our way through the double doors to Peepshow.

My chest swells with pride at another successful club filled with the crème de la crème of society. The club caters to the most wealthy and influential individuals. They prefer the relative safety that one can expect from the ironclad nondisclosure agreement that LEVELS requires every member and their guests to sign.

LEVELS Beverly Hills is the fourth exclusive, luxury, members-only BDSM/dance club with Global and Local All Access Membership or Dine & Dance Membership. The layout mimics the other clubs. A main entry foyer has two sides with two greeter stations for access to Dine & Dance levels and BDSM levels, an All-Access member, can choose from any of the seven levels: 7th Sky Lounge that offers a stunning view of the Hollywood Sign, a bar, restaurant by day dance club by night, coverable pool that's open for the summer, and a glass-retractable roof; 6th and 5th multilevel dance club with two bars and a lounge for food and drinks; 4th Level 4 Restaurant and bar open for breakfast, lunch, and dinner; 3rd has twelve private suites for members to continue their pleasure apart from the BDSM levels; 2nd Peepshow for BDSM with seating alcoves, main stage, performance rooms, and a bar that serves non-alcoholic mocktails; below ground the Cellar BDSM dungeon with mocktails bar. The Dine/Dance members only have access to the party levels—Sky Lounge, Dance Club, and Level 4 Restaurant.

"Ah, Malcolm, you married a real beauty, mate."

I glance to my left to find an Australian actor with the latest box office hit action movie grinning at my wife. A growl rumbles deep in my chest.

Of course she's beautiful and oozing sexy in her Swarovski crystal embellished sheer floor-length gown with a slit to her crotch covered by a minuscule G-string. Her tan accentuated by the whiteness of the beading. Fuck-me mules make her toned legs go on for miles. Her upswept hair reveals her evening collar while her left hand glitters with her full wedding jewelry.

I bring it to my lips and kiss her rings as I eye the actor.

"Yes, and all mine, *mate*," I smirk.

I give zero fucks he's a member; she's my wife!

"Hey, there's a woman eye fucking you," Harris interjects and turns the actor toward some fictitious fan.

He bites the lure and hurries off without a backwards glance.

My Angel giggles and says, "Okay, My Caveman! Let's find the happy couple."

"Good idea," Harris chuckles. Then adds with a wink, "I'll see you guys around."

My Angel kisses his cheek, and he laughs at whatever she whispered to him.

I arch my eyebrow in question, and she shrugs.

"He saved you from acting possessive because of a member, Mr. Steele," she says, then tugs my arm. "Now, come on."

I spank her ass and murmur in her ear, "So you think you are in control, Naughty Girl. When the ceremony ends, I will remind you who is the Dom and who is the sub."

My wife shudders and bites her plump lower lip with downcast eyes.

I chuckle darkly and place my hand on her hip to guide her through the guests.

* * *

"You cheated, Malcolm! You're supposed to go around the *outside* of the buoy, and you know that, big cheater!"

Haley shouts as she storms towards me already on the beach, having left my Jetski on the sand.

We've been on Baz and Lola's Bougainvillea Cay—their private island in the Bahamas—for a couple of days. It's our first Thanksgiving as a family with My Angel and her parents since my accident prevented our gathering last year.

More specifically, it's an island within the chain of the Exuma Cays known as the yachting, sailing, and fishing paradise of the Bahamas. The location offers an ideal spot for relaxation and fun activities.

The forty-million-dollar investment of Bougainvillea Cay lies in one of the most beautiful parts of the Bahamas. It features over five hundred acres of lush, tropical land with a network of paths and walkways. Surrounded by crystal clear turquoise waters, it boasts many white sandy beaches, three inner lakes, and different elevations for stunning views. An airstrip for us to fly in and out with ease makes it perfect for quick getaways. Another plus is its proximity to STEELE Exumas should we wish to use the recreational, spa, or dining facilities.

Two properties round out the island. A palatial two-story, ten-bedroom beachfront villa with saltwater pool, four guest cabanas, and a caretaker's house and an actual castle built by an Englishman in the 1930s. With Leonie doing the design through her STEELE division, they rebuilt it into a spot for the kids to take over. The perfect solution as they grow into teenagers and want their space apart from the adults.

Our parents and the rest of us siblings built our villas along the coastline that features natural coves for privacy. With his STEELE division, Roger created a clubhouse on the largest beach for our family to gather. They added docks with lifts for sailboats, Jetskis, and other water toys.

Bougainvillea Cay is the Steele Caribbean retreat. A spectacular place for our family to gather for Thanksgiving and during the winters, as we do at Steele Southampton in the summers and *Chalet de la Joie* for the holidays. Laucala Island will host Memorial Day and anytime our family—Steele, Knight, Beaulieu—needs a tropical respite.

I race towards Haley and lift her off her feet before she can duck away. Spinning her in the air, I tease her about being my little sister and to respect her elders.

Haley huffs, but giggles when I tickle her silly.

I drape my arm over her shoulders, and we walk back to

the others gathered on the sand. My eyes meet Lachlan's, and I arch my eyebrow at him in challenge. My little sister, fucker.

She squirms from my embrace and hustles to him.

He smirks over her head at me, and I curl my lip in warning.

"Who's ready for some grilled lobster and shrimp?" My father calls out from the pit we dug for cooking on the beach.

Sun made her famous potato salad, and Josy baked her equally loved double-chocolate soufflés. Not to be outdone, Lola made delicious fried chicken. They teased Leonie was best left with tossing the green salad since she's famous for burning water.

"Hey, babe, go get your food. I'll watch Mini Malcolms," I tell My Angel as I drop onto the oversized blanket beside her.

"Thanks, my love. I'll make you a plate, too," she says before she kisses my lips.

I've noticed she's been hungry lately but can't seem to hold down her food. I know how much she loves lobster, so I hope she can enjoy it.

Elio crawls towards the red sock puppet as I dangle in front of them as they laugh with drool dripping down their chins. Selina's first tooth popped up a week before Elio's. At seven months, they amaze us with their growth and development every day.

"Oh, so you want to play, do you?" I coo at them when Selina rolls to her belly and follows her brother. "Well, come and get it."

We play until My Angel returns with our plates and my mother with bottles of water.

"Here, your father and I will watch our grandbabies

while you eat. He's been nibbling on the food while he grilled, and I already ate," my mother offers with a smile.

"Thanks, Mom," I say as My Angel nods around a mouthful of food.

After she finishes, I clear our plates and cheek on Mini Malcolms. They're being spoiled by both sets of their grandparents who shoo me away.

"Come on, My Angel. Let's go for a walk on the beach," I tell her when I return to the blanket.

"Good idea! I'm stuffed!" She giggles, patting her belly, then takes my proffered hand.

We stroll along the shoreline as the waves of the Caribbean Sea lap around our feet. The white-powered sand scrunches beneath our feet with each step.

I tilt my head back with my eyes closed to revel in the warmth of the sun's rays on my face. When I open my eyes, my gaze lands on My Angel.

She stares at me with such blatant love, my heart stutters in my chest. Then she smiles, and her beauty outdoes the surrounding nature. She's brighter than the sun could ever be.

I scoop her flush to my body, not wanting an inch of space between us. My mouth slants over hers as I kiss her passionately. We remain locked together until we need to catch our breath.

My wife cups my face and brushes her thumb over my bottom lip, just as swollen as her from our kiss.

"I love you beyond words," she whispers.

A lump forms in my throat, and I bury my face in her neck as my heart races.

She tangles her fingers in my hair while she soothes me with more words of love.

Once I regain my ability to speak coherently, I lift my eyes to hers.

"I love you so much it hurts sometimes, and I can't express myself with words. Thank you for loving me, My Angel. For giving me Selina and Elio. This is the best Thanksgiving of my life," I confess.

Tears fill her eyes. Now, it's her turn to bury her face in my neck, too overcome for words.

I hold My Angel in my loving embrace as the breeze carries the sounds of our family's laughter to us.

Family first.

STARR

And here I thought I would always be the doula and never the mama. I am eternally grateful for Selina and Elio. But another set of twins? So soon?! Mini Malcolms are eight months barely. Dear God and every deity in every religion's pantheon: help me.

I nod when Dr. Sánchez confirms my inkling I may be pregnant again. Then I nearly fall off of the examination table after she points to two little blips on the ultrasound monitor. She turns up the sound, and their heartbeats fill the room.

Then fill my heart with immense love.

A mama of four, I think as I trace their shapes with my fingertip on the screen. Growing up, I wanted siblings.

Now my children will each other—not to mention their six cousins. And Haley and Harris haven't even begun their families. The Steele grandkids will be as abundant as the family's billions!

"You know the routine, Starr. Not much has changed with the process in eight months," Dr. Sánchez teases.

I smirk and take the images she printed for me. Instinctively, my hand caresses my slightly raised belly—goop and all.

Dr. Sánchez leaves me to clean up before I join her in the office.

I tell her I'll have to schedule my follow-up appointments for after Malcolm and I return from Europe and New York City. With my parents and Mini Malcolms, we fly to Verbier for Christmas and New Year's tonight. Then we plan to stay overseas for business while my parents return home.

I assure Dr. Sánchez I'll ask Leonie's OB-GYN to see me when we get to Paris. On the way back to the West Coast, we're stopping in the City for more business and to move into our East Coast residences. If necessary, I can see Lola's doctor.

Dr. Sánchez laughs at the OB-GYN in every city and tells me to get adequate rest. Then she laughs again when I tell her Malcolm will probably put me in a bubble with my feet up all day!

If I'm not ready for another unexpected pregnancy, I won't blame him if he's not, I giggle as I drive home in my Tesla. During the ride, an idea forms on just how to tell Malcolm the good news. I make a stop at the craft store and smile when the clerk gives my bundle to me.

* * *

I CAN BARELY CONTAIN my excitement as our family gathers in the great room of *Chalet de la Joie*—Leonie and Roger's multimillion-dollar chalet in Verbier, Switzerland—for Christmas Eve.

Verbs, as the in-the-know jet-set call it, is a town in the Swiss Alps. A part of the Valais canton in the southwest of Switzerland, France borders Verbier to the west with Italy to the south. It's the most exclusive ski destination in the world.

It's the winter version of Monaco, with the difference being people who go to Monaco want to watch or be watched. Whereas Verbier has an understated style where wealth is glamorous, stylish, and tasteful. People are here for the reasons one goes to a ski resort—the superb skiing. Not to mention the phenomenal bars and restaurants; the après-ski is perfect for party lovers. Verbier is a glamorous winter playground.

The luxury chalets occupy the area south of the Médran lift. They're slightly away from town along Rue de Médran, where the extra space means they are rarely overlooked and have a private, exclusive vibe. The residential compound is opposite to the STEELE Verbier that's closer to the heart of the village square. The concept is for the STEELE Verbier Chalets to access the resort for its five-star amenities. The most important include the luxury thermal bath spa and the three Jackson Corporation restaurants headed by *The Sexy Chef*.

The massive chalet fits right in with its comfy and chic custom build featuring all the top amenities and accoutrements expected by a posh family. Five stories, twelve bedrooms, sixteen bathrooms, four fireplaces, an oversized ski room, and the usual entertainment rooms including a sixteen-person cinema room, game room, gym, and wine-tasting cellar. The indoor-outdoor heated pool pavilion with spa is an added bonus. Staff quarters are above the six-vehicle garage.

We just finished le *Réveillon de Noël* for the Christmas meal: the dishes included Beluga caviar, foie gras, oysters, lobster, scallops, fresh truffles, roast goose, venison, and cheeses. We ended with the paramount French Christmas dessert *la bûche de Noël*—the Yule log. All the while, a selection of wines and champagne pleased our palates—well, everyone but me.

To continue with French tradition from Leonie's French upbringing, we're about to exchange our first gifts. The beautifully decorated eighteen-foot tree has a vast number of gifts beneath and around its base. The colorful boxes of all shapes and sizes fill the space.

Mariah Carey's "All I Want for Christmas Is You" plays in the background from Leonie's favorite Christmas playlist. The classic songs of Nat King Cole, Johnny Mathis, Céline Dion, Gladys Knight and the Pips, Frank Sinatra, and, of course, the Trans-Siberian Orchestra who performed at her Winter Wonderland Wedding. The sizable stone hearth has a blazing fire and Christmas stockings for each child.

My grin widens as I hand Malcolm's present to him.

"Thank you, My Angel," he says with twinkling eyes.

He holds up two mini red stockings and frowns, glancing towards the fireplace.

"Selina and Elio have stockings already on the mantle," Malcolm says, perplexed. "And these have MM III and MM IV written on them. Why did you—"

A shriek comes from Haley.

Everyone turns in surprise.

She's bouncing and clapping her hands. Her dove gray eyes shine with jubilance. Then Lola and Leonie clap as they grin knowingly.

A slow smile of dawning spreads across Malcolm's face. He drops the stockings in the box as he jumps up and kneels before me. Tentatively, he places his hand on my lower belly, then gazes at me as he bites his full lower lip.

I nod and put my hand over his.

He lets out a whoop and pulls me onto his lap, covering my mouth with his.

The room erupts with shouts from our family and with

barks from The Twins' Bichon Frises and Slade's Siberian Huskies.

"Hold on a minute. Two stockings, Starr?" My father asks.

Malcolm jerks back from our kiss and stares gobsmacked at me.

I nod and whisper, "Merry Christmas, baby."

His chiseled jaw drops to the floor.

"Holy shit, Malcolm! Super Sperm Man!" Harris chortles.

"Yeah, you win, bro!" Sebastian snorts. "Hands down, the winner!"

"Absolutely!" Roger guffaws. "Always doing it your way!"

I worry my lower lip with my teeth, nervous about Malcolm's silence.

"Don't hate the playa; hate the game, my brothers!" He quips gleefully.

Then he cups my chin and murmurs, "The best Christmas gift ever, My Angel. Thank you."

"Oh, sweetheart, that's amazing!" My mother says as she dabs her eyes with my father's handkerchief.

He rubs her back and exclaims, "Indeed! Excellent news!"

Shelley and Morgan add their congratulations and hugs.

"This calls for some Champagne, *non?*" Guy asks as he strides to the bar.

We toast—me with sparkling water in my flute—to more grandbabies, as Shelley says.

"When did you find out?" Malcolm asks as he caresses my belly, lying in bed later that night.

He stares down at me as he leans on his elbow. Platinum grays search my sorrel browns.

I stroke his cheek with my thumb. So gorgeous my husband.

"The afternoon before we left. I've been experiencing pregnancy symptoms but wanted my doctor to confirm. I wasn't sure how you'd feel so soon after having Selina and Elio and getting married..." I trail off.

Malcolm puts his fingertips over my mouth to hush me and shakes his head.

"My Angel, I know I behaved like an ass when you told me about being pregnant the first time. And I will forever kick *my ass* for my abysmal behavior and pray you forgive me truly"—he presses his fingertips when I open my mouth—"However, never feel you cannot come to me about anything. Especially about being pregnant. I'm grateful for all the children you will give me, my love."

I try to blame the raging hormones for the tears that spill from my eyes. But they're really because of his beautiful words.

"Shush, baby. Happy tears, I hope?" He asks.

I nod.

"Words, wife. I will have your words," Malcolm admonishes me with a smirk.

"Yes, husband... *Daddy*," I add coyly, knowing how the moniker turns him on.

Malcolm growls and pulls me beneath his hard body. His kisses increase in ferociousness as his arousal amplifies. His knee drives my thighs apart as he fists his turgid length directing it to my weeping pussy.

We groan as one when one demanding thrust breaches my folds to wedge him deep inside of me.

I cry out in passion, and Malcolm stiffens.

"Oh, fuck! Did I hurt you?" He asks with panicky eyes. "Damn! I didn't mean to be so rough. Did... Did I hurt the babies?"

I would laugh if he weren't so alarmed. Instead, I reach between us to angle his bulbous tip to my seam.

"No, you feel wonderful, my love. I'm not fragile, and the babies are safe within my womb. No need to worry," I reassure him. "Now, fuck me, Mr. Steele!"

Hesitantly, he slides inside inch by tortuous inch.

The pace nearly kills me, so I grip his firm butt cheeks to drive him forward as my hips thrust up. I stare into his wide eyes, then throw my head back on a moan as I impale myself on his ginormous dick. My chest heaves as my back bows from the bed.

"Oh, Malcolm! Fuck. Me. Hard!" I demand. "I need you!"

He blinks, then shifts to his knees as he grasps my ass, lifting my lower half from the bed. I wrap my legs around his hips and offer another plea.

Malcolm bites his lower lip. The veins in his neck strain as he withdraws to his tip. One snap of his hips and he impales me again with a grunt. He pauses to gauge my reaction, and I throw my arms—crossed at the wrists—over my head to grip the headboard.

"Ride me, Mr. Steele… Fuck. Me. Raw. Now…" I grit out as I pin him with my eyes.

He narrows his and tightens his grip.

"Take it, Mrs. Steele! Every fucking inch!" He growls.

I cry out in wild abandon with a white-knuckle grip on the slats as my head tosses side to side, and my heavy tits bounce with each brutal thrust.

"YES! YES! YES!" I cry each time Malcolm re-enters my pussy.

He grunts and growls, shifting positions to increase his penetration, determined to obey my command. His primal roar of release sparks another spasm of my inner walls around his thick girth, sucking him in deeper.

Soon I spiral into erotic bliss from the countless orgasms

Malcolm demands from my ravaged pussy. As I float, my thanks go to the architect for his foresight to put sound-proof walls in each bedroom suite!

"Hello there, Demanding Mama."

I grin as my eyes flutter to Malcolm's handsome face hovering over me.

"I thought I was going to need to resuscitate you. Feel better?" He smirks.

I stretch and purr, relishing in the ache in my well-used pussy and our combined wetness between my thighs.

"I didn't clean you off because it pleases me to see my seed drip from your pussy. Reminds me of how I put my babies inside of you… Again," Malcolm says as he trails his fingertip along my swollen seam.

He collects some of our juices and places his finger against my lips.

A moan slips from between them when I lick his digit into my mouth. Then I suck it greedily.

"Good, girl," Malcolm croons with hooded eyes.

I smack my lips and grin.

"You do realize you made good on your promise to"—I tilt my head to the side pretending to ponder—"How did you say it? Ah yes, *put another baby in your belly. In fact, two more for another set of twins.*"

Malcolm snorts and falls onto his back.

I lean up, then straddle his hips and place his sizable hands on my belly.

"According to the timeline, you most certainly did!" I giggle.

He strokes my babies bump and smiles.

"I am a man of my word, My Angel. And this time you'll

get sick of me. That's how attentive I'm going to be to you," he vows.

I roll my eyes, remembering what I told Dr. Sánchez about the bubble. Then I gasp as Malcolm rolls us over and makes good on his attention, too. A true man of his word…

MALCOLM

"*O*ut of the way! Coming through!"

Haley's tinkling laughter trails behind her as she zips past me on the black diamond piste, her fleeting figure a blur on her Rossignol skis.

The sunlight glints off of her silver helmet as she zooms by in an all-white Moncler Grenoble two-piece ski suit with her eyes covered by gray Dragon googles and matching helmet. Haley's long, toned legs help her carve through the fresh powder. She moves with ease and grace down the expert slope since she's skied from the time she could walk.

It's New Year's Eve morning and we're out en masse for an early morning run. The entire Steele clan, Knights, Beaulieus, and Lachlan—fucker—make our way from the top of the mountain piste to the base lodge. It's a popular time to come out, so other skiers bob and weave around us.

And of course Lachlan isn't far behind my little sister. He salutes me as he schusses past on silent skis—emerald green eyes covered by mirrored googles. He and the rest of the Jackson clan along with Lydie's boyfriend Chase flew in two days ago after spending Christmas at their family seat in Scotland. They purchased a residence at STEELE Verbier Chalets last year, close to Roger and Leonie's.

Once we make it to the bottom of the mountain, we'll have brunch on the deck of the base lodge.

"I'm sorry, baby. I don't know how my boot buckle opened. Thanks for fixing it for me."

My Angel's words draw my attention up to her face as I kneel before her, adjusting the catch. With a snap, I rise and let my hands roam over her lush curves—long legs; rounded hips; nipped-in waist; swell of full tits. The black Cordova retro ski suit with contouring white stripes on the sides fits her trim figure in a mouthwatering way. Or rather, in a cock-thickening way...

"My absolute pleasure, Hot Mama," I murmur against her lips before I swipe my tongue inside her mouth for a toe-curling kiss.

I swallow her moans as I tip her head for the best angle to devour My Angel whole.

"Get a damn room, man!" Lucien shouts, as he flies by us.

Our passionate kiss breaks with My Angel's giggles.

"Come on. Let's go," she says as she pulls from my embrace. "No shows on the mountain today!"

When she turns to step into her skis, I slide my hands around her flanks to rest on her lower belly. Despite my insistence she not ski, My Angel reminded me she's perfectly fine and has skied her entire life. When I quipped *not pregnant*, she boxed me upside the head.

"Are you sure you don't want to take a less risky piste?" I ask for the thousandth time. "I'll go down on you—I mean with you..."

She snorts and leans back against my chest, placing her hands on top of mine.

"Slip of the tongue, Mr. Steele?" She asks coyly.

I grind my groin above the swell of her ass. Just the talk of fucking my horny wife makes me hard AF.

"I have a slip of the tongue for you, Mrs. Steele. Would you like to feel it?" I rejoin.

The click of her boot into the ski binding precedes her slipping from my arms. A wave over her shoulder, and my pregnant wife picks up speed.

Fuck!

I step into my bindings and pursue her down the mountain.

Part of my determination to heal was to get back into my extreme sports: heli-boarding; base jumping; fighter-jet flying; name it, I did it. I would not let that ex-psycho-sub keep me from my favorite pastime since I was a teenager.

But marriage and fatherhood have a way of realigning one's priorities. I can't put myself in a position with the chance of danger or to harm myself where I can't care for mine. And with another set of twins due… No fucking way!

I'll stick to the simpler—if you will—extreme sports including cave diving, motocross; MMA; and the like. No more tempting fate with my life.

My Angel… While I know she would never ever put herself in harm's way, I'd rather she hangs out at the chalet or the base lodge… I swear, if I have to rope her up to keep her still, I will!

To assuage my concerns, we had a video conference call with her OB-GYN. Dr. Sánchez confirmed My Angel's perfectly healthy state and ability to take part in any activities that do not cause her discomfort. I thanked the doctor, then proceeded to spank My Angel to test the boundaries of her discomfort…

With little effort I reach her side and wag my finger at her.

She grins and tightens into a tuck, zipping away.

Dammit!

We play cat and mouse as we maneuver around other skiers down the mountain. Breathless, we come to a stop in front of the lodge. Our ski butlers help us remove our equipment and hand us our heated après-ski hats, sunglasses, and footwear.

"Real cute you are, Naughty Girl," I growl in her ear as my warm breath fans across her cheek flushed from our race and the crisp wind. "It must be time for another discomfort test, hmm?"

I add emphasis with a few pats to her round ass.

She shudders and bites her plump lower lip.

My wicked chuckles follow her as we enter the lodge. I place my hand on her lower back and guide her through the great room to the deck, kept warm by heat lamps.

We stop and chat with a few friends and acquaintances, also in Verbs for the holidays. The opening of the STEELE properties attracts many of our social circle. Including those who enjoy their LEVELS memberships. A Verbier location—as suggested by Harris—is in the pipeline. We're awaiting approvals for a location atop the mountain for spectacular views to take the Mile High Club to another level....

Pride swells in my chest when I introduce My Angel as my wife to those unfamiliar with our nuptials. Some eyes appraise her while others try to hide jealousy behind syrupy smiles.

One woman I may have fucked in the distant past dares to whisper how she misses my cock when My Angel greets a friend of hers. I glare at the hussy and slip my arm around My Angel to get us the fuck out of there. Tine to join our family. Pronto.

We settle between Lydie seated with Chase and Baz next to Lola at the table laden with delicious food and steaming beverages. One by one, everyone arrives. Our hunger spurred on by the challenging run.

"So what's next on the agenda, Papa Griswold?" Leonie asks, referring to Roger as Clark Griswold from *National Lampoon's Christmas Vacation.*

Everyone laughs at the running joke, knowing Roger and his planned-down-to-the-minute activities for our time in Verbier.

"Hardy har har, Mama Griswold," he responds, not at all bothered by her teasing. "After this deluxe meal, time for a walk through town. And if you are good… we'll spend the afternoon soaking in the thermal baths at Lavey-les-Bains. *Bien?*"

"Ah, *oui, Mon Cœur!*" Leonie exclaims, clapping her hands and doing a shimmy in her chair.

"Spa Time!" Lydie laughs. "Now I can definitely get on board with that agenda item!"

The girls—including our mothers—chatter on about the benefits of the baths and the beauty products they prefer. The guys turn to talk about the sporting activities Roger has on the list. I'm all for the snowmobiling but decline the off-piste run. Priorities!

The sounds of shouts reach us from the front of the lodge. As the hullabaloo intensifies, people gather at the railings of the deck to get a better view. Whispers of a major crash and an intensive injury make me rise from my seat to get more information.

"They say she hit a patch of ice and flew off the trail headlong—"

"—only the tree stopped her from—"

"*C'est horrible!*"

"I hear she damaged her spine—"

Fuck. Me.

A shudder rips through me as memories of me flying

over the embankment on my Ducati. Then the spinal injury followed by the coma bombards my mind.

"Pray she makes it—"

I shake my head to clear the fog, then continue to the entry of the lodge. A helicopter appears from the left, heading towards the medics surrounding the rescue snowmobile. Covers over the sled attached at the back obscure the injured woman. Nearby, a man gestures wildly while he speaks into his mobile. Another man comforts a woman who cries in his arms.

My body jerks at the unexpected touch of a small hand on my back. I glance over my shoulder to find My Angel watching me with empathetic eyes. I slide my arms over her shoulders and pull her close to my chest, resting my chin on the top of her head.

Eyes squeezed shut against the images; I let her rock me as she strokes my back and whispers comforting words.

Wind from the helicopter blades buffets us and blows loose snow at our feet.

"Come, my love. Let's get back inside," My Angel says as she circles my waist with one arm while her opposite hand rests on my stomach.

"Wait," I tell her, then turn to watch the helicopter lift off.

The couple hurries away—presumably to the hospital. I take My Angel's hand and rush after them, calling out to get their attention. They pause and face us.

"Excuse us. I'm Malcolm Steele and this is my wife, Starr. I'm sorry about your friend," I start as they nod. "Recently I was in an accident with extensive spinal injuries and a subsequent coma. I can give you the contact information for my lead doctor—Dr. Clint Stevens. He's the best spinal specialist in the world."

They thank me for the doctor's contact information, and we offer our prayers for the woman.

Before we return to the lodge, I sent a text message to Dr. Stevens to apprise him of the situation. He responds in moments and promises to reach out to the spinal specialist at the hospital nearby. With their permission, he can assist in the woman's case. I thank Dr. Stevens and ask him to let me know if he has any difficulties. My heart goes out to the woman. I don't want anyone to not have the best medical help possible.

"You are a good man, Malcolm."

My Angel's soft words reel my drifting mind back to the present. I attempt a smile, but my thoughts are in overdrive.

"What happened?" Baz asks as he approaches us with Roger at his side.

I fill them in, and they agree it was good of me to offer the couple Dr. Stevens' information. Since they helped my father to organize the best team in the world for me, they know the importance of getting the right doctors in place at the onset of a spinal injury.

As we rejoin the others, my mind continues to work out the situation. A thought niggles that begs me to suss it out. While we fill everyone in, my mobile vibrates with a text message: Dr. Stevens confirms he's in touch with the family and will help them.

I close my eyes to offer a silent prayer of thanks for the doctor and of healing for the woman.

Roger's intense stare meets mine when I open my eyes. *The Responsible* cocks his eyebrow questioningly. As the middle child, he's always been sensitive to his siblings, and the need to make sure we're okay resonates within him as much as it does within Baz.

I smile and incline my head.

Roger nods in understanding. Then he claps his hands for everyone's attention.

"Time to move to the next item on our New Year's Day agenda, folks. Right this way!" Roger announces with a smirk as like a tour guide, he directs us to leave the lodge.

We laugh at his antics and head to the G-Wagens for a stop at the chalets before we go to the thermal baths.

Yeah, time for some much-needed relaxation in the idyllic setting surrounded by fragrant pine trees and the snow-capped Swiss Alps that Lavey-led-Bains offers.

* * *

"What's on your mind, son?"

Morgan, my mother, Baz, Roger, My Angel, and her parents sit with me in the study, eager to learn the reason I called a meeting the morning of New Year's Day.

At the ring of midnight, I kissed my adorable babies, then left the party to make love to my beautiful wife. After-wards, my mind returned to the puzzle, yet to be solved. The niggle from earlier demanded I figure it out.

So while My Angel slept in a sex-induced coma, I let my mind do its thing. The pieces fell in to place little by little until the 1000-piece puzzle completed itself.

"STEELE Spine."

I allow the name of my new foundation to roll off of my tongue, pleased with the sound. My eyes make contact with each pair, staring at me quizzically.

Okay, so the puzzle—framed and hung on the wall—sits prominently in my mind but not in theirs. Yet.

"STEELE Spine is my new foundation dedicated to spinal research, technological advancement, and treatment with a division to support people who suffer from injuries and cannot afford the best medical care," I pronounce.

Then I shift on the sofa to face my father.

"Dad, you did an incredible thing when you organized the best doctors, researchers, and physical therapists from around the world to heal me. The section of the hospital you had them design a custom facility dedicated to me and to my recovery has the latest equipment and treatments. Even after the initial setup, prototypes arrived and with the team having the freedom to explore their ideas, I was able to be their tester. Hell, the trial neurostimulation therapy the medical team created was an undeniable game changer!" I tell him.

Standing, I raise my arms out to the sides and spin in a circle.

"Look at me! Who would have thought I'd ever recover? It's because of you, Dad. And all of you with your prayers and support,"—I sit and clasp My Angel's hands in mine—"Without you I wouldn't be here now. I want to pay it forward. Give others a second chance at life… at love."

She sobs as tears roll down her cheeks.

I smooth them with the pad of my thumb and tuck her into my side as I face the others.

Even their eyes shine with tears.

"Excellent idea, Malcolm," Peace says in the silence. "So many people can benefit from STEELE Spine. Case in point, the woman injured yesterday. You put her family in touch with Dr. Stevens. Once your foundation goes live, more people will have access to his team's brilliance."

My father crosses the room to pull me into a fierce hug.

"Yes, son. Your mother and I are proud of you and of the thought you put behind STEELE Spine. We will support you in every way," he says gruffly when he releases me.

Everyone adds their impressions of my foundation and volunteer their time and resources.

"I'd be happy to arrange a meeting with STEELE Foundation's team to guide the creation of STEELE Spine. Perhaps while you're in New York?" my mother asks when she hugs me. Her organizational skills and experience rise to the forefront.

I smile down at her and respond, "Thanks, Mom. You have the most knowledge of foundations. So any help you can give to me will be appreciated greatly."

She returns my smile and agrees to be my guru.

We chat some more then everyone goes about their day.

I place a hand on My Angel's elbow to stop her as she walks towards the door.

"Hey, babe, I hope you don't mind I didn't speak with you about the foundation first. I wanted to surprise you with the rest of our family," I tell her earnestly.

She wraps her arms around my waist, squeezing tight and buries her face in my chest. Her warmth seeps through my cashmere turtleneck as I pull her close. Coconut and frangipani fill my lungs as I breathe in her tantalizing fragrance.

"My love, you amaze me with your resilience, perseverance, and thoughtfulness. I sensed you had something on your mind, but I knew you would share it with me when you were ready. So, no, I'm not upset with you at all. In face the exact opposite. STEELE Spine—Strength in its Support," she says as she beams at me.

My heart thumps against my ribcage. My Angel gets me always. I should have known not knowing first wouldn't bother my free-spirited wife.

I nuzzle the tip of my nose to hers.

"Thank you, my love. And you created the slogan!" I chuckle.

She giggles and says, "I know you didn't just marry me for my pussy, Mr. Steele!"

Now my cock thumps against the zipper of my jeans...

STARR

"*Wiggle your fingers. Wiggle your toes. Allow your awareness of your surroundings to return as you lift to a comfortable sitting position slowly; eyes remain closed. Bring your palms together at heart center; repeat the sound of the Earth with me three times. Aum… Aum… Aum… Bow your head; Namaste.*"

"Namaste," I return as I bow to the divine in Anita.

"And cut!" The video director proclaims. "Great shots today, ladies!"

Anita finished teaching a prenatal yoga session to me for our program collaboration in her private studio at Norman Green's Elite Training Facility Paris—her husband's luxury gym in partnership with STEELE International.

Over eleven years ago, Roger met Norman in Las Vegas at a party at STEELE LV after his final KO match. He told Roger he promised his girlfriend, now wife Anita, he would stop with that fight. He was at the top of his game with no more to prove. Norman said it's better to leave on high than get carted away low.

Roger offered him the opportunity to open his chains of

branded gyms globally through STEELE's Entertainment Properties Division. One for underprivileged youth and another as exclusive elite training facilities for the über-wealthy and star athletes. Anita has her eponymous full-service yoga studios in each Facility location besides the food services in both chains.

Now she includes Starr Light Fitness and Wellness locations and fitness retreats as her client handling our cafés, offering meal plan delivery service to clients, and cooking demonstrations at the retreats. Our clients rave about Anita's skills gained through her culinary training at acclaimed Le Cordon Bleu in Paris.

And after a morning of recording sessions, I can't wait to have lunch. Mini Malcolms 2.0 need sustenance!

"Well, that's it for today, Starr. You did amazing, and I'm sure our subscribers will enjoy part two of our prenatal program! You're moving well with excellent coordination and balance. How do you feel now that we finished?" Anita asks. Her chocolate velvet brown eyes study me like the doula she is for me.

I rub my babies bump and grin. Our subscribers loved what Anita and I thought would be a one-off prenatal yoga program they could stream at home. She thought of the collaboration while I was pregnant the last time to increase our viewer bases. And really, to keep me busy after Malcolm told me he needed space...

A shake of my head dispels those negative thoughts. Then I glance at my engagement ring and wedding band as I cradle Mini Malcolms 2.0. That was in the past. We have an unimaginable present and a future filled with more happiness ahead of us. We're determined to focus on the positive.

"Fantastic! As always, your sequences flow so well. Our Zoom sessions are fine, but nothing beats time with you in person. Especially in your gorgeous studio. I love coming here," I respond, spreading my arms to encompass the room.

Anita's studio reminds me of the tranquil ones at my ashram in Rishikesh, India, where I've gone since I was a teenager. The interior's natural materials of stone, wood, and bamboo, warm ambient lighting, and bright yet sophisticated pops of color for the mats and accessories set the peaceful mood. As you enter the space, you forget we're in the still in Paris' bustling business district instantly.

"Good, since we have two more days of shooting! The preliminary footage looks great. After lunch, we'll review what the editor sent for our approval," Anita says as we leave her studio.

After the holidays, Malcolm and I decided to use Paris as our base for business in Europe. He's traveling to Germany, Spain, Italy, and Montenegro to check on his Entertainment Division's projects. I'm staying put while I partner with Anita and meet with Anton and his development team on the status of SLFW's expansion. Since I'll go on maternity leave—again—I want to get as much done as possible now.

Hence the back-to-back filming days for the yoga streaming program.

Anita and I head to the locker room for quick showers before we go upstairs to the rooftop bistro for lunch. It's clear and sunny; a perfect crisp winter's day. In the summer, the staff withdraws the retractable glass roof into its casing. Now the sun filters in through the panes.

"Ciao, *mes sœurs*! How was your filming?" Leonie greets us with double kisses and hugs. "You're as bad as I was working while pregnant with twins, Starr Steele! How does your husband feel about that? Not good, *non*? Roger drove me crazy! So I can imagine Malcolm most definitely…"

I give Leonie an extra squeeze as my heart swells with love for her calling us her sisters affectionately. And for knowing her brother-in-law so well. Who has told me to slow down or else he'll bind me to our bed until I give birth. I giggle at the thought. I could prove promising…

Over the years, along with Lola and Haley, the five of us have grown from friends to the sisters we never had and always wanted. It reminds me of Shelley's sisterhood with Lucie, the Jackson Matriarch. They met as young women in New York City and became fast friends before they married their billionaire husbands and had children who went on to consider themselves cousins. As they say, not sharing DNA doesn't keep their families from being a close-knit group. And that's how my girls and I are now.

"Well, after the night Malcolm and I had at LEVELS Paris, I needed to limber up my sore muscles and re-center my mind… that he blew!" I laugh, mimicking my head exploding.

Leonie and Anita—both members with their husbands—nod knowingly.

"Ah, yes, the post-coital yoga session will fix you every time. I need to add a class to the schedule!" Anita quips.

"*Oui!* And it'll book up fast for instant gratification!" Leonie giggles, then snorts until tears spill from her glowing amber eyes.

Anita and I join in her infectious laughter.

After the server takes our orders of mixed greens and grilled chicken or salmon, we return to more serious topics.

"So, what do you think of my latest Lola's Coterie prenatal designs?" Leonie asks. "Your boobs look amazing in this bra. It's from the collection, *non?*"

While she was pregnant with The Twins, Lola asked her to create exclusive prenatal and postnatal collections of sexy yet functional lingerie and loungewear. Leonie has been the face of the brand since its inception, thanks to Luc's introduction of the two women. *The Lion* megamodel brought her fashion credibility to the company and helped Lola to catapult it into the realms of much sought after high-end retailers.

For the last few years, Leonie's collections sell out as soon as they're put on preorder. I'm just as hooked as the others. I love every single piece!

"Thanks to you! The balconette gives my boobies an extra boost, and the front closure makes it easy to breast-feed Mini Malcolms," I respond. "Plus, Malcolm enjoys the easy access!"

Anita giggles and shakes her head while Leonie sits back smugly.

"*Voilà!* Mission accomplished," she smirks.

The rest of our conversation turns to our children and SLFW's upcoming fitness retreats. With me preggie, Anita plans to guest co-host the events with Adrienne like she did for me last time. I cannot wait to get back on the road. It's been too long since I led a retreat. They're my favorite part of being an instructor. I get to interact with people beyond my studio on Beverly Hills. It's great!

Leonie and I bid Anita goodbye after we review the yoga program film footage in her office. My sister-in-law and I head to Lola's atelier for dress up. Really for work, as I try on more of Leonie's creations for my feedback and her adjustments before the collection goes to the manufacturing stage.

Later we're having dinner with Malcolm and Roger at the three star Michelin restaurant, Kei. Mini Malcolms 2.0 demand delicious Japanese food tonight!

* * *

WARM OLIVE OIL drizzles over my sun-kissed golden brown skin as I lie propped against a nest of pillows on the oversized Hermès towel beneath the trees filled with the ripe fruit. Their fragrant aroma blends with the salty air of the Aegean Sea. Nearby waves lap at the rocky shoreline in a lazy rhythm.

I stretch languorously as Malcolm's big hands massage the oil into my flesh with a sensuous touch.

He trails his long fingers along my flanks; the tips brush the side curve of my breasts, making my nipples pebble tighter. The pressure of his calloused pads form goose-bumps in their wake. He skims my butt cheeks with a feather-light touch.

A brief moment for more olive oil to drip over my body.

Then Malcolm spreads his fingers wide as he drags them along the backs of my thighs. The taut muscles sigh in relief as I relax deeper into the pillow pile. With a gentle touch, he circles the erogenous zone behind my knees. Warm air from his mouth blows across the sensitive area.

I moan softly.

He chuckles wickedly.

Knuckles knead my calves and the soles of my feet to loosen the knots in the overused muscles. The unexpected pain makes me groan. But Malcolm's lips pressed to my heel, followed by the tip of his tongue gliding up the middle of my foot to suck on my big toe sends a shudder through me.

"Mmm… mmm… Malcolm," I murmur, eyes closed in carnal pleasure.

The skin-on-skin connection as he covers my back with his front cocoons me while his hands glide along my arms to the tips of my fingers. More oil coats my skin as he massages the tight muscles of my triceps. Then he planks over me as he laces his fingers with mine and rubs his nose along the side of my neck.

I nearly climax.

"Feel better now, My Angel?" Malcolm rumbles against the shell of my ear.

His massive dick thumps my ass as though seeking entry.

"Even better if you'd make love to me," I purr, turning my head to capture his full lips with mine.

No further invitation needed, Malcolm pours olive oil on to his thick length. I watch over my shoulder impatiently as he rubs it in from root to tip, slowly. His corded forearms flex as his eight-pack abs tighten. The veins on his cock snake around his girth as pre-cum mingles with the fragrant oil. His Prince Albert piercing jewelry balls glint in the sunlight.

"Like what you see, My Angel?" Malcolm asks gruffly.

I lick my lips and nod.

"Such an enticing sight. Help me up, I want to taste you," I respond.

A predatory gleam fills Malcolm's platinum gray eyes as he lifts me into a kneeling position before him. He stands—feet wide apart, muscular thighs flexed, abs taut—ready for me to engulf his turgid dick in my warm, wet mouth.

I brace my hands on his thick thighs and part my lips when he taps the mushroom tip to them. They wrap around his girth as I bring my nose closer to his groin. My gag reflex flutters, but I breathe through my nose and take him deeper down my throat. When his pubic hair brushes my nose, I hum in carnal satisfaction at the feel of every ridge, every vein, and every inch of him.

"Awww…. Fuuuck… Feel… so… good…" Malcolm groans.

His dick lies heavy on my tongue as I roll it around, then withdraw to the tip. I set a steady pace as my head bobs, determined to give him absolute erotic pleasure. It's his turn for bliss. I peek up at him through my lashes when my lips touch his groin again.

Our eyes meet, and Malcolm sucks in a jagged breath.

When I swallow and hum around his girth, his eyes roll back in rhapsody. Unable to relinquish control for long, his firm hand dives into the loose curls, tumbling down my back to guide my pace for his satisfaction. His hips snap as his release draws near, precipitated by the thickening of his impossibly hard dick.

"Fuuuck, Starr!!!" Malcolm's roar punches the balmy air.

A torrent of his hot, salty seed spews down my throat as he grips me by the back of my head to his groin. His massive dick pulses on my tongue with each jet of cum. I swallow every. Single. Drop.

With a feral groan, Malcolm squats before me and cups my flushed face. Wild eyes stare into mine, then he covers my mouth in a savage kiss. His tongue pushes past my teeth and sweeps every corner of my mouth to taste and to conquer. He ends the possessive kiss with nips and licks. Then he sucks his way down my throat and breastbone, leaving his mark.

My back bows when he pulls a peaked nipple into his mouth and worries the sensitive tip with his teeth. He suckles and swallows the milk with zeal as he moans. Two thick fingers tease my swollen clit.

An orgasm builds at the base of my spine. I can already tell it's going to be mind-blowing.

When he drives his fingers deep inside of my pussy, my climax crests, and I ride his digits to the end like the surfers on the Aegean Sea. My screams of passion could shake the olive trees to their roots. Then middle Earth itself as they reach a fevered pitch from the brutal thrust of Malcolm's ginormous dick into my throbbing pussy.

"Uh. Uh. Uh. Uh," I cry out in wild abandon as our flesh smacks together.

"Cum for me, woman. Cum for me now!" Malcolm demands fervently.

He bites my shoulder as he fills me with his seed again. The hot cum drips down my sticky thighs.

Triggered by his release—with a howl—I come undone for my man.

We collapse in a tangle of arms and legs on the blanket, sweaty and panting. Once our labored breathing returns to normal, Malcolm lifts me in his arms effortlessly. He strides through the orchard to the water's edge.

The sparking sea greets us with its cool and refreshing temperature. Sea gulls cry out in the distance—the only witnesses to our skinny dipping. Even so, Malcolm angles my naked body towards his chest until I'm neck deep in the turquoise water. Then he turns me to face out—away from the Greek private island's shoreline.

He surprised me with a trip here for Valentine's Day after we finished our business in Europe. It coincides with our six-month wedding anniversary. I was beyond thrilled.

The secluded, fifteen-acre island features a four-bedroom, six-bath main house, an open-plan beach house, a private church on one end and a Venetian watchtower on the other, a boathouse with piers, and a staff house. The fertile land allows more than just olive trees.

Pistachio trees, a variety of fruit trees including pomegranates, apricots, peaches, almonds, plums, and figs offer tasty morsels. Sturdy pine and cypress trees around the perimeter of the island, as well as hundreds of ornamental bushes of oleanders, bougainvillea, hibiscus, and geraniums add to its unspoiled beauty.

A sated smile spreads across my face as I tip my head back to rest against his chest. The sun blankets us with its warmth. And Malcolm envelopes me with his powerful embrace.

"Happy Valentine's Day, my love," I whisper as our eyes meet.

His sparkle with joy as he brushes his lips on mine and murmurs, "Happy Valentine's Day, My Angel. I love you so much."

MALCOLM

"Listen, take my advice... It's best to leave the women to their activities than to involve yourself in them. And before you ask, no, they won't appreciate your 'help' in any way whatsoever. As the longest married of us, trust me on this one, bro."

"Amen, brother. I couldn't agree more. So newlywed, heed the knowledge of the more experienced of us. Stay out of their way."

"Thank fuck I don't have to worry about this crap..."

My brothers and I chuckle at Harris' response to Baz's advice seconded by Roger on me leaving My Angel and her sisters to their plans for her move into my penthouse at The STEELE Tower. We arrived from Greece two days ago to boxes of her belongings in one of the guest suites. Clothes, shoes, handbags, makeup, the whole kit and caboodle. Not to mention new items for Selina and Elio and Mini Malcolms 2.0.

Instead of freaking out at the vast amount of boxes and the need to put everything in their places, my laid-back wife merely shrugged. Then she called Lola, Leonie, and Haley to give her a hand. They were more than willing to help her. Even my mother and Sun offered to organize the nursery. Leonie reconfigured Selina and Elio's nursery into one for our new twins and converted two guest suites into rooms for our one year olds. Of course she impressed us with her designs—all shades of pinks and cream. My Angel's squeals of delight scared the shit out of me.

We decided to make New York City our primary residence and waited until we arrived here for My Angel to meet with Lola's OB-GYN—Dr. Oscar Rice—for Mini Malcolms 2.0's sex scan. I was more nervous than My Angel. When the doctor announced two girls, it shocked me speechless. Four women at once? Talk about karma…

She must have sensed my surprise because My Angel squeezed my hand and graced me with the most beatific smile. My heart stuttered in my chest. Then tears filled my eyes when Doctor Rice handed the images from the scan to me.

I made a silent vow to never let a man near my three girls until they were forty years old. Take that karma!

Baz also warned me I'd want to rip Dr. Rice's eyes out when he examined My Angel. And boy, was he right. I could barely contain myself. Meanwhile, she was completely blasé about his head between her spread thighs, with his eyes on my pussy. You'd think we were in the Cellar at LEVELS New York and I strapped her to a bench and not an examination table.

So I sit back and clink bottles with each of my brothers as we hang out on the expansive terrace of my penthouse, while My Angel and her sisters handle things.

The spectacular unobstructed view encompasses Central Park to the north, the Hudson River to the west, the East River opposite. The STEELE Tower's remarkable gray-tinted glass mixed-use skyscraper on Fifth Avenue and

Fifty-seventh Street stands in the heart of Billionaires' Row. It serves as our family's residences on the fiftieth through fifty-seventh floors.

My parents live in their duplex penthouse on the fifty-seventh and fifty-sixth floors. Baz and Lola are below in their duplex. The rest of us have floor-through penthouses with mine on fifty-three. Our private family elevator connects our residences to STEELE International's executive floor on twenty-nine.

Our headquarters are on the nineteenth through twenty-ninth floors. The rest of The Tower has commercial and retail spaces and residential properties.

"And the same thing applies when Starr gets out to Steele Southampton. Let her run the show. Give her control or you'll be sorry…" Baz continues with his sage advice.

Again Roger nods and takes a sip of his beer.

"Exactly. When I asked Leonie if she wanted to make changes to our mansion, she was all no, no. The moment she walked in the door, she went on and on about how this would look better like that and that would look better there," Roger shakes his head. "Thanks to Baz's advice, I gave her carte blanche to do as she wished. In the end, all was right in our world. Yup."

"Thank you, oh wise ones," Harris quips.

At the same time, Baz, Roger, and I answer.

"Oh, just you wait and see, Harris!"

"Give it time, bro!"

"You say that now. Just you wait and see. When you least expect it… Whammo!"

He grunts and finishes his beer with a cocky smirk.

I chuckle to myself. We'll see.

* * *

"So, Mr. Steele, we would be grateful for the opportunity to handle STEELE Spine for you. We hope you will allow us the opportunity to bring your extraordinary vision to life and to aid those who can most benefit from the medical care and support STEELE Spine offers."

I turn to my mother to gauge her opinion on this team's ability to manage my new foundation.

We're in the conference room of my offices at STEELE International, Inc. to meet with potential teams to determine the best fit. With my duties at the company, I need the help of capable people to run the foundation. I will remain hands on, but the day-to-day operations will require a dedicated staff.

My mother arranged interviews with several people after she and I met with STEELE Foundation's leaders the other day. They offered sound advice and put us in touch with recruiters who have excellent candidates for the various positions we require. After days of meetings, we've narrowed the finalists to three.

With an imperceptible nod of her head, my mother lets me know the ones before us impress her. I give in to her experience with foundation staff and tell them we'll be in touch shortly. Miles Crawford—my assistant—escorts them to the elevator after we shake hands.

"I believe they will make a good fit for your needs, Malcolm, sweetheart," my mother says when the doors to my conference room close.

"I agree. They appear well informed and have the experience we seek. Do you prefer them over the other two?" I ask.

We spend some time reviewing the three dossiers before we break for lunch. My mom—just like My Angel—doesn't need fancy things, although they enjoy them. So we order delivery from the corner deli. As we nosh on sandwiches and potato chips, we decide to hire the last team.

I'll ask Miles to send them the offer letters. Just in case, we hold the first team on deck should our offer fall through. When Miles leaves us, my mother turns to me.

"Malcolm, I am so proud of you, sweetheart. To take a setback and turn it into an opportunity to help others is commendable," she says, then flicks her shoulders. "Your father and I raised you right!"

We laugh.

But I know she's correct. Never did she allow her children to behave like spoiled, rich kids. We interned at our family's business each summer and during school breaks to learn from the ground up. She and our father made sure we deserved the titles and responsibilities we have now. And both being philanthropists, they encouraged us to give back, too.

I'm the first to establish a foundation outside of STEELE Foundation. Even though each of us has causes we support, SF remains the top priority. Now STEELE Spine. And I'm excited to make a difference in others' lives who experience injuries similar to mine.

"Yes, Mom. You certainly did. And then some," I grin. "Now I have another huge ask of you."

She leans forward with inquisitive dark brown eyes and an arched eyebrow.

"I want to host a fundraising gala at the end of September weeks after your Labor Day event for STEELE Foundation. So no conflict with the dates. I'd love for you to organize the Spine gala, too. Pretty please with sugar on top?" I ask like I did as a kid when I knew I was pushing it with my parents.

Shelley sits back and tilts her head as she considers my request.

Our mother is an exceptional party planner, and if anyone can juggle two major events within weeks of each other, she can. Her two assistants and the vendors she uses ease the burdens for her. After a few minutes, she reaches for her mobile.

"Tabitha, kindly come to Malcolm's offices with Sharon. We have another fundraising gala to plan," Shelley says as she eyes me.

It won't take long for her assistants to arrive. They're upstairs in her home office. If one considers three generously sized rooms an office. An anteroom for two assistants' desks, a sitting area, and a bathroom, a conference room, and her inner sanctum with en suite bathroom comprise Shelley's version of a home office. She runs her private activities from there and her foundation work from that office on the executive floor of the STEELE International corporate office.

"Thanks so much, Mom," I say as I kiss her cheek.

"Well, you know I'll do anything for my babies," she responds with a grin. "Now we get down to business."

I throw my head back and laugh at her abrupt change from motherly to sergeant.

Once her assistants arrive, we discuss my vision and the timeline. My mother thinks a masquerade theme will make a night to generate donations more fun than the typical dinner dance event. Similar to her choice of a Labor Day White Party in Southampton Village culminating in a fireworks display to attract guests. They confirm the gala will meet my end of September date even with only five months to plan. We'll have it at STEELE42 one of our award-winning entertainment venues. It specializes in weddings, parties, and galas for society's best both in the United States and abroad.

I thank my new gala coordinators. Then my mother and

I take my car to the West 30th Street Heliport to fly out to our Hamptons' beach compound. My Angel and her sisters are moving her in to my mansion and she's checking on SLFW Resorts at STEELE Southampton Village's progress. My father and her parents are there too. I'm eager to arrive so I can help—if she lets me. Otherwise, I'll give Nanny Patience the day off and spend Daddy Time with my babies. Well, toddlers since they're one-year-old.

Tomorrow we're celebrating Selina and Elio's birthday. The rest of the family flies in tonight for the festivities. I still can't believe how much Mini Malcolms 1.0 have grown. I used to scoff at parents bemoaning time flying. Now, I understand completely. All the more reason for Daddy Time.

"VERY GOOD, Selina. You're doing well, Elio."

They may do well, but I sure as hell feel sick to my stomach despite their swimming instructors' words of encouragement.

I'm sitting on the bench with a white-knuckle grip on the edge as I watch Mini Malcolms 1.0 during their first lesson at the club's pool. Roger *The Responsible* is alert, but at ease while Rodolphe and Gaspard have their lesson with the two-year-olds. Other parents sit and chat all nonchalant while I can't keep my eyes off of my babies.

And the women can't keep their eyes off of my brother and me. Cue the giant eye roll.

Mothers or nannies, married or single, stare at us openly while they whisper amongst themselves. The sight of two of the STEELE Quaternity—in swim trunks and t-shirts no less—proves too much for the gawkers. When we entered the indoor pool area, silence descended. Then a buzz rose.

After a nod in greeting, Roger and I took seats and focused on our kids.

Who the fuck has time to leer and gossip when your babies are in water deeper than their height?! Give me a break. I have no time.

"Papa! Papa! Regarde moi!" Gaspard calls out when he spies Roger.

He beams as he strides to the edge.

"Excellent travail, Gaspard!" He says as he claps proudly. *"Et toi aussi, Rodolphe!"*

Although identical twins, we can tell them apart by their personalities. Rodolphe has the seriousness of his father, while Gaspard has the playful spirit of his mother. One's eyes watch you with intensity while the others shine with mirth. And we adore them equally!

Frantic splashing draws my attention from my brother and my nephews.

Elio! Fuck!

I run and jump in to the pool as he flounders between two instructors. His head goes under a second time just as I snatch him by the waist. I glare at the two dummies with my son clutched to my chest.

"What the—"

"Malcolm!"

I pivot with a scowl to face Roger, who's standing at the edge of the pool. He shakes his head.

"That's normal. No need to worry," he says calmly, knowing I'm about to go ballistic. "Elio is fine. The Twins behaved the same during their first lessons. Let them finish."

Not placated, I glance around to find Selina. She's watching me from the arms of another instructor. When she waves her little hand and flashes a two-tooth smile at me, my anger subsides. Still carrying her brother, I wade to her and pull her into my arms. I plant kisses on their chubby, golden cheeks and sigh in relief.

My babies are safe and sound.

Thank fuck!

I apologize to the instructors for disrupting the lessons and return Selina and Elio to them, then climb out of the pool.

Roger claps me on the shoulder and smirks.

"You're gonna have gray hair to match your eyes if you stress out like this all the time," he teases.

I grab the wet t-shirt at the back of my neck and yank it off. My arm muscles and my abs flex from the movement. The sound of a gasp makes my eyes jerk in that direction. A brunette gapes at me as her gaze travels from my head to my toes, pausing at my crotch where the wet swim trunks cling to my ample package. The piercing stands out in bas-relief.

Oh, give me a damn break. They must starve these women of a good fuck. I'm off the market. So good luck with that…

Roger snickers as we take our seats again.

I can feel their gazes burning my back as they take in my tattoo. But I ignore them and return to my vigil. I have more important matters to attend to than these horny housewives.

* * *

"WE CLOSED on the Sutton Place duplex in Lola's building. The proximity to the East River gives us the water view we love. It's a sunny, spacious penthouse in a magnificent, Rosario Candela designed building. Leonie agreed to handle the redesign, including a nursery and two bedrooms for

Selina and Elio," Sun says as we eat birthday cake in the living room of my parents' beach house.

"Yes, and the seven-block drive across Fifty-seventh Street from Sutton Place to Fifth Avenue makes for a quick trip to you at The STEELE Tower. We'll be able to take our grandchildren to the zoo in Central Park easily," Peace adds.

Since My Angel and I will live here mostly, her parents decided to become bicoastal. They arranged to work out of their offices in Knight & Knight LLP New York. Their search for a residence took more time given they wanted a penthouse on Sutton Place and those properties come on market rarely.

However, Lola learned of one in her building where she maintains her penthouse, even though she and Baz live in The STEELE Tower. Her realtor keeps her informed of other opportunities in case Lola wants to expand. This residence is on the top two floors and has been owned by one family since the developer erected the building.

"*Oui!* And don't forget Southampton Village. I cannot wait to get started!" Leonie gushes.

"Of course! It was a stroke of luck the family next to the Steele compound moved to Florida and had to sell quickly. Their beachfront property has just the right sized mansion and a caretaker's cottage on it. So our favorite interior designer will handle the gut rehab. Peace and I took a suite at STEELE Southampton for the season or until our renovation completes," Sun tells us.

My Angel leans up from where she's nestled against my side, with Elio on her lap and Selina on mine.

"Mom, you can stay with us. We have plenty of guest suites in our home. Right, Malcolm?" She asks as she glances over at me.

I nod and add, "Certainly. No need for you to stay at the bed-and-breakfast."

Peace shakes his head and presses his palms together at his heart center with a bow.

"Thank you for the offer. But Sun and I don't want to intrude on your new little family. We're fine with our accommodations," he replies.

"Know that you are always welcome," I say as I bow to the light in him.

My father raises his flute of Champagne for a toast.

"Here's to our family being together with East Coast and West Coast homes!" He exclaims as he nods at Peace.

The patriarchs have become friends along with Guy. We're thankful for the growth of our family clan.

MALCOLM

"Ugh! This is when I always get the least attractive. My belly looks like a giant beach ball. My legs tingle and my back aches. Everything is just so damn uncomfortable! On top of that, I'm tired again. And stop looking at me like that, Malcolm Steele! Argh!"

Okay, so Roger and Baz warned me about the third trimester. But damn… My Angel is not having it. At. All.

She refused the nightly massage I give her. She pretty much told me to buzz off and dozed off to sleep curled in a fetal position. When I spooned behind her, she stiffened, then relaxed when I didn't make any sexual advances. Which surprised me since she's been insatiable from the start of our pregnancy.

But hey, I'll take it, especially since I missed being there for her with Mini Malcolms 1.0.

After consulting with my brothers, they informed me My Angel and I are almost overdue for our babymoon. Roger took Leonie to Lucien's Villa die Fiori in Capri at nineteen weeks for seven days, then bought it for her. At twenty-six weeks, Baz surprised Lola with a fourteen-day trip to Bougainvillea Cay he bought for her.

So I knew my game plan: take My Angel some place warm and secluded on the East Coast easily accessible to major hospitals just in case. She can relax without thinking bad about her body changes and the stress of moving, expanding SLFW, raising Selina and Elio, being a new wife, none of the headaches.

I want to give her joy. See her dazzling smile on her gorgeous face. She'll always be a beauty to me!

Now My Angel rests her head on my shoulder as we fly on our Gulfstream G650 bound for STEELE Little Palm Island off the Florida Keys. Within fifteen minutes of take-off, she asked me to join her in the bedroom.

At first I thought she meant for some Mile High action, but she slipped out of her maxi dress and under the covers. As enticing as her round ass in a black lace thong and her grip-worthy hips appeared bent over the bed, I squashed my lascivious thoughts and held her in my arms. Blue balls be damned...

She slept soundly, finally at ease.

I hate to wake her, but we land in ten minutes. She's bound to need to use the restroom and freshen up before we deplane for the brief ride on the resort's water shuttle. I didn't tell her about our destination, only to dress comfortably. I asked Lola and Leonie to shop for her bikinis, sundresses, and sandals. She won't need much else.

"Babe, time to wake up," I murmur as I stroke her soft cheek.

After a bit of coaxing, My Angel wakes and readies herself. When she sits beside me and peeps out the window, a smile spreads across her face.

"The Florida Keys?" She asks.

Of course, being a world traveler, she'd recognize the islands. I nod and she shimmies in her seat.

When we arrive at the resort and spa, the driver takes us to the only beachfront three-bedroom villa on the opposite end of the island to the main property. There's the reception, bar, and restaurant pavilion; close to it is the spa facilities in another pavilion; a pool with a restaurant and a bar next to the general beach. Ten one- and two-bedroom bungalows stand along the shoreline. STEELE Little Palm Island is a boutique property that caters to the affluent who don't have private islands of their own but want the experience.

As the golf cart travels along the paths, My Angel chats with him about the activities and the spa. He's as enthralled by her as me.

I wrap my arm around her shoulder and hold her hand, content to bask in her glory. I won't begrudge him his five minutes. Especially when My Angel glances up at me and kisses my lips. Her sorrel brown eyes dance.

Our single-story villa sits on its private beach with an infinity edge pool, chaise lounges, and a hammock. Palm trees and fragrant flowering shrubs hide it from the rest of the guests. A butler, chef, and a maid greet us. The butler gives us a tour while the maid unpacks our bags and the chef plates our lunch of fresh grilled seafood and vegetables.

By the time we step on to the deck, My Angel seems one hundred percent better. I send a silent prayer of thanks for my sage brothers.

"Oh, Malcolm! This is fantastic! I can't believe you had the girls shop for me! This bandeau bikini is fierce. I don't seem like such a blimp, only sexy!" She exclaims.

My eyes roam over her body. Bouncy silky curls cascading down her back. Lush tits still heavy from breast-feeding and to prepare for Mini Malcolms 2.0. Long, toned legs ending with fire-engine red toenails. My Angel looks good!

While I take in my fill of her beauty, she chatters on about the spa amenities, going for a swim, tonight's salsa dance party, and yoga on the beach in the morning. I grin and nod, equally enthused. We have an entire week to do whatever her heart desires. And I will be sure to fulfill each and every one of them—to the max.

* * *

"Ssssss... Mmmm mmmm... Fuck..."

Slowly, my senses dawn. What I thought was a dream becomes my reality. Hooded eyes open to reveal My Angel astride me, lowering her hot, wet pussy onto my morning wood. Her voluptuous curves steal my breath. Her head thrown back, eyes squeezed shut, mouth slack.

Damn.

I reach for her hips to guide her down my engorged shaft. Each inch draws another hiss from my parted lips.

My Angel feels so damn good...

This is the second morning I've awoken to her taking advantage of my sleeping form but erect cock. And she'll get no complaints from me. No ma'am!

Over the days we've been on our babymoon, My Angel has returned to her usual carefree self. The shadows beneath her sorrel brown eyes have disappeared. The raised shoulders—hunched from stress—lowered after day three. Instead of frowning at the full-length mirror in the bath-room, she grins at it and takes her daily pregnancy selfie. Her prenatal glow adds to her innate beauty.

We've done the entire list of her desires and have a day to spare. She left the agenda blank. But I guess making love to her husband tops the list.

Yessss!!!

"Oh, Malcolm… right there…" My Angel moans as I swivel my hips.

We continue our slow erotic dance melded as one until she can take no more orgasms and I can no longer hold back my release. With one last upward thrust as I hold her still, I erupt deep inside of her greedy pussy. Then pull a sated My Angel into my arms.

THE BRILLIANT SUN glints off of the turquoise waters of the Straits of Florida as the waves lap onto the white sand beach before us. We finished a yoga session and took a dip in the warm water before our couples' massage. The masseuses just set up our tables when we arrived on the deck from a shower—and a steamy romp.

I reach over and skim my fingertips along My Angel's arm. She turns her head and smiles at me as she twines our fingers.

"Hey, baby," she murmurs.

"Hey, My Angel," I respond as I kiss her knuckles. "How do you and my babies feel? You're not uncomfortable, right?"

She yawns, then glances at me sheepishly.

"I take that as your super comfy, yes?" I chuckle.

"Yes, indeed. So good and so serene," she giggles. "This table fits around my babies bump perfectly."

When I made the appointment, the spa manager assure me they could accommodate a pregnant woman's shape and offer a prenatal massage approved by OB-GYNs. I scheduled more treatments from a body scrub to a facial and even a scalp massage to pamper my wife. So today is just the beginning.

"Good. You have a whole lineup of treatments over the

next few days. So get ready for some major indulgences," I tell her.

My Angel nods and sighs as her eyes drift closed.

Absolutely serene. Mission accomplished.

* * *

"THIS IS JUST what I needed! Thank you, my love!"

My Angel's excited peals of laughter make my heart soar. Her dewy, sun-kissed face beams as our bodies grind to the rhythms of the bongos, horns, and guitars blended with the sultry vocals of the live Calypso band.

When she told me she wanted to dance to the Afro-Caribbean music, I called in a favor for the most popular group in Trinidad to fly up and play for us. The resort staff decorated our private beach with bamboo torches, fragrant flowers, a candlelit table set for a delicious seafood dinner, and a stage. It's our last night in paradise, and I want to make it more than memorable.

So I told My Angel to glam it up for the grown and sexy. And boy, did she deliver in spades.

Luxuriant curly hair caught up in a messy bun lengthens her neck where my evening collar, along with her full wedding jewelry on her hand, sparkle in the torchlight. Makeup-free with pouty glossed lips begging to wrap around my more than willing cock. A gold, strapless tube mini dress clings to every one of her bountiful curves with her babies bump on display proudly. So excited by the music, she kicked off her gold strappy sandals to dance in the sand barefoot. My Angel is a stunning vision who rivals any woman on the planet—far from how unattractive she bemoaned before our babymoon.

I'm one lucky man.

"You're welcome, babe. I only want to see you smile, not upset with yourself. Promise?" I ask with a cocked eyebrow.

My Angel lifts her arms around my neck and gyrates her plump ass against the tops of my thighs. I bend my knees to press my hardened cock to the cleft of her ass cheeks and match her erotic rhythm. We continue to sway as we lose ourselves in the other.

Between sets, the singers invite My Angel to the mic. She joins them for an impromptu serenade that makes me want to snatch her from the stage and ravage her. Instead, a cocky smirk spreads across my face.

Yeah, that's my Hot Mama!

"Well, I am always one for business before pleasure. *Da, khlopushka?*"

Anton smirks at Adrienne, then chuckles wickedly when she sputters her sip of Château Lafite Rothschild Pauillac. He wipes the errant droplets of wine from her lips with his thumb, sucks the digit into his mouth, and licks his lips, never taking his glacial blue eyes from her green feline ones.

The seductive gesture darkens Adrienne's complexion from a buttery pecan to a rosy pink from her hairline to her décolletage. She gapes at Anton, then snaps her lips together as she glares at him while dabbing the rest of the wine with her linen napkin.

"*Udovol'stviye sub"yektivno, da?*" She replies in Russian fluently before translating for me. "*Pleasure is subjective, yes. It appears as though Anton forgets his table manners…*"

Malcolm covers his chuckle with a sip of his wine as his eyes flit between the pair.

Anton throws his head back and laughs uproariously.

"*Mne nravitsya, kogda ty srazhayesh'sya so mnoy,*

khlopushka," he says, then leans to her ear and continues in a whisper. "*YA delayu menya tverdym, kak skala.*"

Malcolm chokes on his wine and puts his glass down on the table with a clatter. His eyes bulge, and he speaks something to Anton in Russian.

"My apologies, Starr, I meant no offense to you," he tells me with contriteness. "You, *khlopushka,* know how true my statement is, *da?*"

The last question he smirks at Adrienne, and she shakes her head with pursed lips.

"I'm sure whatever you two are up to makes me no never mind! You can settle the matter later in one of the rooms in the Cellar," I respond, giggling.

Adrienne turns crimson, and Anton guffaws again. Other patrons glance in our direction.

The four of us came to LEVELS New York for dinner at LEVELS 4 Restaurant—business—and for a bit of pleasure later. Even after experiencing the other club locations, the flagship ranks as my favorite still.

Situated in Manhattan's Meatpacking District, Malcolm told me he and Lucien chose the historic location as a play on the area's name. Put a club where men pack their meat into willing women and willing men allow women to pack them with their toys. The theme for the lobby is minimal and industrial. The fixtures and furniture that appear well worn are high-end, modern replicas used to add authenticity without the grime of old pieces.

On the third floor, the bar bustles as usual with the crème de la crème of society. They hobnob with top-shelf drinks. Seating ranges from the leather and black metal stools at the long, reclaimed-wood-covered bar to the dozen high-top tables styled to match. The bar along the right wall features a floor-to-ceiling mirrored wall of shelves of only the best spirits and wines—most are from the Jackson labels. The bartenders serve signature cocktails. Tables on the left complete the layout of the open-plan room. A path between the two areas leads to the restaurant's maître d' station.

Patrons eat delicious meals prepared by chefs trained by Lucien. The menu offers the expected fare typical of Continental cuisine of pastas, meat, and steaks with favorable sauces. *The Sexy Chef* complements the usual dishes with appealing specials that change daily to keep the choices fresh and habitual guests from getting bored.

Plus the client care is impeccable. Model-perfect and well-groomed servers wear spotless, all-black uniforms of a long-sleeved shirt, pants, butcher apron, and shiny Oxford shoes or heels—the de rigueur fashion for LEVELS employees. They provide top-notch professionalism and knowledge of the dishes and wine selections.

Just as with the lobby and the bar, the décor stays true to the original use of the warehouse. Clean lines and antique pieces for the decor: floor-to-ceiling mullion windows allow natural light to filter through to the room during the day, now dimly lit for dinner; light fixtures hang from the ceiling where the dark metal duct work and copper pipes are visible; exposed brick walls; the floor poured concrete; the well-heeled patrons sit on antique leather chairs at wooden tables. The guys really did a great job with their enterprise. Few can pull off and maintain a high-end, respectable establishment, especially one that's a combo BDSM/dance club with a restaurant.

I shake my head and take a bite of my Steak Frites. Delicious, I moan to myself as the succulent meat melts in my mouth.

"Yes, Anton, keep your sexcapades to the other levels and away from my wife's ears," Malcolm rumbles as he spears an asparagus with his fork.

Adrienne cocks her head to dare Anton to respond, then huffs when he winks at her.

I rub Malcolm's muscular thigh beneath the table to soothe my caveman and brush my lips against his ear.

"As long as we keep ours in the Cellar… Sir," I purr, so only he can hear me.

He turns to me with platinum gray eyes darkened to coal by lust and a wicked smirk.

He leans over to bring his full lips against my ear and murmurs, "That I promise, Little One."

My body quivers as his warm breath fans across my cheek. Malcolm never ceases to arouse me, even with a simple vow of pleasure. I trail my fingernail along the growing length of his dick, then tug a ball on his piercing. His dick jumps as he groans softly.

"Naughty Girl," he admonishes me as his sizable hand covers mine.

"Business first, remember?" Anton smirks pointedly.

Malcolm inclines his head in acknowledgement and says, "Touché, my friend."

"Well then, may I have your attention?" I ask, then continue when everyone nods. "Adrienne, you have been my best friend since Stanford B-School and my CMO and general manager of Starr Light Fitness & Wellness Beverly Hills for nine years. From the beginning when SLFW was my dream to the expansion with the international retreats and the resorts you never failed to stand by my side and make SLFW flourish."

I pause to dab the tears in my eyes—damn hormones.

Malcolm rubs my back and kisses my cheek.

"Starr, do not tell me something is wrong with you!" Adrienne exclaims as she reaches for my hand across the table.

I shake my head and clear my throat.

"Oh no, I'm fine! Ignore the hormonal waterworks," I laugh, squeezing her hand. "With Selina and Elio and now Mini Malcolms 2.0 on the way plus more expansion plans for SLFW, I realize I cannot go on as the CEO alone."

I raise my glass of iced lemon ginger tea and continue, "So this decision was a straightforward decision. Adrienne, I would like to offer you a partnership and the position of co-CEO!"

She gasps while Malcolm and Anton clap, then raise their wine glasses in a toast.

"You deserve it, Adrienne!"

"Congratulations, *khlopushka!*"

After a few moments, I quiet them down and raise my eyebrow at a silent Adrienne who sits back staring at me.

"Do you accept?" I ask, hoping she answers in the affirmative. "I mean, just don't leave a preggie lady hanging, no pressure!"

She jumps up and gives me a hug as she agrees wholeheartedly. Servers appear with chilled bottles of Krug Clos d'Ambonnay Champagne and a variety of decadent desserts.

"We'll drink for you, Starr!" Anton teases.

Adrienne adds, "We know it's your favorite bubbly, but oh well, partner!"

"Awww... Don't tease My Angel. Although I must say you are missing out, babe!" Malcolm chuckles.

I laugh and sip my tea, still in a pretty crystal glass.

"And... since I'm based in Southampton Village, you can head the Western Division and I'll head the Eastern Division. Malcolm and I will still be bicoastal. But this way I won't have to travel as much—especially with a brood of four babies! Sounds good to you, Adrienne?" I ask.

She grins and nods.

"Absolutely! It makes the most sense. What about Márcia?" She asks.

Márcia Souza—my administrative assistant and a yoga substitute teacher—acts as another integral part of SLFW. I spoke with her earlier today, and she agreed to move to the Hamptons wanting a change in scenery. She told me as long as she's near the water, she's fine. Since she grew up in Rio de Janeiro, then moved to LA, she prefers to be close to the ocean like me.

She's a Brazilian petite spitfire who says the crazy New York City streets won't frighten her since she's the Queen of Capoeira. I laughed and told her she won't have to worry about that out on the Island!

I recall my conversation with her to the others, and they agree she can handle herself with her defensive moves. Márcia even impressed Borya *The War Defender* MMA champion.

We spend the rest of the time chatting and enjoying one another as we indulge in the tasty morsels and sip Champagne—well, and tea. The boys discuss the merits of various martial arts while Adrienne and I talk about an upcoming retreat in Marbella she's leading with Anita.

I have to admit I'm a tad bit jealous of them enjoying the beauty of Spain's Costa del Sol. Adrienne promises to send photos and videos to make me feel as though I'm with them and the clients. Then I promise her I'll back as soon as Mini Malcolms 2.0 can travel internationally!

So engrossed in our conversation, we startle when Malcolm and Anton rise from the table. We glance up at the men towering over us.

They have determined expressions on their handsome faces. Fierce, hooded eyes stare down at their prey as they place hands on our chairs.

Adrienne and I turn to each other and giggle as they help us rise. Then we shiver when the Alpha Doms murmur their vows of carnal pleasure in our ears.

The night proves full of vows to keep...

"YOU LOOK divine tied to my cross, Little One. All trussed up and ready for your Dom to use you well..."

After we left the restaurant, we walked through Peepshow and down the stairs to the double doors of the Cellar.

Each time I enter the BDSM dungeon, I'm awed by the expansive, grand hall, austere in design. A multi-beamed high ceiling; cobblestone floors; brick walls; lighting that resembles flickering torches in brackets on the walls and in metal stands scattered around the room; an assortment of what looks like Medieval torture devices placed in clusters.

My gaze bounced from one area to another. An older man in one of the several hanging bondage stockades, his head thrown back in pure ecstasy. His engorged dick eagerly sucked by a younger man on his knees. A blindfolded woman in a swing, her thighs glistening with her pussy juices, and stretched wide to accommodate the large man standing between them, aligning her core to his massive cock. Several men and women attached to hooks hanging from the ceiling in varied positions, being whipped by Doms and Dommes with canes, floggers, and paddles extending from their hands. Still others led naked subs by leashes while they crawled on their hands and knees to one of the partitioned rooms for a bit of privacy. Here and there voyeurs stood watching, mesmerized by the decadent sexual activities.

Adrienne and Anton stopped at the bar for mocktails while Malcolm guided me towards the back.

We're in one of the Cellar's alcoves separated from the main hall by heavy blood-red velvet curtains held by metal links suspended from the ceiling. Within each alcove, a multitude of BDSM toys and equipment offer various levels of pleasure and pain. Malcolm chose an alcove with my favorite piece—the St. Andrew's Cross.

The standing wooden cross has red, suede-lined leather cuffs on the four corners for wrists and ankles dominates the area; a leather bench is along the stone wall; an antique wooden chest sits beside the bench; various whips, crops, and a few paddles hang from hooks. Some paddles are smooth wood, while others have holes or studs on their surfaces. The sizes vary from as large as a cricket bat to as small as an oven mitt.

A glance over my shoulder reveals My Alpha Dom chose a flogger with a woven leather shaft and multiple soft leather tails ending in tiny knots. I shudder and flex my pussy walls in anticipation of its erotic bite on my heated skin. My head drops with a breathy moan as my mind creates visuals of what's to come.

"Tell me your safewords, Little One."

My Alpha Dom's command jolts me back to the alcove.

"Green to continue; yellow for a moment; red to stop all play at once, Sir," I pant.

The unexpected soft caress of the flogger on my hip makes me gasp.

"We will push your limits, so be sure to choose the appropriate safeword. I will respect your wishes. Remember, the sub holds all the power, not the Dom. Do you understand, Little One?" He croons in my ear.

I nod.

Then yelp.

"Words, Little One. I will have your words," my Alpha Dom demands with another flick of his wrist.

The tails slip around my inner thigh while the knots find my wet pussy lips.

"Fuck!" I cry out as my back bows, and I pull at the restraints. "Yes, Sir!"

He chuckles wickedly and murmurs, "Happy to have your full attention, Naughty Girl. Now. Hold. Your. Position."

With experienced snaps of his wrist, the flogger punctuates each word as the tails and knots land on the top curve of my ass precisely. My Alpha Dom continues to warm my body up with increasing stings in a pattern that traces my back, ass, and thighs. Even my calves get a taste.

I concentrate on keeping still, but my engorged clit needs relief. Tears prick my eyes, more from the carnal ache than from the pain. I cry out to beg for permission to cum.

The blows stop, and I sag with the belief he will reward me for maintaining form. But my head jerks up when I hear the clipped strides of his A. Testoni Oxfords carry him across the alcove. Another glance over my shoulder reveals him rummaging through the chest. With a satisfied grunt, he rises and returns to stand behind me.

I squeal when three of My Alpha Dom's fingers smack my pussy lips and the tips catch my sensitive clit. Seconds later, a large, ribbed dildo breaches my soaked folds in one thrust.

"Cum," he growls.

My head falls back as my eyes roll up. A guttural scream pours from my mouth as my pussy creams on the toy fucking me with wild abandon. Wave after wave rocks through me. Shameful squelching sounds along with the musky scent of my arousal fill the air around us.

The dildo drops to the floor, and the flogger resumes.

Stunned by the sudden change, I flinch.

"Ah, ah, ah, Naughty Girl. Hold your position or safeword," My Alpha Dom reprimands as the butt of the flogger traces my ass crack enticingly. "The choice is yours."

I clench my fists, determined to go on and my butt cheeks for more ass play.

"Green, Sir," I grit out, head high.

He chuckles wickedly.

Ten more minutes of tortuous shifts between erotic pain and pleasure kept on the edge with not one more orgasm. And I'm ready to explode. Face wet from tears and skin reddened with his marks, My Alpha Dom removes my feet then my wrists from the cuffs.

My climax-starved body drops limp into his powerful arms as he cradles me to his bare chest. Questions swirl as I wonder when he disrobed and where is he taking me. But they're shoved aside when he lays me in a fetal position on the leather bench. With a sigh, I sink into oblivion as his strong fingers smooth a cool gel onto my heated back, buttocks, thighs, and calves.

"Promise kept, Little One," he murmurs against my ear.

Even in subspace, my body quivers in response to My Alpha Dom.

STARR

I toss and turn all night. No matter the position, I cannot get comfortable. The restlessness drives me crazy. Malcolm tried to comfort me, but I wasn't having it. At. All.

It became so bad, he moved to the sofa in the sitting room of the primary bedroom in our penthouse at The STEELE Tower. I tried to persuade him to stay in bed with me. But he didn't want to disturb the bits of sleep that I got. Well… I realize I can't sleep if he's not lying next to me. His presence comforts me. But not him holding me right now.

As I pace back and forth past the double doors to the sitting room, I glimpse Malcolm asleep on the sofa. His long limbs are not at all comfortable as he flips from one side to the other. At one point, his blanket falls off. I pause mid-stride to see if he will reach for it. But he doesn't. So I waddle over to pick it up and drape it back over his sleeping form.

I sit on the chair opposite the sofa and watch him for a moment. I must have dozed off because I awake in bed, and Malcolm is no longer on the sofa. With a groan from the pain in my achy back, I get up gingerly and follow the sound of water to our en suite bathroom.

Malcolm stands at his vanity, shaving two-day stubble from his handsome face. I lean on the doorjamb and watch my man. Even doing banal tasks, he's sexy as fuck. When he nicks his chin for the second time, I go to him.

"Hey, babe. I didn't know you were awake. It's early, you need to go back to sleep"—he raises his hand to stop me from speaking—"And the chair is no place for you to get your rest, Hot Mama. You and Mini Malcolms 2.0 need to go back to bed. Now."

He cocks his head and raises his eyebrow at me, and I mimic his actions with a pout.

"Nor is the sofa for you, Mr. Steele. You need your rest, too."

I take the razor from his hand and move him back from the sink. I squeeze my babies bump between him and my ass against the counter.

Malcolm lifts me and settles me on top of it with ease. I smile at how strong he is again and say a silent pray of gratitude for his recovery. Then refocus on my task.

"Now, allow me, Mr. Steele," I say as I shave his face, careful not to nick his skin.

Malcolm closes his eyes and rests his hands on either side of my hips.

Silently, with a steady hand, I remove the stubble from his cheeks and chin. I rinse the razor and apply fresh shaving cream each time. When I shave all the hair, I put a warm wet cloth over his face. After I'm done, I pat it and kiss the tip of his nose.

Malcolm rinses the rest of the cream off his face and kisses me on the tip of my nose in return.

"Thank you, Mrs. Steele," he says with a warm smile, his gray eyes shine like liquid platinum in his gorgeous face.

I cup his chin and pull his lips to mine, not satisfied with a mere peck. No, Sir!

Malcolm covers my mouth with his and takes control of the kiss as he tilts my head for the best angle. Our tongues dance, and I moan in appreciation. The hormones rage and demand much more.

"What do you want, Little One?" He asks huskily with eyes now darkened by desire.

"You, my love, I want you," I purr, tilting my neck to give him better access as he trails open-mouthed kisses from my ear to my collarbone.

"Mmmmmm… Then you shall have me, Little One," he growls.

Malcolm grips my hips and slides my ass closer to the edge of the vanity. He skims his hands up my spread thighs, taking my silk negligee with him. He lowers his mouth to my puckered nipple and suckles it hard until I writhe on the counter.

He chuckles wickedly against my heated skin.

"Needy, are you?"

I growl and put my fingers in his hair to pull his mouth back to my sensitive bud. Then I groan when he nips it into his wet mouth.

"Yeeesss," I hiss as I drop my head back and lean on my other hand, still cradling him to my breast.

Malcolm continues to lavish attention on each one, driving my carnal lust through the stratosphere and higher.

My pussy clenches on air with each tug. I need more! I sit forward and cup his heavy balls in the palm of my hand, kneading them.

He growls and snaps his hips in sync with my erotic massage. Malcolm loosens the tie on his black silk pajama bottoms, and they slip down his hips to puddle on the floor.

He takes the base of his erect dick in hand and shifts me forward until he impales me on his ginormous shaft.

We groan in unison as he breaches my carnal core. Then take a few breaths as my pussy stretches to accommodate his girth.

Our rhythm is slow and deep. We allow our bodies to connect and to speak for us. Only our moans fill the air, along with the musky scent of our lovemaking.

Malcolm's cock swells, and I squeeze my inner muscles to draw out his release. With a shout he cums, and I follow right behind him with a strangled cry hampered by my teeth on his shoulder. After the intensity of our release, I need to ground myself or float away.

"I love you, My Angel," he murmurs against my damp neck.

I shiver from his breath and bury my face in his silky hair.

"ARE you sure you're okay alone with Selina and Elio? Why don't you let me call my mother or Anita to spend the day with you? You've been out of sorts since last night."

Malcolm's concerned eyes peer at me as I wait with him for the private elevator to take him to his offices downstairs.

I wave my hand at him and smile.

"Don't worry, my love! I am fine; I promise. Go conquer the world, hotshot," I tease as the elevator doors ping open.

Malcolm shakes his head and strides inside. He gives me one final questioning look before the doors close.

With a sigh, I shut the front door and lean against it for a moment. I'm not due for another three days, so I chalk the tiredness up to being ready to give birth soon.

We're staying in the city until Mini Malcolms 2.0 make their appearance. Then we'll go to the Southampton Village compound. Everyone is in the city to await their arrival—my parents, the Steele clan, the Beaulieus, the Greens, and Blair. Adrienne and Billie will fly in together from the West Coast once I go into labor. I love how they circle around to support Malcolm and me. Our family and friends are the best!

I make my way back to the playroom and place the monitor on the table when I enter.

"Mama!"

"Mama!"

Selina and Elio greet me as they toddle over with arms raised.

"Hello, my little loves! You missed me that much? Wow!" I exclaim as they hug my legs. "Well, I missed you even more, sweethearts!"

The morning passes quickly with a few calls from Malcolm, our mothers, and Anita. Lola and Leonie stopped by before they went to a photoshoot for Lola's Coterie. Obviously, Malcolm put the word out to check in on me throughout the day. That man of mine, I laughed to myself each time a call came in.

"Ready for lunch, Selina and Elio?" I ask as I stand from the glider and reach for their hands.

They clap and babble as we make our way to the kitchen. I settle them at the banquette and head to the pantry. As I reach for the bread, a sharp pain stabs my lower back and radiates down my legs. A pitiful whimper escapes my mouth. I clutch my belly with one hand and grapple at the wall with the other when I realize I'm falling.

I drop to my knees with a pained cry. The bracelet on my wrist beeps. A second later, my mobile rings in the pocket of my sweater.

Malcolm. Thank God.

Harris—the tech wiz—created a monitor to track vitals,

particularly for erratic or elevated heart rates that deviate from the norm. Plus, it has a fall detection and a GPS tracker for location of the wearer. He gave one to me. The app connects to the monitor, then alerts Malcolm, Harris, Anita, and my OB-GYN Dr. Rice.

I shift to sit on my butt and accept the call on my mobile.

"Starr! What's happening?!" Malcolm demands over the speakerphone.

I start to speak, but another cramp hits me and knocks the breath from my lungs. Instead, a pitiful moan spills from my lips as I grimace.

All morning my back continued to bother me, but I just assumed it was just my body getting ready for birth. So I ignored the pangs.

Wrong.

"I'm on my way up!!" Malcolm shouts and disconnects the call.

Elio appears at the pantry door followed by Selina. They stare at me, then toddle over to hug me as though they sense my distress. I cradle them to myself and try to hold back the tears from the pain.

"STARR!!!"

My head jerks up to find Malcolm, Anita, and Shelley bustling into the pantry. Malcolm's face blanches.

"What... What's wrong?" I ask as my eyes flit among them.

"Selina, Elio, come with grandmommy, sweethearts. We'll read your favorite books in the playroom," Shelley says as she takes their hands, then looks at me and the floor beneath me. "You'll be okay, Starr, honey."

My heart flips and I gasp when I see red-tinged fluid staining the seat of my white leggings.

Everything fades: Malcolm barking into his mobile;

Selina and Elio crying as Shelley leads them away; Harris appearing behind Malcolm.

"Starr! Snap out of it!"

I turn my head to Anita.

"Starr, listen. We have to move you. The babies are coming. Now."

"WHAAAT?!?!?!"

"NO FUCKING WAY, DUDE!!!"

A blur of activity ensues as Anita wraps tea towels like a diaper on me, then directs Malcolm and Harris to carry me to a guest suite down the hall. Once inside, they lay me on the bed gingerly, and Anita begins to undress me. Harris leaves the room yelling orders into his mobile. Malcolm gets more towels from the linen closet and brings them to the bed.

"It's going to be all right, My Angel. Dr. Rice is on his way with his labor team. Don't you worry. Okay?" Malcolm says.

Despite his attempt to remain calm, his panicky eyes dart around as he takes in the scene.

"AARGH!!!" I cry out when another contraction wracks my body.

Malcolm jolts and reaches for my hand. Then he winces when I squeeze it during the next contraction.

They're coming faster, and I know what that means.

"Starr, you're going into labor. You can do this. Malcolm and I will help you. Ready?" Anita tells me.

I pant and nod.

Malcolm curses under his breath.

"It'll be okay," I assure my panicked husband as I squeeze his hand.

He peeks over at me and leans in to kiss my lips softly.

"I'm right here with you, My Angel. All the way," he responds with a loving smile.

. . .

AND HE WAS HERE for me, from my yells of this being his fault to the cutting of first one, then the other umbilical cord to helping Anita clean our babies. The two of them did it all—well, aside from the labor—before Dr. Rice and his team arrived thirty minutes later.

It surprised them to find me sitting up in bed with Mini Malcolms 2.0 feeding at my breasts. The pediatricians took them for a checkup while Dr. Rice examined me. He commended Anita on a birthing well done and Malcolm on his nursing skills. We laughed at his jokes and sighed with relief when they declared the three of us healthy and able to remain at home. The girls weighing 5.0 and 4.9 pounds.

Then the nurses bathed me and changed me into a nightgown and robe before the EMTs put me on a stretcher to take me to the primary bedroom. Malcolm and my mother carried Mini Malcolms 2.0 along to the bedroom and placed them in the bassinets until later.

Now, I turn to watch Malcolm holding Selina and Elio in his arms as he introduces them to their baby sisters. The sight so poignant tears slip down my cheeks. When a sob sneaks out, Malcolm glances over his shoulder at me.

"Babe, what's wrong? Do you feel all right?" He asks as he strides over to the bed.

I nod, dabbing my eyes with the pads of my fingers.

"I'm just so happy and grateful for you and our babies," I respond. "You're so good to me and a good father, my love."

Tears fill his eyes and a beatific smile spreads across his handsome face. Elio wipes one of Malcolm's cheeks while Selina plants a sloppy kiss on the other.

We laugh at their methods of comfort.

A soft knock on the door draws our attention.

"You're ready for the fam?" Malcolm asks. "They've been pretty patience, My Angel."

"Absolutely! Let them in to see their newest family members," I exclaim.

Malcolm grins and calls for them to come in.

My mother enters first, followed by Shelley close behind.

"We want to check on all of you before we let the others in," Sun says as she hurries to my side.

Shelley nods and asks, "How are you doing, sweetheart? You gave us a fright going into labor alone! Thank God for Harris and his gadgets!"

"We're well! And I know. Plus, if it wasn't for Malcolm and Anita, I don't know what I would have done," I respond, then turn to Malcolm. "You were right, my love. I should have asked Shelley or Anita to spend the day with me—"

"No. Let's focus on the positive, My Angel. You and our babies are healthy, period," he cuts me off with a firm shake of his head.

Our mothers nod in agreement.

"Now, let's get everyone in here so we can name Mini Malcolms 2.0," he finishes.

Once our family and friends gather around us, Malcolm turns to me. Selina and Elio sit on the bed between us while we hold our twin girls.

"My Angel will do the honor of revealing our daughters' names to you," he says before he kisses my forehead.

I close my eyes and breath in his strength. Then open them refreshed.

"Malcolm and I introduce you to Dione and to Iris," I announce.

"Still in keeping with the Knight tradition. Dione is Greek for child of Heaven, My Angel, and of Earth, me since I ground her. Iris is the Greek goddess for rainbow and the messenger of Zeus and Hera who rode a multicolored bridge between Heaven to Earth," Malcolm adds proudly.

"So beautiful."

"Awww, I love it!"

"How clever!"

"They're gorgeous, just like their Hot Mama!"

Everyone congratulates us and welcome Dione and Iris to the family.

LATER, when we're alone, I watch my husband with his babies.

"Hi, Sexy Papa."

Malcolm lifts his platinum gray eyes from staring into the same ones of his youngest daughters. The three of them with their ebony-haired heads close together as they lie on the bed beside me.

Once again, the Steele traits win. Our children resemble their father with my curly hair instead of his waves. As they say, the apples don't fall far from the Steele family tree.

"Hi, Hot Mama," Malcolm replies. Then he raises his eyebrow and adds, "Keep looking at me like that, and I will fill your belly with another two babies right now."

I giggle at his joke, but stop abruptly when he doesn't join in. My eyes scan his face.

"Oh my God! You're serious?!" I exclaim.

Malcolm shrugs.

"You are one *very* Hot Mama, Starr Steele…"

STARR

"Oh, Starr! Elio looks like a Mini Malcolm most definitely. And his sisters are beautiful female versions of your sexy AF man! Damn, girl, I don't see a glimmer of you in your own children! Poor thing."

Billie's laughter rings out in the pergola on the ocean-facing deck of Malcolm and my Steele Southampton Village beach mansion. She's holding Iris dressed in a pink polka-dot-print onesie on her lap while we chat with the girls.

The morning after Dione and Iris were born, we drove out to the Hamptons in a caravan of Mercedes-Benz Sprinters. I didn't want to spend an extra minute in the city with our babies. It's been four weeks since we arrived. And we couldn't be more delighted.

My parents moved into their mansion on the property next to ours earlier than expected. The first two weeks they worked from home to be near their grandchildren on a daily basis. Now they commute via helicopter for the weekends, leaving the City on Thursday evenings.

Shelley and Morgan cannot spend enough time with all ten of their grandchildren. Normally they would go to the

Mediterranean either to their Villa Sogno in Positano or aboard their megayacht *Serendipity*. Now, they want to be near their grandbabies. They bounce from house to house in the compound to visit, or they have the kids over for babysitting at their mansion. They can't get over how in sync the births are allowing for the children to grow up together around the same ages.

Both sets of grandparents spoil the grandchildren. Toys —all developmental—books, tricycles, clothes, you name it; they have them. We've given up trying to stop them. And when Nanny Grace—an early childhood development specialist—confirmed no harm would come of the abundance, the grands went buck wild with more things!

Malcolm took paternity leave from STEELE International for the rest of the summer through September. On occasion, he works from his home office or takes the helicopter into the City for face-to-face meetings. Sebastian and Roger handle the bulk of his responsibilities, similar to the way they stepped up during his recovery. I'm glad he's here with us.

And then there are my girls.

Anita stayed for two weeks before she, Norman, and their girls returned to Paris. I couldn't thank her enough for delivering Dione and Iris for me. She saved us truly. The best doula ever! Malcolm told them they could have use of any STEELE property anywhere in the world for as long as they want whenever they want, and a company jet to transport them. Norman laughed and said he'd be sure Anita was available for all future births. We laughed, but Malcolm stared at me all smugly. He thinks more babies? Not!

Adrienne and Billie landed hours after I gave birth to Dione and Iris. My girls came straight to the penthouse and traveled with us to the Hamptons. For a week they stayed at Anton's and Patrick's mansions before they had to return to the West Coast for business. Two days ago they came back to stay through Labor Day for the STEELE Foundation fundraiser.

Haley and Blair stay in the City to work, then come out on Thursdays with my parents to spend the weekend here. Haley's desire for a baby makes me wonder what's happening between her and Lachlan. We still can't get her to admit much on their relationship… Blair can't get enough of being with all the kids. She gets a giggle out of them calling her Auntie! And what does Luc think about it?

Lola, Leonie, and I spend every day together since they took off August through the week of Labor Day. I'm thrilled since they have a wealth of knowledge they impart on me from their firsthand experience as moms, and especially Leonie as a mother of twins. Even as a doula, I didn't have the physical experience they had until Selina and Elio. So it's great to learn and to share with them: what to do about swollen ankles; the best oils for breast massages; how to soothe teething gums. My sisters help me tremendously.

Now I giggle at Billie and respond, "I know, right! Malcolm struts around like a proud Sexy Papa all day long! He can't get enough of his babies. He only bemoans with Elio about them being the only males…"

Lola joins in the laughter as she nuzzles against Stella's soft ebony curls.

"Tell me about it! You cannot keep Baz from claiming his babies either," she says.

Leonie nods and adds how Roger does not differ from his older brothers.

"I wonder who's next to pop one out…" I say as my gaze bounces among the singles.

Adrienne studies her red-polished fingernails; Billie skims through her iPhone; Blair goes to refill her citrus-infused water; Haley stares wistfully across the sand to the Atlantic Ocean.

Mmmmhmmm.

"Well, don't everyone speak at once!" Lola laughs. "You can hear a pin drop in the middle of the ocean after that comment!"

Leonie pokes Billie and adds, "You don't know what you're missing, *chérie*! We still bring home the bacon, have someone else cook it, and get tied up for dessert! *C'est la vie!*"

The three of us laugh so hard we snort as tears spill down our cheeks. Leonie cracks us up.

"Okay, so what did I miss?"

We shift on the chaise lounges to find Márcia behind us. Her waist-length hair so jet black it appears inky blue in the sunlight. She arches a perfectly shaped eyebrow above one obsidian eye.

"Oooh! She may be the one! A giant Russian!" I laugh.

"Good grief, could you imagine getting a baby by him out of your little—"

"Whaaat?!?!?" Márcia screeches over Lola.

Yeah, and then there's that Russian pair...

We fill her in on our conversation, and she goes mum just like Haley.

We share more fun times before we have lunch. I call for the nannies to come and take all of our babies for their naps along with their dogs. The rest of the afternoon, my girls and I go for a swim, lay out on beach blankets sipping refreshing iced tea, and relax. Nothing beats Girls' Time.

* * *

BLAIR REMEMBERED how I kept a journal to document my pregnancy with Selina and Elio. So she gave a set of beautiful leather-bound journals to me as one of her baby shower gifts for Dione and Iris. The first one has my notes, sketches, and my musings on nearly every page. Each day I update their growth and development: when they first lifted their heads; their sleep patterns; feeding schedule. I even doodle little drawings of them sleeping or with Malcolm and their older siblings.

I love to go back to the first page and read through. Malcolm often joins me to marvel at their progress. Since Selina and Elio, he's become a professional photographer and can't wait to snap shots of his family.

He's kitted out with the top-of-the-line digital camera, various lenses, flashes, you name it. During my first pregnancy, he used his mobile to take pics. Before Dione and Iris were born, Malcolm had a BDSM photographer friend of his who's a member of LEVELS advise him on "nothing but the best equipment." Now Malcolm takes so many shots of us, I feel as though we need to be camera ready all day and all night long!

Not only still shots, but video, too. "It's important to mark milestones and to record our family like my parents did with my siblings and me, My Angel!" He insists each time the camera clicks or starts.

I have to admit I love his enthusiasm and the time we spend going through his many libraries categorized by theme. We have memories we'll cherish forever. He's an amazing father.

My thoughts drift back to our first morning here.

The sunlight streams through the windows and glows like orange fire behind my closed eyelids, still heavy from sleep. For a moment, I lie there. Through the open balcony doors, the squawks of the seagulls as they soar above the ocean in search of their breakfast filters inside. The breaking waves splash onto the private beach in a soothing rhythm that lulls me to sleep once again.

I'm beyond tired and rest some more before I rise for the day.

My attention returns to our suite as I listen for sounds within our primary bedroom and en suite bathroom. The first things I notice are the loss of Malcolm's warm body wrapped around mine and the lack of breathing from his side of the bed. I crack one eye open to glance towards his pillow. An indentation serves as proof he slept beside me. I reach my hand out to touch the rumpled bedding. Cold.

I lift onto my elbows and scan the empty room for a clue to his whereabouts. The sound of his gentle baritone over the latest version of the fancy-schmancy baby monitor Harris created for Leonie originally is the third thing I notice. I pick it up off of the night table and place it on my breasts—heavy with milk—as I lean back against the headboard with a contented sigh.

My husband is with his twin daughters and Selina and Elio.

"—understand your situation... Absolutely... But your Mommy needs her rest, Iris... You and Dione kept us awake all of last night. But that's okay. You realize why?... Because we love you so very, very much, my beautiful daughters. You are two more gifts for us, along with your older siblings Selina and Elio. Right, guys?"

Their responses of dada, dada followed by the rustle of material and the coos of the babies float over the monitor. He's in the nursery next to our suite, with Selina and Elio's rooms on the other side.

I imagine Malcolm changing his baby daughters' diapers or getting them dressed for the day. He's better at coaxing his baby girls into their diaper than I by a long shot!

"Now, you have to feel better, Stinky Butt Monsters..."

I giggle at the nickname Malcolm gave to Selina and Elio and now uses for Dione and Iris. When Malcolm changed his son's *first diaper, he gagged and ran out of the room, holding his hand over his mouth. I laugh harder and snort at the comical memory.*

Not one to back done from a challenge, Malcolm now aces the diaper and dressing routine. The night prior, he selects their outfits for the next day and lays them out on their dressing tables. His attire varies based on the activity: walking on the beach or visiting their grandparents or resting at home.

Again, I crack up at my silly man.

"I appreciate you're hungry, Dione... Yes, okay... We'll sit on the window seat this morning and watch the seagulls eat their breakfast while you eat yours. Deal, Iris?... Good girls... Yes, Selina, you'll eat too. Don't any of you worry about Daddy taking care of his babies. You and your mother are mine and my responsibility. Understand?... Excellent, my little loves!"

Over the last four weeks, we found schedules and routines that work well—and some that were abysmal. The one I recognize Baz treasures the most is his morning time with his babies. A time father and his children can bond alone.

And a time for Mommy to sleep in bed longer. I roll over to my side and place the monitor beside Malcolm's pillow. The hushed cadence of his voice lulls me back to slumber again. My eyes drift shut, and I rest just as my husband knows I need.

I close my journal for today and go in search of Malcolm and our babies.

We have to get ready for our one-year wedding anniversary dinner. Since Dione and Iris cannot fly yet, we decided to have a sunset dinner on the beach—a traditional New England Clambake—with our family, Jacksons, and friends tonight. When they turn three-months old, we'll go to Laucala Island to celebrate as our little family. A week later, the rest of the clan and our friends will join us.

And I cannot wait for perfectly steamed clams, lobsters, potatoes, and corn on the cob topped with melted butter and paired with local beer and white wine make for a scrumptious meal. Dessert options of warm blueberry and apple pies with vanilla ice cream to round out the dinner. Yummy!

I walk outside to the beach and spot the group further along in front of Shelley and Morgan's mansion. My mobile rings in my pocket—Malcolm's ringtone. I smile as I accept the call.

"Hi, my love. I'm on my way now. See, look towards our home," I say, then wave when a figure turns in my direction.

"Oh, good. I thought I'd have to come rescue you, or you ran away from me and the brood I gave to you," he chuckles.

Even though he can't see me at this distance, I shake my head vehemently. No way would I ever abandon our little family. Malcolm and I worked too hard to get this far for us to part, ever. Hell to the no!

"Absolutely not, Mr. Steele! You are stuck with me for eternity," I vow.

Silence descends on the line. I pull the iPhone from my ear to check the call is still live—it is.

"Malcolm? Are you there?" I ask, concerned.

A soft snuffle comes over the line.

Aaaw… He's emotional.

"Oh, my love. You don't have to say a word, I know. I love you so much it hurts. We will never be apart, no matter what may come. You are my soul mate, the love of my life. As I am yours. Let's enjoy our anniversary today and always," I tell him equally emotional.

"I love you, My Angel. Now and forever," Malcolm replies quietly but with conviction.

My heart swells as I make my way to my man and our family.

MALCOLM

"*H*ot damn, Hot Mama! Am I one lucky man or what? Give me a twirl, Mrs. Steele."

I can't control my reaction to My Angel and follow up my exclamation with a sharp wolf whistle. It pierces the air as I lean with my hands in my tuxedo trousers pockets against the doorjamb of her dressing room at our penthouse at The STEELE Tower.

A celestial goddess stands in front of the room's center island putting her pear-shaped diamond earrings on—a stone at her ear and one dangling below. The giant gems sparkle, along with her wedding jewelry and evening collar with a matching bracelet. She peers over her shoulder at me. Dressed in a white long-sleeved gown that clings to her curvaceous ass and hips to skim her thighs and drape loosely at her knees until the hem pools on the floor.

A sensuous smile spreads across her face as her sorrel brown eyes shine brighter than her jewels. She skims her hands along her hips and down her thighs. More to tempt me than to smooth the silk-jersey material. Wordlessly, she turns in a circle, and her red-polished toenails with a glimpse of Swarovski crystal embellished straps peek out from beneath the hem of her gown.

Fuck. Me.

The front of her dress makes my jaw hit the floor.

A wide vee-neck dips to above her belly button to expose an expanse of chestnut-colored skin from her delicate collarbones to the inner curves of her lush tits, down to her toned abs. The vee ends in a circular diamond-crusted white-gold brooch with two dragon heads holding pearls in their mouths. A cutout at the left side of her waist forms a mock belt to hint at more skin.

Curly hair slicked straight and pulled back in a low bun at the nape draws attention to her flawless face with natural makeup and blood-red matte lipstick.

My Angel stuns me speechless.

"My… My… My… look who we have here…" she purrs as she prowls towards me with a glint in her predatory eyes. "Mr. Steele looking every inch the powerful Alpha Dom billionaire in his custom black tuxedo and patent leather dress shoes. He's leaning against the doorframe with his hands in his pockets, smirking at me. A sexy devil, might I add."

As she steps into my personal space, My Angel runs her nude-polished fingernail along my clean-shaven jaw to stroke across my lips. A purr escapes hers as she leans up on her toes to brush her lips over mine.

I hiss in a breath and nip at her lower lip, trying to take back control. With a shake of my head, I refocus and pat her ass.

"Keep that up, Mrs. Steele, and we will not make it to our fundraiser gala," I warn in my most dominant Alpha Dom voice, despite my cock roaring to life at the feel of her melded to my body.

With a coy shrug, she saunters towards the dressing table and throws over her shoulder, "As you wish… Sir."

That earns my temptress another swat on her ass. My cock strains at the back of the zipper as her flesh jiggles against my palm.

Did I say, Fuck. Me. Already?

My Angel tsks at me and rubs the spot, making me want to bend her over the silk-covered chaise lounge and mount her like a feral beast.

Instead, I watch as she slides a zebra wood box from a top drawer of the center island. She ghosts her fingertips over the elegant box, then turns to me with a smile.

"Malcolm, my love, I am so very proud of you and your achievement of STEELE Spine. I want to commemorate the official start of your foundation with a gift that will always remind you of this incredible evening," My Angel says as she presents the box to me.

"Babe, you didn't have to—"

She shushes me with a finger to my lips and with a shake of her head.

I oblige her and press the emblem for the most-coveted watch brand in the world: Patek Philippe.

The click of the closure reveals an extraordinary piece of craftsmanship. My mouth falls open and instinctively I reach out to gingerly touch the watch. And not just any old watch or even any old Patek Philippe.

This beauty is the rare Sky Moon Tourbillon 6002G without a doubt one of the most widely recognized watches the horologist ever made. With its astonishingly intricate engravings adorning its eighteen-carat white gold case, sapphire blue faces and matching crocodile band, the watch elevates the collection to another level. It also features the most complicated wristwatch movement they make. The front displays the time, perpetual calendar with retrograde date, and the phase of the moon. While the dial on the back has a stellar illustration of the northern sky along with indications for sidereal time on a twenty-four-hour scale, time of meridian passage of Sirius and of the moon, plus the angular progression and the phase of the moon. At $2.5 million, it better…

"For you, my love. Allow me," My Angel says as she hands the box to me and removes my Grandmaster Chime 6300A-010—another pricey Patek Philippe at eight-figures —then replaces it with her gift. "When I accompanied Lola to a Phillips auction and saw this piece, I knew it was meant for you, like the meanings of our babies' and my names. You'll think of us each time you check the time, too."

I tilt her face up to look into her eyes, so radiant with her love for me.

"Thank you, My Angel"—I lean down to press my lips to hers—"You and my babies make each second of every day and every evening incredible. I love you dearly."

Our Bentley Mulsanne Duo-tone in platinum and black pulls up to the front of STEELE42, one of our award-winning entertainment venues. It specializes in weddings, parties, and galas for society's best both in the United States and abroad. A buzz surrounds the area with paparazzi and news crews angling for the best shots and interviews on the red carpet. The energy is high and reaches into the luxury sedan, drawing us out as a valet opens My Angel's door and my driver Oscar Carrera opens mine.

The red carpet is bustling with photographers, television crews, and international glitterati. Lights flash and the photographers yell my name to turn my head in their direction.

As I reach My Angel, I can't help but smile at her radiance. She looks spectacular with the lightbulbs flashing off of her diamond jewelry, particularly her hand harness, engagement ring, and wedding band prove to all the world she is mine. I will have the best-dressed woman on my arm tonight.

My Angel smiles as her hand wraps around my forearm and like a pro saunters along the red carpet. When the paps call for her to pose, as a good sub should, she looks to me for approval, then poses like the best supermodel or movie star. My dick weeps for her.

The paps call for me to join her for a few shots. I loop my arm around her waist and settle my fingers on her hip. Then bend down and softly kiss her lips. The paparazzi go wild and scream our names.

I squeeze her hand and put it into the crook of my elbow, pressing it close to my side as we make our way down the carpet, posing for pictures and chatting with reporters.

Leonie and Roger are just ahead of us. When Leonie hears them calling our names, she turns and makes her way back down the carpet towards My Angel and me. Roger grins and strides along with her.

"*Chéri*, this is your night!" She gushes as she double kisses my cheeks.

The megamodel-turned-interior-designer looks fantastic in a gold, silk satin strapless floor-length gown. Her long legs play peek-a-boo with the thigh-high slit. Her smile is as dazzling as the diamonds adorning her body. Leonie tosses her waist-length hair and twinkles her amber eyes as she hugs me close. The paparazzi reach a frenzied peak and thousands of flashbulbs pop.

Baz appears in a classic tuxedo cut perfectly to empha-size his height and muscular frame. He, too, hugs me and congratulates me on my success. Ours, I correct him with a smile. Lola—in a form-fitting black satin one-shoulder gown—gushes with My Angel and Leonie. No one would believe these Hot Mamas have ten babies among them!

Soon the rest of our clan arrives—including Lachlan with Haley, fucker. All of us pose for the cameras. The rarity of all the Steele siblings in one frame will make for excellent social media posts and traditional media coverage. After several minutes, we walk through the doors of STEELE42.

ONCE WE ARRIVE INSIDE, we place our masquerade masks over our faces before we chat with other attendees. I introduce My Angel to key guests and mention her Starr Light Fitness & Wellness locations and international retreats. Women and men want to be at their peak performance and can appreciate access to a notable fitness brand. Some of whom are already familiar with their offerings and have attended sessions or retreats, even streamed them. Their excitement to meet the founder palpable. The men as expected nonchalantly check out My Angel, and I struggle not to flip someone on their ass.

"Oh, Malcolm, this is a beautiful venue. All the STEELE properties are so refined!" My Angel says, looking up at the vaulted ceiling where the constellations twinkle in the dim lighting.

I want to lave her throat and suck on it until I leave my bright red mark as a warning to others to back the fuck off.

"Not as refined and gorgeous as you, though," I reply instead. "But this is one of my favorites. It was a bank and when we refurbished it, we strove to keep the integrity of the space. We kept the original ceiling, columns, teller windows on the sides, the vault, and more original details."

"It's impressive," she murmurs.

Further inside STEELE42, I spot my father deep in

conversation with some prominent businessmen with my mother engaged in conversation with their wives. They exemplify a power couple I hope to replicate with My Angel.

"Mr. Steele, you have news crews to speak with," my assistant Miles says as he steps behind us with the team for STEELE Spine.

"Thank you, Miles," I respond, then turn to My Angel. "Will you join me?"

She smiles and nods as she slips her hand around the crook of my elbow.

We finish the interviews that interspersed questions on my accident and the trial to details on the foundation's mission. The team and I answer the business-related questions with gusto. But deftly avoided substantial responses on my personal life. We keep it simple with I'm thankful for the opportunity to pay it forward and hope to make a positive impact on the wellbeing of others.

The less fodder given to the media, the better. As with most old money families, the Steeles like media coverage to further our business gains, but prefer intimate aspects to remain private.

"Sweethearts, how do you like the gala? Are you pleased?"

My mother materializes next to me, holding her elaborate feathered mask by its silk ribbon-covered handle. I smile down at her and wrap my arm around her shoulders. She's the same height as My Angel and fits under my chin with her heels on.

"I love it! You and your team did a superb job. Thanks so much, Mom," I squeeze her close. "It's even greater than I expected."

"Well, we had to be sure everything is perfect for your new foundation! Your father and I are very proud of you."

She pauses as her eyes mist with tears. She takes a deep breath and I squeeze her again. Her words make even the Alpha Dom in me blink back tears. I strive to make my parents proud of me. It's so good to hear it from both of them.

"Oh, Shelley, this is awesome!" My Angel adds as she takes over the embrace. "I told Malcolm he has a lot to be proud of!"

The most important women in my live chat some more before we spend the evening mingling during the cocktail hour, speaking with potential donors. We place bids on a few interesting items from the silent auction. Then, eating a fantastic dinner—Lucien's catering division handles the food and drink.

Miles appears beside me to let me know it's time for my speech. I turn to My Angel, and she places a light kiss on my lips before she whispers good luck. Then I nod to the other guests at our table and excuse myself.

As I stride to the stage, several guests greet me, and I take a few moments to thank them for coming. When I arrive on the dais, the new head of the foundation introduces me. A round of applause rings out. I wait for the guests to settle before I speak.

"Thank you for joining my family and me for the inaugural STEELE Spine Annual Fundraiser Gala. Before I impress you with our mission to dazzle you for your hefty donations," I pause for their ensuing laughter. "Kindly allow me the opportunity to thank the most important person in my life—my wife of one glorious year with many, many more to come—Starr Steele. Without her unwavering love and support I would not stand before you today."

A spotlight highlights My Angel at our table. Her eyes widen when our family and friends stand and clap for her. She covers her mouth with her hand and fans her face with the other to hold back the tears. Then she stands and inclines her head to me as she claps.

In a clear voice that carries across the space she responds, "Our love and the love of our family will forever strengthen us. We are grateful for you and your vision for STEELE Spine, my only love."

Then she blows me a kiss and re-takes her seat, indicating for the others to do the same.

My heart clenches at her words. When she gives me a thumbs up, I grin and launch into my speech with gusto. And sure enough, by the end of the night we raise over $40 million.

"WELL DONE, MR. STEELE."

My Angel tips her head back to gaze into my eyes as we glide across the dance floor to the music of the live band.

I tighten my hold on her and kiss her full lips.

"Thank you, Mrs. Steele," I murmur against them.

"Shelley enlisted me to help next year since I was too preggie to work with the team this time. I told her I'd love to help my man in any way whatsoever," My Angel says. Then she winks at me, "But what I didn't tell her was there's a fee…"

I cock my head and raise my eyebrow in question.

"As long as you play doctor to my patient at LEVELS New York for a night, I'll consider my services paid in full… Sir," she says as she bites her plump lower lip.

I growl and cover her mouth with mine, drawing the succulent flesh between my teeth for a nip.

She trembles from the erotic pain then mewls when I lap at the bite with the flat of my tongue.

"Consider that a tasty down payment, Naughty Girl," I rumble.

MALCOLM

"*R*eady to take this jump with me, My Angel? With our responsibilities, we don't have to do this, you know. The choice is yours as always, babe."

She slips her googles over her eyes that glow with excitement, then tightens the strap on her helmet. Once again, she gives me a thumbs up and grins.

"I'll jump with you anytime and anyplace, my love. Let's do this like Brutus!" She high fives with me.

I whoop and pump my fist.

This will be my first extreme sport since before the accident. I stopped them; being a father and a husband, not wanting to risk my life when I have theirs to care for. My top priorities. But My Angel surprised me with a skydiving session for our second morning on Laucala Island.

We arrived yesterday afternoon with our babies and Nanny Patience. In a week, our family and friends will join us for the renewal of our vows on the beach. I want to include all of our little ones as we claim our love as a family forever.

But first My Angel and I jump!

A crew member opens the door of the skydiving plane. We're flying over the spectacular Fiji Islands with the Pacific Ocean glittering in various shades of turquoise. Bright blue sky and wispy clouds surround us.

The adrenaline pumps through my veins as I check first My Angel's safety gear then mine. We may enjoy a good thrill, but I will not allow us to take avoidable risks.

The guide gives us last instructions. Then we line up to exit the plane one after the other for the drop zone 300 feet above sea level.

My Angel glances over her shoulder at me and waves. Even though it's not her first jump, my heart still lurches when she leaps from the plane with a gleeful shout.

Her excitement sparks my own.

Up next, I go through my ritual to give thanks for my fearless wife, love to our family, and our safe finish. It's what I do before any of my extreme activities, even when I was a pain-in-the-ass teen. My rebel spirit still exists, but it's alongside my duty to family and self.

A thumbs up to the guide, and I take my jump.

"Whoohoo, baby! Time to rock and roll!" I yell before I follow her out the door with a somersault in the air.

My laughter floats behind me as I soar through the stratosphere. The air rushes past as I hurtle through the clouds. My blood races through my veins as my heart pumps with exhilaration. Damn, I missed this!

I watch My Angel below me and hear her faint laughter carried on the wind.

A shit-eating grin stays plastered on my face as I free fall through the sky at 120 miles per hour. I take in the pristine beauty of the South Pacific. The twenty-thousand feet give me eighty-five seconds to view it all.

I pull on my cords and float safely to the ground under

my parachute. Years of experience allow me to land on my feet at a run.

Damn! That's what I'm talking about! I am back!

The ground team rushes over to help me wrangle my open parachute. They relieve me of the harness, then my helmet and goggles as I remove them. I scan the area for My Angel.

Once I spot her, I thank the team for their help and jog to reach her side. I scoop her in my arms and spin in a circle. Her long, toned legs wrap around my waist as she devours my mouth with hers. I give the passionate kiss back to her in spades.

Our tongues entwine and our teeth gnash. The adrenaline makes us ferocious, starved for the other. My cock hardens to steel and presses against her fiery core through the layers of our cargo pants.

She moans and grinds her pussy to my groin. Then her moist lips blaze a trail to my ear.

"Take me back and fuck me raw, Mr. Steele. It's been twelve long weeks since I had your colossal cock inside of me. And. I. Will. Wait. No. Longer!" She punctuates each word with a snap of her hips.

I damn near cum in my pants. The friction against my aching dick proves too much.

Fuck. Me.

Without delay, I carry her to the awaiting Sikorsky S-92 Executive Helicopter. It'll make for a quick trip back to our side of Laucala island. My long strides eat up the distance, and I climb in the cabin without breaking our contact. I sit on a back seat, and she squirms on my lap, purposefully teasing my cock. It thumps against her pussy, and she mewls in my mouth. I gobble the erotic sound like a starved man.

I untie her pants to slip my fingers between her wet and

puffy folds. My thumb strokes her needy little clit. The calloused pads of two fingers brush just inside of her pussy to skim her G-spot. I apply enough pressure to cause her juices to flow into my palm, but not enough to elicit an orgasm.

As she moans pitifully with her face buried in my neck, I keep her on the edge for the duration of the ten-minute flight. We'll both explode soon enough.

Before the rotor blades stop, I carry My Angel to the door, impatient for the crew to open it. With a brief word of thanks, I step down and stride to the golf cart.

My Angel protests when I sit her on the seat beside me. Then a mischievous gleam fills her sorrel brown eyes. With a smirk she ghosts her hand over my giant bulge. The outline of my ten inches clear along my thigh from the thick root to the mushroom head Prince Albert's piercing jewelry balls.

I grab her wrist and shake my head.

"We do not want a knee-jerk reaction now do we, Naughty Girl?" I reprimand her.

She sits back with a huff and pouts, arms crossed over her tits and eyes forward.

I chuckle wickedly.

The ride is short, and I chase her into the villa and to our primary bedroom. Fortunately, Nanny Pierce has the babies at her cottage for the rest of the morning.

My Angel squeals when I catch and toss her onto the bed. She bounces, then shifts to her knees. She rips her t-shirt over her head and yanks at the tie of her cargo pants. Standing in the middle of the mattress, she shimmies them with her red lace G-string past her hips. She kicks them to land in a pile with her crumbled t-shirt on the floor. She crooks her finger at me as I stand transfixed by the temptress.

"Come here, Sir," she commands me. "Let me help you with all of those pesky clothes."

I nearly trip over my own feet in my haste to reach her.

She giggles and drops to her knees. Equally frantic to remove the offensive garments as she did hers. My Angel tugs my long-sleeved t-shirt from my pants and over my head. Nimble fingers unbutton and lower the zipper on my fly with ease. She bites her bottom lip when she catches sight of my cock's angry red tip poking up from the waistband of my boxer briefs to my navel. Pre-cum drips from the hungry boy.

Her delay breaks my resolve. I grip her shoulders and lower her to the bed. Legs go up on my shoulders as I plank over her with one hand by her head and the other fists around my throbbing dick. So ready and wet for me, I slam home in one brutal thrust.

She screams and arcs her back as she claws the bedding.

I hiss and flex my ass cheeks, bending my knees to increase the penetration.

So fucking tight; her pussy like a vice.

I dig my heels into the floor and wrap my hand around her throat to hold her in place. Thoughts of making sweet love to my wife for the first time since she gave birth dissipate as a red veil of carnal lust drops before my eyes.

Her full tits topped by pebbled brown nipples bounce with each insistent snap of my hips as I drill her into the mattress. Wild cries of carnal pleasure burst from her slack mouth. Head—with mussed curls a halo around it—thrown back. Eyes squeezed shut.

My mind tells me to fuck her until I can't walk. And then some more. Relentless. Possessive. Claiming. Mine.

And you know why?

Because I'm the rebel; the bad boy billionaire playboy of the STEELE family who in the end always knew I would get what I wanted. And I wanted the brown-eyed beauty. Starr Steele—My Angel—is mine all mine to cherish.

Forever.

***

Malcolm & Starr's Story Concludes For Now...

Turn the page for the Steele Family, Author's Note, and Preview of *A Trilogy of Desires Lachlan & Haley Parts I-III*

Join my newsletter bit.ly/CLBooksNewsletter to learn about the next STEELE World couples to have their romances told.

THE STEELE FAMILY

STEELE INTERNATIONAL, INC

Multigenerational, multibillion-dollar business luxury real estate
development and management corporation

Headquarters & Family's Primary Residences:

The STEELE Tower, New York City

A modern, gray-tinted glass fifty-seven story mixed-use skyscraper
on southwest corner of Fifty-Seventh Street and Fifth Avenue
within Billionaires' Row

Global Offices:

- The United States of America (New York City,
New Jersey, Chicago, California, Miami, Las
Vegas)

- The Caribbean (St. Maarten, St. Barth's, St. Lucia)
- The French & Italian Rivieras (Nice, Cannes, Positano, Capri)
- Monaco (Monte Carlo)
- The United Arab Emirates (Abu Dhabi, Dubai)

STEELE FOUNDATION: A STRONG AND SUPPORTIVE HOUSE

Builds and manages attractive, affordable housing for urban, lower-income families

Available for download at **bit.ly/STEELEFamily**

Author's Note

Thank you for reading Parts I-III of Malcolm and Starr's sexy, sizzling romance! I hope you enjoyed the Happy For Now conclusion of their written-in-the-stars love affair. If so, I'd love to hear your thoughts, please share a review at **bit.ly/CLBooksSI7-9Review** and tell your friends.

Wait! What's up with Lachlan and Haley or Billie and Patrick or Blair and Luc?! The STEELE International, Inc. Series gave lots of hints at what's brewing for these lovers...

Click below for the answers to one steamy story featuring forbidden lovers Alpha Dom Lachlan Jackson and shy, tech wiz Haley Steele as their scintillating trilogy introduces the next series in the STEELE World with STEELE International, Inc. - Jackson Corporation A Billionaires Romance Series Crossover Book 1:

A Trilogy of Desires Lachlan & Haley Parts I-III

At **CharmaineLouise.com** take the *Four types of lovers. Which are you?* **Quiz** to match your Sexy Fantasy: sub, Voyeur, Dominatrix, or Dominatrix sub Switch.

At **CharmaineLouise.com** take the *Four types of lovers. Which are you?* **Quiz** to match your Sexy Fantasy: sub, Voyeur, Dominatrix, or Dominatrix sub Switch.

Follow me on social media including my CLBooks Coterie Fan Club below or on your favorite channels below

and subscribe to my newsletter at **bit.ly/
CLBooksNewsletter** for a **Free Book**.

Fulfill Your Desires.
xoxo
Charmaine Louise

bookbub.com/authors/charmaine-louise-shelton
facebook.com/CharmaineLouiseBooks
instagram.com/charmainelouisebooks
goodreads.com/charmainelouisebooks

PREVIEW: A TRILOGY OF DESIRES LACHLAN & HALEY PARTS I-III

1 *3 Years Ago — Southampton Village, NY*

HALEY — *16*

"HI, SEBASTIAN!"
  "Oh hi, Malcolm!"
  "Hi, Roger!"
  "Hey there, Harris!"
  "*Hello* to you guys, too!!"

SHALL I hurl now or later?

Cue the biggest eye roll in history!

If I'd known my friends would go gaga over my older brothers and my cousins, I would've told the girls we'd hang out at one of their beach houses instead of at mine. Give me a freaking break already…

Eyes batting; duck lips in full effect; cheeks flushed; bouncing on their blankets with uncontainable excitement.

Is this what I have to look forward to all summer???

Gag. Gag. Gag some more. Did I say… gag (all caps)?!

"Uh, hi, girls," Sebastian says followed by similarly surprised greetings from the rest of the boys as they stride past in various board shorts, fit physiques on blast.

My eldest brother tosses the football to Roger—my third older brother after Malcolm—then ruffles my jet black, mid-back-length hair that matches the rest of my siblings. Our signature gray eyes—in me are soulful, set in my heart-shaped face with cheeks that display dimples when I smile or laugh—shine with brotherly affection.

"Hey, little sis. Where's your one-piece?" Sebastian asks with a frown at my new hot pink, triangle string bikini. "What's with theses bits of material, huh?"

Before I can respond, my fraternal twin chimes in.

"Oh, she went *shopping* the other day, Baz," Harris says with a smirk. "Who are you trying to impress, little Haley?"

I scowl in consternation at both of them. But once again, I'm cut off before I can even open my mouth.

"Leave her alone, Harris. I think you look nice, Haley. Who says you have to follow the rules?" Malcolm demands, glaring at Baz.

I smile at my rebel brother Malcolm, also known as *The Enforcer.*

He and Baz used to go at it all the time. Malcolm hated they resembled one another from their muscular six-feet-four-inch frames to the stubble on their chins and their dominant personalities. Plus Malcolm felt he had to follow in our eldest brother's footsteps, being a year younger and the second son. At twenty-three and twenty-two, many people confuse them or assume they're twins. Not good at all.

I know how Malcolm feels since I'm the youngest of the Steele clan at sixteen. The *baby* of the family, as Harris likes to point out since he was born a few minutes before me. We are the double surprise for our parents, who had not planned on having more children. Then a twofer to boot. Roger is three years older and had been the baby of the family until Harris and I popped up.

"Shall we play football or bug Haley?" Roger asks, tossing the ball back to Baz as he winks at me.

Roger *The Responsible* takes his role as the middle child seriously. We can always depend on him to keep peace and order under his intense gaze.

I wink back at my savior, but swallow my words around the nervous butterflies that fill my belly suddenly.

"Yeah, leave Baby Girl alone, Baz, and get ready to have your ass handed to you, cuz!"

Lachlan.

O… M… G! Lachlan!

The second oldest of the Jackson clan at twenty—he's two years younger than their eldest sibling Lydie—and Baz's best friend.

My heart skips a beat when he flashes his movie-star smile at me. Everyone says he resembles Cary Grant with his rugged masculinity and gorgeous looks.

His fit, six-foot-four-inch well-formed frame topped by a face so incredible it takes your breath away. Blazing green eyes lock in on you as your gaze takes in his thick, dark brown hair slicked back from his chiseled cheekbones and strong jawline. The cleft chin adds to his heartthrob persona.

"Screw you, Lach! *You* are going down, man!" Malcolm jeers.

Can Lachlan go down on me?

Oops, what??? Where the heck did that thought come

from, Haley Steele! I admonish myself as a hot, crimson flush spreads from my hairline to the tops of my newly developed breasts. I duck my head to avoid my brothers noticing my reaction to Lachlan—especially Baz.

"Yeah, right, Malcolm! We'll see about that, *cuz*!" Lucien retorts as he snatches the ball from Baz and tosses it to his younger brother Laurent, who laughs and shoulders past Harris.

They're the third and fourth of the Jackson siblings at nineteen and sixteen and best friends with Malcolm and Harris, respectively. And just like Lachlan, they share the Jackson family traits of emerald green eyes, dark brown hair, and six-plus feet in height.

I hear the girls whispering about his hint of a Scottish accent—*He's so James Bond, OMG!!!*—and cover up a gag with a cough. An unstoppable eye roll happens behind my glasses, though. I push them up the bridge of my nose.

Yeah, our cousins spend most of the year—and their lives—in Scotland where their family's company is based in Aberdeen at the Jackson Town House. Like the Steeles, they have a multi-generational, multibillion-dollar company. Jackson Corporation's repertoire is fine dining, distilleries, and vineyards worldwide. Their Irish and Scottish family created the finest single malt Scotch Whiskey and became billionaires years ago.

STEELE International, Inc. is my family's luxury real estate development and management corporation based in New York City in The STEELE Tower with offices and properties around the globe. The Tower is also our family's residence on the top three floors of the fifty-seven-story building. Morgan, our father, is the CEO and Chairman of the Board. In time, each of us will take on a leadership role within the company. For now, we intern during our school breaks to learn our family's business from the ground up.

Our mother Michelle—known by friends as Shelley—insists we do more than as she calls it "lounge around the pool working on our tans" in Southampton Village during the summers. As the head of STEELE Foundation, she contributes through our philanthropic arm that builds and manages attractive, affordable housing for urban, lower-income families. My siblings and I help to construct some properties, too.

She and her best friend Lucinda—aka Lucie and the Jackson Matriarch—spent most of their adult lives together, forming a closer bond than they have with their blood siblings and relatives. Incredibly, our mothers met our fathers while working as a shopgirl in a STEELE retail space and as a bartender in one of the Jackson pubs. Both families became super close even without sharing DNA. Hence our cousin relationship and Aunt Lucie and Uncle Connor.

Not that I desire for Lachlan to be my *cuz* or for him to consider me a *Baby Girl*…

While my brothers and I are at our family's private beachfront compound in the Hamptons, our cousins came over from Aberdeen for the last half of the summer. They'll intern at Jackson Corporation's New York City offices while we're at STEELE International. Aunt Lucie uses the same playbook as our mother.

Baz and Malcolm and Roger are on break from Harvard University Business School and Harvard University, respectively. Harris and I are still in high school at Collegiate School and its sister school, The Brearley School. They're all the Steele family's legacy schools.

Lydie starts her first year at Saïd Business School at the University of Oxford in the fall. Lachlan is in his third year and Lucien in his second at Pembroke College at the

University of Oxford. Laurent attends Gordonstoun School. All are the Jackson family's legacy schools.

Tradition ranks high for our families.

"Haley, who is that fine specimen of a man?!"

My best friend Natasha Bond's question and nudge draws me from my musings.

I sigh inwardly and plaster on a smile before I glance over at her.

She's all gorgeous face, long blonde hair, big blue eyes, and willowy figure compared to my only now forming curves and gawky self. She's tall like me, more so since she's two years older at eighteen and not from my genetics. At first it shocked me the most popular girl at school wanted to be friends with me this past year. Oddly enough, others started asking me to hang out for lunch or sleepovers. I'd always been a bit of a loner, so it took me a moment to get used to their constant attention.

"Which one?" I ask with a hint of sarcasm.

My tone goes over Natasha's head.

Did I mention she's not the brightest lightbulb in the box…?

She elbows me with a giggle, and her big boobs almost pop out of her minuscule bikini top—I went with her shopping for my new bathing suits.

"The movie star one with the sexy Scottish accent, that's who!" She giggles as she tilts her chin towards the boys playing near the surf.

I scowl.

My Lachlan.

Could this situation get any worse?!

I choose to ignore her question—rude, yes, but oh well— and rise to get a bottled water from the cooler.

Is Natasha serious with me right now?!

I uncap the bottle and let my gaze drift from my

brothers and cousins—including my man Lachlan—to my friends, who whisper amongst themselves as they point at the sweaty boys and giggle.

With a harrumph, I gulp down half of the bottle.

It's just not fair Lachlan only sees me as a baby girl and not someone he's attracted to, like he's eyeballing Natasha. She's grinning at him all coy like as she adjusts her breasts in her bikini top.

Why can't she back up off of him?!

Since I was little, I used to follow Baz and Lachlan around like a little stray puppy, just wanting to be around my eldest brother, who I've always admired. Until recently when I realized I wasn't just following them to see what they were up to, rather to be near to Lachlan as much as possible. When he returned this summer, something just clicked inside of me. Suddenly, I wanted him to pay attention to me as more than his little cousin or *Baby Girl*.

I even picked out this bikini in hopes he'd see my new curves and want me.

Is it too much to ask for???

LACHLAN — *20*

EVEN WHILE WE PLAY FOOTBALL, my gaze keeps going to the sexy as fuck blonde who all but drops her top for me. Baz sacked me good a minute ago when her feminine wiles distracted me, and I ended up on my ass in the sand.

It's not like I don't get laid whenever I want. Hell, girls—and women I might add—throw themselves at me. A Jackson male with billions in the bank and a more than willing ten-inch cock. Not that I'm interested in settling down with one female at the moment. No, ma'am!

Like my father Connor tells us, "Live life to the fullest, boys. But do not bring home any unexpected bundles…"

Yeah, not something he says to our eldest sibling, Lydie. He's never hidden his intention to marry her off to improve Jackson Corporation's business with some type of alliance. Can you say old-fashioned?

Even though Lydie is older than me and should be the heir to the family's business, our father wants me to take over when he retires. My loyalty lies with my sister. So, we'll see…

But this bird here.

No question. I would shag her in a heartbeat.

But she's Haley's friend, so she can't be of age despite her banging body.

"Pay attention, Lach You dolt!!"

Laurent's fierce growl and shove to my chest returns me to the football game at hand. Right.

"Okay, damn!" I retort, wiping the sand from my hands.

We play some more, and I remain focused despite the wolf whistles from our impromptu cheerleading squad. The Jackson clan wins, and we do a victory dance before both teams dive into the cool Atlantic Ocean.

When I come up for air, the blonde appears and wraps her arms and legs around me like a starfish.

"I knew you'd win!" She exclaims as she covers my mouth with her full lips in a passionate, no-holds-barred kiss.

Well, damn.

I cup her ass and kiss her silly. Not once do I hide the burgeoning erection of my thick cock from her eager, hot snatch. Nor does she try to deny me access to her greedy core. Her hips pump to their own beat.

It's good being a Jackson.

I tangle my tongue with hers as my hands caress her willing body.

"Damn, Lach. Is she even legal?"

Roger's question pulls my mouth from devouring the blonde's.

Damn, is she? I wonder.

She giggles and nips at my ear.

"I'm eighteen. No need to worry," she pants, breathless from my domineering kiss.

When she whispers she's on the pill, my cock twitches beneath the water.

She giggles.

"Um, Natasha. We need to go to the deck. It's time for lunch."

The sound of Haley's soft voice makes me wince. I release the blonde and move away from her guiltily.

What is it about my youngest cousin that makes me feel like I'm doing something wrong or hurting her in some way?

Haley

To see Lachlan kiss Natasha makes me physically ill. I have to do something to stop them from going further. Or I really will hurl all over the sand.

"Um, Natasha. We need to go to the deck. It's time for lunch," I say lamely from a distance, praying he'll let her go.

So unfair.

As though she's a live wire, Lachlan releases Natasha quickly. She tries to cling to him. But he swims away without a backwards glance at either of us.

The butterflies in my stomach sink.

"What, Haley?!" Natasha demands angrily as she storms towards me.

I stare at her with my mouth agape.

"Just because you can't have them doesn't mean *we* don't want a chance to be with them!" Natasha exclaims in a loud whisper as she approaches me. "Did you really think we were hanging out with *you* to be friends?! You're some tech nerd who's boring AF! We knew you have the hottest brothers. And now cousins too? Give us a break for wanting access to them!"

Now my mouth drops to the sand, and my eyes fill with tears behind my glasses.

I should have known it was too good to be true.

Why would the It girls of Brearley want to hang out with me—the geek—all of a sudden?

I've been friendly with girls at school, but not really *friends*. I had hoped to have a real best friend at last. I mean, Lydie is nice to me and all, treats me like her little sister since we're united by the abundance of testosterone around us. But she's so much older and always focused on acing her exams and work at Jackson. We don't spend a lot of time together.

But I guess she's better than this bunch of pseudo-friends…

"Well, you can't cock block us!" Natasha shrills when she stands before me, and the other girls echo her sentiment.

I take a breath to calm myself before I lose all cool points.

"Well, then go!" I retort. "I don't need *friends* like you, anyway!"

The girls glare at me, then gather their things and leave in a huff.

Natasha's icy blue stare sends chills down my spine. But

I glare gray shards of molten platinum at her until she grabs her things and stomps away.

My stomach lurches, and I rush from the beach to my bedroom suite. I've had enough for one day.

LACHLAN

"OKAY, let's go now before Malcolm and Roger notice and want to tag along. I need a drink and to get laid pronto."

Baz says before we creep out of his bedroom suite to go to a party.

We make it out of his rooms and down the dimly lit hallway past his parent's wing.

CRASH!

"Oh! Ow!!"

Baz and I whirl around to find Haley sprawled out on the floor. A crystal vase shattered beside her.

Unbeknownst to us, Haley—who is forever tagging along with us since she was a kid—must have heard us when we passed her set of rooms. This time, it appears she tripped on the rug right outside of their parents' bedroom and knocked the vase down when she reached for the table to catch herself.

"Haley? What the hell?!" Baz whisper shouts.

"Are you all right?" I ask, concerned.

When she turns her heart-shaped face up to me, tears shimmer in her platinum gray eyes behind her glasses. Her cute dimples disappear on her flushed cheeks.

As her chin wobbles, I crouch in front of her and cup her face. My hand tingles from the contact.

"Hey, Baby Girl, don't cry," I murmur as I stroke her cheek with my thumb. "It's okay."

Baz nudges me out of the way and reaches for her. His shocked anger replaced by his big brother concern.

"Haley, are you hurt? Did the glass cut you?" He asks as he checks her out.

"What's going on?"

We jolt at the commanding voice of Uncle Morgan and turn to face the Steele Patriarch.

Aunt Shelley hurries past him and shoos Baz and me away.

Haley's cries must have woken them.

As Uncle Morgan reprimands Baz and me, my eyes flick to Haley, who's being led to her rooms by Aunt Shelley. As they walk away, Haley peeks at me over her shoulder.

My heart skips a beat, and I have a sudden urge to care for her, to protect her.

I shake my head, and I glance away, confused by my reaction.

Baz and I decide to forgo the party. Instead, we hang out at the bar and play pool on their mansion's entertainment level.

"Ha! You lost, again, Lach," Baz guffaws as he takes a sip of his Jackson Special Blend Scotch.

Yeah, my head isn't in the game. It's still churning over the emotions Haley brought out in me earlier. I shake it again and sigh as I take a drink from my crystal snifter.

"What the fuck's eating you, cuz?" Baz asks.

I shrug, then plow ahead despite a niggling not to draw attention to my predicament.

"Doesn't it bother you Haley could've cut herself?" I ask in return.

Baz's eyebrows lift, and his eyes narrow on me. They

turn a stormy gray. Carefully, he places his snifter on the ledge of the pool table.

"What do you mean, Lachlan?" He asks, still eyeing me.

I give zero fucks he's going all Alpha male on me. I'm one too.

"You did not appear overly concerned for Haley, Sebastian," I reply as I place my snifter down.

"Oh, so you think you can take care of Haley better than me?! She's *my* little sister. *I* know what's best for her, Lachlan, not *you*!" He retorts, as his face flushes in anger.

I don't back down. Something urges me to defend Haley even over her eldest brother who I know truly loves her as he does all of his siblings. Hell, he prides himself on being their third parent.

But again, my mind is in a confused state.

"Yes, I can! She's my—"

She's my what? Not my little sister. And from the way my heart stuttered as her soulful gray eyes stared up at me— touching something deep inside of me—she's not just my cousin anymore, either.

As I think more on it, she's been acting differently towards me all summer, not like her usual self over the holidays and last summer. More shy; averts her eyes when our gazes meet; lingers near me with a faraway look on her face. It makes me wonder.

Haley cannot feel the same. Can she?

But she is Baz's little sister—*my best friend's* little sister. And I cannot have her. No matter what deep part of me she's tapped into all of a sudden. No matter what I sense from her. Besides, she's only a sixteen-year-old girl, and I'm twenty-year-old man.

Fuck. Me.

I lift my face towards the ceiling and blow out a frustrated breath.

"Haley is your *what*, Lachlan?"

Baz's menacing tone draws me from my errant musings.

"My youngest cousin who needs to be more careful, cuz," I answer, schooling my face into a stoic expression.

Baz scans my face for any sign of deceit. None found, he nods and racks the balls.

"Ready to lose again, cuz?" He taunts with a smirk.

I return his smirk with one of my own and take a grateful sip of my Scotch.

Crisis averted.

***

Click the Link Below or Visit books2read.com/u/4NjpYo For Your Copy

A Trilogy of Desires Lachlan & Haley Parts I-III

Intrigue My Desires Harris & Kat Part I

Decode My Desires Harris & Kat Part II

Honor My Desires Harris & Kat Patt III

A Trilogy of Desires Lachlan & Haley Parts I-III

A Trilogy of Desires Harris & Kat Parts I-III

Series Extras

Series Playlist

WELCOME TO CHARMAINELOUISE — THE SENSUAL LIFESTYLE

GLITZY. GLAMOROUS. STEAMY.

CharmaineLouise New York, Inc. invites you to indulge in *The Sensual Lifestyle* through **CharmaineLouise Books** and **CharmaineLouise Intimates**. CLBrands immerse you in *Sexy Fantasies* with CLBooks contemporary romance novels and give you *Sexy Under Things & Loungewear* with CLIntimates.

Charmaine Louise Shelton the Founder, CEO & Author of CLNY loves all things classic, elegant, feminine, and of course with an erotic edge! Favorite outfit of choice is a cashmere cardigan, leather pencil skirt, and seamed silk stockings with stiletto heels. Sexy Fantasy Type: sub with a dash of Voyeur. When not writing and designing, Charmaine Louise travels and spends time with her Maltese buddies, ZIGGY and Jynger.

CharmaineLouise — *The Sensual Lifestyle*

~ Visit online at **CharmaineLouise.com**

~ Subscribe to **CharmaineLouise Newsletter**

~ Find us on Facebook **@CharmaineLouiseNewYork**

~ Instagram **@CharLouNY**

CharmaineLouise Books *Sexy Fantasies* launched summer 2020. Sizzling, contemporary romance with your soon-to-be favorite Alpha Doms, Powerful Billionaires, and the women they lust after and love for second chances, insta-love, enemies-to-lovers, and more.

Want to chat it up and share your thoughts with other CLBooks Lovers? Read our blog, join our CharmaineLouise Books Coterie Fan Club and follow us on my author pages and social media to be in the know about the book release dates, exclusive content, giveaways, contests, and more!

~ **Purchase your eBook and paperback novels from my Author Page by clicking here!**

~ Read and subscribe to our blog *The World of Sex*

~ Connect on **Amazon Author Page**

~ **Goodreads Author Profile**

~ **BookBub Author Profile**

CharmaineLouise Intimates *Sexy Under Things &* *Loungewear* debuted in 2003. Inspired by the sensuous sirens and sylph swans of the past and present, the hand crochet cashmere and silk collections are for the sexy: hence, the line names Ginger — Bombshell; Diana — Show-stopper; Jackie — Timeless; Lena — Classic. Also known as The Movie-Star from Gilligan's Island; Ms. Ross The Boss; Mrs. Kennedy Onassis; Ms. Horne.

Do you thrive on seduction and being sexy lounging at home? Read our blog and follow us on social media to receive the tips, the latest additions to the collections, private sales, and more!

~ Read and subscribe to our blog *The Art of Seduction*

~ Find us on Facebook **@CharmaineLousieIntimates**

~ Instagram **@CharmaineLouiseIntimates**

Fulfill Your Desires.

www.ingramcontent.com/pod-product-compliance
Lightning Source LLC
Chambersburg PA
CBHW072033190726
48294CB00005B/1238